THE SCARLET CLOAK

By Peter Shokeir

First paperback edition March 2025

Book design by CoverKitchen

ISBN 978-1-7386765-4-5 (paperback)

ISBN 978-1-7386765-5-2 (ebook)

www.petershokeir.com

PROLOGUE

Fleet Admiral Redwood's aging frame was not used to all this stress, so when he sat down, he could hear his joints pop like firecrackers. What a disgusting noise. He hoped none of the others had heard it. Thankfully, they appeared too preoccupied with their own petty squabbles. Men in military uniforms barked at one another, but they paled in comparison with the politicians who were spewing words at a rate that seemed impossible for a normal human tongue.

The politicians were members of the Western Union Governing Council, which consisted of representatives from all the member nations. This was only a partial council; the full council consisted of over two hundred people. Two dozen members were currently present, half of them physically gathered in a briefing room within the Pentagon, the other half holograms. This meeting was to discuss their strategy for dealing with their two principal enemies: the United Third and the Chinese Empire. All present grasped the reality of the situation. No longer did anyone deny what was going on.

World War III had begun.

The hijacking of *Leviathan* had started it all. The Chinese Empire and the United Third had been blamed for it and the attack on Rome that left ten thousand dead. President Jacob Hynes had been among the casualties. As a result, a new president had come into power, the same president who had declared war on the Chinese Empire and called this meeting.

Harold Powell raised his hand. "All right, settle down."

The room went silent. Everyone sat around a conference table, Powell at the head of it, his hologram shivering as he examined his cronies with a cocky smile. He was the new president of the United States and head of the Western Union. He had only been in office for six months now but wielded his power as if he had been in charge for years.

Redwood felt a touch of revulsion go through him. He always knew Powell was no good. Hynes had wanted to sack Powell after they found out the United Third's leader, Incognito, was a former Western Union scientist. Powell had been Incognito's boss and was also in charge of the Keymaster Project. Although the project resulted in the supersoldiers that helped the Western Union conquer South America, these supersoldiers eventually went rogue and created a criminal organization known as Cloak. So not only was Powell responsible for Cloak, but he had also allowed Incognito to come to power. Such debacles could not be overlooked.

But now that Powell was president, he was nearly untouchable.

"Let's put all this foul business to rest," Powell had told Redwood. "We can't say anything without hurting ourselves. That would be bad now that we're at war."

Redwood felt another touch of revulsion. How could he have let this happen?

"Let's begin the meeting," Powell told the partial council. "These are crucial times right now. This war may determine who shall lead the world for the next century, and if we're gonna come out on top, we need to develop a solid game plan for dealing with our enemies. That is why we're all here today.

"Currently, an operation is in the works to capture Incognito. For security reasons, only a handful of people know the precise details, but we will briefly review the operation. This meeting, however, is primarily to discuss strategies for dealing with the Chinese Empire. I'll hand over the meeting now to General Kazakov, who can speak on this in depth."

General Ivan Kazakov stood up, holding a tablet computer in his gnarled hands. His hologram was poorly transmitted. Static consumed half his body. In charge of the Western Union's non-peacekeeping land troops, Kazakov was a wrinkled old prune of a Russian with a nose that looked like the curved beak of a hawk.

"Thank you, Mr. President," Kazakov said before looking down at his tablet. "So far, no actual battle has occurred due to nuclear deterrence. There have been several border skirmishes between East and West Russia. Otherwise, the Chinese Empire has not retaliated violently to our declaration of war. But in response to our naval fleet protecting Australia, the enemy has deployed an opposing fleet surrounding the..."

Redwood paid attention, but Kazakov's briefing added nothing new. Everyone at the table knew the situation. They all knew the Chinese Empire had almost no air force and a pitiful navy compared with the Western Union. The Chinese also had only a fourth of the world's land area in their possession, while the Union held the rest. Even Japan, with initial resistance, had finally allied with the West.

But the Chinese had a major advantage, which was population. Their army was massive, supposedly made up of over a billion soldiers, although Western analysts estimated it was three hundred million at most. Even so, there was no way the Western Union could possibly win the war with land engagements alone.

The Western Union also had to contend with the United Third and enforce law in the Occupied Territories, wasting precious resources and military assets that could be better used against the Chinese Empire. If they were going to win this war, Redwood knew they needed to first defeat the United Third and pacify the Occupied Territories. The best way to do that was by removing Incognito.

And that was where the Helmet Man came in.

***

"All right, we're only twenty minutes away from landing," the pilot said.

Her copilot nodded. "President Powell's peeved he didn't make it to the council meeting on time. Hope he doesn't sack us."

"It's not like he *has* to be there in person. With holograms these days, I'm starting to think showing up in the flesh is just a formality."

"Does this mean we'll soon be out of a job? I was already worried, what with how good autopilots have become, but now..."

The pilot was about to give a witty reply when an alarm started blaring.

"Hey, what—?" the copilot asked before sudden turbulence interrupted her.

On reflex, the pilot looked out her left window. The moon provided some much-needed visibility that night. She saw an escort fighter jet emerge from the clouds.

It was on fire.

The copilot gaped. "What the—!"

A beam of yellow light slammed into the fighter jet. It was ripped in two, the flaming remains falling to the earth.

"Evasive action!" the pilot screamed. She grabbed the controls and turned the plane right in order to stay away from whatever had shot down that jet.

A second shockwave hit them. A jet to their right was attacked. It was soon riddled with holes and covered in sickly yellow flames. The jet went down, leaving behind a trail of black smoke that stained the moonlit sky.

"They're dropping like flies!" the copilot cried.

"Arm the emergency defense system," the pilot ordered. "A distress signal should already have been sent out."

The entire plane rattled. The pilot shook her head, trying to get rid of the double vision that plagued her. She noticed that her copilot was as pale as a sheet.

"Get your head out of the clouds!" she snapped. "What's wrong with you?"

The copilot answered by opening her mouth, making a sound similar to a death rattle. Tears began to flow from her quivering eyes. They were focused on the entity before her.

The pilot saw it too and stopped breathing.

A figure stood on the nose of Air Force One. It wore a dark cloak that fluttered in the wind. Despite the fact that they were thousands of feet in the air and flying at six hundred miles per hour, the figure was perfectly poised, perfectly still.

The pilot's eyes were transfixed by the silver helmet.

It gleamed in the moonlight.

Before she could scream, the figure fired a beam.

***

"Hey, why's the plane—?" Powell cried before his hologram shivered and lost color. It quickly disappeared altogether.

The entire council was silent and stupefied. Redwood found himself immobile and unresponsive. The new vice president, Bartley Reynolds, reacted first. He was a fat man who jumped up to his feet with surprising speed.

"What is this?" he bellowed. "Is it transmission troubles, or did something happen to Air Force One? Get someone in here this instant!"

As if on cue, a gang of Secret Service agents ran into the briefing room. The leader of these agents spoke with a layer of controlled terror in his voice.

"Sirs, Air Force One and its escorts have all been taken down."

Nobody in the room thought they had heard that correctly, so the agent repeated himself.

"Air Force One is down. We need to get you all to a bunker. Now!"

***

A minute later, Redwood was running through the halls. Secret Service agents pushed him along and shoved government workers out of the way. Alarms rang. Everyone moved with purpose.

"Have we confirmed if the president is alive?" Redwood asked as he ran.

"Sir, we don't know anything about that," one agent said.

"Can you at least find—?"

The ceiling exploded inward. Bureaucrats screamed and scattered backward as fragments of plaster showered down on them. Redwood and the agents covered their eyes. They wouldn't have been able to see even if they tried, for a cloud of dust hung in the air, obscuring what had crashed through the roof of the Pentagon.

A smoldering carcass was thrown out of the dust cloud. With a disgusting crack, it hit the floor, clothes still smoking.

One agent recognized the body, his face devoid of any emotion. "Powell…"

A woman screamed. Redwood looked at what she was pointing at. Then he reacted in a way that both shamed and confused him.

He screamed too.

The figure stood where the ceiling had collapsed. He wore a black cloak that concealed his entire body and dragged along the floor. The symbol of Omega, a bloodred horseshoe, decorated the back of the garment. But nobody really paid attention to the cloak. All eyes were on the silver helmet.

"The Helmet Man…" an analyst croaked, shivering out of control.

"No…" his colleague said. "That isn't a man."

Temple was six and a half feet tall, but the elongated helmet on top of his bulging neck made him appear more than eight feet in stature. The helmet was perfectly smooth, silver in color, and impossible to take off. But unlike the Helmet Man, Temple's helmet was tall, cylindrical in shape, and rounded at the top. To Redwood, it looked like a column of pure malice. Others saw it as a brutal tool of defilement. But what they all had in common was the primal fear that grew within their guts.

"Run."

Redwood turned to the agent next to him.

"You heard me," the agent whispered.

And that was what Redwood did. He ran. Everyone else remained still, transfixed. But then, after five seconds, one woman started scrambling to her feet. This caused a chain reaction. Dozens of people scuttled away from the harbinger of evil like frightened hermit crabs. The Secret Service agents, however, raised their firearms.

A pale hand with black nails emerged from Temple's cloak, pointing accusingly at one of the agents. His index finger glowed yellow for a split second before firing a beam. Light tore through the agent's chest, leaving a smoking hole. Another beam came forth. Then another. And another. In a few moments, all the agents were dead. It happened so fast that not a single retaliatory bullet had been fired.

The remaining people screamed and ran even faster. Their efforts were futile. Temple's light beams hit them in the back. Corpses thudded to the floor at a wicked rate. Some even caught fire from the heat of the beams. The screams were soon cut off. A hard silence fell.

Temple glided forward over the corpses like a wraith.

"Freeze!" a security officer cried from down the hall. The officer and his two comrades wore tacky uniforms and carried submachine guns. Although they had ordered Temple to freeze, they didn't give him the chance to comply and fired instead.

Temple raised his pale hand. A wall of pure light appeared before him. It was square in shape, semitransparent, and glowing yellow. It shielded him from the bullets, which hit the wall and disintegrated on impact. The security officers kept firing until they had no more ammo. After their weapons went quiet, the wall protecting Temple disappeared. He fired beams again. The men died. Temple moved on.

Moving through the Pentagon at a deliberate pace, Temple came across more fleeing people and shot his beams. One went through a woman's head. Two burned through a man's torso. And so on. There was no warning or discrimination. Their killer didn't even bother to slow down and admire his handiwork.

Temple entered a bare hallway with several bureaucrats fleeing down it. He was about to finish them when overhead doors at both ends of the hall slammed down, sealing the exits. The bureaucrats trapped inside banged against these doors and pleaded for release.

They would soon have it.

White gas filled the hallway, nerve gas to be precise. The bureaucrats grabbed their throats as they choked on death. Temple, meanwhile, appeared to be unaffected at first but then started to sway, the gas working through his skin. Temple fell to his side, banging against the wall. He tried to lean against it for support but soon went to his knees.

"Do you think that did him in?" an officer asked. He and his colleague sat inside a security office on the other side of the Pentagon, having just taken matters into their own hands.

"Let's pray so," the colleague said, eyeing with dread the live security feed on his holographic monitor. "Otherwise, we just killed five people for nothing."

Then Temple's cloak caught fire. Yellow flames covered his body, and his veins glowed. He started to get back up. The remains of his burnt cloak fell from his shoulders, revealing the monstrosity that lurked within.

The officers watching the feed lost all color in their faces.

Temple was built like a bodybuilder, muscles large and bulging. Without the cloak, he wore only skintight black shorts and his silver helmet. Like his hands, Temple's bare feet had black nails that accentuated the paleness of his skin. Each foot was missing a pinkie toe. He also had no nipples or a navel. The veins on his skin soon stopped glowing. They were black as well. Whatever flowed through Temple's veins, it was not blood.

Temple dug his heels into the floor and charged forward. He moved so fast that he was just a blur to the cameras.

The beast collided with the door and burst through it. Temple skidded to a stop. He had broken into a cafeteria. Trays of food sat unattended on the tables, hastily abandoned by government employees smart enough to evacuate.

But the cafeteria wasn't unoccupied.

Two dozen armed soldiers wearing gas masks and green uniforms stood before Temple. They all fired at once. Temple raised his palm and conjured a wall of light that blocked the bullets. With a wave of his fingers, the wall sped forward at the soldiers. Most of them managed to roll out of the way, but a few were completely reduced to ash. Another had his arm disintegrated, and he fell, squealing.

The wall disappeared. As the soldiers got reoriented, Temple came at them.

The veins on his forearms and fists were glowing, a cruel heat radiating off them. A soldier raised his automatic weapon, but Temple grabbed it. The gun melted away in his grasp. Temple punched the soldier right through the chest, his fist coming out the other side. The soldier gaped in surprise and agony. Temple pulled his arm out, leaving a cauterized hole. The soldier tumbled down and died without a sound.

Another soldier fired a few bullets that missed their mark. Temple backhanded him, taking his head off. He tore the arm off another soldier. The unfortunate soul screamed and stumbled backward. Temple silenced him with a punch to the head, which left a smoldering hole where his face was supposed to be.

"Die!" a half-crazed soldier bellowed. He fired his grenade launcher. Temple erected a light wall with one hand. The grenade hit the wall, exploding on impact. The flames only managed to curl around the wall's sides. Temple sent the wall flying at his attacker, who was burned out of existence.

More bullets came. Temple made a small, circular shield of energy to protect himself. He threw more deadly blows, fired more beams, and plowed through his foes. After a minute of chaos and screams, he had taken out all of them.

Except for one. The last soldier shot Temple in the back five times. It was the same one who had lost his arm in the initial assault. Temple stumbled forward but then spun around and put a beam through the soldier's skull.

The cafeteria was then silent. Temple touched one of the wounds. His fingers were stained with black blood. The bullet wounds glowed for a moment before healing. Temple wiped his bloody fingers on his silver helmet, leaving three horizontal lines where his face would have been. It made for fine war paint.

Temple moved on. He encountered little opposition but plenty of victims. They all burned. They all fell. They all died. Some screamed, some pleaded, some cried, and others vomited. But a few laughed. Oh, how they laughed.

Now Temple was in the central courtyard with the night sky overhead. The moon was full and juicy, the white eye absorbing all the hate, all the pain.

Snipers positioned themselves on the roof of the Pentagon and aimed down at the courtyard. They would all shoot at once. There was no way the enemy could block all these bullets. There was no way.

Temple stopped walking and flexed his muscles. His flesh was now glowing, fists clenched tight and veins coming alight. This wasn't like the glowing from before either. It was like the sun, bright and hot. The grass around him ignited. The windows shattered inward. The snipers caught fire. They cried out in agony, but it wouldn't last long. Temple kept getting brighter, and brighter, and brighter...

And then he burst.

The light exploded outward, decimating the inner walls of the Pentagon. Concrete shattered. Metal melted. Bodies burned. The outer walls of the Pentagon exploded. Debris flew everywhere. Police cars and military personnel were gathered outside the Pentagon to confront the threat, but all they could do was fall back. A huge piece of concrete crushed a car. Another flattened a walker. Seven people were killed from the fallout. They were, however, only a minority when compared with the hundreds that had still been inside the building.

The Pentagon was collapsing. It was now nothing but a pile of rubble. Yellow flames continued to burn away what was left. A shape flew from the remains. It left in a flash of light and soared through the air at supersonic speeds.

Temple was gone.

Redwood stood in the panicked crowd, agitated beyond belief. He had made it out, but he still felt burned. And despite the collective delusions of Redwood and the other onlookers, there was no escaping the truth.

The world would burn. Humanity would submit.

The Omega Lord would rise.

CHAPTER 1

Seven Months After the Pentagon Attack

"So, if you follow my tips, you'll keep those limbs of yours!" Hank Powers laughed. "Any questions about land mines?"

The cadets didn't have any. Most of them were quite pale.

Powers laughed again. "Hey, I never said war was pretty. Come on, some of you must have questions." He glanced around the classroom. Powers was still thrown off by how young these cadets looked. Most of them were barely in their teens. If the Western Union was going to stand a chance against the Chinese Empire, they needed more soldiers. It didn't help that the situation in the Occupied Territories was deteriorating more each day. Powers himself was on standby, waiting to be briefed on a big operation that was about to take place. Since he had nothing else to do until then, he had volunteered to be a guest speaker for navy cadets. One might wonder how anyone could learn from such a blustering man. The answer was they didn't.

"Seriously, someone ask a question already!" Powers barked.

A girl raised her hand. She was very timid and slouched in her chair. Her head had been shaved, presumably because it had been genetically altered to have an unnatural color. The military no longer had tolerance for such blatant individuality. Powers could still tell from the stubble that it had been neon green.

"Sir, I have a question," the girl said. "You mentioned something about how soldiers usually force civilian vehicles off roads that aren't wide enough to pass on."

Powers furrowed his brow. "Yeah, go on."

"But that means the cars being forced off might drive over a land mine."

"What are you getting at?"

The girl gulped. "I'm just wondering … is that … moral?"

Something snapped inside Powers. "You ungrateful brat! This is war! Who cares if we blow up a couple of terrorists? Don't you get it? You and your family are gonna be speaking Chinese if we don't toughen up!"

The class jumped in their seats. The timid girl shriveled up.

Powers cleared his throat. "Whoa, uh…"

Looking more confused than angry now, Powers could only stare at the floor.

"Class dismissed," he muttered.

The class got up and left, the girl who got berated being the first out the door.

For several minutes afterward, Powers stood with his fists clenched. He imagined the Pentagon on fire, almost as if he were there. Then he thought about Incognito and the destroyed fleet. And the Helmet Man. That Helmet Man…

Powers punched the wall until his fist broke.

***

"You're late," Camilla Ryder said.

"Sorry about that, boss," Powers said. "Lost track of time at the cadet school."

They stood in an airplane hangar filled with walkers and hundreds of people bustling about. Ryder examined Powers' injured hand with dull and emotionless eyes. She would have been quite beautiful if it weren't for that.

"What happened to your hand?"

"Oh, that." Powers raised his cast. "I … punched some stairs, yeah."

"Well, I hope those stairs deserved it."

"So, what's happening, boss? Where's that Keito at? Lazy bum is never around."

"Keito could not make it. He has already received his assignment for the upcoming operation and is preoccupied with executing it."

"And the other pilots? I read their profiles. Bunch of weirdos, if you ask me."

"You will meet them at the briefing, and I would advise you to refrain from besmirching your comrades. It could taint the team dynamic."

"Sure thing, coach. What is this 'upcoming operation,' anyway? Judging by all these walkers and soldiers, we're about to kick some Chinese ass."

"Wrong. Our main objective is to capture Incognito."

***

"Robby, can you please pass me the laser rifle?" Dr. Plato asked.

An android that looked like a possessed crash test dummy handed him the rifle. Dr. George Plato, a thin man with a patchy mustache, took a moment to inspect the rifle. Over a hundred military personnel sat inside the hangar while the military police watched over them from the sidelines. The listeners all leaned in, more so to get a better look at the speaker than anything else. Dr. Plato was perhaps the most valuable scientist the Western Union had. He had single-handedly created the modern-day walker and numerous other weapons for the military. He used to be a recluse, but ever since the war began, the Western Union had been running him ragged. He looked so tired that many in the audience thought he was about to keel over.

Ryder and Powers took seats near the front. Ryder remained as stoic as ever while Powers stole glimpses of his teammates who sat beside him. They had only given curt greetings before the briefing started, so he was forced to recall their profiles from memory as he sized up each one of his four new comrades.

The one sitting closest to him was a thin black woman with short hair and an inquisitive expression. Carol Kennedy. A novel rested in her lap, some chick book written by Jane Austen, Powers observed. Apparently, this Kennedy liked to read a lot. Powers had even caught her sneaking in a few pages before the briefing began. He just hoped she didn't try reading *Moby Dick* or something while they were on a mission together.

Garcia Cruz, another teammate, leaned back in his chair with a wide yet relaxed smile. He almost appeared to be daydreaming, but his attentive, kinetic eyes proved otherwise. Powers couldn't remember if he was from Spain or South America. Either way, Cruz was unusually handsome for a highly decorated serviceman. The bigwigs usually put pretty boys like him in the movies to promote the military. Seems this Cruz preferred excitement over glamor.

Powers had a hard time getting a look at Diya Patel, who sat to the left of Cruz. According to her profile, her parents had fled India as refugees, like many who wished to escape the brutal rule of the Chinese Empire. Again, highly decorated, but Powers couldn't get the image of her as a cheerful preschool teacher out of his head. This impression was solidified when she caught him looking at her and gave him a wave, along with a giddy grin.

The last teammate was the only one Powers felt confident in at first glance. Duncan York sat with his arms crossed and head leaned back. Aviator sunglasses concealed his eyes. His scrawny arms were covered in tattoos while his crew-cut hair was so fair, it was almost white. Powers thought York had the most impressive résumé of all, even on the same level as his own, but he felt no jealousy. It was just good to have a verified pro in his corner.

Powers then realized he had missed a whole spiel from Dr. Plato. He decided to wait until later to inspect his new squad.

Dr. Plato talked some more before aiming his laser rifle down a firing range and pulling the trigger. A burst of red came from its tip. A scarecrow standing downrange had a hole burned through its chest. Then it combusted, burning away in a matter of seconds.

"Incognito has the ability to make himself intangible," Dr. Plato told his audience. "That means he can move through solid objects, remain unaffected by physical attacks, and even fly. This intangibility reduces friction to zero, so Incognito can move at impossible speeds. Gravity does not affect him either. He can also make anything he touches intangible, rendering objects weightless. This is how Incognito managed to lift an aircraft carrier."

People in the audience murmured. Powers gritted his teeth. Having personally witnessed Incognito decimate a fleet of Western Union ships outside the Neutral Zone, he knew exactly what Dr. Plato was talking about.

"However, after analyzing the footage of Incognito's rampage, we have discovered several weaknesses of his," Dr. Plato continued. "First, he seems to get weaker the more he uses his powers. This was demonstrated by his decreased speed toward the end of his rampage. Second, he appeared to have been dodging certain attacks such as missile strikes. We believe that Incognito is vulnerable to heat and electricity. This is why I have been focused on developing energy-based weapons, lasers in particular."

Carol Kennedy raised her hand and sat up straighter.

"You have a question?" Dr. Plato asked.

"Are any of our walkers equipped with these laser weapons?" she inquired.

"Yes, all the ones being used for this operation have laser rifles instead of standard machine guns. Same with the unicopters. Any other questions?"

One corporal spoke up. "Dr. Plato, how did Incognito obtain his powers?"

A military policeman answered by cocking his gun. The corporal shut up.

After several more minutes of orientation, Dr. Plato ended with an ominous warning.

"Remember, all this information is highly classified. Any leaks could compromise this operation. Disclosing this material to any unauthorized personnel, whether an enemy agent or a family member, is punishable by death."

The audience left the briefing in a state of submissive fear, making sure to keep their mouths shut. Powers and his new teammates remained behind, standing in front of the emptying room while Ryder brought Dr. Plato over. Powers and the others stood to attention.

"At ease," Ryder said.

Her subordinates complied. Dr. Plato stepped forward to speak.

"You all have customized walkers," he said. "Powers has had his for the longest. I built Hornet as a trial project, but the military found my custom walkers too gaudy for their uses. However, with the recent emergence of ... 'enhanced individuals' and our war with the Chinese Empire, the military has allocated the funding for more walker development and the formation of the Specialized Walker Squad, or SWS for short."

"This squad is made up of special operatives with no rank and no official affiliation to any branch of the military," Ryder interjected. "This allows for greater flexibility and secrecy in our activities. We will require both for the foes we shall face."

Dr. Plato swept his tired gaze over the squad. "You have all been selected as the most qualified candidates. For the four who have just received their walkers, I will take the time to walk each one of you through their special features."

Duncan York raised his hand, his aviator sunglasses glinting. "May we speak freely?"

"Granted," Ryder droned.

"Have you decided who will lead this squad, ma'am?"

"Are you requesting the job?"

"Of course. I am the most qualified."

"Hey, watch it, buddy!" Powers yelled. "I was here long before you."

"You also made a fool of yourself in Japan," York retorted.

Powers turned to him, growling. "What did you just—?"

"Enough, Powers," Ryder said. She turned to York. "Powers has already been selected for the role. You will obey his orders and show the proper respect."

"As you wish, ma'am," York said.

Garcia Cruz laughed with white teeth. "Well, it appears we have a little friction in our squad already, but what do expect with such a diverse bunch?"

"Civility," Kennedy replied curtly.

Cruz laughed again. "Perhaps you are right."

"After you are all done speaking with Dr. Plato, you will practice drills together with your walkers," Ryder said. "This squad needs to be prepared to confront Incognito and his agents. We shall meet again after the drills. Dismissed."

The walker pilots dispersed. Powers and York exchanged cool stares before walking off in opposite directions while Cruz and Kennedy went to change into their flight suits.

Diya Patel, however, went up to Dr. Plato and shook his hand.

"Doctor, I must thank you again," she said, her expression warm and eyes watery. "My husband and children have never been prouder. Of course, I can't tell them everything, but still, to be selected for such a squad is so..."

"You're welcome," Dr. Plato said with a withered smile. "And I'm glad you have made your children proud. That makes me ... happy."

Patel's grin faltered for a moment, but she quickly recovered. "I must get ready for practice. Thank you again. I will treat Garnet well."

Dr. Plato gave a half-hearted wave to Patel as she left.

"Very informative presentations," Ryder told him.

"Part of the job, I suppose," Dr. Plato said, eyes downcast. "I finished your walker too. You should try it out, though I'm still a little shocked that you want to go onto the battlefield. I thought you worked behind the scenes."

"I can do both."

Dr. Plato gulped. "Ms. Ryder, you're the one who captured the Helmet Man. You must know about my daughter. She... I..." He gulped again. "Please, save her."

"I cannot promise that. Gilda Plato has betrayed the Western Union. If she should get in the way of Incognito's demise, I will have no choice but to kill her."

"Well, if you can't save her ... then make the Helmet Man suffer."

A ghost of a smile appeared on Ryder's lips. "Yes, I believe I can manage that."

CHAPTER 2

Thousands of feet below the ocean's surface, *Tortuga* rolled onward, looking for the next spot to drill. There was still plenty of oil beneath the bottom of the ocean. The trick was getting to it. *Tortuga* was able to do it easily, drilling for new oil wells and hooking pipelines up to them. The thing was the size of an office building. It used to be the largest vehicle in the world until *Leviathan* was built. Its boxy body was supported by two large tank treads that rumbled across the seafloor. *Tortuga* served two purposes. The first was to get oil.

The second was to be a prison.

Controlled and operated by the Western Union, *Tortuga* was one of the world's most secure facilities. What harder place to reach than the bottom of the ocean? Outer space, perhaps, but that was even more impractical. Oil drilling made the underwater prison at least somewhat economical, especially since the prisoners were used as unpaid labor.

Tortuga's inmates included terrorists, rebels, political prisoners, and even former leaders of conquered nations. What they all had in common was that the Western Union wanted them out of the picture, so they were sent here to work and die. Only several prisoners had ever left *Tortuga*, and none had ever escaped.

At least until now.

***

Sitting at the table, Abrafo poked at his food, losing his appetite the more he looked at the concoction. It was grayish, mostly fluid, but had green chunks as well. He forced himself to eat despite his disgust. Drilling for oil worked up an appetite.

Most of the other prisoners seemed to be going through a similar thought process, reluctantly eating. The entire cafeteria was filled with prisoners of various ethnicities. Some were black, some Middle Eastern, some Asian, a few even Western, but all of them were filthy and beaten down. A guard went by. The prisoners lowered their heads, hands quivering as they reached for their plastic sporks. Only the daily screenings of sitcoms about well-to-do families and mundane situations gave them the faintest comfort.

Then Abrafo's eyes settled on a man sitting nearby, an Asian with an athletic build. Abrafo could tell this man still had pride. More than that, he seemed to have a sense of purpose. Could he be useful?

Abrafo lumbered over and plopped down next to the Asian. Abrafo was Nigerian and over six feet tall. A diagonal scar marred his face. Most people, including his fellow prisoners, were immediately intimidated by him. But not the Asian.

"You must be new here," Abrafo said. "You speak English?"

The Asian didn't seem to hear him, too focused on eating his slop.

"What are you in for?" Abrafo asked. "Must be something very nasty for you to end up in *Tortuga*. For me, I was caught planting a bomb at a military base. Too bad it didn't go off. Western swine…"

"Hey, what are you doing there?" a guard yelled. He held a stun baton. Sparks came off its end.

"Just saying hi to a friend," Abrafo said innocently.

The guard shocked him with the baton. Abrafo fell to the floor, convulsing for a second before throwing up his inedible lunch.

"Don't get smart with me," the guard said. "I heard you bragging. Next time you mouth off like that, I'll be inclined to put you in solitary."

Abrafo got off the floor and wiped the vomit off his lips. He shot a look to the Asian, but the man had not stopped eating, unconcerned.

"You got something to say?" the guard asked, his face red with anger.

"Sir, forgive me," Abrafo growled, barely containing his own anger. "I just can't help myself sometimes. It is my nature."

"Of course it's your nature," the guard shot back. "But you need to rise above it."

A bell rang, signaling the end of lunch break. Like zombies, the prisoners rose and headed back to work. The Asian rose as well, not even acknowledging Abrafo as he left. Abrafo wanted to throw up again. It seemed this man was planning on being a model inmate. The Westerners often got prisoners to rat on each other and act servile by bribing them with beer and fast food. How many burgers had it taken to buy the Asian off?

"See, that one knows his place," the guard said, pointing at the departing man. "Why can't you be that well behaved?"

Later, while Abrafo was helping other prisoners carry barrels of drilling fluid, he felt someone brush past him. It was the Asian. Abrafo felt tempted to spit on him, but he noticed that the Asian had slipped something into his pocket. Discreetly, he took it out and saw it was an access card the guards used to get into restricted areas. Abrafo smiled. That man must have pickpocketed the guard earlier in the cafeteria.

Perhaps this man could be trusted after all.

***

Warden Welsh stood on the bridge with a raised chin as his guards manned stations and checked a variety of instruments. All the problems of both a prison and an underwater vessel. Welsh never understood how he kept pulling it off. He briefly marveled at his own abilities as he watched one particular screen that showed a Kurdish man with burns on his arms receiving a cheeseburger for his cooperation. Welsh snorted. Savages were so easily bribed.

"Sir, there's an energy surge from the supermax section," a guard said, his panel blinking like crazy before him.

Warden Welsh chuckled. "Him again, huh? He hasn't done it lately. I wonder if we need to give him a refresher."

Another guard laughed. "That sounds like fun."

Welsh and two guards took the elevator down to the supermax section, which housed *Tortuga's* most dangerous and valuable prisoners. These prisoners were confined to their cells for the rest of their natural lives. Welsh didn't normally go down there unless he felt like letting off some steam. But today he *really* felt like it.

The elevator stopped. Welsh and his men got out and walked to the thick door at the end of the hall. Two armed men in shockproof suits guarded the entrance.

"Open the door, boys," Welsh said. "Somebody needs a talking to."

After a complicated procedure, the door swung inward. Welsh walked to the doorway, but he was smart enough not to enter the cell.

"I thought you knew better than to act out," Welsh told the prisoner.

"What? What did I do?"

"You know what you did. Quit using your powers."

"You may chain my body, but you can never chain my spirit," the Helmet Man said in a constipated voice. "Your pleasure dungeon has no effect on me."

"It's nice to know that prison hasn't ruined your sense of humor, but I have a feeling it will in time."

Slate stood in the cell, wearing nothing but baggy shorts and an irremovable silver helmet. His pale, muscular body was covered in scars and burns, many of them recent. Despite this, he seemed in pretty good spirits. Two beach-ball-sized metal spheres covered his hands. Conductive tethers connected them to the wall. All of his energy was diverted every time he attempted to use his powers. The tethers also prevented him from getting close to Welsh. Nevertheless, the warden made sure to keep back.

"Hey, could you take these things off my hands?" Slate asked. "It's really hard to scratch myself and do ... other things."

Welsh grinned. "Didn't I ask you to stop using your powers?"

"Yeah, but I thought you might have changed your mind."

"I didn't." Welsh snapped his fingers. One of the guards wearing a shockproof suit entered the cell. He held a hot branding iron.

"Torture doesn't work on me," Slate said. "You should know by now."
Welsh licked his lips. "Well, it works for me."

When Slate first arrived on *Tortuga*, he had never expected it to be this bad.

Torture was one thing. At least you got to interact with someone. But during the first few months of his incarceration, he often found himself alone for weeks at a time. He tried to cause as much of a ruckus as possible by gathering up his energy and releasing it all at once, hoping it would get someone's attention. When it did, the visits were often unpleasant, but at least they broke up the monotony. A few scientists in shockproof suits occasionally came to take a blood sample and perform tests on him. Slate didn't mind, even enjoying the company. The scientists largely ignored his crude comments, however.

He missed the others. Gilda, Straper, Thomas, Naomi... Were they doing okay? He suspected they were lying low, maybe even plotting to break him out. The Helmet Man had little reason to worry about them. He was more concerned about himself. How long would the Western Union keep him locked up? Would they kill him once they conducted all the experiments on their wish list? Even if they decided to spare his life, they had no intention of ever letting him roam free again.

Six months went by, and Slate grew more restless with each day. It got to the point where he tried to chew his own arms off, only to realize he couldn't due to his helmet.

"Ugh, I'm so bored!" he finally cried. "This may be the worst torture you could inflict on me. Bastards didn't even give me a TV."

"Technology corrupts, young man," a voice said.

Slate almost jumped from his skin. "Ah! Ghosts have come to molest me!"

"Do not flatter yourself."

"Hey, that's kind of hard for a narcissist to do."

The voice laughed. "My, it is nice to have someone to talk to."

"All right, who are you?" Slate demanded. "You're no ghost."

"I may be one very soon," the voice said. "For now, I am only a prisoner."

"Wait, you must be in the cell next to mine. I couldn't hear you before."

"But I could hear you," the voice said. "I have trained myself to be extra perceptive. Perhaps you managed to do the same."

Slate thought about that for a second. It was true that he was starting to notice things that he hadn't before, such as the small creaks and moans of pipes. But he was also starting to sense something less tangible. He didn't know how to explain it, but he felt as if something was moving through the walls, a kind of energy. It took him a while to realize that he must be sensing the electricity going through the wiring in the walls. It was more than odd.

"You might have a point," Slate said. "Hey, you may find this hard to believe, but I have superpowers. I can shoot electricity and beams and even fly. What do you think of that?"

"Not impressed," the voice grunted.

"Hey, don't deny my natural prowess!"

"You are a clumsy oaf. Only in attack power and endurance do you excel. Your defense and precision need much work."

"How can you tell that? Psychic powers?"

"Your abrasive personality and the fact that you took so long to hear my voice are more than enough evidence."

"All right, what's your point?"

"I want to teach you how to be more contemplative. If you wish to become stronger, you first need to become smarter, more patient."

"Okay, sure. It's not like I have anything else to do."

"But I have conditions. You must call me Shifu and obey all my instructions."

"Sounds kinky. Anything else?"

"Yes, one more thing. I would like to see the sun again one day. For over thirty years, I have been in this cell. It is not pleasant. The sun sounds so lovely right now. Just once more before I die will be enough to satisfy me."

Slate was mortified, an emotion he didn't feel often. Thirty years? It had been six months since he was incarcerated, and he already couldn't stand it.

"That won't be a problem," Slate told the voice. "Just keep me occupied so I won't go crazy." He paused. "I mean crazier."

"My young student, I do not think you could be less sane even if I tried."

For the next several months, Slate was far less bored. He did try to bother the guards every now and again but mainly focused on working with his new teacher. His first exercises consisted of keeping his body still, emptying his mind of all erratic thoughts and becoming hyperaware of his internal state. That was perhaps the most difficult part of his training. It wasn't in his nature to be contemplative. He wanted to pace around or punch something. His teacher was all that prevented him from doing that.

"Do not wander! Listen! Think!"

Shifu instructed Slate about being aware of his physical self and focusing his energy on certain points of his body. As long as he didn't discharge, the conductive tethers attached to his hands wouldn't divert his energy. Shifu also taught him how to speak Mandarin. Slate managed to pick up the language, but it raised some questions about his teacher.

"You're Chinese, aren't you?" he asked one day. "So am I."

"It took you too long to figure that out," Shifu huffed. "As for your race, I could honestly not care less. Good students are determined solely by their work ethic."

"You must have also worked for the Chinese Empire. Can't say I'm a big fan."

Shifu sighed. "I will not argue with you, but please understand that you cannot blame the Chinese people. They are only trying to survive."

"I don't have a beef with them. It's that emperor and his flunkies who push my buttons. They worked with Cloak to do some pretty nasty stuff."

"Yes, Cloak. You have told me much about them. I cannot speak on behalf of Cloak, but maybe I can for the Chinese Empire, although it is a long-winded defense."

"Go ahead. We have plenty of time."

"Perhaps later. Now back to work!"

"Geez, for once I'd like some straight answers."

It took much time, but the Helmet Man learned all he could from his teacher. Meditation, patience, control... In response, a seriousness started to grow within him. Slate didn't know what to make of it. He only knew that he had Shifu to thank. The old teacher had shown the Helmet Man a side of himself he never thought existed. As a result, he had new abilities that made him more dangerous than ever.

He was ready to fight Cloak again.

Now all he had to do was break out of jail.

***

"Suppertime," Abrafo growled.

The Asian opened his eyes and rose from his bunk. Abrafo wheeled a cart into his cell. The doors slammed shut behind him. He dropped the tray with a clatter in front of the Asian, whom he had learned was named Toshio.

"We have a few minutes," Abrafo told him. "Had to bribe a guard."

Toshio eyed his slop. "Bribe? With what?"

"With another prisoner." Abrafo chuckled without smiling. "Only thing we have to trade down here is our bodies. No cigarettes, no booze, maybe some junk food... But it is still a prison. You can always bribe a guard."

Toshio shoveled down his slop with a spork in half a minute. Sunday was the only day the prisoners had for themselves, even though they were not permitted to leave their cells during this time. The guards merely wanted them to recuperate at least somewhat before the grueling work schedule resumed for another week.

"Your gift earlier has already been a big help, but I still need more convincing," Abrafo said. He held his hand out. "Did you do what I asked?"

Toshio nodded, reaching inside his shoe. He took out a severed pinkie toe and handed it over. Abrafo examined the appendage before dropping it in the toilet. With a sneer, he flushed the evidence away.

"Do you think they monitor what we flush?" Abrafo asked. "Or do you think they just dump it all into the ocean without checking?"

"Both are possible," Toshio said.

"A man of few words. I like that. Too bad the owner of that toe wasn't the same." Abrafo reached into his cart and tossed Toshio a pamphlet filled with Western propaganda. It was the only reading material allowed in *Tortuga*. Toshio finished his meal and peeked between the pages of the pamphlet. He read the hidden note and then promptly ate it. Abrafo nodded before sitting down. He stared at the bare wall.

"Tell me, what do you miss the most?" Abrafo asked.

"On the outside?" Toshio closed his eyes. "My wife."

"Would you like to see her again?"

Toshio opened his eyes again. "Yes."

"And are you willing to kill?"

"Yes."

"Then welcome aboard."

CHAPTER 4

Shifu looked down at his skeletal form. His prison uniform hung from his frame like a poncho. He was still able to raise his arms, but he had lost the strength to stand over a week ago and now could only sit in the corner of his cell. A part of him wished he could cry, but he was too old and tired to shed tears over a lost cause.

The guards had last fed him almost two weeks ago. Shifu prided himself on his discipline, but the small bowl of beans had been immediately devoured, and he would not be fed again unless he could supply the guards with useful information.

Shifu had spent decades in this cell. He had memorized every crack and felt every groove his walls, floor, and ceiling had to offer. It had been a hollow existence. The worst, however, had come only in the last year. The guards had a renewed interest in anything he knew about the Chinese Empire and its revered leader. They had interrogated him, tortured him, and even tried to bribe him with petty pleasures. Now they starved him.

But Shifu had already given in. That was the true horror of his situation. He had disclosed all the useful information he could offer about the Chinese Empire long ago. Anything else he knew was likely of little consequence or completely outdated. The guards must know. They knew he could tell them no more, and yet they insisted on continuing the punishment. They did this on sheer principle alone. They needed to know that all avenues had been explored, that all measures had been taken against the enemies of the Western Union.

Shifu couldn't imagine his life lasting much longer. He couldn't imagine feeling the sun on his leathery skin again. He couldn't even dream of it. Only images of its lunar counterpart occupied his sporadic and restless slumbers. And while awake, he could only imagine his soul slipping away and stone-faced guards cremating his body. No one would mourn him.

Was this fate deserved? Shifu reflected on his life. He had not been a good man before his incarceration. A sane man, perhaps, surrounded by madmen. But he had been cruel. He had ordered death. He had even condemned some to the same fate he now suffered. Knowing his own sins, he found it hard to hate his captors. He was too weak for hate anyway.

Shifu now only had one single goal before he died, and that was to impart whatever insights his mind had grasped during his imprisonment, to know his stay in this world was not all inflicting pain and pain being inflicted upon him. This one hope had proved elusive for him as his body withered and his death neared.

Or at least until the Helmet Man arrived.

"Can you hear me, Shifu?" Slate asked.

Shifu forced himself to speak. "No more lessons for now."

"It's been a while."

"Practice instead."

"I've practiced enough, and I think I've learned all I can from you."

"Is that so?"

"Just want to thank you. You know, teaching me. Also..."

"Yes?"

"This was nice. Talking... I'm not used to talking normally with people. My helmet... This damn helmet... You don't see it. You just hear my voice. I'm glad."

"Glad..." Shifu felt the corners of his mouth twitch into a smile.

"So, it's true? You got no more lessons, old man?"

"Yes, I have no more lessons."

***

The self-driving car sped down the highway. Admiral Redwood took in the passing scenery, although it was a futile task to do so at these speeds. All the sleek cars, guided by computers, drove at hundreds of miles an hour. These superhighways crisscrossed North America and Europe, making travel easier than ever. Of course, planes and ships were still needed for voyages across oceans.

Redwood wasn't alone. Two Secret Service agents sat in the front of his car, and two other cars were escorting their vehicle. After the attack on the Pentagon, there was no more fooling around. The Western Union had been on edge ever since that day. People were jumping at the littlest things. There had been crackdowns on any voice of opposition. Unity was the only way the West would survive. Anything threatening that unity would be neutralized.

The car began to slow down once it entered the city limits. Miami was looking more like New York each day, in Redwood's opinion. Skyscrapers were popping up everywhere, covered in holographic advertisements. Half of these advertisements featured either a scantily clad woman or a burly soldier pushing some product.

"Times are tough… A woman's gotta look good for her soldier boy."

"Coke's red, like the Chinese! Drink Pepsi instead!"

Recruitment centers had been set up throughout the city. The lines of drafted teenagers seemed never-ending. Redwood would sometimes see a group of protestors with picket signs, but the police quickly dispersed such gatherings. Redwood sighed. On some level, he agreed that lowering the enlistment age had been a bad move. Kids shouldn't have to spend their youth learning how to fight. But he also knew that the survival of the Western Union depended on bolstering their ranks. The Chinese Empire would not be beaten easily.

The car dropped him off in front of a military base. After a series of checkpoints, Redwood reached the inner sanctum of the base. He noticed that people gave him a wide berth. Eyes stole glances at him whenever he wasn't looking, but the worst glances came from those who didn't even bother to hide their curiosity.

Redwood knew the rumors that had been spreading that he had seen the Pentagon attacker firsthand. He had only described the perpetrator to a few people, each one of them agreeing with him that whoever the attacker was, he was not the Helmet Man. But the perpetrator had a silver helmet as well. Was he another supersoldier created by the military? What was that monstrosity? Redwood started sweating. The memory still ate at him.

He entered the command center, where soldiers manned rows of computers, holographic maps floated in midair, and a platform gave anyone on it a bird's-eye view of the center. The bustling room was filled with an anxious energy. Very soon, one of the West's greatest enemies would be eradicated. Taking Incognito out of the picture would be the best way to pacify the Occupied Territories. It hadn't gotten to the point of total revolt, but there had been riots, protests, and even the murder of peacekeepers within safe zones.

Three people and two holograms were already on the platform. Both Vice President Reynolds and General Kazakov were there in person. One hologram was of Charles Cromwell, general of the Western Union Air Force, a beautiful British man with golden hair and blue eyes, the perfect poster boy. The other hologram projected the image of Astrid Herman, a German with short gray hair and general of the Western Union Peacekeeping Forces. Her forces had been trying to capture Incognito for years. Her anticipation was palpable.

The final figure was someone Admiral Redwood was all too familiar with.

"Good day, Mr. President," he greeted coolly.

***

Something was wrong.

The Helmet Man hadn't heard his teacher speak in over a week. That wasn't normal. Shifu did have naps but for no more than four hours at a time. Slate wanted to pace. Had he somehow earned himself the cold shoulder? Or was it something worse?

"Hey, guards!" Slate shouted. "The guy next to me might be sick or something! Geez, the service here sucks. Guess I can't expect much, what with the government running this place and all, but still."

Slate had been yelling for hours now, with no response. He had even let off some big electrical surges to show that he wasn't joking around. Why weren't they coming? Maybe it was time to escape. It would only—

Slate realized he was no longer alone. "Great, it's *you* again."

"I'm impressed," Incognito said. "You noticed my entrance rather quickly. I thought your incarceration would have dulled your senses."

Incognito wore his iconic white suit with gold buttons, had his long gray hair in a ponytail, and held a scythe. The mask he wore was white, oval in shape, and covered in black Arabic calligraphy. The cell had no bulbs, so the only illumination came from a flashlight that Incognito held. Black eyes peered at Slate through the dim light.

"Oh, my knight in shining armor!" Slate cried in fake pleasure. "Take me away from this wretched place so we may frolic!"

"Revolting fool," Incognito hissed. "Perhaps you don't wish to be rescued."

"Well, guess I'm happy someone came, but did it have to be you?"

"Yes. Now, I must free you from your restraints. Lazing around is not an option."

"Hold on, we need to go rescue someone else. I'm also kind of naked except for these rank shorts. Could I get a shirt or something?"

"You are in no position to demand anything of me. Be grateful I'm dragging your carcass out of here at all."

Out of nowhere, a loud hum filled the room.

"I'm afraid neither one of you is leaving."

Slate and Incognito snapped their heads toward the hologram that had appeared.

"I didn't think any of the Keymasters were still alive," Powell said, clasping his shimmering hands together. "Seeing you and Slate in the same cell makes me feel all fuzzy inside. It's like a family reunion."

"Hurry up, you filth!" a guard shouted. "Get those pipes hooked up! That sub needs to be filled. Hustle now, hustle now!"

Dozens of prisoners dragged thick yet flexible pipes to hook up to the wall. Every month, a submarine came to drop off supplies and pick up oil. Offshore pipelines were more efficient for transporting oil, and the submarine had to deliver supplies anyway, so it would often take some oil with it upon leaving. Abrafo was one of the men tasked with hooking up the pipes. He stared coldly at Warden Welsh, who was too preoccupied with directing his guards to notice.

"I cannot wait to see that man burn to a crisp," Abrafo murmured.

Toshio nodded, helping lift the pipe. Abrafo had finally allowed him into his inner circle. Despite being quiet and withdrawn, Toshio had been of unfathomable help to Abrafo, first with the key card, then with helping him recruit other prisoners, and finally with assisting in what was about to be accomplished today: freedom.

"You're not pulling your weight," a huge guard growled, zapping a prisoner with an electric baton. "Anyone else want a taste?"

The pipes were all in place. The submarine was already docked with *Tortuga*, so all that had to be done now was pump the oil.

"Prisoners, get back!" a guard ordered. All the prisoners complied, retreating from the pipes and lining up against the wall.

"Is it time yet?" one prisoner whispered.

"Wait for the humming," Abrafo told him.

The pumps turned on. Oil began to fill the sub. But although the pumps hummed, that was not the signal. The prisoners exchanged glances. What was taking so long?

"Hey, what are you cretins doing over there?" a guard demanded. The guard and his cronies walked over, their batons spitting out sparks. Abrafo cursed to himself. When was Incognito going to make his move?

Then the humming started. It was soft, but Abrafo could hear it, as did the other prisoners. The conductive mesh had turned on, signaling Incognito's arrival.

The riot could begin.

Abrafo dashed for the pipes while the other prisoners charged at the guards. There were lots of shouts and screams, fists and batons flying back and forth, but Abrafo paid them no mind. He had a task to accomplish. A guard tried to tackle him, but he dodged and reached the pipes. Abrafo grabbed the nearest one.

"Stop that prisoner!" Welsh yelled.

It was too late. One of the pipes had purposefully not been clamped on properly, which allowed Abrafo to easily tear it out of the wall. Oil gushed from the pipe. Abrafo aimed the stream of oil at a group of guards, who were instantly drenched.

"Shut off the pipes!" Welsh shouted. The flow of black liquid stopped. However, one of the guards covered in oil was stupid enough to turn on his electric baton, hoping to take out his anger on some of the prisoners.

"No, wait a—!" a fellow oil-covered guard cried, but he was interrupted by the sudden burst of flame. The fuel-covered guards were now on fire, screaming in agony.

"Put out that fire!" Welsh ordered. "Hurry!"

The guards aflame ran around in circles, their screams only getting louder. Most of the guards were too busy fighting the prisoners to help. Abrafo, Toshio, and a dozen other prisoners used the opportunity to run for the nearest door. They managed to open it thanks to the key card supplied by Toshio and fled the area. Sprinting through the halls, Abrafo knew that they needed to take control of the bridge. If they could do that, they could make *Tortuga* surface and—

Toshio moved fast. Half of the prisoners were already knocked out by the time Abrafo noticed that a sword had extended from Toshio's sleeve. Did he have a weapon this entire time? Had he been working for the guards all along? Abrafo didn't even have time to come up with any answers or feel betrayed as the back of the sword knocked him out.

Guards arrived. They gaped when they saw that all the prisoners had been incapacitated.

Only Keito Kusanagi remained standing.

"Good work," Welsh said, arriving at the scene. "We've smoked out all of Incognito's dogs. But I wasn't expecting my men to be roasted alive." He kicked Abrafo in the ribs. "Kusanagi, how come you didn't know about the oil attack?"

Keito shrugged. Abrafo hadn't told him everything.

"I'd like a spoken answer!" Welsh barked.

As requested, Keito spoke. "You will secure all the prisoners," he ordered. "I will deal with the Helmet Man."

***

Powell's hologram shivered as he snickered. "Long time no see, old friend. I thought you were dead till I found out you were the Western Union's boogeyman. To think Incognito was a former Keymaster all along."

Incognito didn't reply. He only stared holes into Powell.

"Powell, you slime!" Slate yelled. "Think you're untouchable, huh? Just wait! I'm gonna bust out of this dump, fly to Washington, and spank you silly right in the Oval Office. You think you can keep me locked up here for over a year and laugh in my face?"

"Obviously, yes," Powell said. "Slate, you've done it again. Thanks to you, Incognito is ours. That humming you just heard is the conductive mesh getting charged. The mesh lines the cell's walls and the entire hull of *Tortuga*. Incognito will be unable to phase out of your cell without being electrocuted."

"Wait, how did Incognito even know where I was?"

"I purposely leaked the location of *Tortuga's* resupplying. I knew Incognito wouldn't let his prize slip away from him. Why, he destroyed a fleet of ships just to rescue you before. But this time, the Western Union was prepared for him."

Slate giggled. "Wow, am I that special? I always knew I was pretty!"

Powell blinked. "You're a really disturbed individual, you know that?"

"Sorry, I repressed that knowledge."

"Powell…" Incognito seethed.

"Ah, I see someone's happy to see me," Powell jested.

"So, you managed to follow in your father's footsteps," Incognito spat. "If it weren't for nepotism, you would never have crawled from the sewer to the position you now hold. Of course, what else can I expect from the West?"

"Nepotism can only get you so far. I certainly have enough talent to outwit you."

"You think you have me trapped? I have foreseen this."

"And I have foreseen that you have foreseen this."

Slate cocked his head. "Wait, what?"

Powell ignored him and resumed taunting Incognito. "I knew some of the other prisoners would try to help Slate escape and that you would lend them a hand. That's why I planted a mole here. Your men have already been captured."

"That wasn't my plan," Incognito said. "Do you really think I would entrust this operation to underlings I barely even know? They were just decoys."

"A decoy for what?" the president asked.

An explosion shook *Tortuga*, nearly knocking Slate over.

Powell's smile faded.

"Could I get a little warning?" Slate whined. "Terrorists have no manners."

"What was that?" Powell demanded.

"That would be the submarine," Incognito told him.

***

"What do you mean the submarine exploded?" Welsh questioned.

The guard at the monitor had gone pale. "Sir, not only has the submarine exploded, but now there's a hole in *Tortuga's* hull."

Welsh and several other guards were on the bridge, trying to take control of the situation. One holographic screen showed an entire hallway being flooded. Another revealed that half of their food supplies were now submerged. That conniving Incognito must have planted a bomb on the submarine. Just after they quelled a riot, another disaster had struck.

"Seal off the breached area!" Welsh ordered.

"Sir, we already have," a guard said. "But the explosion has compromised *Tortuga's* structural integrity. We need to surface."

"No, we evacuate!" Welsh yelled. "We'll use the escape subs!"

"There's no time, sir. We need to surface."

Welsh snarled and punched a console. This couldn't be happening. The president himself had told him not to surface under any circumstances. But Welsh wasn't going to die over this, not in a million years. Medals were nice and all, but living was nicer.

"Fine, start the detachment process," Welsh ordered. He turned to another screen, which showed a strike team assembled outside the Helmet Man's cell. They were equipped with shockproof suits and laser rifles.

"Where's Kusanagi?" Welsh snapped. "He should be with the strike team."

"Sir, he's getting his repulsion pads from lockup."

Welsh gritted his teeth so hard, they might have shattered.

"Ready for detachment," a guard said. "Warden, it's your call."

"Do it," Welsh growled. "Do it before I blow a blood vessel."

***

The main body of *Tortuga* began to detach from its giant tank treads. Inflatable pontoons erupted from its sides, lifting the prison up toward the surface. It left its tank treads on the seafloor. They would only slow its ascension.

Western Union submarines started to close in on *Tortuga*, readying their torpedoes. They had warned *Tortuga* not to surface, but their warnings went unanswered. Incognito could not be allowed to escape. They would blow *Tor-*

tuga out of the water if necessary.

But then torpedoes struck two of the Western Union's subs, disabling them. The other subs had no time to react before they too were struck.

"Where are those torpedoes coming from?" a submarine captain demanded. "How did the enemy sneak up on us like that?"

"It must be Incognito's stealth sub," an officer said.

"Find that sub and blast it away."

"What about *Tortuga?*"

"The surface forces will have to handle it. Just keep us alive."

***

Captain Young-Bum shook his head as he observed his torpedoes strike the subs. He may have been a criminal, but he did not enjoy taking life. Wasn't the sea bloody enough already?

"Captain, two Western subs have taken serious damage," said a crewmate manning a control panel. "The rest are on high alert now. If we fire any more torpedoes, we run the risk of the enemy pinpointing our location."

"Do not fire again unless those subs attempt to harm us or *Tortuga.*" Captain Young-Bum turned to face his guest. "Has Magenta been launched yet?"

"They left a few minutes ago," said Kevin Straper, standing next to him. He showed no excitement for their success against the attack subs. Captain Young-Bum could not help but feel pity for this young man.

What had happened to make him so dead inside?

***

"You think you outsmarted me?" Powell spat.

"It wasn't difficult," Incognito said.

"I still have you trapped in that cell. I can flood it with nerve gas anytime I want. You won't get the better of me!"

"You know, I've been musing on a mystery for quite a while now. How did you manage to survive the attack on the Pentagon? Could it have something to do with those secret little projects of yours at Cheyenne Mountain?"

Powell's face went from red to white in a matter of seconds.

His hologram disappeared.

"Talk about dodging the question," Slate said. "Okay, get me out of here already!"

"Patience, you wretch." Incognito sliced his scythe through the air. The tethers hit the floor with a thump. He was about to perform another trick when the gray metal spheres covering Slate's hands shattered into hundreds of pieces. Slate then punched the wall and sent a sudden surge of energy through the conductive mesh. The humming stopped, the mesh melted and was no longer electrified. The nerve gas dispensers were also offline. Incognito took a step back. His eyes darted from side to side.

Slate chuckled. "Scared you, didn't I?"

"Insolent buffoon. Do not think I am cowed so easily. I'm merely surprised that your powers have increased so dramatically."

"Yeah, but those tethers were still a pain in the ass, so thanks for the help. Now let's get going! Oh, and a bunch of guys are outside the door, so be careful, I guess."

Slate waltzed to the cell door before abruptly kicking it down with a laugh. "Wonder if Naomi remembers that date she promised!"

CHAPTER 6

"This isn't happening!" Powell snapped, reentering the command center in a fiery rage. "Incognito pulled one over on me!"

The entire room was in a state of frenzy with officers running back and forth. Holographic screens displayed images of *Tortuga* rising through the murky depths of the sea, inching closer to the surface with each passing minute.

Beet red, Powell stomped back onto the platform. He vented his anger by kicking a console and swearing up a storm. Redwood and the other military leaders kept their distance. They could make an educated guess on how the president's private negotiations with Incognito had gone. Still, to see Powell lose his cool like this...

"Is *Excalibur* in position?" Powell asked, calming down a little.

"Sorry, sir," an officer said. "It'll be ten minutes before it's in range."

"Son of a... Deploy the unicopters and that walker squad! If that Incognito wants a fight, I'll give him the fight of all fights. He's better dead and useless than alive and free."

"Mr. President, we should keep our distance from *Tortuga* and fire at it from afar," Redwood said. "That way we can keep Incognito and the Helmet Man pinned down while we wait for *Excalibur*."

"No! I won't risk letting that scumbag slip out of my fingers. I want Incognito's head on my desk! I want to dangle his lifeless corpse for all to see!"

Redwood wished to object, but the other military leaders offered no support. With little other choice, he zipped his lips.

***

The strike team hesitated as they pointed their laser rifles at the cell door. They had been briefed on the abilities of the Helmet Man and Incognito, but nothing could prepare them for the reality. It would be suicide to enter the cell. They would wait for those freaks to step out.

"Keep your cool, men," the team leader said. "Just stay vigilant."

The cell door flew off its hinges and crashed into four men, who were pinned beneath its weight. The others stumbled back.

"Shoot!" the team leader yelled.

The men fired, but the lasers only hit the back wall of the cell.

"Where did they go?" the team leader questioned.

"Look behind you," Slate told him.

The remaining men barely had time to turn around before Slate bumped his fists together. All the men's hearts stopped. They grabbed their chests and fell to the floor.

"That was efficient," Incognito said, standing next to Slate. With the conductive mesh no longer working, Incognito had phased through the floor, taking Slate with him, and appeared behind the strike team. Then Slate used his new attack on them, and for some reason Incognito could not grasp, their shockproof suits had not been able to protect them from it.

Slate bumped his fists together again. All the men on the floor convulsed, their hearts restarting. They were still unconscious, however.

"What are you doing?" Incognito snapped.

"I promised my friends a long time ago that I wouldn't kill any Western Union soldiers," Slate said. "Unlike you, I keep my promises."

"Western filth should not be spared, especially in a combat scenario. Now hurry up. Don't you wish to rescue a fellow prisoner?"

Slate smacked his helmet. "Oh, right. I forgot. Wait here a sec!"

The Helmet Man rushed to the neighboring cell and kicked the door down. He jumped inside, only to find a shriveled old man curled up in the corner.

"Shifu!" Slate yelped. He scooped up the old man in his arms and tried to shake him awake. "Geez, looks like you've just been embalmed. Come on! Wake up already!"

Shifu's eyes rolled up to gaze at the Helmet Man.

Slate relaxed a little, nodding. "Great, yeah, you're awake. It's good to meet you in person. Almost thought I'd never get the chance."

"Ah ... I ... you..." the old man wheezed. "You managed to escape?"

"Yeah ... well, I'm out of the cell." Slate chuckled, although it rang hollow. "Man, your heartbeat is weak. We gotta get you some help. Maybe a bath too."

Shifu smiled, toothless. "I am afraid I won't get my last wish."

"What, seeing the sun? Don't worry. The sun's overrated anyway."

"Slate, you told me about your father. Find him... Family is all that matters. My father ... my father is the emperor. You know this?"

"I guessed," Slate said, his voice grave.

"He was corrupted by power. He ... he banished me after I told him he had gone mad. I ... I was captured by the West ... and now..."

"It's all right. I've got you now."

"I ... I still love him," Shifu whispered, still smiling. "No matter what ... don't stop ... loving your father... It is your only defense..."

Something in Shifu's voice made the room grow cold.

"Defense against what?" the Helmet Man asked.

Shifu gulped, his smile fading. His frail body shivered. With his last breath, he answered Slate's question.

"The moon..."

A gasp escaped. Then Shifu's body went still.

Slate held on to him, his helmet tilted downward, brooding. A moment passed before he put the old man down and got back to his feet.

"Welsh..."

***

"Send all available guards!" Welsh ordered. "Don't let Incognito escape!"

"Sir, Incognito and the Helmet Man are nowhere to be found."

"Then find them!"

"There's no need for that," Incognito said, now standing on the bridge.

Welsh and the guards jumped. Slate had also appeared. He was now wearing a prisoner's jumpsuit and shoes he had found lying around. He bumped his fists together, stopping the hearts of all the guards except for Welsh. The men fell like rag dolls. Welsh yelped. Slate bumped his fists again and restarted the guards' hearts, but the men were in no state to be of any use.

That just left Warden Welsh.

Welsh sweated. "Hey now..."

"You tortured me and never once laughed at my jokes," the Helmet Man said. "That's something I might have forgiven. But when you starve an old man to death in his cell, that's when I take the gloves off."

Slate grabbed Welsh by the throat and lifted him off the floor.

"Wait ... please..." Welsh gagged. "Don't kill me..."

"I don't kill Western Union soldiers," Slate said. "But that doesn't mean we can't have a little pruning session..."

Welsh's face turned purple. "No, please... Kill me instead..."

"Well, for once, I'm glad you refrained from killing the Western scum," Incognito said. "Do as you wish. We still have time."

Slate dragged Welsh away.

***

"The unicopters and the Specialized Walker Squad have been deployed," an officer said. "All ships are giving *Tortuga* a two-mile berth."

"Good," Powell grunted. On the holographic screen before him, *Tortuga* could be seen rising out of the sea. The giant metal box made waves as it broke through the surface. Massive pontoons kept the prison afloat. Powell then saw Incognito and Slate phase through the top of *Tortuga*, now in plain view for the satellites to see.

"You two will be sorry that you poked your heads out," Powell said. "It'll only make it easier to cut them off."

"Sir, we have visual confirmation of a hostile," another officer said.

"I can see that," Powell snapped.

"No, it's a walker, a flying walker. Sir, it's approaching *Tortuga!*"

"It's Plato's traitor brat!" Powell shouted.

"Why did we not detect it until now?" General Kazakov asked.

"That walker must have advanced stealth capabilities," General Cromwell said, brushing his exquisite blond hair back. "It must also be Incognito's getaway ride. Alert our forces."

"I give the orders!" Powell told them. "Blow that purple cow out of the sky! Show her what it means to betray me."

"Hold on," an officer said. "It seems that *Excalibur* is finally in position, sir."

"Good, prepare to fire! We can be rid of Incognito with one shot."

***

It was a particularly sunny day. The sea stretched out in all directions. A few Western Union ships could be seen in the distance. Slate seemed disoriented and oddly quiet after emerging on top of *Tortuga*. Incognito noticed this and did not like it. Had the death of that Chinese prisoner affected him *that* deeply? He could not afford to have the Helmet Man behaving so dour and sluggish. Perhaps the arrival of his comrades would energize him.

"Our ride is almost here," Incognito said. "Look to the horizon."

Slate noticed that a walker was flying toward them. He raised his head as his dark mood dampened. It only now occurred to him that he was free and had friends waiting for him. He could enjoy the tropical sun and its warmth. But Shifu...

Then he sensed something else coming.

"Ah, crap," Slate groaned. "More trouble..."

"What is it?" Incognito asked.

"A lot of enemies are coming this way, unicopters and walkers."

"I do not see anything. They must be using cloaking technology. Well, such cheap parlor tricks clearly do not work on you, so we have nothing to worry about. Go meet up with your friends. I shall wait here and—"

A sword almost took Incognito's head off, but he ducked in the nick of time. He swung his scythe in retaliation. The swordsman jumped back.

Slate laughed. "Keito, nice to see you again!"

Keito Kusanagi now wore a black jumpsuit and repulsion pads on his feet. He did not return Slate's greeting.

"You must be the mercenary who has been causing my lackeys so much trouble," Incognito said. "I have no time for this. Be gone already."

Keito did not comply. He kicked the deck. The repulsion pad on his foot accelerated him forward. He swiped his blade, but Incognito blocked it easily. Keito's sword happened to be electrified, so Incognito's intangibility could not protect him.

"Slate, stop this fool's heart," Incognito ordered.

Slate chuckled, flying away. "Nah, catch you later!"

"Worthless baboon..." Incognito muttered to himself, blocking another of Keito's attacks. No matter. This fight shouldn't last long. He could be faster than the speed of sound if he had to. There was no way the swordsman could beat him, but he wanted to avoid using his powers, for his body suffered each time he did.

Keito kicked again and flew up into the air. Incognito scoffed. He had enough. It was time to end this fight. He lifted his scythe, preparing to strike.

That was when *Excalibur* fired.

Slate was already halfway there to meet the flying walker when a bright flash came from the sky. White light consumed everything. An oppressive hum blanketed the area, overshadowing even the sound of the prison being ripped apart. Slate shielded himself with his arms. The heat was intense, even from this distance.

The white light faded almost as fast as it had come. Half of *Tortuga* had been vaporized. The other half barely managed to stay afloat.

"Slate!" a voice yelled.

The Helmet Man turned to find the flying walker levitating before him. Magenta, a humanoid mecha, had thin limbs and dragonfly wings that kept it airborne. However, it now also had a large, awkward box attached to its back. Slate didn't know what the purpose of this box was until it opened up.

The box was carrying a passenger.

"Now *this* is who I want to rescue me," Slate declared.

"Good to see you again, Helmet Man," Naomi said with a smile, floating out of the passenger box in a white gown not fit for combat. It had been over a year since Slate had interacted with the opposite sex, and in his mind, this was a fine way to resume the practice.

"I saw the bright light," Naomi said. "May I ask what that was about?"

"Oh, yeah... I think Incognito just got vaporized," Slate said.

Naomi's smile faded. "Let's hope not. Otherwise, we won't survive this."

Gilda sat in Magenta, relief flooding through her as she saw Slate hover in front of them. His irritating mannerisms assured her that this was indeed the Helmet Man. Peace of mind had eluded her for the past year since Slate had been captured, and she hadn't gotten one good night's sleep in six months. What had made it worse was Incognito would not rescue Slate for one year as punishment for disobeying him.

Now, after months of hardship and vigorous training, Gilda was at last reunited with her comrade. Smiling yet tired, she asked Tim, her autopilot, to turn on the loudspeaker.

"No problem, Ms. Gilda," Tim said. "You're loud and clear."

"Slate, welcome back," Gilda said. "How was prison?"

"The showers weren't as bad as I thought they'd be," he said. "What's up with you?"

"I don't think we have time for small talk and witty remarks," Naomi said. "Our employer may just have been vaporized."

Gilda doubted Incognito was dead, but it couldn't hurt to hope.

"Who cares?" Slate asked. "Don't tell me you're getting all teary-eyed over that piece of work. It took months for him to rescue me from that hellhole."

"It's actually been a year," Tim said.

"A year! Wait, who are you?"

"I'm Ms. Gilda's autopilot. Don't you remember?"

"You know, I don't think we've ever had a conversation."

"Slate, the Western Union is coming for us," Naomi said. "Incognito was our ace in the hole, but now we might be on our own."

"Whatever," Slate scoffed. "What can those weaklings do?"

Missiles appeared out of nowhere. Literally. There were at least thirty of them, and they were all headed toward Slate.

"We got to move," Naomi said.

Naomi and Magenta started falling back.

Slate, however, did not budge. The missiles were only seconds away.

"What are you doing?" Naomi yelled. "Move!"

"I'm tired of this," Slate said. "I'm tired of letting them walk all over me."

The Helmet Man raised his hand. Electric arcs spewed from his fingers, dancing through the air. The electricity hit the missiles before they even got close to him. All of them exploded. Flame and shrapnel flew everywhere. A few chunks of metal came at Slate, but they too were struck by lightning and destroyed before inflicting any damage. The sky was soon calm.

The Helmet Man lowered his hand.

"Uh, wow," Gilda muttered. "Nice one."

"You've gotten stronger," Naomi said, awestruck, though she tried not to show it. "I thought being in *Tortuga* would have made you weaker."

"Like I said, I'm tired of this," Slate told her. "I ain't running no more."

"Slate, don't kill any of those soldiers," Gilda said. "You promised, remember? They're just doing their job."

"That excuse is getting old," Slate snapped. "Fine, I won't. But that doesn't mean I can't teach them a lesson."

A burst of red light came from thin air. Slate managed to dodge it, though he could feel the heat of the laser as it skimmed by him. Dozens more came.

"Where are they coming from?" Gilda asked, Magenta maneuvering out of the line of fire. She definitely wasn't tired anymore.

"There must be unicopters nearby using cloaking devices!" Naomi shouted back, also taking evasive action. She dropped down, a laser flying overhead. Then she flew to the right, avoiding yet another laser. She put on goggles while doing this. "Gilda, switch to infrared. Don't kill them, you two. Just disable these enemies."

Gilda put on a devilish smirk. "Well, I guess I'm okay with that."

"All right, I'll disable them real good!" Slate yelled.

Gilda switched to infrared. What was revealed made her smirk evaporate. She knew that four aircraft carriers and six smaller warships were circling *Tortuga* from afar. What she hadn't known was that ten unicopters were heading their way, all sporting laser rifles.

A squad of walkers were coming as well. Two walkers with wings flew toward them while two more walkers skimmed across the water on giant motorized surfboards. All these enemies had been cloaked, but now they were visible to Gilda.

She almost wished she hadn't turned on the infrared.

***

"When will *Excalibur* be ready to fire again?" Powell demanded.

"Sir, we will need another ten minutes to recharge," an officer said.

Beads of greasy sweat rolled down Powell's forehead. *Excalibur* was a space station that harnessed the sun's rays in order to fire a high-energy beam. One of the reasons the Western Union had been so interested in the Helios Tower project was for the military applications of the technology. Because of this investment, the Western Union may have just killed Incognito. But Powell wasn't going to take any chances. He wanted *Excalibur* ready to fire again just in case that freak managed to survive.

And should that fail as well...

"Gentlemen, I'm afraid we may need to resort to our final option," Powell said, though without much reluctance in his voice. If anything, he was tranquil.

"Mr. President, what else is there?" Redwood questioned. "We've already launched all our elite forces and fired *Excalibur*."

Powell chuckled. "Little do you know, Redwood, but *Tortuga* has a nuclear device within it. This was installed should a prison break seem imminent. After all, *Tortuga* does house some of the Western Union's most dangerous enemies. Extra precautions had to be taken."

All the color left Redwood's face. No one else looked too thrilled either.

"That—that's insane," Redwood said. "Our soldiers are within the blast radius. If you detonate that device, thousands of our own could be killed. And we have a nonnuclear pact with the Chinese. Setting off that bomb during wartime could trigger a nuclear exchange."

"Incognito must be stopped at all costs," Powell said. "The Chinese aren't stupid. They won't risk nuclear annihilation. The worst that'll happen is the Chinese will assume we're conducting nuclear tests and conduct some of their own in response."

"Then you clearly don't know the Chinese Empire," Redwood said. "Emperor Long is insane. His subordinates will do whatever he commands."

"I agree," General Herman said. "Our military cannot afford any more losses. Setting off that nuclear device will destroy five percent of our naval forces."

"I agree with the president," Vice President Reynolds said. "Killing Incognito will reduce hostile activity in the Occupied Territories by fifty percent at least, freeing up a good thirty percent of our forces. Even if we lost twenty percent, it's still a net gain."

"Such a disgusting way of thinking," General Kazakov spat at the vice president. "The lives of my soldiers cannot be spent like money."

"It doesn't matter what we desire," General Cromwell said. "President Powell is head of the Western Union. This decision is ultimately his."

"That should already be obvious to everyone here," Powell snapped. "If Incognito's still alive, I'm nuking him to kingdom come."

***

More lasers were fired, but Slate easily dodged them, sensing his enemies coming from a mile away. He kept close to the sea's surface as he flew toward the nearest aircraft carrier. The invisible unicopters followed him in hot pursuit and continued to fire their laser rifles. Most of the lasers hit the water, sending steam billowing up.

Slate didn't really fight back, except to shoot a bolt at a laser rifle, shorting it out. The unicopters began to pull back. They were giving up on their prey.

"Didn't think I'd win so easily," Slate hooted. "But hey, I'm not complaining."

The aircraft carrier's guns fired, all aimed at the Helmet Man.

"Okay, *now* I'm complaining," Slate said.

All of its mounted laser rifles fired as well.

"Damn it! Would you quit it already?"

Raising his hands as he flew, Slate was able to stop the projectiles with his powers. Electricity shot from his fingertips and set off all the projectiles that came too close to him. The air was turbulent with flames and shockwaves, but the Helmet Man kept flying regardless. He only dodged the lasers, which were coming at an alarming rate, but he maintained a swerving flight pattern that threw off the aim of the laser rifles.

Slate reached the carrier and landed on it with a thud. At least twenty men on the flight deck were helping launch unicopters. They stopped working and scurried backward at the sight of the Helmet Man. The sunlight reflected off his silver helmet.

"I told you to quit it," Slate growled.

Armed men came rushing from the control tower. They seemed scared, but that didn't stop them from firing their machine guns. Slate sighed and raised his hand. None of the bullets hit their mark, despite some of them being tracker bullets, electric sparks shattering them before even getting within a foot of the Helmet Man.

"Bullets don't work!" one man cried.

"Damn right," Slate said, pounding his fists together.

Everyone gasped and fell to the flight deck. Slate pounded his fists together again, restarting their hearts. Then he put his hand on the flight deck and sent a burst of energy into the ship. Arcs of blue energy danced across the hull. Sparks flew off the control tower's antenna. The unicopters and jets still on the flight deck belched smoke. Slate stopped. The entire aircraft carrier was now damaged beyond usefulness and repair.

"Man, this is too easy," Slate said. "Almost boring."

A black shape flashed by. Slate, sensing it, rolled out of the way. The shape struck right where he had been, leaving a large hole in the flight deck.

"That got the blood pumping!" Slate yelped, hopping back to his feet.

A laser almost did him in, but he flew upward. The laser hit a unicopter that Slate had been standing in front of instead, melting it into a useless pile of molten metal. Just as he was getting his bearings, the black shape zoomed past, almost slamming into him. Slate charged up his hand and fired a beam, but the black shape was already behind him. It fired lasers from a distance and flew around Slate so fast that it was invisible to the naked eye. It took all his agility to dodge the lasers, weaving left to right and changing altitude in an instant. He had a few brief moments to fire a beam or shoot electricity, but his foe kept moving at unearthly speeds, hoping to wear down the Helmet Man.

Slate groaned. How was he supposed to defeat an enemy he couldn't even hit? What would Shifu tell him to do at a time like this? Be patient and observe, probably.

"Can't exactly do that now," Slate said, but he would try regardless. The enemy was quick. That was obvious. He concentrated hard, trying to sense what that thing was. It was big, dark, artificial, and lethal. Could it be...?

"A walker!" Slate yelled, snapping his fingers. It was a flying one like Gilda's. Maybe he could stop the pilot's heart.

"Man, I've been giving more people heart attacks than a fast-food joint."

Slate flew after the thing, barely able to avoid the lasers. It was only a matter of getting close to the walker and using his heart-stopping technique. Then he would win.

Lasers flew at him from behind. It seemed that unicopters had come to assist their comrade, but they were no threat compared with the walker. Slate disabled their laser rifles fast by firing some bolts. The walker took advantage of this distraction and flew in to finish him off.

"Gotcha," Slate said, about to pound his fists.

But then a violet blob of sticky matter hit him in the chest. The wind would have been knocked out of him, if he breathed at all. He spun out of control. Four more blobs collided with Slate and clung to him. With a groan, he realized what this stuff was. It was the same substance that had been used to capture him in the first place, some rubbery goop that prevented him from using his powers due to its insulating properties. He soon found his limbs stuck to his sides. He began to fall from the sky toward the sea.

As Slate fell, the black walker sped at him. Metal fingers plucked him from the air. An odd feeling came over him. Something wasn't right about that walker. He sensed some strange energy flowing through it. It felt too familiar. It felt like...

"Hey..." Slate said, dazed. "It's me..."

"Not quite," Camilla Ryder said from her walker's loudspeaker. "After all, you're one of a kind, Helmet Man."

CHAPTER 8

The unicopters were focused solely on Slate. That much Gilda could be thankful for. However, all the cloaked walkers were pursuing her and Naomi, which sucked dearly. The two walkers on the water might not be a problem, but the airborne ones...

"Gilda, let's split them up," Naomi said over the radio. "We need to keep them occupied until Incognito reappears."

"What if he doesn't?" Gilda asked, more concerned about having to stay in a war zone than whether or not Incognito was still alive.

"If Incognito's dead, we'll soon be too."

The two walkers on surfboards fired at them from the sea's surface. Lasers skimmed past both Magenta and Naomi, though they dodged them almost as well as Slate had. Naomi threw some punches of compressed air that hit the largest walker. Its surface was dented, but the only lasting damage was to the pride of Hank Powers.

"Damn psychic lady!" Powers yelled. "Whatever. She can't do much damage unless she gets closer. Cruz, stick with your lasers. This one can stop bullets with her mind."

"What an interesting first day on the job," Cruz said as he surfed next to Hornet in his orange mecha, Tangerine, although one couldn't tell its color while it remained cloaked. "What about the Plato girl? Do we leave her to York and Patel?"

"What, this one ain't enough for you?"

Invisible blows struck Cruz's walker, causing its window to crack.

"I think I'm more than entertained already," Cruz said with a smooth smile.

The two flying walkers, meanwhile, came at Gilda from opposite directions. She fired bullets at their wings, but they evaded with minimal effort. One of the walkers extended a vibrating sword from its arm and swung it.

"That's Sapphire!" Gilda yelled, moving Magenta back to avoid the blade.

"The same one from *Leviathan*," Tim agreed. "Cyphrus was piloting it before, but who's inside it now? Whoever it is can really fly that thing."

Gilda had Magenta dodge another slice. "Shut the hell up, Tim! I can't concentrate."

York remained impassive, his raptor eyes hidden behind aviator sunglasses, as he commanded his walker to swing its sword yet again. He also fired a laser, only for Magenta to move to the side and throw a kick. His walker blocked it with its free arm.

"Patel, what are you waiting for?" York snapped.

"You are too close!" she yelled over the radio. "The heat would damage you as well!"

York had Sapphire dodge another kick. "Just do it!"

Giving in to the request, Patel gunned her cloaked walker forward. Garnet was red and about as slender as Magenta. Its most distinguishing feature, however, was the deep grooves etched across its armor. Patel pressed a button. The grooves began to glow. The air shimmered around the walker. Its cloaking device shut off, leaving the mecha visible.

"Ms. Gilda, that walker's temperature is rapidly rising," Tim warned.

Gilda scowled and aimed her cannon at Garnet's wing. The shell shot out and whistled through the air. Patel smiled as she twisted a dial.

A wave of heated air slammed into Magenta. The shell, meanwhile, exploded from the heat before it could even reach Garnet. Gilda shook in her seat and yelped. York also grimaced as he shook, but he got his wits about himself faster and swung his sword at Magenta. The blade managed to hit the left wing. Gilda cursed but spun Magenta around for a kick. It struck Sapphire straight in the back, sending it flying toward Garnet.

"Patel, watch out!" York yelled.

Panicking, Patel told her walker to do an emergency temperature drop of her walker's armor, but it was still piping hot as Sapphire crashed into it. One of Sapphire's wings was bent, while Garnet had its entire front smashed in. The red walker spiraled out of control.

"Patel, do you need help?" Cruz asked, gaping at the sky.

"Ignore her!" Powers yelled. "Focus on the floating chick!"

Naomi dodged another laser blast from Hornet. Tangerine threw a punch, which nearly grazed her. She smirked and sent another telekinetic blow.

Then four more arms came out of Tangerine's back. The walker now had as many limbs as an octopus.

"I don't like to be all hands with a lady," Cruz said over his loudspeaker, "but you've been far too frisky for me to be chivalrous."

"A gentleman never makes bad puns," Naomi teased.

"Quit hitting on that lady and kill her!" Powers yelled.

Tangerine threw a barrage of blows at Naomi. The six arms were also equipped with laser rifles, which fired whenever they had a clean shot. Naomi worked hard to dance through the air to avoid the blows and lasers while Cruz's fingers did a dance of their own on the controls in order to control his walker's six arms. His eyes never stopped following Naomi. Even a computer would be envious of his calculation.

"Don't forget about me!" Powers yelled, his walker throwing a punch. Naomi almost had to laugh. She easily floated to the side. Hornet's fist flew by her and slammed into Tangerine instead. Cruz gasped as his walker tried to steady itself on its surfboard.

"Cruz!" Powers cried. "You'll pay for that, woman!"

"You boys need to learn some teamwork," Naomi said. "How about—?"

A green walker shot out of the water. It threw a kick and struck Naomi on the side. She got knocked back and felt a wave of pain go through her head and shoulder. Her powers only managed to soften the blow some, but she didn't think anything was broken.

"Kennedy, glad you could make it!" Powers shouted.

"Perhaps a woman's touch is needed," Cruz said.

Kennedy didn't indulge in banter. Her green walker landed on the water and moved across the sea's surface like a skater. Emerald was the world's first submersible walker, having the ability to go a thousand feet deep, and could run on water if moving fast enough due to its abnormally light and aerodynamic structure.

Emerald threw another kick. Naomi went up, avoiding it, and tried to send a telekinetic blow, but the walker sank like a rock into the sea, the invisible blow doing nothing more than splashing water up. Five laser blasts erupted out of the blue depths. Naomi almost got fried. Emerald shot back out of the sea and threw a punch.

"Come on, Cruz!" Powers yelled. "Let's help her mop up this mess!"

"Sir, look out!"

Garnet crashed into the sea next to Hornet. A cloud of steam rushed out in all directions. Cruz struggled to keep his surfboard from tipping over. Tangerine was not made to operate in the water, so taking a dip was a no-go. That meant he couldn't rescue Patel either.

"Kennedy, go after her!" Powers ordered.

Emerald did just that and sank again.

Meanwhile, Gilda fought to keep her walker airborne, despite its damaged wing, but gravity soon prevailed. Magenta's descent could only be slowed by its one good wing.

"Mayday! Mayday!" Tim screamed.

"Quiet!" Gilda barked. "We need to land, but there's only sea for miles."

"You'll need to land on one of the Western Union's ships," Tim said.

"Yeah, that'll work out nicely," Gilda scoffed. Then her eyes settled on the one place that wasn't crawling with Western Union foes.

Tortuga was still afloat, but only just. Its remaining pontoons were covered in burns and looked ready to pop at any time. A good portion of *Tortuga* had been vaporized when that beam came from the sky, so Gilda could see the insides of the prison. Some prisoners were jumping out of *Tortuga*, only to drown in the sea. Ignoring the shiver that went down her spine, she flew Magenta over to *Tortuga* and landed on it with a thud.

But she wasn't the only one who had landed there.

"Plato!" York yelled. His walker sped toward her with its blade raised.

Gilda, however, dug Magenta's hand into *Tortuga*'s surface and tore off a huge panel of metal. She got her walker to throw it like a Frisbee. Sapphire flicked its sword and swatted it out of the air. It then fired lasers. Magenta skidded to the right, the lasers flying past, and fired its cannon in retaliation. York avoided it, his walker now before Magenta.

"Just keep it up for a little longer," Gilda told herself. "Just wait for—"

Six metal hands grabbed Magenta from behind, restraining its limbs.

"You are one dangerous little girl," Cruz said through his loudspeakers.

"You think that'll hold me?" Gilda spat.

Sapphire pierced Magenta's side with its sword. York flipped a switch. A charge went through the sword and into Magenta.

"Ms. Gilda!" Tim screeched. "Overload! Over—"

Tim's voice ceased. The entire walker powered down. Tangerine kept its grip on the now-dead Magenta while Sapphire circled around the two walkers. Gilda growled and kicked her console. How was she already beat?

"Nice try, girl," Cruz said. "We know all your walker's weaknesses."

Gilda saw that her radio was the only instrument still working, so she flipped the switch and talked into it. "Who is this?" she yelled.

"So, you're Gilda Plato," York said through the radio. "To think we'd have to sully our hands with a traitor like you."

"I couldn't care less what you think!"

"Don't waste your words on this one," Cruz said. "She is far too proud to hear them."

"You're right," York said. "But perhaps she'll hear out someone else."

A weird dial-up tone came out of the radio. Gilda's eyes narrowed.

The dial-up tone ended. A new voice spoke.

"Gilda, this is your father. Can you hear me?"

Ncame from her mouth.

"Gilda, are you there?"

"Yeah ... is that really you, Dad?"

Dr. Plato sighed. "You're alive. My little girl..."

A few tears managed to escape Gilda's eyes.

"Gilda, you've been through so much," Dr. Plato said, sounding pretty teary-eyed himself. "I know how close you were to Henry Marker, how upset you were after the Bunker attack, how you wanted to make things right. I love you. Do you know that?"

"I do... Love you too."

"I'm sorry I wasn't there for you," Dr. Plato said, sounding small. "Work has always been my main focus. Perhaps if I had been a better father, you wouldn't have been foolish enough to run off with enemies of the Western Union."

The heartfelt reunion was over. Rage woke Gilda up.

"Dad, you don't get it," she protested. "The Western Union has been lying to the world. They created Incognito and Cloak. It's been Cloak that I've been fighting, not the Western Union. Cloak was responsible for the attacks on the Bunker, the Pale Pyramid, the Helios Tower, and *Leviathan*. And that's just the beginning. They've been working with the Chinese Empire. If Cloak isn't stopped, who knows what'll happen?"

"A child shouldn't be concerned with such matters, even if they are true. Incognito and the Helmet Man are monsters for using you."

"Look, you're right about Incognito. It was a mistake ever to trust him. But Slate—I mean, the Helmet Man—is different. He's only trying to help."

"Gilda, you might be executed for what you've done!"

"I think it is time we ended this conversation," Camilla Ryder said. Her walker landed on *Tortuga*'s flat top. Much like Gilda's walker, Obsidian was slender and had long legs. It could also fly. Two wings retracted into the black walker.

"Ryder..." Gilda snarled. "So, you're here too. What's that piece of crap you're flying?"

"Young lady, you're already in trouble," Dr. Plato said. "Stop this—"

His voice was cut off. Gilda was saddened to hear it go.

"I thought your father could talk sense into you," Ryder said. "I was wrong. I shall have to use Obsidian to discipline you on his behalf."

Inside her walker, Ryder wore a black jumpsuit, her blonde hair tied back in a ponytail. Her doll-like eyes were locked on Magenta.

And her walker held a squirming figure in its claws.

"Slate!" Gilda yelled. He had just got out of prison, only to be recaptured. Was this what they called cruel irony? It sure felt like it.

Ryder made sure to hold the Helmet Man tight. "Incognito is dead, both you and the Helmet Man are captured, and it will be only a few short moments before your other companion and the *Eodum* are also defeated."

Slate wriggled around. He was encased in the hardened goop that had hit him earlier. A few bolts of energy came off him, but nothing that could do any damage.

"You crazy lady," Slate growled. "What's with your walker? It feels so much like me. Did the Western Union use my DNA for something? That's patented!"

"If anyone holds a patent on your DNA, it is us," Ryder told him in her blank voice. "The Western Union made you. We can do with your blood as we see fit."

"So, you admit it," Gilda said. "You admit the Western Union created the Gifted."

"For the sake of justice," Ryder said. "But I will not argue ethics. All I am doing is waiting for reinforcements."

Slate snickered. "Hey, so are you gonna lick me like last time?"

Gilda, despite the situation, did a double take. Same with Cruz.

"That was a unique moment of weakness for me," Ryder said, although if one looked real closely, one could tell she was blushing, only just.

"That's what all the ladies say!" Slate laughed. "Wait ... that's not funny."

"Ma'am, I believe Powers is approaching," York said.

"Excellent," Ryder said, getting back to her regular abnormal self.

A bulky yellow walker got on top of *Tortuga*. It carried a limp figure wrapped in a white gown. The walker lumbered over next to Obsidian and dropped the body before it.

"Naomi!" Gilda screamed. No, this wasn't right...

"I am surprised at your efficiency, Powers," Ryder said. "But where are the others?"

"Kennedy messaged me," Cruz answered. "She has rescued Patel. They are headed back to the nearest aircraft carrier."

"Good to hear that none of your squad has perished. And it looks like I can bring Ms. Plato back alive to her father. He will be very..."

Ryder trailed off, thinking for a moment. Her lifeless eyes then snapped to the limp figure. She got her walker to reach down and tear away the white gown.

Underneath it was an unconscious Hank Powers.

The yellow walker punched Obsidian before it had a chance to ready its weapon. The force of the blow was so strong that Ryder's walker flew off its feet and collided into Sapphire. Both the mechas fell into a pile of tangled metal limbs.

"Ma'am!" Cruz shouted before Magenta broke free and fired its cannon. The shell destroyed Tangerine's left leg. Cruz cried out as his walker fell backward.

Smirking, Gilda couldn't help but be proud. Magenta just needed a moment to reboot. Someone had made improvements on her walker to compensate for its weaknesses. She could only imagine the expression on Slate's face when he saw who that someone was. Then Gilda felt stupid as she remembered how no one could even see Slate's face. Not enough sleep...

York made Sapphire stand up and moved in to attack Gilda and whoever was piloting Hornet before noticing something that made him screech his walker to a halt.

"Impossible!" York shouted. "How did he escape?"

The Helmet Man dusted off the burnt crumbs that had once been the hardened goo. He had channeled his energy to his extremities so he could produce a tremendous amount of heat, burning away his restraints.

"You almost had me fooled with your act," Slate told Naomi. "But I always had faith. I was just waiting for you to make a move before I escaped from that crap."

"I bet you only just now thought up a way to free yourself," Naomi scoffed from inside Hornet. She now wore a white flight suit that had been underneath her gown.

"You hijacked a walker to sneak up on us," Ryder said, her own walker standing back up. "I didn't think any of you were that clever."

"Not all of us," Naomi said. "Just me mainly."

"Ma'am..." Cruz said, his walker still down.

"You are still outgunned," Ryder told Naomi. "I would advise surrender."

"Ma'am, look!" Cruz yelled, his suave voice cracking.

Ryder turned her walker around to see what had spooked him.

An aircraft carrier was levitating hundreds of feet above the sea.

It hung there for another five seconds before dropping on top of a smaller ship, flattening the vessel. Even from this distance, the sound was brutal and loud.

Everyone besides Ryder was dumbfounded.

"Incognito managed to survive," she said. "We are all going to die."

"What?" Powell screamed. "Incognito is still alive? That little... Fire *Excalibur* again! Send that sucker to oblivion!"

"Sir, some of our ships will be destroyed as well," General Herman warned.

"That's a price I'm willing to pay," Powell shot back, his eyes wild and hands shaking. "Those soldiers signed their lives away to me. I will dispose of them as I see fit. Now fire *Excalibur* again, or I'll have you all shot!"

***

A second aircraft carrier was lifted out of the sea. Fighter jets, unicopters, and dozens of crewmen toppled off its flight deck and smashed into the water below. The massive ship swung like a baseball bat, swatting away four airborne unicopters. They were reduced to wreckage. The carrier was finally and roughly deposited back into the sea where it proceeded to sink. York found himself fixated. Cruz muttered a Hail Mary.

"All those people..." Gilda whispered.

"I gotta stop him," Slate said.

"Hurry and be careful," Naomi said from inside Powers' walker. "Incognito might end up killing himself if he continues."

"I'm counting on it," the Helmet Man spat, shooting up at incredible speeds.

"You shall not escape," Ryder said, flying after him. But Hornet grabbed Obsidian's leg before it could go very far. Ryder tried to pull her walker free, to no avail.

"I think we should let the boys play by themselves," Naomi told her.

Slate left the others behind, heading for another aircraft carrier being lifted out of the sea. Flying around the floating ship, it took him a moment to find his rescuer.

Incognito had his scythe embedded in the hull of the carrier. Like the ship, he was floating. Slate also noticed that Incognito's left arm was missing. A shrieking marine from the carrier fell past him, plummeting into the sea.

"Uh, it seems you have your hands—sorry, *hand* full," Slate said. "You might want to take it down a notch because, you know, you might die and stuff."

Most of Incognito's clothes were scorched, as was his mask and ponytail. The stump of his left arm had been cauterized. Incognito had only dodged the full brunt of *Excalibur's* beam by a millisecond. He was neither happy nor forgiving.

With a flick of his wrist, he tore his scythe from the aircraft carrier. It stayed in the air for a second before falling into the water upside down.

"Hey, don't make me put the hurt on you, old man!" Slate snapped.

"Western scum..." Incognito hissed. "All of them need to drown like rats."

Slate was about to give a witty reply when Incognito flew right at him. He smashed into the Helmet Man, and they both flew back several hundred feet.

"What's the big idea?" Slate yelled.

A beam of light erupted from the sky. It struck right where Slate and Incognito had been. A huge section of sea evaporated. Steam erupted in every direction. A tidal wave as tall as a building was formed that capsized two smaller Western Union ships. The light disappeared, leaving behind a massive amount of collateral damage.

Incognito pushed Slate away.

"Oh ... thanks for the save, I guess," Slate mumbled.

"Foolish swine. Did they really think the same trick would work twice on me?"

"Still, one hell of a trick."

Incognito didn't privilege Slate with a response. He was too busy watching the black submarine emerging from the water.

"The *Eodum* is here," Incognito said. "At last, we can leave."

"Yeah, about that..." Slate said. "We still have a lot more enemies to deal with. In the meantime, another beam might get lucky and blow us away."

"No, it's over. The Westerners have reached their limit."

***

"It's over," Redwood said. "We've failed."

Everyone in the command center stayed quiet, except for Powell, who was grinding his teeth down to the gums. The holographic screen showed images of sinking aircraft carriers, crumpled unicopters, and floating corpses.

"Tell our men to pull back," Kazakov ordered in an unsteady voice. "We need to preserve as much of our forces as we can for—"

"I didn't order you to pull back..." Powell said, wrapping his hands around a nearby chair, squeezing it with incomprehensible outrage. "Keep fighting... Wait for *Excalibur* to recharge... Can't stop till he's dead..."

"Sir, that won't work," General Cromwell said. "I'm afraid—"

"Then we nuke them!" Powell bellowed, making everyone jump out of their skins. "Nuke them all! Incinerate their flesh! Detonate *Tortuga's* nuclear device!"

Redwood and the other generals exchanged glances. Even Vice President Reynolds looked unsettled.

"Sir, I'm afraid that's impossible," an officer said.

"And why might *that* be?" Powell snapped.

"Because ... it was destroyed when *Excalibur* was fired at *Tortuga*."

"Then we'll fire a nuke from one of our nearby subs!"

"The Chinese might think we're attacking them," Redwood said. "To fire a nuclear missile would be suicide. And our men are still out there."

"I have no use for failures!"

"Then we have no use for *you*."

Powell spun around, ready to pounce, but a fire was gleaming in Redwood's eyes, a fire that broke Powell's rage for a second.

"What was that?" Powell whispered harshly.

Redwood narrowed his eyes. "Under section nine of the Western Union Charter, the head of the Western Union—i.e., the president of the United States of America—can be impeached if there is a majority vote by the Western Union Governing Council."

A stone-cold silence gripped the room for an entire minute.

General Herman then spoke. "The Governing Council will need to be fully assembled in order to have an official impeachment. However, for a temporary suspension, we five will suffice."

"Nonsense!" Powell barked. "Guards, get in here!"

The doors to the command center burst open. Five men rushed in. They wore green uniforms and carried compact machine guns.

"Arrest Redwood!" Powell ordered. "If he resists, shoot to kill."

The men started to approach Redwood when Kazakov stared daggers at the guards, stopping them in their place.

"You will not obey Powell," Kazakov told them. "We generals forbid it. The president is no longer in a proper state of mind. Isn't that right, Cromwell, Herman?"

General Cromwell was relatively new to the game, but he did know when to abandon ship. He nodded to Kazakov. "Yes, you are sadly correct."

Herman sighed. "I agree. President Powell is no longer fit for duty."

Powell's anger was fading, replaced by confusion. He turned to his vice president, but Reynolds could only shrug.

With initial hesitation, the guards now pointed their weapons at Powell.

"Guards, escort the president to his quarters," Redwood said.

It was very difficult for him to hide the satisfaction in his voice.

***

The *Eodum* pulled up next to *Tortuga*, and the hatch to the submarine opened up. Abrafo and a good many other prisoners were the first to board. Abrafo and his men had been put in a holding cell after their failed mutiny, but when *Excalibur* was fired, their cell door was blown off its hinges, giving them the opportunity to escape.

Naomi and Gilda boarded next. Magenta landed on the *Eodum's* back and sank into the vessel via an elevator. Hornet, however...

"I have no use for this now," Naomi said, getting out of the big yellow walker.

Powers, still lying on top of *Tortuga*, woke up, muttering to himself.

With little reverence, Naomi waved her hand at Hornet. It was knocked overboard and crashed into the water.

"Ah, my walker!" Powers yelled, now wide awake. "You witch, you'll pay for that! I have never been so tempted to smack a lady!"

"You shouldn't be tempted by things you can't possibly achieve," Naomi said, wagging her finger with a smile. "Besides, you'd only hurt yourself with that toy."

"Harassing my men is unforgivable, even if they are simpleminded," Ryder told her.

Powers nodded. "Yeah, you tell—hey!"

"Don't provoke them, Ryder," Redwood ordered over the radio. "We don't have the tactical advantage. Let them go."

"The Helmet Man cannot escape," Ryder said, focused on Slate, who could be seen approaching. "I could destroy that submarine with a single shot."

"Incognito has won," Redwood said. "That is the unfortunate reality. We also have some problems with the chain of command that need to be addressed. We'll get another chance to destroy Incognito, but we blew this one."

"We cannot let this opportunity slip by."

"Ryder, if you so much as threaten Incognito or one of his thugs, I shall personally activate the self-destruct system within your walker. Am I clear?"

"I understand my position," Ryder said, but she kept her eyes on the Helmet Man.

Slate landed on the *Eodum*. Naomi was waiting there for him. All Western

Union forces, with the exception of Ryder and the SWS, kept their distance from the submarine, although they were still on full alert. Naomi surveyed the sea around them. Three aircraft carriers had sunk, tens of unicopters were destroyed, and countless bodies littered the water. Half of *Tortuga* had also been annihilated. The prison floated dead in the sea as smoke rose from its wound.

"We did a serious number here," Naomi said. She wasn't smiling anymore.

"I didn't want any of this," Slate said.

"Is that so? Prison really has changed you, for the better too."

"I don't know about that. All I know is we need to get back to fighting our real enemy. Maybe these dead soldiers would forgive us if they knew what we were about."

"I sincerely doubt that," Naomi said. She climbed into the submarine. Slate followed her. "Yeah, no redemption for us."

***

A short time later, the *Eodum* submerged, leaving behind the desolation. Naomi led Slate through the submarine. She kept her mouth shut.

Slate turned to her. "So, where are you taking me?"

Naomi continued to be silent.

"Oh, that's how it is. Fine, keep quiet. I don't have to talk either." He was quiet for five seconds. "Yeah, how'd you like that? Not so nice, is it?"

Rolling her eyes, Naomi opened the door to the common room. Slate stepped inside. He noticed food had been put out and had already been substantially sampled by two people.

Kevin Straper finished off a cracker. "Hey, Slate! You're out of the can."

"Good to have you back, Helmet Man," Gilda said, leaning against the wall.

It was apparent even to Slate that Gilda and Straper had grown over the past year. Straper's once horrid acne had faded away, and his lengthy blond hair was now tied behind his head. Gilda had become more muscular, her purple hair slightly longer. Dark circles under her eyes revealed a lack of sleep. Gilda and Straper didn't seem like the innocent misfits he had grown attached to. Now they bared more of a resemblance to veteran soldiers. Slate's initial cheer at seeing his young friends was ebbing into dark realization.

"Got nothing to say?" Gilda snorted. "That's a first."

Slate decided to play along. "Nah, just admiring how ... mature you've gotten!"

"Whoa, pervert alert!" Straper exclaimed. "That's our Slate, I guess!"

Gilda shot Slate a dirty look, but she couldn't really stay mad.

"I'm glad you're enjoying yourself," Naomi said, giving Slate her own dirty look. "But I think our reunion will pale in comparison with this."

She gestured to a doorway on the other side of the room. An old man emerged. He wore khaki shorts, a Hawaiian shirt, and a warm smile.

"Incognito told me you hadn't changed much," the man said. "But my word, Slate, you haven't aged a day. And here I am, almost as old as the Chinese emperor himself."

Slate was speechless. This was what dreams were like. He grew weak at the knees, disoriented. This was too good to be true. After all this time, his search was over. That man... He was much older, but there was no mistaking. It must be... It was definitely...

Slate dared ask the question.

"Dad...?"

***

Miles from where *Tortuga* had surfaced, a lone marine grasped a life preserver. His arms were getting weaker by the minute. He barely had the energy to yell anymore. That monster, that fiend known as Incognito, had flipped over the aircraft carrier that he was on with that weirdo ability. What made it even worse was that he saw the terrorist escape on his submarine, along with the Helmet Man. So many dead, so many friends, and for what?

The marine knew he didn't have long to live. He could feel himself getting colder, almost as if he were covered in snow.

Then something dawned on him. It took a while to notice, but he wasn't in the water anymore, and the coldness was now bone-chilling in strength.

The marine snapped his eyes open and looked around. He was resting on a giant slab of ice. He felt the cold surface in disbelief. How could this be? This was the Caribbean Sea, not the Arctic... Maybe the ice came from one of the sunken ships. Yeah, that could be it.

"Goodness, you must be tuckered out if you're A-okay with lying on ice!"

The marine yelped. Sitting up, he saw a thin young woman standing on the block of ice with him. She wore a leather outfit that consisted of black go-go boots, skintight pants, fingerless gloves, a vest that showed off her bony arms, and a black cape that nearly touched the ice. The cape's collar pointed up, overshadowing the back of her head. The young woman also had spiky gelled hair and an angular, androgynous face. The marine couldn't help but think how his sister had looked just like that during her teens, except for the cape. The marine tried to shake his head clear. He must have drunk too much seawater.

"Oh, my, such a catastrophe..." the young woman moaned. "Aircraft carriers sunk, buoyant corpses looking like bloody lily pads, and so much *burning*... Oh, but orders are orders. Can't have Sebastian mad at me."

"Who the hell are you?" the marine muttered.

With surprising force, the young woman grasped the marine's arm.

"They call me Ember," the assailant whispered. "But you can call me lover. Now, let's get to the juicy part, the part where my heart can't stop beating..."

A piercing cold wrapped in pain went through the marine's arm. He let out a scream that made Ember bite her lip in excitement. It took only a second for the marine's arm to freeze solid and be covered in a blue frost.

Ember giggled. "I wish I could savor this, but I have a job to do. Pleasure before work and all that. So, tell me, did Slate manage to escape?"

The marine didn't respond beyond giving a stunned look. At least his nerves were too damaged to feel any more pain, a small blessing.

Ember snapped her fingers. "Ah, that's right. You lesser life-forms know him only as the Helmet Man, a silly yet delicious nickname. All right, so did *the Helmet Man* escape?"

"Eat me," the marine seethed. "Eat me, you freak…"

"Well, if you insist," Ember said, snapping the marine's frozen arm off. It wasn't painful, but the imagery and the snapping were too much. The marine hurled.

"Eww, that's disgusting!" Ember cried, grimacing. She proceeded to lick the severed limb like a popsicle.

"You're not human!" the marine cried, now dry heaving.

Ember tossed the arm into the sea. "Of course I'm not, cutie. I'm a superior being. You saw what I did. I'm … Gifted. Now talk, if you please."

"The Helmet Man got away, along with that Incognito," the marine spat. "You must be working with them! Just you wait! Just you—"

Ember grabbed the marine's neck and absorbed all the heat from it. A moment later, the marine was frozen solid, a frosty corpse.

Yawning, Ember stretched her legs and "accidentally" kicked the body into the sea.

"Whoops, clumsy me!" she yelled. "Better get going. Need to get back to the Forbidden City by the end of the week. My Mentor beckons!"

She crouched down, and flames began to swirl around her. She launched herself upward, leaving a trail of fire in her wake, laughing maniacally as she flew to her master.

CHAPTER 11

Manned by three astronauts, the space station known as *Excalibur* was established as a deterrent against Chinese aggression. Theoretically, it could have been used to decimate the Forbidden City, home of the Chinese emperor. However, that was no longer possible.

A blue semitransparent dome covered the red palace. It was a force field, generated by cutting-edge technology that even the Western Union did not possess. The massive concrete expanse of Tiananmen Square stretched out far into the horizon, having been expanded after the formation of the Chinese Empire. Normally, the square was completely barren, but it had been filled to the brim for the past year.

Three hundred thousand Chinese soldiers stood in ranks around the palace, as well as three hundred walkers. Tents were situated around various points of the square, some devoted to providing food for the soldiers, others to cleaning chamber pots. The walkers were rusted and almost archaic in appearance. It would have been almost more suitable to use old-fashioned tanks. The soldiers themselves were grubby and nearly dead on their feet. Most of them didn't have guns, merely rusted swords. The Chinese Empire was purposefully kept in the dark ages. Much of China didn't even have electricity. Only the industrial areas of the subservient nations had any real technology. Even then, the empire kept tight control of those areas.

The Black Lotus and some imperial research facilities, however, did possess advanced technology, used only with special permission from the emperor himself. Even knowing this, the Western Intelligence Service still debated internally over how the Chinese Empire managed to get its hands on a force field generator.

The generator, in fact, had been a gift.

A gift from Cloak.

***

The agents of the Black Lotus entered the throne room. First to enter was Lily, a young woman wearing a red pantsuit, her hair in two buns. She had snake-like eyes and a depraved smirk, but it faded when she glimpsed at the throne.

Poppy followed her. He wore a conical straw hat and a balaclava. His irises looked like red petals coming off his pupils. A giant bald man with hams for fists came in after, his name being Pansy, but he was anything but. He often served as the emperor's personal bodyguard. Next was a little girl known as Thistle. Long black hair hung off her head like a funeral veil, and she emitted a low buzz like an angry beehive.

"I don't want to be here," Thistle whimpered to herself.

"Hush up," Poppy hissed.

Mistress Lotus herself rolled in. Her body was a black metal ball, four feet in diameter. A carving that resembled her old face was etched on its front, a carving of a lotus on the back. All the Black Lotus agents were cyborgs. They had given up their human bodies in service of their emperor. They were also the children of Mistress Lotus and the emperor, making them loyal to a fault. Although the emperor detested modern technology both on ideological grounds and on a psychological level, he made allowances when it came to his own security and sometimes the military. It also helped that the Black Lotus agents looked deceptively human, with the obvious exception of Mistress Lotus. And at the end of the day, insanity was not logical.

The agents lined up in a rank before the throne and knelt. Mistress Lotus rolled to a stop between them and the throne. The carved face stared at her sovereign.

"Emperor, the Black Lotus has assembled at your request," Mistress Lotus boomed. "Please, make use of me and our children."

Emperor Jin Long laughed and coughed at the same time, making a wet noise. For years, he had not been in good health, mentally or physically. He was now worse than ever. Red robes hung off his frail form. The robes themselves reeked of something spoiled. The nails on the decaying ruler's hands were talons, yellow and pointed. His beard was greasy and had bits of food in it. Attempts had been made to bathe the emperor, but each attempt ended with him having a fit and ordering someone's fingers to be fed to the pigs living behind the palace. Now nobody tried to clean him anymore.

The emperor had something, however, that did look fresh and new. It was his look of devotion. It was devotion to his lord. It was devotion to his Mentor.

Temple stood behind the throne, looming over it. Bloody war paint had been freshly drawn on his towering silver helmet. A dark cloak hung from his broad shoulders, covering his brutal form. Ever since Temple's arrival, the emperor had become entranced with the helmeted beast, obsessively so. The emperor fawned over Temple, keeping him close, fingering his cloak, touching his chest. He even occasionally stroked the silver helmet. It caused the emperor to pass out from euphoria every time he did it.

Everyone had the same thought whenever encountering Temple: Was that the Helmet Man? But nobody thought that for long. To mistake Temple for the Helmet Man would be like mistaking a wolf for a dog, a beast for a tame animal. There was no reason to Temple, only a will, only cruelty.

The four agents of the Black Lotus stayed on their knees, even though the urge to flee was ever-present. Lily's smirk was gone now, replaced by a nervous twitch of the lips. Poppy mentally repeated a Chinese proverb he had heard as a child. It was a feeble comfort. Pansy remained still, frozen in the yellow headlights. Thistle continued whimpering. The guards lining the walls managed to be even stiller. The only time they moved was when one of the guards collapsed and began convulsing or if a guard decided to disembowel himself with his own sword. It had become a regular occurrence.

"I am pleased to see you all assembled here," Sebastian said in fluent Mandarin. "Your emperor has summoned you to assist in several operations that could determine the outcome of our war with the Western Union."

The second-in-command of Cloak stood to the left of the throne. His folded hands rested on top of a white cane. Sebastian wore his usual blue suit and round sunglasses. He always had that awful grin, as though he knew something hilarious was about to happen.

High General Chao Xing stood to the right of the throne, a hairless young man with a swirling dragon tattoo on the back of his head. Xing was fascinated. Terrified and fascinated. He was terrified of Temple, an unpredictable and malicious being with titanic power. His fascination was all that kept him sane, kept him from going off the deep end. How was it this man called Sebastian remained unaffected? How was it this man could actually tame Temple? How was it the almighty Chinese Empire could fall to one being?

It was terrifying and fascinating.

Cloak now controlled the Chinese Empire.

When Cyphrus and her cronies first contacted the empire, Xing was not trusting, to say the least. They were creations of the Western Union, mass-murdering criminals. Associating with them was ill-advised.

However, Xing had managed to work this unwanted partnership to his advantage. Because of Cloak, he had been able to get rid of Mao Long, former prime minister and former heir to the throne. No way would Xing let such a monster become the next emperor. He had hoped that after the emperor's passing, he himself could rule the empire using a puppet ruler. Then the Chinese people would at last get what they deserved: peace and prosperity.

But Xing would easily have preferred Mao Long any day over Cloak.

A man less than three feet tall stood next to Sebastian. He had a shaved head and an indifferent expression. Geppetto was another one of the Gifted who had betrayed Sebastian in favor of Cyphrus. Xing believed that after the foul woman died, Geppetto had no choice but to go back to Sebastian. Could he be a potential ally? Possibly...

"The Black Lotus will stay in the capital until further notice," Sebastian said. "With luck, we shall stop the West before it has a chance to strike."

"Yes, Prime Minister," the Black Lotus acknowledged in unison.

"We are at war, and war is hell. Lucky for you, hell is Cloak's specialty."

***

Five minutes later, Xing found himself walking down a hallway. Sebastian strolled beside him. Ten guards marched ahead. Pansy followed Sebastian, pushing the emperor on an ornamented wheelchair, while Geppetto and Mistress Lotus tagged along. The other cyborgs had gone to their quarters. Temple kept to the rear, stalking them. Xing tried to ignore Temple but was unsuccessful. Maybe he couldn't do anything about the beast, but he could at least try to squeeze information from Sebastian.

"So, Prime Minister, I have heard rumors that you are developing some sort of weapon that will assist the empire," Xing said. "Most likely, you plan to use it on the Western Union's fleet protecting Australia. Am I correct?"

"I couldn't say," Sebastian said. Despite being blind, he had no trouble navigating the halls, hardly even using his white cane.

"There have also been rumors of the Helmet Man escaping *Tortuga*," Xing continued. "I know Cloak has been after the Helmet Man for some time now. Are you planning to capture him soon? Perhaps I can assist."

"No thank you," Sebastian said. "I can't have your inept digits meddling around in the Mentor's affairs. How about we head to the interrogation chambers in silence from here on? Your voice is rather irritating, I'm afraid."

Xing kept his mouth shut, doing his best to hide his frustration. It had been a desperate move to pester Sebastian with questions like that, but what else could he do? He had tried nearly everything to purge Cloak from the Forbidden City. His most ambitious attempt had been seven months ago when he and the other high generals tried to convince the emperor that Cloak was nothing but a leech. Xing had pointed out how Cloak was abusing imperial resources for its own purposes, how the Gifted were spawns of the West, and how they seemed to be giving orders more often than the emperor himself. For a moment, the emperor had been somewhat convinced, outrage sparking in his eyes. Xing briefly felt hope.

But a mere week later, Temple destroyed the Pentagon.

"This is a gift from the Mentor," Sebastian had told the emperor in a silky voice. "Watch the West burn. Enter the temple. Embrace your lord."

Sebastian now turned into a room with the emperor and his posse following. Xing stopped before doing the same and grabbed Geppetto.

"May I have a word?" Xing asked.

"Don't even try it," Geppetto said.

"Wait, I—"

"Don't even try it," Geppetto repeated, his eyes sunken. "There's no escape. Just let it happen. Don't even try to resist."

Xing decided to forego subtlety. "I cannot allow this to happen to my country," he hissed. "Does giving up even make it better?"

Geppetto stared lifelessly at him. "No, but I'm too tired. I'm just ... too tired."

After a moment, Geppetto went into the room. Temple was the only one who remained behind. Xing felt a newfound chill.

Temple turned to him.

Xing almost cried out, but he kept his head and joined the others.

"Glad you could make it," Sebastian said with his usual smile.

The room had a one-way mirror that looked inside a dark chamber, where a man was curled up in the corner, muttering to himself. He wore rags and appeared malnourished. Burns covered his limbs.

"Him again?" Xing asked. "He cannot tell you anything."

"He's a general of the Western Union and a former companion of the Helmet Man," Sebastian said. "I'm sure he knows something. Besides, I'm curious why the Western Union sent him here in the first place."

Geppetto, Mistress Lotus, and Pansy were dead quiet as they faced the chamber. The emperor, however, snickered in anticipation from his wheelchair, drool leaking from the corners of his mouth. Xing just closed his eyes.

Sebastian pressed the intercom button. "Had a good sleep?"

"Johnson? Johnson, is that you...?"

"No, just me," Sebastian said with mock sympathy. "I have more questions for you."

"Questions? I ... I didn't study..."

"No need for that. We're more than happy to give you a refresher."

"I ... I can't remember ... really ... honest..."

The door to the chamber opened. The beast entered.

"I can't remember! Not again! Please, I can't remember!"

Sebastian chuckled. Xing's stomach turned.

Temple took his time with Eisenhorn.

"You wanna hear about that trek through the Sahara again?" Slate asked. "How about my trip to Japan? Or the time I fought a hippo?"

"I think I've heard enough of your stories," Oscar Radcliffe said. He sank into his armchair, having listened to Slate for five hours straight. "Perhaps it's time you talked with your friends. You've barely spoken to them since you were rescued."

"All right, it's just that you're my dad and all. I thought you'd give your own son the time of day. Just saying…"

"Don't pull that card on me," Oscar snapped. "Now go hang out with your friends, or I'll put the smackdown on you."

"Child abuse!"

"Get moving!"

Slate screamed like a brat and ran out of the room waving his hands.

Oscar sighed. "He hasn't aged a day … and he's *still* a pain in the ass."

"That's what makes him so special," Naomi said, walking into the sitting room where Oscar and Slate had been talking. "If you have any buttons that can be pushed, Slate will make sure to pound on them until they're broken."

Oscar smiled. "I feel old just being near the boy. We only realize how precious our time is when standing next to something immortal."

"Slate is far from immortal," Naomi told him.

"He's the closest thing to it."

"I suppose. Did you tell him where you've been?"

"Just that I have been helping Incognito fight Cloak. He seemed satisfied with that answer. He mostly wanted to talk about himself anyway."

"I bet. Anyway, I need to meet Incognito in the infirmary. He's out of surgery and wants to discuss what we'll be doing once we reach Egypt."

"That man never takes a break," Oscar huffed. "But I guess his obsession is the only thing keeping him alive now."

"Pretty soon, even that won't be enough," Naomi warned.

***

Five minutes later, Naomi entered an infirmary filled with fretting stooges. In the center of it all was Incognito, lying in his bed, wearing a hospital gown and his mask. His scythe was leaning next to his bed within arm's reach. Three doctors fawned over him. They checked his IV, monitored machines, and did all sorts of tests. The rest of the men were prisoners that had escaped from *Tortuga*. One of them was Abrafo, who kept close to the bed. They strived to make sure that Incognito was well protected. Naomi thought all they were doing was giving Incognito a swelled head, although they probably couldn't make it any worse at this point.

"Everybody out," she said. "Right now, even the doctors."

"We can't leave him," a doctor said. "He's in dire condition."

"Incognito has nothing to fear," Abrafo said. "Not while we are around."

"Oh, are you going to flex until he gets better?" Naomi jabbed.

"You best listen to her," Incognito said. "All of you leave, except for the woman."

Abrafo and his men slunk out of the infirmary, dragging along the doctors with them. The room was now empty save Naomi and her employer. Bandages were wrapped around the stump where Incognito's arm used to be, but that was the least of his medical problems.

"They were unable to use growth patch technology on me," Incognito said. "I shall have to get a bionic limb."

"Being Gifted has its drawbacks," Naomi said. "So, how did you lose your arm?"

"Damn that mercenary... When *Tortuga* was struck by the orbital weapon, Keito Kusanagi grabbed me as I made myself intangible. I noticed this as I tried to move out of the line of fire, so I slowed down in hopes of shaking him off."

"Then your arm was incinerated," Naomi said. "Did Kusanagi die?"

"I'm not sure. Having a limb burnt off distracted me."

Naomi ignored his snarky comment. "What's the plan now?"

"Everything has been arranged. By the time the Western Union even learns of the gathering in Egypt, it will already have ended. With this rally, rebellion shall ensue. There's only one uncertain variable."

"You mean Slate?" Naomi asked, her voice growing strained. "Was it really necessary to put the others through all that? Did Thomas—?"

"For the greater good, my dear. And the greatest good is to destroy the greatest evil."

***

The cleanup would take days. It should have taken weeks, but they were only planning to gather the materials they could salvage and the bodies of their comrades. Everything else would be left to the sea. They had no time to be environmentally friendly. There was a war to fight.

Fishing nets and scuba divers kept pulling up corpses. Meanwhile, a crane vessel was tasked with lifting Hornet up from the bottom of the sea. Its crane now lowered the yellow walker onto the deck. Seawater trickled from the cockpit.

"It doesn't look bad at all," Powers commented. He laughed, though it sounded hollow. "Just pump out the water, buff out a few scratches, and it's good to go."

"Idiot," York muttered as he leaned on a railing next to Cruz. They had gone to visit Patel in the infirmary, and she had told them she would be out within three days. Kennedy was nowhere to be found, busy reading in her quarters. Now Cruz and York were spending time observing their blundering superior.

"I was giving him the benefit of the doubt," Cruz said. "But now..."

York spat over the railing. "He allowed himself to be captured and hit your walker while you were busy fighting that floating woman. The man's losing his edge."

"That would imply he ever had an edge."

"No, Powers has a strong record. I think he just let it get to his head. Now he's making stupid mistakes. Ryder should have noticed this by now."

"Ambitious, are we?"

"So? You hope that mouth breather remains our squad leader?"

"Well, I'm not thrilled with the prospect, but I would never question the wisdom of Ms. Ryder. She did capture the Helmet Man, after all."

"I have worries about her too."

Cruz sighed. "Yes, we chose a rather unusual assignment, haven't we?"

Meanwhile, Camilla Ryder watched the cleanup effort from the deck of a warship. *Tortuga* would have to be decommissioned, since it was beyond repair, as were the sunken aircraft carriers. Many of *Tortuga*'s prisoners had either escaped or died, but a few had been found among the survivors. Corpses were laid out on the decks of the ships. They had run out of body bags an hour ago. Ryder witnessed many soldiers crying. One of them cradled a body. Another called the widow of a dead marine to offer his condolences.

Throughout all this chaos and pain, Ryder felt only the occasional twinge of sorrow. She didn't even have the emotional capacity to feel disgusted with herself. It was like being dead sometimes, but as she observed all the pain these people were experiencing right now, she thought that perhaps she wasn't so unlucky after all.

Two medics nearby were placing a man on a gurney. His eyes were unfocused, his body was limp, and drool dripped from his mouth.

Ryder approached them. "This is Warden Welsh, I presume?"

"Unfortunately," one medic said. "He had his mind completely pruned. The guy's brain-dead now. Poor sucker."

Pruning was a procedure that erased the memories of a subject. Ryder knew plenty about pruning, having inflicted it on countless others. On rare occasions, one may even have their entire memory wiped, turning them into a vegetable just like Welsh.

"The Helmet Man did this?" she asked.

"That's what the witnesses say," the other medic said. "I didn't know *Tortuga* had its own pruner. The higher-ups must have kept it under wraps."

"Better take him away," Ryder told them. "He will need to be put on life support."

The medics nodded and rolled the gurney inside the ship.

Someone staggered next to Ryder, stealthy despite his condition.

"Kusanagi, you should not be out of the infirmary," she said.

"There are others who need the bed more than I do," Keito replied. He was covered in burns from head to toe, but the growth patches on his skin ensured that he would fully recover by the end of the week.

"Of all the Western Union's forces, you were the only one able to wound Incognito, taking his arm, no less," Ryder said.

"I would have lost if not for *Excalibur* and Incognito's own restraint. That man has powers no mortal should possess. I am lucky to have survived the encounter."

"You are being modest."

Keito closed his eyes. "I also doubt that I will be able to defeat the Helmet Man."

Ryder turned to him as if she had just awoken. "How powerful has he become?"

"So powerful that only someone like Incognito could stop him now. Even your impressive walker might not be enough."

"Ms. Ryder, may I speak to you?" a new voice asked.

Ryder and Keito turned around to see a man approaching them.

"Yes, you are Vincent Quinn, aren't you?" Ryder asked.

Quinn laughed. "I'm privileged that the famous Camilla Ryder knows my name. I've come to retrieve you by request of President Powell."

"Wasn't the president taking a leave of absence?"

"Yes, but this is unofficial business, at least officially." Quinn laughed again.

"President Powell would like a private conversation with you. It'll be a two-day trip on your part."

"Where are we going?" Ryder asked, not sounding the least bit interested.

"We're going to Cheyenne Mountain, Ms. Ryder," Quinn told her.

***

Ryder was not impressed. Most others would be if they took the tour she was about to go on, impressed and horrified.

"Powell has been here for almost eight months," Quinn said as they walked down a barren hall. "He's grown fond of the place. Treats it almost like his personal castle."

"That is not possible," Ryder said. "Powell has been traveling all over the Western Union nonstop since he took office. I have personally seen him touch people, so he couldn't have been using holograms."

Quinn smirked. The two of them were strolling through the Cheyenne Mountain Complex. Made during the Cold War, the bunker had once housed the North American Aerospace Defense Command, or NORAD. The Western Union now used it as its top research facility. It was a city within a mountain, made up of several buildings built on top of a thousand giant springs designed to absorb the shock of a thirty-megaton nuclear blast. Dr. Plato worked here full-time, along with dozens of other scientists who rarely saw the light of day.

"Is he using body doubles?" Ryder asked. "That is the only explanation."

"In a sense, they are body doubles," Quinn said. "But that's just the tip of the iceberg. Perhaps the president can explain things better."

They entered a large hangar. Three walkers stood in it. They were all stripped down to the bone, their inner workings exposed. A team of scientists was fiddling around with wires and computers. Clumsy androids assisted with the heavy lifting. Dr. Plato was supervising, clearly sleep-deprived. He glanced over at Quinn and Ryder and nodded weakly.

"A pleasure to see you again, Dr. Plato," Ryder said. "I am sorry for your troubles."

"My daughter is still in the hands of Incognito," Dr. Plato said.

"I could not help your daughter. She is strongheaded."

Dr. Plato sighed. "I know. Too much like her mother, that one."

"A tour will occupy our minds," Quinn interjected.

"If I must," Dr. Plato said. "All right, I guess we can start with these things." He gestured to the stripped-down walkers. "These are the same type of walker as your Obsidian, Ms. Ryder. I call them Archangels. We created a biological nervous system for these walkers using the Helmet Man's DNA. Because of this, these mechas have a virtually inexhaustible power supply and a substantially quicker reaction time than any normal walker."

"They're perfect killing machines," Quinn said.

Dr. Plato shook his head. "Not quite. Their metal frames can only handle so much. We had to build limits into the Archangels. If I am correct, the Helmet Man has nearly unlimited potential. That's why we're working so hard to create our own Helmet Men."

Ryder seemed intrigued or at least didn't look so vacant anymore.

"That got her attention," a bemused voice said.

Ryder turned around and saw a man about her age enter the chamber. Wearing light blue robes with closed-toe slippers, he had a lean build and long, dark hair that went well past his shoulders. His face was smooth, handsome, and youthful. She had no interest in romance anymore, but she did recognize his attractiveness.

"Ryder, good to see you," someone else said from the right. It was Powell. He wore a disturbing grin only a madman would make.

"You came just in time," the robed man told Powell. "What's your number again?"

"Number twelve, Mr. President," Powell said.

"Twelve already? Geez, we have to make you things last longer. Well, you seem to have gone rabid, Old Yeller. There's only one solution to that."

The robed man took out a gun and shot Powell.

Ryder started to move, planning on taking out the robed man, but Quinn put a hand on her shoulder. He did not appear concerned.

"I'm sorry you had to see that," a voice said from behind Ryder.

She spun around. Her eyes widened. It was perhaps her biggest reaction in years.

Another Powell was standing before her now. He didn't have a mad smile like the Powell who was lying on the floor. This Powell walked over to Ryder and chuckled.

"Number thirteen, right?" the robed man asked.

"Yes, Mr. President," the new Powell said. The scientists tinkering with the walkers didn't even bother to look over. This had become a regular occurrence.

"Mr. President, could you perhaps have 'disposed' of number twelve elsewhere?" Dr. Plato asked, his face pale. "We're trying to work here."

The robed man laughed. "Yeah, I got carried away. Hope you can forgive me. I just wanted to play a little trick on this lovely flower. Seeing the famous Camilla Ryder react like that was definitely worth the mess."

"I would like to know what has just occurred," Ryder said, settling back into her emotionless demeanor.

The robed man put his gun away. "Take a wild guess."

"That is not a body double," Ryder deduced, looking at the dead Powell on the floor.

"It's a clone," the robed man said. "Both Powells you see are obedient replicas."

Ryder looked at him. "And who are you?"

The robed man chuckled. "My dear Ryder, you're looking at the real deal."

The *Eodum* was starting to feel cramped, especially with dozens of muscular fugitives wandering around. The former prisoners of *Tortuga* were restless and unoccupied. Unlike virtually any other prison, boredom was a luxury that was seldom given to them in *Tortuga*. They were used to either working or being tortured. Finding themselves with nothing to do seemed to make them angsty. Gilda and Straper kept to their common room, but they didn't think these men would try anything, not with Incognito or Slate around. Every time Slate walked by, the men would fall silent and make room for the infamous Helmet Man, and they did just that as Slate and Naomi went to the common room.

"Move it! Coming through!" Slate hollered. "Your idol is here! Yeah, I killed the president. I crashed *Leviathan*. I blew up the Helios Tower thingy. Fear me! Love me!"

"So, it's true," one of the men muttered.

"He *does* wear a helmet," another whispered.

Naomi kept her head down, hiding her red face. How could anyone believe this idiot was a terrorist mastermind? Slate had changed out of the prison jumpsuit and now wore his usual getup, a black vest over a black long-sleeved shirt, black pants, black boots, and black gloves. Even though Slate didn't see color, he sure seemed to love his black.

They entered the common room and locked the door behind them. Slate stretched his limbs and chuckled. Straper watched TV, and Gilda slept on the couch. Sweat was pouring off her head, words escaping her lips every now and again.

"Mom..."

"Gilda, get your lazy ass up!" Slate yelled right next to her head.

She jumped awake. Terror was plastered on her face. Irritation quickly replaced it.

"The gang's all here!" Slate cheered. "Except for Thomas, that is."

Thomas was the long-lost British prince who was kidnapped as an infant by Cloak. Through a series of experiments, Thomas had become invulnerable to physical harm, although he still needed air and food. Slate and the others had found him on a deserted island filled with theme-park androids and rescued him. Everyone had kept quiet about Thomas, and Naomi knew that the Helmet Man was starting to notice.

"He's waiting for us," Naomi told Slate, not exactly lying.

"That's pretty vague," Slate said. "Okay, fine. What's been going on with you guys, then? It's been over a year, though I bet it was dull as hell without me."

Naomi let out a breath and rubbed her eyes. Straper lowered his head, lost for words. Gilda, who was no longer irritable, was the one who finally got the ball rolling.

"Do you know about the war?" she asked.

Slate rubbed his helmet in puzzlement. "Uh, what war?"

"Figures," Straper said. He snickered, but his heart wasn't in it.

"Well, he *has* been in solitary confinement for over a year," Naomi pointed out. "Slate, after *Leviathan* was hijacked, the Western Union blamed the United Third and the Chinese Empire for the attack on Rome."

"Hang on, that was Cloak's fault!" Slate yelled.

"Yes, but it's true that the Chinese Empire was involved. It's also true that the military found you near the crash site, where you were subsequently arrested. And let's not forget the fake Helmet Man who appeared on TV to make demands. That's more than enough to implicate the United Third. You're working for Incognito, after all."

"Not something I brag about."

"Neither do I. Anyway, with President Hynes's death, Powell became president soon after, and during his inauguration, he declared war on the Chinese Empire."

"Powell..." Slate growled. "He's even worse than Incognito, if that's fricking possible." He told his friends how Powell had let Cloak hijack *Leviathan* so that President Hynes would be killed, leaving the Oval Office for the taking.

"Dude, Powell's a total psycho!" Straper exclaimed. "He let thousands of people die just so he could become president?"

"That's insane," Gilda said. "I knew the Western Union could be shady, but this..."

"He was also in charge of the Keymaster Project during the later years," Slate said. "I knew him a little. Never liked the guy. Too willing to cross a lot of lines. Man, I bet the whole Western Union has gone to shit under Powell. How bad is it?"

The room was silent. Nobody knew how to describe it, but Naomi gave it a shot.

"There have been many laws passed in the Western Union," she said. "Censorship has increased, there are fierce crackdowns on any objectors, and children as young as fourteen are being conscripted into the military."

"Yeah, that sounds bad," Slate said.

"Everyone is paranoid," Gilda said. "I can't blame them. The Pentagon got bombed. A lot of people died. No one knows who did it, or at least the news isn't saying, but everyone is either blaming the Chinese or Incognito. In the Occupied Territories, the peacekeepers are shooting anyone who looks suspicious on sight, even in the safe zones."

"I saw it happen," Straper said. "Incognito had me go ... uh ... incognito. I had to wander around Istanbul without being seen. It was a training exercise, I guess. Anyway, a Turkish guy took something from his pocket. A peacekeeper thought it was a detonator, so he put one right through the guy's head. Turned out the guy was just grabbing his inhaler. A riot broke out after that. I was lucky to get out of there alive. Not very pretty."

Slate clenched his fists. Not only did that recap tell him how bad things had gotten, but it gave him a hint of what his friends had been through for the past year.

"Enough of this crap!" he exploded. "What the hell did Incognito make you do? Where's Thomas? What's Incognito planning? I didn't break out of prison for *this*. We're supposed to be fighting Cloak, remember?"

"Slate, we haven't heard anything about Cloak since the war began," Naomi said. "The last solid piece of intel that I heard was how the Chinese Empire executed Cyphrus. What happened to the remaining Gifted is a mystery."

"You're saying Cloak's finished? I don't buy it."

"Neither do I, but the war has restricted travel and the flow of information. Fighting Cloak has become even more difficult than before."

"Then what have you been up to all year? Have you just been diddling around or—?"

"Incognito is about to make his move," Gilda told him.

Slate stopped his ranting. "What do you mean?" he asked, though he had already figured out the answer himself.

"The United Third is finally going to implement its master plan," Gilda said, her hands shaking. It wasn't clear if they were shaking from fear or rage. "The Occupied Territories are going to revolt against the Western Union."

***

"I suppose you're wondering what happened to me," the young Powell said. He walked down a long hallway next to Camilla Ryder. Quinn and Dr. Plato followed them.

"The thought had crossed my mind," Ryder said. "I assume your new appearance isn't strictly cosmetic."

"No, it isn't," Young Powell said. "I don't just look younger. I *am* younger. And if all goes according to plan, I'm going to stay this way forever."

"How exactly did you manage this?"

"It's all thanks to the Helmet Man. Dr. Plato and other scientists have been working on some personal projects of mine for quite a while now. The trouble is these projects could never get past the theoretical phase because we were missing a critical piece to the puzzle. But at last, DNA samples were harvested from the Helmet Man during his stay in the slammer. What we've been missing is accelerated regeneration. It's one of the reasons why I wanted to capture the Helmet Man so badly."

"So, the Helmet Man's DNA has given you eternal youth?" Ryder asked, looking bored and tired despite the fairly interesting conversation. "It sounds dangerous to be meddling with science of that nature as well as experimenting on yourself."

"There were a few side effects, but it's a small price to pay for immortality."

They entered a cool room. Fifty glass tubes stood against the walls. Each looked big enough to hold a person. Ryder walked up to one and examined it without much enthusiasm. Looking inside the tube, she could see a dormant humanoid figure. The figure had few features, having more in common with a faceless mannequin than an actual person. It appeared to be made out of transparent red gel with white dots suspended within it. A particularly large white dot floated right in the center of its head.

"We have a few other rooms like this one," Young Powell said, standing right behind Ryder, almost pressing against her. "Bizarre, huh?"

"Mr. President, I ... hah ... wanted to talk to you!" a woman interrupted.

Ryder turned to see a young lady in her late twenties running toward them. She had a strained smile. In an offhanded sort of way, one might say she was pretty.

"Natalie, you've arrived just in time," Young Powell said. "Camilla, this is the scientist responsible for my youth. What a goddess!"

"Oh, please, Mr. President..." Natalie said, blushing and looking at her feet.

"Perhaps Natalie would like to continue the tour from here," Dr. Plato said. "I need to get back to work, if that's all right. This isn't my area of expertise anyway."

Young Powell nodded. "Sure. Quinn, escort Dr. Plato back."

"Are you sure?" Quinn asked, glancing at Ryder.

"We're all friends here," Young Powell assured him. He smiled, but his eyes were full of impatience. Quinn didn't question it. He and Dr. Plato left.

"I guess it's only us three now," Young Powell said, putting his arms around both women. Ryder glanced at him. She now strongly suspected that Powell had done more than just become younger. He had also altered his features to make himself more attractive. This observation was made in the most clinical of senses.

"Uh ... so ... uh ... where should I begin?" Natalie stuttered, slipping out from under Powell's arm. "Ah ... yes, the clones ... right... You see, Ms. Ryder, these gelatin people you see in the tubes are made from the same substance as growth patches. Nanotechnology, you see ... the nanobots, they ... uh..."

"Take your time, Natalie," Young Powell told her.

Natalie blushed again, her entire face as red as a cherry. "Yes ... well ... the nanobots are given instructions to rebuild a person based off ... uh ... their genetic code. Yes ... ah ... they do it much like how growth patches regenerate missing limbs and whatnot. The problem was ... however ... that it's difficult to grow a person from scratch. We needed the Helmet Man's DNA to stabilize the process. Otherwise, the clones would simply ... hmm ... fall apart... Yes, we can also make it so the nanobots build the neurons in such a way that, you know, the clones already have memories, as well as make them obedient and loyal. It's like reverse pruning. We're putting in fake memories rather than ... uh ... removing real ones."

"These things are proto-clones," Young Powell said. "We call them Tabulae Rasae. That's Latin for 'blank slate.' Clever, ain't it?"

"I thought up the name myself!" Natalie burst out, forgetting herself for a moment. She blushed yet again and covered her mouth.

Young Powell laughed. "No need to worry about modesty. You of all people have earned the right to brag."

Natalie blushed so hard that steam nearly came from her ears.

"I was told you are attempting to make an army of Helmet Men," Ryder said. "Have you succeeded in making clones of him yet?"

Young Powell sighed but maintained his smile. "We've tried, but the Keymasters were very protective of their supersoldiers. Those jackals made it so that replicating their DNA would be nearly impossible. It was to prevent our enemies from creating supersoldiers of their own should they capture one of ours. We tried to clone the Helmet Man several times, but the clones barely get halfway through forming before turning into a puddle of crap."

Young Powell walked over to a door and opened it. He led Ryder inside with Natalie following close behind. Inside this new room was a giant circular tub built into the floor. The liquid inside was spinning like a whirlpool. Electric sparks came off it every now and then. It was silver in color.

"We call it pandorium," Young Powell said. "This is what the Helmet Man's headgear is made of. The liquid has got to be constantly charged and moving. Otherwise, it'll harden into unbreakable material."

"What are its properties?" Ryder asked.

"It's attracted to psychic energy." Young Powell shrugged. "I know, sounds dumb, but it's true. It also acts as a perfect insulator. The pandorium helmet limits Slate's powers. If that helmet should break, we'd all be screwed. I suspect that's why Cloak's after him. They want to harness his power and do nasty things with it."

"This pandorium is for the army of Helmet Men you wish to make?"

"I pray we won't need it, but better safe than sorry. Any more questions?"

Ryder thought deeply for a moment before speaking. "During the Pentagon attack, a body double of yours was reportedly killed by the perpetrator. It was a clone, correct?"

"Good thing the clones had already been put to use by that point," Powell said. "I might be dead otherwise."

"So, not only do you use the clones as body doubles to avoid assassination, but you also use them to hide the fact that you have become immortal."

"The citizens of the Western Union would be a bit befuddled if they found out about my 'condition.' Besides, the people aren't ready for immortality."

"But you are?"

Young Powell stopped smiling. His face was now dead serious. Natalie squeaked and backed away from him.

"Do you know why you're here?" Young Powell asked Ryder. "The *Tortuga* disaster has put my political future in jeopardy. I didn't expect one of my clones to malfunction like that. The worthless lookalike made everyone think I went bananas."

"I'm so sorry, Mr. President," Natalie whimpered. "I told you the clones had a short half-life. I ... I didn't think... Please, forgive me!"

"No, don't go blaming yourself, Natalie," Young Powell said. "Those clones should have been replaced every month, not every six weeks. Ryder, I must confess that the clones we've created don't last very long. Even with the Helmet Man's DNA, their bodies simply aren't stable. Insanity is one of the first symptoms of breakdown. Now Redwood and the others are using this opportunity for a power grab. I might get impeached, and should they find out what I've been up to in Cheyenne Mountain..."

"You want me to spy on Redwood," Ryder said, not sounding the least bit surprised.

Young Powell smiled again. "Would you do it? You could be immortal."

"Living holds no pleasure for me," Ryder said. "Why would I wish to do it forever?"

"Nothing gives you pleasure anymore?" he asked, moving closer to her. "What about the Helmet Man? I heard you licked him when making the arrest. Interesting... Must have been a real rush, being so close to something so volatile. I bet you like hunting him, don't you? You like the chase. It makes you feel alive..." He leaned in, whispering in her ear. "Well, I could make it so you always feel alive."

"I only serve the Western Union," Ryder said.

"Ryder, I *am* the Western Union. You can serve the Union *and* hunt the Helmet Man. Anything for the hunt again, right? It's the only thing that jolts you. And you can't possibly believe that Redwood would make a good leader. Sure, he's reasonable, at least seemingly, but he shows far too much restraint in the heat of battle. Rather than letting you go after the Helmet Man and

Incognito, he threatened to blow you up!"

Ryder raised her chin slightly.

Powell grinned wider. "The Western Union needs strength now more than ever. I can offer that. I can protect the people, not just from the Chinese or Incognito but also from themselves. You've seen the worst of people. You know they can't be allowed to do as they please. That's why you are so loyal to the Western Union, right? It put the world back on track after the Choke, after the human race almost lost it all. But just wait … things will disintegrate again without me pretty soon. You can stop that, though. All you need to do is tell me how Redwood plans on attacking the Chinese. Then I'll grant your wish."

Ryder backed away from Young Powell. Her dull eyes sized him up.

"Answer one more question," Ryder said.

"All right, shoot."

"Few people know what actually happened at the Pentagon," Ryder said. "The public was told it was a bomb. Only a handful of government officials know the real truth, that a man in an elongated silver helmet was responsible."

A dark look went over Young Powell's face, a glimmer of fear as well.

"My question is this," she continued. "Is he stronger than the Helmet Man?"

Powell frowned. "Well … that's possible. Probable, even. Why do you ask?"

"Because I might want to hunt down this new Helmet Man instead," Ryder said with an almost unnoticeable glimmer in her eyes.

***

Hours later, Young Powell paced his personal quarters. His miniature palace was lavishly decorated with silk sheets, ornate furniture, and oil paintings. Natalie had just left to resume her research. She was becoming clingier each time she came here. *What an idiotic girl,* Young Powell thought, although she was an easy way to pass the time. All women were feebleminded, in his opinion. Even that Ryder was easily fooled. She completely believed that his clone had malfunctioned. Young Powell knew he didn't always act best under pressure.

Neither did his clones. Appealing to her disgusting obsession with the Helmet Man was a big help as well. He snickered. Now that he'd had his pleasure, it was time for business.

Young Powell pressed the intercom button. "Quinn, get me a secure line. I wish to contact our secret friend. We haven't really been on speaking terms, but now might be the time to reignite our relationship."

"Sir, the line is ready and safe," Quinn said.

"Excellent," Young Powell said. He turned the intercom off and pressed the button next to it. A holographic phone popped up and started ringing. Young Powell decided to have a drink. He walked over to the fridge and took out some chilled wine.

As he poured it into a glass, a surge of energy came from his hand. The glass shattered, cutting his hand. Wine spilled all over the floor.

Young Powell swore. He hastily wrapped his bleeding hand with a towel. This was becoming more frequent. Natalie had warned him that the Helmet Man's DNA might do strange things to his body, but this? Deciding to look on the bright side, the president wondered with a smirk if he might be able to shoot lightning soon. Maybe he'd shock Redwood...

The holographic phone continued to ring. Young Powell started to wonder if it was going to be answered. But sure enough, it was. The phone stopped ringing. A man with a twisted grin materialized into the room.

"Mr. President, you look absolutely dashing," Sebastian said. "What's your secret?"

"That secret isn't going to leave my lips anytime soon," Young Powell said. "But I got another secret that might interest you."

"Do you think that's appropriate?" Sebastian asked. "We are at war, after all. You want the world. Cloak wants the world. Our goals are incompatible."

"Not quite as incompatible as you may think."

"Aren't you upset we tried to kill you?"

"The important thing is you failed. Listen, I called because I want to neutralize Fleet Admiral Redwood before he becomes a problem for me."

"Oh, how exactly are you planning on doing that?"

"Redwood is about to wage an assault on the Chinese Empire, leaving me out of the loop." Young Powell scowled. "And *nobody* leaves Powell out of the loop."

CHAPTER 14

Ever since he was imprisoned in his torture chamber, General Randolph Eisenhorn had preferred being asleep to his agonizing reality.

It was only because of Klara that Eisenhorn had lasted this long. Every time he fell asleep, Klara was there. He always awoke on a small island made from white sand, a sea of pitch-black water surrounding the island, the sky illuminated with stars and planets. He didn't care about any of that so long as Klara was there.

She was always dressed in an odd assortment of mismatched and colorful clothing. A multicolored scarf covered her head, concealing all but her eyes. She also wore red shorts over white long johns, big yellow sneakers, a green long-sleeved shirt, and blue mittens. Sometimes she would talk. Other times she would say nothing at all.

"You're doing quite well," Klara said. "Pain can be overcome."

"Easy for you to say," Eisenhorn spat, but there wasn't any real malice in his words. All his troubles had begun when the Helmet Man showed up. Eisenhorn had been in charge of a cadet training facility at the time. Then Cloak killed all his cadets. Then Johnson died. Then the Western Union sent him to this depraved madhouse as an ambassador. Why they chose him, a crazy old man, to represent the West was anyone's guess.

Eisenhorn first met Klara in a dream. Even now, he didn't know if she was real or just a figment of his decaying mind. But there was no denying that she had predicted an assassin would try to kill him with a syringe. When Eisenhorn had awoken, he found that Klara's prediction had come true. He had barely survived the attempt on his life and accidentally killed the assassin. On Klara's instructions, Eisenhorn then hid the syringe in his room. He wasn't sure if it was still there. The Chinese had moved him to a different room after the episode. He had hoped that in return for helping take down Mao Long, Xing could pull some strings so that he could get his old room back.

Then Cloak arrived.

There had been a coup. Everyone was frightened. All the servants whispered to one another, pale-faced and wild-eyed. Even the soldiers were jumpy. Shu, Eisenhorn's personal caretaker, had visited him regularly, often looking like she wanted to cry, but an unearthly tension always prevented her from doing so.

"They killed another," she whispered, wrapping her arms around herself. "The head cook was accused of attempting to poison the emperor. He was executed. That man... That man with the helmet did it. Why doesn't he speak?"

Eisenhorn quickly ran out of reassurances and wisecracks. He had been confined to his new quarters, but every glimpse of the outside world told him that things were going downhill. His old friend Hynes had died, and that scumbag Powell was now president. Shu didn't know anything else except that the Western Union had declared war on the Chinese Empire. That was the only good news for Eisenhorn. He might have even been glad if the Western Union decided to nuke the Forbidden City, except that Shu was here, not to mention himself. Shu had made this madhouse bearable for him. Every time he was about to go on a racist rant about the Chinese, he remembered Shu, and occasionally Xing or Slate, reminding himself they weren't all bad.

Then the night came when Eisenhorn was taken.

It was fast and swift. He had been sleeping, about to meet Klara once again, when five Chinese soldiers burst into his room. He managed to knock some teeth out and break a nose, but they eventually subdued him.

That had been eight months ago.

"I never heard of someone daydreaming inside a dream before," Klara said.

Eisenhorn shook his head, his attention on Klara once again. Like Shu, Klara had kept him from going even madder. It did irk him that she wasn't spilling the beans on what she wanted that syringe for, what her true identity was, how she could show up in someone else's dreams and predict the future, or even her ultimate reason for helping him.

"Just lost in thought, I guess," Eisenhorn said. "Klara, I don't know how much more I can take. I'm not ever gonna get used to this torture."

"You must endure," Klara told him.

"I don't have to do squat! Give me answers, and I might be a little more cooperative. Better yet, why don't you take off that stupid outfit?"

"I don't want to," she whispered.

"I wouldn't mind seeing how pretty you are underneath that getup," Eisenhorn sneered. "I haven't had a proper date in years."

"That's uncalled for," Klara whimpered.

For a moment, Eisenhorn felt kind of guilty, but then he remembered his predicament. This woman had no right to complain.

"Tell me what you're doing inside my head," Eisenhorn snapped. "You don't know how horrible it is, being tortured by—" He paused, anxious. Silver flashed through his mind. He fell to his hands and knees, the sand coarse yet soothing.

Klara shuffled over to him. "I'm sorry that I can't tell you everything. I told you already that I can't risk letting the enemy get its hands on any information."

"What about that syringe?" he asked. "I haven't said a word about that."

"It's true. You haven't. But there's too much at stake to risk giving you the full picture."

"But don't I have a right to know what I'm risking my ass for?"

"You've never had that complaint with the Western Union."

Eisenhorn got back to his feet. "That's different. I knew all I had to know. I was fighting for freedom, for justice, for world peace. We were gonna set the world straight after the Choke, show them foreigners how to run their countries."

"I also thought that at one time. Little did I know that those ideals were simply an excuse to gain more power, conquer more countries, build more weapons..."

Eisenhorn was about to yell a reply when the island began to shake.

"The dream is ending," Klara said. "We need to be patient, Randolph, because we're only going to get one chance to strike. But time is running out. You must get your hands on that syringe again. Without it, all is lost."

"Klara, you vague woman! This conversation isn't over! What's that syringe supposed to do? It won't just kill me, will it? Tell me! Tell me what it's for!"

But Eisenhorn didn't get his answer. The world simply went black.

***

"Wake up!" a voice cried.

Eisenhorn's eyes snapped open, his arm lashing out on instinct. He almost hit Shu in the face. She yelped and cowered back.

Eisenhorn groaned and rubbed his forehead. "You better be real..."

Shu's surprise wore off. A small smile surfaced on her face, but it was one of pity rather than relief. Eisenhorn's entire body was covered in small burns. He was clearly malnourished, ribs now visible. The interrogation chamber he was in had a one-way mirror looking into it, as well as a pile of rags for sleeping on and a bucket for waste. It smelled almost as bad as the slum outside of Cairo that he had driven through with Johnson and the Helmet Man.

"I cannot believe you have survived so long," Shu said, kneeling beside him. "I have seen many tortured, but never someone I cared about."

"This ain't torture..." Eisenhorn said, getting up on his knees with great effort. "Try having one of those vegan diets. Now *those* are torture! I like my steak ... with barbeque sauce and mushrooms and—" His stomach growled.

"Here you are," Shu said. She lifted a bowl off the floor. Eisenhorn recognized the bowl as his own, but he wasn't paying attention to that. His interest was solely on its contents: fresh milk. Without even thinking about it, he grabbed the bowl and slurped the milk back as though it might evaporate at any moment.

"Slowly..." Shu urged. "You have not had anything to eat in days. Just sip it."

"Easy for you to say," Eisenhorn said, but he reluctantly complied. He quickly finished his milk, although it only seemed to make him hungrier. Was a steak too much to ask for?

"What's Xing up to now?" he asked. "He better be getting me out of this cell. I thought the little weasel was on my side."

"He is doing his best," Shu said. "Master Xing is the only one who is trying to stop those foreigners from controlling the empire. Ever since the new prime minister arrived, things have been worse than ever. I do not know what is happening outside the palace, but I am lucky not to have been executed already." She gulped. "They whipped me once."

Eisenhorn nodded, looking down at his own body.

"Oh, sorry," Shu said. "I am not trying to say my suffering has been any—"

"No, that's fine..."

Shu examined him. "Do they always burn you?"

"No, that ... that silver devil doesn't do it every time. Sometimes he just stands there. To tell you the truth, I'd rather be burned. At least then..." Eisenhorn started to hyperventilate. He fell on his side, gasping like a fish out of water.

"Please, calm down," Shu told him. She started stroking his back, muttering a song underneath her breath. After a moment, Eisenhorn got control of his breathing. His eyes were still full of panic.

"Listen," Shu said. "Master Xing wants to know the real reason you came to the Forbidden City. Depending on your answer, you may be freed. Xing might not have the influence he once did, but he still has many friends."

"Why can't you people just leave me alone?" Eisenhorn muttered. "Everyone hates me... They all just want to use me. Hynes, Klara, Xing... even Johnson wanted to control me ... keep me locked up with those brats. Even you, Shu, you lying woman ... feeding me that crap ... trying to get me to spill my guts so I can stop being useful and get wacked off."

"Don't say that," Shu said, acting stern, though there was a touch of pleading to her voice. "I am not using you."

"Then why am I here? Why do I have to live like this? Goddammit, I'll kill you all! Not just you revolting Chinese, but all those spoiled cowards back home. Just nuke yourselves! Wipe humanity out! Do it! Do it!"

Shu was even more terrified than when she had been whipped. She was about to say something when the cell door flew open and two people entered.

"What's are you doing here?" Lily snapped in Mandarin. "No visitors allowed! Prime minister's orders!" She gave Shu a swift kick in the ribs. Shu suppressed a cry. Lily raised her foot, but Shu scurried out of the room before another kick could come.

Poppy stood next to Lily. He looked down at Eisenhorn, his strange poppy-shaped irises catching the general off guard, silencing him. Before Eisenhorn could say anything, Poppy bent down and swiftly injected something into his neck. Eisenhorn fell into a deep sleep, no dreams to be had, and thus no Klara.

"You don't need to waste expensive drugs on him," Lily scolded Poppy. "Just knock him out with your fist."

Poppy closed his abnormal eyes. "Such brutal methods are beneath me."

Lily looked ticked and inquisitive at the same time. "You think you're better than me, little brother? It's about time I smacked your fat head again."

Ignoring her, Poppy bent over and picked up the bowl next to Eisenhorn. Despite being indoors, Poppy still wore his balaclava and conical hat. He did, however, lift his balaclava enough so that his lower face was exposed. Poppy sniffed the bowl.

"She has been giving the prisoner food," he said.

"That's against the prime minister's orders," Lily noted.

"So it is, and she couldn't have gotten the guards to cooperate on her own. This must be the work of Xing, if I had to guess."

"Do we report this to that prime minister of ours?"

"No, we will report it to our mother. She does not trust the foreigners."

Lily smirked. "I never thought Mistress Lotus would betray the emperor."

"She wouldn't. As long as the emperor lives, she will never go against Cloak. However, knowing the emperor's condition..."

"Do you think we could defeat Cloak?"

"We would all die, most likely," Poppy told her. "But it would be better than listening to one more word of that blind man's drivel."

"I do not know how long my crew can take this," said Captain Young-Bum. "It is one thing to transport a small group of passengers, but having the *Eodum* filled to the brim with dangerous fugitives is completely another matter."

"Have I not paid you a fortune?" Incognito questioned. "Did I not save your wretched life from the Chinese Empire? Do you think I am incapable of controlling my subordinates?"

Young-Bum thought of Incognito's inability to control the Helmet Man, but he kept that comment to himself out of self-preservation. "My men are having a difficult time keeping this crowded submarine in order, and we are running low on food."

"Food is not an issue. We shall arrive in Egypt shortly. You will deposit us there and go back to the hole you came from until I need you again."

Captain Young-Bum nodded, not satisfied but realizing that arguing any further would be futile, even dangerous. He left the infirmary and shut the door behind him. Incognito sat in a chair next to his bed, dressed but still hooked up to several machines. His missing arm was all the more obvious now that his coat had an empty sleeve.

Oscar Radcliffe, meanwhile, sat on the bed. "Do you ever take that mask off?"

Incognito took a moment before replying. "No."

Oscar laughed. "Must be uncomfortable to sleep with one on."

Incognito did not respond.

Oscar sighed. "Small talk was never your specialty, but now you're absolutely no fun at all. You really have lost your soul."

Again, Incognito did not respond.

"Slate and the others will not be controlled so easily. All you are doing is pushing them away. We need them, and they need you. Don't make this difficult."

"This is the only way to make them learn," Incognito told him. "I've tried the carrot. Now I must use the stick."

"Too bad your carrots were rotten," Slate growled.

Oscar and Incognito turned to the door where the Helmet Man had burst in. Two burly men tried to restrain him, but Slate headbutted one of them and nonlethally shocked the other. The two men collapsed in a heap. Slate stepped over them casually.

"Slate, what's the matter with you?" Oscar yelled. "This violent display—"

"Sorry, Dad, but I got a few bones to pick with this creep," Slate said, pointing a finger at Incognito. If Incognito was worried, he did not show it. He merely stayed in his seat and glared at the Helmet Man.

Oscar stood up. "That's enough, Slate. If you want your questions answered, this is not the way to go about it."

Slate ignored his father. He kept walking until he stood in front of Incognito. The terrorist rose from his chair and grabbed his scythe.

"Ask your questions, Helmet Man," Incognito said. "Perhaps my answers will illustrate your position more clearly."

"What have you been doing to my pals?"

"Ah, you've noticed a change in them."

"What did you do, you piece of shit?"

"All I have done is shown them the true face of their decadent empire."

"We had a deal. You said my friends wouldn't have to fight the Western Union."

"And they didn't. I only sent them to the front lines so they could witness the bloodshed firsthand. Anyway, I'm not even obligated to continue following our agreement, since you, against my wishes, ran away to fight Cloak on *Leviathan*."

"I guess letting millions of people get gassed to death ain't a concern of yours."

"Not if they are Western vermin corrupted by ignorance and greed."

"If you think people are that stupid, give them a book or something. How are people supposed to learn if you kill them all?"

A deep quiet gripped the infirmary. Incognito stared at Slate for a tense moment before he began to unplug the tubes and wires that bound him to the medical machines. After fully disconnecting himself, Incognito started pacing the room, using his scythe as a walking stick, his eyes fixed on the Helmet Man.

"Why do you hate the West?" Slate asked. "What makes them worse than the people living in the Occupied Territories? How can someone as smart as you be a racist?"

"Don't tell me you don't hold any prejudices. Someone as single-minded as you must surely have some."

Slate raised his hands. "What can I say? I hate everyone equally."

Oscar smiled despite the situation. Incognito didn't find it as funny.

"I hate Westerners for many reasons," Incognito said. "But the primary reason I detest them is their numbness, their lack of feeling."

Slate made a raspberry. "What are you babbling about?"

Incognito stopped his pacing and turned to Slate. "The West knows no empathy. They do not understand the suffering of others. Individualism and consumerism inspire selfishness. Westerners are addicted to their own comfort. It's not that they don't know that genocide is being committed, that starvation is common, that children must fight in wars. What they can't do is feel pity, to understand the pain of the weak. Apathy is the enemy, Helmet Man, and apathy is what the West is. I once tried to play on their terms, but then I saw what horrors the West was capable of. Then I realized there was no saving them."

"Cloak is the enemy."

"Even if we succeed in destroying Cloak, how long will it be before the Western Union attempts to make more supersoldiers? My sources tell me Powell may be doing just that."

"Not everyone's like Powell."

"But the West has allowed him to come to power. Evil triumphs when good men do nothing, but could one even be called a good man if he allows evil to succeed?"

"Doesn't the same apply to you? You didn't try to stop Cloak from gassing Paris."

"I never claimed to be a good man. Who needs redemption? There is too much to do."

"What are you planning? What part do you think I'm gonna play? Not that I'm gonna do anything you say ever again."

"I wouldn't be so sure of that, Helmet Man, especially since you still have not asked the question that matters most to you."

For a moment, Slate didn't know what Incognito was talking about, but then he had a cold realization. Now more than ever, Slate wished that he had never been locked away. He spoke in a calm and deadly voice, his body still as stone.

"Where's Thomas?"

Oscar lowered his eyes. Incognito didn't reply immediately, seeming to savor the moment.

"He is being kept somewhere far away from here," Incognito said. "I suppose you could call him collateral. Or, if you prefer, a hostage. Consider your other friends in the same position, although they aren't nearly in as much danger as the dear boy. Many enemies of the West would love to get their hands on the long-lost British prince."

"You knew?" Slate snarled.

"Almost immediately. Did you think I wouldn't be able to figure out the boy's identity? I considered the possibility of using him as a bargaining chip against the Western Union, but then I realized that using him against you would be far more rewarding."

"He's invulnerable. I'm not worried about him."

"Most traditional forms of abuse may not harm the boy, but he is vulnerable to suffocation and starvation, as I found out personally through experimentation."

"You're gonna die..."

"Even if you did have the power to kill me, my death would mean the death of the young prince. This, my dear Helmet Man, is the price for betraying me."

"Why do you even want me?"

"Because you're faceless. I want to put into power a leader who is not constrained by race, who all non-Westerners can identify with, who will live forever to enforce my vision."

Slate turned to his father. Oscar just kept his eyes down.

"Helmet Man," Incognito said. "The lives of your friends hinge on your actions. If you truly care for them, cooperation is your only option."

Slate would have tried to clobber him had he not realized the delicate position he was one. For once, the Helmet Man restrained himself. But it wasn't easy.

"What do you want me to do?"

"Patience, boy," Incognito said. "You will know soon enough."

***

The next day, the *Eodum* surfaced from the depths of the Mediterranean Sea. A tugboat docked alongside the submarine, and everyone boarded it except for Captain Young-Bum and his crew, who couldn't have been happier to be rid of their passengers.

Half an hour later, the tugboat docked at an Egyptian harbor. No Western Union peacekeepers were anywhere nearby, and anyone who normally frequented the harbor had long since vacated the premises. Abrafo and his cronies got off the tugboat first and led the group down the rotting docks. Incognito, Slate, and the others followed, nobody making so much as a peep. Something was brewing and only Incognito had a solid idea of what that might be.

A convoy of trucks was waiting for them near an abandoned warehouse.

At least thirty well-armed men were waiting there too. They seemed to be a mix of Africans and Middle Easterners. The leader of these men approached Incognito. Slate, Gilda, and Straper recognized him. Whether they were happy to see him was ambiguous.

"My friends, it is good to see you," Barir said.

"Does he really think we're his friends?" Gilda asked Straper.

Straper replied with a lame shrug. They had crossed paths with Barir shortly after the Bunker was attacked. Gilda hadn't seen him for some time now, but she couldn't say that she had missed him in any respect.

Abrafo laughed. "Is that you, Barir? I thought you would have been blown up by now."

Barir laughed back. "No such luck. You were hoping my position was vacant?"

"I would have liked the promotion." Abrafo walked over and clasped Barir's hand. They both seemed to be in a cheery mood. Nobody else was.

"Barir, did you complete the tasks assigned to you?" Incognito asked.

Barir stopped his bantering with Abrafo. Now he was nothing but business.

"Yes, Incognito," he said with the utmost respect, even bowing a little. Gilda rolled her eyes. "In fact, we could begin in a few hours, unless you wish to rest first?"

"No, I want to get this over with. Be quick about it."

Barir made a little bow again, evoking another eye roll from Gilda.

Everyone got inside the trucks. In a few short hours, Incognito would begin the first phase of his final plan. Gilda tried not to think about it as she took her seat. She didn't want to imagine what she might have helped create, what the world might soon be reduced to. She couldn't escape, not even in her dreams.

Reality was everywhere. The truth was undeniable.

***

"I'm sorry, Slate. I'm so sorry."

Oscar had been repeating these words for some time now. To Slate, they were hollow at best. Gilda and Straper stood nearby, silently looking down at the floor. Naomi was next to the Helmet Man and had a hand on his shoulder. Oscar stood on his other side. The chatter of a massive crowd could be heard from beyond the golden curtains.

"I'm sorry, Slate. I'm so sorry."

"Stop saying that," Slate told his father. "It's not helping anyone. Besides, there's only one person to blame for all of this."

"I have known the man you call Incognito for nearly sixty years," Oscar said. "Perhaps if I had been a better friend…"

"Dad, cut the crap. It's not your fault."

"This isn't right," Gilda said. "I'm just standing here."

Straper didn't say anything. He only took a deep breath through his nose.

Naomi smiled. "Slate, this is the most mature thing I've ever seen you do. I know you're hurting, but this is for Thomas, remember?"

"Yeah, for the kid," Slate said. "Man, the old me would be going on a rampage right now, punching people, kicking babies, lighting stuff on fire…"

"I must admit, I almost wish you were doing that right now," Naomi said.

"What, even the baby-kicking part?"

She snickered. "Maybe not *that*."

"It's time," a cold voice told the Helmet Man.

Incognito appeared behind him. If Slate didn't know any better, he would have thought Incognito was the world's healthiest man, as well as the world's most wanted terrorist. Incognito stood straight with a scythe in one hand, though he didn't use it to support himself. Nothing was noticeably wrong with his posture or breathing. It was like he had been miraculously rejuvenated, if only temporarily. He had also replaced his missing arm with a bionic one made out of hard plastic. With his gloves on, one couldn't even tell the arm was false. So much confidence radiated off him that one could almost see it.

"So, I don't have to say anything?" Slate asked.

Incognito shook his head. "Not this time. But you will eventually."

Slate sighed. He left his friends and followed Incognito at a slow and steady pace. They walked through the curtains. The noise of the crowd was now almost deafening.

Thousands of people saw the Helmet Man and Incognito emerge onto the stage and began cheering. The stage shook from the noise. The crowd was a mix of ethnicities, many Arabs, others African, some Turkish or Persian. Most of them wore dirty and worn-out clothing, but a small fraction wore expensive garments. There was no real common characteristic among these people, except for one.

They all despised the West.

"The United Third has assembled," Incognito said, his voice booming from countless loudspeakers. "Now, at long last, our revolution can begin."

It had taken all the United Third's influence and resources to set up this rally. The problem wasn't so much the rally itself. Keeping it hidden was the main challenge. If the Western Union had found out about this gathering, they wouldn't have hesitated to firebomb everything in the area. But Incognito had been careful. He arranged discreet transportation networks, paid off corrupt Western Union officials, and made sure to silence anyone foolhardy enough to try sabotaging his plans.

"This is Jeff Springer, reporting!" an oily man onstage exclaimed. He held a microphone and wore a strained smile. "This is truly a historic moment. Incognito has finally revealed himself to the world, accompanied by the Helmet Man. Now he shall give a speech to his loyal followers. Oh, and ... uh ... death to the West!"

Springer's legs were shackled to the stage as if he were a performing animal. The United Third had kidnapped him only yesterday. The news anchor had been spewing Western Union propaganda for years. To have him start speaking on Incognito's behalf not only demoralized the West but also gave this rally more credibility.

A seven-foot-tall terrorist had been pointing his television camera at Springer, but he turned it toward Incognito and the Helmet Man as soon as they got onstage. Incognito cleared his throat. The crowd would be addressed in English, since that was the only common language among this diverse audience. Dozens of United Third agents acted as translators for those who were not acquainted with the tongue.

"For centuries, the West has plundered our lands, corrupted our youth, and spat on our beliefs," Incognito said, his voice firm and icy. The crowd's cheers died down. Now they only listened. Slate brooded behind Incognito.

"Ever since its inception, the Western Union has continuously waged war on the rest of the world," Incognito continued. "You've seen the results. Safe zones have been erected throughout the Occupied Territories, where Westerners and a few of our own have taken refuge, though most of our brethren struggle just to make a living wage within these zones. Everywhere else is poverty-stricken and war-torn. Starvation and mass murder are everyday occurrences. The West manipulates us into fighting among ourselves, allowing them to control us easily and exploit our natural resources like the profiteers they are. Should they continue their gluttonous campaign, we will forever be their lapdogs, every ounce of our culture eradicated. This has already happened to all of Latin America. But we have seen past their propaganda, have we not? We know who the puppet masters are. The Western Union is preoccupied with the Chinese Empire. Now is the time to strike.

"I have made plans for our revolution. However, these plans are dependent upon *you*." Incognito pointed at the crowd. "One man cannot change the world alone. Perhaps I could have assassinated their leaders or destroyed their cities, but what would that have accomplished? Such actions would only stir the hornets' nest. It is *you* who must stand up. It is *you* who must put an end to the West. It is *you* who must change the world. I, Incognito, and the rest of the United Third, beseech you all to put an end to your petty differences. Whether you are Algerian, Ethiopian, Iranian, or Somali, we must be united if we wish to purge our lands of Western decay. Only through unity can we have freedom. Only through freedom can we have dignity."

Incognito stopped his rant, letting his words sink in.

"Show us your face!" someone in the crowd yelled.

Others soon chimed in.

"Show us your face, coward!"

"Who hides behind a mask?"

"You want me to be brothers with these filthy sub-Saharans?"

"Sub-Saharans? I dare you to say that again!"

"Who are you, really?"

"Why does that man wear a silver helmet?"

"Jeff Springer, reporting! The United Third rally has taken a turn for the—"

"Quiet, Western pig, or you shall be shot!"

"The Western Union will destroy us all!"

"Incognito does not believe in the words of the Quran! Do not follow him!"

"Show us your face, coward!"

The crowd was becoming dangerously restless. Fistfights broke out. Enraged spectators threw curses at the stage. Some of Incognito's loyal subordinates tried to restore order, tearing men apart from each other and issuing hollow threats, but a riot was certain to break out soon if the situation continued to deteriorate.

Incognito pulled a remote from his pocket and pressed a button.

The loudspeakers emitted a horrible screech. Everyone cringed. Babies cried. The elderly howled. Springer even dropped his mic so he could cover his ears.

Incognito released the button. The screeching stopped. The crowd was back under control, but they still looked ticked.

"I see many of you are distrustful," Incognito said. "That was to be expected. I didn't think you'd follow me without explaining my plan further."

"It is not your plan that bothers us," a man spoke up. "It is your lack of commitment. Everyone here is risking their lives while you remain safely behind the scenes."

Incognito glanced over to his right. He and Slate weren't the only ones onstage. About a dozen men sat on chairs near the side. All these men were influential supporters of the United Third. Among them were two oil tycoons, three warlords, a former Saudi prince, and seven leaders of other terrorist organizations with allegiances to the United Third. They were all plump and richly dressed. The man who spoke was the plumpest of them all. He had a well-trimmed beard, a skullcap, yellow robes, and a polite smile.

"The man who just spoke is Karim Hassan," Springer told the camera, having picked up his microphone. "Hassan is the one of the most wanted terrorist leaders in the world, his bounty second only to those of Incognito and the Helmet Man."

"What you propose is ambitious yet preposterous," Hassan told Incognito. "There is only a minuscule chance of success, but you ask us to take all the risk while you sequester yourself away from the turmoil you have induced."

"What about you, Hassan?" Incognito questioned. "Do you personally go to the front lines rather than feed that substantial gut of yours?"

"Everyone knows who I am. The Western Union hunts me down like a wild animal even as we speak. But unlike me, you have never been seen in person before now. Come to think of it, how do we even know you are the real Incognito?"

Some people in the crowd nodded in agreement. Springer kept his mouth shut, for the cameraman was giving him a deadly stare.

"It does not matter," Incognito said.

Hassan raised his eyebrow. "I believe it does matter. Your followers—"

"These people are not my followers."

Hassan laughed. "Oh, then whose are they?"

Incognito pointed at the Helmet Man. "They are his."

Everyone in the crowd started to murmur. Hassan frowned and looked to his peers sitting nearby, but they were just as confused as he was. Slate didn't say anything. He kept quiet and still. That was all Incognito had asked him to do.

Incognito started to speak again. "I am dying. I am an old, sick man who hasn't much time left, perhaps a year if I am fortunate." He walked over to Slate and put a hand on his shoulder. It took all of Slate's restraint not to send a thousand volts into him.

"It is the Helmet Man who shall lead you after I have gone," Incognito said, squeezing Slate's shoulder. "He of all people knows the cruelty of the West. For you see, the Helmet Man was a supersoldier created by the Western Union."

The crowd looked startled, to say the least. Hassan's lips thinned.

"Yes, the helmet he wears is not a disguise but a prison," Incognito said.

"When he was a child, Western scientists encased his head in metal and forced him to commit murder. Can you imagine the betrayal, let alone the pain? He trusted those men. He put his faith in them."

Incognito let go of Slate, which was probably a wise move because Slate was shaking uncontrollably. Who gave that creep permission to tell his life story?

"I know perfectly well what pain he had to endure," Incognito told the crowd, "because I was one of the scientists who created the Helmet Man."

If the crowd was startled before, they were completely baffled now. Jeff Springer looked like he had just laid an egg. Even Slate was taken aback, his anger ebbing. Why would Incognito tell the world he used to work for the Western Union? It was plain stupid.

For a moment, nobody uttered a word. Then Hassan spoke up, clearing his throat.

"Excuse me," he said. "But I believe you just admitted to having worked for the Western Union as a scientist that experimented on children."

"I take no pride in the offense."

The crowd was silent no longer. It was outraged. Teeth were bared. Things were thrown. Guns were even pointed at the stage.

"You lied to us!"

"We trusted you!"

"My husband died in your name!"

"This will not be tolerated!"

"Kill the fraud!"

"Death to the deceiver!"

"Enough!" Incognito's voice boomed over the loudspeakers. The crowd was once again pacified, at least momentarily.

Incognito then did something that would be forever engraved in these people's memories, something that would turn the tables in his favor, something that would mean the start of a revolution.

He took off his mask.

The crowd gasped.

"See what I have sacrificed!" he yelled. "See what I have done! This was not for redemption. This was to ensure that the enemies of humanity would be vanquished. This was for the new world, the new order!"

The mask fell from Incognito's grasp and clattered on the stage.

"Look at me! Look at what I have become!"

Some women in the crowd fainted. Springer's face turned deathly white. Hassan grabbed his stomach, jogged over to the side of the stage, and vomited out his lunch.

There was not one inch of Incognito's face that looked human anymore. Cancerous bulges that squirted pus and bled pink blood covered most of it. The remaining areas were transparent. Portions of his pulsating brain could be seen through his glassy skull and plastic-wrap skin. How he still managed to have hair on his head was a miracle. His eyes had also remained untouched, those piercing black orbs that gazed into the heart of the crowd.

"This is my punishment!" Incognito cried. "This is my hell! This is the price I must pay for my crimes. This is what I am willing to endure for us to triumph. If this still doesn't convince you, then behold!"

Armed guards led three prisoners onstage. A forklift carrying a large object followed them. The prisoners, who wore bags on their heads, were forced to kneel before Incognito. The forklift lowered the object onto the stage.

Incognito approached a prisoner and tore the bag off his head.

"This man is Rear Admiral Basinger," Incognito said.

He tore off another bag.

"This woman is Colonel Riza."

He tore off the final bag.

"And this man is General Cromwell."

The crowd was floored, especially by the reveal of Cromwell. The young, blond general no longer looked handsome, now sweaty and pasty. It was obvious from the smell that Cromwell had soiled himself at some point. He looked at Incognito. His terror vanished as his patriotic fervor took over.

"Scum!" Cromwell shrieked. "Scum! You're scum!"

Incognito stared at him with nuclear intensity. "One and the same," he whispered.

With guillotine efficiency, Incognito beheaded Cromwell with his scythe. Blood soaked the stage. The severed head hit the wood with a thump.

"Impossible!" cried a man in the crowd.

"He killed one of their leaders!"

"This man is a miracle worker!"

"Jeff Springer, reporting! Incognito just beheaded Cromwell!"

"The United Third shall rule!"

Incognito moved on to Rear Admiral Basinger.

"I wish I could see how you'll die," Basinger growled. "Just you—"

The scythe lopped his head off. The crowd went wild.

Incognito approached Colonel Riza.

"You can't change the world," Riza spat.

"Then I shall have to destroy it," Incognito said. He sliced through her neck. And Slate did nothing.

Incognito, now with blood splattered all over him, staggered over to the large object on the forklift. He touched it reverently, gazing at the crowd.

"This is an atomic bomb."

The crowd heard these words, but they did not register.

"You heard me," Incognito said. The object he touched was a metallic box covered in colorful wires. People now kept a close eye on it, as though it might explode at any second.

Incognito patted the device. "I have begun to assemble a nuclear arsenal. This is the first bomb that I have acquired, with great difficulty, stolen right from under our enemies' noses. After all, one must have nuclear weapons in order to be considered a superpower."

Now the crowd was really bewildered.

"In order for this revolt to be successful, we must be united," Incognito explained. "We must seek to become a new superpower. We shall become the Saladin Federation."

The crowd exploded into shouts and conversations, some sounding enthusiastic, others skeptical. Was Incognito really planning to create a superpower? Was such a thing possible?

"We can do it," he told them. "We have just beheaded three of their leaders, the Chinese Empire probes their borders, and now we have nuclear weapons."

Many started cheering.

"Already, we have begun operations devoted to pushing out the Westerners from our lands. First, we shall take the safe zones. Then we shall take their military bases and everything else that is rightfully ours. You have the means, but do you have the resolve?"

People shouted in agreement. There was lots of clapping.

"Now is the time of the Third World, the time of the brown and black and yellow man. Now is the time to seize control. The United Third shall prevail. The Saladin Federation shall rise. Let the final jihad begin! Death to the West!"

"Death to the West!" the crowd chanted. "Death to the West!"

It was contagious. Incognito raised his fist. Now the whole crowd was chanting. The influential supporters of the United Third stood up and started clapping. Hassan wiped the vomit from his mouth and reluctantly joined in.

"Death to the West! Death to the West!"

"Springer here... I think ... this is war ... a war we might lose. Oh, no..."

Slate did nothing. He could only stand there as the world crumbled.

"Sir, do we shoot?"

"Give me a sec, soldier! I'm waiting for HQ to respond."

"The gate's gonna come down any minute, sir!"

"Give me a damn second!"

An endless slum surrounded Cairo. Refugees who could not enter the city were made to live there until a spot was made available.

But now thousands of souls tore at the fence surrounding the safe zone. The fence had been electrified, shocking dozens of refugees to death. However, so many people grabbed the fence at once that it just couldn't cope, eventually shorting out. Incognito had promised them a better world, and they weren't about to pass it up.

Peacekeepers in sky-blue uniforms stood far back from the fence with their machine guns raised. Walkers equipped with tear gas, flash grenades, and ultrasonic cannons had arrived to assist with crowd control, but even with these reinforcements, it was doubtful they could hold back the mob.

"Sir, what do we do?" the soldier asked again.

"I just got word from HQ," his superior said. "Don't fire unless they breach the fence."

"By then it'll be too late!"

"Follow orders, soldier!"

"To hell with orders! Shoot the savages!"

"Don't you dare shoot those—!"

With a prolonged groan, the fence came down.

The mob surged forward. The peacekeepers fired without warning, without discrimination. Dozens of refugees fell to the ground, their bodies riddled with bullets, but hundreds more followed. The mob had breached the city. Most of the peacekeepers were either beaten or trampled to death. Some refugees had guns and used them on the walkers. The mechas held out for a while but were soon overwhelmed.

A holographic ad featuring a sensual woman flickered nearby.

"Times are tough... A woman's gotta look good for her soldier boy."

***

"ATTENTION, AN EVACUATION HAS BEEN ORDERED. PLEASE MAKE YOUR WAY TO THE NEAREST RALLY POINT."

The voice recited this command in an endless loop from loudspeakers all over Cairo, though nobody could hear it over the panic. The streets were filled with fleeing people. Some carried bags, others children. Peacekeepers did their best to maintain order, an uphill battle at best. Fights broke out over who got to be evacuated first. Priority was given to government officials, children, and pregnant women. Evacuation points were hastily erected. Every unicopter and plane available was ferrying people out of the city. A human ocean swirled around a landing pad. Each person fought and prayed to be next in line as a unicopter landed.

"I better get overtime for this," the pilot said.

"Why are we evacuating?" his copilot asked. "Can't the military do anything?"

"Reinforcements are coming, kid. Don't worry. This revolt won't last—"

"Death to the West!" a man with a grenade launcher yelled before blowing up the unicopter. It was officially chaos. People tried to get away from the burning wreckage, but the crowd was thicker than tar and moved just as fast. The man with the grenade launcher tried to fire again. A peacekeeper shot him before he could. The man fell. A child started to cry.

"Remain calm, people!" the peacekeeper shouted.

They did anything but that.

***

On the other side of the city, a squad of peacekeepers engaged in a firefight with a group of United Third terrorists. The peacekeepers were squatting behind an armored van. From the looks of it, they had the upper hand.

"Keep hammering them!" their sergeant told them. "They'll lose heart!"

A nearby trash can with a bomb hidden in it exploded, killing half the squad. The terrorists had no problem finishing off the remaining peacekeepers.

***

Two peacekeepers escorted the Western Union ambassador down a hallway, almost knocking over an elderly Egyptian janitor who was mopping the floor. They were taking the ambassador to the roof where a unicopter waited. The embassy was under heavy assault from all sides. No longer could Cairo be considered a safe haven.

"How could this happen?" the ambassador asked. "The United Third isn't capable of this kind of attack. The entire city... You sure it's happening everywhere?"

A peacekeeper nodded. "Istanbul, Baghdad, Lagos, Casablanca, almost all the cities in the Occupied Territories are revolting."

"What about South America?" the other peacekeeper asked.

"Not them," the first peacekeeper clarified. "They've been pacified for decades."

"And Israel? I heard they haven't got any uprisings."

The first peacekeeper was about to reply when a bullet went through his head. The ambassador screamed while the second peacekeeper whirled around, pistol at the ready. The janitor from before held a small gun, having hidden it in his mop bucket. In their rush to evacuate, neither peacekeeper had wondered why a janitor had still been working despite an evacuation order. This proved to be fatal.

It was on reflex, but the peacekeeper managed to shoot the janitor square in the chest. Staggering backward, the janitor fired multiple times, hitting both the ambassador and the second peacekeeper. All three men fell to the floor.

No one survived.

***

A teenage boy hurled a Molotov cocktail at a storefront. It erupted into flames upon impact, setting the store alight. An amateur sniper gunned down two peacekeepers before a unicopter arrived, killing the sniper with a volley of machine gun fire. A machete cut off a peacekeeper's arm. A suicide bomber disabled two walkers.

Anarchy ruled the streets. This mayhem lasted for two days. The remaining peacekeepers had lost all hope of getting reinforcements. The United Third had also managed to hack many of the drones. Mobile mines known as Pinocchios latched on to Western Union soldiers rather than terrorists. A squad of computer-controlled walkers assisted the United Third in its assaults on the Western Union embassy. Drone jets shot down unicopters, one of the drones even flying itself into a skyscraper when it ran out of ammo.

At the dawn of the third day, the chaos subsided. The evacuation order was finally silenced. It was soon replaced by a new voice on the loudspeakers, one that did not urge abandonment but proclaimed victory.

"Cairo is ours," Incognito declared, his voice echoing across the city. "The Westerners have fled. The Saladin Federation controls these lands now. Much hardship is ahead, but beyond that is freedom. We shall bring liberty to our people and death to the West."

"Death to the West!" the people chanted. "Death to the West!"

That chant was no longer a hollow gesture. There was confidence in those words. Incognito had shown these people what was possible.

They could end Western civilization.

***

Admiral Redwood was being driven slowly through an endless horde of protesters. The rabid people shouted at Redwood's car. Only a handful of overwhelmed police officers held them back. Many held picket signs with various slogans. *BRING OUR TROOPS HOME. NO TO WAR. THE WEST NEEDS REST.* They all wanted the same thing, which was to end the fighting. Redwood believed this was easier said than done. Would Incognito and the Chinese give up if the West put down its arms?

More police officers came to assist in crowd control. Redwood had been asked if lethal force should be used. He quickly shot down the idea, much to the resentment of several government officials. Redwood knew why some of these protestors were here. The *Tortuga* incident hadn't gone unnoticed by the public. The news was falsely reporting that all the troops killed by Incognito had died during a training exercise gone wrong, but rumors were spreading, nonetheless. It didn't help that the Helmet Man was at large once again, although many newscasters were claiming this Helmet Man was not the original.

But people weren't stupid. They knew *Tortuga* had a prison break, and when that many soldiers died in such an ambiguous way, citizens were bound to ask questions. Now there were outright revolts in the Occupied Territories. Thousands may be dead, and millions of Western Union citizens were fleeing the region. Hell, General Cromwell was executed on live television. Redwood still felt ill from watching that.

And Incognito had revealed that he had once worked for the Western Union. Again, the media did its best to discredit such claims, but the damage had been done. Not only did this mean the government couldn't use that information to discredit him anymore, but the very citizens of the Western Union would question the reliability of their government even more for having produced their own worst enemy. Redwood could barely believe the situation. Damn Powell... If only they had revealed the truth themselves, Incognito wouldn't have been able to turn his own weakness into an advantage.

Now people were scared. Conscripting teenagers and cracking down on dissenters also wasn't a good way to earn the people's trust. In truth, Redwood couldn't blame people for being afraid, not when there was plenty to be afraid of.

But then there were "attention-seekers" who simply liked to yell a lot and stir up trouble. They made people paranoid and violent. One attention-seeker was a thin man in a robe who referred to himself as Mr. Preacher. He had a scraggly beard and twitchy eyes. Mr. Preacher stood on top of a van, giving yet another barely coherent speech.

"The government! Nothing but lies! Armageddon is coming! End of times! The moon will teach us! Don't listen to Powell! Listen to the moon!"

Redwood would have paid him no mind under normal circumstances. He was just another loon who forgot to take his medication. But what worried Redwood was that many in the crowd were listening, actually listening! When people started to listen to nonsense like that, it was time to get worried. Perhaps he would have this Mr. Preacher arrested, but there were much more pressing matters to deal with first.

The car reached the gates, which only opened wide enough for the vehicle to squeeze through. A protester tried to climb the fence, but a police officer pulled him down and struck him with a baton. The car made it through the gates. It took another ten minutes to get through all the other checkpoints. Redwood started to regret not taking the unicopter, but at long last, he arrived at the Eisenhower Executive Office Building. He would much rather have had this upcoming meeting at the Pentagon. Too bad it was no longer standing.

He thought of that other Helmet Man again, shuddered, and closed his eyes.

***

"So far, most major cities have fallen under the United Third's control," General Herman said. Her voice was steady, but she couldn't keep her eyes from watering with rage. "Any city that hasn't fallen within Africa and Western Asia is experiencing significant unrest. It is unknown how many minor cities, towns, and villages have fallen under the United Third's control, but it is safe to assume many have."

Everyone at the table was quiet. Generals Redwood, Herman, and Kazakov were present, as were Vice President Reynolds and John Mathews, director of Western Intelligence. Several world leaders also sat at the table via hologram, including the British prime minister and the recently appointed Japanese prime minister, the last one supposedly killed by the Helmet Man and his associates. For obvious reasons, Powell was not attending the meeting, now confined to the Executive Residence of the White House.

Kazakov spoke first. "General Herman, you are in charge of peacekeeping. How do you account for Incognito's overwhelming success? We suspected that the United Third had less than a few thousand members, but now it looks like they number over a million."

"Most of the insurgents are not experienced combatants but are radicalized civilians," Herman said. "Incognito also seems to have many sleeper agents who are allowing these revolts to go as smoothly as they are."

"There are rumors that Incognito has obtained an atomic bomb," the British PM said.

"Yes, I saw the video being broadcast by the United Third. It is revolting."

"How did we not know Jeff Springer had been kidnapped until the video was aired?" the Japanese PM asked. "He is the Western Union's top newscaster."

"We believed he was kidnapped only the night before."

The British PM cleared his throat. "Excuse me, but we were talking about the *atomic bomb.* Are these reports accurate, and if so, when and where will Incognito use it?"

"Incognito claimed to be in possession of an atomic bomb during his rally. We have taken inventory and found that none of the Western Union's atomic weapons have gone missing. Perhaps Incognito obtained it from the Chinese, but he could also be bluffing."

"He wasn't bluffing about Cromwell," the British PM spat.

"All our women weep for their lost Adonis," Reynolds said, suppressing a blech.

The British PM ignored him and went on. "With his so-called powers, Incognito could easily have swiped a nuke from under our noses. He was able to kidnap Cromwell and Springer without us even knowing till the last minute. Now even our own safety can't be guaranteed."

Herman didn't know how to respond to that. She gritted her teeth.

"We are all to blame for this," Redwood said. "We underestimated Incognito and allowed him to slip through our fingers."

"That was Powell's doing," Director Mathews interjected.

"It doesn't matter who's at fault here," Redwood told him. "At least not now. Herman, continue your report. What about our refugees?"

Herman seemed to regain control of herself. She smoothed out her uniform and continued. "A majority of them are fleeing to southern Europe. Many were also going to Israel, which has yet to experience any major revolts. This is probably due to them being a full-fledged member of the Western Union. However, Israel has officially stopped taking in refugees as of this morning, with the exception of those with Jewish heritage."

"That's absurd," Reynolds grumbled.

Herman sighed. "Israel is a small country and only has so much room to accommodate this influx of people. It also isn't known for its trustful nature. It wishes to weather the storm on its own. I cannot say I blame them. After all, for every thousand refugees they take in, one of them could very well be a United Third terrorist."

"Can we not force them to accept refugees?" the Japanese PM asked.

"No, again, Israel is a member nation. We would have to violate a number of agreements in order to strong-arm them. It is a challenging matter."

"Not to mention that damn lobby," Reynolds muttered.

"There's also the matter of the drones, which are killing our troops left and right," Kazakov said. "How did the United Third hack into our military networks? This breach of security is without a doubt due to negligence, criminal negligence."

Herman frowned but answered anyway. "We believe there were still access codes we did not know about that Zaidi Industries programmed into our machines. We contacted Victoria Zaidi. She claims to know nothing."

"You trust that girl?" Kazakov cried. "Do you remember what her brother tried to do?"

"Enough!" Redwood shouted, standing up abruptly. "Kazakov, behave yourself. If you have another outburst like that, I won't hesitate to have you thrown out."

Kazakov gaped, as did everyone else.

Redwood deflated. "It's clear we're all tired. Let's take an early lunch."

***

Redwood absentmindedly sipped a cup of coffee in his temporary office, hoping dearly that he wouldn't be interrupted. His old office had been far more spacious and welcoming, but after the Pentagon was destroyed, Redwood had been forced to set up shop at the Eisenhower Executive Office Building. Not only was his temporary office half the size of his old one, but he was also sneezing more often. Mold? Redwood found himself not caring about that. All he wanted was one moment of quiet before resuming his hellish day.

Someone knocked on his door. His wish for peace had clearly been ignored.

Redwood let out a ragged breath. "Come in."

Director Mathews entered the room, making sure to shut the door softly behind him. Soon after its formation, the Western Union had consolidated all Western intelligence agencies into a single one called the Western Intelligence Service. This made Mathews, who now headed the organization, one of the most feared men alive.

"That was some meeting," Mathews said. "It's not even noon and already people are biting each other's heads off."

"Everyone's tense," Redwood said, sipping more of his coffee. "So am I."

Mathews smiled faintly. "I want to talk about Powell."

"There's nothing to talk about. He's out of the loop."

"For now, but do you really think it'll last? How are we supposed to explain to the public why we're impeaching the president during wartime? Do we tell them that Powell wanted to drop a nuke on a super-terrorist who can lift aircraft carriers out of the ocean?"

"I'll think of something," Redwood said, finishing his coffee. It had been too bitter.

"Powell still has a lot of support within the government, even with the *Tortuga* fiasco. The right-wingers love him. Don't forget that."

"There's no way I'm letting that psychotic blowhard back into office. I'll see him thrown in prison for the way he's behaved."

"I doubt he'll be prosecuted for anything. At best, he'll pull a Nixon on us and resign, but that's being hopeful. At worst, he'll be back in office within weeks."

"You're kidding."

"Powell's cronies have been using these revolts in the Occupied Territories and Cromwell's death against you. They claim Powell needs to be put back in power immediately in order to avert disaster, that you are an incompetent pacifist."

Redwood rubbed his eyes. "I'm aware of the rumors. I just don't pay them any mind."

"Maybe you should. You might end up in handcuffs otherwise."

"Please make your point, Mathews, so you can get out of my office."

Mathews looked directly into his eyes. "Powell cannot continue to be our leader, not with these revolts going on, not when we are about to make our move against the Chinese."

Redwood gave himself a moment to process these words. He wanted to be sure he was reading between the lines correctly. Once sure, he spoke in a low, careful voice.

"It won't come to that."

"We may not have another option," Mathews said. "Powell might very well be back in office by the end of the month. We need to act before he can do more damage."

"Leave my office."

Mathews sighed but complied regardless. He opened the door, the hinges not even squeaking. "Consider it, Redwood."

"It won't come to that."

"You were always the optimist, weren't you? I never was."

Ever so gently, Mathews closed the door.

CHAPTER 18

Xing realized his foot was tapping. An anxious tic, no doubt. He forced himself to stop. Weakness could not be shown. Xing ran a hand over the back of his head, caressing his dragon tattoo. Some small part of him was superstitious, and that small part believed his tattoo gave him the power to perform feats no normal man could. If he were going to purge Cloak from the Forbidden City, he would surely need this power.

"Very punctual," a scratchy voice said. An old man, although not nearly as old as the emperor, hobbled over on his cane. He had white whiskers that hung to his chest and small, piercing eyes. "Pardon my tardiness. I was delayed."

"That's quite all right," Xing said. He stood in the lush courtyard surrounding the palace. Today was quiet, the sky electric blue from the force field that encased the Forbidden City. The only sounds came from outside the palace walls, where thousands upon thousands of soldiers stood in rank. A few attendants had been pruning the bushes, but Xing had shooed them away earlier. Sensitive conversations could now be held.

"Let us take a stroll around," the old man said. "I need to get the blood flowing, take in the fresh air, admire the gardens."

"We have the entire courtyard to ourselves," Xing said. "Let us take the path to the right. I do not wish to pass the Traitors' Garden again."

"Neither do I. Lead the way, then."

Xing obliged. They strolled slowly, passing a variety of flowering shrubs. Two kingfishers flew out of a small pond when they went by. The force field prevented them from soaring into the heavens, causing them to squawk in protest.

"High General Zhou has received orders from our new prime minister," Xing said. "She is to patrol the Arctic Ocean with a small fleet of ships."

"Intriguing," the old man said, feeling a fern with his limp hand while passing. A bronze Buddha statue sat in the shade nearby. It bore a suspicious likeness to Emperor Long.

"Most of the Black Lotus agents will be accompanying Zhou," Xing said. "Only Pansy will remain here to act as the emperor's personal bodyguard."

The old man delicately picked a flower as he walked and sniffed it. "One cannot live as long as I have in this political jungle without developing foresight. I know your chances of success, and they are not favorable."

"You can't possibly be content with Cloak's rule."

"No, but I would rather live under Cloak than in the Traitors' Garden."

"Temple will also be going with them."

The old man stopped in his tracks. His heart seemed to skip a beat.

"Perhaps," he muttered. "Yes, our chances still aren't good, but much better."

Xing smiled on the inside. So, now it was "our chances" instead of "your chances." Good, he was making progress.

"Those soldiers outside the palace are all loyal to you," Xing said.

"They are loyal to the emperor," the old man corrected.

"But being their direct commander, if you tell your men that devious foreigners are holding the emperor captive, they will believe you. Our prime minister did not trust any of my soldiers to guard the Forbidden City, rightfully so. High General Duan, this means you are the only one who can purge the capital of Cloak."

Duan stroked his mustache. "What is to stop that silver devil from simply returning to wipe us out?"

"Not to worry. Even devils can be killed."

***

Ember strolled through the Forbidden City like she owned the place. In a sense, she kind of did, or at least Cloak did. She had fallen in love with the Forbidden City the moment she arrived. Nobody complained whenever she killed a random servant, someone was always getting tortured, and the décor was to die for. Red everywhere! It was too bad she couldn't stay here much longer, but the Mentor needed her. There was wickedness to be done.

After finishing up her picnic in the Traitors' Garden, Ember walked swiftly to her next destination. On his way, she blew a kiss to a passing guard. If the guard hadn't remained stoic, she might have been tempted to freeze something important off.

Ember reached a large door and flamboyantly flung it open.

"The gang's all here!" she yelled, bouncing into the room. "Or at least who's left! My, we're an endangered species. Four Gifted dead and two AWOL. Ah, wait, I meant five dead! Keep forgetting about Void. You know, the one Slate killed over twenty years ago?"

"Yes, I recall," Sebastian said. He sat behind an oversized desk, his hands folded and his smile just as slimy as ever. Geppetto stood to his right. Apathy had been painted on his face for months now. He still retained that look, but disgust briefly radiated off him upon seeing Ember.

Geppetto had never liked her and doubted anyone else did either. Her indulgent behavior and sadistic tendencies had caused a great degree of separation between her and the other Gifted. Ember often went on solo missions and could disappear for months at a time on whatever secret errand Sebastian had assigned her. She was the black sheep of the family, the Prodigal Daughter. In some ways, she was more of an outcast than the Helmet Man.

There were two things, however, that kept Ember in the good graces of Sebastian. The first was her loyalty. Obsession was a strong word, but it fit perfectly when it came to Ember's devotion to the Mentor. She would kill—no, she would *die* for her Mentor. The Mentor, whom Ember had never even met or seen, had always been a constant authority figure for her, albeit an unseen one. But every now and again, she would get a glimpse of the Mentor, though *never* literally. A dream, perhaps, or maybe a bit of information Sebastian let slip. Yes, that was enough for Ember, at least for now.

The second thing that made Ember valuable to Cloak was her raw power. Possessing the ability to absorb heat and spit it back out as fire, she was a fearsome opponent, once having killed three hundred armed men single-handedly during the Nigerian Genocide. Out of all the Gifted, only Slate matched her in terms of combat ability.

No, there was another. One that didn't match but dwarfed Ember's power. As much as Ember thought she was the hand of the Mentor, it was this other who truly held the post.

Temple stood in the corner. Three horizontal streaks of fresh blood dripped off his silver helmet. Geppetto eyed the helmet from the corner of his eye. He knew he couldn't use his powers to control Temple, even if the beast wore no helmet. Standing in his presence was like being near a nuclear reactor about to explode.

"Oh, how's my big boy doing?" Ember shrieked merrily, causing Geppetto to cover his ears. She sprinted across the room and skidded to a stop in front of Temple.

"Sebastian, what have you been feeding him?" Ember asked. "He's gotten bigger, I can tell. And look, he made a mess again. All that blood!"

She has an attraction to that thing, Geppetto thought. *What a freak.*

"Temple doesn't need to feed," Sebastian said. "At least not in the traditional sense."

Ember didn't seem to hear him. She was too busy analyzing Temple's sculpted body. Some of it was visible through the front opening of his cloak. Muscular flesh. White skin. Black nails. So unique ... so deadly... Ember caught another glimpse of her Mentor. So close... Ember reached out, her hand shaking like a leaf, lips quivering...

Before Ember's fingers made contact, Temple grabbed her throat with one hand. The iron grip immediately turned her face red. Temple lifted her off the floor. Her legs danced frantically in the air as the grip tightened.

Sebastian chuckled, leaning back in his chair. "Look, but don't touch. I thought you knew the rules by now, Ember."

Ember's face was turning blue. Her bloated tongue stuck out. Geppetto gulped. As much as he hated Ember, he almost felt like intervening.

Just as Ember's suffocation seemed imminent, Temple let go. Ember crashed to the floor and gasped for air. She spoke after a moment of recovery.

"Ah... Oh, yes... That's the good stuff... Oh, yes... You shouldn't have stopped... Just getting warmed up..."

Geppetto's mouth fell open. She *liked* it? Any ounce of sympathy he had felt disintegrated. *Psycho, a true psycho*, he thought.

"Can't have you dying on us, Ember," Sebastian explained, like he would to a spoiled child. "The Mentor has need of you." He briefly turned Geppetto's way. "*Both* of you. No one else can be trusted, least of all any agents of the Chinese Empire. Anyway, Ember, I need you to go break bread with a potential ally of ours. I know you're not the best person for the job, given your excesses, but we are short on manpower."

Ember rubbed her throat and got back up. "Oh, Sebastian, you're too cruel. I wanted to go to the Arctic. All the fun's going to be there."

"All work and no play make Ember a dull girl," Sebastian said. "But all play and no work make Ember a lazy girl too. And in my opinion, you've been playing far too much."

She pouted. "I've done plenty of work."

"This is not a debate, I'm afraid." Sebastian maintained his smile, but there was a touch of impatience in his voice. "Complain again, and Temple will resume strangling you, except he won't stop this time."

Ember scrunched up her nose. "Fine, meanie! You've officially ruined my day. I hope you're happy!" She spun on her heel and marched out the room, her cape fluttering.

Sebastian rose from his chair and grabbed his white cane. "Geppetto, why don't we go out on the balcony? More privacy for us."

That sounded more like an order than a request, so Geppetto obeyed without complaint. He followed Sebastian out the door to the balcony. They were so high up that Geppetto was able to see over the palace walls and take in the massive army standing guard right at their doorstep beyond the semi-transparent force field.

The sea of red soldiers did not look as formidable as when they had first arrived. Their uniforms were nothing but rags that hung off malnourished bodies. A strong wind might very well blow them all away. Despite entire platoons being devoted to waste disposal and chamber pot cleaning, the stench had become monstrous. The only barriers holding the stink back from engulfing the Forbidden City were the force field acting as an air purifier and the well-maintained gardens producing an array of fragrances.

Sebastian walked over to the railing. "We haven't spoken privately, just the two of us, in quite some time. Two years, if I remember right."

"Three years," Geppetto corrected, not bothering to hide his distrust.

"My, then this conversation is long overdue." Sebastian waved Geppetto over. "Come, stand next to me. Enjoy the view for both of us."

Geppetto felt like a timid deer as he walked to Sebastian. The railing was just a bit taller than Geppetto, so the vertical metal bars gave him the distinct feeling that he was in a cage full of rabid animals.

A bark made him jump out of his skin. Speaking of rabid animals...

"Pleasant walk?" Sebastian asked the newcomer.

A yellow Labrador retriever happily barked a reply. It could have been mistaken for a normal dog, but Geppetto knew better. How many palace servants had been eviscerated because of that mutt? It had to be at least twelve. What was its name anyway? Sebastian had never told him. Geppetto sincerely wished at that moment that he could control animals like he could humans. He would never feel safe around this mutt otherwise.

Sebastian scratched behind the dog's ear. "I know that things between us have not been amicable. Don't worry. I've forgiven your trespasses against us. Cyphrus could be very convincing when she wanted to be, though not convincing enough in the end. I'm only sorry that Atlas was unable to survive."

"No, you're not," Geppetto said. Sebastian had made it almost sound like it was Atlas's own fault for dying. Unlike Sebastian, Atlas had cared. Geppetto had let Atlas down by talking him into teaming up with Cyphrus. Worst of all, he had long ago given up trying to avenge Atlas because he had no idea who was at fault anymore. Was it Repulsa who killed him? Cyphrus who tricked him? Sebastian who used him? Slate who led the charge? Incognito who lured Repulsa away? The Mentor who set all this in motion? Himself? Did it even matter?

Sebastian stopped scratching his dog, much to the canine's disappointment.

"Ember was right," the blind man said. "The Gifted are an endangered species. Just as well. Our Mentor will soon no longer need us. However, that time has not yet arrived. That is why I have begun to supervise you and Ember more closely, to ensure nothing ill befalls the remaining Gifted."

"Very thoughtful. What next, pension plans?"

Sebastian laughed. "No, but I have something even better."

Geppetto saw that Temple had not followed them out onto the balcony. How did he not notice until now? It was as if Temple's presence had been an unseen weight that had subtly stopped crushing him. Perhaps this was why he now acted so cocky, more talkative. Had this been Sebastian's intention?

Sebastian laughed again, this time more ominously. "Geppetto, I'm going to give you answers."

CHAPTER 19

O*h, lord...*
      "Wake up, cadet!"

Gilda's eyes snapped open. The rifle shook in her quivering hands as she lay on the ground. It was scorching outside. Sweat dripped off her brow.

"Shoot like you mean it, cadet!"

Gilda aimed her rifle, trying to shake off her grogginess. She would take out that tin can in one shot. Maybe then the instructor would shut his mouth.

"Fire at your own time!"

Where was the can? Gilda couldn't find it. There was only a whirlwind of sand.

"I said fire at your own time!"

But she couldn't see the can. Where did that oaf instructor put it?

"Earth to Plato! Fire your weapon!"

She saw something, a silhouette in the whirlwind.

"Shoot your weapon now, Plato! What are you waiting for, Christmas?"

The whirlwind started to die down. Her trigger finger twitched in anticipation. She was more than ready for that tin can to come into view.

The whirlwind was gone. What was concealed was now revealed.

It wasn't a can.

Oh, lord... Oh, lord... Oh, lord...

"You will shoot," Incognito hissed. "Kill the boy."

Henry Marker stood far downrange, right in Gilda's sights. He had his hands folded in front of him, smiling shyly. He hadn't aged a day since he died.

But Gilda had.

"Henry!" Her heart pounded like mad. The rifle slipped from her palms and fell on its side with a soft thud.

"Not going to shoot me?" Henry asked.

Gilda looked up. Henry Marker was no longer downrange. He was in front of her. She yelped. He had moved so fast! Rolling onto her back, she attempted to flee the scene by doing an embarrassing crab walk. She fell on her rear after scuttling just a few feet.

Henry laughed good-naturedly. "You're afraid of *me?* That's a first."

Gilda turned red and got to her feet. Questions such as how her long-dead friend had come back to life did not pop into her mind. But she did recognize where she was. It was the rifle range near the Bunker.

"He's a handsome one," a woman said, wrapping her arms around Henry from behind. She had brown hair and wore a black dress. Gilda recognized her. She felt a surge of emotion, a mix of rage and despair.

"You should have let me kiss you," Henry said. "You really should have."

"There's no point in being a prude, Gilda," the woman said, stroking Henry's chest. "You're going to die soon anyway if you keep following that Helmet Man."

It was *her.* Gilda's mind did not compute.

Oh, lord... Oh, lord... Oh, lordy lord...

"You got nothing to worry about," Henry said with a big clown smile that was a real rarity these days. He closed his eyes, blind but smiling. "I just wish we could kiss again. We dead would do anything to feel alive again. *Anything...*"

The woman's eyes rolled back. The sky became pitch-black.

Oh, lord... Oh, lord... The sun is no more...

Gilda screamed. It was a scream that she had never thought herself capable of producing.

The woman's eyes were—

Henry opened his mouth. Out came the voice of Legion.

Blood spurted from Gilda's ears. The voices were eating her brain. *Her brain.* She kept on screaming, but she couldn't hear her own voice anymore. Nobody else could either.

Oh, lord... Oh, lord... The moon is full...

***

"Guys, she's awake!" Straper yelled, breaking into a smile.

Gilda sat up like greased lightning and sank her teeth into his neck.

"Ah, Gilda!" Straper cried. "Get off! Get off!"

The teeth drew blood. In a panic, Straper punched the side of her head. She wouldn't budge. Her feral eyes were focused on nothing.

"Let go, girl!" a large man barked. The man and his muscle-bound associates tried to pull her away from Straper. One man forced her lower jaw open. The other thugs then tore her off Straper. She convulsed and chomped her teeth together.

"Don't hurt her!" Straper told the men. He touched his bleeding neck. It wasn't too bad. Gilda hadn't punctured an artery, but it was a close call all the same. The men did their best to keep her restrained. She calmed down little by little. It took another minute for her struggling to stop. She was breathing heavily, eyes darting but lucid. She eventually relaxed. All the same, the guards kept a good grip on her.

"Gilda, what the hell is wrong with you?" Straper demanded.

"I ... huh ... I ... what..." Gilda was attempting to form a coherent sentence, but Straper's punch had jumbled her brains.

Straper huffed and touched his neck again. Blood dribbled onto his shirt.

"You can vamoose now," he told the guards. "I can handle her from here."

"What if the bitch goes rabid again?" a guard asked.

"Hey, I said leave it to me! You want to piss off the Helmet Man?"

The guards looked at one another and then looked down at Gilda, who was still catching her breath. Against their better instincts, they let her go and shuffled out of the room.

"Incognito will hear of this," another guard warned.

"He's got a revolution to run, pal," Straper told him. "I don't think he cares if one of us had a bad dream."

The guard sneered and closed the door.

"Straper..." Gilda said, still lying on the floor. "Straper... I bit you... I ... sorry..."

"Hey, don't sweat it," Straper said, producing a growth patch from his pocket and putting it on his neck. "I'm just glad you're okay and that you don't wear braces."

Gilda's mouth formed into a withered smile. With Straper's help, she climbed back on the sweat-drenched bed and lay down on her stiff back.

"Man, Gilda, I knew you were having bad dreams lately, but nothing like *this*," Straper said. "You were screaming so loud that we thought you were being attacked."

Gilda gulped dryly. "This dream ... it wasn't like the others."

"What was it about?"

"I think I had a dream like this a long time ago," Gilda said. "It was ... yeah ... when Cloak captured Slate and me, on the plane, after the Pale Pyramid collapsed. It was vaguer that time, though. Most of my dreams for the past couple of months have mostly been me reliving bad memories." She gulped. "But this dream wasn't a memory. It was new."

"Maybe it's stress-related?" Straper suggested. He gave a snort. "I mean, what could be stressful about our situation?"

"I don't think that's it," Gilda said, sitting up. "Or at least I don't think that's the only reason. Maybe ... I don't know. Maybe it's guilt. Because of me, both of us are working for the United Third. I convinced you. You tried to talk me out of it, but I insisted."

Straper nodded, lowering his eyes. "You sure did."

"I mean, we helped a lot of people, but was it worth it in the end? Incognito is stronger than ever. Things are escalating everywhere. I think we might have something to do with it. After Slate left, things got tough ... real tough. Incognito sent us on all those surveillance assignments. I saw a kid get killed, Straper. I saw dogs get sicced on people. All that chaos ... and we had something to do with it."

Straper clenched his fists. "I guess..."

"When Incognito finally announced a rescue mission for Slate, I thought things would be different. But they've only gotten worse. Doubts... I've got nothing but doubts now."

"Yeah, maybe..." Straper said. "Maybe you deserve those dreams."

"You might—" Gilda paused. "What did you just say?"

"I said you probably deserve to have those dreams," Straper said. He tried to sound like he was joking, but something in his voice gave him away. "I wish I could have those kinds of dreams. At least I'd be getting punished."

"You think my dreams are a good thing?" Gilda questioned.

"Well, where exactly were you going with that fricking monologue of yours, then?"

"I don't know, but not there! I'm just trying to find out why I'm going crazy, and you're being a total tool. Where's the compassion? I need your help."

"You want my help? Okay, how about some advice? If we really wanted to put a stop to Incognito, let's stop pussyfooting about it. Let's go join up with Slate and kill the guy. We'd save millions of lives, yet you and Naomi are too chicken even to consider it. Fricking geez... I thought at least Slate would be the man around here, but even he's a coward now."

"Slate isn't a coward. He's trying to protect Thomas."

"One kid over the entire world? Everyone we ever knew?"

Gilda teared up. "What the hell happened to you? When did you become so cruel?"

"Nobody is clean anymore! The Western Union is Nazi Germany right now. Everyone's a killer. All we can do is make sure we kill the right people."

"Straper..." Gilda began.

Straper walked to the door. "Nuts to this. I'm going back to my room."

"Straper, get back here!" Gilda shouted with more worry than hate.

But Straper ignored her. He was careful to slam the door behind him.

***

Naomi rapped on the door. No response. She waited a few seconds before knocking again. Again, no response. She was getting peeved but controlled herself.

"Slate, it's me," Naomi said. "Can I come in?"

There was only silence for a moment.

"Free country," a voice grumbled at last. "Wait, no it isn't."

"It's in a state of anarchy," Naomi jested. "That's about as free as you can get." She was trying to make light of the situation as best as she could. It didn't seem to be working. Sighing, she turned the knob and slipped into the room. The lights were turned off, but she could make out someone sitting on a bed.

"Mind if I turn on the lights?" Naomi asked, flipping the switch, illuminating a barren bedroom with rocky walls. "Sorry, that was more of a rhetorical question. Isn't it a bit strange to be sitting alone in the dark?"

The Helmet Man was slouched over. "What's the point of light if you can't even see?"

"That's still no reason to be gloomy." Naomi strolled over and plopped herself next to Slate on the bed. It hadn't been slept in. Not surprising, since he required no sleep.

They had been cooped up in the United Third's headquarters for over a week now. It was located underneath a Congolese rainforest, in an abandoned mine, to be exact. Incognito was keeping them here under lock and key to make sure they didn't interfere with his plans. Ever since they arrived, Slate had secluded himself in his room. Oscar Radcliffe had tried talking to him but in the end decided to give Slate some personal space. Naomi had also tried talking to Slate several times, but to no avail until now.

"You may not believe it, but you did the right thing," Naomi told him. "Thomas is alive because of you. I didn't think you had it in you to restrain yourself like that, to keep yourself from attacking Incognito right then and there on that stage. You always surprise everyone, Helmet Man, and that's what makes you so dangerous."

"I don't feel dangerous right now," Slate said. "I feel neutered. Sure, I saved

Thomas, but I also let that psycho have his way with the world. Incognito is rotten to the core. How can his followers possibly believe anything he has to say?"

Naomi raised an eyebrow. "How is it you don't understand by now?"

"Oh, and what exactly don't I understand?"

"As cruel and cold as Incognito is, his lies have bits of truth baked into them."

"Are you gonna start giving a speech about how evil America is? Give me a break. I've had enough of those."

"It's not just America. The Western Union has always viewed itself as the savior of the world. Westerners' technological superiority has left them all with swelled heads, and because they have the ego and the tools to go with it, they try to force their vision on the rest of humanity. It's foul. It's practically racism. In fact, it often takes that very form."

Slate waved his hand. "Every fricking country thinks it's the best."

"Not every country controls two-thirds of the world."

"All right, you need to put your tinfoil hat on. I seriously don't care about any of this."

"You don't care? You don't care why the Western Union is taking over the world, about why the Gifted were created? You don't care why you got liquid metal poured over your skull when you were an innocent boy? You don't care why Houdini had his eye scooped from his skull? You don't care why Geppetto was forced to perform tricks or else get electrocuted by a shock collar? You don't care why Sandtrap was disfigured when he—?"

Slate grabbed her arm, taking her off guard. It wasn't a rough grab, however. That was the surprising part. It was soft. Naomi blushed on contact.

"I care," he said. "I've always cared. I just didn't want to. When I grew up, I always saw people laughing things off. No matter how bad things got, you could always laugh it off. It became my motto, my way of life."

Slate let go of her. Naomi almost missed his touch, but she had too much pride to say so.

"But now I know there are some things that shouldn't be laughed off,"

Slate said. "Messing with people I care about is one of them. I don't care how justified Incognito thinks he is. He's crossed too many lines."

Naomi stared at him. She let his words roll around in her head before responding.

"You're right," she said. "You're absolutely right. Incognito is only convincing these oppressed people to become the very thing the Western Union believes them to be, violent and weak-minded. We can't let him destroy the Western Union. We can't let him turn these people into monsters like us."

Slate touched his helmet as though it was an old war wound. "What's Incognito planning? What does he want me for?"

"I only have a rough idea," Naomi said. "But I believe Incognito wants a perfect society. He thinks that the values of the Third World are superior in every way to Western values."

"No new news to me."

"Then perhaps this might be. Once Incognito unites the Third World under the Saladin Federation, he will eradicate the rest of humanity and leave you in charge of this new federation as an immortal king."

Slate scratched his helmet. "Wait ... Saladin Federation ... immortal king ... eradicate humanity! Ah, shit! That's a bad thing!"

"It *is* a bad thing," Naomi agreed. "It's an unspeakable, unfathomable thing."

Slate was speechless, which was becoming a common occurrence lately, one he did not like. He took a moment to formulate a coherent question. "Just how is Incognito gonna pull something like that off?"

"I have no idea, but I don't doubt for a second that he is capable of doing it. His determination is unwavering."

"And you were helping him all along?" Slate snapped.

To her credit, Naomi looked ashamed. "I never thought he would get this far. The fact that he's still alive is unbelievable."

"You said before that you wanted to kill the Mentor. You thought only Incognito could do it, and that's why you're working for him. But you can't seriously tell me your revenge is worth being a part of *this?* To think you were defending the cretin only a minute ago."

Naomi closed her eyes. "Slate, please, listen ... my mother..."

"You haven't changed a bit. You're no different from the rest of the Gifted. You had the nerve to hate me, to think you were superior. But I never stooped as low as you. Not ever!" He got up from the bed and marched to the door. "I don't care if Incognito is holding all my friends captive. I'm putting an end to him, once and for all!"

Making a dramatic exit, Slate burst out the door and stormed down the hallway.

That was when Naomi began to cry.

CHAPTER 20

The jungle emitted a variety of noises, like the buzzing of insects, the calls of birds, and the rustling of leaves. The ill-tempered henchmen found no difficulty in ignoring these sounds as they dragged a pair of Arab men behind them. They might as well have been in a vacuum.

Following them were more henchmen hauling a family of three and a lone man. The family was American, a couple and their daughter. The lone man was black and wore a white coat. Out of all the prisoners, he appeared the calmest, which was not calm at all. How could one keep a level head when being brought before the infamous Incognito?

Barir stood next to Incognito, surveying the clearing in the middle of the jungle, where their prisoners would be inspected. Near its edge was a twenty-thousand-gallon tank of purified water. The underground headquarters of the United Third lay hidden beneath their feet. Incognito had been commanding his loyal followers from the seclusion of his headquarters. The Western Union still had many troops in the Occupied Territories, and the cities that had been taken over by the United Third remained in turmoil. It would be some time until Incognito could publicly take command of anything.

Barir knew that Incognito needed to be kept safe, since he was the heart of this revolution. Even so, Barir did not favor this tactic. Wasn't Incognito validating all of Hassan's criticisms? Was he letting everyone else do his dirty work while remaining hidden? Barir silenced those thoughts. He couldn't believe for a second that Incognito would be afraid to sully his hands. After all, he was about to execute these prisoners with his own blade.

The two Arabs were dropped in front of Incognito. Disdainfully, Incognito poked one of the men with the butt of his scythe.

"This is truly revolting," Incognito said. "Our own brethren were assisting subhuman Westerners. Did they promise you Walmart gift cards in exchange for your servitude?"

One of the Arabs stared daggers at Incognito. "That American over there has been my friend for almost a decade. He gave me work when no other would. Am I to repay him and his family with a bullet to the head?"

"If that man happens to be one of the largest weapons manufacturers for the Western Union, then yes, you should have shot him. Do you realize how many of your own people have died at the hands of this profiteer?"

"How many have died at *your* hands?" the other man spat. "We have been trying to forge peace with the West for years. You only justify their contempt of us."

"I have no time for the ramblings of Uncle Toms. Gag them."

The henchmen jammed cloths into both their mouths. The two prisoners didn't give much resistance except to glare.

Incognito turned to the lone man in the white coat. "Where did you find this one? I never expected you to come across him again."

"He was stationed on the military base where the family was hiding out," Barir said. "I thought he could be useful to you when dealing with the Helmet Man."

"That is where you are wrong, Barir. We only need the brats."

Dr. Samuel Taylor chuckled. His captors shoved him to his knees. He went down, still chuckling as he found himself facing death, scythe and all.

"You were of some help during the Helios Tower fiasco," Incognito told Taylor. "As such, you will be given a swift execution."

"I never imagined I would find myself in such an insane situation again," Taylor said with an amused smile but fearful eyes. "Gilda and Kevin ... nice to know they're still alive. Slate took care of them, despite your efforts."

"Gag this one too," Incognito ordered.

His men obeyed, shoving a cloth into Taylor's mouth.

"Let us proceed with the executions," Incognito said. "But spare the child and take her away before the gruesomeness begins."

"No!" her mother screamed. She wrapped her arms around her frightened daughter. The father did the same.

"Do you want her to see you get beheaded?" Incognito inquired.

"You're not taking my daughter away!" the mother shrieked.

Incognito almost reeled back. "You would permit your own daughter to witness your execution, all to keep her close for comfort? Selfish Westerners…"

Barir leaned toward Incognito, whispering in his ear. "Must we kill the mother?"

"The fact that I'm sparing their brat is more mercy than these befouled creatures deserve," Incognito said, not bothering to whisper back. "Now do as I instruct."

The henchmen pried away the parents, who were both screaming as loud as they could. The girl started to cry as Barir walked over and grabbed her hand.

"Hurry, child," he told her. "You must not see what is about to happen."

Incognito approached Taylor and raised his scythe. "Feel honored to be slain by me. Your death shall be clean."

"Can't say the same for you," Slate snarled.

Incognito's eyes widened. The Helmet Man bumped his fists together.

Staggering backward, Incognito grabbed his chest. His cold heart ceased to beat. Not wasting any time, Slate ran up and punched Incognito square in the mask, causing it to crack. Incognito lost his grip on his scythe and fell on his back.

The Helmet Man shook his head. "You really had that coming."

Meanwhile, Barir's heart might as well have stopped too. "No, this is unthinkable!" he cried. "Quickly, shoot the Helmet Man!"

The henchmen didn't seem to hear Barir. They only stared at Incognito's limp body, stupefied. The prisoners wore similar expressions.

But Taylor only chuckled again through his gag.

Slate chuckled too. "What? What did I do?"

"What are you waiting for?" Barir cried. "Shoot him!"

The men shook their heads clear and took out their handguns.

Slate barked a laugh. "You clearly have no idea who I am, do you?"

Incognito's eyes snapped open. "Do you know who *I* am?"

Slate swore and leaped forward on reflex. That didn't stop the swinging scythe from cutting his back. Blood sprayed from the wound, but Slate paid it no mind. He regained his balance, twisted around, and fired a bolt of energy at his attacker.

Incognito, however, sank into the ground before the bolt could make contact. The bolt merely hit the soil, scorching it. The terrorist had vanished.

"Get these prisoners out of here!" Barir ordered his men. "Incognito shall take care of the Helmet Man!"

The henchmen quickly led the dumbfounded prisoners, including Taylor, back toward the entrance to the mine. Barir also left, dragging the American girl with him, screaming way too loud.

"Hush up!" Barir shouted, but that only made it worse.

The Helmet Man ignored them. He was tense and alert, his arms outstretched as though he was trying to walk across a balancing beam. Incognito's prosthetic limb had been designed so that it could restart his heart should he suffer cardiac arrest. Slate wanted to kick himself. It was stupid to think an opponent like Incognito would be taken down so easily. Now the element of surprise was gone. Where did that geezer run off to anyway?

Slate sensed an attack, able to pick up the subtle vibrations, and flew up as a scythe swiped at his legs. Incognito floated out of the ground like a specter, silent and lethal. In a flash, he was in front of the Helmet Man and started swinging his scythe so fast that the human eye could barely pick it up, twenty swings per second, maybe more. It was impossible for Slate to dodge them all, even with his superhuman speed. He flew left, down, up, left again, right, up even higher, receiving dozens of small cuts despite these quick maneuvers.

This midair battle lasted for about ten seconds before Slate tried to kick his opponent. Incognito flew backward, not taking any damage.

"You're throwing away your future," Incognito growled.

"Please, I know what you want with me," Slate said. "You're planning to turn me into some kind of king for your new world. Look, if I wanted to be a king, I'd have gone out with Thomas's mom. Hey, I wonder if she's single..."

Incognito squeezed his scythe's handle. "Is this really the time for jokes?"

"How else am I supposed to piss you off?"

"I thought you would understand. You of all people know what atrocities the West has committed. You have seen the hatred. You have seen the contempt. Most importantly, you have seen the apathy. I even left you to rot in *Tortuga* in hopes that you would finally come around, but despite all my efforts, your delusion remains boundless."

"You left me in *Tortuga* on purpose! Do you even know how to make friends?" Slate focused all his energy into his arm, preparing to fire a beam, but before he could even aim his arm, Incognito flew toward the tank of water below them. He stabbed his scythe into the tank's side, lifted it off the ground, and flung it at the Helmet Man.

Slate fired his beam just as the tank was halfway through its arc, only seconds away from slamming into him. The beam struck the tank, annihilating it. He sped backward to avoid the debris and scorching steam.

A palm tree almost struck Slate upside the head. Incognito had swung it, his scythe embedded in the trunk. Not wanting to give up on a good idea, he swung the tree again. Instead of dodging, Slate fired a bolt of electricity at the trunk. It caught fire. If he could damage Incognito with his lightning bolts, maybe a little fire could work as well.

Flames quickly consumed the palm tree. Tsking in annoyance, Incognito yanked his blade from the flaming tree and let it crash down into the clearing below.

However, the smoke had obscured his vision, so he wasn't able to see Slate fire another beam. It didn't hit Incognito, but it did singe his hand, causing him to drop his scythe. The blade clattered to the ground far below.

"You're unarmed now!" Slate shouted, flying toward Incognito with a charged fist.

"Fool, I still have one good arm left," Incognito told him, aiming his prosthetic limb that had transformed itself into a compact laser rifle. Without hesitation, he fired it. The laser went through Slate's shoulder.

"Ugh, that's a foul!" Slate croaked. He was no longer flying and was losing altitude fast. He managed to summon up a burst of energy, slowing his descent somewhat. That didn't stop him from getting hurt as he crashed into the ground.

Incognito swooped down. He snatched his scythe up and landed before the limp Helmet Man. The tip of his blade poked Slate in the neck.

"Would you believe I was restraining myself to ensure I didn't kill you?" Incognito asked. "No, you probably wouldn't, not with that Western arrogance of yours."

"Screw you," Slate groaned.

"Go ahead, recite your one-liners. They're all you have now. With you at my mercy, I can say this with due pleasure: you belong to me."

"That's enough," someone spat.

Incognito turned to see that Oscar Radcliffe had arrived. With him was Barir, along with twenty armed men. Gilda and Straper were also there. Dread was etched on their faces as they saw Slate pinned down by his masked foe.

"Do not meddle in this matter," Incognito warned.

"I should have meddled sooner," Oscar said. "Release him!"

"Am I to do this out of the goodness of my heart?"

"Look where you're standing."

"Self-reflection was never my strongest—" But then Incognito took a literal look at where he stood and went rigid.

"Go ahead," Slate told him. "Stab me. I'll fry you to kingdom come."

"You..." Incognito growled. How could he not have noticed until now? He had always been so careful of his surroundings. However, not only had Slate managed to sneak up on him, but Incognito now also found himself standing in a large puddle of water. It must have come from the tank the buffoon had destroyed earlier. Any moment now, the Helmet Man could send his energy into the puddle and electrocute him to death.

"It's a draw," Oscar declared.

Incognito pulled his blade away from the Helmet Man's neck and speedily floated a good distance away from the puddle. Touching down on dry ground, Incognito squeezed his scythe's handle stronger than a vice grip.

"Doesn't anyone understand?" he asked with calm anger and quiet desperation in his words. "Is the divide between the world and me so large?"

"I understand," a voice spoke up. "I just don't condone. Not anymore."

Naomi approached Incognito. Her face was blank and her eyes cold. Thomas held her hand.

"Looking good, kid," Slate said as he struggled to his feet, his clothes soaked.

"Slate, are you okay?" Thomas yelled. He tried to pull away from Naomi, but she kept a good hold on his hand.

"What is *this?*" Incognito demanded.

"I figured out where you hid Thomas," Naomi said. "My years with Cloak taught me a few things. You think all your men are loyal, but you're wrong."

"We are all loyal, you shrew!" an armed man shouted.

Barir glared at the man, a silent warning.

"It's over," Naomi continued. "You tried everything in your power to bring Slate to your side, all the same tricks that would have worked on you or me. What you failed to realize is he isn't anything like us. He was buried under the ground for twenty years. He's a stranger to this time, an outsider. He's unbiased. He sees everything for what it truly is. If anything is going to set the world right, it'll be him, not us with our distorted perspectives. Yes, there is lots of evil in this world, but there is a lot of good too. What you plan..."

Incognito looked at her with an intensity that would make a lesser person wilt away. But Naomi didn't back down. She kept her face blank and her eyes piercing.

Slate hobbled over toward Naomi and stood next to Thomas. The boy was obviously nervous but smiled at Slate anyway. The young prince also seemed well fed and unharmed.

"I thought you tortured the kid," Slate said.

"That's the impression I wanted to give," Incognito told him. "Harming children, even an abomination such as this one, is not to my liking."

"What a sweet guy you are."

"It appears we are at an impasse. What do you propose?"

"My friends and I leave for good, Naomi and my dad included. Taylor too. You also got to keep yourself from targeting civilians. That means you can't put into effect that master plan of yours. In exchange, I won't stop you from playing war. Hell, you can take over the entire Third World for all I care, but I'm through."

"What if I were to refuse those absurd terms?"

"Then you'd have to force us to stay, but we'd probably end up killing each other. That means the Western Union wins. That means Cloak wins. You ain't stupid enough to refuse my terms. At least this way you still have a shot at freeing your people."

Incognito kept still and silent for what seemed like hours. His eyes darted toward Barir, who gave his leader a defeated look in return. Then he looked at Oscar, but his old friend only shook his head. He finally settled his eyes on Naomi.

"What happened to your conviction?" he asked her. "What happened to your drive for revenge? Without me, you have no hope of killing the Mentor."

"There's the easy way, and there's the right way," she told him. "I still wish for nothing more than to kill the Mentor, but I'll do it with someone I respect, someone who will help me move on and let me live my life. I never thought such a thing would be possible until recently, but now that I know it can be done, that's the path I wish to follow. Let me ask you, do you wish to live your life? Do you wish to move on, to be redeemed?"

"You know the answer perfectly well," Incognito snapped. "Fine, if that's your wish, then go. I have no use for those not willing to die for their beliefs, so be gone. Leave this place. You and the other roaches have three days to do so. Make use of them."

Incognito stormed off, his lackeys following him. Barir quietly considered

Slate and his friends before leaving as well.

Gilda and Straper ran over to Slate. They seemed both shocked yet satisfied with the outcome. Oscar stayed where he was, his age more pronounced than usual.

"That's what I'm talking about!" Straper cheered. "Glad you finally showed him!"

"Nobody likes a suck-up," Slate jabbed. "How are the rest of you guys?"

"Excellent!" Thomas yelled.

"Not treated too badly?" Slate asked.

"No, it was mostly just boring. And lonely..." Thomas perked up again. "But you're back, Slate! You're back and here to stay!"

"You bet, kid." Slate turned to Gilda. "What about you?"

"Honestly, I don't know," she said, her lack of sleep evident. "Did you say something about Taylor?"

"You mean Dr. Taylor?" Straper asked. "What the hell is he doing here?"

"Barir and his boyfriends kidnapped him," Slate said. "Don't worry. We'll get him back to where he belongs. You two knuckleheads should see him before then."

"Yeah, definitely," Gilda said. "It'd be nice to see a familiar face."

"What about us?" Straper asked. "Looks like we're unemployed. What now?"

"Let's get our stuff packed up," Naomi said. "We'll decide what to do from there."

Gilda and Straper left to do just that.

Oscar walked over to his son and touched his shoulder. "I'm proud of the way you handled that, son. You've finally matured."

"That's a backhanded compliment if I've ever heard one," Slate said.

"It certainly is. Listen, when you get the chance, I want to talk to you and your friends. It's about time I answered your questions."

Slate pumped his fist. "Ah, yeah! Exposition, here we come!"

Oscar shook his head and laughed. Then he too walked off.

Slate now turned to Naomi. Thomas stood awkwardly between them, not sure what the cause was of the sudden tension in the air.

"Look, about our last talk…" Slate mumbled.

"No, you spoke the ugly truth," Naomi said, putting a hand on his bicep. "I couldn't expect anything else from you."

"Doesn't mean I had to be such an ass about it."

Naomi smiled. "Actually, that's exactly what it means."

Thomas giggled. "You said a swear."

Slate chuckled. "Yep. Speaking of ass, I sure do smell like it! That water must have mixed with some crap in the ground. Gotta change my clothes."

Naomi's smile turned devilish. "I could help with that."

It was as if someone had pressed the pause button on Slate's life. He stood frozen in place, stiller than any mime could ever hope to be. The tension that had been polluting the air before had been replaced by a new kind of tension, a good kind.

Slate spoke at last. "I'd like to thank the Academy…"

CHAPTER 21

Temple loomed over the Arctic.

The air felt far colder around the silver devil, adding to the already frigid temperatures. The unicopter's side door was open. Icy wind blew into the fuselage. None of the other occupants dared complain, save one.

"It's chilly," Thistle whimpered. "Mother, it's chilly."

"Hush, child," Mistress Lotus commanded in a low tone. "You have a coat. Wrap your arms around yourself. Warmth will come to you."

Poppy watched this exchange. Mistress Lotus could not wrap her arms around her child. She had long ago given up her flesh for her lover. It would have almost been romantic if the sacrifice had been mutual. He felt like spitting at the mere thought of it.

All the agents of the Black Lotus, excluding Pansy, had been flying around in this unicopter for over twelve hours. The aircraft had solar panels so they could be airborne indefinitely. Poppy shivered at the thought, or maybe it was just the cold.

Lily sat next to Poppy. They wore thick coats, like Thistle. Mistress Lotus didn't need one, but her spherical body was strapped down to prevent her from rolling around. Thistle kept close to her mother, crying silently. The crying itself wasn't anything new. Thistle was still young and sensitive. Poppy suspected she would grow out of it when her kill count reached the hundreds. Even so, her crying was abnormally shrill today. Poppy knew why.

Temple stood in front of the open doors. He wore only his fluttering cloak, shorts, and helmet. The cold did not bother him, for he was cold. He was cold, waiting, searching... Poppy and his kin had been told to attack the enemy only after Temple made the first move. It was unclear what they should expect. For all Poppy knew, this could be a death trap, but the emperor had given direct orders. Disgusting old man…

"What are you doing?" Lily hissed at him in their tongue. She was usually quite giddy before combat missions like this one, but now she was somber. "Are you daydreaming? Cloak's creature is right there."

"Do you love Father?" Poppy asked.

"What? Don't get me killed, nitwit."

"I asked you a question. Do you—?"

Temple stepped out of the unicopter and fell toward the sea, hundreds of feet below.

As if a spell had been lifted, Thistle started sobbing. Her long hair wrapped around her tear-stricken face like a cocoon. She also made a low buzz like an electric shaver.

"Calm, girl," Mistress Lotus said. "The emperor himself, your father and creator, has given us this mission. Your life is his. He did not ask you to cry. He asked you to follow that abomination into battle, and so you shall."

Poppy almost laughed at those words. Did it really matter what the emperor wanted? After all, he wasn't the one giving the commands anymore.

***

Camilla Ryder stared out the window. There was nothing to look at but endless ocean and the occasional iceberg. Cloaking technology had rendered their entire fleet invisible. Even with that precaution, the ships were careful to move slowly to avoid making waves.

"Calm before the storm," Vice Admiral Lexington mused. He had a pencil-thin mustache and a scrawny build. Lexington had been keeping close to Ryder ever since the voyage began. Last night, he had visited her quarters, asking in a breathy voice if there was anything she needed. Ryder said no and closed the door. That didn't seem to discourage him.

"Only two days till we reach East Russia," Lexington whispered, standing near Ryder as she looked out the window. She didn't acknowledge his presence, but he kept talking anyway. "I have a nice bottle of wine. When you get off duty, perhaps I could interest you in a glass?"

"I don't drink," Ryder told him. "Not anymore."

Lexington licked his teeth. "Oh, but this is a special occasion... You and I are about to make history, Ryder. Why not celebrate with wine?"

"Hope we're not interrupting anything, boss!" Hank Powers shouted.

Powers thundered onto the observation deck, dressed in an uncomfortable blue uniform, the seams nearly bursting from his bulbous muscular build. Keito Kusanagi followed behind. The swordsman wore a dark outfit with a sword on his hip. His burns had been healed, and he looked no worse for wear. The rest of the SWS had also arrived. York stood with a straight back, Kennedy held a thin copy of *Bill Budd,* Cruz maintained his typical good humor, and Patel wore her cheerful smile, already having made a full recovery.

"You ruffians better get a move on," Lexington snapped, wiping his sweaty hands on his pant legs. "Ryder and I were having a private chat."

"She asked us to come here, pal," Powers told him.

"Yes, I did," Ryder confirmed.

Lexington scrunched up his nose. "Oh, how I pity you, Ryder, forced to deal with an ignoramus and his diversity squad. Make sure to put them on the front lines. They'll be useful shields for all the worthwhile soldiers."

Powers took a step forward, his nostrils flaring. Keito, unbothered, put an arm in front of his comrade to prevent any unpleasantness.

"I have to return to my post and make sure that nearby Chinese fleet doesn't cross our path," Lexington told Ryder. "Tell me if you ever wish for a transfer. Good stock like you shouldn't be babysitting this gang of misfits."

With those chivalrous words, Lexington strolled out of the observation deck. None of the squad was sorry to see him go.

"That pompous sleaze!" Powers yelled, punching the air. "Thinks he's better than me! Ever since the war started, bastards like him think they can start speaking their mind."

"Take a moment to calm down," Ryder told him. "That is an order."

Powers' shoulders sagged. "Guy must have friends in high places…"

"Let us not waste time discussing the vice admiral," Ryder said, turning to face her subordinates. "I assembled the squad here to assign your tasks. Keito, you will be on standby for the remainder of the night."

Powers sniggered. "Well, R & R is a pretty important job too."

"I would like a private word with you before that," Ryder said. "York, you will be conducting patrols around the perimeter of the fleet with Kennedy and Patel."

"Does this mean I get my beauty rest?" Cruz asked.

"For now. You'll switch with Kennedy in four hours, and Patel will switch with Kennedy in another four hours, and then back to you. York, I'm leaving you in charge of the squad for the next twelve hours. You asked for the responsibility, and now you will receive it."

"Thank you, ma'am," York said. "I am grateful for your confidence."

"Whoa, hey!" Powers protested. "I'm the leader of this squad! I should decide who gets to replace me when I'm taking a break."

"We will discuss that during our private talk," Ryder said blankly.

Powers turned red. He turned to his squad to gauge their reactions. Patel and Kennedy avoided eye contact. Cruz kept his amusement hidden as best as he could.

"If there are no more questions, you are all dismissed," Ryder said.

Keito turned on his heels and left the room. Cruz, Patel, and Kennedy followed. York smirked at Powers before leaving as well. Powers wanted to knock those aviator sunglasses off his smug head, but he knew better than to act out now.

When the door closed, Ryder resumed looking out the window. "Powers, tell me what ails you."

Powers glanced around, laughing a little. "Uh, you mean 'ale,' like beer?"

Ryder wasn't amused. She was incapable of it. "No, I mean, why have you been more unreliable than usual lately?"

"Hey, don't question my patriotism!"

"Patriotism and competence are not one and the same. I wish to know why you broke your fist. I also wish to know why you allowed your walker to be hijacked by that woman so easily during the *Tortuga* incident."

"I told you already, I punched some stairs ... by accident! And that woman! Yeah, that freak! But she got the jump on me, and I wasn't the only one taken out."

"You also struck Cruz's walker. That was an amateur mistake."

Powers clenched his fists. Anger was building in him again, except that he couldn't direct it at anyone but himself.

"Powers, you have not yet been discharged because of your exemplary record, our lack of soldiers, and my personal assurances to Admiral Redwood. Those reasons, however, will offer you no more protection from this point forward. I expect immediate improvement."

A few tears escaped Powers' eyes, but they dried up within seconds.

"And you still need to tell me what is wrong, Powers."

Powers relaxed a little. His fear was now visible to the naked eye. "Those things ... those animals..."

"You are talking about the Gifted."

"Illusions, that's what I thought. Bunch of parlor tricks, that's what I said. But no, there ain't no way you could fake this."

"This behavior of yours got worse after the Pentagon attack."

"It was the straw that broke the camel's back. First the Helmet Man, then Incognito, then *Leviathan* ... Rome ... the war..."

Ryder stared at him with empty eyes. Her silence was piercing.

"I'm an ant," Powers said in a child's voice. "I'm an ant against giants. Incognito, the Helmet Man, that flying woman, the second Helmet Man, they're gods. I can't touch them. All my life, I thought I was the top of the food chain. But I'm puny... Nothing I do will matter. Maybe if I'm lucky, they'll let me live."

"That goes for the rest of us."

"Doesn't make it any better."

"No, but it means you are not alone. One ant cannot match a giant, but—"

"Yeah, yeah… I know the speech, teamwork and all that. And here I thought the West was supposed to be all about individualism and stuff." Powers felt like punching a wall again. "I see kids joining the army and people being threatened with guns. All these sacrifices aren't gonna mean squat in the end. It doesn't matter if we make the hard choices or not. Do we even make those kinds of choices ourselves? Are we giving up our humanity for nothing?"

Ryder kept quiet for a couple of seconds, her blue eyes examining Powers from head to toe. He needed reassurance. He needed help. Hank Powers was still salvageable.

"Powers, I find you immensely attractive."

Powers raised his eyes in swift confusion. "What the…?"

"That was the primary reason I first recruited you." Ryder moved toward him. Powers took a step back. Ryder put a hand on his enormous chest. A shiver went up his spine.

"I have not felt a true emotion in almost seven years," she said. "I have only felt occasional ripples of feeling in my psyche. I am blank. I am not whole." She started to press herself against Powers. "But you make me a woman."

Powers jumped back. "You're crazy!"

Ryder took a step toward him.

"I always knew you were off," Powers said. "But not *this* off."

"Powers, you speak your mind. Your blood runs hot. That is why I need you. You think having no emotions is a blessing?"

"That–that Spock guy seems to do just fine."

"That is a misconception," Ryder said, caressing the side of her dead face. "The worst feeling in the world is not feeling at all. I have tried nearly everything to feel again. My experiments with medication, illicit drugs, and alcohol proved unsuccessful. My duty to the Western Union was my only salvation, my only way to feel. That is until a year ago."

"So … I make you feel?"

"Precisely. You see, you *do* hold importance. You are necessary. You are not all bravado. There is a purpose to your existence."

"Uh, thanks..."

"That being said, I cannot have you failing me. If this abysmal behavior continues, I will leave you. Then you will truly have nothing."

"Boss, you need help."

"I can help myself just fine."

It was official. This woman was beyond him. Powers tried to dig deeper anyway. "Hey, boss, your condition, how exactly..."

Ryder considered answering, but light flashed on the other side of the observation window. An explosion followed. Sirens squealed.

A beam of yellow light had just hit an invisible ship.

"Red alert, we are under attack!" a voice cried over the intercom. "I repeat, we are under attack!"

Beams of light, at least two per second, brought the warships out of hiding. For every beam that came down, a ship's cloaking device got fried. Most of the beams hit the control towers. Some hit rotors. In half a minute, almost the entire fleet was visible.

Ryder gazed out of the window, remaining stoic in the face of chaos. "Powers, move out," she ordered.

Powers didn't waste any time gaping. He wasn't so easily stupefied these days. Floating aircraft carriers can do that to a guy. He dashed out of the observation deck.

"The therapy worked," Ryder told herself. She followed Powers.

Keito was already on the move. He ran onto the fight deck of the aircraft carrier with his sword drawn. The Arctic cold didn't faze him in the slightest. Unicopters and fighter jets were taking off. Ships readied their guns. Soldiers were putting out fires caused by the beams. A lot was happening. The beams had stopped. Every ship had been hit. Where was the enemy? Up above? Very likely.

"Looks like the invasion's off," Powers said, rolling up inside his oversized walker, which held a giant surfboard. "Admiral Redwood ain't gonna be happy."

Their fleet of fifty-five ships was exposed. They had hoped to travel from Alaska to the Sea of Okhotsk, where there were relatively few Chinese patrol ships. From there, the invasion force would have to move stealthily southward through East Russia and strike Beijing, using a device invented by Dr. Plato to pierce the force field protecting the Forbidden City. If they could capture the emperor, the entire Chinese Empire would crumble, the Western Union winning the war. They hoped to avoid notice until they were less than a hundred miles away from Beijing. Their cloaking technology had made this plan feasible.

But now all was revealed.

The other specialized walkers rolled in behind Hornet. Tangerine was the only other one to hold a surfboard, while Sapphire and Garnet had their wings extended. Kennedy was the last to arrive in her green walker.

"Manage to finish your chapter?" Cruz teased.

"Sorry for the delay," Kennedy said. "And no, I did not."

"All right, lay off her!" Powers yelled. "We need to be prepared for—"

The aircraft carrier started tipping. Powers' walker almost fell over.

"Are we sinking?" he exclaimed.

No one answered, but the entire squad was already staring at the cause of the tipping. Keito was the only one to recognize it. Even though he had seen something similar before in the Neutral Zone, it still wasn't something he could easily brush off.

A mountain of water grew out of the ocean. It had to be at least three hundred feet tall. Its diameter was comparably smaller, around seventy feet, but in absolute terms...

"Guess I'm not used to this crap after all," Powers whispered.

"What do we do, Powers?" Patel almost screamed.

"Fire at the fricking thing!"

Western Union ships fired at the mountain of water. The walkers joined in immediately. Explosions blanketed the mountain, evaporating chunks of it. It did no good. The mountain regenerated itself. Eight liquid appendages then grew from its sides, each thicker than the trunk of a giant sequoia.

"Report," Ryder commanded. She rolled up in her own walker. Obsidian looked meaner than ever, moving with the grace and precision of a surgeon.

"The Black Lotus is attacking," Keito said. "Mistress Lotus has revealed herself. The others have not, but they may be near."

"How did the Chinese know we were coming?" York asked.

"Now is not the time for speculation," Ryder said. "A small Chinese fleet is nearby. We need to defeat the Black Lotus before those ships arrive, or we will be overwhelmed for sure. Powers, you and your squad assist the navy in their battle with Mistress Lotus. Keito and I will handle the other Black Lotus agents. Now move out."

Powers grunted in understanding. He commanded his walker to jump off the aircraft carrier. Hornet hit the water with its surfboard and rode it toward the liquid behemoth. Cruz followed in the same manner while Kennedy skated Emerald across the water at high speed, having no need of a surfboard. Keito kicked the flight deck, the repulsion pad on his foot accelerating him twenty feet up before he kicked again. The remaining three walkers flew straight upward before Obsidian flew in a different direction.

The invasion might be off, but the war was definitely not.

Ryder reached the clouds. She wanted to survey the area. The Western Union had very limited information on the Black Lotus. Ryder knew it was made up of Mistress Lotus and her four children, who had cybernetic enhancements that gave them superhuman abilities. It was theorized the emperor had created the Black Lotus after hearing rumors that the Western Union had made supersoldiers of its own. It was also theorized the Chinese had obtained this cyborg technology from scientists within the Western Union itself. Of course, these theories were strictly speculative.

Something caught Ryder's eye, something in her periphery. Obsidian's sensors didn't detect anything, but her eyes never failed her. It was something black, something formless.

A fighter jet fell from the sky. The black something was latched on to it. Ryder couldn't wrap her mind around what it was. She could only describe it as living smoke.

The black smoke let go of the fighter jet and formed into a sentient whirlwind. The falling fighter jet hit the ocean, the unconscious pilot dying on impact.

Ryder had a good idea what that thing was now. She fired her laser. The smoke fluidly avoided it. She fired two more laser beams. Again, the smoke dodged them. It started circling Obsidian like a hungry shark. It appeared to have no long-range attacks at its disposal. As long as Ryder maintained her distance, she would be out of harm's way. But her attacks weren't making contact. How could she destroy it?

The smoke vanished, dissipating in a second.

Ryder was alone. She didn't like it.

Alarms started blaring. She wasn't afraid, only alert. She checked her gauges. Obsidian was overheating. Black smoke seeped out of the vents and filled the cockpit. The skin on Ryder's face started to tingle. Then it started to itch. Then it burned.

Darkness closed in. The living smoke encompassed her.

***

Keito propelled himself through the air, kick by kick, and landed on one of the aircraft carriers. The water mountain was starting to swing its many limbs at the ships near it. Two vessels were capsized, four others taking on a significant amount of water.

Thirteen ships, as well as Hornet and the other walkers, blasted away at the monster. *That battle seems as hopeless as someone trying to fill a pail with no bottom*, Keito thought.

A red shape sped over his head. He drew his sword. The enemy had spotted him. Fleeing was pointless.

A woman landed on the flight deck before him.

"Waiting for me, handsome man?" she asked in fractured English.

Keito raised his sword. He wasn't feeling talkative.

"Good, Keito Kusanagi don't diddle around," Lily said. Lengthy blades extended from her palms. "You're world's greatest swordsman? Well, I greatest swordswoman!"

***

"York! Patel! Distract that thing!" Powers ordered.

Sapphire slashed at a water tentacle. "We're already doing that!" York yelled.

"Well, keep doing it!" Powers yelled back. "Cruz and I will attack from the surface. Kennedy, use this opportunity to finish Mistress Lotus. Our intelligence says she should be controlling it, and your walker is the best one for the job."

"Understood," Kennedy said. Her green walker stopped skating and sank. Its jets propelled it through the water faster than a sailfish. Emerald circled behind the liquid monster and shot out of the water. In an almost death-defying stunt, the walker began skating up the monster's back.

"Whoa!" Powers shouted. "That's even cooler than I'd thought it'd be."

A liquid limb nearly slammed into Garnet, but the walker became superheated, and the water evaporated before touching it. A shell whizzed past far too close and struck the creature.

"Those ships need to watch where they aim," Patel snapped.

"I know it sucks, but we got to keep this thing pinned down," Powers said as he fired shells of his own. They all struck the water monster. A column of water almost knocked Hornet and Tangerine off their surfboards.

"Hurry up, Kennedy!" Powers bellowed.

Emerald reached the small of the creature's back and fired torpedoes into it. Deep inside the mountain of water, Mistress Lotus sensed the oncoming projectiles and redirected them into each other with a strong current. Even so, the resulting explosion jostled her around. The entire titan shook and grew smaller. The shells from both the ships and the walkers continued to hammer away. Cruz whistled in triumph.

"Go catch her, York!" Powers yelled.

York fully understood the order when he saw Emerald plummet downward. The water monster had shaken the walker off its side, and the mecha didn't have wings.

"York, hurry!" Powers shouted.

Sapphire dove toward the falling walker. Columns of water blasted out of the creature's side, but York maneuvered his walker around these attacks in a series of close calls. He crashed into the plummeting Emerald. Kennedy cried out from the impact, but Sapphire now had a firm hold of her walker.

"Keep at it!" Powers told Cruz and Patel. "This thing's on its last leg."

York turned his head and saw that the water monster was on the ropes, now more of a hill than a mountain. Powers especially seemed to throw everything he had at the enemy. He easily dodged each time a water tentacle swung down. During all this, Hornet never ceased firing shells. York didn't want to admit it, but he was impressed. There was a reason why Ryder chose Powers as team leader, why he was often considered one of the best walker pilots alive.

York scoffed. "Still think I'd do the job better."

"Powers, they're here!" Patel cried.

Two shells struck near Hornet. Powers growled as waves crashed into his walker, water droplets sprinkling down around the yellow mecha. He was just about to yell at the friendly fire, only to realize it wasn't friendly fire.

It had come from a fleet of red ships.

"Guess this is what a world war looks like," Powers said.

***

Ryder grasped at the control panel. Her vision became blurry. Was this her punishment? No, she had done nothing wrong, only her duty. If anyone was going to punish her, it would be her superiors, not this phantom.

One of her hands found the button she was looking for. She didn't know if it would work, but there wasn't anything else to try. She pressed it.

The lights on Obsidian's control panel flickered off. The smoke in the cockpit was cleared immediately, leaving only a layer of black dust on the floor.

Ryder coughed out some of the dust. Fresh air entered her lungs. She had triggered an electromagnetic plus. She figured the Black Lotus was somehow controlling the smoke and that it was likely susceptible to such an attack. Sure enough, her theory had panned out. A good chunk of Obsidian was organic, so not all of its essential functions had been affected. However, her radar and radio were toast, not to mention her targeting system. She would have to exercise more caution when dealing with her remaining enemies.

Those yellow beams... The Black Lotus wasn't the only threat hidden in the clouds. The second Helmet Man who had attacked the Pentagon was with them. That must mean the Chinese Empire was behind the Pentagon's destruction. This revelation only made Ryder more confident in her choice. The enemies of freedom were working together. They could not succeed.

Yet they could not fail.

***

Keito blocked another attack, then another, and another. Lily continued this barrage at a hectic pace. She was a cyborg and did not tire. Her two swords often came down at the same time, but Keito either managed to block both with his sword or only blocked one while dodging the other. She spun like a whirlwind. He jumped back and threw three ninja stars at her. She knocked them out of the air with one blade.

Lily laughed and snorted. "That all you got? I thought you were able to take on Helmet Man. Guess I expect too much from Japanese."

Keito frowned. He kicked the deck of the ship and flew upward.

Lily's snakelike eyes locked on Keito. "Anything you do, I do better!"

She kicked the flight deck, flying thirty feet up in less than a second. Keito's arm was cut as Lily flew by. He barely managed to block her other blade.

"I got pads installed after you did," Lily taunted.

She repelled herself back toward Keito, but he kicked at her as she approached, hoping to knock her out of the air with his repulsion pad. He only grazed her with the gust of air, but that was enough to throw her off balance. She was caught in a momentary free fall before using her repulsion pads to stop her descent.

This window of opportunity was too tempting for Keito to pass up. While Lily was still correcting herself, he came at her with full force. He didn't just swing his sword through the air. He *cut* the air. His katana moved with such speed that even Lily had a hard time anticipating where it was going. She only just deflected it.

Keito wasn't finished. He sliced again, faster than before. Lily almost got hit that time. He seemed to swing his sword twice more, but she couldn't be sure. Her sadistic smile was starting to fade. How was this man so fast?

One of Lily's blades shattered. Her eyes widened, and her grin was gone, replaced by an expression of bewildered shock.

"You broke it," she whispered in disbelief.

Keito stabbed her through the chest. The tip of his katana came right out her back. Blood gurgled from her mouth as she fell thirty feet. She hit the flight deck, and she hit it hard. The fall itself did no serious damage, seeing as her skeleton was metal, but she shuddered again as a spasm of pain went through her frame.

Keito landed before her. He flicked his blade, flinging the blood off it.

Lily struggled to lift herself. She wasn't bleeding as much as a normal person would have, but that didn't mean her wound was benign.

"You ... you think you're so tough?" she asked. "My father ... emperor ... divine being... Gave me perfect body... Made me god..."

"Gods must bleed easily, then," Keito said. "Surrender."

Lily's legs shook like petals, but she was able to get to her feet. She raised her one remaining blade and smiled weakly. "You think you slayed me? I slay you... You aren't..."

Lily seemed to be thinking of a clever comeback. But something distracted her mid-thought. She was only mildly perplexed at first.

Then her revived smile melted away. Her mouth parted, her breathing became more rapid, and her eyes widened again, but they weren't wide with shock this time.

They were wide with primal terror.

Lily slammed her foot into the deck, jumping up twenty feet, and fled the scene.

Keito blinked. He was just about to go after her when a coldness slipped inside him. It was below freezing outside, but this new cold was not a sensation he could shrug off. His eyes grew large, the grip on his sword tighter than ever.

Temple stood behind the swordsman. Fresh blood dripped from his helmet.

CHAPTER 23

Ryder flew her walker low, scanning the area for Black Lotus agents. The mountain of water that had been attacking the fleet was starting to merge back into the ocean, though that didn't stop the ships and walkers from hammering away at it.

However, the fleet of Chinese Empire ships had finally arrived and exchanged fire with several Western Union ships. One Chinese ship was on fire. A Western vessel started to sink. This was a historic moment. The Chinese Empire and the Western Union were engaging in hot war after decades of using underhanded techniques and proxies against each other. Nobody had thought it would have ever come to this.

Ryder would have assisted her comrades under normal circumstances, but an even more pressing situation had caught her attention.

Two figures were fighting on a nearby aircraft carrier. At least thirty corpses and two half-melted unicopters were scattered across its flight deck. Reinforcements must have attempted to intervene. Moving her walker in closer, Ryder noticed that one of the fighters was Keito. He was dashing about at a frantic rate. The other fighter seemed sluggish by comparison, yet he managed to avoid Keito's sword every time.

Ryder squinted. That man... He wore a silver helmet.

Something stirred inside her. She gasped. Something *actually* stirred inside her. She took a deep breath. This was what she wanted, wasn't it? Yes, of course it was.

Whoever or whatever that man was, Ryder would have him.

***

Keito stumbled. Another beam had burned through his calf.

He squeezed his eyes shut, suppressing the pain. A fist backhanded him, knocking two of his teeth loose. He jumped up and swung his sword. His opponent stepped to the side, almost lazily, successfully avoiding the blade. A beam of light hit Keito's last repulsion pad. He landed roughly, twisting his ankle.

Temple kneed him in the chest. Keito felt two of his ribs break. In retaliation, he tried to swipe at Temple with his sword. It bounced off Temple's helmet, the silver devil having used it to block the blade. Temple straightened his neck out afterward. Joints popped.

Despite Keito's normally cool demeanor, he was getting desperate. Even the Helmet Man had some weaknesses, but this new Helmet Man was different. It was only good for killing. Keito could not imagine it doing anything else.

Keito decided to put all his energy into one last assault. He sliced his katana through the air multiple times, moving like a blender. Just one cut. He only needed one.

But Temple either sidestepped the slices or blocked them with his elongated helmet. Keito's attacks soon became slower, less accurate. It didn't even seem like Temple had to put any effort into dodging them anymore.

Keito felt his leg give out. He could block out the pain, but the damage was done. His legs were riddled with burnt holes. Before he could fall to his knees, Temple slammed his fist into his face, also punching his gut for good measure. Keito collapsed on his side, his body broken in countless ways. He barely managed to hold on to his sword.

With one hand, Temple grabbed Keito by the head and lifted him off the deck. He then shot a beam through his torso. The swordsman screamed, squeezing the handle of his sword even tighter. Another beam ripped through him, this one much lower. Keito was no longer screaming. He was crying. The third beam went through his shoulder, but he refused to let go of his sword. That's what this beast wanted, wasn't it? No ... he would never submit.

Temple squeezed Keito's skull. There was audible cracking.

Just as Keito thought his skull was about to cave in, Temple stopped squeezing and conjured up a wall of light. A laser came from the right. The wall stopped it, but Temple had to exert himself, his white muscles bulging.

Keito's eyes widened. Temple was distracted. Here was his opening. In the blink of an eye, he sliced his sword through Temple's wrist. Keito dropped on the deck, the severed hand still clutching his head. The wall of light vanished. Temple staggered back. Black blood poured from his stump.

Another laser came down, forcing Temple to jump backward. Ryder was careful not to hit Keito. Obsidian fired more lasers, blasting away at the aircraft carrier's flight deck. Temple was able to avoid them every time, but Ryder had him on the run.

Temple didn't stay on the defensive for long, firing beams at Obsidian. Ryder was able to fly out of the line of fire but had a hard time manually targeting him. His movements were becoming erratic. He also kept close to Keito to make her aim more carefully. Temple may have been a beast, but he wasn't a stupid one.

After a minute of this, Temple created a glowing disk. It was semitransparent and about the size of a trash can lid. He tossed it at Obsidian like a Frisbee. Ryder had a strong suspicion that the disk could cut through her walker. However, it seemed to be slower than Temple's beams. She moved to the right, out of its path.

The disk exploded. Ryder had not expected this but wished she had. Obsidian spun out of control, Ryder struggling with the controls.

Temple flew at Obsidian, reaching it within seconds. He grabbed the walker's wing and ripped it off like a child torturing a fly.

Ryder felt a jolt. Her walker was free-falling. She was barely able to land on the aircraft carrier, her walker skidding to a stop. Obsidian aimed its laser gun at the sky. However, Temple had already landed on the ship, right in front of her walker.

Ryder quickly adjusted her aim and fired a laser. Temple dashed forward, the laser hitting the flight deck instead. While running between Obsidian's legs, he punched through its left ankle. The walker tumbled to its side onto the flight deck. Temple fired twenty beams at the downed walker. Obsidian's armor was thick enough to protect Ryder, but the walker wouldn't be getting up again anytime soon.

With his opponents helpless, Temple took the time to regenerate. His stump glowed yellow. The bones grew first. Then came the flesh. Finally, the skin and nails reappeared, the new hand of Temple squeezing in triumph.

"Hang on, Ms. Ryder!" Cruz yelled.

Tangerine landed on the deck to the left of Temple while Emerald touched down right before the beast. Powers, York, and Patel were still busy chasing away Mistress Lotus, which left only Cruz and Kennedy to assist their own mistress. They had both been confident that they could handle this situation alone.

But now...

Kennedy found the joints of her fingers locked into place. A fine sheen of sweat now covered her face. She had always prided herself on her logic and objectivity that bordered on escapism. That was why she enjoyed reading. That was why she made a fine walker pilot.

But now...

Temple glided toward her.

"Kennedy!" Cruz drove his walker between Temple and the green walker. Tangerine extended all six arms. Emerald remained stationary.

Temple flew at them.

"You cockroach!" Cruz screamed. Tangerine rained down punches and laser blasts, leaving holes and scorch marks on the flight deck. His fingers danced and his eyes darted. He pushed himself and his walker to the brink as they executed an all-out bombardment.

And yet Temple dodged every attack. The cloaked menace had only been temporarily stalled but inched closer and closer with every millisecond. Cruz had stopped breathing by this point. His face became blue. His eyes watered. His fingernails bled. Vomit came up. That was the last thing Cruz tasted before Temple reached his walker and shot a beam clean through the cockpit. It went straight through Cruz's head, between those darting eyes.

Temple flew up and kicked the walker with the force of a wrecking ball. Tangerine flew backward into Emerald. Kennedy at last unfroze and began shrieking at the top of her lungs. Images of the demon pounded away at her psyche as the two walkers toppled off the deck, crashed into the ocean, and sank out of sight.

Temple returned his attention to Obsidian and drifted toward the walker. His pace was slow yet unwavering. He grabbed the cockpit door and tore it off.

But Ryder was ready. She fired her machine gun. A few bullets ricocheted off Temple's helmet, but most of them went through his torso. His body jerked about. Black blood squirted from his wounds. Ryder continued firing. She only stopped when she ran out of bullets.

Temple snatched the machine gun from her hands. His heat melted it into goop. He ripped Ryder from her seat and threw her out of Obsidian. She tumbled onto the deck. Temple's wounds lit up, healing instantly. His cloak was riddled with bullet holes and stained with blood, but he was otherwise unmarred. He stood over Ryder. The air was colder than ever.

"Get back..." Keito wheezed. He was limping over, barely able to lift his sword. Camilla Ryder was his employer. It was his duty to serve her, to protect her. He could care less about the Western Union. Ryder was the one he was indebted to. He could not—

Temple shot a beam through his chest. Keito fell, moaning. Temple paid no mind to him. Ryder was his object of focus. He brought down his foot on her leg, breaking it. She yelped. The pain was nothing compared to what she was feeling inside. Yes, she was feeling! It was a mix of emotions. Her face twitched like mad. One might have mistaken it for a seizure.

Next, Temple knelt and twisted her arm behind her back, yanking it out of the socket. She let out another yelp, greater than the first. In her state of mind, it was a complete wonder how she managed to get the small knife from her pocket. She stabbed it into Temple's neck repeatedly until the blade broke.

More black blood flowed from Temple. It dripped all over Ryder, staining her clothes. But he did not heal this wound. Instead, he grabbed her jaw and pried her mouth open. She was helpless to resist as the ichor filled her mouth. It was bitterer than anything she had ever tasted. And it was warm, almost hot.

Temple let go. Ryder vomited the blood, spewing it across the deck. Unicopters were approaching. Temple was uninterested in them. This woman was still breathing. There was still time to take her to Hell.

A bullet struck his back. He stood up, searching the area.

The bullet exploded. White light consumed half of his body. His left arm was gone, as was a good portion of his torso. The dark cloak burned. The flesh of Temple was blackened. He stumbled to the side.

Something flashed by. Keito had used his last ounce of strength to take advantage of Temple's moment of weakness. He staggered to a halt several feet away from him. Unable to do any more, the swordsman passed out.

Temple stood still. The fire burned away the last of his cloak.

His head toppled off his shoulders.

The helmet hit the flight deck. Temple's body collapsed. The severed head rolled off the edge of the flight deck and plummeted into the ice-cold water.

***

Poppy put his rifle away, satisfied that his target was dead. Although Keito Kusanagi had the honor of delivering the final blow, Poppy knew Temple's defeat would not have been possible without his personal assistance. For that, he could be proud.

Lily climbed back into the unicopter, bleeding heavily and grimacing. Thistle was busy weeping in the corner.

"You got nothing to cry about," Lily spat in Mandarin. "You didn't get stabbed."

"Be nice to your sister," Poppy told her. "Now let's pick up Mother. The battle is won."

Lily shot him a dirty look as she patched herself up but said no more. The pilot changed course, decreasing in altitude so they could retrieve Mistress Lotus.

Poppy took satisfaction in knowing the foreigners would soon be purged from the empire. His mother had done nothing to stop Cloak. Only Xing was taking any action. Xing had asked him to kill Temple during the chaos of battle. Poppy had been skeptical. He wanted Cloak gone as much as Xing, but betraying his mother was not something he would do easily. Xing had finally convinced him after explaining how he would deal with Sebastian on his end. Poppy almost snickered at the thought.

The Chinese Empire did not forgive, and neither did he.

***

Three unicopters landed on the flight deck. Marines jumped out, guns locked and loaded. Half of them surrounded the remains of Temple's body and riddled it with bullets. They weren't taking any chances. The rest of the marines brought out stretchers for Keito and Ryder. As Ryder was being moved onto one, she grabbed a marine by his arm.

"The battle..." she said, emotionless again, but that didn't stop her from feeling pain.

"We're retreating," the marine said. "Orders from Washington. The Chinese fleet has withdrawn for now. That water creature also isn't anywhere to be seen. But the element of surprise is gone, and we'll be done for if more enemy ships come."

"Then..."

"Sorry, ma'am. The invasion has failed."

As Ryder was loaded onto a unicopter, she guessed to herself how many soldiers had been killed. Hundreds at least, including Cruz, maybe Kennedy. Craning her head, she took a long look at Keito and his broken body as he was loaded onto a separate unicopter. She now had a perfect visualization of what the fleet had been reduced to.

And she had made it all possible.

CHAPTER 24

"Union Network has confirmed that over two thousand military personnel have perished in the Arctic Ocean," the anchorwoman said. "President Powell has yet to address the nation."

Redwood sat in his cramped, dark office, watching the news on a holographic screen. He had whiskey in a coffee mug. It was his only comfort right now.

"Fleet Admiral Redwood has also yet to comment about the failed invasion. Vice President Reynolds is putting the blame on Redwood's 'ham-fisted' approach to dealing with the Chinese Empire. Many also claim the revolts in the Occupied Territories have only gotten worse due to Redwood's diversion of military resources and pacifist tendencies."

Redwood sighed and sipped his drink. He had seen this propaganda machine tear apart people in a second flat. Never before had he personally been in the grinder, until now.

Outside, the crowd of protesters had swelled since news of the failed invasion came out. Redwood could see them through his window. Thousands of people held picket signs, screaming and shouting half-baked criticisms. Riot walkers kept the crowd back with tear gas and ultrasonic cannons. Any protester who attempted to climb the fence was shot by snipers with rubber bullets. Police were considering whether to start using real ones.

"Heathens control the government!" Mr. Preacher cried. He was on top of a truck with a megaphone in his hand. Those who weren't protesting listened to him. "The moon will strike them down! Have you had the dreams?"

"We'd like to take this moment to send our thoughts and prayers to Jeff Springer, our beloved anchorman, who is being held prisoner by the United Third," the anchorwoman continued. "Any information about his whereabouts should be reported to the authorities."

Redwood's phone rang. It was a secure line. He snickered with little enthusiasm. When was the last time he had gotten an actual phone call? These holograms were everywhere nowadays. He muted the TV and picked up the phone.

"Admiral Redwood speaking..."

"Judging from your tone, I take it you saw the news."

Redwood sighed. Was Mathews going to start harassing him too? "I don't have to watch the news. Looking out the window is more than enough."

"I warned you, didn't I?"

"You sure did. Now Powell and his cronies are using the failed invasion against me. I expect he'll be back in office any day now. Ridiculous... I wasn't even in favor of the invasion, not with the Occupied Territories in such a bad state."

Director Mathews didn't reply at first. He seemed to be keeping quiet in order to stress an unspoken point. Redwood had a good idea what it was.

"Remember our conversation in your office?" Mathews asked.

"I told you it won't come to that, and I still stand by those words."

"It *has* come to that. How exactly do you think the invasion failed? The Chinese knew where the fleet was going. Someone leaked our plans."

"It couldn't have been Powell. He wasn't privileged to that information. Only a handful of people were."

"Including you."

Redwood got angry. "So were you."

"Sorry, I'm not your enemy, but you know what I'm saying. Someone could have given Powell the information. We can't trust anyone."

"But not even Powell would—"

"Powell tipped off the Chinese Empire so he could discredit you and regain control of the government. I know it in my gut."

"I'm sorry if a gut feeling isn't good enough for me," Redwood snapped. "I need more evidence before I could even consider *that*."

"You don't have to consider it," Mathews told him. "It's already done."

Redwood's heart stopped. The mug slipped from his fingers and shattered on the floor. The carpet greedily absorbed the alcohol. "You didn't..."

"I did. I'm doing. Don't watch the news. It won't matter by tomorrow morning."

Ever so gently, Mathews hung up the phone.

Redwood unmuted his television, not taking Mathew's advice.

He instantly regretted it.

"This is Union Network. Breaking news, President Powell has died in a car crash. At around 11:00 p.m., the president's limousine malfunctioned, causing it to accelerate to four hundred miles per hour. It drove straight off the side of Superhighway 89, killing the president and four other passengers on impact. Yes, the president is in fact dead.

"Foul play has yet to be ruled out, though officials say a computer malfunction is likely responsible. How this devastating loss will affect the Western Union during this time of war can only be speculated. More details soon to come."

***

Xing wished he could have played a more active role.

But he had to be content with staying on the sidelines. If the plan should fail, he needed to stay alive so he could fight another day. Of course, if the plan did fail, he had no idea what else there was to try. For all he knew, this could be his last shot at defeating Cloak.

Emperor Long sat at the head of the table. A rich assortment of food had been laid out before him. Shu spoon-fed the emperor, careful not to make eye contact with him. He choked down a smidgen of mush, but the food mostly fell from his mouth, dropping back onto the plate. The emperor caressed Shu's lower back. She did not protest. Xing observed the emperor's wandering hand venomously. Nevertheless, he kept his lips sealed.

Sebastian sat on the other end of the table, sipping water. His cane leaned against the table near him. The yellow dog was curled around his feet. Guards stood near the door, as did numerous attendants who would run to the emperor's aid should he desire anything. As for Xing, he had the dubious honor of sitting beside the emperor.

Pansy, the Black Lotus agent serving as the emperor's bodyguard, stared daggers at Sebastian from the corner. Xing was somehow relieved to see this. It seemed that Mistress Lotus did not trust Cloak any more than he did. Regardless, she would not act against Cloak unless her emperor was dead or commanded it. That was why Xing did not confide in the Black Lotus about his plans, with the exception of Poppy.

"I wonder what's delaying High General Duan," Sebastian said, putting down his glass of water. "At this rate, his dinner will get cold."

"High General Duan has been busy ever since the foiled invasion," Xing said. "The Western Union is fortifying its West Russian border. Shots have even been fired."

"I suspected such retaliation would occur," Sebastian said, scratching his dog. "Yes, all the Mentor's predictions are coming true."

Xing wanted to laugh. Did this slime not know Temple had been toppled?

"For now, I believe the Chinese Empire should refrain from attacking the Western Union," Sebastian continued. "We will wait for the United Third to weaken them even more before making our move. The emperor agrees."

More food dribbled from the emperor's mouth. He wasn't listening.

Sebastian chuckled. "We'll just take that as a yes. Anyway, I wish to inform you that I plan to install conductive mesh in a majority of the palace's walls."

Xing raised his nonexistent eyebrows. "You wish to install more electrical devices in the Forbidden City? Prime Minister, I am worried we are headed down a slippery slope."

"The emperor needs all the protection Cloak can offer him. Best get used to it. This is only the first of many renovations to come."

High General Duan marched into the room. His expression was fiery, to say the least.

Sebastian clucked his tongue. "You're late for supper. That's no good. The emperor demands his generals eat with him."

"I have no appetite," Duan told him, looking more youthful than ever. He was not even using his cane. "Emperor, I beg your forgiveness."

Twenty soldiers rushed into the room. They held machine guns.

Not taking the time to look surprised, Pansy sprinted over toward his emperor, determined to protect him. One of Duan's men shot Pansy with a strange-looking gun. Nothing seemed to come out, but Pansy went limp and dropped to the floor. Shu yelped while the emperor howled and pointed an unkempt fingernail at Duan.

"Traitor!" he hissed, food flying from his mouth.

Duan had tears in his eyes. "Emperor, forgive me."

The soldiers, who also looked tearful, disarmed the remaining guards in the room. The attendants did nothing except cower.

The emperor howled again. Xing stayed still with his hands folded.

"Emperor, I do this for you," Duan said. "I do this for the empire." He pointed at Sebastian. "This foreigner, this spawn of the West ... he does not care about the Chinese. He does not care about the empire. He does not care about you, our divine emperor. He will bring ruin to us. Everything you have built will crumble. Please, Emperor, heed my—"

"Do you think your emperor doesn't know that?" Sebastian interrupted.

High General Duan turned to him. "What did you say?"

"Your emperor knows his people starve," Sebastian said. He grabbed his cane and got up from his chair. His dog also stood up with a dumb grin. "Your emperor knows I bring only evil to these lands. He knows his servants are torn apart by beasts. He knows the Mentor is the harbinger of death. He knows. He just doesn't care."

Sebastian walked over to the far side of the room and pulled back two lush window curtains. From the window, one could see over the palace wall and through the force field that protected the Forbidden City, where hundreds of thousands of soldiers stood in ranks. They were hungry and disease-ridden but were still an imposing force.

"I have told all those soldiers about your treachery," Duan told Sebastian. "I have also taken control of the force field generator. I can take down the field and order those men to swarm the palace at any time I desire. You have no Temple to hide behind, nor do you have any of your comrades here to assist you. Cloak will no longer be allowed to leech off the empire. You will no longer warp my emperor's mind. The Chinese shall prevail!"

"You put an awful lot of thought into this failure," Sebastian said. He pulled a slender object from his pocket. Duan's eyes widened, as did the eyes of his men. Xing tried to remain calm, but this unforeseen development put even him on edge.

Sebastian had taken out a detonator.

"What is that?" Duan demanded. "Are you planning to use that on us?"

"No," Sebastian said. "Just them."

He pressed the detonator.

Outside the force field, jet-black mist spewed from the ground. There were at least thirty points of origin for the gas, ensuring full coverage of Tiananmen Square. The soldiers kept in ranks, though many drew their weapons as panic settled in.

A thousand men collapsed on the pavement and grabbed their heads in agony. Primeval cries escaped their throats. Eyes rolled back. These men were followed by thousands more who did the same. Before long, all the soldiers in the square fell. It was an ocean of human misery, limbs flailing as countless minds were torn apart.

Xing gaped. Shu sobbed. High General Duan shivered, as did his men. Thousands upon thousands of men were losing their souls before their eyes.

The emperor laughed.

Sebastian continued to grin. "You see? He truly doesn't care."

Nobody knew how to respond.

"This is the weapon that I have been developing," Sebastian told them. "More accurately, it's a variation of a weapon that Cloak already developed.

The mind-control nanobots were thought to be useless after the Western Union discovered a vaccine and its leaders were inoculated, but the vaccine was never distributed within the Chinese Empire, was it?"

"You demon," Duan whispered.

"The force field will protect us from the nanobots," Sebastian said, "though it'll be a few days before anyone can safely leave the Forbidden City. The men outside have become mindless supersoldiers, equipped with unnatural strength and able to follow basic commands. Since I needed to make a large quantity of nanobots, their programming was made simpler in order to make their manufacture financially feasible. Those men out there won't be able to speak or engage in complex thought ever again. I have truly made them into killing machines."

"Demon!" Duan cried. "Men, blow him away! Kill the swine!"

His men were eager to obey the command. They fired.

At the last moment, Sebastian took out something that had been hidden in his cane.

A sword.

His arm was a blur. He was knocking the bullets out of the air with his blade. They piled up around his feet as he continued swinging the sword at an unnatural pace.

Duan's men soon ran out of ammo.

Sebastian stopped moving his sword, his grin larger than ever. "Looks like you are out of bullets." He appeared on the other side of the room. "You should have used them better."

Beads of sweat rolled down Duan's forehead. He turned to see what had happened to his men. When he saw, he took a breath, almost choking on it.

All his men had been beheaded. Their bodies hit the floor. Heads rolled away. Blood was everywhere, pooling around the corpses. Duan felt his ankles give out. His Achilles tendons had also been cut. Duan fell face first, breaking his nose. He let out a shriek.

The emperor was laughing uncontrollably now. Snot dribbled from his nostrils. Shu covered her mouth, her sobbing turning to horror. Xing buried his face in his hands.

"Do you see what you must do now?" Sebastian asked, sheathing his sword. "Killing me won't be enough to fix your empire. Do you know what has to be done?"

Duan muttered a few curses, unable to get off the floor.

"I see," Sebastian said, his smile thinning. "You haven't learned anything. The Mentor would be disappointed."

Sebastian snapped his fingers. His yellow dog pounced on Duan. The man's screams lasted for a good two minutes.

"Servant, alert the guards downstairs," Sebastian told Shu over the sounds of torture. "Tell them to clean this mess up. And alert the technicians. Pansy needs to be rebooted. Who knew he had such an Achilles' heel?" Sebastian had to laugh at that one.

Shu practically sprinted out of her seat to escape the room.

Outside the Forbidden City, the soldiers had stopped squirming and were standing back up, veins black and eyes bloodshot. Hundreds of thousands of mind-controlled slaves now guarded the emperor. It was yet another gift from Cloak.

Sebastian walked over to Xing, who still covered his face in despair. The second-in-command of Cloak leaned in close to Xing so he could whisper into his ear.

"Nice try."

CHAPTER 25

"They say President Powell's dead," Redwood said, looking out his office window, the protestors as rabid as ever. "I'm not sure myself. For a while, it seemed like he died during the Pentagon attack, yet he made a public announcement three days later. I suppose we'll have to wait for the DNA test to confirm it's him."

Camilla Ryder stood on the other side of his desk, hands behind her back. Her arm had been popped back into place and her leg had been healed, though she still had a slight limp. The fleet had just returned to America, beaten and bruised. Ryder had flown to Washington to update Redwood on the situation. He wanted to hear it straight from the horse's mouth.

"If Powell really has perished, it will be yet another devastating blow for us," Ryder said. "I heard protests and riots have broken out in every Western Union city."

"Not every city. Just most of them." Redwood paused for a moment before continuing. "Ryder, if the report is true that you and Keito Kusanagi killed the second Helmet Man, I am legitimately impressed. At least some good came out of this disaster. The victims of the Pentagon attack have been avenged thanks to you."

"Thank you, sir."

"The fact that this second Helmet Man was working with the Chinese Empire means they were the ones behind the Pentagon attack. Those damn supersoldiers... They wouldn't be around if it wasn't for Powell."

"He merely did what was necessary," Ryder said.

Redwood stiffened. "An investigation is being conducted to determine how the Chinese Empire learned of our attempted invasion. We're considering every possibility, no matter how inconceivable. Everyone with knowledge about the operation is considered a suspect."

"Even me?" Ryder asked.

Redwood turned to Ryder, his face stone cold. "I heard you visited Cheyenne Mountain."

Ryder didn't answer. Her expression was passive.

"Vincent Quinn, Powell's lackey, picked you up," Redwood said. "He took you to see Powell, the real Powell. What exactly did you two talk about?"

Again, Ryder played dumb, or perhaps she wasn't acting at all.

Redwood continued to glare at her. "Ever since the Pentagon attack, I've suspected something strange has been going on with Powell. Tell me, how can we trust our leader when we don't even know where he is? I'm still not precisely sure what he's been up to. You probably have a better idea, don't you?"

The protestors continued to chant. Even so, their voices now seemed muted.

"Ryder, I brought you here to my office because I can't even trust the military police to take you into custody," Redwood said. "That's how paranoid I am right now. And I wanted to speak with you myself, to see if you could defend yourself. Go on, Ryder. Argue your case. Let's hear what you have to say."

Redwood didn't speak for a full minute. Neither did Ryder. They both just stood there, looking at each other. Redwood's eyes were full of emotion, hate in particular. Ryder's eyes were filled with nothing.

"What is the Western Union?" she finally asked.

Redwood's frown grew. "I want an answer, not a question."

"This is my way of answering. After all, answers usually just lead to more questions. Why not cut the middleman out?"

Redwood felt like spitting on the floor. "You want to know what the Western Union is? It's all the nations of the Western world joined together in an effort to help humanity. We seek to end war and poverty. We seek to make the world a place worth living in. Through the use of force and diplomacy, we are reclaiming the world from tyranny and ignorance. Incognito and the Chinese Empire stand between us and world peace. And if the invasion had been successful, we would have been one step closer to our goal, our ideal world."

"You are wrong."

"Oh, you deny the accusation against you?"

"No, I deny your conception of the Western Union. We are not trying to achieve peace, nor are we trying to create a utopia." Ryder took a step closer to Redwood's desk. "We are trying to create a never-ending state of war."

Redwood's eyes narrowed. "I beg your pardon?"

"We must always be at war," Ryder said, her words robotic and her logic cold. "It doesn't matter who the enemy is, but blood needs to be shed. True, the Chinese Empire will eventually crumble, and Incognito will be slain. However, we will always need an enemy, something to unite us, something to justify the people's lack of freedom. They seek safety from 'foreigners' and 'terrorists,' not even knowing what such labels actually mean. They know only that 'foreigners' and 'terrorists' are bad, that they cannot be reasoned with, that they must die. Governments were not made to protect people from 'outsiders,' but to protect people from themselves."

"What are you blathering about?"

"Before the Great Choke, the world was peaceful and prosperous, but with one virus, all of that was taken away. Anarchy, war, starvation, and chaos resulted. The poor response allowed the Choke to take a billion lives. The Western Union puts the blame on corporations, but the real enemy was liberty. The real enemy was freedom."

"Are you calling *freedom* evil?"

"Without structure, without leadership, people are frightened animals. But united, we can cure any virus, topple any regime, even stand against the heavens themselves. And in order to be united, in order to be willing to surrender our freedom, we must have a common enemy. Your ideals are sentimental. The only true justice is to turn chaos into order. That is my justice. That is why you are not fit to be our leader, Redwood. You do not understand that peace, at least complete peace, leaves us vulnerable to the cruelness of reality. You have always held me back, kept me from crossing lines that did not even exist. Powell may be simpleminded, but at least he understands the true purpose of the Western Union. In short, you're too soft."

"That's no excuse to kill your comrades!"

"They signed their lives over to the Western Union. We may dispose of them as we see fit. If we ask them to die in vain, they'd best do it."

Redwood snatched a handgun out of his desk and pointed it at Ryder. "That can't be all. You're just making excuses. Powell must have offered you something."

"Powell did offer me the chance to pursue the Helmet Man without any restrictions. Yet another incentive for me."

"What would your squad think if they saw you right now?"

"Good soldiers obey their superiors no matter what. Their opinions are of no concern."

"Then why are you betraying me, your commander?"

"As of now, you are no longer my commander."

Five Secret Service agents, all armed, crashed through the door. Redwood jumped in his shoes and dropped his gun. Ryder kept her detached cool.

"Admiral Redwood, you are under arrest for treason," an agent said.

"Preposterous!" Redwood yelled. "Is Powell behind this? I knew the lunatic wasn't dead. Men, this woman in front of me was responsible for the failed invasion."

"They know," Ryder said.

"What, that's impossible! There's no—"

Redwood stopped shouting his objections. Instead, he noticed agents. They all wore intense expressions, their eyes almost as empty as Ryder's.

"Sir, Director Mathews has already been executed," the agent said. "We know you played no active role in the assassination attempt, but you still had knowledge of the plot."

Redwood felt his head get fuzzy. "Do you really want Powell to continue running the Western Union? Knowing what he's done? He'll kill us all!"

"Sir, please calm down."

"Like hell I'll calm down!"

Ryder picked Redwood's gun up off the floor. "Admiral, although I do not agree with your philosophy, I admire your dedication to the Western Union. As such, I convinced Powell not to execute you. Instead, you shall spend the remainder of your life in exile."

"This ... this isn't the Western Union! This isn't America!"

"I have to go visit the hospital now," Ryder said. "We are worlds apart, Redwood. I wish you could have seen past the fantasy."

Pocketing Redwood's gun, Ryder walked out the door.

"Your brains are scrambled, Ryder!" Redwood yelled after her. "I can't wait until Powell gets tired of you. You won't be exiled! That's for sure!"

An agent cleared his throat. "Sir, I'm going to have to ask you a few questions."

Redwood clenched his teeth. He was breathing heavily.

"Sir, have you ever actively conspired against the Western Union?" the agent asked.

At first, it looked like Redwood wasn't going to answer. Then he grunted, "No..."

"Have you ever withheld vital information?"

"No."

"Sir, we know you did. Didn't Mathews visit your office recently?"

"He was vague..."

"Sir, have you ever owned a copy of the Quran?"

Redwood felt sick. "No."

"Do you consider Emperor Long divine in status?"

"No."

"Have you ever engaged in incorrigible activities?"

"What?"

"In terms of romantic relationships."

Redwood felt even sicker. "That's none of your business."

"Answer, please."

"Incorrigible to you, perhaps."

"So, that's a yes?"

The questioning continued. After a while, Redwood barely paid attention to the agent. He gazed out the window, the protesters still angry and chanting. Maybe they could rush the fence and knock it down like the refugees in Cairo did. The protestors would swarm the Eisenhower Executive Office Building and kill everything inside, purge the whole mess.

Redwood then noticed one of the picket signs.

It had a symbol on it.

He shivered involuntarily but figured it must be a coincidence. Then he saw some of the other signs. If it really was a coincidence, how come so many other signs had that symbol? For the love of... They numbered in the dozens, maybe hundreds. How could he be so blind? It was right outside his window!

"Sir, you look pale," the agent said. "Please, take a seat."

Redwood settled into his chair. Surrounding the building were hundreds of picket signs with bloodred horseshoes painted on them.

It was the symbol of Omega.

"End of days! End of Days!" Mr. Preacher cried. "Obey! Obey the moon!"

***

Keito Kusanagi had countless tubes coming in and out of him. He was covered in stitches and scars, some new but many old. But Powers was especially curious about the Japanese lady sniffling at his bedside.

"That is Kusanagi's wife, Asami," Ryder told him, reading him easier than a book. "She is upset about his slow recovery."

"I don't get it!" Powers barked. "With all our technology, he should already be better. You got your arm dislocated and a leg broken, boss, but you're fine now!"

"Please, keep your voice down," a nurse said. She wore an all-white outfit and held a touchscreen tablet.

"Uh ... sorry, I'm just a little confused," Powers said, going slightly red. The nurse was pretty cute. "Can you explain to me what's wrong with my pal?"

"The doctors aren't sure," the nurse confessed, scanning her tablet. "We were able to heal some of his injuries, but all his burns have been resistant to growth patches. It could be that radiation is impeding the patches, though our Geiger counters haven't picked up anything."

Powers laughed. "Geez, you're smart."

"Would you please leave the room?" Ryder asked the nurse. "I need to speak to my subordinate and Mrs. Kusanagi privately."

"Just don't be too long," the nurse said. "The doctors will be doing another round of tests anytime now. We're very busy, as you can imagine, what with both the failed invasion and the revolt." A tear escaped her eye. She wiped it away. "Oh, sorry. I'm still so sad about Cromwell. Such a handsome man ... beheaded by that maniac..."

The nurse left, much to Powers' disappointment.

"This news will be announced to the public shortly," Ryder told Powers and Keito's wife. "I wanted you both to hear it from me. Today, Admiral Redwood was arrested for treason."

Asami Kusanagi covered her mouth. Powers' reaction was much less delicate. "Not Admiral Redwood!" he cried. "Say it ain't so!"

"Settle down," Ryder said. "He will not be executed, merely exiled."

"Well, that doesn't make things much better!"

"Excuse me, but what does this mean for my husband?" Asami asked.

"Now that one of our leaders has been exposed as a traitor, security will become even tighter," Ryder said. "The fact that Keito Kusanagi, a foreigner, was admitted into a military hospital is highly unusual. I suspect that he won't be allowed to stay much longer."

"Then we'll just move him back to Japan," Asami said.

"Their medical technology cannot help your husband."

"What do you suggest?" Asami asked, squeezing Keito's limp hand.

"I have a close relationship with the president now, and given your husband's past contributions, perhaps we could arrange other accommodations for him or have the military make an exception. For now, Powers shall guard both of you until Keito recovers."

Powers gawked. "I will?"

"Orders are orders," Ryder said.

Powers zipped his lip, but he kept his scowl exposed.

"Thank you, but I can handle myself," Asami said. "Protection is not necessary."

"Yes, I have read your background. Your résumé is almost as impressive as your husband's. Regardless, you are a stranger to our land and require a guide."

"Then I accept your generous offer."

"Excellent. Powers, let us meet with your squad now. Mrs. Kusanagi is allowed to stay for the testing. We are not."

Ryder and Powers exited the room and walked down the spotless hallway until reaching a waiting area. York sat in a chair with his crossed legs on the table. Patel knelt beside Kennedy. She appeared to be consoling her comrade but stopped when Ryder approached.

"Are you still shaken, Kennedy?" Ryder asked.

While everyone else wore blue uniforms, Kennedy had donned white pajamas and slippers. She held a copy of *The Catcher in the Rye.* As a nervous tic, she rubbed one of its pages between her fingertips. Her face, meanwhile, was straining to stay neutral.

"I ... I haven't been able to read since the invasion," Kennedy said. "That man ... that helmet ... I couldn't ... I couldn't help Cruz."

"He died protecting his comrade," Powers said. "That's one hell of a manly way to die. And we don't blame you for freezing up. That thing was vicious. But it's dead now."

"But I didn't—"

"It's over now," Patel told her, putting a hand on Kennedy's knee. "You did your duty. Now you must take time to recover."

"Yes, you will be put on leave for the time being," Ryder said. "Patel and York, I will see you both tomorrow afternoon at fifteen hundred hours in our

Washington hangar. You will both be briefed on your next mission."

York swung his feet off the table and stood up. "What about Powers?"

"That will be discussed at the briefing. Dismissed."

Powers once again suppressed his irritation. He expected York to shoot him a smug smirk, but to his credit, York remained somber in light of the situation. York then gave Kennedy a pat on the shoulder, pocketed his hands, and walked away.

Patel gave Kennedy a brief hug. "You are brave, much braver than I would have been. Do not forget that."

Kennedy hugged back but did not speak. Patel smiled sadly and left as well.

"Doctors gonna let you go soon?" Powers asked.

"Eventually," Kennedy said. Then she stayed silent.

Powers sighed. He and Ryder left the sitting area. They made their way down several more halls. Powers didn't know where they were going. Ryder was leading the way, perhaps aimlessly for all he knew. Still, it wasn't like he needed to be somewhere.

"I didn't know Keito had a wife," Powers said. "Good for him."

"His wife was kidnapped by a criminal gang several years ago," Ryder told him as they kept walking. "Even with her combat skills, they overpowered her. They held her hostage in an effort to control Keito Kusanagi. They wanted him to eliminate their enemies. Their plans failed, however, when I intervened."

"Is that why Keito works for you?"

"After I returned his wife, he pledged his sword to me. The Western Union was skeptical at first, but they were more accepting once they saw the extent of Kusanagi's abilities."

Powers stopped walking. Ryder also stopped, turning to him.

"Is something the matter, Powers?" she asked.

Powers sighed. "This stuff with Redwood ... I don't like it. The Western Union is changing. People are changing. They're scared, real scared. So am I."

"Good. Fear is what keeps people in line."

"I thought fear made people go crazy."

"Then you are wrong."

Ryder then stood to attention. Powers did the same on reflex.

"Powers, I will not see you again for some time," she said. "President Powell has given me a mission. To be more precise, it was a mission that I requested personally."

"You're leaving?" Powers asked. "Without Keito or me? Don't you need me around? Was it something I did? Look, I know I was on thin ice with you before, but I thought I put on a pretty good performance during the invasion. And back on that ship, didn't you tell me—?"

"I need you here," Ryder told him. "But thank you for your concern. And this is not a reflection of your standing with me. York and Patel are adequate enough to assist me with the task ahead, and I do not require a squad leader with only half a squad."

"But I still got the job, right?"

"You will resume your duties once the current situation stabilizes."

Ryder gave Powers a salute. He returned one.

"Boss, before you go, I gotta say that I'm proud to be your lackey," Powers said. "You and Keito killed the monster that destroyed the Pentagon. I didn't think us regular guys could do anything against those freaks, but you proved me wrong."

Ryder looked away from him. Powers thought for a moment that she was embarrassed. But she couldn't get embarrassed, could she?

"Thank you, Powers. Now, if you'll excuse me, I have two Helmet Men to hunt down."

Ryder marched away, leaving her subordinate behind. Powers grinned for a moment.

Then he started to puzzle over her parting words. *Two* Helmet Men? Wasn't there only supposed to be one left?

"They killed it," Powers told himself. "They must have killed it."

CHAPTER 26

General Eisenhorn spat sand from his mouth. "Klara, you're starting to piss me off!"

"You've been very aloof lately," Klara told him. As usual in all his dreams, Eisenhorn was sitting on a small island made of sand, an endless black sea surrounding him and his companion.

"Sorry I'm not a pleasure to be around," Eisenhorn grumbled. "You must have a hard time being vague and unhelpful. What a burden."

"Unhelpful? Didn't I save your life from the assassin?"

"Yeah, only so I could live the rest of my days in a Chinese torture chamber."

"You don't seem to..." Klara trailed off, lost in thought.

"Nuts to this," Eisenhorn said, wiping the sand off himself. He started walking toward the black water. Maybe he could wake up by dunking his head in it.

"Stay away!" Klara screamed.

Eisenhorn froze. Klara's eyes had become huge. Even underneath all those clothes, it was clear that her body was tense.

The general grinned. This was her weakness. "Relax, Klara. I'm just gonna wet my feet. Don't get many baths these days."

"Randolph Eisenhorn, you stay away from that water," Klara ordered.

"Girl, you sound just like my mother, only with less slurring."

"Please, don't!"

"Then tell me what's going on! Who are you? What's the syringe for? What happens when I inject myself with it? Does this have something to do with Cloak? Does it have something to do with the thing that burned me?"

Klara was tearing up. "I can't tell you! Have faith!"

"Blind faith is the reason the Chinese Empire is so warped." Eisenhorn was only vaguely aware of the hypocrisy in his words. "That's it! Time to get my feet wet."

"No!" Klara tried to grab him, but he knocked her back. He lumbered toward the edge of the island, planning to walk straight into the black sea.

A scream came from the water.

Eisenhorn fell. His eyes rolled back. Goose bumps dotted his skin. He should have known *never* to go near the shore. He had broken a taboo. More screams came from the water, some far, others *very* close.

"Get back!" Klara cried. "It will consume you! You shall be converted!"

You shall be converted...

Klara was fading. "It's a sea of evil! We will drown in it!"

The world began to crumble.

Eisenhorn screamed. Out came the voice of Legion.

***

Eisenhorn woke up. His body seized up, not letting him breathe. It was a full minute before he could relax. He started panting. Oxygen filled his lungs.

"I ... I almost drowned."

"Relax. You are on dry land now."

The general should have been startled by the voice that spoke up, but he was more exasperated than anything. "Xing, about time you showed yourself."

High General Chao Xing leaned against the wall of the interrogation chamber. He looked the same as Eisenhorn remembered. Something was missing, though. Despite being barely in his twenties, Xing had always seemed like a man, but now he looked like a beaten child. It was Xing's confidence. It had dried up.

"When I was a boy, I thought the emperor was the greatest man ever to live," Xing began. "Every day, my mother would pray to a Buddha statue that bore his face. I always joined her, at first out of love for my mother, then out of love for the emperor himself. My father was the high general of the homeland before I was. He told me I would get to visit the Forbidden City with him one day. You couldn't imagine the joy I felt when I heard that. I was so happy."

"Past tense," Eisenhorn said.

Xing sighed. "Yes, past tense. When I was fifteen, I finally visited the palace. I went through all the ludicrous security measures, was coached by my father extensively in order to make sure I observed decorum, and arrived in the throne room to find..."

"A demented old man," Eisenhorn finished.

"I could have handled it if that were all. If he had just been elderly and incompetent, I might have been content. No, it was his cruelty, his hatred, his spitefulness that sickened me. Was this the man I've been worshiping all these years? Was this the savior of China? Was I just blind? Was my faith being tested? It took me years to realize it wasn't my lack of faith that was the problem. It was everyone else's faith. My mother and father were blind. They were all fools. I stopped hating the emperor and hated them instead. *They* let him live. *They* let him rule. *They* let him abuse his subjects."

"Geez, sorry your country is so screwed up."

Xing turned to Eisenhorn with his chin held high. "I am proud to be Chinese. I love my people. I never wanted to be born anywhere else."

"Whatever. Didn't mean any harm."

Xing relaxed some. "No, of course you didn't. I shouldn't expect you to readily sympathize with the Chinese people. Not when their government is torturing you."

"What are you doing here, Xing?"

"I don't know myself. Someone to talk to, perhaps..."

"What about Shu? You can't talk to her?"

"It would be improper to be consoled by a servant, although this isn't exactly proper either. As well, the emperor has grown ... attached to her. Many of his wives and concubines have either been killed or committed suicide. He needs replacements."

Eisenhorn shook his head. "No, don't tell me these things. Don't tell me..."

"I don't know what to do. I have tried everything. I was originally waiting for the emperor to die so I might then guide the empire to prosperity. But now Cloak is in control. If I don't act soon, it will mean China's end."

"Wish I was dreaming," Eisenhorn muttered to himself.

Xing almost fell over from the revelation he had at that moment. "A dream... Yes, I had one too. But it would never work. Not in a—"

The door to Eisenhorn's chamber opened.

"Visiting hours are over," Sebastian said with a smile.

Eisenhorn's depression and confusion turned into fury. He turned his eyes to Sebastian, that grinning lunatic. Yeah, *lunatic* was the right word. That man was the reason behind this insanity. He was the face behind the curtain, him and his mystery boss. Eisenhorn wasn't sure of much anymore, but he was definitely sure this man needed to die.

Not thinking straight, Eisenhorn got to his feet. He was thin but had ferocity on his side. He screamed and charged at Sebastian.

Then he saw Temple.

The shadow of his helmet fell upon Eisenhorn, who skidded to a stop as his fury turned to jelly. He collapsed in a heap.

Xing couldn't believe it. Poppy had told him this thing had been beheaded, that half its body had been blown apart beforehand.

Yet here Temple stood, right behind Sebastian.

"Xing, you must inform me before you go visiting prisoners," Sebastian scolded, taking immense pleasure in it. "It's very naughty to sneak behind your superior's back. You're lucky we're short one general. Otherwise, I wouldn't be so forgiving."

Sebastian waved for Xing to come. Like a trained dog, Xing slunk out of the room, keeping his eyes down as he passed Temple, though not able to suppress a shiver.

The door was closing now. Eisenhorn's fear had not abated.

Sebastian laughed. "See you tomorrow, General..."

***

"These terrorists, these foreigners, do you know what they believe? They believe man was never meant to walk on the moon. They believe man was never meant to cure diseases. They believe man was never meant to live past seventy. They believe man was meant to dwell in huts, to wallow in dirt, to live like animals."

President Harold Powell's voice echoed across the Western Union. The people needed reassurances. The *Tortuga* incident. The revolts. The failed invasion. The attempted coup. It was too much. People sat in their homes with their eyes glued to holographic screens. They were letting their fear turn them into sheep. There were many who resisted, turning off their TVs in disgust, but not nearly enough.

"These ignorant beliefs are just reflections of the foreigners' hidden envy," Powell said. "They want our technology. They want to be civilized. But they don't want to put in the hard work. They think firing a couple of missiles and throwing a few Molotov cocktails will get them a free meal ticket.

"They're wrong! I will not stand for it. The previous administration was too soft on these undesirables. Over the years, Hynes grew far too complacent. A remnant of this ignorant era, Admiral Redwood, plotted against me with the help of Western Intelligence Director Mathews. The invasion failed because of them, because they thought we could reason with the Chinamen. But despite what these misguided fools believe, we can't reason with Chinamen. We can't reason with terrorists. They can only be beaten! They can only be conquered!

"I have ordered the recommissioning of *Leviathan*. It has already begun retaking Istanbul from Incognito and his infantile 'Saladin Federation.' He wants a jihad, does he? Then we'll give him a crusade in return, one those foreigners and their sand god will never forget.

"Trust in your government, Western Union! Trust in me, as you did my father, and as you did Andrew Usher, the first head of the Western Union. All you protesters out there, I understand your pain. You asked for results. I will give them to you. We will retake the Occupied Territories. We will conquer China. Incognito will be beheaded like he beheaded our beloved Cromwell. Emperor Long will be torn apart by our machine-gun fire. Trust in your government, Western Union! Trust in me!"

***

Incognito sat in an armchair, his scythe close at hand, listening to Powell's hateful speech as the dialysis machine did its work. At last, the Westerners had shown their true colors. This was the good news.

The bad news was *Leviathan*. The Westerners had finished repairing their war machine and were already putting it to work. The United Third was losing its grip on Istanbul. Of course, Incognito had known that the Western Union would retaliate and recapture some of its territory. Such news was no surprise. It was Slate and that woman's insubordination that baffled him. Had he not shown them the cruelty of the West? Were they that blind to the crimes of the Western Union? Did they not realize that only he could defeat Cloak?

The loss of Slate was a disappointment, but Incognito knew the cause would survive. He would just have to adjust his plans accordingly, like he did when the war started earlier than anticipated. The people of the Third World would not have an immortal leader, but the West would still be obliterated. That would be enough for him. He could die knowing that his mission had at least been partially fulfilled.

There was a knock on his door.

"Enter."

Two burly guards restraining a South Asian man came into the sparse room. Their captive was twitchy and nervous, with a starved face.

"You wished to see me," Incognito said. "Careful what you wish for."

"Please, sir, I have a message," the captive whimpered. "Only you were to see it."

"Tell me, why should I not shoot the messenger?"

The messenger gulped, lips quivering. "The message ... it's..."

"Kill him outside."

"It's Temple!"

Incognito instantaneously materialized in front of the man. The dull side of his scythe's blade jammed into the messenger's throat, causing him to gag. Blood trickled from Incognito's arm where the dialysis tubes had been. He paid it no mind.

There was only one thing on his radar.

"You lie," he hissed.

The messenger was scared to death, as were the guards who held him. "Please..." the messenger wheezed. "The message ... hologram ... projector..."

But Incognito was already holding the projector. The messenger almost fainted when he noticed this. When did the phantom have the time to pickpocket him?

"Lock him up," Incognito ordered his stunned guards. He took his scythe away from the messenger's throat. "I will decide what to do with him later."

The guards took the terrified messenger away. The door slammed shut behind them.

Incognito weighed the portable hologram projector in his hand. It was spherical, a newer model. He activated the projector by throwing it. In the middle of its arc, it stopped in midair and cocooned itself with a projection of a hairless Chinese man.

"Greetings, Incognito," the projection said. "You likely know who I am already, but allow me to introduce myself. My name is High General Chao Xing of the Chinese Empire, and I am in desperate need of your assistance."

"Taylor," Gilda whispered.

Straper grinned. "Good to see you, Doc."

Taylor found himself grinning too. He spread his arms. Both Straper and Gilda embraced him. In silence, they stayed that way for several seconds until Taylor pulled back from them. His grin dimmed as he examined both his former cadets. Then he turned to Thomas, who sat on the couch in the corner of the cavern that acted as a sitting room. An abandoned mine filled with terrorists wasn't the ideal spot for a reunion, but it would do.

"Who is this boy?" Taylor asked.

Gilda and Straper looked at one another and began to laugh.

Taylor sighed. "That's not a good sign."

With no other idea on how to explain the past two years, Gilda and Straper sat down on the couch with Thomas and started from the beginning. Taylor sat across from them in a wooden chair as they divulged how the United Third had trained them, how they uncovered Cloak's plot in Japan, how they ventured into the Neutral Zone, how they stopped Cyphrus and *Leviathan*, how Slate had been captured, how Incognito had exploited them for the next year, how they recently rescued Slate, and what Incognito was now up to.

Taylor listened initially to these stories neutrally. His first major reaction was when Gilda explained who Thomas actually was. For the next ten minutes after that, he could do nothing but stare at the young prince.

Thomas shifted in his seat from embarrassment. "Um, Mr. Taylor?"

"It's 'doctor,' dude," Straper interjected.

"Right... Dr. Taylor, could you please stop looking at me?"

Taylor blinked. "Sorry, you just bear such a resemblance to the queen."

"You know my mom?" Thomas whimpered.

"No, but I still remember the kidnapping. The nation was devastated. I always wondered what had happened. But I never thought Cloak could be..." Taylor turned to Gilda and Straper. "Please, continue."

They could have reminisced for hours but stuck with the basics and left out some pretty substantial details such as the mountain-sized water monster and the mechanical dinosaurs. They didn't want to overload Taylor, but their efforts were in vain. He became largely stoic unless letting out a laugh at one of the anecdotes involving Slate. He also tightened his lips slightly whenever Naomi or Incognito were mentioned. Gilda could tell he had no positive feelings for either one. She couldn't blame him for detesting Incognito, but she found herself saying more nice things about Naomi than ever before. Taylor only knew of Naomi as Repulsa, who had helped slaughter a hundred cadets with the other Gifted. Having felt similarly about Naomi in the past herself, Gilda knew it would be tough to turn Taylor's opinion.

When they were finished, Taylor leaned back in his chair and smirked. "You've been busy," he declared.

Gilda and Straper laughed hard. Taylor laughed as well, but with less vigor.

Thomas sat up on the couch. "Um, Dr. Taylor?"

Taylor turned to him. "Yes, your ... Royal Highness?"

"Don't bother with that," Straper said. "Just call him kid. Or brat."

Taylor rolled his eyes. "What did you wish to ask, Thomas?"

"You're from Britain, right?" Thomas asked. "That's where my mom's from."

Taylor smiled until his teeth showed. "You could say that."

"So, how much do you know about Britain? I've never been there. Naomi showed me pictures, like ones of those red buses and the guys in the tall, furry hats. My—"

"I'd be happy to talk about home," Taylor told him. "But first, I'd like to speak with my friends in private if possible."

"Oh, great!" Thomas exclaimed, his timid demeanor vanishing. "Don't worry. I can wait. Thanks, Dr. Taylor. I've got so many questions."

"Actually, Naomi asked us to watch over him," Gilda said. "We shouldn't leave him alone, especially since he's been kidnapped for a month."

"I told you, I'm fine," Thomas said. "It was just boring. They kept me in a room like this one and gave me food and toys. Really, it's okay!"

"He is a hardy kid," Straper said. "You know … in every way."

Taylor shook his head. "Enough, my head is about to explode. Thomas, please go."

Thomas nodded and got off the couch, but before he left, he ran up and gave Taylor a quick hug. The doctor returned it gladly. Then Thomas ran out the room and shut the door behind him. Taylor stared at the bare door for a moment before turning to Gilda and Straper.

"Is he really invulnerable?" he asked.

"He'd definitely be happy to give a demo," Straper said. "Naomi's actually trying to get him to act more normal. You know, learn to blend in and stuff."

"Yes, this Naomi sounds like an interesting character," Taylor said coolly.

"Enough about us," Gilda said. "What have you been up to? And how do you still remember us? I thought for sure the Western Union would have pruned you."

"A woman named Camilla Ryder wished to keep me around as an 'expert' on Slate," Taylor said. "Do you know who she is?"

"Yeah, we met her," Gilda fumed.

Straper shrugged. "Meh, she's hot."

Gilda punched him on the arm. Straper moaned and rubbed it.

Taylor chuckled. "I thought you two grew up. Anyway, the Western Union assigned me to a military base in Central Africa. I wasn't allowed to leave, but I was kept busy treating injured soldiers and being interviewed countless times on my experiences with Slate."

"Did any of the others avoid getting pruned?" Straper asked.

"General Eisenhorn wasn't either. I believe he is on some sort of diplomatic mission right now. Union Network has been pretty sparse on the details. Victoria and Goldberg, unfortunately, underwent the procedure. From what I've heard, they're doing fine otherwise."

"When did the United Third kidnap you?" Gilda asked.

"Last week, shortly after the revolts began. The United Third attacked our base with hacked drones. Many perished. Only a few were captured, including me. Our captors initially only wanted my medical expertise, but Barir eventually heard about my capture and took me to the United Third's headquarters. Then Incognito tried to execute me."

"And Slate saved you," Gilda finished.

Taylor nodded, but he didn't offer a verbal reply. Instead, he sat in thought while Gilda and Straper waited patiently for him to go on. He finally did.

"I heard your story," Taylor said. "Now I want your explanation."

Gilda and Straper frowned and turned their eyes downward.

Taylor frowned too. "Well?"

"We should never have joined Incognito," Gilda said. "I'm sorry. I was so angry at Cloak, so angry at myself. And Henry ... I missed him so badly."

"We're done," Straper said. "I told Gilda already we can't let Incognito use us anymore. She wasn't listening, but I think we're both on the same page now."

Gilda shot him a look but continued. "We're leaving with Slate soon. We'll keep fighting Cloak and hunting the Mentor, but on our own terms. Incognito can go to hell. The Western Union too. I don't want any part in their stupid war. They're both full of it. They're both cruel. Maybe Incognito is worse, but I can't go back to working for the military. Powell..."

"I'm not a fan of Powell either," Taylor said. "And if what you say about him is true..."

"We can't go back, Taylor," Gilda said. "But we're not staying here either."

"We'll make sure Incognito lets you go too," Straper added. "The United Third is just worried about what you might know."

"I was blindfolded here," Taylor said. "The location of their headquarters remains a mystery to me. However, forgive me if I do not give my hopes up. Incognito was close to chopping my head off. As for your decision to join the United Third ... I've decided not to judge you. Who could blame you for choosing the wrong path while so young and traumatized? And it seems you need no convincing about Incognito."

Straper snorted. "Definitely not."

"Thanks, Taylor," Gilda said.

"But I'll give you two a warning," Taylor said. "You're both about to become adults. The next path you choose will determine the rest of your life. I personally advise you to hand yourselves over to the Western Union, if not simply to see your loved ones again."

Gilda remembered her father and bit her lower lip.

"Slate is truly impressive," Taylor said. "But he's no guardian. He cannot give you what you need. Neither can Naomi, if that is her real name. The time for excuses is over. From this day forward, you are both responsible for your own actions."

***

The Helmet Man reached out but hesitated.

"It's fine," Naomi told him. "I don't mind."

Slate put his arm around her as they walked. "Thought you'd swat my hand away."

"We're on a date," Naomi said. "And you've been patient."

"Patience ... who'd have guessed?" Slate mused. They made their way through the jungle on a narrow path. A gaggle of United Third recruits had been spying on the odd couple for several minutes before an instructor yelled at them. Otherwise, the United Third gave them a wide berth. It seemed Incognito wanted to avoid another incident.

"Never been on a stroll before," Slate said. "Or a date."

Naomi glanced up at his silver helmet as if trying to find his hidden eyes. "You've never been on a date? Does that mean you're...?"

"Nah, my dad introduced me to a few chicks in the past. Had to prune them afterward, but it was cool of him, I guess. Mind if I ask about your love life?"

"I've had a few loves, all of them fleeting," Naomi said. "My life is too transient and violent for anything long-term. The occasional fling was all I could hope for. The other Gifted were worse. Houdini and Cyphrus bought their companionship and disposed of it immediately. Ember only ever had victims. Sandtrap couldn't have romance, while Sebastian merely didn't want it. Atlas was oddly innocent, almost infantile, and focused only on eating. The only one with even a remotely normal love life was Geppetto and his own brief flings. We weren't built for romance, it seems. Only killing."

"I don't know about that," Slate said. "Look what we're doing now."

Naomi blushed. They reached a ridge that overlooked the Congolese rainforest, which hid not only the United Third but also countless refugees fleeing the revolts. Naomi could see smoke rising from several campfires. Greenery concealed all else.

"Enjoying the view?" Slate asked her.

"Yes, thank you for taking me here. I know you can't enjoy panoramas."

"At least we didn't go to a restaurant."

"Because you can't eat?"

"No, because of your appetite. You'd eat me into the poorhouse."

Naomi snickered. "Do you even have any money?"

"I can always bum a few bucks from Straper."

They stood there for the longest time, letting the sounds of the jungle wash over them. Naomi eventually leaned against the Helmet Man. She placed a hand on his chest.

"I'm ready to go back now," she whispered.

Slate put his hands on her shoulders and turned her so they could face each other. "You sure about that? You don't have to do me any favors."

Naomi pressed up against him. She looked up at the silver helmet and saw her own dark eyes stare back in the reflection. Slate tilted his head downward. She had his attention.

"You're doing me the favor," she whispered even quieter.

Slate reached around and placed his hand on the small of her back. They stayed that way until the sky turned red. Evening had come. It was time to go back. They separated from each other, only for Slate to put her arm around her again as they walked down the slope.

"I'm doing the favor," Slate muttered to himself.

CHAPTER 28

"Y ou wanted to see me, old-timer?"

Oscar sighed but also smiled. "Kids today and their manners."

Gilda entered the large garage, hands in her pockets. "Come on, kids were always punks. Don't act like it's anything new."

"No, but it still annoys the hell out of me." Oscar waved her over. The garage was filled with United Third walkers in need of repair, plus a variety of tools and equipment that took up every available corner. There was barely room to move around, let alone do any actual work. Oscar didn't mind, but Gilda sure did.

"What's going to happen to Magenta?" Gilda asked, making her way through the maze of junk. Oscar was sitting on a metal container the size of a trunk.

"Take a wild guess," Oscar said. "Incognito isn't going to let you take away a valuable piece of hardware that doesn't even technically belong to you. You stole it, after all. And it is Incognito's money that paid for Magenta's repairs and maintenance. Besides, how would you be able to maintain it without the United Third's resources?"

"I guess you're right. Geez, I must have always taken Magenta for granted, like every kid my age had one."

"That might very well happen if this war gets any worse."

Gilda tried not to look annoyed. Slate's dad could be a real bummer. "Can I say bye to Magenta, maybe take it out for one last flight?"

"Afraid you can't. Incognito's orders. But you can say bye. Your walker's right here." Oscar patted the container he was sitting on.

Gilda gasped. "Holy—! Did you crush it?"

"Certainly not. I would never destroy such a wonderful machine. It's just more compact now, easier for storage and travel."

Gilda walked up to the container. She felt its contours with her rough hands. "But Magenta's so big. How'd you pull this off?"

"I took out all the unessential systems, replaced its armor with a more flexible variant, and added some extra joints to its skeleton."

"All the trouble this could have saved us…"

"It's still fairly heavy, and the new armor won't be as durable. On the plus side, Magenta is even faster than before."

Gilda smiled angrily. "Of all times to give it an upgrade, why now?"

Oscar laughed. "Sorry, didn't think Slate would go berserk, at least not so soon. Probably should have expected it, knowing him."

Gilda's smile faded as did her playful anger. "Mr. Radcliffe…"

"Call me Oscar. I don't deserve the respect."

She ignored the self-effacement. "Could you tell me about Slate?"

"Please elaborate."

Gilda massaged the back of her neck. "Well, I just don't know much about him. What was he like as a kid? Who were his friends? Was he always such a piece of work?"

Oscar shook his head. "I think it's best if Slate tells you all that himself."

"Well, whenever he does talk about his past, it's usually about how bad it was. But it couldn't have been *all* bad. There must have been some good moments, right? Even the other Gifted must have been a little happy. There must have been some good moments."

Oscar deflated, gazing at her with drooping eyes. Gilda stiffened. She must have gone too far. Who was she to pry into the past? Didn't she already know enough about Slate?

"I'll tell you this about my son," Oscar said. He smirked. A few of his teeth were missing. "That boy is one of the smartest people I've ever met."

Gilda blinked. "I … beg your pardon? Slate is one of the smartest people you've ever met? This coming from a guy that managed to fit a walker into a suitcase?"

A small laugh escaped Oscar. "You seem surprised."

"Look, I won't deny the man has his moments, but he acts like a nitwit ninety-nine percent of the time. He can't even read. He's just so ... crude."

"Is he crude because that's who he is or because that's who he wants to be? You've seen the man in action. He's a genius when it comes to fighting and often has great insight. Yes, he doesn't have book smarts, only because he actively avoids that sort of thing. I guess you could say he's inhibiting himself."

"But why would anyone do that?"

"To be more relatable. Slate makes himself idiotic in order to fit in better. His powers and helmet made him different enough already. He didn't want to be abnormally intelligent to boot, so he made himself into what he thought other people wanted him to be."

"That's..." Gilda began, her voice soft. She stumbled to find the right words. "That's ... that's just sad."

Oscar sighed. "Yeah, that's the word ... sad." He caught himself. "Sorry, I'm being depressing again. It's become a bad habit of mine. Here, I got you a present." He took a portable hard drive from his pocket and handed it to her.

"Thanks," Gilda said, taking it. "What's on it?"

"It's Tim."

Gilda did a double take, holding the hard drive at arm's length. "You put my walker's autopilot on here?"

"A copy, to be precise. I thought you'd miss him. Now you can take him with you."

"Oh, well, thanks again," she said, pocketing the hard drive. In truth, she wasn't much in love with Tim, though he was nice enough. He was just the third wheel of the group, not even a living thing. The very fact that Tim could be copied was a testament to his artificiality. Still, the gesture was nice. She gave Oscar a small smile.

"Mr. Radcliffe!" Barir shouted, entering the garage with two guards.

Gilda scowled. "This guy again..."

"What is it, Barir?" Oscar asked, not seeming too thrilled to see Barir either.

"Incognito wishes to speak with you," Barir said in a stern yet urgent voice.

"He can wait."

"I'm afraid he can't. He said it was about Temple."

If Oscar Radcliffe had still been sleepy, the rush of adrenaline made sure that wasn't the case anymore. It was as though he had been struck by lighting.

"Hey, Oscar," Gilda asked. "What's this Temple?"

Oscar squeezed his hands into fists. "My greatest sin…"

***

Two hours later, Straper entered a conference room with a spring in his step, approaching a long table with chairs surrounding it. He and the others had their belongings packed and planned on leaving the United Third's headquarters tomorrow. Naomi had already set up a place for them to live for a while. He was only here now to listen to what Oscar had to say, yet another reason for his good mood.

Straper sat down, leaning back in his chair. "Fantastic, we're about to get answers. Happy day, happy day!"

"It's both frightening and exciting to have someone give us the full picture," Taylor agreed, arriving behind Straper and sitting down. "Maybe we'll even learn who this Mentor is."

"Yeah, and it's all thanks to Slate. He finally had enough of Incognito's crap and knocked him down a peg. Glad everyone is seeing things my way now."

Taylor's cheer ebbed, but he said nothing. He had considered not attending this meeting to avoid giving the United Third another reason to kill him. But he couldn't help but worry about Gilda and Straper. He had a feeling this wouldn't just be an information session.

The rest of the group soon entered the room. Gilda somberly took a seat between Straper and Taylor.

"Is something the matter?" Taylor asked.

"Something got Oscar spooked today," Gilda said, more to herself than Taylor. "I think it has something to do with Cloak, something about a Temple."

"Hmm... I suppose we'll soon learn about this 'Temple' too."

Thomas plopped down across from Gilda. He had spent the afternoon jumping on land mines for fun. Naomi wanted to stop him but gave up after seeing how happy he was. Taylor had also watched out of curiosity, only to end up a shaken wreck by the end of it.

"Sorry about your walker," Thomas said, sounding more upset about it than Gilda. "It was so cool. I wish I could've piloted it."

"Great, now you're making me miss it," Gilda said. She reached over the table and messed up his hair. They both found themselves beaming.

Naomi came into the room, laughing. Slate followed. He whispered into her ear. Naomi laughed yet again. Slate touched her shoulder.

Thomas smiled and sat up. "What's so funny?"

"Yeah, you two gonna let us in on the joke?" Straper asked.

"Nah, it's at your expense," Slate said. He whispered something else to Naomi. This evoked yet another wave of laughter, which she tried to hide as if her mouth were full of food.

"You two need to settle down now," Oscar said, walking into the room, but he had a wilted grin. "We have much to cover."

Naomi got ahold of herself and sat with the others while Slate leaned against the wall behind her. Gilda glanced over at them briefly but made no comment.

Oscar took his place at the head of the table. "I would first like to start this meeting by saying how proud I am of you all. Each one of you has been fighting an enemy that has proven to be as dangerous as it is ambitious. Every one of you, especially Slate, has done a great service to humanity. Thank you. Thank you, all."

"Teacher's pet..." Straper said under his breath.

"Neapolitan got nothing to do with this!" the Helmet Man snapped.

Taylor sighed. "The term is 'nepotism.' Learn proper English already."

Oscar cleared his throat. "I think it's unfair that you have all fought for so long without knowing what exactly you are fighting against and why."

"Hey, I know all I need to know," Straper said. "Cloak kills people. We kill them."

"Don't interrupt the man," Gilda scolded.

"Lay off me, geez!"

"Knock it off, you two," Naomi ordered, thumping their noggins together with her powers. They moaned and rubbed their heads but spoke no more.

"Things have changed," Oscar continued, making sure that nobody else was going to start talking. "I originally wanted to just tell my story, but now I also want to make an offer. Incognito is about to enter the room—"

"What!" Straper snarled. "I ain't working for that psycho again."

"We want nothing to do with him," Gilda spat.

Naomi frowned. "Your offer doesn't interest us if Incognito is involved."

"Dad, I know this guy used to be your friend, but cut the cord already," Slate said. "It's not enough that he's a mass-murdering racist. He's also a total tool."

"Just give me a chance to explain," Oscar said. "This is a proposal. Nobody will force you to do anything. Incognito was wrong to manipulate you all. I was personally appalled by his actions. However, he may have found a way to take down Cloak for good. After I tell you all I know about Cloak, I will explain the offer in detail."

"The answer is no, old man," Slate said, walking up to Oscar. "I don't care if Incognito offers me the Mentor's head on a silver platter. He can't be trusted."

"Naomi, please talk some sense to this boy," Oscar told her.

"I'm right behind Slate," she said. "He's making nothing but good points."

Oscar's face darkened. "Incognito knows where Temple is."

The words didn't register to Naomi at first. It was a gradual process. Her irritated expression gave way to a blank stare. Then her eyes widened. Sweat beaded on her forehead. She looked at Slate's silver helmet. A pulsating coldness grew inside her.

Take her! Take her, you beast!

"Slate," she whispered. "I need to hear this offer."

CHAPTER 29

"You all know the basic story," Oscar said. "Over fifty years ago, the Western Union secretly started the Keymaster Project. The Western Union was having great difficulty holding the lands it was conquering. It needed an ace in the hole. It needed to take warfare to the next level. The military recruited numerous scientists to create biological weapons that could turn the tides of war. We first experimented with animals, creating birds that were able to take down small aircraft, dogs that could each maul a dozen armed men to death, termites that ate metal, fish that acted as living naval mines..."

"Exploding fish?" Straper asked, gawking.

Oscar chuckled. "Yes, exploding fish."

Everyone else sat in silence. Slate had agreed to hear out Oscar's proposal after Naomi changed her mind. The others did the same, although they muttered in protest.

Incognito entered the room and took a seat near Oscar. Nobody acknowledged him, and he did not acknowledge them. His black eyes were focused on nothing.

"The Western Union, however, was not content with animal subjects alone," Oscar continued. "They soon asked the Keymasters to begin human trials. Like with the animals, we had no success with turning normal humans into supersoldiers. They had to be born. So, we started from scratch. We used the DNA from numerous donors to create our supersoldiers, enhancing the genes that were responsible for psychic energy."

"Psychic energy?" Taylor asked. "Forgive my rudeness, but you must be joking."

"I'm not. Regular humans only generate a minuscule amount of psychic energy, but the Gifted are able to generate exponentially larger quantities that could be expressed in a variety of ways such as teleportation or telekinesis. It was trial and error, but we managed to create humans who could perform feats we had thought only gods were capable of."

"If you could only create supersoldiers from scratch, how do you explain this guy?" Gilda asked, pointing a finger at Incognito without looking at him.

"Incognito found a way to turn himself into a supersoldier on his own. He destroyed all his research afterward. Not even I know how he did it, which is probably for the best."

"This is likely why Powell wanted to catch me alive," Incognito added. He was on his best behavior so far, but nobody was giving him the benefit of the doubt.

"I'd like to know more about how you created these supersoldiers," Taylor told Oscar. "This sounds completely unbelievable."

"I don't want to get too wrapped up in the technical details," Oscar said. "I don't think any of your cohorts care about that. Also, it would be dangerous to tell you how we precisely did it. Countless entities would torture you for that kind of information.

"But here's the CliffsNotes version. The Keymasters implanted altered genetic material into the eggs of several volunteers. These volunteers were healthy women with life sentences. They were offered freedom should they survive the pregnancy. Only one did, but surprisingly, there were no miscarriages."

Naomi trembled. Slate touched her shoulder. It helped a little.

"The supersoldiers we created surpassed all our expectations," Oscar went on. "Once they got into their teens, we started using them on the battlefield. Before that, the Western Union was highly unsuccessful in keeping hold of any territory in South America for long. It was the supersoldiers who decimated the enemy. The Western Union was then able to dedicate more of its resources toward occupying Africa and the Middle East as well as conducting its cold war with the Chinese Empire. Soon, the last major pockets of rebels and drug lords were extinguished. South America belonged to the West."

Incognito's grip on his scythe tightened.

"It was time for a change of scenery," Oscar said. "The supersoldiers were no longer needed in South America. They were to be relocated to a special facility."

"The Bunker," Gilda said.

"Correct. It was my idea. I had hoped this new environment would be more nurturing for the Gifted, a school rather than a lab. They were never treated as well as I wished, but things became ... unbearable for them after Slate's fight with Void."

"Is Void the supersoldier who almost killed Slate?" Gilda asked.

"Yes, the one who put him in that twenty-year healing coma. Void had gone on a rampage, killing hundreds of civilians. Do any of you recall the Los Angeles earthquake over twenty years ago?"

"Only vaguely," Taylor said. "Was the earthquake a cover story?"

"Yes. It helped that there actually was a minor earthquake that occurred shortly before Void's rampage, though the damage it caused was inconsequential. It took a lot of pruning and media manipulation, but the cover-up worked. Void was killed by Slate. However, Slate himself almost died from his wounds and was forced to go into hibernation so he could heal."

"How did he end up buried near the Bunker?" Straper asked.

"To be honest, I'm not quite sure," Oscar said. "But don't get ahead of me. I've still got much to tell."

"Why did Void go on a rampage?" Thomas asked. The others had debated whether or not he should hear Oscar's tale. In the end, they decided he had the right to know. So far, he was handling himself well.

"Mental instability," Oscar said. "Void was always very introverted, not soldier material. Slate was like that at one time too, but he got over it. Void never did, unfortunately, and couldn't live with the pressures of being unique."

"I think 'unique' is the wrong word," Slate muttered.

"It's the perfect word," Oscar snapped. "As I was saying, things became a lot worse for our supersoldiers. The higher-ups in the government were afraid, deathly afraid. Not only were they afraid of the public finding out about the supersoldiers, but they were also afraid the supersoldiers would turn on them.

Some even suggested that the supersoldiers be put down to ensure the security of the Western Union."

"That obviously didn't happen," Slate said.

"No, it didn't. You and the supersoldiers were too valuable to be killed. However, many believed the supersoldiers needed to be ... disciplined. What occurred after that ... it's not for the faint of heart to hear."

"Tell them," the Helmet Man demanded. "Tell them what you did. The Gifted haven't been acting out for no reason. They're pissed, and so am I."

Oscar licked his dry lips. "Neither I nor Incognito had any real say in what happened. I suppose we could have resisted harder or protested more. We were at least partially responsible, that I'll admit to. Those supersoldiers ... those children were ... tortured. There's no other word to describe it. Tortured..."

"If you're not responsible, who is?" Slate questioned. The other stole glances at him. He wasn't joking around, like usual. It made them uncomfortable.

Oscar's mouth thinned. "I told you, I held some of the responsibility."

"Then who held the rest of it? Come on! Give me a name! Who—?"

"Alphonse Schmitt."

It was not Oscar who said this, but Incognito. The terrorist mastermind kept a firm grip on his scythe, tapping the fingers of his free hand on the table.

The name meant nothing to Gilda, Straper, Taylor, or Thomas.

But the Helmet Man knew it.

"Him..." Slate muttered, shaking his head. "That guy... Almost forgot he existed. Maybe I wanted to forget him."

Oscar looked away from his son. Small tears escaped his eyes.

"Do I really want to ask?" Gilda said.

"I'll ask," Taylor said. He breathed in, like he was about to jump into a pool. "Who is Alphonse Schmitt? Is he a Keymaster as well?"

"I only met him a few times," Slate said. "Not right in the head, that one."

Straper groaned. "Great, if Slate's saying that..."

"My memories of life before the Gifted escaped are foggy at best," Naomi said, her hands folded so tight, she was bound to break a finger. "But my worst were those of Schmitt."

"He better be dead," Slate said, pacing around the table. "If that guy's still alive, then the world really doesn't deserve to keep spinning."

***

Geppetto had multiple layers on, yet he still shivered out of control. "Turn up the heat. It feels like something important is about to freeze off."

"Sorry, sir, but the heater is turned up all the way," Killian said. He and five other armed men were traveling with Geppetto across the frozen wasteland of Antarctica. Killian had a small goatee and a shaved head. Geppetto had heard of Killian before, a reliable mercenary with many notable accomplishments under his belt. Killian had been off the radar for years, presumed dead, but it seemed he had been secretly working for Sebastian all this time.

Now Geppetto found himself stuck with Killian and his men inside a snowcat heading to the middle of nowhere. Killian was driving the vehicle while Geppetto sat shotgun. A fierce snowstorm kept visibility low, so Killian was extra cautious while driving. Not only was it cold, but it was also boring. Killian didn't look like the kind of guy who would appreciate small talk, but Geppetto decided to initiate a conversation anyway.

"So, what other work have you done for Sebastian?"

Killian shook his head. "Can't answer that, sir. Not without Sebastian's approval."

"Forget it," Geppetto huffed. He tried to fall asleep so he could get his mind off the cold, but a swarm of anxiety-inducing thoughts kept him from losing consciousness. He particularly thought about the recent conversation with Sebastian. There was so much the blind man had revealed, so much still waiting to be uncovered...

"Geppetto, I'm going to give you answers," Sebastian had said as they stood together on the balcony overlooking Tiananmen Square.

Geppetto had almost burst into hysterical laughter. Answers, really? He had learned long ago that asking the big questions was pointless.

"You don't seem convinced," Sebastian said. His yellow dog growled.

Geppetto felt like kicking it. "Can you blame me? After years of teasing the answers, you're suddenly going to tell me what's going on?"

"What better time than now?" Sebastian asked, waving his arms around him. "The Mentor is about to play a more direct role in Cloak's affairs. When that happens, we will be unstoppable. It's the beginning of the end, Geppetto. I don't think it will be detrimental to our plans if I tell you this information, at least not anymore."

Geppetto wasn't buying any of it. Should he just walk away? No, the offer was too tempting. It couldn't hurt to have Sebastian give him the rundown. Sure, why not?

"How much do you know?" Geppetto asked.

"Enough," was Sebastian's murky answer. "But even I don't have the full picture. Only the Mentor knows. Pawns don't need to know the game plan, you see, though I always saw myself more as a bishop than a pawn."

Great, so no real answers were to be had. Geppetto decided to continue regardless. "All right, here's my first question. Temple ... is he the Mentor?"

Sebastian started slow clapping. "Very good, Geppetto. I was expecting a much more obvious one than that. You seem to have put a lot of thought into it."

"Are you going to answer or not?"

"Yes, I will. However, the question you asked cannot be answered with a simple yes or no. The nature of Temple is not so cut-and-dry. He could be best thought of as the Mentor's proxy, a blunt instrument for our leader to communicate and act through. The physical form of Temple is not the Mentor's, but the energy Temple wields and even his very will are. In summation, the answer is 'kind of.'"

Geppetto gaped. An actual answer! However, the revelation brought up a host of questions. He had known that if the Mentor did exist, their leader would most certainly not be normal. But from what Sebastian just told him, it seemed the Mentor was far less normal than Geppetto had ever guessed.

It was time to ask the ultimate question. "Then ... if that's the case ... who ... or *what* ... is the Mentor?"

The yellow dog barked angrily and sprinted back inside the palace. Sebastian, gazing at nothing, paid no mind.

"That is something you'll have to discover for yourself," Sebastian finally answered, oddly contemplative. It gave Geppetto the creeps. "I honestly don't give much thought to the Mentor's true nature. It seems so irrelevant. All that matters is our master's objective."

Geppetto didn't like that answer as much as the first one. It was too vague for his tastes. Despite that, he still felt as if he had one more piece to the puzzle.

"Then what is the Mentor's objective?" he asked, staring into the horizon, out toward the end of the world. "What's Cloak's purpose? What have we been working toward all these years? Why all the death? Why all the misery? Why all the suffering? Why does the Mentor torment us? Why, Sebastian? Tell me. Tell me *that*, at least."

Sebastian's smile seemed to flicker, but only for an instant. He put his hand on Geppetto's shoulders and turned him around so they were facing each other. Geppetto looked up at him. The perpetual grin on Sebastian's face now had a warmness never before seen. A rush of blood went to Geppetto's head. His legs wobbled as if he were a rickety table.

"The Mentor seeks to bring meaning to our suffering," Sebastian revealed at last, his words careful and engrossing. "Everything ill that has ever befallen you, all the years of pain and hardship, it all meant something. It all had a purpose."

"No, it was to keep us in line," Geppetto objected. "That was it. The military, you, the Mentor... All of you just wanted to control us, turn us into slaves..."

"That's the shallow answer," Sebastian told him, squeezing his shoulder. "It's true on some level but shallow all the same. The Mentor has discovered the deeper answer, the true meaning of your suffering. Now the Mentor seeks to ensure that your suffering has not gone to waste. Not just the Gifted, but all of humanity's pain serves a purpose. There is a reason why people suffer.

There is a purpose to evil."

Now Geppetto found himself on a quest to discover the ultimate design of the Mentor. Sebastian had told him to go to Antarctica. There was only white in every direction, with the occasional rock poking out of the ice. Neither the Chinese Empire nor the Western Union felt like fighting over this desolate and dead continent, so it belonged to no one. If there was an end to the world, it was somewhere close by.

"We're here," Killian said. The snowcat came to a crunching stop. Geppetto forced himself awake. He peeked out the window, seeing only more snow.

"Excuse me for asking," Geppetto said, "but what's so special about 'here'?"

Killian shrugged. "These are the coordinates Sebastian gave me. Now we wait."

"Wait for what?"

Killian shrugged again. "Something, I guess."

A bark echoed from outside. Geppetto snapped his head toward the sound. To the far left of the snowcat, a yellow dog sat in the snow. It panted happily at the arrival of the newcomers.

"It's Sebastian's dog!" Geppetto shouted. "What the hell is that mutt doing here? Did we take it along with us?"

"No," Killian said, staring at the dog. "I double-checked our cargo before we left. It must have come here some other way."

The dog barked again and bounded off, disappearing into the storm.

"Guess we follow it," Killian said.

The snowcat pursued the dog. How that dog managed not to freeze to death out there perplexed Geppetto. It would make sense if it had been a husky, but Sebastian's pet looked like something you would buy for your kid at the pet store. There was something off about that dog, something otherworldly.

They followed the dog for half an hour. The storm was picking up as well, so the snowcat had to stay within twenty feet of the dog or risk losing its trail.

"This is all elaborate and tedious," Geppetto said, rubbing his shivering arms. "Definitely Sebastian's style. Whatever's out here, it must be important."

Killian squinted. He had caught sight of a dark object up ahead. The dog was barking and running around the object.

"We're stopping," Killian said. "Get ready, men!"

The snowcat came to a halt. The five men in the back checked their rifles. Geppetto didn't feel much safer with them around. After all, they were mere humans.

Rushing out of the vehicle, the men scouted the area and gave the thumbs-up when they were done. Killian and Geppetto got out. The wind hit them like an icy slap to the face. Geppetto realized he should have put on snowshoes. The snow was almost up to his belly button, making it nearly impossible to walk. He might as well have been swimming through it. Killian might have assisted him, but Geppetto had more dignity than to ask.

Geppetto waddled over to the dark object that had attracted the dog. Killian walked close behind, his men flanking their sides for protection. The object was twelve feet in height, jet-black, and tubular in shape. It had a rounded top.

Geppetto stopped in his tracks. A new kind of coldness gripped him.

The monolith had the same shape as Temple's helmet.

"Sir, are you okay?" Killian asked him.

"Yeah, I can handle myself. Let's just find out what that thing is."

Killian nodded, but he kept an eye on the monolith. The storm seemed to settle down the closer they got to the object, as if the wind knew better than to come close.

They were now only a few feet from the object. The air was still here. It was quiet. It was dead. The monolith was man-made. It did not belong here. They were upon it now. Geppetto put his small hand against the monolith's surface. He expected some kind of reaction. At first, all that happened was that more heat escaped his body.

Then the monolith started rumbling. Geppetto jumped back. Killian and his men raised their weapons. Geppetto thought it was the dumbest thing he ever saw someone do. What were they going to do, shoot it? *Go on, try and fail!*

The rumbling stopped. Creaking replaced it. The monolith was opening.

Harsh fluorescent light poured out. A man holding a bottle stood inside the monolith.

"Well, if it isn't my favorite little munchkin," the man slurred. "Did Sebastian finally let you into his inner circle? Course he did. No other reason you'd be here."

The fear and even the cold left Geppetto. His mind didn't recognize the voice at first, but his body did. It went tense. His gut turned upside down. Rage started to boil inside him, a rage that had been dormant for years. He pawed unconsciously at his neck. No, it was *him*. Of all people, it was *him*. After all these years, *he* was still alive.

Geppetto screamed at the top of his lungs.

Alphonse Schmitt gurgled out a laugh. "Look, he remembers me."

CHAPTER 30

"What exactly did this Schmitt do that made him so bad?" Straper asked. "Did he hit you guys or something?"

Taylor felt like hitting Straper himself. "You know, a little tact never hurt."

"I'm sick of wasting time. I want straight answers."

"He didn't do anything bad to me," Slate said. "But every time I met the guy, I always got the feeling that he wanted to."

Straper snorted. "What about you, Naomi? How did Schmitt hurt you?"

Naomi turned pale. "I would rather not say out loud."

Everyone else gave Straper the stink eye.

"What? Just asking!"

"I don't want to dwell on this conversation," Oscar said. "There is much we still have to discuss. Where was I?"

"I think you were about to tell us where it all went wrong," Gilda said. Her arms were crossed so tightly that they turned red. "Tell us about Temple."

Naomi went even paler than before. Oscar bit his lower lip.

"Tell them," Incognito hissed. "Tell them what we created, what the West brought forth into this world."

Oscar stopped biting his lip. A line of blood dripped down his chin. He began to talk slowly, measuring every word. "Most people with any knowledge of the Keymaster Project believe only ten supersoldiers were made. From oldest to youngest, there was Void, Slate, Houdini, Geppetto, Cyphrus, Sebastian, Sandtrap, Repulsa, Ember, and Atlas."

Gilda leaned in closer. "Are you saying there's another supersoldier?"

"Yes, an eleventh supersoldier was made, another Helmet Man."

Slate became alert, but he refrained from making a witticism.

"This supersoldier was known as Temple." Oscar paused for emphasis.

"Temple was the most unique creation of the Keymasters in that Temple was created without the use of a surrogate mother. He was born fully grown in a vat, not made for combat but for information gathering. We created Temple with the ability to read minds, and not just one mind at a time but billions of minds simultaneously."

"You're kidding!" Straper cried.

"What in heaven's name did you make *that* for?" Taylor demanded.

"Temple was the ultimate surveillance device," Oscar said. "Why tap phones when you could read minds? Using a complicated interface, we could tell Temple to search for the location of a specific person. We could determine who was a spy and who wasn't. We could even predict terrorist or military attacks before they happened. The Chinese Empire wouldn't have been able to make a move without the Western Union knowing.

"And that's just the tip of the iceberg. The emotional state of entire populations could be analyzed. The Western Union could see if Tibet's population was willing to revolt against the Chinese. Temple could have rendered the Western Intelligence Service completely obsolete. With Temple, the Western Union would have been invincible."

Oscar paused again and covered his mouth, remembering the fire. He muttered some words before moving on. "Temple changed. I don't know when it started happening, but it happened. He was always dangerous. We had to put a pandorium helmet on him. Otherwise, anyone who came close to him would go mad. Before he donned the helmet, several of the Keymasters became schizophrenic just by being in the same room with him."

"Is *that* what Slate's helmet is for?" Straper asked, scooting his chair away from the Helmet Man.

"Stupid boy," Incognito scoffed. "You would have gone insane long ago if that were the case. No, Slate's helmet was meant to keep his powers restrained. His nervous system, charged with psychic energy, attracts electrons. We shielded his brain so he wouldn't be able to gather energy as easily."

Slate did not chime in, but he did touch his helmet self-consciously.

"He is correct," Oscar said. "Slate's helmet was meant to keep something out. Temple's helmet, however, was meant to keep something *in*. We thought putting a helmet on Temple would be an adequate enough safety measure. It wasn't.

"One day, Temple came to life. Before then, he had merely been a piece of meat. There was no life in him, no consciousness to speak of. Even an insect had more of a will than Temple. We just put wires into his body and had our computers give commands to his empty mind. However, soon after we started to transport our supersoldiers to the Bunker, Temple started moving on his own. He ... he killed everyone."

Oscar stopped talking and sank into his chair. Words refused to come from his mouth. He squeezed his eyes shut.

Incognito took over from him. "Temple killed all the Keymasters. He killed all the soldiers. He killed everyone, except for Radcliffe and me. By that time, I had already given myself superhuman abilities, so we were able to escape. If only I had mastered my gift sooner, the nauseating creature wouldn't have stood a chance against me. The other supersoldiers, meanwhile, used this opportunity to escape. A plane had been transporting them, but it disappeared without a trace.

"The government went into a state of panic. Not only were all their brilliant scientists killed, but their supersoldiers had also gone rogue. Covering their tracks was all the cowards could do, so they destroyed any evidence that the Keymaster Project had existed, including files, animal test subjects, and anyone deemed a security risk. I'm not sure how many wretched souls the Western Union pruned or how many were killed. I assume several dozen at least. Oscar and I were among the targets. They weren't sure if we were still alive, since they failed to find our bodies, but they were taking no chances. They wanted our heads.

"So, we fled. I managed to settle Radcliffe into a reasonably comfortable safe house where he could lick his wounds. Afterward, I scoured the world, searching for any trace of the supersoldiers. The Western Union did the same for a time, but they eventually gave up, deciding to focus more on preserving their plausible deniability."

Incognito stopped speaking. He scanned the room with cold eyes. Everyone was waiting for him to continue, but he remained quiet. It took about a minute for someone to get fed up.

"That can't be it!" Thomas cried, smacking his hands on the table. "That's no way to end a story. You didn't finish it right."

"What did you expect, happily ever after?" Incognito spat. "Life rarely ends that way, boy. The best one can hope for is a bittersweet conclusion."

"Lay off him," Gilda said. "He's right. You haven't finished the story. What about Slate? How did he end up buried near the Bunker?"

"Haven't you been listening, girl? Radcliffe already told you that we don't know. Slate's unconscious body was being transported on a separate plane that crashed over the Sahara. What happened after that remains a mystery."

"So, this Temple is the one behind everything," Slate said. "He must be the Mentor. He's the one I gotta beat the crap out of."

Taylor blinked several times. "Is that all you got from this?"

"What else is there to know?"

"To be honest, I don't even know if Temple and the Mentor are one and the same," Oscar said, breaking his silence. "Does the Mentor even exist, or did Sebastian invent this elusive figure as a way to control the other Gifted? I'm not sure. But if the Mentor is real, I have a theory who it might be."

Everyone seemed interested in this topic, even Incognito.

Oscar felt the eyes on him. He forced himself to relax. "I originally thought Temple spontaneously obtained his powers, that Sebastian used this opportunity to help the other supersoldiers escape. However, from what Incognito has recently told me, it appears that Sebastian and Temple are working together. It could be that Sebastian has found a way to tame the beast, but I have an alternate theory. I believe that someone gave Temple his powers. I believe that someone uses Temple as a puppet and gives orders to Sebastian. I believe that someone was a Keymaster."

Oscar glanced at Incognito to see what his thoughts were. Incognito didn't give a verbal reply but nodded slightly. Oscar looked away and said it out loud.

"I believe the Mentor is Alphonse Schmitt."

***

"Of course I'm not the Mentor!"

Alphonse Schmitt didn't say this as though he were offended. His reaction was like that of someone who had been mistaken for an attractive celebrity.

Geppetto had managed to ask only one thing since he got onto this small elevator: "Are you the Mentor?" He was utilizing all his self-control not to scream again. He wouldn't dare show any more weakness in front of this trash.

Killian and his men were waiting up on the surface. So was that yellow mutt. The elevator was only big enough to hold two people. It felt like being trapped in a coffin with Dracula, though Geppetto thought that was an unfair comparison. Dracula had charm.

"I can't believe Sebastian sent a dwarf to keep me company," Schmitt slurred, taking another deep gulp from his unmarked glass bottle. It didn't take a genius to figure out what was in it. "What is he going to send next? An elf? A centaur? Still, I suppose you're better than that superskank. I can't stand her hideous voice."

It was impossible to tell how old Schmitt was. He could have been anywhere from forty to seventy. Pale skin was stretched across his face, looking like it might tear in half at any moment from the tension. His red, plump lips were in a constant state of pouting. They made Geppetto think of slugs. Schmitt's hair was steel-gray, thick with grease, and combed back sharply. His white suit was well made but in desperate need of a wash. He needed a shave as well, his stubble as sharp as porcupine quills. His stink filled the elevator. Geppetto's hatred was wrestling with his disgust. It looked like the match would end in a draw.

"Nearly out of my medicine," Schmitt said, peering inside his bottle. "On my last crate. Canned goods are running low too. Almost happy you showed up. This one-sided conversation alone is doing wonders for me."

Geppetto forced out another question. "Ember knows about this place?"

"What do you think the skank was doing while you and that traitorous tart tried to take over Cloak? Sebastian can't always come here. He had to put his trust in one of the others. Houdini was the first choice. The man was loyal, but his temper made him unreliable. We had to settle for the loose woman. Houdini... We shouldn't have made any Arab subjects. Breed like rats already. Caucasian supersoldiers were the way to go. Come to think of it, I don't know how we ended up with you. I must have spilled some booze in a test tube. No ... wasn't drinking back then. Wasn't as bored."

It was too easy, too tempting. Geppetto could take control of this slime that stood next to him. He could make this man bash his head against the wall until his skull cracked like a walnut. Sebastian wouldn't like it, but who cares what he wanted? Geppetto had once respected him on some level because he had supposedly done away with the Keymasters. Now it turned out that he had kept the worst one alive all this time. Only Geppetto's desire for answers kept him from inflicting his wrath upon Schmitt.

After two agonizing minutes, the elevator came to a stop. Schmitt shuffled off first, Geppetto following a good distance behind. They were now in a barren hallway with concrete walls. The temperature here was much warmer compared with the outside, but Geppetto could still see his breath. Schmitt gave the tour as they went farther.

"The Russians made this love nest centuries ago," Schmitt wheezed, coughing up phlegm before continuing. "It was during their cold war with America, back when they thought they could take over the world. Ridiculous. Those commies couldn't even get their trains to run on time!" Schmitt took a swig from his bottle. "Anyway, when the Soviet Union rightfully caved in on itself, this place was abandoned. Actually, it was forgotten, but I found it again. Had to go into hiding after you creatures went rogue. Good place to lay low. Been here for twenty fricking years, and it's just as mind-numbing as you'd expect."

They reached the end of the hallway. A solid metal door with a relatively new keypad blocked the way. Schmitt stared at the keypad for a few moments before doing anything. Then he tapped in a code with a shaky finger. The door unlocked.

Schmitt licked his teeth. "Almost forgot the code. Haven't been outside in a while. The frostbite isn't worth the fresh air." He pushed the door open halfway and slunk through the opening. Against his better instincts, Geppetto followed. It took quite a while for his eyes to adjust. It took even longer for his nose to do the same. The light was dim, the air was damp, and the smell was horrendous. It stank of filth, sewage, and blood.

"Try not to step in any puddles," Schmitt said. This didn't stop him from stepping in some brown water himself. He didn't seem to care. "I'm not the only one here, by the way. There are about a dozen others, maybe just ten now. You could call them my lab assistants. Not a very useful bunch. Just lie around most of the time."

Geppetto started to make out his surroundings. They were in some sort of locker room. Five shriveled things that had once been men were curled up in the corners, lying on top of soiled rags. They were even filthier and more unshaven than Schmitt was. They didn't react as Geppetto and Schmitt walked by them.

Schmitt kicked one of the creatures in passing. "They were scientists once. All of them have different reasons for being here. Gambling debts. Fleeing from Chinamen. Got mixed up with the wrong crowd. The reasons range from pitiful to tragically hilarious. They all sought asylum, a place to hide. Sebastian gathered them up and brought them here. I actually wanted Dr. Plato to come join me. We even kidnapped that manly daughter of his. What was her name? Ah, I remember ... Gilda Plato. Fugly little brat. But I saw a recent picture of Repulsa. Now, why couldn't all my supersoldiers look like that? A shock collar on that one..."

A few more minutes, Geppetto told himself. *Just a few more minutes.*

They entered the next room. It was filled with empty cans and buckets of whatsit. Their contents looked like water but definitely didn't smell like it. They moved through several more rooms, each in dire need of cleaning.

At last, they entered a room that looked somewhat clean. It had two tables covered with wires and circuit boards. A metal sphere sat in the center of the room. It was without doubt the cleanest-looking object that Geppetto had seen since he entered this foul place. Yet when he looked at the sphere, he got the same feeling he did whenever he was around Temple, like something cold was slipping inside him, making itself at home.

"This is what I've been working on for seven years now," Schmitt said, pride swelling in his voice. His bottle was now empty. He set it gently on a table and approached the sphere with reverence. After fiddling with the panel on top, he pried the mysterious machine open.

"Come." Schmitt waved to Geppetto like he was expecting him to do a flip as well.

Geppetto closed his eyes, imagining Sebastian's dog was tearing Schmitt apart. He approached the sphere. It was almost as tall as he was, but he could see inside it if he stood on his toes. Its innards were an incomprehensible mess of electronics and metal parts. Smack-dab in the middle was a transparent orb with a gray blob suspended in its center.

"I call this a node," Schmitt said. "The orb you see in the middle was made by Zaidi Industries. I couldn't make the component on my own, not with my limited resources. The whole Helios Tower fiasco was all about obtaining this small but essential component. The Gifted were told it was a weapon. It's much more than that, I can assure you. It's a superconductor, one that conducts psychic energy. The rest of the sphere, all the circuitry and whatnot, serves to focus the energy, funnel it. This is only a prototype. The Mentor requires at least a hundred more, not to mention everything else needed to complete the Requiem Array. The cost could be in the trillions. It took over a billion dollars just to build this doohickey alone. In reality, most of Cloak's profits go to funding my little project."

So many answers were coming from this man's mouth. *Keep going,* Geppetto wordlessly urged. He wanted the old drunk to keep going, to spill his guts out. Then he could literally spill them out.

"You're a quiet one, aren't you?" Schmitt noticed, shutting the metal sphere. "Not that I'm complaining. A man's voice coming from a child's body is almost too amusing to take. If you had any pride, you'd have snuffed yourself by now."

Same to you, pal, Geppetto wanted to say. Instead, he asked another question. "What's the Requiem Array?"

"Something the Mentor commissioned me to make," Schmitt said. "To be precise, the design of the device came to me in a dream. Divine inspiration, it was. I only have a vague idea of what its purpose is. It's *catastrophic.*"

"Have you met the Mentor?"

"Not personally, no. I have only received dreams and interacted with Temple, just like Sebastian. I don't know if the Mentor is simply keeping a low profile or if that's the only way our leader can communicate with us. I suspect the latter."

"Where has Temple been all these years?"

"Mostly here with me. He occasionally went out to do an errand. Temple acted almost like a lab assistant, doing a lot of the literal heavy lifting. He's also the reason my other lab assistants don't last very long. Either Temple kills them or they just lose their marbles. Weak-minded fools... That never was a problem for me. It's only recently that Temple has exposed himself so fully to the world."

Geppetto was getting close to something. At least he hoped so. "Why is that? Why has Temple come out of hiding?"

"Two reasons, munchkin. The first is Cloak needs the help. Without Temple, Cloak wouldn't be running the Chinese Empire right now. Most of the Gifted are either dead or have allied themselves with Incognito. That means it's time to take out the big guns."

"What's the other reason?"

Schmitt laughed to himself, his teeth yellow yet flawless. "Temple has gotten stronger. Oh, yes... He's gotten much stronger ever since World War III began. He's now an army unto himself. I no longer have to shelter him like some fragile baby bird. He's left the nest, a chick turned bird of prey."

"You've been *protecting* Temple?"

"Temple is the key. So is Slate. For what, I do not know. All I know is that Sebastian had a dream, a vision. Sebastian—no ... *the Mentor* seeks the Helmet Man. Even the Requiem Array comes second to this, and so do you. Then again, you always came in short."

Schmitt laughed again. He put a clammy hand on Geppetto's shoulder. Geppetto shook it off. He didn't care how good the answers were. This man would not touch him.

The Keymaster's smile turned to a comical scowl. "You better play ball, dwarf. I might get Temple to skin you otherwise. He listens to me, you know? A being with that kind of power takes orders from *me*. If Temple is a god, then I have become greater than a god. That warrants at least a modicum of respect from you."

Geppetto didn't care about answers anymore. He had more than enough. He willed his mind to take control of Schmitt, to turn this sadist into a puppet. This would be satisfying. He could imagine all the Gifted, even Slate and Repulsa, cheering him on. *You're not going to hurt us anymore, old man,* Geppetto almost said out loud. This was a long time coming.

Bash your head against the wall, Geppetto willed.

Nothing happened.

Schmitt sighed, wishing he had another bottle. "That's the problem with you Gifted. You're all so reliant on your powers. What would happen if they didn't work, huh?"

Schmitt kicked Geppetto in the face. Blood squirted from Geppetto's nose as he hit the floor, screaming in frustration and pain.

Something was glowing in Schmitt's pocket. He took it out and put it on his finger. It was a ring of some kind. The stone in the center emitted a harsh yellow light.

"My ring uses a variation of the superconductor made by Zaidi Industries," Schmitt said. "I had the material specially commissioned. It absorbs all psychic energy within a certain radius. Your powers won't work here, dwarf."

"You son of a…"

"It's time I left this Popsicle stand," Schmitt said. "Sebastian sent you here to give me a ride to the Chinese Empire, though Killian and his men will have to kill all my remaining lab assistants. Doesn't feel right to leave them unsupervised."

Geppetto stopped using his powers. It was useless, and he couldn't physically take on Schmitt, even if he was an old drunk.

The ring on Schmitt's finger stopped glowing. Geppetto rubbed his neck. A handful of boiling tears escaped his eyes.

"Schmitt…" he hissed.

"One other thing, dwarf. You forgot to call me Daddy Schmitt." The Keymaster snickered. "You haven't forgotten your training already, have you?"

"So, you don't know for certain who the Mentor is," Taylor said.

Oscar frowned but nodded. "That's correct."

"Do you know why Cloak's interested in me?" Slate asked. "I know I'm amazing, but this obsession is getting out of hand."

"They might want to recruit or study you," Oscar said. "To be honest, I'm not exactly sure why they're after you either. Any more questions before we move on?"

"Yes, I have one," Gilda said. "I don't know if I'm overstepping my boundaries, but why did you take so long to show yourself? When Slate joined the United Third, you had months to visit him before the Western Union caught him. Didn't you want to see him?"

Oscar went bright red. Slate turned his silver helmet toward Gilda. She jumped a little in her seat. Was the Helmet Man mad at her?

Straper shifted in his chair. "Geez..."

"I purposely prevented Radcliffe from seeing him," Incognito said. "I presumed Slate's search for his long-lost father figure was a major motivation in his war with Cloak. Revealing Radcliffe could have caused him to become disinterested."

"What!" Slate yelled. "You..."

"That's just cruel," Gilda said.

"Despicable," Taylor spat.

"Slate, don't!" Oscar shouted, almost begging. The Helmet Man had charged his arm up and was now aiming it at Incognito. The terrorist wasn't cowed in the slightest.

"Please, Slate," Oscar beseeched. "You still have to hear our proposal."

"We ain't interested," Straper said.

"Sorry, Oscar," Gilda said. "We're not going to be roped into helping Incognito again."

"What if I told you that Cloak is stronger than ever?" Oscar asked. "What if I told you that Cloak is controlling the Chinese Empire? What if I told you that Cloak was behind the Western Union's failed invasion?"

"It wouldn't make a difference," Slate said, his arm glowing brighter by the second.

"Wait, is it true?" Gilda asked. "Has Cloak taken over the Chinese Empire?"

"It's true," Oscar said. "Temple is exerting some sort of influence over Emperor Long. Sebastian now makes most of the decisions. Not only has Cloak taken over the Chinese Empire from the inside, but it has also been behind every major strike against the Western Union since the war began. Both the attack on the Pentagon and the thwarting of the West's attempted invasion are Cloak's doing."

"I knew Cloak wasn't finished," Gilda growled.

"What do they hope to achieve?" Taylor asked.

Oscar gave them a disturbing answer, eyes downcast. "For lack of a better term, they are after world domination."

Slate dropped his glowing arm. It had gone limp. Oscar's statement earned a variety of responses from the others as well.

"You're joking."

"Shit."

"What! There's no way they can pull that off."

"I don't know what else it could be," Oscar said. "They obviously want the Chinese Empire to win the war."

"Could they do it?" Gilda asked. "Could the Chinese win the war? Is Cloak really capable of taking over the world?"

"They've already taken control of the Chinese Empire," Oscar said. "That's a good fourth of the world already, not to mention at least half the human population."

Thomas stiffened. "Is that what Cloak's after? Does the Mentor want to rule the world? Is that why all those people had to die?"

"I don't know," Oscar said. "It could merely be a phase in Cloak's ultimate plan. What I do know is they can't be left to their own devices, and the Western Union is too overwhelmed and unreliable right now. That means we have to stop Cloak ourselves."

"That's what I'm gonna do," Slate said. "*Without* Incognito's help."

"Listen to me, Slate!" Oscar shouted. "Incognito has been contacted by elements within the Chinese Empire who also seek the downfall of Cloak. They want his help. Specifically, they want him to defeat Cloak and secure the emperor. Once he does that, a coup will take place that'll put the right people in charge, people who will end this world war."

"Who exactly asked for Incognito's help?" Taylor asked.

"It's too risky to give you any specifics, especially since you haven't yet accepted our offer, but we were hoping Slate, Naomi, and any other volunteers would accompany Incognito on his mission to stop Cloak once and for all."

"Why did they ask Incognito?" Gilda asked. "Can't the Chinese deal with Cloak themselves?"

Oscar felt like shaking them all. "You don't understand! Emperor Long is like a god to his people, incorruptible and all-powerful. Many can't even imagine the emperor falling under anyone else's influence. They think he is the one making all the decisions. Perhaps Emperor Long believes it himself. The emperor hasn't been of sound mind for years. It was probably easy for Cloak to take control of him, and if they have the emperor, they have the empire. We not only have to destroy Cloak, but we must also make sure the emperor is handed over to some of his more moderate and level-headed countrymen."

"So, you want us to help Incognito get the emperor for himself?" Slate asked. "Oh, wow! I don't see anything wrong with that at all!"

"I couldn't care less about the Chinese Empire," Incognito said. "In fact, I don't care if you traitors decide to join me or not. I can handle this myself."

"You aren't helping!" Oscar yelled. He turned back to the others. "Incognito's abilities are unmatched. He is the only one who can fight Temple. Slate, it is true that you're stronger than ever, but you're still not strong enough. Temple is a beast, a juggernaut. He brought an empire to its knees. He even destroyed the Pentagon single-handedly for the sole purpose of winning over the emperor's favor."

"One guy destroyed the Pentagon!" Straper cried. "That's crazy!"

"Remember Keito Kusanagi, Slate?" Oscar asked, his eyes wild. "Remember that Ryder woman and her black walker? Temple beat them both at the same time, as well as two other customized walkers. I don't mean he just beat them in battle. He *beat* them. From what I've heard, Keito is barely alive. A walker pilot was killed. Another is in the hospital. Temple probably could have killed them all. He chose to torture them instead. They did manage to behead Temple, but his severed head simply grew a new body."

Taylor and Gilda exchanged glances, petrified.

"He's not exaggerating," Naomi said. She hadn't spoken in a while. "Temple is unlike any other enemy we have faced. He's ... fearsome."

"Sounds like my kind of opponent," Slate said, cracking his knuckles. "Forget Incognito. I can kill Temple myself."

"Did you even hear me?" Oscar snapped. "Temple beat both Ryder and Keito. You were barely able to fight only Ryder when you were escaping from *Tortuga*."

"Hey, she caught me off guard! I could have taken her in a fair fight."

"And what will happen if Temple catches you off guard? He won't give you a fair fight, I can tell you that. Even if you have Naomi and the others helping you, Temple will beat you. I'm not sure if even Incognito can take down Temple by himself. Our best shot of slaying the beast is if we all work together."

"I don't need their help," Incognito said. "These wretches would only get in the way."

"Reverse psychology, eh?" Slate observed. "Your mind tricks won't work on me anymore, Incognito. I won't do it!"

"Good, I shall be rid of your idiocy."

"You two are unbelievable," Oscar said. "Maybe the reason Cloak's been so successful is because both of you can't cooperate."

"I have no time for this tripe," Incognito said. "Not when I'm trying to establish a superpower and wipe out Western civilization. You ingrates decide what you're going to do by tomorrow morning. I will face Temple, with or without you."

Incognito hobbled out of the room with his scythe and slammed the door behind him.

"Why do people even follow that guy?" Gilda muttered.

"If we're lucky, Incognito and Temple will kill each other off," Straper said.

"As you can see, Incognito isn't asking for your help," Oscar said. "I am. Because of me, a gang of killers is terrorizing the world. I must make amends. I know none of you owe me any favors, but I truly believe this is the only way to stop Cloak. You have all come this far, haven't you? Just take one more step, and you'll reach your goal!"

"Nice try, old man," Slate said, sounding more exhausted than angry. "I know you and Incognito go way back, but that racist kook can't be trusted. But thanks for the info. I'll make sure it's put to good use."

Oscar wanted to get mad again, but he too was exhausted. Instead, he left them with parting words. "Think it over. I'll hear your final decision tomorrow." He got up from his chair. "It just seems such a waste to give up now, after you've all fought for so long. Perhaps I'm asking too much. Either way, the only people who are able and willing to stop Cloak are Incognito and those in this room. I'm not asking you to follow him, only to join him. Like me, he has much to atone for. He may not be looking for atonement, but he needs it. I wonder, Slate, if the same goes for you?"

Oscar left the room, leaving the Helmet Man and his comrades to consider his offer.

It did not take long for most of them to make up their minds.

"I assume we all feel the same way?" Gilda asked everyone else.

Slate, Straper, and Thomas nodded. Taylor tilted his head back.

"No," Naomi said. "We do not all feel the same way."

Gilda and Straper shot her looks. Thomas sat up with wide eyes.

Slate kept his cool. "You want to help Incognito?"

"I want to help myself," Naomi said, her flesh shaky but her voice strong. "I was willing to part with Incognito because I was starting to think this day would never come. Now it seems I shall finally meet my maker."

"Are you going to leave us?" Thomas asked, trying not to sound distressed.

"I won't leave unless Slate decides to come with me," Naomi said, rubbing the boy's shoulder. "I don't want to face this alone."

Slate smacked his helmet in exasperation. "Great, first Dad, now you!"

"Why are you doing this?" Gilda questioned. "I thought you were better than this, Naomi. You're just giving in!"

"I'm not giving in!" Naomi screeched. The chair Gilda sat on briefly levitated an inch off the floor before dropping back down. Her purple hair now stood on end.

Slate grabbed Naomi's arm. "Easy there!"

A vein throbbed on her forehead as if it might burst at any moment. Taylor and Straper moved back. Thomas whimpered.

Naomi grabbed Slate's arm. "I need to tell you something."

Slate cocked his head. "What, now?"

"I need to tell you everything."

"Okay..."

"I need to tell you my story."

"Yeah, sure... How long will this take?"

"I don't know. An hour, I suppose."

Slate turned to the others. "I'll hear her out. We meet back in an hour."

Gilda waved them off, too tired to argue.

***

An hour later, everyone was back in the conference room. Gilda, Straper, and Thomas were more restless than before. Taylor just seemed impatient.

Naomi shuffled into the room, worn out. Her hair was frizzy, and she smelled of ozone. Slate came after her, more worn out mentally than physically. Naomi lowered herself delicately into a chair, and Slate took his place standing behind her.

"Naomi doesn't want me telling you everything," Slate said. "Not yet. What I will say is she has every reason to want Temple dead."

"So, she's met this Temple before?" Taylor asked.

"Yeah, and she's seen his power. We're dealing with a new kind of baddie here, someone who isn't going to give long monologues or hatch some evil plan. This guy is after blood. I'll have to throw everything at Temple in order to beat him. Naomi will have to help me every step of the way. And I can't believe I'm saying this, but I'll need Incognito's help too." It took Slate a moment to utter his next sentence. "But I won't need you guys."

Straper was the first to object. "Hey, what just happened here? First you want to kill Incognito. Now you want to team up with him again? Geez, Naomi must have really rubbed you the right way."

Slate took a step toward him. "Watch what you say, punk!"

"I thought we were going to take Cloak down together," Gilda said, looking hurt. "I thought you were going to let me decide my own destiny. Now we suddenly can't go along with you just because Naomi told you her sob story?"

Straper snorted. "Jealous much?"

"Shut up, Straper! You're such a turd."

"You kids will only get in the way," Slate said. "I can't babysit you and fight Temple at the same time."

"That never stopped you before," Gilda snapped.

"Well, maybe I'm changing. If I am, it's for the better."

"None of you should be going," Taylor said. "Even you, Slate."

Slate scoffed. "What are you, my dad?"

"No, but I care about Kevin and Gilda, and they care about you. I don't know you as well as they do. I do know that while your helmet may be unbreakable, inside you're shattered. These two want to help heal you. However,

I'm afraid Oscar does not."

"What did you just say about my dad?" Slate questioned.

Taylor kept his gaze on the Helmet Man. "Oscar is a weak man, a guilty man. He's more concerned with fixing his own mistakes than he is with your well-being."

"Keep talking, pal! Keep talking!"

"I will. Slate, you don't have to fight in order to feel wanted. Your father, however, thinks otherwise. He wants you to risk your life cleaning up his mess. He wants you to fight a foe the likes of which you've never faced before. Everyone else you've fought has either been weaker or has gone easy on you. Incognito, for all his faults, pulled a good many punches when you attacked him. Temple won't. And Oscar knows that."

Slate grabbed Taylor's throat. He squeezed until Taylor's tongue stuck out of his mouth.

"You just show up and talk that shit," Slate hissed. "Who the hell are *you?*"

"Slate, stop!" Thomas screamed.

He did, but reluctantly. Taylor pulled away, coughing.

"He was trying to help you!" Gilda cried, smacking Slate's arm. "We all are!"

"Nobody talks about my dad that way," he said. "Not even you people."

"Screw you, Slate!" Straper yelled. "I respected you, man. I wanted to be you!"

"No one should want that."

"Mom, please don't go!" Thomas sobbed. He buried his face in Naomi's chest. Tears wetted her blouse.

"I'm not your mother, Thomas," Naomi said, but she held him anyway.

"No, you are... You're all I have. Don't go. Don't let that monster kill you. Stay behind. Please, Slate ... you too... I can't lose you both."

"Thomas, I have to do this for myself and for the good of the world," Naomi said.

"Oh, please," Gilda said. "You could care less about the world. This is all about you and your stupid revenge. You're doing this for all the wrong reasons."

"Yeah, would you be risking your life fighting Cloak if you didn't have this personal beef with Temple?" Straper asked Naomi. "Would Slate have had such a quick change of heart if you hadn't become his girlfriend?"

"I told you to watch it!" The Helmet Man grabbed Straper by his shirt, his silver helmet only inches from the young man's face, reflecting the rage.

"Go on," Straper snarled. "Kill me. The world's become shit anyway."

"Straper, there's no point," Taylor said in a raw voice, rubbing his neck. "He's clearly made up his mind."

Slate let go of Straper, who kept his distance from Slate and wore a wounded look. The Helmet Man rested his hands on his hips. He paced around for a second, kicking at the floor. He stopped, deep in his own head for a moment.

"Fine, maybe I don't have a right to tell you guys what to do," Slate said. "If any of you want to join me on this mission, I'll accept it. But I chose this path for myself. You'll all have to do the same. Make up your minds by tomorrow morning. Just remember that this battle won't be like any of the ones before."

"Just go," Taylor said, still rubbing his neck. "No more speeches."

"I understand your concerns," Naomi said, accidentally sounding condescending.

"That doesn't mean you care." Taylor coughed again. "This behavior doesn't surprise me from a former member of Cloak, a killer for hire, dragging children to war … but I expected more from Slate. I guess I set my expectations too high. In the end, you're both just murderers. You don't care about what's right. You only care about what's convenient. You'd both be better off with Cloak, with your own kind, doing your Mentor's bidding."

"Goodbye, Taylor," Slate said. "If I ever see you again, I'll kill you."

CHAPTER 32

"Those cursed Westerners... Istanbul has been retaken already."

"It's because of *Leviathan*. The tides of war turned in their favor when they put that machine back in the sky."

"We need to solicit help from the Chinese. The enemy of my enemy is my friend."

"The Chinese? They don't even have enough weapons to arm their own troops."

"Besides, we don't need help from those imperialists."

"Agreed, they're as bad as the Westerners."

"My grandfather is Chinese! Watch your words!"

Incognito listened to the bickering in a detached manner. He wasn't the only leader of this revolution. The round table was full of men from a variety of backgrounds. They had pooled their resources with the United Third and thus believed they deserved some role in the decision-making process. So far, there hadn't been a lot of deciding. Barir was also there, sitting across from Incognito. He made sure to keep silent.

"Incognito, what are you planning to do about this situation?" Karim Hassan asked. The fat man was eating a jar of olives, his plump fingers covered in their juices.

"It would be foolish to waste troops on retaking Istanbul," Incognito said. "The city is too close to Europe, and our troops are spread out thinly as it is. As such, we must declare the city lost, as well as the rest of the country."

"You are handing over Turkey to the Westerners without a fight!" a man cried. "This is my home you are talking about!"

"I am not giving up. I am merely being a realist. We should focus on keeping the rest of our territory and building the government for the Saladin Federation. We will make our stand in Aleppo, *Leviathan*'s next target."

Hassan sucked his fingers clean. "Syria? I doubt they'd advance so soon."

"My informants say otherwise. All those in favor?"

More than half the men raised their hands. Hassan was one of the few who didn't.

"Good, I shall give the order for our troops to fall back to Aleppo," Incognito said.

"Before I forget, we should address the issue of suicide bombings," said a former Saudi prince. "Many of our agents—"

"Troops," Incognito corrected. "We are a superpower. We call them troops now."

"Yes, troops. Well, many of our 'troops' still perform suicide bombings."

"You must admit it is highly effective when it comes to scaring those Westerners," Hassan said, belching. Several of the men laughed.

"But it's not good policy to blow up your own army," Incognito said. "Let it be known this council formally prohibits suicide bombing in all forms. All those in favor?"

Everyone raised their hands, some more reluctantly than others.

"A petition has also been presented to us," the prince went on. "Many are displeased that no women are on this council."

"That shall be considered on a later date," Incognito said. "There's already much to cover on the agenda. We don't need you to keep adding things. And I find it a tad ironic that a former Saudi prince is preaching feminism. Such hypocrisy does not impress me."

The prince wasn't happy, but he didn't bring up the subject again.

Incognito rose from his chair with the help of his scythe. "Before we move on, I have an announcement to make."

The council started murmuring. Hassan polished off his olives. Barir rubbed his beard.

"I shall be gone for several weeks," Incognito said. "Until my return, Barir will lead this council and take over all military operations for the United

Third."

The murmuring turned to yells of outrage.

Hassan laughed. "You cannot be serious? Right when the West is about to attack us, you run off on a secret errand. Where are you going?"

"To the Chinese Empire," Incognito said. "I shall attempt to form an alliance with them. It will benefit the Saladin Federation greatly."

"I heard a demon now rules the Forbidden City," a warlord said.

"You are not far from the truth."

"If we are to keep the Westerners from taking more of our territory, we need your leadership, Incognito," the prince said. "Please, don't leave us in our time of need."

"It's time you all started fending for yourselves anyway. I'm not going to live for much longer. I was hoping that I would have an heir by now, but it seems fate had a different plan. Perhaps it is the people, not I, who need to choose the next leader of the Saladin Federation. But until I pass away, I reign supreme. Anybody who objects to my decision might as well try to kill me right here and now. Go on. I'm waiting."

The entire council remained seated. Nobody was stupid enough to try that, though Hassan secretly hoped that someone was and managed to get lucky.

Incognito sat back down. "Let's move on to the next item on our agenda. That Western news anchor, Jeff Springer, is starting to become more trouble than he's worth. All those in favor of his execution?"

***

Barir waited until everyone except for Incognito had left the room. He approached his leader, bowing in respect.

"Spare me the formalities," Incognito huffed. "Speak your mind."

"I am honored that you chose me to fill your role."

"But?"

"But this can only be temporary. I am not leadership material."

"You may not be a good politician, but you are a good soldier. Simply focus on keeping Syria out of Western hands until I get back."

"There is more…"

"Of course there is."

"You have always known how I feel about your master plan, about how you wish to deal with the Westerners."

"I do. You object to it, and I continue to tell you it's the only way."

"It is genocide. The Saladin Federation cannot be founded on such bloodshed. It goes against everything Saladin himself believed in."

"I am the only one who will bear the burden. And you forget, Westerners are not people. They are self-indulgent animals. Their souls have been irredeemably tainted from their culture of excess and ignorance. That is, if they ever had souls to begin with."

"I agree that the West should stay out of our lands, but isn't this plan excessive in itself?"

"They won't suffer for long. It will be quick and efficient."

"Incognito, I will fight the Westerners to my dying breath in order to defend my home, but I cannot assist you in such a plan."

Incognito sighed. "You are right, Barir."

"I … I am?"

"Yes, you aren't leadership material."

***

Ryder snapped to attention.

"You've proven yourself very useful to me," Young Powell said, sipping wine. He sat in a large plush chair within his quarters in Cheyenne Mountain. It was practically a throne. Natalie stood next to the chair, also holding a glass of wine. She was already tipsy.

"Sir, it is an honor to serve the Western Union," Ryder said.

"Well, you also had some personal motivations, didn't you?" Young Powell asked.

"I wanted to speak to you about that, sir."

"Don't worry, Ryder. I'll keep my word. Your walker has already been repaired by Dr. Plato. And from now on, the only superior you answer to is me. All the Western Union's resources are at your disposal."

"That sounds adequate, sir."

"You're welcome. Quinn has some leads on the Helmet Man's whereabouts. Go speak with him before you leave."

"I'll do just that, sir. And the matter of Keito Kusanagi?"

"He'll be moved to a private hospital. It's probably a good idea for Powers to keep guarding Kusanagi and his woman. I don't like the idea of leaving those Japs unsupervised."

"Is that all, sir?"

"One more thing, Ryder." Young Powell took another sip of wine. "It's likely, in your pursuit of the Helmet Man, that you will come across Incognito."

"Should I avoid engaging him solo?"

"That might be a good idea, but I also want you to catch him alive."

Ryder's face stayed blank, but she felt her left eyebrow twitch. "Sir, we tried to do that before. It resulted in three destroyed aircraft carriers and hundreds of dead men. I will be lucky to survive an encounter with Incognito, let alone capture him."

"Do it, Ryder." A spark came off Powell, Ryder noticing this with detached curiosity. "That man has something in his noodle I want, and what Powell wants, Powell gets."

"I shall try my best, sir."

"That's all I ask. Now get lost."

Ryder saluted him and left his quarters.

"She's a scary woman," Natalie said, pouring herself another glass of wine.

"Yeah, she hasn't been right in the head in years," Young Powell said. "She used to be a pretty emotional woman, giving heartfelt speeches, crying over her dead men, though I only met her a few times before she changed."

"What happened?" Natalie asked, sitting on Powell's lap.

"That's not something I'd like to discuss in front of a lady." Powell kissed her. She kissed back poorly. During the kiss, Powell's mind wandered to terrible places, first to Ryder, then to the Helmet Man, and finally to Temple.

Temple... Did Ryder really kill him? Good riddance. That thing was why the Keymaster Project had ended the way it did. Powell, like the others, had thought Temple was the key to the Western Union's domination of the world, but now the Chinese had gotten hold of him. Maybe it was a mistake to give Cloak information about the invasion, even though it had been a onetime thing. Young Powell knew now that Cloak needed to be destroyed. The Gifted had been useful, even after they went rogue, but now they had to be put down.

Powell had only met Temple once, back when the beast couldn't move, when he was just a piece of meat that could spy on people. It had easily been the most unpleasant experience of his life. He had wanted to see Temple in the flesh, to be shown his true power. Alphonse Schmitt, a man who had always given him the heebie-jeebies, demonstrated how Temple could operate. Type in some numbers, scan a picture of a wanted terrorist bomber, press a button, and presto! Powell now had the exact location of the bomber. However, once the results came back, a sudden coldness grew inside him. Something *died* within him. Temple's helmet seemed to vibrate. The wires entering his body made it look like he was rooted to the ground, like he was a tree of knowledge. Powell had felt his bladder emptying itself. Schmitt laughed. Powell tried to strangle him but ended up slipping on the floor wet with urine.

"Ow, you're hurting me," Natalie whimpered. She pulled back her head. Blood stained her lips. It was the lipstick of the devil.

"You are mine," Young Powell said, red staining his lips as well. He shivered, all the way to his bones. "Yes, you belong to me... You belong to the God of America."

***

"Our sources claim that Incognito is taking a leave of absence," Quinn read from a holographic display projected by his watch. "The exact reason for this leave or where he plans to go are unknown. Also, the Helmet Man is said to be accompanying him."

"From my observations, it appears the relationship between Incognito and the Helmet Man is a strained one," Ryder said, looking over her walker. They were in the underground hangar where Obsidian was being stored. Ryder planned to meet up with York and Patel and then leave for Turkey tomorrow. She did not wish to delay the hunt any further.

"You think that's the key to taking them down?" Quinn asked, turning off his watch.

Ryder examined her cockpit. She could no longer see signs of damage, though the memory of Temple still lingered within her mind. "I believe the Helmet Man's comrades will prove to be his weak point, the two teenagers especially."

"Sounds like a plan."

Ryder climbed down from her walker. "Before I leave, I wish to speak to Dr. Plato. Where might I find him?"

"He's in his office, if you want to talk with him now."

"Indeed, I do."

***

Five minutes later, Ryder rapped her fist on Dr. Plato's office door.

"Hmm... Who is it?" a voice grumbled from within.

"Camilla Ryder. May I enter?"

"Huh? All right, give me a second..."

Dr. Plato opened the door. His face was gaunt, and he smelled like an old shoe.

"Sorry, my office is messy," Plato said, cleaning out the inside of his mouth with his tongue. "Do you want to talk somewhere else?"

"Your lack of hygiene is of little concern to me."

"Then come on in."

Ryder walked into the room, immediately noticing the rank smell. The wastebasket was overflowing with crumpled paper. Junk-food wrappers and bottles of prescription pills covered his desk with a stone Budai statue sitting in the center of the chaos. She also noticed the couch in the corner was covered in dirty sheets. It seemed Dr. Plato was sleeping here.

"Sit," Dr. Plato said, clearing off wrappers from a chair. "I can't get much sleep anymore. Been having strange stress dreams lately. Working myself to exhaustion is the only way I can get any shut-eye. Powell wants those Archangel walkers flightworthy by the end of next month, so I'm not short on things to do."

Ryder seated herself. The chair had something sticky on it. The seat of her pants was already glued on. She eyed the Budai statue. The fat, laughing man was a stark contrast to the scraggly and dejected appearance of her host.

"Dr. Plato, why do you work for the Western Union?"

Dr. Plato closed his office door. "That's an odd question."

"Perhaps I should rephrase my inquiry. Why do you work for the president?"

"That's a bit complicated," Dr. Plato said, settling himself into his office chair. "I'm aware you made a deal with Powell. I also made a deal of sorts with him long ago."

"May I ask what it entailed?"

"I'd rather not say, but I will tell you that I did it for my daughter. I wanted her to grow up without a besmirched reputation. I wanted her to turn out different than her mother or me. Gilda wanted that too, I believe. Maybe that's why she ran off. Maybe that's why she hates me."

"The United Third is known for recruiting vulnerable youth. Would you describe your daughter as being vulnerable?"

"Yeah..." Dr. Plato nodded sadly. "I failed, didn't I?"

"Yes."

Dr. Plato laughed. "Honest, I like that. Nobody around here is honest anymore. Powell is always lying through his teeth these days, even to himself. I don't know if he's going to save the Western Union or be its ruin. But I owe him, and I guess he's better than Incognito or the Chinese. The world needs someone with a firm hand to run it, keep this craziness in check."

"I agree. Those are the same reasons why I follow him." Ryder got up from her chair. "If I should get the chance, Dr. Plato, I will try to capture your daughter alive."

"Thank you. You have no idea how much that means."

"Until next time."

Ryder left the office, leaving Dr. Plato to brood on his failures.

"Are they leaving already?" Taylor asked.

"The sooner the better," Gilda told him. "That's what Naomi said."

Taylor nodded, staring at the floor. He sat on his bed with folded hands and a meditative expression. Gilda and Straper had decided to visit his spartan room in hopes of smoothing things over with him, but they weren't expecting any miracles.

"Can they be convinced to stay?" Taylor asked, knowing the answer already.

"They made up their minds," Gilda said.

Straper snorted with a half smile. "It ain't easy to talk Slate out of something once he's made up his mind."

"An astute observation," Taylor said.

Gilda cleared her throat. "Look, about what Slate told you ... he didn't mean it. He's just frustrated about the whole situation."

"*He's* frustrated?" Taylor snapped, looking up. "What about me? Incognito apparently wants to keep me here until Slate gets back. *If* he gets back. I've become collateral while he goes on a self-indulgent crusade with that woman of his."

"Slate will make sure you go free," Gilda told him. "We'll make sure."

"Forgive me if I doubt your word, or your Helmet Man's."

"Hey, you got to admit, you were pretty out of line back there," Straper said. "You told Slate his dad didn't love him. How the hell is someone supposed to react to that? He probably shouldn't have grabbed you like that, I guess, but come on."

"Perhaps I was out of line ... but what about you two? What about Thomas? Did Slate give any thought to your well-being when he made his decision?"

"He thinks what he's doing is right," Gilda said. "I don't know. Maybe he is. Incognito is a monster, but at least he has limits. Cloak is something else."

"It's hard to compete with a man who wants to wipe out an entire civilization."

"Yeah, Cloak ain't nearly that bad," Straper said.

Gilda's dreams ran through her mind again.

Oh, lord... Oh, lord... The sun is no more...

"I'm not so sure about that," Gilda said. "Maybe..."

"What, you want to go on this mission?" Straper questioned.

"Slate, Naomi, and Oscar all think it's a good idea."

"They all have hidden agendas," Taylor said. "Just like Incognito."

"Slate's our friend. He's saved our lives at least a hundred times."

"I thought Slate wanted us to stay out of the way," Straper said.

"He doesn't want us, but I think he needs us. I mean, are we just going to stay behind?"

"Yes, stay!" Taylor cried. "Incognito is using you yet again. You personally admitted that joining the United Third was wrong. It's time to learn from that mistake."

Gilda furrowed her brow. "I don't know if we did the right thing then. We'll probably never know. But I'm starting to think that staying here is even worse than not going. Incognito can't be left alone. Neither can Cloak or the Chinese Empire. And Slate needs our help."

"Incognito is a master manipulator. He's made fools of you before, and he'll do it again."

"Maybe Incognito *wants* us to stay here," Straper said. "Think about it."

"What's with your sudden change of heart?" Taylor fumed.

"Oh, um..."

"I'm confused, Taylor," Gilda said, raising her hands, looking at her palms, wanting to grab her own face. "I don't know what's right or wrong. It's all gray. I can't even sleep anymore. I'm being attacked from all sides, even from the inside. Just tell me what—"

"I know what you're feeling," Taylor interrupted. "I know ... because I've felt that before. I've felt rage. I've felt injustice. I've felt guilt. I've felt all of it. That's why you must listen to me. You talk about Henry and how much his death affected you." He leaned in toward her. "Well, I've lost people too. I lost everyone I loved."

Gilda dropped her hands and stared at Taylor. The anger was still on his face, but his eyes had begun to tear up. Her chest grew heavy just looking at him.

Straper forced himself to speak. "What are you talking about, Doc?"

Taylor covered his eyes. "I had a family, a wife and a son." He breathed out. "My wife died when my son was a toddler. A peacekeeper shot her. We lived within a safe zone in Central Africa. The soldiers there were nervous of anybody dark-skinned." Taylor had to laugh. "I grew up in England. It was insane. My son... I wanted to move away after my wife died, but I was still in the military, and there were so few doctors around..."

Taylor stopped for a moment, covering his mouth with a closed fist. Then he continued. "Other children regularly picked on my son for his race. I talked to the school several times, but each time they threatened to escort me off the property."

"That's horrible," Gilda said.

"How come we never heard of this before?" Straper demanded.

"The military kept it quiet," Taylor said, his eyes red. "I thought things would change with a black president, but Hynes was so right-wing that most people thought he was an outlier, an abnormality. The situation reminded me of Margaret Thatcher. Nobody thought she was a typical woman, just an outlier. Do you kids even know who Thatcher is?"

"No," Gilda admitted. "Please, go on."

"Yes ... well, my son soon stopped hanging out with the other children from the Western Union. Instead, he became chums with the native children. His mood improved, so I didn't think much of it. I even supported it."

A few tears came from Taylor's eyes. He wiped them away. "It turned out, however, that terrorists like using children as suicide bombers." More tears came out. He didn't bother to wipe these ones away. "These terrorists regularly recruited native children, but when they met my son, they knew he could get closer to sensitive targets than any of the other children. It was a golden opportunity. Soldiers hesitate before shooting a child, even if the child has a bomb strapped to his chest. The soldiers hesitated. My son didn't."

"Taylor, I..." Gilda thought she had the words but didn't.

"What the hell?" Straper asked himself under his breath.

"Listen to me, you two," Taylor said. "Incognito is warping your minds like the terrorists who warped my son's mind with their false promises and cheap trickery. I want to learn from my mistakes. I won't turn a blind eye again. I'll keep you two here no matter what, even if I have to use force. Even if I have to defy Slate."

"It's not the same thing," Gilda said. "I'm sorry you lost your wife and son, Taylor, but we're not children. You can't fight Slate. You'll only get hurt."

"This path will bring you no closure," Taylor warned with wide, tearful eyes. "It will bring you no fulfillment. It will only deepen the hole in your soul. It's an addiction. I see it in you. I see it in Slate and Naomi too. And I especially see it in Oscar Radcliffe. I know what he has become because I almost became it myself."

"Taylor..."

"Incognito ... I had begun to sympathize with his views. I was almost tempted to join the United Third. Because deep down inside my soul, I hated the Western Union. I hated it with all my heart. It's ... it's a hideous feeling."

Gilda and Straper were suddenly aware of a great divide between themselves and the man sitting before them. It was a canyon. Where did it come from?

Taylor shuddered. "I often go out of my way to hate Incognito because sometimes ... when I'm at my lowest ... I root for him." Taylor shrank. He was aging before their eyes. "Don't go. Please, don't go... For my sake... For your sake..."

Straper's eyes were focused on a spot on the wall. Anxiety built within him. Gilda also felt anxious. She gritted her teeth and made eye contact with

Taylor. Gazing into his eyes, her feelings became clear to her.

"I've made my choice," she said.

***

Slate tossed a bag into the back of the seaplane. "Geez, you packed a ton of crap. Who needs six pairs of shoes for a secret mission?"

"Each pair is more useful than the last," Naomi said. "One for running, one for hiking, one for combat, one for casual use, and two for formal occasions."

"Be more low-maintenance, like me. I don't even have extra underwear."

"That's going to change very soon if you want this relationship to last."

"Best knock it off before Incognito arrives," Oscar said. He was dragging a suitcase full of electrical equipment behind him. The private airfield was mostly deserted except for a few United Third agents fueling up the seaplane, which would take Slate and the others to rendezvous with the *Eodum*.

Thomas pouted next to Naomi. "I want to go with you guys. We just got back together."

"At least I know you'll be safe," Naomi said, petting his head. "Well, as safe as one can be during World War III. Barir promised to look after you, and Dr. Taylor will be here to keep you company. Don't worry. We'll get you a souvenir."

"Yeah, I'll bring back one of the emperor's wives for you," Slate told him.

"I'm still a kid!" Thomas yelled.

"Fine, more for me."

Naomi smacked Slate with her telekinesis.

"Ouch, not in front of the boy!" he shouted.

Thomas shrugged. "I don't mind."

"Little snot! Do you condone domestic abuse?"

"I truly forgot how annoying you could be," Oscar grunted, putting his luggage in the plane. "We're going to leave soon. Want to say goodbye to the others?"

The Helmet Man switched personalities in an instant. He went from being the class clown to the somber veteran. "No, not unless they come to see me."

Oscar nodded and turned his attention back to his bag. Thomas resumed pouting. Naomi only let out a breath and smiled. "If you think that's best, I'll support your decision," she told the Helmet Man.

Slate nodded. "Thanks. Sorry about getting moody all of a sudden."

"Actually, I sometimes prefer you this way. Your perpetual high can be quite grating."

Slate then noticed a car driving onto the airfield. It was about half a mile away but moving fast toward them. "Is that the man of the hour?" he growled.

"No, Incognito will have at least a dozen men with him," Oscar said. "The approaching vehicle is too small to fit that many people. It must be your friends."

"They're coming to say their farewells," Naomi said. "You okay with that, Slate?"

Slate crossed his arms. "We'll see."

The car stopped next to the seaplane. A brief yet tense moment passed before the car's doors swung open. The occupants unloaded.

"Are you two here to send me off?" Slate questioned.

Gilda and Straper walked up to the Helmet Man. Both wore stony expressions.

"Our bags are in the car," Gilda said in a firm voice. "A truck will be coming shortly with the new compact Magenta."

"We've decided to go with you," Straper added, clarifying the obvious.

Slate studied them as a general would his soldiers.

"We don't trust Incognito," Gilda said. "But we trust you, Slate. Maybe Naomi did sway you, but your other reasons for doing this mission are just. Cloak can't win. I don't know if Incognito is worse than Cloak or not, but I know you're better than all of them."

"Taylor tried to convince us not to go," Straper added. "I think he's got some good reasons. It's just that those reasons are his and not mine. Sitting back and doing nothing is a crime on its own. Sometimes, our gut is the only thing we can trust, and right now it's saying I should follow you to the bitter end."

"We've come too far," Gilda said. "Let us help you, Slate. Please."

Slate had listened attentively to their words. Two trucks were approaching from a distance. The clock was ticking. He didn't have much time to think.

Like Straper, he decided to go with his gut.

Slate grabbed Gilda and Straper each by the shoulder. He pulled them close, the two almost tripping over their own feet. The smooth, flawless silver helmet leaned in. A harsh whisper vibrated off the Helmet Man.

"First chance I get, I'm gonna kill Incognito," he told them. Gilda's and Straper's eyes widened. "Incognito will be weakened after Cloak is defeated," he went on. "That'll be the time to strike. Naomi's gonna help me. We're planning to make it look like the enemy did it so the United Third won't come after us, but this is bound to be a suicide mission. If you want to help, just nod. Otherwise, you two have no business coming."

Neither Oscar nor Thomas heard any of that. Oscar was too far away and preoccupied with adjusting his luggage while Thomas threw pebbles. Naomi also made sure the air didn't vibrate around Oscar or Thomas, further impairing their hearing.

Gilda and Straper took a quick moment to look shocked, but the trucks were almost here. They nodded discreetly.

Slate nodded back. He let go of them and turned his attention to the newcomers. The vehicles came to a stop, their engines quickly dying. Burly men stepped out. Abrafo was among them. He had an oversized machine gun strapped to his back.

"Why are the Western brats here?" Abrafo said, glancing at Gilda and Straper. "Do not tell me they are coming with us. This is not a daycare."

Gilda's annoyance was evident, her surprise from earlier wearing off. "If this was a daycare, I'd tell you to take a nap."

"Leave the one-liners to me," Slate said, reverting back to his usual persona. "Where's the old fart at? Did he need a diaper change?"

"I use a catheter," Incognito seethed, getting out of one of the trucks. "Any other bodily functions you wish to discuss? I know a base creature such as yourself must experience sheer delight whenever there is toilet humor."

"I love you too. Hobble over so we get out of here already. World War IV will have already started by the time we leave."

Abrafo kept himself from striking the Helmet Man, knowing that would be foolish. Incognito simply shot Slate a chilly look as he made his way to the plane.

Oscar approached Incognito, wanting to escort him to the aircraft.

"Appears the Western brats have decided to tag along," Incognito breathed. He seemed tired already. Tying up loose ends had drained him.

"I heard Dr. Taylor will remain in your custody," Oscar said. "The others aren't happy about it. Taylor also tried convincing them not to go with you."

"I expect nothing else from brainwashed brethren. He has forsaken his roots."

"Hey, you piece of shit," Straper spat, having overheard the conversation. "Taylor is braver than you'll ever be. Show him some respect."

Incognito raised his scythe, planning to use the sharp end.

Slate smacked Straper upside the head. Incognito's thugs laughed, Abrafo laughing the loudest. Straper's face flushed red. He only stood the indignity because Slate might just have saved his life. Incognito lowered his weapon, having saved face in front of his subordinates. He paid Slate and his friends no further consideration as he entered the plane. Oscar followed him.

"Get on board as well, you two," Naomi told the teenagers. "And please, try not to antagonize a man who can destroy an aircraft carrier on a whim."

Straper wiped away tears of rage as he stormed onto the plane. Gilda kept her head down and boarded as well. Abrafo and the other men started loading equipment. Another truck arrived, this one carrying the compact Magenta. Slate observed them quietly. Naomi leaned against him while Thomas stood before her.

"Long ago, my mother showed me what I truly meant to her," Naomi said, mostly to herself. She placed a clammy hand on Thomas's shoulder. "That moment defined who I was ever since. It has led me to this very moment, and now it's going to lead me to the heart of the scarlet empire, to Temple, to the end."

Slate raised his head. "And to the Mentor..."

***

Karim Hassan took a huge bite from his chicken leg. He wore a bib in order to keep his expensive robes spotless. The dining hall he sat in was covered in pillows, with Hassan sitting on the biggest and fluffiest of them. Serving boys wearing loose silks and blank expressions were lined up along the wall, holding trays of fruit. A table of food stretched out before Hassan. His guest was on the other side of it.

"Chicken is a universal food," Hassan explained through a mouthful of the stuff. "Westerners eat it. Muslims eat it. Jews eat it. Asians eat it. Only vegetarians refuse to eat the beloved animal, but I do not consider them proper people. It is also a miracle food. You can get more meat per acre with chickens than you ever could with beef."

"I could make a nasty joke but shall restrain myself," Ember said. She lay on her side, her black cape folded neatly in the corner. She took an unnecessarily huge bite from an apple while eyeing one of the serving boys. "Delicious ... the forbidden fruit."

"Please, eat more," Hassan said. He was now gnawing on the chicken bone in an attempt to get at the marrow.

"Tempting, but I've got a figure to worry about." Ember finished off her apple, even eating the core. She took another look at the serving boy. "Well, seconds couldn't hurt."

"That can be arranged," Hassan said with skin-deep warmth.

"I heard apple seeds have cyanide in them," Ember said. "If that's the case, I like to think I get a little bit deadlier every time I eat one of these scrumptious morsels."

Hassan tossed the remains of the chicken bone behind his shoulder. "An interesting idea. I personally believe if everyone ate chicken, the world would be at peace."

"What about those vegetarians you detest so much?"

Hassan shrugged. "As I said, I do not consider them proper people."

Ember flashed her pearly whites. "Now *that* is something I could get behind."

"I am glad you feel that way." Hassan started on another leg. "I am also glad Cloak has decided to pay me a visit. I have been a loyal customer of yours for some time, and now that Cloak has secured a high place in the Chinese government, I wish to become a loyal ally."

"A high place?" Ember hooted. "We're running the show!"

"Even better. Incognito has proven himself to be a poor leader. As such, I believe it is time I take the reins. The Saladin Federation would profit greatly from an alliance with the Chinese Empire, especially if we wish to see the Western Union defeated."

"I'll relay the offer, but what I really came for was some intel."

"I was about to get to that. While I do not know where Incognito is now, I do know where he will be and also approximately when."

"They're planning to attack us already? Good for them."

Hassan raised his eyebrows. "You expected this?"

"Oh, yes. In fact, we're counting on it!"

"It's time to dream again."

Eisenhorn was getting wise to Klara's routine. He expected to feel the coarse sand against his cheek, to see a starlit sky, to have Klara refrain from giving him any real answers.

But none of that happened.

Eisenhorn awoke in a perfectly white room. At least he thought it was a room. It was just all white around him. He got to his feet.

"You've noticed the change."

The voice came from behind him. He turned to see Klara. She looked the same as ever, the mismatched clothes coiling around her like the bandages of a mummy.

"Yeah, I noticed the change!" Eisenhorn yelled. "What happened to the sand? What happened to the ocean? What happened to the sky?"

"Occupied," Klara told him.

Eisenhorn threw up a laugh. "A dream can't be occupied. It ain't an airplane bathroom."

"It's not just a dream," Klara said. "It's a perspective, a state of being."

"No, I won't do this again!" Eisenhorn yelled, crossing his bony arms. All his muscle had been stripped away, leaving him gaunt and half dead. The Chinese Empire was whittling him down to nothing. Klara wasn't helping. Temple made it worse.

Klara moved in closer. "Randolph, I understand your situation must infuriate you. Truth be told, I also grow weary of waiting, but too much is at stake to risk acting now."

"Why can't I just die? Huh? Why can't I just die? You're no use. All you do is pester me with these pointless dreams. Johnson is dead. My cadets are too. The Western Union has left me to rot. Xing is useless. And Shu ... I can't believe it." Eisenhorn shrank down several sizes. "I guess it never would've worked. She saw me for what I was, an old and broken man. It was her job to be friendly to me. But the emperor? He's even older. Better than me, I guess. Yeah, better than me. She needs to be with her own kind. That's the real problem."

"If you really believe that, then I truly feel sorry for you."

Eisenhorn knew he would be crying if he were still in good health. The tears had dried up. Why couldn't he be healthy and young while trapped in this dream world? Reality was seeping in. Or perhaps it was the other way around. Perhaps the nightmares were escaping.

"The empire grows corrupt," Klara continued. "The West also crumbles from the inside. But Cloak grows stronger, as does its leader."

Eisenhorn's self-hate turned outward, back into regular hate. "So, this is about Cloak!"

"Yes, and we will have to sacrifice both our lives if we wish to stop them. We must also, above all else, get that syringe."

"But what's so important about the syringe?"

"It is a trigger." Klara paused for a moment. "It will detonate the bomb in your head."

The bomb dropped. He didn't know what to make of it at first. A bomb in his noodle? No, the idea was ludicrous. He laughed. This wasn't just a dream. It was a bad dream, and a bad joke to boot. He laughed again, this time with more desperation.

Klara did not laugh.

Eisenhorn's laughter stopped. His mouth went dry. "A bomb..."

"The Western Union put it there," Klara said. "The man who tried to assassinate you over a year ago was an agent of the West. You were to be destroyed, along with the emperor and the rest of the Forbidden City. I prevented that from happening."

"Hynes... He sent me on a suicide mission."

"I thought you were willing to sacrifice your life for the Western Union."

"I am, but I deserve respect!"

Eisenhorn huffed and puffed in anger. Klara watched passively for a moment.

"Hynes did not do this to you out of spite or hatred," she said. "He did this for the Western Union. In fact, he was fulfilling *your* request."

Eisenhorn's face couldn't get any redder. "What? I don't remember that!"

"Before the bomb was implanted in your brain, you assured Hynes that this was what you wanted, to be useful again. He complied. You were pruned before the procedure to prevent you from divulging information that could lead to the mission's failure."

"This... This was what I wanted... Yeah, I can see that. I can see Hynes doing this favor for me. Good old Hynes! But you prevented me from completing my mission. You're the reason there's a war going on!"

"This war is nothing," Klara said. These words came from a small voice, but the weight of them could not be ignored. "Your pain is nothing, not to our enemy. Our suffering is merely a means of satisfying its hunger and fulfilling its evil ambition."

Klara gestured to her right. Eisenhorn turned to see that the white void was no longer so white. A blemish in the infinite drew his eyes. A black circle, a *perfect* circle, dotted the ground several yards away from him. It looked like something Bugs Bunny would hide in.

Eisenhorn began to waddle toward it.

"Look into it," Klara whispered. "Gaze into the abyss, into the eyes of the enemy."

*****

Gilda awoke, or seemingly awoke, to find herself lying on an island.

It was made of white sand. A black ocean surrounded her. A starlit sky provided the illumination. The air was crisp and chilled. Goose bumps gave her skin the consistency of a fleshy gravel road.

"You've grown up."

The woman loomed before her. She wore her usual black dress. Gilda didn't cry out this time. She only shuffled backward like a crab until she slipped and fell on her backside.

The woman laughed. "You were never the graceful one in the family."

"You're not my mother!" Gilda screamed. "She's dead!"

"Marker kissed you without your permission," the woman said. "He tried to use you like a tool, didn't he? It's not his fault. All men are like that. Disgusting, aren't they?"

Gilda moved away from her, getting dangerously close to the black water.

"You know what's even more amusing? *You liked it.* You acted like you hated it, but you liked it all too well. Men may be disgusting, but so are women in their own unique way. The victim always escapes the blame, despite playing their own little role."

Gilda wanted to get as far away from this apparition as possible, but she was too close to the water. She was much more afraid of *it* than her mother.

"Sorry," her mother said. "I'm not dressed for the occasion." She raised her wrists. Needles were sticking out of them. Blood stained her dress. The garment became scarlet. She closed her eyes. Gilda stopped breathing.

"So arrogant, so ignorant..." her mother went on. "Only the lord can be without shame. We are all worms under the eyes of the lord. Men, women, big, small, victim, monster... It does not matter. All will tremble under the gaze of the moon."

With closed eyes, her mother approached.

***

"Gaze into the abyss," Klara urged, terror lacing her voice.

Eisenhorn knelt next to the hole in the ground. It was as black as the ocean surrounding the white island. It was dark and empty enough for the mind to draw its own pictures, to induce hallucinations in the careless and weak-minded.

Eisenhorn was both.

"You must understand," Klara said, careful not to fall prey to hysteria. "I have tried to convince you, but now I must show you. I must show myself, remind myself why I have given myself, body and soul, to the cause. All one needs to do is gaze at our foe to witness the totality of our enemy's vision, though even I don't comprehend the scope, the finality of it."

Something blinked into existence, into the void. Eisenhorn didn't notice at first, despite it literally staring him in the face. It was a more gradual realization, all the more chilling.

"Klara..." he murmured.

The moon stared out from the abyss. It was a flawless moon, seemingly made from white marble, polished smooth by the tides of time.

Eisenhorn's own two eyes could not break contact.

Klara crouched next to him and whispered into his ear. Every syllable she spoke brought her one step closer to insanity.

"Oh, lord... Oh, lord... The sun is no more..."

***

Gilda knew she had nowhere to run.

So did her mother.

"I am a tool," her mother said. "I am befouled. I am imperfect. I am weak. I am nothing. But *we* are pure. *We* are whole. *We* are creation *and* ruination. *We* will topple the heavens. *We* will fulfill our purpose."

Gilda sat up, not under her own volition. Tears bubbled from her eyes.

"I don't even have to force you," her mother said. "You answer when spoken to."

Her mother's eyes snapped open.

Gilda let out a silent scream. Now she *couldn't* forget.

The moon had her.

Her mother's eyes were white. Pupils were a thing of the past. Irises were *so* last season. These were the whitest eyes you could imagine. Balls of ice, that was what they were. They were staring at Gilda. She knew it would be too good to be true if they weren't.

Gilda tried to scream again, but this time something did come out. Black blood boiled out of her esophagus, cascading from her mouth. Her eyes rolled into the back of her head. Only white orbs stared out of her sockets now.

It was the gaze of the moon.

***

A scream erupted from the hole.

It sounded familiar to Eisenhorn. He couldn't place it. It made his hair stand on end. It also aroused something foul and deep within his being.

"What the hell am I looking at?" he asked.

Klara couldn't help it anymore. Fear overtook her. Her eyes rolled into the back of her head. Whiteness now stared back. She then answered him.

"Omega..."

Once again, something blinked into existence. And again, Eisenhorn didn't notice it until it was too late. It was a second moon, placed to the right of the first pale orb. A part of him died right then and there, never to regrow or come to life. If his soul was a flower, then a petal had fallen off it, leaving the bloom debased and befouled.

Those weren't moons staring back at him.

They were a pair of white eyes.

A taloned hand emerged from the void.

Child...

Gilda usually slept on her back, so she nearly drowned when she threw up. Fortunately for her, Naomi had been lying in the bed next to her and was only half-asleep, too restless to slip away, when she heard an unsettling gurgle. She saw Gilda twitching on her bed, the contents of her stomach spilling out the sides of her mouth.

Naomi was still groggy, but she had enough sense to wave her hand. Gilda flipped upside down, and an invisible smack on the back cleared her throat. After her coughs turned into gasps, she let out several guttural screams.

"These aren't your typical bad dreams," Naomi muttered, getting out of bed.

It took a few minutes to clean up Gilda and another couple to calm her down, but even then, the feral look in her eyes refused to go away. Gilda now sat on the edge of her bed. Her expression of terror had devolved into one of apathy, remembering that she was on the *Eodum* and sharing a cramped cabin with Naomi. They were heading to the Indian Ocean, just beginning their first leg of their journey to the heart of the Chinese Empire.

"It's the first night of our mission, and you're already having a nervous breakdown," Naomi said. "What use are you going to be without any sleep?"

"My dream…" Gilda said. Several incomprehensible words escaped her mouth before she gave up. She rubbed her eyes and more carefully thought out what she was going to say. "My dream was real…"

She expected Naomi to give a snarky reply.

Naomi didn't. "Did you dream about the moon?"

Gilda almost screamed again.

"I take it from your reaction that this is the case," Naomi said. "It's nothing. The news has been reporting it since before the war. Scientists speculate it has to do with stress. Thousands of people throughout America have been having these dreams, not to mention the rest of the Western Union. They aren't sure if it's strictly a Western phenomenon or if the rest of the world has been experiencing this too. The Occupied Territories are too volatile right now to do these studies, and the Chinese Empire wouldn't even know how to conduct them.

Gilda shook her head, not believing it at first. Then she vaguely recalled a news report that talked about lunar-related dreams. Naomi wasn't making this up.

"But ... it felt so real..."

"You've been under more stress than most," Naomi said. "It doesn't help that you bottle up your feelings." She rubbed her eyes. "Look, I'm not used to being a shoulder to cry on, but I'm willing to give it a shot if you let me."

"I'm fine," Gilda said a bit too quickly. Naomi frowned. Gilda decided to say it again, slower this time. "I'm fine."

"You better be," Naomi told her. "I can't have you endangering the mission. If I feel you're only going to be a burden, I *will* keep you on the *Eodum* while the rest of us go on without you, even if Slate objects."

"I'm fine," Gilda repeated, almost convincingly. "I'm not great, but I'm fine."

"We'll see." Naomi climbed back into bed. "I'm going to sleep again. Replace your sheets. You don't have to go back to sleep tonight, but at least lie down. We have a big day tomorrow, and the days are only going to keep getting bigger."

"Okay." Gilda started to gather her sheets when a question began to gnaw at her. "Naomi, have you been having dreams about the moon too?"

"One," Naomi said, not going into further detail. "Goodnight, Gilda. And for goodness sake, sleep on your side if you think you're going to vomit again."

***

Gilda didn't sleep another wink that night. The circles under her eyes were getting noticeable. Regardless, she was wide-awake for the briefing about to take place.

Eight people, including her, surrounded a table covered in maps and diagrams. She sat next to Straper and Naomi. Slate stood next to Naomi, drumming his fingers impatiently. Oscar sat across the table while Abrafo stood near Oscar, shooting inhospitable glances toward the Helmet Man and his friends. Captain Young-Bum also stood near the table. He was only going to be with them for the first leg of their journey, but he still wanted to be kept in the loop. After all, he was risking his life, crew, and submarine to transport these notorious individuals.

The terrorist mastermind himself sat at the head of the table. The armchair that Incognito occupied seemed to be devouring his frail frame, but his cold eyes and honed scythe reminded everyone not to underestimate him.

"Let us begin this preliminary briefing," Oscar said, shuffling through some papers. "First, let me say how grateful I am to—"

Incognito banged his scythe on the table. "Skip the platitudes."

Oscar's face reddened. "We won't go into any specifics today. Only Incognito, Naomi, and I will know the full details until we deem it necessary to inform you."

"What's the deal?" Straper asked. "How can we contribute our input if we don't know what the plan is?"

"We don't want the entire mission to be compromised should one of us get captured," Naomi said. "While we do trust you, the Chinese Empire has rather persuasive methods of torture. You won't be able to keep a secret for long."

"In any event, the day we are dependent on your input is the day the world will truly be doomed," Incognito added.

Straper suppressed a growl. "Slate, back me up here."

The Helmet Man raised his hands. "Hate to say it, but the guy has a point."

"Thanks a lot."

"Quit your bickering," Abrafo warned. "This is no soap opera."

Slate gasped. "Unless one of us happens to be … pregnant! Dun, dun, dun!"

"I think I've had enough stupid for today," Gilda said. "Just get on with it, Oscar."

Oscar waited a moment to make sure no one had a follow-up joke before continuing. "While we can't go over the specifics of the mission, we ought to go over the profiles of some of our enemies."

"Like powers and weaknesses?" Straper asked.

"Precisely." Oscar got out a remote and pressed a green button. The room went dim. A holographic screen appeared over the table. It showed a rough sketch of an ancient old man sitting on a throne.

"No recent photos exist of the emperor," Oscar said. "But this sketch is pretty close to what he looks like. The emperor is over a hundred years old. He is physically frail and, due to his advanced age and position of absolute power, psychologically unstable. His extended contact with Temple may have further deteriorated his mental state. The emperor himself shouldn't put up much of a resistance. On the contrary, we must take great care, since the stress of his capture might kill him, and we need him alive."

"But you will have to get past his guards first," Young-Bum warned.

"Yes, a significant challenge." Oscar clicked to the next screen, which showed the five cyborgs of the Black Lotus. Again, this was merely a sketch. "The Black Lotus is made up of five cyborgs. They are only answerable to the emperor. However, we must now consider them pawns of Cloak, since Sebastian is controlling them through the emperor. There does seem to be some tension between Cloak and the Black Lotus, but not enough to exploit."

The screen zoomed in on the first Black Lotus agent.

"This is Poppy," Oscar said. "You've encountered him before in Japan. He's all organic except for his cybernetic eyes, which give him superhuman vision. When it comes to long-range combat, he's practically invincible. The only way to fight him is up close."

The image shifted over to the second agent.

"You haven't met her, but Lily will be very difficult to deal with. Her entire skeleton has been replaced with a titanium alloy, nearly unbreakable. She has abnormal strength and recently had repulsion pads attached to her feet, similar to Keito Kusanagi's. Swords also extend from her hands. And she's quite psychotic. Be careful with her."

The third agent was presented.

"You also haven't met Pansy," Oscar said. "This man is characterized by his quiet demeanor and keen observation skills. He also has a nearly unbreakable skeleton, though he can take much more damage than Lily. He's virtually bulletproof. Pansy has also recently become the emperor's personal bodyguard. Undoubtedly, we will encounter him during our mission. If our information is correct, he is also equipped with a rocket launcher in his right arm."

"Cool!"

Everyone shot Straper a look.

"What? It is!"

Oscar shook his head and clicked his remote. The screen showed the fourth agent.

"This one you've met. Mistress Lotus, the leader and the mother of the other Black Lotus agents. She is by far the strongest and most intelligent of them all, as well as the most devoted to the emperor, her husband and the father of the other Black Lotus agents."

"What a family," Slate said.

"Look who's talking," Oscar replied. "Mistress Lotus can control all water within two hundred meters. When we reach the Forbidden City, the only major body of water will be the moat surrounding the palace, so that's fortunate. Her metal shell is sturdy, but Slate's beams seem to be strong enough to pierce it, as demonstrated during their encounter in the Neutral Zone. I don't know what kind of effect her powers will have on a person. After all, the human body is mostly water. I would assume it would be extremely painful to be ensnared by her. I advise that none of you encounter Mistress Lotus without backup."

The last Black Lotus agent appeared on-screen.

"They're using a little kid!" Straper cried.

Gilda shook her head in condemnation.

"Yes, she is the youngest Black Lotus agent, turned into a cyborg only two years ago," Oscar said, looking sadly at the holographic screen. "Being the youngest, we don't have much information on her or her abilities. All we know is she has suffered extreme trauma, and her mother is coercing her into assassinating others. Rumor has it she's quite good."

"The Black Lotus really is the Chinese version of the Keymaster Project," Slate said, arms crossed and voice hard.

Oscar shifted in his seat. "Well, not even we used children *that* young for combat."

It was a feeble defense, but Slate didn't pursue the subject.

"This sounds like a whole lot of trouble," Straper pointed out. "We haven't even covered the Gifted yet, and I already don't like our chances."

"Then crawl under your bed and die," Incognito told him.

"We have a countermeasure," Oscar said quickly to avoid an argument. "The emperor, while knowing the Black Lotus is loyal, still did not fully trust them, so he had special guns designed. These guns are able to incapacitate the cyborgs, temporarily or permanently depending on the setting. But the emperor's paranoia will prove to be his downfall. Our ally in the Forbidden City will supply us with these weapons, and one was used on Pansy during a failed coup two weeks back, so we know they're effective. However, each weapon was made to fire only once, and we will have only three at our disposal."

"Three guns for five superhuman cyborgs," Gilda noted with a sigh.

Oscar laughed. "No, more like three *shots* for five superhuman cyborgs. You'll have to find a different way to kill the other two cyborgs. I suggest not using these guns on Poppy. A regular gun will do for him. Mistress Lotus, Pansy, and Lily will have the honor instead. Hopefully, we won't have to kill the child. If we do, I hope it won't be too difficult."

"This mission is sounding more pleasant by the second," Naomi said. "How about we move on to the Gifted? I can take over from here."

Oscar shrugged. "Be my guest."

Naomi ripped the remote from his hands with her mind. The old scientist practically had a heart attack. He scowled as it landed gently in Naomi's open palm.

"First up is Geppetto," she said, clicking the remote to reveal a blurry photo of her former comrade walking down a crowded street. "He's a dwarf, not hard to identify. He has the power to take control of anyone's voluntary functions. Although I'm not certain about his range of control, I'd say he can finely manipulate a person up to a kilometer away. Being two kilometers apart results in a complete loss of influence."

"I think he's going to be the biggest problem," Straper said. "Only Slate isn't affected by this guy's powers. Hell, I don't think even Incognito is safe."

"We have already taken steps to ensure I do not fall under the dwarf's spell," Incognito snapped. "The rest of you will have to make do."

Oscar huffed. "Everyone else will have to use long-range attacks when dealing with Geppetto. And try to nonlethally incapacitate his victims if you can."

"I make no promises," Incognito told him.

"Of course you don't," Naomi said, rolling her eyes. "How about we move on?"

She clicked the remote. A close-up photo of a young woman in heavy makeup dominated the screen. Her face was splattered in blood, and she was making a kissy face.

"Who is this freak?" Abrafo snarled.

"Ember's her name," Naomi said, not sounding like she had many fond memories of her. "She's by far one of the strongest Gifted. She's also the most insane. This picture is a selfie taken during the Nigerian Genocide five years ago. Ember took a very active part in the killings. She has the ability to soak up all the heat within a couple yards of herself and can freeze people and objects if they are close enough to her. She can then release this heat in the form of fire and even use this ability to fly. So, like Geppetto, we should try to take her on from a distance. By no means should you allow her to capture you alive. She'll torture you for information. Then she'll just torture you for fun."

A sketch of a man materialized on-screen. He wore a slimy grin and round sunglasses.

"This is Sebastian, the second-in-command of Cloak. He is the only one of the Gifted with no code name because he is considered a failed experiment. The Keymasters merely gave him the name 'Sebastian,' a mundane name for a mundane failure.

"However, it has recently been confirmed that he does, in fact, display superhuman skills. He managed to deflect machine gun fire with a sword."

Nobody gasped in surprise. They were too used to this kind of bizarreness.

"The Keymasters gave Sebastian heightened senses and reflexes," Naomi said. "But he had to get his optic cords severed since his brain couldn't process all the extra input his eyes were picking up. The seizures he had as a toddler nearly killed him.

"Sebastian is one of our primary targets. For all practical purposes, we should consider him the nerve center of Cloak. If he dies, Cloak dies. Our hope is to capture him alive, but do not hesitate to kill him if necessary. Out of all our enemies, he is by far the cleverest and is a master manipulator. Do not listen to anything he has to say.

"Now, for our main adversary..."

Naomi clicked the remote. She couldn't contain her tremble.

The sketch that replaced Sebastian's was substantially cruder by comparison. It was a vortex of dark and foreboding colors, lots of grays and blacks and bloody reds. And silver. The figure embedded within the swirling mess looked like it was both carefully and hastily drawn, if such a paradox was possible. It had a dark, misshapen body and a head entombed within a towering helmet. Blood stained the silver prison.

A vacuum had sucked out all the life in the room. A thick sheet of perspiration covered Abrafo and Young-Bum. Oscar stared for only a moment at the screen before turning his eyes downward. Gilda felt a shiver travel up her spine, only for it to hit her gut and cause her to gag. She half expected black blood to come up. Straper tried to smile, hoping to lighten up the situation, but his grin came across as forced and even unnerving. He immediately stopped. Incognito, meanwhile, tightened his grip on his scythe as he kept his eyes locked on the screen. He may have felt fear if his hate wasn't so great.

Naomi felt a tear come to her eye.

Take her! Take her, you beast!

The Helmet Man touched her shoulder. She looked up to see her own rattled reflection in the silver helmet.

"I can't see the screen," he told her. "Lucky me."

The tension left her body. She wiped the lone tear from her face and gave Slate a ghostly smile. Then she turned away and continued presenting.

"Temple is without question the most fearsome enemy we will encounter," she said. "He was made to act as a surveillance device that could read the minds of billions of people simultaneously. Since then, his abilities have evolved for unknown reasons. He is now able to fire concentrated energy beams and create energy barriers that can be used as shields. He also has the ability to fly and release massive amounts of energy to cause widespread destruction. Perhaps most frighteningly, he has regenerative powers that surpass any of the Gifted. Atlas needed constant feeding in order to regenerate. Even then, he required transplants for missing body parts that regenerated improperly. None of these shortcomings impede Temple. He managed to regenerate his entire body from a severed head.

"But he may have a weak spot. Temple uses psychic energy to regenerate, which can only be created by neural tissue, so destroying the brain ought to be fatal for him.

"The obvious problem is his helmet. Like Slate's, it is nearly indestructible. The only way to get to Temple's brain is by going under his helmet. We'll have to pin him down and go through the base of his skull. It's going to be messy, and Temple won't let it happen without a fight. Nobody, and I mean *nobody*, is allowed to face him alone. If you spot him, run. After you've safely gotten away, contact the rest of the group so we can plan accordingly. Temple will only be engaged if Slate, Incognito, and I are all present. I would prefer to have Gilda and her walker there too. The rest of you will stay out of the way.

"Because of the danger, our aim is to kill Temple and nothing else. Capturing him alive would prove foolhardy. We wouldn't get information from him anyway, though it may be possible to get something from Sebastian. Perhaps then we'll be one step closer to revealing the true identity of the Mentor.

"Now then, let's go over some of the minor details…"

***

The briefing was dismissed an hour later. Naomi was stacking some papers when Oscar walked up to her. His face was still pale from the drawing of Temple.

"You drew all those sketches, correct?" he asked.

"I'm afraid so."

"And Temple's?"

"I drew that soon after I met him. I rarely drew from then on, despite my affection and talent for sketching."

"Naomi, that picture … you must burn it. You must destroy all copies. You must *never* let it see the light of day again."

Naomi nodded. "I was going to do that right away."

"Burn it… Burn it till there's nothing."

Once again, Gilda found herself lying in bed. Fatigue plagued her. It was only fear of the dream world that kept her from shutting her eyes. Drowning in vomit wasn't the way she wanted to die. She was too young even to be thinking about dying.

"Go to sleep," a voice ordered from the dark. It seemed Naomi couldn't sleep either.

Gilda felt tempted to call out her hypocrisy. "Can we talk for a bit?" she asked instead. "It might help take my mind off things."

"Talk? About what?"

Gilda shrugged. "Tell me about your life with Cloak. You don't have to talk about the bad stuff. Just talk about the dull things if you have to."

Naomi laughed. "There are no dull moments in my life. I'm having trouble remembering the last time I was bored."

"Then tell me about the least painful things."

"Are you trying not to hurt my feelings?"

"Well, every time you mention Cloak, you start acting mopey."

"Can you blame me?" Naomi asked, her humor turning sour. "Any good memory I ever had as a child is subsequently followed by a horrible one. I can't even remember eating my first piece of pizza without also remembering Ember setting a waiter on fire for forgetting her slice."

"All right, I'm sorry you feel that way, but I can handle it."

The lights went on. Gilda expected to see Naomi standing next to the light switch, only to remember she was telekinetic.

"What do you mean you can handle it?" Naomi asked.

"I mean I want to listen."

Naomi frowned. "I don't understand. Why do you want to hear these horrible things? Do you find it entertaining?"

"I don't, but I want to be a good friend, so I'll listen."

Naomi wore her perplexed expression for a moment before it faded away into a look of touched melancholy. Gilda kept her hands folded over her chest as she burned a hole in the ceiling with her eyes.

"I don't mind at all," Gilda assured her. "Growing up, I never got to talk about these sorts of things. When I was little, even a small 'hello' from my mom was a huge treat for me. Dad wasn't around much either, but Mom was almost *never* around. I didn't complain. Both her and Dad had important military jobs. I knew they had to work long hours.

"Then I overheard an argument between them. I wasn't snooping or any-thing. It was tough *not* to hear. You couldn't really call it an argument either, because my mom was doing all the yelling while my dad just timidly criticized her before finally giving up. I was young, but I got the gist of what the prob-lem was. Dad figured out Mom wasn't really working late. She was partying late with guys that weren't my dad."

Naomi sat up in her bed. Her perplexed look returned with a vengeance.

"Mom moved out soon after without so much as a goodbye," Gilda went on. "I once asked Dad where she went, and he had to leave the room to cry. Then the military police showed up on our doorstep a few months later. Mom had overdosed on narcotics while at a party."

Gilda closed her eyes and took a violent breath. "I went out of my way not to cry at the funeral. I made inappropriate jokes for the next several weeks about her being dead and deserving it. I only stopped when I made Dad cry harder than I ever saw him cry. Then I realized Mom wasn't the only one to blame. It was him as well. He was too weak to keep the family together. All he could do was make a deal with the Western Union so my mother's record could be wiped clean. She could rest in peace with a wholesome reputation. Dad thought that would make everything better. It didn't."

Gilda turned her head to make eye contact with Naomi. "I swore I would never be like her. Same with my dad. They're both so weak. I wish I could flat-out hate them, but I can't. They're my parents. I love them, but I'm also disgusted by them. Maybe I betrayed the Western Union just so I wouldn't be like them. Maybe I don't have a boyfriend so I won't be like my mom. Maybe I'm assertive so I won't be like my dad. I'm not a spitting image of my parents. I'm their shadow, their opposite. That may be a good thing or a bad thing, but as I grow older, I think it's becoming a worse thing. Now my own dreams are mocking me. They make me realize how pathetic I am. My dreams make me feel weak. They make me feel dead.

"Well, I told my story. Now tell me yours."

Naomi stared at her for half a minute. Gilda returned the favor. Not even the mechanical noises of the submarine could break the silence between them.

Naomi finally walked over and sat next to Gilda on the bed. She took a moment to gather her thoughts before she spoke.

"Okay, now I'll tell you mine."

NAOMI'S STORY

My memories of life before the Gifted rebelled are fragmentary, and I believe some are even confabulated. The ones I know are real are the ones of extreme cruelty, the kind that children can't even begin to process until they are grown up.

Alphonse Schmitt wasn't the only inflictor of pain back then, but he was the best at it and the worst of them. He told me that when I got older and lost some baby fat, we could have some real fun. That was the only reason he showed restraint against me.

I also can't remember the rebellion itself very well. It was a blur of screams, waiting, and hunger. I was *so* hungry. A plane had been transporting the Gifted to the Bunker. Sebastian killed the pilot and the soldiers on board, and our plane was rerouted. It was equipped with highly efficient solar panels, which meant we could fly indefinitely. We stayed airborne for three months. Despite carefully rationing our food, it ran out after the first month. Then we ate something foul. I think it was a person. None of the Gifted ever talked about it again.

Where would we go? Sebastian had the answer. He always had the answer, like he was getting them from some all-knowing third party. That was probably why a few of us believed him when he told us about the Mentor. But I didn't believe. Not right away.

We were to hide out near the border that cut Russia in two. Around this time, the Chinese Empire was invading every piece of land that didn't have a Western Union flag on it. They took almost all of Russia, which had refused to join the Western Union up until that point. The Russian government and its nuclear arsenal had fallen into disrepair in the fifty years following the Great Choke, making it unable to effectively resist the Chinese invasion. When the Chinese expanded past the Ural Mountains, getting dangerously close to

Europe, the Western Union intervened on behalf of the westernmost part of Russia, effectively annexing the region. After the country was officially split, thousands of refugees attempted to cross the border into West Russia. Because of all the refugees and lack of jobs, crime was rampant near the border, as was human misery. It was the perfect place for Cloak's inception.

Although he referred to himself as our "second-in-command," Sebastian was our leader for all practical purposes, despite that Houdini, Cyphrus, and Geppetto were older than him. Houdini was hot-tempered, Cyphrus vain, and Geppetto unwilling. Plus, Sebastian was too good at his job to be denied it. He was fourteen years old.

Cloak started, like everything else, small. Sebastian loaned out Cyphrus, Geppetto, and Houdini to West Russian crime bosses. We quickly made our mark, but the Western Union was still looking for us, so we had to be careful. We were to kill anyone who saw us using our powers. The youngest of us—Atlas, Sandtrap, Ember, and myself—were not allowed to leave the warehouse where we lived unless one of the older Gifted accompanied us. Ember didn't take to that too well. After a few unwanted fire alarms, we made an exception, Sebastian giving her personal errands to run. What those errands were was anyone's guess.

I had to entertain myself during the early years. I was self-taught as well. I quickly picked up reading, writing, and several languages, including Russian, but math was never my strong suit. Atlas didn't do much talking. He mostly just ate and slept. Geppetto was the only one he opened up to. Geppetto often told stories to him. I would usually sit in and listen.

"Let me tell you about Slate," Geppetto said with wonder. "He was the second oldest Gifted and by far the strongest. He always wore a silver helmet and made everyone laugh. The Western Union constantly had him fighting South American cartels and rebels, so I only met the guy once, but I felt like he could've been my older brother. One day, he..."

Many of his stories were about Slate, who became something of a hero to us. Slate managed to be so happy, despite leading such a miserable existence.

If he could be happy, why not us? I think we all envied him at one time or another. I often drew pictures of Slate fighting bad guys and saving the day. Some of my drawings had him fly down to rescue me from Houdini and Cyphrus as they were about to beat me up. It was silly, but I was a young girl. I think I even might have had a crush on him during my formative years. It would not last.

Geppetto and Atlas bonded over these stories. Bonding... I guess that's the right word. I tried some bonding of my own with Sandtrap, who had been bedridden since before the rebellion. He was covered in burns and had no limbs. Growth patches have no effect on the Gifted, so his mangled body was beyond repair. There was talk of putting him out of his misery, but Sebastian had faith.

It was seven years after the rebellion before Sandtrap could move on his own with his powers. Before then, I was his only real companion. I read to him. I bathed him. I changed his bedpan. I almost connected with him. But he was just so broken, so we never truly bonded. When I heard he died during the Helios Tower incident, I felt a mix of relief and sorrow. Sebastian was wrong. We should have killed him.

I had just about as much success bonding with the other Gifted. They were either too busy with their assigned tasks or too caught up in their own personal grievances. I liked Geppetto and Atlas. I pitied Sandtrap. The rest of the Gifted meant little to me. Cyphrus treated me like a rival and constantly put me down. Houdini bit my head off every time I tried to talk to him. I didn't even bother trying to be friends with Ember. As for Sebastian, he kept himself sequestered from the others unless it was business. I almost never got to see him. When I did see him, I could tell he saw me more as a tool than a person.

Once I started to become a young woman, the day came when I received my first mission. It was small and unimportant, but I was excited, nonetheless. Sebastian told me that I had to pickpocket a West Russian gangster from a distance using my powers. The gangster had an incriminating photo of a local politician that we needed to obtain. Houdini would supervise me to make sure I didn't do anything foolish.

The streets of Kazan were covered in dust, the storefront windows in desperate need of a wash. All the pedestrians looked like they were chain-smokers. Yet I was ecstatic. In my eleven years of life, I had rarely ventured out into the real world filled with real people. Despite the rundown state of this neighborhood, I thought I had just stepped into paradise.

"Stop your daydreaming and keep vigilant," Houdini snapped. He looked much younger than he did when you met him, Gilda. His hair was jet-black, and he had no beard. An eye patch covered the horrid accessory in his eye socket, and his clothes were those of a vagrant. I wore similar clothes. I looked much too young for my age. My giant Bambi eyes were those of an infant, and I had greasy pigtails that could be mistaken for rat hair.

"Where's the man you want me to steal from?" I asked.

Houdini almost hit me right then and there on the street, but that would attract attention, so he settled for shaking me violently. "Stupid girl! Don't announce your crimes!"

"Sorry!" I yelped. In truth, I wasn't sorry, but Houdini stopped shaking me when he noticed a group of men walking down the street.

"Do you see them?" he asked. I nodded. There were four of them. Three skinny men in cheap suits flanked a corpulent man in a thousand-dollar outfit.

"The fat man is your target," Houdini whispered. "The photograph should be somewhere on his person. Be discreet. Your powers haven't fully matured yet. That won't happen until puberty. But you should have enough strength for this. Do not fail, or I shall beat you."

That was enough incentive for me. I walked away from Houdini, going toward the men. As I approached, the fat gangster made a remark in Russian. All the henchmen hooted. I knew enough Russian to know a crude joke had been made at my expense.

As I went by, I felt up the fat man's body with my mind. He probably thought it was the wind, because he didn't seem to notice or care. I sensed something in the pocket of his pants. It must have been a Polaroid, the picture I had to retrieve.

I was very stealthy. I didn't just yank the photo from his pants. I made it fall out, seemingly naturally, to the concrete. Using my mind again, I created some wind to distract the henchmen. The photo was also blown away. The gangsters didn't notice as it sailed into a narrow alley. I approached the alley briskly yet calmly and snatched up the photo before some real wind could blow it away. Mission accomplished.

Then things went wrong. I was making my way back to Houdini, who was leaning against a brick building, not at all impressed. I found it ironic that he was so critical of my vigilance yet didn't notice the oncoming car before it slammed into him. He flew forward and crashed into some trash cans. I heard a sharp crack.

The barrel of a machine gun poked out the car's window. It was pointed right at the gangsters I had just robbed. They only had time to reach into their jackets and widen their eyes before the machine gun tore through them and painted the sidewalk red. The fat man got the brunt of it, his thousand-dollar suit now about as expensive as the rags I wore. The gangsters fell to the ground. I couldn't scream. It was caught in my throat. That didn't stop the nearby pedestrians from doing so. Everyone sane enough was running away, save me.

Two men in balaclavas jumped out of the car. They ran over to the fat man's corpse and started searching it. They were after the photo. Houdini lay in the street, unconscious and with blood dripping from his mouth. I panicked. Would they try to kill me if they found out I had the photo? Would Houdini blame me for how he got hit by the car? I didn't like any of these questions. I decided to book it like everyone else had.

I ran for about ten blocks before I stopped. It hurt to breathe. I was also lost. Where was the warehouse the Gifted lived in? I couldn't get back without Houdini's help. I was also hungry and sleepy. I started to cry.

"There you are!" a voice shrieked in English.

A thin woman with silver hair and a wrinkled face ran up toward me. She was in her forties but had aged poorly due to bad genetics and a hard life. I was too tired to avoid her. I fell to my knees and cried some more.

The woman embraced me. She was hysterical now, laughing and sobbing simultaneously. It felt like hugging a skeleton, yet I stopped crying.

"You are alive!" the woman cried. She held me out to appraise my appearance. Her smile widened. Hot tears spilled from her red eyes. The woman acted like she knew me, but I had never seen her before in my life. Had she mistaken me for someone else?

The woman noticed my confusion. Her smile became a knowing grin. "Oh, my child, you couldn't possibly remember me. But I could never forget you, not even when they tried to erase my mind. It was love that kept the memory of you within me."

"But who are you?"

"Naomi, darling... I gave birth to you. You are my child."

NAOMI'S STORY

My self-proclaimed mother took me to her home. It wasn't much, just a crummy apartment with a few worn-out pieces of furniture. She lived alone and didn't bother to keep the place very clean. Although not a pigsty per se, there were places that hadn't been dusted in a while, and the windows needed wiping down. It was all depressing.

The woman sat me at a kitchen table covered in coffee stains and fed me goulash. It wasn't very good, but I was hungry, and she had put lots of effort into making it. I even had seconds. She didn't eat any herself. All she did was watch me with baggy eyes and a tired smile.

After eating, we sat in silence for a few minutes. The woman stared at me with fond eyes. I kept mine downward, examining my faded sneakers. She must have been waiting for me to speak. I finally worked up the nerve to do so.

"What's your name?" I asked in a timid voice.

"Nina," the woman said, saying the word slowly. It must have tasted like chocolate to her. "My last name means nothing to me. I have had so many husbands that I can't even remember what it is anymore."

"My name's Repulsa."

She gasped. "How horrid! Those scientists know nothing about naming things. They vomit out Latin and call it eloquent. Such despicable creatures they are!"

I giggled. The woman called Nina giggled as well. It was a giggling party.

"What name did you call me earlier?" I asked.

"Naomi," the woman purred. "It is a better name, no?"

"Yeah, I like it." I paused for a moment. "You can't be my mother."

The woman leaned forward. "And why is that, darling?"

"The ladies who gave birth to us died right after." I covered my mouth as soon as the words came out. I had just divulged Cloak's secrets to a stranger. Houdini would whoop me good for that. Then I remembered his unconscious body bleeding in the street. Was he dead?

The woman nodded. "Most of the mothers perished. All of them, in fact, save me. Those government pigs did not expect me to live, so they tried to erase my mind and dump me back where I came from. But I remembered."

She knew too much about the origins of the Gifted to be just some crazy lady off the streets. I was intrigued. Could this woman really be my mother? I decided to pry. "But the women that had us were all criminals."

The woman sighed. "I led a rebellious youth. I was involved with anti-Western movements. I thought joining the Western Union was a travesty for Russia. I still believe that. The police regularly beat us. We were blacklisted from traveling and finding decent jobs, but people still managed to resist. I resisted too much. I accidentally killed a police officer during one of the protests. I was sentenced to death. Men in suits came to visit me the day before my execution. They wanted me for a potentially lethal experiment. I would be pardoned for my crimes if I survived it. To their credit, they kept their end of the bargain."

I didn't believe her just yet. "How come the pruning didn't work on you?"

The woman shrugged. "It did work in a way. I forgot my sister had a baby. The pruning machine must have made a mistake. Good luck for me. My sister is dead now. So is her baby. Killed in a political rally turned riot. Bad luck for them."

"But even if you did give birth to me, you're not my mom. I was made from a bunch of people's genes. I only grew in you."

The woman got out of her chair and knelt next to me. Then she grabbed my shoulders and looked me in the eye. "You are my child," she said with utter conviction. "I recognized you right when I laid eyes on you. I didn't even need to see you pickpocket that man with your powers to confirm it. That is the power of love, Naomi. The Western Union impregnated me and tore you from my breast. Naomi, darling, I named you the moment I saw you. Naomi, you have my eyes. You don't have my genes, but you have my eyes. Naomi, darling ... I love you."

She cried. She kissed me. She held me. She loved me. I was never treated with such affection in all my life. Not by the Gifted. Not by the Keymasters. A long-dormant longing woke within me. All my skepticism faded away. This woman was giving me something I had forever ached for. She was giving me a family. She was giving me love.

"Mom..." I whimpered. I started to cry too.

I spent the night with her. I slept next to her. I ate her terrible food the next morning. She told me stories. I told her my stories. Some were about Slate. She didn't care much for them, or for Slate and the other Gifted, or for Cloak.

"You must leave them," she told me. "You must leave them and stay with me."

I told her I couldn't. She was sad. I told her that I'd visit. She stopped being so sad.

I left my mother in the afternoon. It was the hardest thing I ever had to do. I went back to the scene of the crime, expecting to find a chalk outline where Houdini had fallen. There wasn't one. There weren't any corpses either, or any blood for that matter. Everything looked normal.

But I only had to wait for five minutes before a car pulled up. Cyphrus was driving it. She must have used her powers to spot me through a security camera. There was at least an inch of makeup over her face, covering her scars. She was dressed like a spoiled teenager and acted just like one.

"Get in," she hissed.

I complied. As I took my seat, she wrinkled her nose. "You smell terrible," she told me. "Houdini's alive, no thanks to you. He barely made it back to the warehouse in one piece. I even had to drive out to this hellhole and look for you. Well, I'll make sure to enjoy myself when Houdini beats you for your insolence."

Next thing I knew, I was standing next to Houdini's bedside. Cyphrus and Geppetto were also present. Geppetto didn't look much different from what you remember, except he had hair. Sebastian entered the room, wearing that grin he always wears. He was young but carried himself like an adult. Like Geppetto, he didn't look much different from how he looks now. Sebastian always had one of those faces that never seemed to age.

"Stupid girl left me to die," Houdini wheezed. There were bandages wrapped around his head and throat. A cast also cocooned his right leg. He glared at me with his one eye while clenching his fist. "Come over here so I can strangle you…"

"It was your own fault for not noticing the car sooner," Sebastian said.

Geppetto snickered. "How'd this happen? Can't you teleport?"

"I'm not about to use my powers in public," Houdini snarled.

"That's enough," Sebastian told them as though he were breaking up a schoolyard quarrel. He turned to me. "Good work, Repulsa. That was a fine performance for your first mission." He held out his hand. I thought he wanted me to take it at first. Then I remembered the photograph and blushed. I took it out. It depicted a graying man with a much younger girl, far too young, kissing and doing all kinds of things.

Sebastian took it and slid it into his coat pocket. "Thank you, Repulsa. You are already producing tangible results. I expect great things from you."

Cyphrus snorted. "Aren't you going to punish her? She disobeyed orders."

"Lay off the kid, will you?" Geppetto said. "She did her best." He gave me a smack on the back. "Just got scared is all. Nobody saw you use your powers, did they?"

"No," I lied. "I tried to get back to the warehouse for help, but I got lost and spent the night at a bus station. Then I asked for directions and found my way back to where the gangsters were killed. That's when Cyphrus picked me up."

"What a load of crap," Cyphrus sneered. "You're hiding something."

"Forget about the girl!" Houdini hollered. "What about me? I demand justice!"

"I've already sent Ember to deal with the men who attacked you," Sebastian said. "They were hired by the politician in the photograph. He wanted to get rid of the leverage against him. Have no fear. Our employers want us to send copies of the photograph to this politician's colleagues and opponents, as well as his wife and children. His life will effectively be destroyed, and I suspect he'll commit suicide out of shame, and if he doesn't commit suicide, we will *make* him commit suicide. Is that to your liking, Houdini?"

"It will do," Houdini grumbled.

"Splendid. Now rest and heal. You'll be back in top form soon enough. Cyphrus, I have another mission I wish to discuss. Please meet me in my office immediately. Geppetto, go check up on Atlas and Sandtrap, see how they're faring. As for you, Repulsa, you can get out of those clothes and take a bath. Then you may have the rest of the day off."

Everyone left the room at the same time. I was about to head for the bathroom when Sebastian grabbed my shoulder. He whispered something into my ear.

"The Mentor is watching..."

I did not know what to make of that, so I just slipped from his grip and kept walking.

I spent the next few days in a state of euphoria. I had a mother who loved me. None of the other Gifted could say that. I wanted to flaunt it in their faces. Then I saw Atlas weeping in the corner. He was a few years younger than me but already exceeded me in height and weight. I patted him on the back, but he only continued to cry.

"Geppetto isn't coming back till next week," he sniveled. "I'm so lonely..."

I didn't feel much like gloating after that. Instead, I felt a deep shame that I can still feel to this day. Atlas didn't have a mother to love him. None of them did.

It was easier than I thought to sneak out. After only a week, I couldn't wait any longer. I had to see my mother. She had given me detailed directions to her place. Once I found a street with a familiar name, it was a cinch to get to her apartment.

I was always careful to go only when the other Gifted were preoccupied. It wasn't like we were kept under guard, but the place often felt like a prison.

Going to see my mother was like digging out of Alcatraz for me. I was always worried Sebastian or one of the others would find out about my excursions and what they might do to my mother if they did. It turned out I had an ally. One day, Cyphrus cornered me and asked where I had been the entire afternoon as she hadn't been able to find me.

Sandtrap, who lay nearby, answered. "Cleaning ... windows... Working ... hard..."

Cyphrus didn't seem satisfied by that answer, but she didn't pursue the subject further. I always loved Sandtrap for that.

The visits to my mother were always grand. She would swoop down and smother me with affection. It was embarrassing, and I loved every second of it. We ate her terrible food. We watched her mediocre soap operas. We both learned to play chess. She taught me some basic math and history. She brushed my hair with reverence. It was all so magical. I felt emotions I had never felt before because of her.

There was only one thing that got in the way of our joyous time. One day, I used my powers to grab a glass from the top self. My mother saw this and slapped me hard. I dropped the glass, it broke, and I cried. She told me never to use my powers in her presence again. She told me government pigs had put this power in me and pig's blood now coursed through my veins. She said she wouldn't blame others if they hated me for it and that I would have been burned at the stake if I had lived a thousand years ago. I hated my powers from then on.

Still, it was mostly good. Our arrangement was draining but doable. Sebastian and the others didn't seem to suspect a thing. My mother loved me dearly, and I loved her. We kept this up for about four months.

One day, I knocked on her door. She opened it. I expected a smile from her. I got a frown. She beckoned me in. I sat at the table, expecting a sloppy dish of goulash. Instead, I got a sloppy dish of reality. I asked what was wrong.

"Darling, you torture me!" my mother wailed. "You live with criminals, abominations against nature. I cannot stand to see my Naomi fall prey to these villains. And this Mentor of which you speak… I get cold sweats every time you mention the name!"

"Sorry, Mother," I said. "But it won't be easy to run away from the other Gifted. They'd hurt you if they ever caught us."

"Do you wish to stay with them rather than your own mother?"

"No…"

"Do you want to let that pig's blood in your veins turn you into a murderer? Do you want to turn into a pig? *Do you?*"

"No! Please, I'll go with you. Wherever you want."

My mother embraced me. "That's all I wanted to hear. Don't worry, my darling Naomi. Momma will keep you clean and safe. Just listen to Momma."

And listen I did. She told me we would leave tomorrow night. My mother had to pack her belongings and withdraw what remained of her meager savings. I would also need to pack whatever possessions I had. I didn't own much, just some clothes and books. A small backpack sufficed for me. Before I climbed out the window and ran into the darkness, I visited Sandtrap in his bed. He was the only one of the Gifted I knew wouldn't rat me out.

"I'm leaving forever now," I said, kissing his scarred forehead. "Thanks for lying."

He wheezed in pain. I kissed him again. That was all I could give him.

I met my mother in front of her apartment building. She had her bags and wore a tattered coat. She also wore an irritated scowl.

"You are late," she told me. "Our train leaves in twenty minutes."

"I came at seven. I followed your instructions."

She sighed. "Forget it. We must run to the station."

So, we ran. Our luggage bounced. People stole glances at us. We didn't care. We kept running. My mother tripped several times, but I helped steady her with my powers. She didn't notice. Otherwise, she might have stopped to scold me.

We were running through a desolate park. The homeless slept on rickety benches. More dirt than grass could be seen. There was still some snow under the trees, the white fluff accumulating dirt and dog urine. Soon, we entered the heart of the park. It was black and empty. Not even the vagrants dared venture here.

"Hurry, my child!" my mother gasped. "We must make our train!"

Then she screeched to a halt. I stopped as well. I glanced at my mother. She was slack-jawed, reminding me of how I looked when doing long division.

I turned my head to see where she was looking. I wore a neutral expression for a moment. Then I broke out in a big grin.

"Don't worry, Mother! I know who that is. I told you about him, remember? It's Slate! He's alive and came here to help us. See, look at his shiny head!"

Temple blocked our path. Fresh blood trickled off his silver helmet.

NAOMI'S STORY

My mother took a step backward.

Temple took a step forward.

I grabbed my mother's hand. It was as limp as a dead fish. "Hey, is that you, Slate?" I yelled. No reply. "Geppetto told me all about you! Have you got any jokes to tell?"

"Darling..." my mother whimpered.

I turned to her. Then I screamed. I had never seen someone's eyes go so big or a face go so pale. Her hair had gone from silver to white in an instant. I thought such a thing could not happen. It could. The corners of her mouth were turned down as far as they could go. My mother wore an upside-down smile. She took another step backward.

Temple took another step forward.

"Darling..." my mother whimpered again. "Darling, what have you done?"

I let tears stream down my face. "Mom, I—"

"Darling, what have you done to me!"

A wall of yellow light materialized behind us, blocking our exit. Temple floated forward, like he didn't even need his feet for walking anymore.

"Stay back, you beast!" my mother yelled. "What do you want with me?"

Temple stopped moving. He shrugged off his black cloak, wearing only skintight black shorts underneath. A muscular body with black nails and veins was exposed to us, his skin whiter than my mother's hair. But he had no hair. He had no nipples. He had no navel. He had no soul. The shadow of his silver helmet fell over my mother. Her lower lip quivered.

"Are you after her?" my mother asked the monster. "Are you after the girl?" She tore her hand from mine. "Is that all this is about?"

Temple walked toward her. He cracked his neck.

My mother grabbed me by the scruff of my shirt. "She's the one you want, isn't she? That's all this is about, right? Yes, I'm right! She's yours! Take her! She's not my real daughter. I just birthed her. She ruined me! I couldn't have any more children after her. No man wanted me. It's all her fault!"

Temple stopped three feet away from us. His knuckles cracked.

I looked up at my mother. "Mom! What are you saying?"

My mother tightened her grip on my shirt, choking me and silencing my pleading. "I'll leave here," she begged. "I promise never to bother you people again. I was just playing house. I just wanted to feel young again!"

Temple raised his arm, fingers outstretched.

She shoved me toward him. "What are you waiting for?" she sobbed. *"Take her! Take her, you beast!"*

Temple grabbed me by the scalp. He lifted me off the ground with one hand. His other hand grabbed my mother's face.

"No!" she screamed, the hand of the Mentor muffling her voice. He threw both her and me to the ground. Skin scraped off my cheek. Temple knelt beside us. He put a hand on my head, pinning me down. He did the same to my mother using his four-toed foot.

"Stop, you're hurting me!" my mother cried. "I don't want to die like this! I want to die old in bed. Don't kill me! Not like this. Please!"

Temple made sure my mother and I were facing each other. I tried to squeeze my eyes shut, but his fingers pulled my eyelids open. I could only see my mother's face, wrinkled and contorted into an expression I can't even begin to describe. Temple's foot was driving her head into the dirt. She screamed some more.

"You!" she spat at me. "You and your pig's blood! You brought this on me. You should have died in my womb as nature intended, you pig!"

The sound of her skull cracking was audible over her screams.

"Pig!" she shrieked.

Another crack.

"Pig!"

One more crack.

"Piiiiiii—!"

No more head. Temple tore his foot away. The blood had drenched him up to his knees. It had drenched me from head to toe. Light radiated off Temple, burning the blood off his person. I could not do the same.

The moon was full that night.

I didn't move. I didn't cry. I don't think I even breathed. I lay there like roadkill, gaping with a glazed countenance. I felt as though a million cold eyes were sizing me up, looking upon my debased person.

The wall of light vanished. Temple took his hand off my head. I wasn't aware of the pain ceasing. Then he set nearby bushes alight. The fire spread. I heard shouts. Familiar voices.

"Is that Repulsa?" Ember asked, wearing a pink shirt and jean shorts. She had the body of a boy and the eyes of a crazed cat. "Is she dead?"

"No, she's breathing," Houdini told her. "There's another one. Ugh... I don't think I need to check *her* pulse."

They both knelt by me, looking surprisingly concerned. Ember cried melodramatically. Houdini slapped her upside the head, but the fight did not escalate from there because they had caught sight of Temple.

They let their jaws drop. Temple was just a silhouette to them. The flames of the fire burned behind the beast. His helmet gleamed like a jewel, his body the absence of light. Ember and Houdini couldn't take their eyes off him. They were transfixed. They were his.

After a long moment, Temple walked into the flames. He was gone. His cloak had been left to burn on the ground, the red horseshoe embroidered on it also gleaming briefly before the inferno consumed it too.

Houdini carried me home. I was a corpse. I don't remember the next few days. I woke up covered in an itchy blanket. Bandages were wrapped around my face and head. Sebastian sat next to my bed, his smile as wide as ever. I was still a corpse.

He clucked his tongue and shook his head. "I suppose we all have to learn the hard way now and again. I don't think you need any more punishment than you've already had. I'm just glad you're home, safe and sound." He laughed. "What were the chances you would encounter that woman? Our lord must have planned this from the beginning. Now you see, Repulsa. Now you see what we are trying to teach the world. It will be a hard lesson, but they will learn. Oh, yes, they will learn."

He stood up and patted my shoulder. I simply stared at the wall.

"And don't forget," he said, "the Mentor is watching."

CHAPTER 37

Naomi stopped her story and covered her mouth, suppressing tears.

Gilda didn't know how to react. She had never heard such a story before. Her family troubles were nothing in comparison.

"For years, I didn't know my mother's murderer had been Temple," Naomi said, wiping her eyes with a quick movement of her finger. "I thought Slate had killed her. I don't think I ever hated anyone so much in all my life. Even when I found out the truth, that it was a different Helmet Man who ruined my life, I still hated him. It's hard to let go of hate, you see, even when you should know better. It was unfair, it was cold, but I couldn't help myself."

"Is that why you tried to kill him at the Pale Pyramid?" Gilda asked, her voice weak.

"Yes. All those stories Geppetto told me made me believe Slate was my personal savior. Instead, he became my personal devil. Even though I now care for him and cherish him, I still find myself sometimes tempted to hate him again. It's terrible... I've just hated for so long. And that silver helmet ... it can't ever come off."

"What happened after that?"

"I grew up. I killed people. I became a pig. My mother was right. The Gifted were abominations. We were born to kill, and we die terribly. No one deserves to live that life. I often contemplated suicide. I sometimes put a loaded gun between my teeth. On rare occasions, I even pulled the trigger, only to stop the bullet with my mind before it could hit the roof of my mouth.

"The last time I tried this was five years ago. I had just come back from the Nigerian Genocide. So many dead children. As I squeezed the trigger in my hotel room, a blade pressed against my throat. I dropped the gun. Someone had snuck up on me.

"'If death is what you wish for, that can be arranged,' the voice hissed. 'If this is merely performative, then hear me out, woman.'

"I jumped out of my chair. I was now in the presence of the Grim Reaper.

"'I've been observing you closely for quite a while,' Incognito told me. 'I considered killing you, but that would be doing you a favor, it would seem.'

"'Who the hell are you?' I demanded.

"'They call me Incognito. I don't care for the name myself, but it will suffice.'

"He already knew about my mother and told me it had been Temple, not Slate, who murdered her. He offered me a chance to kill Temple. So, after some initial hesitation, we formed a partnership of sorts. He wanted Sebastian, but I couldn't hand him over, since he was always on the move. That's why we hoped to nab him after the Helios Tower was destroyed, along with whatever he had Lawrence Zaidi build for him. Then you and Slate came into the picture. Then I went berserk. And that's the end of my story."

Naomi leaned back. She glowed divinely, perhaps due to catharsis. Gilda admired her for a moment before shaking her head clear.

"So, you blame Temple for what happened," Gilda said.

"I blame the Mentor," Naomi told her. "No one else."

"But your mother…"

"My mother was weak. She did love me, but she loved herself more. Life had been hard for her. I was her last chance at happiness, yet I was also where it all went wrong." A fire entered her eyes. "But I could never hate her. I could only pity her. If I did hate her, I would only be stooping to her level. I will never let that happen. I will never be her, but I will love her all the same. I told you this story because you seem to have gone through something similar, that you would understand. Can you?"

Gilda nodded. "Yeah, I think so."

Naomi let the fire burn. "It's the Mentor who's behind it all. It's the Mentor who controls Temple. It's the Mentor who killed my mother. When I looked at Temple, I also saw a dark shadow standing far behind him. It was taller than any skyscraper or any mountain climbed by man. It had dead white eyes. It looked down at me. It laughed at me. It has to die."

"You dreamed about the eyes too," Gilda said. "The moon eyes."

"Yes, I did. But let's not talk about them anymore. They exist only in dreams."

Naomi flicked off the lights with her mind. They settled themselves into bed.

Gilda cleared her throat in the dark. "Naomi..."

"Yes."

"I love you."

The darkness was silent for a moment. Then a reply. "I love you too."

"Slate loves you too. We all love you. Thomas, Straper ... we're your family."

"Thank you. You don't know what that means to me."

"Think nothing of it."

"Goodnight."

"Pleasant dreams."

***

A knock on the door woke Incognito.

"Enter," he snapped.

Oscar entered the room, which was filled with medical equipment. Incognito lay in a small bed, his scythe within reach. As always, he wore his mask.

"I want to talk," Oscar said. "About everything."

"Then this conversation will be long indeed," Incognito said. "Speak."

Oscar closed the door, sat on a chair, and ran his knobby fingers through his beard. "Naomi and Slate are a couple now."

"We made the Gifted sterile. No need to worry about them breeding."

"Poor Naomi ... no wonder she's so attached to Thomas."

"What, do you want more of those creatures scurrying about? Don't be foolish."

"Such spite ... such contempt..."

"They're spawn of the West, unnaturally birthed by vile women."

"Tell me, what comes first, the destruction of the West or the destruction of Cloak?"

"They are not mutually exclusive goals."

"I'm starting to doubt that. Remember the Helios Tower incident? Instead of rescuing Slate and Gilda, you could have followed their plane to Sebastian's location. But you wanted to free Slate immediately so you could let him stop the Helios Tower from being blown up. You wanted to win him over, to get him to join your cause, to become your symbol."

"Oh, would you have been willing to put his life at risk?"

"I know my son. He would have wanted it that way."

"And was refusing to see him what he wanted as well? You and I both know I lied when I told Slate I kept you from seeing him. I didn't want to push him away by having him hate you as well. The truth is you were too ashamed to face your fake son, or perhaps you were ashamed of him. You only worked up the nerve to show yourself after finding out he had been locked away in *Tortuga* and that you might miss your one chance to mend fences."

"Shut your foul mouth. I had my reasons for not wanting to see Slate until recently, and you still haven't explained your own actions during the Helios Tower incident."

"I saved Slate because I couldn't risk Sebastian getting his hands on him. We don't know what could have happened. Besides, Sebastian would have been careful. Following the plane would have been foolish. I had a plan set up, and I didn't wish to spoil it."

"Well, your plan failed. Sebastian is still on the loose, and despite what you think, Cloak is a far bigger threat than the Western Union. Your prejudice clouds your mind."

"What about *your* mind? Is it not clouded with guilt over how you toyed with nature, about how you birthed monsters?"

"My guilt is what drives me."

"And my so-called prejudice drives me. Oscar Radcliffe, you have always had opposing forces battling within your soul, likely due to your mixed heritage. An Iranian mother and an English father... My goodness, what a mess."

"Are you going to wipe me out along with all the whites?"

"No, but your weak nature requires constant correcting."

Oscar stood up. "Incognito, you cretin! Are you going to back out on us the moment you see a chance to take the Western Union down a peg? All my years of atonement will not be thrown away because of your bigotry!"

Incognito folded his hands and narrowed his eyes.

Oscar deflated. Anger turned to sadness, rage to regret.

"Jericho..." he whispered.

The dull side of the scythe's blade rammed into his neck, pinning him against the wall. He gasped. A bloated tongue stuck out of his yellow-toothed mouth.

"Do not *ever* use that name," Incognito said, making sure to lean in on the scythe harder as he said these words. Oscar gagged again. "You cannot say it without suffering a steep price, and not even your precious Helmet Man will have time to save you."

Incognito pulled his scythe away. Oscar gasped, which hurt dearly but felt good at the same time. He slid down the wall until he was sitting on the floor.

"Feel honored," Incognito said. "I would have killed anyone else for that transgression. You are my only friend."

Oscar managed to rasp a sentence. "We're not ... we're not friends..."

"No, but you'll have to do."

***

The Helmet Man felt the electricity flow through the *Eodum*. Outside the submarine, the sea currents flowed as well, the creatures within the murky depths living short and pointless lives. He leaned against the cold wall as everyone else slept. He wanted to go to Naomi, to sense her breathing and feel her pulse, but Gilda was with her. Patience wasn't his virtue, but he had learned to wait.

Shifu was at least partially successful in that department.

The Chinese Empire was drawing nearer. Slate was Chinese himself yet felt no sense of homecoming, only a dark cloud that grew with each passing minute. Shifu had taught him much and had been his companion when there was no one else to fulfill the role. Slate was indebted to him. If his teacher's homeland could be helped, he should at least try.

Great, where was the clown everyone loved to laugh at? Then again, that love only ran skin-deep. He was changing, becoming harder and colder. The jokes were not coming to him as easily. He would have to force them out. Although he didn't have to rely on humor anymore, his friends would still need his levity in the trying times to come. The electricity danced between his fingers. Death was waiting for him.

And so was the Mentor.

CHAPTER 38

"I miss Naomi," Thomas said again, drooping like a burdened tree branch.

"I know," Taylor said. "She'll be back in a few weeks. Then it will all be over."

"It'll never be over."

Taylor didn't have a reply to that. They were playing checkers in a small rec room, though it was more of a cave than a room. It didn't even have a door. The United Third's underground headquarters would be the safest place to hide, Naomi had told them. The Western Union didn't know its location, and that meant Cloak probably didn't either. The only threat was Incognito's own men, but as long as Taylor and Thomas didn't do anything to aggravate them, they should be safe. Taylor found this to be of little comfort.

"Do you hate Slate?" Thomas asked.

Taylor had suspected this question was coming. He had prepared a response but still found it difficult to get anything out of his mouth.

"Slate and I..." he began. "I said things I wish I hadn't. He did too, I believe."

"Are you guys going to be friends again?"

"No, I don't think so. We've gone down different paths that will likely never intersect again. He's doing what he thinks is right, and I'm doing what I think is right. When it comes to these kinds of matters, no single answer will ever suffice."

"Oh." Thomas thought about this for a moment. "That's stupid."

Taylor laughed softly with a half smirk. "Yes, you're probably right."

He moved one of his checkers. Thomas quickly captured it.

"Are you trying to play, Dr. Taylor?"

Taylor shrugged. "Not really."

Thomas shook his head. "I don't want to play either."

"Let's put it away, then."

"Yeah… Have any more stories about Britain? Any about my mom?"

"I'm afraid you've heard them all."

"Those were good stories…"

"Hey, can I get out of the dress now?" a voice asked.

Taylor and Thomas sat up. They recognized the voice immediately.

"Hush up!" a guard shouted back. "Move faster!"

"Do you think walking in heels is easy?" Jeff Springer yelled. Two imposing men led Springer down the hall. The anchorman wore a pink tutu with pointe shoes, even makeup and a curly blond wig to complete his appearance. His execution had been postponed. The United Third freedom fighters were just too in love with seeing the former voice of the Western Union make a fool of himself on live television. The Western Union had long since blocked these broadcasts from the airwaves of its citizens, for obvious reasons.

Springer and his guards marched past the rec room. Taylor and Thomas watched discreetly as the guards threw their captive in a cell and locked the door.

"Poor man," Thomas said.

"I don't care much for him," Taylor said. "He spouts a lot of nonsense and riles people up to dangerous effect. Still, I don't think anyone deserves to be treated like that."

"Even Incognito?" Thomas asked.

Taylor couldn't resist a smile.

Thomas started to droop again. "Can we go see Mr. Springer?"

Taylor felt the need to raise an eyebrow. "That's an odd request."

"I feel bad for him," Thomas said. "He doesn't have any friends here."

Taylor nodded. "Okay, fine. Let's go now."

"Really?"

"Yes, really."

They left their game of checkers and went to the humiliated news anchor's cell. A guard stood in front of the cell door. He looked at them sternly and crossed his arms.

"We're friends of the Helmet Man, you know," Taylor warned the guard.

The guard scrunched up his nose but stepped aside. Taylor opened the door and entered with Thomas. Jeff Springer sat on his single cot. There was also a bucket for waste and a jug of water. He had taken off his wig and removed most of the makeup. He was sniffling.

Taylor coughed. "Excuse me, Mr. Springer?"

Springer sorted himself out. "I ... uh ... didn't expect visitors."

Taylor closed the cell door. The guard didn't stop him from doing so, but he didn't seem too pleased about it either.

"Hello, Mr. Springer," Thomas said. "You're a TV star."

"Yeah, I guess I am," Springer said. He wiped his red eyes clear. "So, you're my number one fan, huh?"

"Well, I wouldn't go *that* far."

"Thanks, kid." Springer turned to Taylor. "What's this about? Another interrogation?"

"The boy just wanted to see how you were doing," Taylor said. "He was worried. His name is Thomas, and mine is Taylor. How are you?"

"Other than being kidnapped, wearing a dress, having to poop in a bucket, and awaiting execution, I'm perfectly fine. But hey, thanks for worrying."

"I'll talk to Barir, see if we can work something out."

"Yeah, well, forgive me if I don't have faith in your persuasive abilities."

"Perhaps it was a mistake to come here. Come on, Thomas."

"Wait, hold on there!" Springer yelled, raising his open hands. "I think we got off on the wrong foot. I don't think you two are associated with Captain Cuckoo and his band of misfits. I've seen you walking around here. You stick out like a Chinaman in the Pentagon. Sorry, too soon? I like edgy humor. Can't do too much of it on TV, what with censors and all."

"Who's Captain Cuckoo?" Thomas asked in all seriousness.

"Just one of Incognito's many clever aliases. Look, you two work for the Helmet Man, right? Not Incognito?"

"Well, I only knew the Helmet Man briefly," Taylor divulged.

"Oh, didn't know that. Yeah, I met the Helmet Man once. Well, I didn't 'meet' him, but I was a commentator for that big rally Incognito held. Some of my best work. Too bad it probably meant the end of the free world."

"Why are you cooperating with Incognito?" Taylor asked.

"Why? Because I like my limbs attached to my body."

"But you will never be a news anchor again after this. Your image is in the toilet. Parading you around in a dress is just icing on the cake for the United Third."

"Don't remind me. I mean, what did I ever do wrong? Sure, I said crazy stuff on TV, but you need to do that in order to get people's blood pumping. You can't be calm and logical when going to war. You have to be aggressive and dimwitted."

"Who says we had to go to war? Violence should be a last resort. The Western Union has been too reliant on coercion for quite some time, and you've played an active part in President Powell's warmongering."

"Don't even get me started on that guy, and I don't need this spiel about journalistic ethics. I took that class and slept through it! But I never killed anyone. I don't make the news or choose what I say on the air. I'm just in it for the cash and babes. Is that so wrong? Rhetorical question. Yes, I know it's wrong, but don't knock it till you try it."

"So, you say stuff for money even when you know it's wrong?" Thomas asked. "That doesn't sound like a nice thing to do."

"Where did you come from, kid? Under a rock?"

"No, a deserted island, apparently," Taylor said.

"I'm not sure if you're joking, Mr. Taylor."

"I am not."

Springer looked at Thomas again, more closely this time. "Hang on a sec, is this the long-lost British prince that Incognito is keeping captive?"

Taylor almost had a heart attack. How did this man know? If Springer knew, who else did? Assassins could be coming after Thomas this very moment.

Springer noticed Taylor's reaction. "Wait, it's true!" He then remembered the guard outside and lowered his voice. "I thought that was just some crazy rumor, like how Incognito can walk through walls and lift aircraft carriers."

Taylor cleared his throat.

"Ohgoodgodyoucannotbeserious," Springer blurted, speaking too fast to be intelligible. "Oh, shit. Oh, hell. Oh, sweet mercy. I don't want to know any of this. Oh ... you gotta get me out of here. You got to get me out of this nuthouse."

"The United Third would kill us if we were to attempt something so foolish. I won't put myself or Thomas at risk like that."

"You think he's safer here? This place could be firebombed at any time. The Western Union is looking for it like the Spanish looked for El Dorado. Once they find it—and they will—everything here is going to be a pile of ash, you and the kid included."

"What are you proposing?" Taylor snapped. "Should I try to smuggle him out of here and put all my other friends in jeopardy when Incognito finds out?"

"Yeah, and smuggle me out too while you're at it! That kid's a hostage as long as he stays here. And need I mention the firebombing again?"

"We're hiding from something far worse than the Western Union."

"And what might that be?"

"Cloak."

The name was familiar to Springer, but it took him a moment to recall the information. "Those guys? They're real? They're not an urban legend?"

"Yes, and deadlier than you can imagine. If they get their hands on this boy, they could use him as leverage against the Helmet Man."

"Well, he's a prince, right? Just take him to his mother. If he's not safe with the queen, where *will* he be safe?"

"Cloak got to him once. They can do it again."

"Is that what happened to him? Never mind. Like I said, I don't want to know. Taylor, listen to me. I'm going to die if I stay here for much longer, and so will you and the kid. That's why we have to split now. All you need to do is get us to a village with a phone. Then I can get us papers and transportation.

Incognito will never be able to find us. I guarantee it."

"I'm sorry. I don't know why I even indulged in your game of hypotheticals. It's not even my place to take Thomas anywhere."

"Come on! Don't you Brits have some kind of duty to your queen?"

"I think we're done here." Taylor rapped on the door. The guard opened it with his nose still scrunched up.

"Hey, don't leave me here!" Springer yelled. "At least get me some pants!"

Taylor and Thomas went back to the rec room and sat back down to their game of checkers. Thomas was keeping quiet, looking at the checkerboard with an intensity uncommon in most boys his age.

"What do you think about what Springer said?" Taylor asked.

"What do you think?" Thomas parroted.

Taylor thought he knew. The answer had been so clear at first. It was too dangerous to try escaping, especially with a child in tow. They would surely be caught. Then again, Incognito wasn't around, and Taylor seemed to have some leeway around here. Springer had every motivation to escape, but what if he decided to hand them over to the Western Union? Taylor had no doubt the Western Union would prune him this time, if not worse. And once the Western Union found out about Thomas's invulnerability, they might consider experimenting on him, even if he was the queen's son.

Also, the lower ranks and bureaucracy of the Western Union were likely filled with informants working for the United Third, the Chinese, or perhaps even directly for Cloak. The only way he could consider handing himself over to the Western Union was if he handed himself over to an individual in the higher echelons who could protect him. As for Springer, Taylor would have to find some way to ensure he cooperated. He wouldn't be able to escape the region without some resources, and Springer likely had some at his disposal. Some ideas were already taking shape in Taylor's mind. Yes, maybe it was possible...

But even then, would it really be what was best for Thomas? He had never met his mother. What if he didn't like her? What if she didn't want him? Would he really be safer in the queen's care than here? And he hadn't even considered what Slate's or Naomi's reactions might be. Slate would probably kill him, as would Naomi, should he try to take Thomas away. They both loved the boy, but Taylor didn't believe they would make good parents. They were too damaged, too absorbed in their suicidal quests. They both chose to go with Incognito, even though they had only just been reunited with Thomas after he was kidnapped. In the end, it came down to who would best take care of him and where he would be the safest.

Could Taylor simply flee while leaving Thomas behind? But the mere thought made his stomach twist. No ... he had already lost his son, not to mention Gilda and Straper and all those cadets at the Bunker. He would not fail another child. Thomas could not be left to suffer.

"I think we have to tread carefully," Taylor replied at last. "Your thoughts?"

Thomas put a fist under his chin, reminding Taylor of that famous statue. "I don't want to leave Naomi or Slate," he said. "I'll miss them."

"I understand."

"But I always wanted to meet my real mom," Thomas went on. "And I don't want Incognito to use me against Slate again. I don't want to be a problem for anyone."

The boy's thoughtfulness impressed Taylor. Truly prince-like. Was royal blood a real thing? It was certainly a romantic idea.

"You want to start a new game of checkers?" Thomas asked.

Taylor smiled. "Sure."

Thomas made the first move.

***

Istanbul looked like it had been through hell. The streets were filled with rubble and corpses, empty metal husks that had once been cars continued to smolder, and the storefronts that still stood all had shattered windows. The trash of war littered the city, empty cartridges, unexploded ordnances, and plain old human waste commonplace. Camilla Ryder was now being given the grand tour of this pacified yet still dangerous war zone by Colonel Villefort, a Frenchman with thick eyebrows that took up much of his forehead.

"It is corpse cleanup now," Villefort told her. "Almost all the hostiles have been eliminated. Just a few hiding in the buildings now. Do not worry, Ms. Ryder. We are about to conduct our final sweeps. Civilians can then move back into the city and start working again rather than laze around. Times of war can easily be mistaken for extended vacations."

"I do not think that is a mistake many people make," Ryder said, taking in the ruined city with unfeeling eyes. Western Union soldiers were scattered everywhere, and an occasional walker stepped past. Some soldiers conducted bomb sweeps. Others took pictures of the carnage, made notes on touchpads, or put charred items in plastic bags. The unluckiest servicemen had to toss hundreds of human bodies into the backs of dump trucks. Many soldiers couldn't get through the first shift without fainting, throwing up, or taking a swig from a flask.

"Describe to me in detail what occurred here," Ryder said.

Colonel Villefort lowered his eyes, remembering things that were far too easy to recall. "It was fast. That was the best and worst thing about the attack. A quick death for the enemy, but it was so brutal and efficient, like we were making sausage.

"We were told to hold our position outside the city. We could hear gunshots and the howls of those savages from over a kilometer away. *Leviathan* then came from above. Its automatic guns managed to kill over a thousand combatants per minute. Enemy air resistance held out longer than anticipated. Several hijacked drones and enemy-manned unicopters took out five of our platoons, but *Leviathan* soon wiped them out of the sky. After the guns stopped firing, the city was as silent as death. All this happened in five minutes."

"I am satisfied with the results," Ryder said. She halted, as did Villefort. It was nearly impossible not to stop and take in the desolation. The Hagia Sophia had all but collapsed in on itself. It was now just a couple of walls holding up half a dome. Restoration of the landmark would take years, if it was even salvageable.

Villefort shook his head. "Barbarians… Why destroy something so beautiful?"

"How will the United Third react to our victory?" Ryder asked.

"They are planning to make their stand in Aleppo. Most of their forces have fallen back there already. They gave up a lot of territory, but it was a wise move. There must be moles in our intelligence network, because Aleppo was *Leviathan*'s next destination."

"Incognito is rumored to be abroad somewhere," Ryder said. "Who will be commanding the United Third's forces in his stead?"

"A man named Barir. He is an intelligent individual, holds lots of respect, but many doubt his leadership abilities."

"Does this Barir have a last name?"

"Not that we know of. As you likely know, many members of the United Third only go by their first names in order to protect their families. A curious practice. It must be confusing, what with all the Muhammads."

Ryder tilted her head back toward the sun like a solar panel adjusting itself so it can absorb as many rays as possible. It made her blank face glow. "Where do you suspect Incognito has gone?"

"Intelligence suggests he may be trying to form an alliance between his future Saladin Federation and the Chinese Empire. The very idea makes my guts twist up. I suppose it has always been the men versus the animals, only now the animals are traveling in packs."

"Where would you suggest I go next?"

"South Korea. It is the closest Western Union nation to Beijing. If Incognito is planning to visit the Forbidden City, you might be able to intercept him from there before he enters Chinese waters. The main problem will be detecting that stealth submarine of his. Naval mines would be the best preventative measure."

"I heard shots have been fired across the Korean Demilitarized Zone."

"Yes, but no deaths, thank heavens. Of all the places World War III will be fought, it won't be there. It's too much of a death trap for either side to have the advantage."

"Colonel Villefort, I thank you for your time and advice."

"Anytime, Ms. Ryder. I expect you will put in a good word for me with the president. I hear you are his new favorite. You are one of the big shots now, as you Americans would say."

Ryder turned to Colonel Villefort. It would be presumptuous to say she looked sad, yet the utter blankness of her features could easily lead one to that conclusion.

"Do not elevate me," she said. "I am just one of many."

***

York sat on a fallen pillar with his elbows on his knees. The glaring sun reflected off his sunglasses, making his eyes appear to glow. He had been advised not to leave the makeshift base but found himself unable to comply. As the battle was raging in Istanbul, he had felt a familiar need for adrenaline. It pulled him to the carnage. This need was one of the reasons he had joined the SWS. Of course, he was merely a witness to the current conflict. Ryder needed him fresh for the mission. A brief excursion was all he could indulge in.

"Are you busy?" a voice asked.

York didn't bother turning his head. Patel made her way toward him with doleful eyes. He hadn't expected her to leave the base. Despite her obvious talent, York had never been able to shake the impression that she was unfit for the squad. Her gooey kindness felt misplaced in a combat scenario. Still, walker pilots were often oddballs.

"You can have a seat," York told her. "Did you fly your walker here?"

"No, I walked like you," Patel said, sitting next to him. "Now that Cruz is dead and the others are grounded, we are the only members of our squad left."

York snorted. "A squad with only two people?"

"I'm sure we will get more members soon. Perhaps Kennedy will also re-cover. And Powers ... I'm not sure. Do you think he is a good leader?"

"No. One passable performance doesn't exonerate all his buffoonery."

Patel sighed. "This destruction..."

"War is almost never clean."

"I know that much. But still ... such excess."

"If you're having doubts, you're free to quit."

"It is natural to have doubts," Patel almost snapped. "Chinese soldiers once whipped my father half to death for not slaving away fast enough in the shell factory. My mother saw her brother and his friends lined up and shot for possessing modern electronics. I know what the real world looks like, and I fight for the Western Union because it was my parents' salvation, because it has been the salvation of so many suffering people."

Patel looked back toward the ruins of Istanbul. "But now I see the West compromising itself. I see it forsaking all the values that made it a utopia. And for what? Security? Supremacy? I am not fighting for this."

"You don't get paid to second-guess," York said. "You don't see the big picture."

"Who does?" Patel asked. She got up and left without another word.

York showed no signs of doubt. His sunglasses hid his eyes well.

Sebastian took in the scenery, but not through sight. He listened to the metal clang and the steam hiss. He smelled the soot and all the other pollutants lacing the atmosphere. He could taste them too. He even felt the toxins brush up against his skin. It was like hugging a giant dust bunny. Mumbai was a factory city that made shells and gunpowder for the Chinese Empire. All the subservient nations of the empire had been given the supposedly demeaning industrial jobs. The Chinese themselves were almost exclusively either soldiers or farmers.

Sebastian stood atop one of the few remaining skyscrapers left in Mumbai. Most of the city was covered in grimy factories. Legions of workers marched in and out of them, the steam whistles signaling a shift change. These people lived short, hard lives. Most of them didn't reach the age of fifty. They worked all day and slept together in overcrowded apartments that were almost a hundred years old. Nearly everything was gray. Even the Arabian Sea in the distance seemed bleak and dead. All the subservient nations of the empire had been drained of their life and pride. Their inhabitants had become beaten slaves and lived like vermin.

Only a handful of Indians lived in luxury. Long ago, Emperor Long had brought back a modified form of the caste system. Those who proved their worth and loyalty to the empire were granted special privileges and became noble in status. Many of these nobles lived in the Taj Mahal or other luxurious accommodations. These higher caste members were even crueler to their own people than the Chinese soldiers who patrolled the streets.

Sebastian continued to grin his everlasting smile. He could feel the evil writhe around him as if he were in a pit of black snakes.

"What a filthy place," Ember said, covering her mouth and nose. She stood next to Sebastian, having recently been reunited with her superior.

"How did the meeting with Hassan go?" Sebastian asked, adjusting his sunglasses. "The information you gave me was superb, by the way."

"Why, thank you, Sebastian. The meeting went splendidly. The fat man knows how to please a guest, I can tell you that. I really should have stayed for seconds..."

"And spoil the main course?"

"Oh, don't tease me," Ember said, feeling flushed already. "Will Geppetto be here? He's always such a downer."

"Yes, as will Schmitt."

Ember made a face. "Fantastic. Simply marvelous."

"His lack of people skills is burdensome, even for me," Sebastian admitted. "But Schmitt has proven himself multiple times to be an irreplaceable asset to Cloak and the Mentor. Even I might be less valuable."

"How is that creep more important than *me?*" Ember cried.

Sebastian didn't bother to answer. His acute ears heard the ring of the elevator on the other side of the roof.

The elevator was packed, reminiscent of a clown car. Five Chinese soldiers came out, along with High General Fang, who was in charge of all the empire's territories south of China. He was short and plump, boy-like in appearance except for a greasy mustache, likely grown for the sole purpose of offsetting his boyish looks. Fang was the brutalist among the high generals. His ruthless methods could only be emphasized by how the emperor had ordered Fang to restrain himself while purging the empire of Muslims. With the emperor's own bloodlust well known, this was a truly disturbing fact.

Mistress Lotus followed, rolling out so fast that Fang and his men were nearly flattened. Poppy and Thistle emerged next. Thistle kept her head down, and Poppy held her hand. Lily was the last to exit the elevator. She walked stiffly, still injured from her encounter with Keito Kusanagi. She stared daggers at anyone she passed.

"Why have you summoned us, Prime Minister?" Mistress Lotus boomed in English. She came to a stop in front of Sebastian, as did everyone else. "My children and I were heading back to the Forbidden City when you requested our presence in Mumbai."

"My ships have changed position without my authorization," General Fang snarled, his small eyes sizing up Sebastian. "I command my troops. Do not circumvent my authority."

"Why aren't we meeting in war room?" Lily questioned, her scowl a mix of pain and irritation. "And why we speak in foreign tongue?"

"Yes, I'm already sick of you butchering the English language," Ember said.

"Think you're tough?" Lily questioned. Her one good blade extended from her hand.

Ember perked up. "A fight already? Well, good thing I'm all rested up!"

"No more bickering, you two," Sebastian said, sounding amused. He turned to the others. "Thank you for meeting us here. It provides the best view of the sea and the mayhem to come. Also, thank you all for speaking English. Ember hasn't picked up the tongue yet, though it seems a few others here also have problems with second languages."

Lily scowled even harder. Her blade nevertheless retracted.

Sebastian continued. "I called you all here today to warn you of an impending attack."

"An attack!" Fang shouted. "Another thing I was not warned about until the last minute. This is unacceptable! The emperor will hear of this!"

"Settle down. Incognito and the Helmet Man are planning to enter the Chinese Empire through Mumbai. They will use the stealth submarine to approach the land undetected and then obtain new transportation somewhere within the city. Of course, I only became aware of this information a few days ago."

"That makes no sense," Fang said. "Why would they try to sneak into our territory through such a populated area?"

"Well, General Fang, you keep your borders well guarded. It wouldn't matter where they landed. The city also provides them with the opportunity to get in touch with their contacts and obtain supplies. Besides, the harbor is constantly congested with vessels and transport submarines. If someone were to spot Incognito's transport, it would likely go unnoticed."

"Why did you not warn us until now?" Poppy hissed.

"I found it necessary to keep this 'on the down-low.' You see, I've begun to grow tired of Incognito and the Helmet Man. They have some sort of grudge against Cloak. Now it seems they also hold a grudge against the empire. That's why the emperor and I decided to lure them in, only to crush the fools right as they set foot on our doorstep."

"The emperor knew of this?" Mistress Lotus asked, skeptical and cold.

"Of course," Sebastian said. "I would never go behind his back."

"Where is your pet?"

"Temple will stay by the emperor's side in Beijing to ensure his safety. But I'm sure the combined strength of the Black Lotus and Fang's forces will be more than enough to contend with Incognito and the Helmet Man."

Contempt thickened the air. Poppy and Lily had to restrain themselves from pouncing on the two Gifted. Fang was tempted to order his men to shoot.

Mistress Lotus wrapped herself in a deep silence. It would have intimidated most people, but Ember was yawning, and Sebastian continued to smile.

"I do not like you, Prime Minister," Mistress Lotus told Sebastian. "I never liked you. I do not trust you either. You are a dishonest and dangerous man. Such an individual should not hold the power you do. I detest you and wish only death upon you."

Sebastian chuckled.

"But I must obey my emperor, my beloved and all-knowing husband," Mistress Lotus continued. "He clearly sees something in you and that pet of yours I never will. However, if I ever get hold of concrete evidence that you mean to harm the emperor, I shall promptly crush your skull and feed what remains to your dog before I kill it as well."

"Hey, where is that dog of yours, Sebastian?" Ember asked.

"I believe he's with Geppetto right now," Sebastian said.

"Did you even listen to a word my mother said?" Poppy spat.

Sebastian shrugged. "Sort of."

A ringtone interrupted the exchange. Sebastian took out his cellphone and answered it. After listening to the automated message, he started to laugh. "Ah, the underwater sensors have detected the stealth submarine nearby. I didn't know if they would work or not, but it seems Schmitt pulled through again. Lucky us."

"They managed to get *this* far?" Fang exclaimed. He swore in Mandarin and spat on the rooftop before switching to English again. "Where are they now?"

"About twenty kilometers away," Sebastian said. "Have no fear. The ships I moved should be dropping depth charges on them right about now."

***

Slate, Naomi, Gilda, Straper, Abrafo, and the rest of Incognito's men were all dressed in drab clothes that smelled worse than they looked, an achievement worthy of note. Naomi and Incognito inspected the others, trying to find flaws with their disguises.

"It will have to do," Incognito said, already sounding tired of the whole affair. Oscar stood to the side, keeping quiet and out of the way.

Naomi put her hands on her hips. "Everyone will keep their heads down at all times, and make sure to shuffle your feet when walking, like you're wearing shackles. Do not make eye contact with anyone, and only speak when spoken to by imperial soldiers. We are going to unload the submarine in an abandoned port. From there, you will be loaded in the back of a truck, disguised as Indian workers, and just in case the authorities stop us, you all have your backstories memorized."

"Yeah, I only skimmed mine," Straper said.

Slate chuckled. "Same here."

"Even a clown would find your antics tiresome," Incognito said. "Radcliffe and I will be in a hidden compartment between the front seats and the back of the truck. We will go to the rendezvous point, where we will switch trucks and pick up supplies before driving out of the city. It will be a long drive before we meet up with the helicopter."

"Don't you mean unicopter?" Straper asked.

"Many in the empire live without electricity or running water. I doubt they would have unicopters or shopping malls. Sorry to disappoint you."

"You don't sound sorry," Straper muttered.

"The helicopter will fly us to Nepal," Naomi said. "For security reasons, I won't divulge any more details until we've reached our destination."

Abrafo nodded. "Good plan, except we do not look Indian."

"You'll be wearing these," Naomi said, holding metal collars. "These will disguise you and also translate everything you say into Mandarin, the official language of the empire."

"I recognize those," Gilda said. "We used them when in Japan. I didn't—"

The submarine jolted, knocking everyone off balance. Slate and Naomi managed to stay standing. Incognito just barely steadied himself on his scythe. The others hit the floor hard.

"Can't Young-Bum steer this thing straight?" Slate complained.

As if waiting for his cue, Captain Young-Bum burst into the loading bay while everyone was getting back up. "That was a depth charge. The Chinese know our position."

"Isn't this supposed to be a stealth submarine?" Incognito questioned. "Don't tell me I wasted all that money on a submarine that was only *slightly* undetectable."

"The Chinese couldn't possibly have the technology to detect us," Young-Bum said. "Then again, the Black Lotus is fairly high tech."

"No, this reeks of Cloak," Naomi spat.

"I concur," Incognito said. "Young-Bum, can you get us out of here?"

The submarine shook again, more violently this time, but they were prepared for it.

"The Chinese have us surrounded," Young-Bum told Incognito. "Retreat is impossible. I thought it was a patrol fleet, like the three others we passed under. Then that depth charge was dropped. But at least we are not facing the Western Union. They would have sunk us by now."

"Forgive me if I'm not thrilled by that news. What do you suggest?"

"We must evacuate. It is our only chance of survival."

"No, you need to get us to Mumbai," Oscar said.

"We are only a few kilometers away. You can practically swim there."

Another depth charge exploded. This one almost ripped the *Eodum* in two. A stream of water spewed out of the wall, soaking Gilda and Straper.

"Man, I hate water!" the Helmet Man whined. "Except if it's a wet T-shirt contest!"

Naomi felt like slapping him, but she was too distracted by her wet shoes to care.

"I vote we get the hell out of here," Straper cried, now dripping.

Gilda flicked her hands free of water droplets. "I wouldn't mind that."

"Young-Bum, evacuate your men," Incognito said. "We are leaving."

CHAPTER 40

Binoculars were of no use to Sebastian himself, but he did have a pair on his person. He held them out to High General Fang. "Take a look at the ocean, General."

General Fang snatched up the binoculars and did so with little enthusiasm. It only took a moment for him to spot his ships on the horizon. "The enemy managed to get this far into our waters!" he exclaimed.

"Yes, but the good news is we know where they are," Sebastian said with cruel cheer. He was a glass-half-full kind of guy. "Mistress Lotus, you and your children can head out to sea to ensure everything goes swimmingly. No pun intended."

Mistress Lotus brooded inside her shell, contemplating the many ways she could kill the grinning man before her. "Lily, you are far too injured to be of any help. Go inside and wait for the battle to conclude."

Lily didn't protest, but her face twitched into a bizarre expression of rage.

"Poppy, stay on the roof and snipe from here," Mistress Lotus said. "If fate is in our favor, you may be able to kill them all without the rest of us having to fight."

Poppy nodded, already checking his rifle to ensure its combat readiness.

"As for you, Thistle, attack anything airborne," Mistress Lotus said. "Fang will ensure the air is kept clear of our aircraft."

"My pleasure," Fang said. "Just do not let any of them escape."

Thistle wrapped her arms around herself, but she didn't respond otherwise.

Sebastian snickered. "I appreciate the professionalism."

"Your appreciation means nothing," Mistress Lotus snapped. Then she rolled forward off the roof and fell like a rock. It had to be at least a forty-story drop.

"Whoa, she's going to crack like an egg!" Ember yelled, peering off the building's edge to see Mistress Lotus's descent. "Looks like she'll be served up scrambled!"

But Mistress Lotus did not splatter as Ember predicted. Her metal body slammed into the concrete, the pavement cracking upon her impact. The black ball appeared to be undamaged. She merely rested there for a moment.

Then she took off, rolling at least a hundred miles per hour toward the sea. She maneuvered easily through the sparse traffic, passersby barely catching a glimpse of her. In less than a minute, she reached a wooden pier and kept rolling until she went off the edge of the pier and dropped into the ocean.

Sebastian raised his eyebrows. "Impressive."

Ember made a raspberry. "I would have rather seen her crack open."

Thistle started to cry. Her cries turned to screams. Black smoke poured from her mouth, curling around her. Ember yelped, but nobody else was bothered by the almost paranormal event unfolding before them. The smoke took off, flying toward the impending battle.

Ember laughed in surprise. "Now *that* was impressive!"

General Fang didn't bother with any parting words. He spat on the rooftop again and marched back to the elevator. His men followed. Lily limped after Fang, giving Ember and Sebastian dirty looks.

Poppy lay on the roof and began fiddling with his scope.

"Isn't that uncomfortable?" Ember asked him. "A mat couldn't hurt."

"Leave him be," Sebastian said. "Say, do you want to join the fun?"

Ember screeched louder than a banshee. "Yesohyesohyesohyes!"

Sebastian chuckled.

"I get to fight Slate!" Ember shouted. "Oh, Sebastian, do I have to worry about killing him? Please tell me I don't!"

"Go all out," Sebastian said. "You couldn't kill him even if you tried."

"That sounds like a challenge!"

Ember blasted off as a rocket would, a trail of orange flames and smoke following her, and sped through the air toward her quarry.

Sebastian leaned on his cane. His amphibious smile was now as wide as it could get. All he could do now was enjoy the show.

***

"I swear, if someone farts in here, we're all gonna die," Straper mumbled, squished up between Oscar and Gilda. "You know, if the depth charges don't get us first."

"Would you quit screwing around?" Gilda snapped. "And move your knee!"

The *Eodum* had been carrying three smaller submersibles in its loading bay. All of them were now in use. Captain Young-Bum and his men were in one sub, and Abrafo and his United Third henchmen were in another. Slate, Naomi, Gilda, Straper, Oscar, and Incognito were in the third. They barely had enough room to breathe and couldn't move their limbs. What made this all the more uncomfortable was that Incognito's scythe was also wedged in there with them, so they all had to be careful to avoid the blade. Oscar had already cut his bicep on it. The cargo space, meanwhile, contained the compact Magenta, medical supplies for Incognito, and miscellaneous weapons and equipment. By no means was there room to spare.

"You know what would help?" Slate asked in a constipated voice. "We should all take our clothes off to help with the claustrophobia. I'll go first."

"Do it and I shall beat you within an inch of your life," Incognito promised.

"I can barely steer this thing," Naomi said, hunched over the submersible's controls. "No matter. We should reach the dock in about five minutes."

"How can we be sure our plan hasn't been compromised?" Oscar asked, his face pressed against a cold window that only offered a view of the ocean's gray and sterile depths.

"We can't. We may have to find an alternate route to the rendezvous point."

"And what if that's compromised too?"

"Then we are all going to die," Incognito said flatly. "Quit worrying."

A depth charge nearly killed them all, but fate had another plan. They were only jostled about. However, a stream of salty water spewed into the submarine, getting everyone wet.

"Crap, we're taking on water!" Gilda yelled.

"I suppose I'll have to intervene," Incognito huffed.

"No, you have to conserve your strength!" Oscar told him.

"Yes, I better conserve my strength as we all drown."

"If you die, the mission will fail before we even reach the Forbidden City."

"Then what do you suggest?"

"Slate and Naomi will protect us. You just take them up to the surface and come right back down immediately."

"Very well, then." Incognito grabbed Naomi and Slate by the scruffs of their neck and made them and himself intangible. All three of them floated upward, phasing through the roof of the submersible.

"Man, that'll always freak me out," Straper said.

Gilda shrugged. "At least it's less crowded now."

***

Incognito floated out of the ocean's surface and released his passengers. Naomi and Slate had to start flying on their own. Neither of them was wet, though Naomi hadn't been able to breathe for a moment. She took a ravenous breath, only to cough on the polluted air.

"A little warning before you pull that crap again," Slate said.

"Meet us at the rendezvous point," Incognito said, ignoring the comment. "Do not die, or I shall be rather annoyed."

The phantom descended into the water again, not even making a splash.

"Can we kill him sooner than we planned?" Slate asked.

"I'm tempted to say yes," Naomi said, still catching her breath.

"Hey, let's try not to kill any Chinese soldiers," Slate told her. "I mean, Gilda doesn't want me to kill Western Union soldiers, so why not Chinese ones too? Most of them are conscripted and just trying to feed their families, after all."

Naomi smiled slyly. "Why, Helmet Man, it appears you *do* have a soul."

"Don't worry. I'll make sure to kill plenty of people later to make up for it."

"I'm sure you will." Not wasting any more time on banter, Naomi flew away to engage the ships farther out to sea. Slate would take on the ones closer to land.

Seven warships were within his vicinity. They were painted red and covered in equally red rust, so their decrepit nature was not so apparent at first glance. Each one had four gun turrets, which all aimed and fired at the Helmet Man.

Slate flew low and skimmed the water, avoiding projectiles as they slammed into the surface of the water. He fired several beams. A few of them hit the turrets while the rest struck the water, creating steam that served to decrease visibility for the warships. A few sailors cried out as they were mildly scalded.

Slate flew up, admiring his handiwork. "Just think of it as a sauna!" he yelled at the ships below. "It's a great way to get chicks to take their clothes off!"

"You think you're going to get that far on a first date?" a shrill voice questioned.

A fireball nearly cooked the Helmet Man alive, but he had sensed the newcomer approaching and flew out of the way.

"Who the hell are you?" Slate demanded.

"Surely you've been anticipating our meeting," Ember said. She floated, her hands and feet shooting out steady streams of flames to make this feat possible.

Slate scratched his armpit. "Nope, don't think so."

"How dare you? The glorious Ember presents herself before you, prime and ready for combat, and you can't even acknowledge me!"

"Lady, I barely use good manners on my friends. What makes you think I'm gonna be a gentleman to a chick who's planning to burn me alive?"

"Because we have a bond," Ember purred. "I felt it a mile away."

"Look, I'd totally hook up with you, but I got another gal in my life, so I'm just gonna stop your heart now." Slate was about to pound his fists together when the temperature dropped, his hands going numb. He flew back on instinct. A thin layer of ice had grown over his gloves. Slate swore. His heart-stopping technique wouldn't work until his hands had defrosted.

Ember blew fire from her mouth. Slate dropped down, the flames licking the top of his helmet. He sent electricity through his fingers in hopes of heating them up. Another burst of flame. Slate dodged to the right. More flames. He went up higher. The Helmet Man shot clumsy electric bolts at Ember, who dodged them playfully.

"I call this one the hot tamale!" Ember cried. She twirled around, creating a tornado of fire that soon expanded. Slate shot a beam at the water. This resulted in a wave that blocked most of the flame, but his left leg still got burned.

"I hope you're just warming up!" Ember taunted. "As for me, I was ready before we even started. Now come to Mommy!"

"Damn it! Where were you when I was single? We can still fight to the death, but could you stop with the insinuations? It's too fricking sexy!"

"If you want to be the dominant one in this relationship, you have to earn it!"

This flirting was cut short by a submarine falling out of the sky.

The *Eodum* crashed down into the ocean, nearly squashing them. Filthy water sprayed everywhere. Ember coughed as she was drenched. Slate retreated, doing his best not to get caught in the spray. The *Eodum* sank out of view, gurgling bubbles as it made its final descent. If anyone had still been on board, they would most certainly be dead.

Ember examined herself. "Oh, poo! Now I have to get this dry-cleaned."

The Helmet Man then noticed the mountain of gray water that had grown out of the ocean a hundred feet away. Two thick liquid limbs came out its sides. Mistress Lotus had thrown the *Eodum* to get his attention. It worked.

"Swell," Slate huffed. "How could I forget you?"

"Watch where you throw submarines!" Ember yelled at the water giant. "My life is not acceptable collateral damage!"

A water limb swung down at the Helmet Man. He flew out of its way, the limb crashing into the ocean. The other limb tried to swat him out of the air. It almost succeeded, clipping his side. He only had time to straighten his flight path before Ember threw more fire at him.

"Water, fire, and lightning!" Ember screamed with a manic grin and bulbous eyes. "Just throw in some rocks and a gust of wind, and we'll have all the elements!"

***

Naomi was barely aware of Slate's predicament. She had problems of her own.

Her fight had started off easy. She had redirected the shells fired at her from a warship toward other warships' turrets, destroying them. She kept her promise not to kill any Chinese soldiers, though she may have maimed a few. What mattered was that she had tried her best.

Then a lone bullet undermined her confidence. It almost took her head off, her mind catching it only on reflex.

The bullet exploded in a white burst. It nearly set her hair on fire. She shielded herself with her arms, disoriented from the blast. Another bullet came. She caught this one too and flung it away before it had a chance to explode.

Both bullets had come from land. A few blurry skyscrapers were the only landmarks that she could make out from this distance. It was Poppy. It had to be. He was the only sniper that could aim so accurately from so far away.

Naomi deflected another bullet. This one didn't explode. It released compressed gas with a hiss. She used her mind to create a whirlwind, blowing the gas away from her as she flew in the opposite direction. Whatever that gas was, it probably wasn't healthy to breathe in.

Then something dark moved in to cover her face, a black mask attempting to snuff the life out of her. She twirled, using her powers to repel the intangible enemy. The black smoke was blown back but then became snakelike in its shape and movements. It darted after her. A bullet came. She deflected it. The smoke came too. The warships started firing again.

"Maybe we need Incognito here after all," Naomi told herself.

Geppetto kept to his side of the boat. That was hard, considering Alphonse Schmitt's side had the bathrooms. Geppetto had decided to avoid going over there by urinating over the boat's rail into the water. He would hate to be a fish right about now.

They were traveling in the yacht that once served as Cloak's headquarters. Two small gunboats had been escorting them ever since they entered Chinese waters. The Chinese Empire had taken possession of the yacht when it captured Cyphrus, only to give it back to Cloak when Sebastian took the post of prime minister. One of Killian's men was now driving the yacht while the others walked around the boat with loaded guns, expecting trouble at any time. Killian himself stood next to Geppetto, smoking a handmade cigarette.

"You'll kill yourself with those," Geppetto said. His nose was still throbbing from Schmitt's kick, but it wasn't broken, and the swelling had gone down.

"Not the way I make them," Killian said, inhaling again. He held the smoke for a moment before blowing it out. He seemed to savor it so much that Geppetto was almost tempted to bum one off him, but he could already hear one of Schmitt's mocking jabs. Something like, "Hey, those will stunt your growth!"

"I've been avoiding the subject, but how did it go with killing Schmitt's lab assistants?" Geppetto asked. "I can't imagine they put up much of a fight."

Killian took another long drag. "I think it almost went too easy. Don't like it when they go down easy. They were practically begging for it."

"What do you think of Schmitt?"

"I beg your pardon?"

"What's your impression of him?"

Killian took one final drag before tossing the stub of his cigarette into the water. "I think the man was already unpleasant before he spent twenty years in some bunker in Antarctica. Now ... well, let's just say I have a policy never to work with the kind of person Schmitt is, the kind of person who enjoys the ugly side of our business far too much."

"I couldn't have put it better myself."

A jolt went through Killian. Becoming a hardened mercenary once again, he took out pocket-sized binoculars and used them. "Sir, I think this might interest you."

Geppetto frowned as Killian handed him the binoculars. Raising them, he saw for himself what had spooked Killian so much.

Mumbai could be seen from the yacht, as could a giant made of water. Lightning and fire streaked across the sky. The sound of warships' gun turrets became more audible as they approached the almost surreal battle that took place in the distance.

"Slate..." Geppetto muttered.

"Who?" Killian asked.

"The Helmet Man. Slate is his real name, if you could call it that."

"One of you guys?"

"Not anymore. Ember must be fighting him. Probably enjoying it too, the psycho bitch. I think the water giant is Mistress Lotus."

"The rumors about the Black Lotus were true, then," Killian mused.

Geppetto didn't like this in the slightest. What was Sebastian pulling? He must have called all his stoolies here to take on Slate and his friends. Was Sebastian going to capture Slate, or did he have some other goal in mind?

"We should approach cautiously," Geppetto told Killian. "I don't want to get caught in the middle of that."

"Quit being a coward," an impatient voice slurred. Alphonse Schmitt shuffled toward them, holding a bottle of rum he had raided from the liquor cabinet. Sebastian's dog followed behind. The mutt yipped mindlessly at the clashing titans.

"Stay on your side of the boat," Geppetto warned.

"This little border of yours was drawn unilaterally and arbitrarily," Schmitt scoffed, rashly swinging his bottle through the air. "Now listen up, because I'm about to tell you how a genius like me figured out how to detect that stealth sub."

Geppetto wasn't the least bit curious, but Schmitt went on with his monologue anyway, taking a clumsy swig from his bottle.

"It's rather clever," Schmitt said. "You see, I'm not detecting the sub but the freaks in it. I threw together some psychic energy detectors for Sebastian at the last minute. They're not very sensitive, but they don't have to be. Three people with abnormal levels of psychic energy can easily be detected, so Sebastian had the Chinamen drop these detectors around the ocean floor near Mumbai, and there you are. Not bad for a rush job."

Schmitt checked to see if there was anything left in the bottle. There wasn't. He tossed it in the ocean. "Keep going, Killian. I want to see these gods rip each other apart. Can you believe it? I helped create two of those divine beings over there. Hell, I created a pantheon!"

"I'm not going to risk my life just so you can have a front-row seat to that craziness," Geppetto said.

"Settle down there, little one. If you get any grumpier, you're going to have to start hanging out with Snow White. Killian, who ranks higher, me or short stuff?"

"Sebastian said your orders overrule his," Killian told Schmitt, although he didn't seem to relish the prospect.

"Fantastic. Common sense on Sebastian's part." Schmitt snatched the binoculars away from Geppetto without so much as a please and pressed them against his eyes. His pouted lips curled into a delighted sneer. Sebastian's dog kept on yipping.

"My God, it's just like watching an opera," Schmitt whispered.

***

The water monster's arm almost smashed into Slate again. The other arm came down from above. Ember flew alongside it, absorbing the heat. The liquid arm solidified into solid ice. Slate fired his beam, which shattered the ice in an explosion of a million fragments that could have been mistaken for a snowstorm.

The other arm came back around. Slate used his beam to sever it off the giant's shoulder. The detached limb smashed into the filthy ocean.

"I know you like this!" Ember shouted, tossing more flames. "Fighting is in our blood. Let it run hot through your veins. Let the sea of guts and fire carry you away!"

She grabbed something out of the water monster and threw it like a javelin. It was an icicle with a deadly point flying straight at Slate's chest, but he caught the icicle with one hand at the last second and squeezed it until it snapped.

"I've got bigger fish to fry than you," Slate said. "Quit wasting my—"

A liquid limb smashed into him before he could finish that sentence. He had been so preoccupied with Ember that he didn't notice the water monster had regrown one of its limbs.

Abruptly, the Helmet Man stopped moving. He was frozen within a block of ice. Oppressive cold blanketed him. He could barely sense Ember's giggles. It was taking all his energy not to be frozen solid himself.

The block of ice dislodged from the giant's arm and fell to the ocean. It made a surprisingly small splash, more of a plop. The ice block bobbed up and down for a moment before Ember landed on top of it. She pressed her hand against the ice and melted a good portion of it until Slate's helmet was exposed.

"Don't want to melt too much of this ice away, do we?" Ember cooed. She let flames curl around her neck like a scarf. "The devil ... trapped in ice at the very bottom of Hell yet surrounded by an everlasting inferno. Yes, you are the devil, Helmet Man." Ember started to caress the silver helmet. "And I am the inferno..."

Slate spoke reasonably. "Help, I need an adult!"

"We're both adults here. You know what, I don't think I'll kill you. Why not burn your limbs off and deliver your charred yet living remains to Sebastian? Imagine all the rewards and goodies the Mentor will give me for my evil deed."

A floating warship bashed the water giant, creating a boom that a thousand drums could never hope to reproduce. With the jolt disorienting Mistress Lotus, the water giant almost dissolved right then and there. The warship now had the appearance of a crumpled tin can. All its crew was dead.

Incognito had grown impatient.

He was hovering several hundred feet in the air, as was the warship. The intangible terrorist had embedded his scythe in the side of the vessel, lifting it out of the ocean and using it as easily as one would a bat. He couldn't see well through the filthy water, so he wasn't able to target Mistress Lotus directly. His only option was a blunt one.

Mistress Lotus got her head back in the game, though she lacked what one would conventionally call a head. She commanded her water giant to swing an arm at the floating specter. Incognito and the warship were already intangible, so the limb merely passed through. He took another swing at Mistress Lotus, making the warship briefly tangible so it could give her a serious beating. The two collided, creating another boom that made ears bleed.

On land, thousands of Indian workers stopped to gape at the biblical brawl. The Chinese soldiers tried to whip them back into shape—literally—but they only had to take one look at the fight before becoming entranced themselves.

Even an irreverent creature like Ember was awed by such a spectacle. She had to remember to blink. "We must have someone film these things," she muttered.

Slate liked how distracted Ember was. It gave him time to gather up some energy and release it all at once. The ice exploded. Ember lost her balance, throwing flames in the air. The Helmet Man didn't put much thought into what he would do next, only brute strength. He reeled back and kicked Ember in the chest so hard that she seemed to skip across the water like a well-thrown stone. She sank into the water as all stones do, no matter how well-thrown. There was no sign of her after that.

Slate sent at least a thousand volts into the water, hoping it would finish off his enemy. Incognito, meanwhile, continued to beat the water giant with

***

Naomi knew running away was no option. Poppy's bullets kept whizzing by, the enchanted smoke continued to hound her, and now the warships were firing missiles. She disabled a few with her mind, but that was tiring and merely delayed the inevitable. The Black Lotus was persistent, as were those Chinese warships. This was too much. How could she think at a time like this? If only there was more risk of collateral damage on the Black Lotus's part.

Wait, maybe she was going about this all wrong. It wasn't her style to punch her way out of a situation. That was Slate's style.

Some semblance of a plan formed. The smoke was closing in. As soon as another missile came within her vicinity, she detonated it with her mind and created a wind that redirected the flames toward the black smoke.

The smoke tried to steer clear. It failed. The flames consumed the apparition. The black smoke was gone, as were the flames. All that was left was regular smoke that choked the air.

This smoke proved to be Naomi's salvation. She blew it everywhere until she was concealed. Poppy would not likely be impeded by such a nuisance, but the warships might be.

Then her knight in shining armor arrived.

"Guess you're not dead yet," Slate said, flying through the smoke to meet her.

A bullet flew past Naomi, too close for comfort. "Slate, Poppy's shooting at me! He's doing it from the farthest skyscraper to the right."

"On it!" Slate aimed with care and fired his beam. It cut through the smoke like a hot knife through butter and drew a glowing blue line across the sky.

***

The beam of energy hit the skyscraper. The roof crumbled beneath Poppy. He had to roll leftward to avoid falling to his death. Sebastian shielded himself with one arm from the flying debris. The roof kept collapsing until a quarter of it was gone.

Poppy got to his feet. His flower-shaped irises locked on Sebastian's foul smile. Was he actually amused by all this? He ought to shoot him right where he stood. Better yet, Xing should have succeeded in having him killed. It didn't make Poppy feel better that Temple was still alive, despite the beast being beheaded.

"I think we better cut our losses and make a tactical retreat," Sebastian told Poppy. "Let Fang and his forces contend with the Helmet Man."

***

The warship fell from the sky and hit the water with a bang. Mistress Lotus had fled the scene, her water giant merging back into the ocean, the waves calm once more.

Incognito grabbed Slate and Naomi by their collars. "You both took too long," he hissed at them. "We are running behind schedule."

"I didn't ask for your—" Slate began, but Incognito had already made them intangible, and they flew into the ocean. The warships caught a brief glimpse of them and fired some shells at the water, hoping to smoke them out. It was no use.

The battle was at last over. Incognito had seen to that.

***

Two young Chinese sailors helped Geppetto onto the deck of the warship, doing a poor job of concealing their curiosity. He almost laughed. *What, have these kids never seen a dwarf who can possess people?*

Killian and two of his men also came on board, much to the disdain of the Chinese sailors. Western mercenaries on a Chinese vessel? They couldn't imagine a greater outrage. But they had more pressing concerns.

"Where is he?" a high-pitched voice howled. "I'll kill him and all his in-bred friends!"

The Chinese sailors had fished Ember from the water, much to their regret. As soon as she regained consciousness, she froze one sailor solid and burned another until only blackened bones remained. Now she was staggering around, spitting fire and flinging flames. Dozens of sailors surrounded her, keeping several feet back with raised swords and rifles.

"Slate!" Ember foamed. Her eyes bugged out. She was sweating like crazy. "Get back here! Get back here and kill me, you animal!"

"Settle down," Geppetto told her. "Or I'll have to take over your body."

"No, I've been humiliated!"

"You're only humiliating yourself further. Stop, I mean it."

Ember tossed fire at Geppetto, who ducked in the nick of time. Losing patience fast, he seized control of her. The crazed young woman's limbs snapped to her sides with great resistance. Her mouth struggled to form words.

"Killian, we're going to have to transport her," Geppetto said. "Make sure our—"

Alphonse Schmitt strolled past, holding a silver gun, and approached Ember with something that could be mistaken for courage but was in fact sociopathic indifference. Then he put the gun to her head and pulled the trigger.

Ember fell face down. Geppetto staggered back in shock. The Chinese sailors started gibbering. Killian took out another cigarette.

Schmitt knelt and put a shaky finger on Ember's neck. "Good, got the dosage right," he said, snorting his nose clear of mucus. "Can never be too sure with tranquilizers. Good thing I have experience with these. Used them all the time on you supersoldiers."

Geppetto forgot his shock and remembered his loathing. "I thought you killed her."

"I've worked too long and hard on you miracle babies to toss you in the river. Killian, dump this skank on the boat. Ugh ... this one was always a handful. The trick is to burn her before she burns you."

Schmitt got up and stretched. He noticed Killian smoking. "Hey, Killian. One more thing. Make sure not to give any of those coffin nails to the Oompa Loompa. His growth is already stunted as it is."

Geppetto clenched his fists as Schmitt laughed his way back to the yacht.

CHAPTER 42

Visibility was near zero. The snow fell so hard that the soldiers had stopped bothering to keep the road clear. This was typical of the Himalayas, one of the worst places to be stationed. To serve here meant you were either incompetent or untrustworthy.

Major Shin was both. He had indulged too heavily in the empire's coffers and had governed Chiang Mai, a city in Thailand, so poorly that his citizens had to eat insects just to survive. Now he was in command of less than a hundred troops, tasked with maintaining and patrolling a seldom-used road. It was always cold, his men were either drunks or slackers, and everything was in short supply, from socks to food. Shin thought often of deserting, but he had seen what happened to those who deserted. On a good day, it was medieval.

He sat in a small shack next to the road, shivering and suffering from frostbite. Ten of his men were with him while the others were either on patrol or causing mischief in a nearby village of only fifty inhabitants. The road went along the side of a massive mountain, frequently suffering from avalanches and bad weather. Shin was too lazy and unmotivated to keep the road in good shape, so it was nearly useless.

"Sir!" a soldier shouted.

Shin turned his head to see what the fuss was about. Two headlights pierced the snowstorm. The vehicle soon appeared, a large truck covered in rust and belching exhaust. Shin felt his day get noticeably better. He recognized the truck and knew what it held.

The truck stopped. Shin came out of his shack, trudging through the snow, his men following behind him with rifles. He reached the truck and tapped on its window. It rolled down, and the face of a jaunty Indian driver poked out.

"Major Shin, my friend, it is good to see a yeti hasn't eaten you!" the driver yelled over the snowstorm.

"Not even a yeti could live out here," Shin said. "I hope you brought more tea, Sanjay. We ran out last week."

"Yes, and plenty more goods. Reading material too."

"Half my men cannot even read. Food and drink are what they desire."

Sanjay laughed. "Simple pleasures for simple men."

"Which boxes are ours?"

"Everything but the wooden crates. Those are for the monastery."

"Those holy men better not be getting all the good supplies. Men, unload the truck! We are going to eat well tonight."

The soldiers were quick about unloading as the snow had started falling harder. It only took fifteen minutes before Sanjay was ready to depart again.

"Try to come back sooner next time," Shin told him. "Supplies are always low."

"I will try," Sanjay said. In truth, this would be his last trip up the mountain.

The truck drove away without any major incident. Everyone hidden behind the wooden crates relaxed as the shack disappeared into the storm behind them.

Straper rubbed his hands as if he was trying to start a fire. "Dude, my fingers are about to freeze off, not to mention my other parts."

"This cold is piercing," Oscar grumbled. "It doesn't matter how many layers we wear."

Five of the six stowaways were swaddled in thick clothing. Gilda and Naomi kept close together. Oscar and Straper did the same. Incognito sat on his own with an electric blanket covering him. Oscar regularly fed him soup and checked his temperature. Incognito did not care for the attention. Slate and Straper's snickering only made it worse.

They had almost failed to sneak out of Mumbai. The Chinese Empire had locked down the city almost immediately following the battle. A backup plan had been in place for such an eventuality, but now they were behind schedule.

It was uncertain whether Abrafo or the other United Third members had survived the battle, since they had failed to make the rendezvous, and the fate of Young-Bum or his crew was also undetermined. Incognito was displeased to hear this. However, no one suggested aborting the mission. Nobody wanted to give up, not after all the hardships.

"Poor Young-Bum," Gilda said, her lips blue. "We would have heard from them by now if they were still alive, right?"

"I'm not sure," Naomi said. "Perhaps they are only temporarily hindered, or maybe they don't want to risk contacting us for fear of compromising the mission."

"Abrafo and the others would have been of great use to us," Incognito said. "But their deaths will serve to further motivate me."

"Glad they could be of help," Slate said, putting his feet up. He was the only one not affected by the cold. The energy that flowed through him provided enough heat to warm up a house. His comfort proved unbearably irritating to the others.

"That was the last checkpoint," Sanjay told his passengers. "It is smooth sailing from here unless there's an avalanche. Hey, you want the heat turned up?"

"We could have had the heat turned up?" Straper practically shrieked.

"Of course. No need for you to all freeze to death back there."

"Do it!" Gilda shouted, frustration almost driving her insane.

Slate laughed. "Nah, I think we're good. Actually, could you turn on the AC?"

"Ignore the buffoon," Incognito ordered. "Increase the heat."

Sanjay did as he was told. Then the truck gave an unwelcome response.

It stopped moving.

"What happened?" Incognito snapped.

"The engine has stalled," Sanjay said, though his good cheer still remained. "I will take a look at it, but we are only twenty kilometers from the monastery. We should be able to hike there if needed."

"In this weather?" Gilda cried.

"Not an option," Naomi said. "We're behind schedule already."

"Can't Incognito just fly us up there?" Straper asked.

"I am not a taxi service," Incognito seethed.

"He needs to use his powers sparingly," Oscar reminded Straper. "Every time he does, even for the briefest instant, his life is put in jeopardy. Frankly, I'm surprised he didn't die in Mumbai after that display of his."

"Still, walking would suck," Straper said.

Slate chuckled. "Walking doesn't sound too bad. Ain't no skin off my back."

Everyone turned to look at him, an idea forming in their heads.

The Helmet Man went stiff. "Uh-oh."

***

Despite the Taj Mahal being one of the world's most iconic buildings, it had been rendered inaccessible to the West for decades due to the Chinese Empire's isolationism. The mausoleum now served as a palace of pleasure for the higher caste members of India and other influential leaders of the empire.

Geppetto sat in perhaps the nicest room he had ever been in. It was massive and decadent, filled with cushions, piles of food, and attractive youths dancing in skirts. Several dozen other guests shared the room with him. They seemed too intoxicated or distracted to care about anything. Killian and his men were resting somewhere else. Ember was still too upset to indulge. She was no longer in a manic state, now merely pouting as food and male dancers were steadily offered to her. She turned them all down.

"How can I enjoy myself at a time like this?" she cried, sprawled over a cushion next to Geppetto. "I can't stand it! I lost! My one talent is fighting, and I was completely blown away by that brute."

Geppetto took a large gulp of wine, finishing his cup off. "If the Taj Mahal can't cheer you up, I don't know what could."

"Seeing Slate's muscular body covered in third-degree burns would do the trick."

"That I can't help you with." Geppetto wanted another drink. He only had to raise his hand for a moment before an attractive girl filled his glass. Not the worst place to be, he concluded, though he could have done without the present company.

Schmitt sat ten feet away from Geppetto and Ember, too close for Geppetto's tastes. The Keymaster took one bite out of a morsel of food before tossing it over his shoulder, the servants quickly cleaning up after him. Now he was gulping down alcohol and grabbing a Chinese dancer by her leg. She didn't resist but struggled to maintain her fake smile.

"You know, I don't care much for creatures such as yourself," he said, treating her to a yellow smile. "But you don't look like a twelve-year-old boy, unlike most of your kind. Maybe if you put a bag over your head, we could work something out."

"He could charm a snake," Ember said with a scrunched-up face.

Schmitt's smile turned into an exaggerated sneer. "What'd you say, skank?"

He let go of the Chinese dancer, who was happy to flee. All the other dancers and singers went about their business. Some patrons briefly emerged from their stupor to look concerned, only to fall right back into it.

"You heard me!" Ember yelled. "Don't think I forgot how you shot me in the head or all the disgusting things you did to me and the other Gifted. Sebastian's mercy is your only safeguard against my flames, you icky thing you!"

Geppetto let his mouth drop open. For the first time in his life, he started to like Ember, though even Darth Vader was nice compared with Alphonse Schmitt.

Schmitt got to his feet at once. "You don't want to push me, skank."

"Quit calling me that!" Ember whipped her hand at Schmitt, hoping to burn a limb or two off. Geppetto wasn't surprised when nothing came out.

"What ... what the hell?" Ember questioned, staring at her hand. She felt like a crocodile without teeth.

Schmitt walked up to Ember and slapped her. The blow was so strong that she fell on her back. Blood dripped from her mouth.

"Burn before you get burned," Schmitt said, fingering the glowing ring in his pocket. "My lessons have been forgotten, it seems. No matter. As long as Daddy Schmitt is around, I'll always be happy to give you a refresher."

Geppetto threw his drink at Schmitt.

The Keymaster's pants were soaked. Schmitt went silent and looked at his wet crotch in calm disbelief. Then he looked at Geppetto. "Bad mistake, dwarf..."

"That's enough horseplay," Sebastian said, entering the room. He grabbed a drink from the tray of a passing servant and sipped it with great care. High General Fang followed behind him, wearing a scowl that could only be matched by Schmitt's own.

Ember got off the carpeted floor, wiping the blood from her mouth. "Sebastian, there you are! This fiend needs to be put down. He took my powers away. My powers!"

Sebastian put a hand on her shoulder. "They are only temporarily suppressed, I can assure you. I hope you are all rested. We have a tremendous task ahead of us. After the events in Mumbai, I cannot emphasize enough how the emperor's safety is our top priority. That is why I have asked General Fang to command the troops surrounding the Forbidden City."

Fang spat on the floor. A servant ran over to wipe it up. "I detest the idea of commanding such docile creatures," he said. "Those mind-controlled soldiers lack bloodlust. Why must I take charge of those useless things?"

"Because your ruthlessness is notorious even outside the empire," Sebastian said. "You were personally responsible for wiping out most of the Muslims in the Chinese Empire."

"Good for him," Schmitt said, gulping down another drink.

"They had refused to acknowledge the divine status of the emperor," Fang snarled. "I would have killed all the Christians too if the emperor had let me."

"Such zeal will be needed when facing Incognito and the Helmet Man," Sebastian said. "Who better to protect the emperor?"

Fang made fists with his small hands. "Does the emperor will this?"

"Naturally."

"Then there is no room for debate..."

"Good. The Black Lotus has also left for the Forbidden City. I don't want to pull any punches when dealing with Incognito and the Helmet Man."

Fang gestured to the other members of Cloak. "What about them? What about *you?*"

"Ember and Geppetto will be stationed at the Yantai military base. As for myself, I have to run some errands before returning to the Forbidden City. Relax, I will soon return to help govern. It must be chaos there without me."

General Fang spat on the floor again before storming out of the room. A servant cleaned up the spit as Sebastian turned his attention to his subordinates. "Ember and Geppetto, you will go to the base I just mentioned. I will explain the details later in a more private setting."

"That means I can stay here and get drunk," Schmitt said. "Yay, me."

"For now, if you already completed all the tasks that I assigned you."

"Give me something harder next time."

Both Geppetto and Ember gave Schmitt the most hateful looks they could muster. They would be more than glad to part with the Keymaster.

"Don't get too comfortable," Sebastian cautioned Schmitt. "Another assignment will soon fall into your lap. I have a feeling you're going to enjoy it."

***

Xing had gone through the plan at least a hundred times in his head and was still not at ease. Relying on foreigners was not an optimal solution, especially ones as unpredictable as Incognito and the Helmet Man, but he had exhausted all alternatives.

All these doubts, however, were quelled every time he walked around the Forbidden City. Death hung in the air. The servants and soldiers were all on the verge of madness. The legions of mindless soldiers outside the Forbidden City did little to make anyone feel secure. They were automatons at this point, possessed by Cloak's nanobots. They answered to only one master, the same master the emperor now answered to.

It was rare for anyone to enter the emperor's private quarters besides a handful of servants and guards. Even Xing rarely ventured into such sacred ground. He now sat on an armchair a few feet away from the emperor. Pansy hovered close by. He had become edgier ever since being incapacitated by High General Duan and his men.

Temple stood behind the emperor's small throne, the shadow of his silver helmet shading the emperor better than any palm tree. The three diagonal lines of blood painted on the helmet had long since dried. It would need a fresh coat very soon.

A holographic screen floated in front of them, displaying the battle between Mistress Lotus and Incognito. The emperor watched with crusty eyes and amazement as Incognito worked over the water monster with a warship. Xing was amazed too, though he was more amazed that the emperor had allowed a hologram projector to be installed in his private quarters, only sixteen months after refusing a heart rate monitor. If Cloak was able to convince the emperor to get over his phobia of modern technology, what else could they convince him to do? Xing knew he had to put an end to this.

The video stopped playing. The emperor howled and gnashed his teeth. Xing wasn't pleased either. Incognito and the Helmet Man had been discovered before even setting foot on empire soil. Everything seemed to be falling apart already.

Sebastian's hologram replaced the screen. He wore that same expression as always. "As you can see, Emperor, Incognito and the Helmet Man have decided to attack the empire. What's worse, Incognito's abilities are even more fearsome than we thought, as are those of the Helmet Man and Repulsa. Emperor, I fear for your security. The Black Lotus was your greatest defense, yet they were no match for the dreaded Incognito."

Pansy frowned but offered no rebuttal.

"We still have our force field, the conductive mesh lining the walls, and the countless enhanced soldiers guarding the Forbidden City," Xing told Sebastian. "And do not forget about Temple. Besides, the Helmet Man and Incognito have a long way to travel from Mumbai to Beijing, separated by millions of troops and numerous other barriers. We do not even know if they are heading for the Forbidden City."

"Still, we thought the Black Lotus could not be defeated," Sebastian said. "Now here we are. Emperor, Cloak believes you need to consider additional security measures. For that, we will need your full trust and cooperation."

"The emperor has already put his full trust in you," Xing said.

"Emperor, the Mentor values your loyalty," Sebastian addressed, no longer paying attention to Xing. "However, the Mentor suspects your loyalty may only be skin-deep. I've had to assure our leader this is not the case."

"It is *you* who must be loyal to the emperor!" Xing barked, just realizing he went too far.

Sebastian's smile started to turn sour. "I think you best leave."

Xing wanted to protest, but Temple turned toward him. That was his cue.

"You best leave too, Pansy," Sebastian ordered.

Pansy obeyed, making less of a fuss than Xing but still disgruntled. Soon, only the emperor and Temple remained in the room with Sebastian's hologram.

"Mentor..." the emperor wheezed. "Mentor..." He grasped at Temple's cloak. The cloth slipped through his gnarled fingernails, forever eluding him.

"Yes, I believe that you believe," Sebastian said. "But in order for you to prove it, you must trust your lord with all your body and soul."

"Mentor..." the emperor said. "Mentor... Mentor..."

Sebastian's flickering hologram leaned in toward the emperor. At the same time, Temple's shadow grew colder and more defined.

"My dear emperor," the blind man whispered. "I require your nuclear launch codes."

"Can we at least dump some luggage?" Slate howled.

"Everything we packed is critical!" Oscar yelled from the truck. "Keep pushing."

Slate grunted some obscenities but continued to push the vehicle forward. Sanjay was unable to get the engine started, unfortunately for the Helmet Man. But thanks to Slate's abnormal strength, they were making decent time.

"How about you jerks get out of the truck?" Slate shouted at the occupants.

Straper snickered. "Sorry, sprained my ankle!"

"And as Radcliffe said, I must conserve my strength," Incognito said, not having to raise his voice over the wind to be heard. "We're slowing down. Pick up the pace."

"Fine, I'll help," Naomi said with a bemused smirk. She used her powers to help clear snow off the road and move the truck, easing the burden on Slate.

It was another two hours before their destination came into view. The monastery hung off the mountain's edge and was the size of an average house, its paint worn away by the weather. Two hundred stone steps connected the isolated monastery to the unmaintained road below. Slate shoved the truck up to the foot of the stairs before collapsing into the snow.

"Out of service," he groaned.

Incognito was the first out of the truck. "Quit lazing around," he told the Helmet Man. "Unload the truck and be quick about it." With the help of his scythe, Incognito began to climb up the steps to the monastery.

Much to Slate's relief, he didn't have to do any unloading. Naomi carried the heavy stuff with her mind, including the compact Magenta, while Gilda and Straper took all the lighter items. Oscar only took up the sensitive equipment that needed to be handled with care. It was a long time before Slate felt like getting up and climbing the imposing stairs himself.

The monastery's interior, at first glance, held no surprises. It was sparsely furnished and smelled of incense. Two stoic monks, bald and wearing orange robes, were waiting for their guests. They were identical twins, and each had skin smoother than a baby's bottom.

After the group unloaded their luggage, they were seated at a small table in a cozy room and served tea. Incognito raised his mask and sipped his drink through what remained of his lips. It wasn't easy to ingest anything when one had to look at that, but everyone managed. Slate was unable to partake, so he waited until the others finished.

"Okay, tea party's over," Slate said at last. "Let's talk business."

"I suppose I will be heading for my room now," Sanjay said, having joined them after checking over the truck. "I was told I had to remain here at the monastery until you all completed your task, presumably to ensure secrecy."

"You presume correctly," Incognito said.

Sanjay nodded and left them to their business. The two monks each took a seat.

"We think you should first discuss your plan of attack," the first monk said.

"Then we will explain your method of transportation," the second monk added.

"Hold on, you guys are monks," Gilda said. "I'm no religious expert, but does helping us conflict with your vows or something?"

"We are not monks," the first monk said. "This guise is simply a way for us to conduct our activities on the mountain without interference from the soldiers."

"We *are* Buddhists," the second monk explained further. "And lay people are allowed to defend themselves if provoked."

"And the Chinese Empire has undoubtedly provoked us. Besides, how can one be a proper monk in a place such as this?" The first monk pointed at the Buddha statue nearby. Its face had the likeness of Emperor Long.

"Enough of your prattling," Incognito told them. "Radcliffe, begin the presentation posthaste. We need to make up for lost time."

"Agreed." Oscar put his phone on the table, and it projected a three-dimensional map of the Forbidden City. The palace was enclosed by a semitransparent blue dome and surrounded by a sea of soldiers.

"This is the Forbidden City," Oscar said. "It is perhaps the most secure location on Earth, even surpassing the White House and *Tortuga* in terms of impenetrability. A force field, a moat, a fifty-foot wall, and three hundred thousand soldiers all protect the palace, which also has a mine-laden concrete expanse surrounding it for miles. I should mention the soldiers are all infected with the kind of mind-control nanobots you encountered in Japan and on *Leviathan*."

"That sucks," Slate commented.

"You bet it sucks," Straper said. "I remember how freakishly strong and resilient those mind-controlled guys were. How can we take on a million of them?"

"Three hundred thousand," Oscar corrected.

"Splitting hairs, brah!"

"We can't forget about the Black Lotus and the Gifted either," Gilda said. "This plan of yours better blow me away, because I'm losing confidence fast."

"Well, the force field is our biggest obstacle," Oscar said. "It's the reason Incognito can't simply fly into the Forbidden City, seeing as he's vulnerable to energy. The field comes down momentarily when people and supplies go in and out the palace, but this is done sporadically and rarely. Also, many of the walls of the palace have been laced with electric mesh to prevent Incognito, should he get in, from moving freely within the palace. That's why we have to sneak in through a secret route."

Oscar pressed a button on his phone. The hologram expanded to reveal the underground levels of the palace. A long tunnel extended from the lowest level. It was so long that the hologram was unable to project all of it.

"This is our way in," Oscar said, pointing at the tunnel. "It happens to be the longest tunnel in the world, over two thousand miles, much longer than the Channel Tunnel that connects England to France. The original was built by the former communist government before the Chinese Empire was founded. After the Great Choke and Jin Long's ascension to power, the tunnel was altered so it would connect the Forbidden City and a secondary palace in Nepal. This serves as an escape route should the need arise. It never has. Also, magnets bend the force field around the tunnel, preventing it from blocking the way. It's the only hole in this otherwise impenetrable barrier."

"So, how are we going to get into this tunnel?" Gilda asked.

"We'll go over that later. Once we enter the palace, Incognito will take out all the soldiers stationed by the underground tunnel entrance. We will then meet Chao Xing, one of the empire's high generals and our ally. Without him, this mission would not have been possible. He will inform us where the emperor is and give us the special guns we can use against the Black Lotus. Gilda and Straper will guard the tunnel entrance. This job is crucial. If something goes wrong, that tunnel will be our only escape route."

"We'll protect it," Gilda told him. "Count on it."

Straper gave a thumbs-up.

Oscar nodded. "Good. Naomi and I will secure the force field generator. If we can keep it on, the soldiers outside won't be able to storm the palace. It will also prevent the emperor from escaping."

"The greatest defense makes for the greatest prison," Naomi mused.

"Couldn't have put it better myself."

Slate raised a hand. "Hey, what about me?"

"You'll escort Naomi and me until we exit the underground levels. After that, we go our separate ways, since you'll have the task of capturing the emperor."

"Great, I've always wanted to kidnap a world leader."

"You will be forced to take on the emperor's personal guard. Slate, I must emphasize that you must not harm the emperor under any circumstances. He is our bargaining chip, understand? And should Temple be guarding the emperor as well, avoid a confrontation at all costs and retreat to inform the rest of us."

"Gotcha. Don't kill the old guy. Don't fight the evil twin."

"What about Incognito?" Gilda asked. "Isn't he going to help capture the emperor?"

"As I mentioned, much of the palace walls have conductive mesh in them," Oscar said. "Incognito won't be much help searching the palace and so will be waiting with you. However, there is one spot the force field doesn't cover, and that's the tunnel entrance we'll be using. If outside forces learn of an attack on the Forbidden City, they might use this tunnel as a means to aid the emperor. Incognito will prevent this."

Straper was more confused than usual. "Aren't Gilda and I protecting the tunnel?"

"You are protecting the tunnel from forces within the palace. Incognito will protect the tunnel from forces *outside* the palace, should the need arise. Of course, while the tunnel is a major weak spot, it is the only area we have to protect."

"This is the only aspect of the plan I do not agree with," Incognito told Oscar. "If Temple is lurking somewhere within that madhouse, I should be on hand at a moment's notice."

"We will all be carrying communicators, so if one of us spots Temple, we can warn everyone else. The ideal outcome is to secure the force field generator and take out most of the Forbidden City's security before engaging him, and if we capture the emperor, the outside forces will be even more reluctant to intervene."

"Okay, let's assume we capture the emperor, secure the palace, and kill Temple," Gilda said. "What then?"

"We will pretty much be on security detail," Oscar said. "We'll make sure people can't get into the Forbidden City and that the servants, captive guards, and everyone else behave themselves. Abrafo and his men were going to help with that, but seeing as they're not here, we'll have to make do. Xing is going to pretend to be one of our captives and negotiate with Incognito on behalf of the empire. After forcing a few concessions from the empire, we will make our retreat."

"Is that it?" Straper asked. "I thought we were going to stop the Chinese Empire."

"Our goal is to defeat Cloak, not the Chinese Empire," Oscar said. "If we're lucky, we can capture Sebastian, but we may have to eliminate him along with what remains of Cloak. They're too dangerous to be left alone with the power they have right now. Other than that, all we are doing is putting the empire in the hands of High General Xing."

"We should help out the people living in the Chinese Empire," Gilda told him. "We have the opportunity to change their lives for the better. How do we know if Xing really wants what's best for his people? He could be even worse than the emperor for all we know."

"The white man's burden," Incognito scoffed. "What a naïve little tramp you are."

"Watch your mouth," Slate snapped.

"I don't need to take that kind of crap from you," Gilda told Incognito. "I know I'm right. These people need help."

"They need to help themselves," Naomi told her.

Gilda's anger fizzled away. She gave Naomi a betrayed look.

"Wait, are you agreeing with this creep?" Slate asked Naomi.

"I'm afraid I have to," Naomi said. "Who are we to tell the Chinese people how to govern themselves? Isn't that what the Western Union is trying to do to the rest of the world and what the Chinese Empire is trying to do to its subservient nations? If China is going to change for the better, it must come from within. And I am not thrilled with the idea of Incognito telling the Chinese how to run their government."

Incognito eyed Naomi for a long moment but made no rebuttal.

"Oh," Slate said. "Good points all around."

Gilda rubbed her arm. "Yeah, I guess that makes sense. Sorry, I got carried away."

"Apology accepted," Naomi said. "You just had the urge to right an injustice, and there are certainly worse urges to have."

"Wisely said," Oscar said. "Now if there are no other questions, I think we will let these monks show us to our transportation."

***

The monks took them to a cellar and through a trap door that led into a network of underground caverns, which were surprisingly warm. The caverns weren't massive, but they were extensive. Only the monks' lamps and the electric discharge from Slate's hand provided light for them to see, so they took it slow and steady.

It was a good twenty minutes before they reached a hole in a rock wall. They climbed through it and entered a man-made tunnel. When Gilda looked down one end of the tunnel, she could see only blackness. The tunnel was covered in smooth metal, so smooth that everyone had to keep hold of a railing the monks had installed to prevent them from slipping, though they still did plenty of that. Straper nearly broke his leg, and Gilda bumped her head on the wall. Incognito had the most trouble, but he asked for no help, and nobody offered it. The monks were the only ones who had an easy time with it, calm and perfectly balanced.

Slate almost fell for the eleventh time. "Geez, it's like a fricking ice rink."

"This surface is ultra-slick," Oscar announced as if he was giving a tour. "No friction. It's made that way so the pod can go as fast as possible."

Pod? That sounded pretty high tech to Gilda. "Is that our transport?"

"Yes, you see those strips?"

The others looked, noticing shiny strips going down both sides of the tunnel.

"Those are the rails," Oscar continued before almost slipping again. He regained his balance and trudged on with a grimace. "The pods themselves are, in essence, projectiles being fired by one big electromagnetic gun."

"How fast can they go?" Gilda asked.

Oscar winked at her. "With one of these pods, you could travel from Los

Angeles to New York in less than an hour."

Both Gilda and Straper had to whistle at that.

Their treacherous journey concluded when they reached a bullet-shaped contraption that blocked most of the tunnel. It was perfectly smooth and about the size of a small bus.

"This is our ride," Oscar said.

"We have been planning this for quite some time," the first monk said. "General Xing is a very careful man. He suspected that the Forbidden City may need to be forcibly taken one day, even before the arrival of Cloak."

"He tasked us with breaching this vast tunnel and building this pod," the second monk added, putting his hand on the pod's flawless gray surface.

Gilda examined the inside of the pod. It had twenty seats and a space in the back for cargo. "Won't the Chinese be able to detect this pod coming?"

"Xing has that covered," Oscar said. "At least I hope so. We believe Xing to be trustworthy. Otherwise, we wouldn't be here today."

"I do not trust him," Incognito grunted. He almost slipped on the tunnel surface again but caught himself on the railing. "But I am confident I can kill him anytime I wish. Xing knows this too. Betrayal will not come easily for him."

Gilda didn't know how anyone could stand to be around such an obnoxious ass. "How long will it take for the pod to reach the Forbidden City?"

"Fifty minutes at maximum speed," Oscar said. "The g-force shouldn't be lethal, but this trip will be far from comfortable. Be ready for the worst."

Naomi also looked inside the pod and checked the safety straps. It didn't look like a complete death trap. "I suppose it's time to start loading our equipment."

"When are we leaving?" Slate asked.

"Tomorrow morning," Oscar said. "Use this night to rest up and prepare yourselves. We are about to put an end to Cloak."

Naomi put her head through the curtain, expecting Gilda to still be awake, which she was. Gilda lay on a mat, staring at the ceiling with her hands folded across her chest. It was the pose of a corpse displayed in its casket.

"At least you're trying to rest," Naomi said. "Have you been counting sheep?"

Gilda flexed her entwined fingers. "Does that make me the shepherd?"

"I suppose…"

"I'm just talking nonsense now. Sorry, I guess I'm tired."

Both of them could hear Straper snoring in the next room. It served as a comfort, like waves against white shores.

"He's getting his sleep," Naomi said. "I've noticed his mood has improved. Same with Slate. It must be because they've gone back into their regular routine of adventuring rather than sitting still under Incognito's thumb."

"They think this kind of lifestyle is normal," Gilda said.

"Do you think this is normal?"

"No. Not even close."

"Me neither, but let's be grateful for Straper's improvement. You know, Gilda, I think he might be hurting as much as you are. He just shows it differently."

"I'm afraid," Gilda confessed, changing the conversation.

"Of sleeping?"

"Of course."

Naomi went through the curtains and touched her shoulder. "Everyone needs sleep. Only Slate doesn't, and even he needs downtime. Don't be afraid to lower your guard, Gilda, because if you have it constantly up, it will fail when you really need it."

Gilda nodded slightly. "I'll try."

"Good. I think you should lie on your stomach, remember?"

"But I feel vulnerable that way."

"I'll be nearby. Now sleep. Bad dreams don't always come."

Gilda nodded again and rolled onto her stomach, much like a flipped tortoise. Then she forced her eyes shut. Despite her resistance, it only took a moment to slip into unconsciousness.

She had no dreams that night.

Naomi slunk out of her room. She planned to go visit Slate but noticed Oscar was hunched over some medical supplies, including a syringe full of yellow liquid.

"What's that you have there?" she asked.

Oscar jumped but smiled when he saw it was only her. "Ah, it's for Incognito. Should he need a pick-me-up. It enhances psychic energy briefly, but it takes a terrible toll on the body. You and Slate must not use this under any circumstances. This injection would almost certainly kill Incognito should he use it."

"Not something to put in your morning coffee, then."

"Definitely not."

"You should sleep."

Oscar lowered his eyes. "I can't... How could I possibly sleep the night before my redemption? I spent the first third of my life accumulating knowledge, always anxious to utilize it, to make my mark. The second third of my life was devoted to the Keymaster Project and Slate, causing untold damage to the world. Now, the last third of my life has been devoted to undoing this damage and killing my rebellious creations."

"And what happens after you've redeemed yourself?"

"I couldn't care less, so long as all those monsters are dead."

Naomi frowned. "Slate and I happen to be these 'monsters' you speak of."

"Well, you know what I mean."

"Get some rest. For your son's sake."

"Okay, I'll try."

And so Oscar tried, though he would fail in the end.

Soon after Naomi left Oscar, she was sidetracked yet again.

"Wench, I must speak with you."

Incognito had been waiting for her. He was leaning on his scythe, his body wilted and fatigued. Naomi had no desire to converse with her former employer. She had taken his verbal abuse and condescension for far too long. She kept on walking.

Incognito instantly appeared before her, blocking her path. She skidded to a stop.

"Accept this gift, and I shall never engage you in casual conversation again," Incognito said. He took a silver locket from his pocket, dangling it as if tempting a cat.

Naomi scoffed and snatched the locket out of his hand with her mind. It landed in her palm. It was expensive, made from real silver. She felt its surface. Its smoothness was only surpassed by Slate's helmet. She snapped the locket open to see what was inside. There was a name etched in it. She scoffed again when she saw it, but then her eyes settled on a picture. The sight of it almost made her vomit her heart out.

"You have no idea how difficult it was to obtain that photo," Incognito told her. "All records of your mother are gone, and she has no living relatives. Nobody remembers her, nobody loves her, save you."

"You bastard…"

"Despite my grandest efforts, I cannot help but sympathize with your plight. White mothers are often unable to love their offspring properly. How could she love a child not even of her own stock? That is why I have always felt pity for the children of the West. And you, my dear, are quite literally a child of the West, born from imperialism and illusions of racial superiority, created for the sole purpose of conquest."

Naomi moved fast, slapping him as hard as she could. His mask nearly flew off. She had used her real hand. It was a special occasion.

"Don't pretend you know anything about my mother," she told him, tears threatening. She held them back, but she couldn't stop her eyes from glistening. "You aren't my father. You don't have a daughter. You have no one. You made that choice long ago. You are going to die alone. Nobody will weep for you. Nobody will mourn you. Your subordinates will secretly relish your demise and fight among themselves until the power vacuum has been filled. And there will be no Saladin Federation. The West will live on, and you will not. And if anyone will remember you, it will only be to spit on what you stood for."

She was tempted to slap him again, but it would have been redundant. The next course of action was obvious. She walked away.

The Helmet Man was sitting against the wall when Naomi stormed in. She had calmed some but was still pretty steamed.

"Something wrong?" he asked.

Naomi shook her head, not in response but in an attempt to clear her head. She fingered her locket for a moment then answered, "I think Incognito was trying to be nice to me."

Slate sat there for a moment before saying, "Screw him!"

Naomi smiled, her mood improving. "My thoughts exactly. Mind if I sit down?"

"Yep. I mean, no, go ahead."

"Try not to think too hard," Naomi teased. She took her seat next to the Helmet Man, not wasting any time to put her head against his shoulder. He smelled of ozone.

"Are we ready?" she asked.

"Ready as we're ever gonna be," he said.

"Is this really the end?"

"I don't know. I sure hope not. I kind of want to live after this."

"Are we still going to be killers?"

"There's still Powell and the Western Union to deal with, not to mention the remains of the United Third after we ... do the deed."

"Is all that our responsibility?"

"Maybe, if things get as bad as I think they will."

"And after that? What kind of lives could we possibly lead?"

"I don't know. A family?"

"We can't have children." Naomi didn't bother to hold back her tears this time.

"But we have Thomas."

"It's not the same."

"It'll have to do. We could set up a place to live somewhere in the middle of nowhere. My dad could be the grandpa. I'm sure he'd like that."

"They'll never stop hunting us." Naomi didn't specify who might want to hunt them. To her, everyone wanted to cut her open and see her secrets spill out.

"Then we'll keep running," he told her. "We'll live on. Long after the Western Union crumbles, after the Chinese Empire is just a brutal page in history, after Cloak and the Mentor are no more, we'll live on."

"No," Naomi whispered. "No, *you'll* live on. You'll live on forever. I'll be dead one day, and you'll find someone new. You'll always find someone new."

"Don't talk about yourself that way."

"It's the truth. You'll probably only be with me out of pity when I start to turn gray. Then you'll find someone else after I die. You'll always find someone new."

"I'm not like that."

"You don't have to lie, Helmet Man. I know what I am."

"I'm not like that..."

***

The fake monks spread sand over the floor of the ultra-sleek tunnel to prevent anyone from slipping as they loaded equipment. Naomi took her time fitting the compact Magenta into the back of the pod.

"It's been a real hassle transporting your walker," she told Gilda. "It'd better be useful."

"You mean *I* better be useful?" Gilda deduced.

Naomi laughed. Gilda laughed too.

Incognito scoffed as he stepped into the pod. "When you hens are done clucking, there is work to be done."

Naomi and Gilda scowled briefly before going back to work. But before Gilda could go far, Oscar leaned discreetly toward her as he loaded medical supplies. "He always had a hard time getting a date," he whispered.

Gilda grinned. Incognito dating?

Everyone and everything was soon loaded onto the pod with no major setbacks. They all buckled themselves in. One of the monks swept up the sand while the other one gave some last words of advice to the passengers.

"Make sure your safety belts are buckled. Keep your arms at your side and your heads against the headrest. Ensure all loose articles are securely fastened. Do not get up from your seat when the pod is in motion. And please, no smoking."

"You sound like a flight attendant," Gilda mumbled.

"Do we get any peanuts, brah?" Straper asked.

"I admire all of you," the monk told them. "The people of the empire will forever be in your debt. Give my best wishes to High General Xing."

"Let's be on with it, then," Incognito snapped.

The monk nodded and sealed the door shut. For the next five minutes, the passengers sat in the dimly lit pod. There was no conversation. It suited them all just fine.

Then the humming began.

It started off small. Then it got loud. Really loud. Something electrical started buzzing as well. A thousand bees couldn't match it.

"I can sense the electricity," Slate said. "Each side of the tunnel has it flowing in a different direction. I think a field is about to be generated."

"Is this gonna hurt?" Straper asked, already knowing the answer.

The buzzing was overpowering now.

The Helmet Man chuckled. "You better believe it."

And then they were launched.

CHAPTER 45

Oscar was right. It wasn't a comfortable ride.

But it wasn't lethal either. That would have been too merciful. The pod rocketed forward and continued to pick up speed for the next twenty minutes. Gilda felt as if a giant foot was stepping on her. Straper was pretty sure he heard a few of his bones crack. Naomi and Oscar felt similarly. If Incognito had a difficult time, he didn't show it, but this trip was undoubtedly taking its toll on his already frail body. Even Slate was beginning to feel sore.

The electric hum increased proportionally to the acceleration, which meant regular conversation soon became impossible. Why hadn't the monks told them about the sound? They would have worn earplugs if they had known it was going to be this bad.

During the ten-minute period that made up the middle of their voyage, they finally stopped feeling like they were being turned into pancakes. The pod was going at a constant speed now, though the sound was still intense.

Then came the deceleration. This was nearly as bad as the acceleration. The straps dug into their flesh, and their necks threatened to snap forward. But the worst part wasn't the physical pain. It was the knowledge that they were on the last leg of their journey. Countless enemies waited for them at the Forbidden City, the silver devil being the worst of them all. The humming did decrease as they slowed down, but the steady dwindling of white noise seemed only to emphasize the calm before the storm.

An instrument beeped, signaling their impending arrival.

"There can be no snakes in my Eden," Incognito muttered. No one heard him over the humming. It didn't matter. His words were meant only for himself.

Incognito lost substance. The straps couldn't hold him back any longer. He flew through them, grasping his scythe, which had been tied to the floor. His inertia shot him out of the pod. Phasing through its metal hall was effortless for him. He was in the tunnel now, soaring faster than any living bird could. He saw the light at the end of the tunnel. The end was near. Just one more battle. Just one more sacrifice. He could manage that much.

Incognito entered the Forbidden City's loading bay. It was deep underground and the size of a modest airplane hangar. Half a dozen pods were lined up along the right wall.

Two dozen guards had been posted in the loading bay. They were not slacking, but they were also not prepared. One guard caught a glimpse of the blur that was Incognito, raising his eyebrows and his gun. Incognito didn't give him time to finish doing either. He cut the guards to ribbons. There was no resistance. All two dozen men dropped to the concrete floor, blood spattering over the walls, painting the loading bay a bright red.

The pod arrived. It was moving at a crawl now. Large mechanical clamps caught the vessel, halting it. Incognito checked his blade. Not a drop of blood on it. The g-force hadn't severely affected his body either.

The pod door opened. Slate was the first to get out. He noticed all the dead guards. "I expected this, but I still can't stand you."

"Was I to give them a slap on the wrist?" Incognito glanced around. "Where is Xing? The worm should be here."

"I ... I am over here." High General Chao Xing emerged from the shadows. His face had no color. He covered his mouth. "The guards ... I told them to leave, but they refused. Orders from the emperor himself. Such bloodshed..."

"And there shall be more to come," Incognito told him. "Do not feign ignorance. You knew who I was. You knew what would happen to your countrymen should they choose to oppose me."

Xing gulped and smoothed his suit out. "I understand, but I wish for casualties to be kept to a minimum. If the situation was reversed, you would expect the same of me."

"I would expect you to do your job. May I ask what that nonsense in Mumbai was? Cloak knew we were coming."

"They did not find out from me. I can say that much."

"I shall pretend for now that you speak the truth. Now tell me where Temple is."

"With the emperor, as are four members of the Black Lotus and thirty members of the imperial guard, all in the throne room. The youngest member of the Black Lotus, Thistle, is outside the palace, aiding High General Fang."

"What is Fang up to?"

"He is commanding the three hundred thousand soldiers outside the palace. Such an unpleasant man... I never cared for him myself. He always spat on my floor."

"What about the rest of Cloak?"

"Unfortunately, save Temple, the Gifted are not in the Forbidden City."

"I beg your pardon?" Incognito took a step forward. "The whole reason we came here was to do away with those curs."

To Xing's credit, he didn't flinch. "I promised you Temple only."

"He's got you there," Oscar said, unloading supplies. Naomi helped him. Straper was checking over his rifle and handgun. He had his war face on. Gilda fiddled with the compact Magenta, planning to make it not so compact. She stopped briefly to examine Xing. He was a world leader, yet he didn't seem much older than she was. It didn't inspire confidence.

"Here are the firearms I promised," Xing said, pointing to a small crate.

Oscar went to it and took out one of the guns. It had the appearance of a toy, plastic and nonthreatening.

"These guns will help you defeat the Black Lotus's cyborgs," Xing said. "The switch on the side changes the setting from stun to lethal. I advise the lethal setting. But this gun will only briefly incapacitate a normal person, even on the lethal setting, so don't waste it on them. Remember, each gun only has one shot."

Oscar passed the weapon to Slate. "Here you are."

"Yeah, I won't need this," Slate said, tossing the gun over his shoulder. It clattered on the floor, almost sounding like it broke.

"Be careful with that!" Oscar yelled. "Such impulsiveness!"

Xing blinked. "I did not imagine the Helmet Man to be so ... casual."

"Fella, believe me, you haven't seen me casual," Slate said. "I still have my pants on."

"I too will not require a gun," Incognito told Oscar. "Give it to the weaklings. They need all the help they can get."

Straper and Gilda tried not to look irritated but failed miserably.

"Fine," Oscar snapped. "Naomi, can you take one at least?"

Naomi shrugged. "I'll be glad to. Let boys be boys."

An alarm blared. Red lights flashed. It threw everyone off. Gilda and Straper went tense. Naomi and Oscar just deflated.

Slate rubbed the back of his neck. "Don't think *that* is supposed to happen."

"Explain yourself," Incognito hissed, grabbing Xing by the neck.

"This ... shouldn't be happening..." Xing wheezed. "One of the guards ... must have gotten away from you..."

Incognito tightened his hold, causing Xing's face to turn red. "No one escapes me. Neither will you if this is some elaborate ruse."

Incognito let go. Xing kept himself from gasping. That would have been a sign of weakness. He merely treated Incognito to a cool glare.

"If I wanted you dead, I would be very far away, and the deed would already have been done," Xing said. "I suggest you all hurry. Your enemies now know you are here."

***

Shu fell again. Her face was already swelling up.

"Sorry, hit you again!" Lily yelled in Mandarin, not really sorry at all. "The emperor wants you pretty, but I still don't know what he sees in an old hag like you!"

The emperor licked his dry lips. Snot dribbled out his left nostril. Shu had been entertaining him for some time now by having to spar with Lily. It always ended with the cyborg knocking her down and leaving a new injury. For the emperor, it wasn't as entertaining as bearbaiting, but it had its moments.

Mistress Lotus and her other two children silently watched this performance. Poppy felt a wave of disgust as he watched the ancient fool amuse himself. Pansy did not seem to have an opinion one way or the other. Mistress Lotus also seemed indifferent, but Poppy suspected she disliked all the attention the emperor was showing this servant woman, even if it was negative attention. Oh, how his mother's devotion sickened him so…

Temple stood behind the throne. The guards occasionally stole a glance at him and soon after wished they had not. His mere presence seemed to make the match between Lily and Shu more perverse, almost sacrificial.

The alarm went off. Mistress Lotus swiveled around to face the throne room door. The alarm had been recently installed. She never anticipated it would be used.

"Invaders," she declared.

The guards readied their weapons. Poppy took his rifle off his back. Pansy cracked his knuckles. Lily smirked. They had all been standing by the emperor's side for half a day now. His paranoia had never been greater. His throne was drenched in sweat and smelled almost as bad as he did. He let out a cry and flailed his limbs about. Shu scurried off to a corner, covering her battered face as the alarm persisted.

The alarm had not stirred Temple even an inch. The lack of response from him somehow made the room colder. The emperor grasped at Temple's cloak, desperate for the monster's power.

"Inform High General Fang of this disturbance," Mistress Lotus ordered a guard. "Have him put his troops on high alert."

The guard nodded and ran out of the throne room. Immediately afterward, seven other guards ran in. They were quivering and sweaty.

"Ma'am, this is no false alarm," one of them told Mistress Lotus. "We believe intruders have entered the palace through the emergency escape tunnel. The computer reported that a pod was approaching, but we were told it was just a system test."

"Told by whom?" Mistress Lotus snapped.

"It ... it was in writing... It had the emperor's seal..."

"A traitor is in our midst," Mistress Lotus seethed. "This may be the work of Sebastian. It explains why he has yet to return to the Forbidden City. He may even be working with Incognito and the Helmet Man. His actions in Mumbai could have been to avoid suspicion."

Poppy almost agreed with her, but then a thought struck him. Was Xing behind the attack? It was possible. Poppy shared Xing's hatred of Cloak and had even plotted with him to undermine the Black Lotus and the emperor, but he would never stoop so low as to ask foreigners for help. If Xing really were responsible, Poppy would make sure the Traitors' Garden would soon have another occupant.

"What is our next course of action?" Poppy asked his mother.

"Same as always," Mistress Lotus said. "We protect the emperor."

"I'm so ready for a good fight," Lily said with zeal. Her wounds had healed via growth patches, and the technicians under the employment of the Black Lotus had replaced her broken blade with a new one. They assured her it couldn't be broken. She had tried it out on a few of the technicians just to be safe, but it had yet to prove itself in true battle.

"A good warrior does not seek fights," Mistress Lotus told her. "There are already too many of them on our doorstep."

"This one *is* on our doorstep," Lily argued.

"Do not let your desire for combat distract you. Go to the force field generator. Turn it off so Fang and his forces may assist us."

"You got it, Mother!" Lily sprinted out of the throne room, knocking aside two guards.

Mistress Lotus turned to her two remaining children. "Poppy, Pansy, remain here with the emperor and seal the doors. Only open them for me and no other."

"Where are you going?" Poppy asked, not bothering to hide his impudence. If his mother had only acted against Cloak sooner, this could have all been avoided. He may have been disappointed with himself for failing to kill Temple, but it was nothing compared with what he felt now for his mother. How could such blindness be respected?

"I am going to take the offensive," she said. "I will not sit here and let enemies of the emperor track their dirt into his domain. They will face me and fall."

The emperor let out a terrible scream. Mistress Lotus rolled to his aid, going so fast that she left skid marks on the floor, and stopped at the foot of his throne. "What is wrong, my emperor?" she asked.

He mewled and began to utter one word repeatedly. "Mentor! Mentor! Mentor!"

Mistress Lotus quickly noticed what had upset him. Temple was moving away from him, gliding away, to be precise. He made his way to the doors.

"Where are you going?" Mistress Lotus questioned.

Temple ignored the cries of the emperor. Sympathy did not impede him.

"Guards, stop him," Mistress Lotus ordered.

The guards were not too thrilled to obey, but they did. They surrounded Temple, swords drawn and guns pointed. Only one soldier was bold enough to take a step toward him. His hands shook so badly that he could hardly point his sword.

He would be punished for his brazenness. A fist darted out of Temple's cloak and punched the guard right through the head, briefly poking out the back of his skull. The action was so swift that even Poppy barely saw it. The hand retracted, hidden away beneath the cloak once more. The hole where the guard's face used to be had been cauterized. It only squirted a little blood as the corpse fell to the floor.

The guards were wise enough to fall back several feet. A few of them dropped their weapons in shock. One even stabbed himself in the chest with his own sword, escaping a horrid fate that may have befallen him otherwise. This guard fell too.

"Enough!" Mistress Lotus spat. "Guards, keep away from him. He is clearly set on leaving. I do not trust him near the emperor anyway."

Temple continued onward, gliding out of the throne room before disappearing from sight. The remaining guards sighed in relief.

"Cowards," Mistress Lotus muttered. She consoled her emperor. "Have no fear, my husband. I will deal with the intruders and any enemy under the guise of an ally. I will always be devoted to you. I will always be your wife. We are lovers. We will soon rule this world together for all time. You are divine. You cannot die."

The emperor calmed down a little and gnawed on his shriveled hand.

"Now may we act against Cloak?" Poppy barked. "Give the order to have Sebastian and his worms killed. His beast just abandoned us in our time of need. What more evidence do you need of Cloak's treachery before—?"

"Silence!" Mistress Lotus boomed, the floor shaking from her voice. Shu yelped, curling up in the corner as best as she could.

Poppy wished to say more, but Pansy put a hand on his shoulder. Poppy growled. His own brother was just as deluded as his mother.

"We do not pretend to know better than the emperor," Mistress Lotus said like she was stating a common fact. "It is our duty to serve, not to rule. His acceptance of Cloak has given us many victories over the Western Union. They are losing the war. We are winning. Our emperor's judgment is not impeded."

Pansy nodded. Poppy squeezed his rifle until he heard it creak.

"Keep the emperor safe," their mother continued. "Should any intruders breach the throne room, take the emperor to his underground bunker and seal the doors. If the bunker is compromised, go to the pods and flee the Forbidden City."

"But the intruders will likely be guarding the tunnel," Poppy said. "That's where they are entering from, after all."

"Then you will fight them to protect your father."

"Why bother protecting him if he cannot die?" Poppy questioned.

Mistress Lotus stayed silent for a moment. Then she answered in a dead voice, "I do not care if you are my child. Say such blasphemy once more and

I will inflict my full wrath upon you. It was the emperor who gave you your rifle, your eyes, your food, your home, your very life. Show him respect, ungrateful wretch. Do your duty."

CHAPTER 46

Gunshots woke Eisenhorn from his half sleep.

He had kept himself from truly sleeping for over a week now. He didn't want to see Klara. He didn't want answers. He didn't care if he couldn't escape the hell he was in anymore. After that dream, he never wanted to sleep again. Every time he closed his eyes for more than five minutes, he felt a stab of pain and terror in his gut. It would move up through him until he almost vomited it out. Then he would grasp his throat and choke.

That dream... He would *never* go to sleep again. That was final. Eisenhorn once heard you could die of sleep deprivation. Fine, whatever. Better than having that dream again. He envied insomniacs. They didn't have to face the moon.

Then he remembered what had woken him up. The gunshots. He became aware of the alarm. More gunshots. The sound of footsteps. A few screams. What he heard did not frighten him. It would be hard to top that dream he had. If anything, he welcomed this new development. Maybe the Western Union had gotten the upper hand and was launching an all-out attack on the Forbidden City. Perhaps it was a coup. It could also be Cloak. This last thought dampened his spirits a little, but he was still perked up.

The door...

Eisenhorn thought he heard something. He shook his head.

The door...

This time he knew for sure he had heard something. He glanced around his unpleasant residence. Where did the voice come from?

Go to the door, Randolph...

He recognized the voice this time. "Klara? That you? Woman, you better not be a figment of my imagination! Am I asleep or what?"

The door, Randolph...

Eisenhorn found this all fishy, but he decided to obey the voice in his head regardless. He got up on his thin legs and went to the metal door.

"Okay, now what?" He felt stupid indulging these hallucinations. He usually only indulged his delusions.

No answer.

"Klara, quit lazing around!"

Hand...

"What?"

On the door... By the lock...

Eisenhorn had no idea where this was going. He put his right hand on the door, near the heavy lock that was his first major obstacle to freedom.

Close your eyes...

Eisenhorn did so. "Now what?"

Now dream...

He didn't dream, but something else happened. His right hand grew numb. It wasn't because the door was cold. The cause was internal in origin. Now his hand was burning. It was hot. It was on fire. His yelp was only stopped by the piercing headache he suddenly got. A warm fluid dripped from his nose. Blood.

"Klara!"

The pain stopped, as did the burning and numbness. A large snap made his heart skip a beat. A whoosh of air followed. He opened his eyes.

The lock was gone, as was a good chunk of the door. Eisenhorn had seen several heist movies in his lifetime, all of them he liked well enough. One part he always enjoyed was when the cat burglar cut the glass in a perfect circle. Looking at the door now, he was reminded of such a ludicrous cinematic moment. The hole in the door was perfectly round, like a cat burglar had at it with a welding torch. He could stick his hand clean through it.

"Klara..." Eisenhorn had seen many strange things in the past few years, and this was certainly on the list. Klara had done this somehow. But why? Was it...?

Eisenhorn pushed on the door. It swung open with little resistance.

He was about to blow a gasket. Why hadn't Klara done this sooner? Then he felt more blood trickle from his nose. He tilted his head back to stop the bleeding. Maybe Klara couldn't have done whatever she did just now without hurting him. He also guessed she only chose now to help him because something was brewing in the Forbidden City, distracting the guards and Cloak. Escape was now feasible.

This wasn't the time for contemplation, though. This was the time to run.

Eisenhorn did just that. He darted out of his cell and did not slow down even to consider where he was going. He slammed through doors. He felt his feet hit the floor. He didn't care about being fatigued or conspicuous. He was free. He was free! He couldn't help but cry, despite it going against his masculine ideals.

"Klara, you magnificent conjurer!"

A guard ran by him. Eisenhorn skidded to a stop. The guard hadn't noticed him, but Eisenhorn once again became aware of his predicament. Guards were everywhere on high alert. The alarm was still blaring, which would help conceal the sounds he was bound to make, but that wouldn't be enough of an advantage. He needed to be careful. More than that, he needed a plan. He needed to know where to go.

It only took a moment's thought to determine his destination.

The syringe. Ever since that dream, Eisenhorn had been convinced. Klara didn't need to explain the importance of the syringe any longer. He knew all he had to know. It was the only thing that could stop whatever he had seen in his dream. That hand... Those eyes... They belonged to something. They belonged to the enemy.

They belonged to the Omega.

He had to go to his old room. He had stashed the syringe there over a year ago. It was still there. It must be.

But where was the room? Eisenhorn had a poor understanding of the Forbidden City's layout. He had scarcely been out of his torture chamber or previous accommodations. Even then, he was often moved around with a bag over his head. Asking for directions probably wasn't a good idea, so he decided to search the palace until he came across a familiar area. The trick was to avoid capture until then.

A sword jabbed him in the back. Too late.

Eisenhorn raised his hands. He glanced over his shoulder. Five guards, three with swords and two with machine guns, had snuck up on him.

"Take it easy there, fellas," he said calmly.

The guard who had him by sword point yelled something in Mandarin, though the general recognized a few swears here and there. The sword pushed harder into his back, piercing his ragged clothing and digging into his skin. He growled like a bulldog. No way was he going back to his cell. He would rather die taking these men on.

The guards dropped their weapons in order to clutch their chests. They went down hard and fast.

Eisenhorn rubbed his back, perplexed and relieved, thinking these men were dead. But they convulsed again. A few gasped. One moaned.

"This is *way* too easy," a constipated voice said.

"Believe me, it's going to get a lot harder," a woman said. Eisenhorn liked this voice but didn't recognize it. He did, however, recognize the former. There was no way he could forget a voice like that. Flashbacks bombarded his fractured mind.

The Helmet Man strolled down the hall, doing a little jig at one point. A woman in white walked by his side. A toy-like gun hung from her shoulders. She moved with more purpose than her counterpart. A jittery older man wearing a large backpack followed close behind them. This trio was the definition of oddball.

"Some kind of hallucination," Eisenhorn muttered. He eyeballed the silver helmet again, was reminded of Temple, and shivered.

"Hey, pal, you don't look so hot!" Slate yelled at him. The three newcomers stopped in front of him. The woman looked at him with mild pity, noticing his gaunt and unsanitary appearance. The jittery old man kept a good distance away. Eisenhorn paid him no mind. Slate was the real object of interest.

"Well, I never expected to see you again," Eisenhorn said, straightening his posture. "That is if you aren't a hallucination of some kind. Heard you ran off with Incognito. I better have heard wrong, boy. Still, it's good to see a familiar ... uh ... face."

Slate tilted his shiny head. "Who are you again?"

Eisenhorn went red. "What! You don't recognize me? How dare you? After all we went through! Traversing that forsaken desert and fighting those super-human freaks should have ingrained me in your memory for life."

"I know him," the woman said, putting a finger under her sharp chin. "He's one of your companions you escaped with from the Bunker. General Eisen-horn, I believe."

The old man with the backpack gasped at the mention of Eisenhorn's name. The general hardly noticed. He was too ticked at the Helmet Man.

Slate wagged his finger. "Yeah, now I remember. He was the only one in the group crazier than me!"

"Hey, I resent that," Eisenhorn spat.

"How come you remembered him and I didn't?" Slate asked his female counterpart.

"Because you have a selective and unreliable memory," she said. "I was also Houdini's go-to lady at the time, so I have an intimate knowledge of your companions."

"You're one of the Gifted!" Eisenhorn cried. "I knew you were too pretty to be trusted!"

"I used to be a part of Cloak. Now I'm working with Slate. I regret the deaths of your cadets. I could not stop it from happening in time. Forgive me."

"Her name's Naomi," Slate said. "She's got superpowers like me. She's cool. And she's mine, so quit giving her pervy glances."

"I'll look at her however I want to, cretin!"

"Man, I must have repressed you. Oh, Gilda and Straper are here too."

"Who the hell are they?"

"Cadets from the Bunker."

"My cadets are here too? Good lord, what would Johnson think?"

"Incognito's also here, so you'll have to deal with that."

This was too much for Eisenhorn. He needed to sit down.

"We're here to destroy Cloak," Slate said. "Believe me, I don't like Incognito either, but I'll take care of him later. Oh, here's my dad! Call him Oscar!" He grabbed the jittery old man by the shoulders, presenting his pseudo-father to the general. Oscar was too stunned to offer up a decent greeting. The same went for Eisenhorn.

"I'm sorry to interrupt your reunion," Naomi said. "But more guards will be coming soon." She kicked one of the unconscious guards to emphasize the point. "General, do you know how to get to the loading bay?"

Eisenhorn rubbed his head. "No ... sorry, lady. I need to get to my old room. I left something important there. Can't remember where it is, though."

"I don't have time to show you around. Just wait here."

Slate shrugged. "You can come with me. I'll appreciate the conversation."

"Sounds like you're getting the better end of that deal," Eisenhorn said.

"Hey, I'm the only one who gets to tell jokes at other people's expense!"

"He has a dangerous mission," Naomi told Eisenhorn. "You shouldn't go."

"Oh, where are you headed?" Eisenhorn asked the Helmet Man.

"To the throne room. I'm gonna punch the emperor right in the kisser."

"Don't tell him that," Naomi snapped. "And you're not to harm the emperor."

"The throne room..." Eisenhorn had never been inside, but he had once passed the large doors when they were shut. He might be able to find his room from there. "All right, I'll take you up on your offer, Helmet Man. Just watch my back, and I'll watch yours."

"Sounds like you're getting the better end of *that* deal," Slate said.

Naomi sighed. "Just go. Oscar and I need to get to the force field generator."

Slate marched down a hallway to his right. "Okay, see you, babe! You too, Daddio!"

Eisenhorn turned to Naomi. "You could do better, sweetheart. Trust me."

He then ran after Slate.

Naomi rubbed her eyes. "I hate coincidences. They usually mean trouble." She saw Oscar was still uneasy. "Are you okay?"

Oscar shook his head. "No, I'm not. Let's just get to the generator. I must speak with General Eisenhorn later. I have something important to tell him."

***

"So, what are you doing in the Forbidden City?" Slate asked Eisenhorn. "Take a wrong turn at Albuquerque?"

The general remembered the black hole. And the eyes…

"Hey, I asked you a question, old-timer!" Slate yelled.

"I … I'm an ambassador," Eisenhorn muttered. He grabbed his side in pain. He had a hard time keeping up with the Helmet Man, who was walking at a brisk pace. Eisenhorn's gut hurt too. The blood from his nose had run down the back of his throat and irritated his stomach, as if being half-starved wasn't bad enough.

Slate laughed. "You, an ambassador? No wonder World War III started."

"It doesn't help that you've made a mess of things. Working for Incognito? The nerve! Nobody has common sense these days. Nobody!"

"I'll give you that. If you think I'm annoying, just wait till you meet Incognito."

The general frowned. It wasn't in his nature to be deceitful, but he didn't know what the Helmet Man would do if he found out about the bomb in his head. Eisenhorn didn't think he would kill him, but he sure would try to stop him from setting it off, or at least his girlfriend might. That was why he had decided to keep that info to himself.

Eisenhorn was definitely going to inject himself. He might try to warn the Helmet Man and his friends beforehand. It might even be possible to convince them to take Shu and Xing with them. However, if it came down to it, he would be willing to inject himself and let the others die. Cloak needed to be stopped at all costs. That dream had been convincing.

"More guards," Slate said. "Leave it to me."

Ten palace guards in red uniforms screamed and came at them with raised swords. Slate bumped his fists together. The guards fell on their faces. He bumped his fists again, bringing the guards back from the dead. They were too incapacitated to be any sort of threat. By Eisenhorn's estimate, Slate had taken down around fifty guards since he had met up with him.

"How come you ain't killing them?" he demanded. "Are you an imperialist sympathizer?"

"What, you think I'm doing it because I don't want to hurt my fellow countrymen?" Slate scoffed. "I don't know why I'm being so merciful. Maybe I don't want to have double standards. I try not to kill Western Union soldiers either."

"You're gonna have to kill sometime, son. Better not wuss out at the last second."

"Hey, this 'wuss' just took out ten armed men! And keep up! You're falling behind."

Eisenhorn was panting so hard, his throat hurt. His stomach growled too. Burning this much energy and using such atrophied muscles was going to kill him if he wasn't careful. Only thoughts of Shu, Klara, Johnson, and the syringe kept him moving.

They were getting close to the throne room. They were also encountering more guards, so many that the Helmet Man was always bumping his fists, careful to always restart his victims' hearts. A few guards with guns got some shots off before going down. Slate made the bullets explode before they had a chance to hit either Eisenhorn or him.

The floor was soon covered with dozens of unconscious bodies. Guns and swords slipped out of limp hands, making a constant clatter that meshed well with the screams and yelps of the soldiers. Eisenhorn had tried to step over them but gave up pretty quickly, settling for stepping only on their nonsensitive bits. It was a dreamlike scenario. He looked around, expecting Klara to pop up. The exploding bullets were like firecrackers. The red-clad bodies that kept piling up made him think he was wading through a sea of blood.

The massive doors to the throne room were now visible. A hundred guards stood in front of them. They were armed to the teeth and scared out of their minds. A line of men stood in front of their comrades, holding up bullet-proof shields.

But the Helmet Man had no need for bullets. He bumped his fists. The hundred men fell. A dozen guns went off before they did. Only one bullet made contact, since Slate was starting to get a little worn out. It bounced harmlessly off his helmet, as he knew it would.

"Good warm-up," Slate said. He restarted all his enemies' hearts and stretched his arms.

"I need booze," the general murmured.

"That's the spirit."

"Spirits? You got any?"

Slate and Eisenhorn traversed the mountain of moaning men. Weak hands grasped at the Helmet Man's ankles. He easily kicked himself free. The duo reached the throne room doors. Slate examined the obstacle and pressed his hand against the wood.

"There are a lot of baddies in there," he said.

Eisenhorn almost asked how he knew that, only to remember this weirdo "saw" differently. "Who's in there?" he asked instead.

"A bunch of guards, one huge guy, another with a rifle, and some old dude sitting in a big chair, the emperor probably." Slate paused. "Temple isn't here. Guess that means I can go in."

Eisenhorn was so relieved that he wet himself a bit. "I'll man the fort. Go on in, son. Kick some Chinamen ass."

"Racist old fart, I already told you I'm Chinese."

"When did you start giving a damn about being politically correct?"

Slate had a witty reply, but he wasn't able to get it out. Something was fast approaching. He kicked Eisenhorn out of the way with only half a second to spare.

A black metal ball slammed into Slate. He was thrown back twenty feet and crashed through small doors that led to a balcony. He found himself lying on it, sore all over.

"Guess the easy part's over," Slate groaned.

"You guessed correctly," Mistress Lotus boomed. She rolled faster than a sports car, not the least bit concerned about the guards getting crushed under her bulk, and collided with him. Both of them smashed through the railing and toppled off the balcony.

"The Chinese Empire does not forgive, Helmet Man!"

It took General Eisenhorn a full minute before he could get his head back on straight, his chest still aching from the kick. He was lying on top of several unconscious guards. He sat up, coughing up a lung. Slate was nowhere to be seen. Eisenhorn wasn't worried. That nitwit could handle himself, and he had his own hide to worry about.

A rusty and prolonged creaking grabbed his attention.

The doors to the throne room were opening.

Eisenhorn wasn't a coward. Under normal circumstances, he would have taken on the emperor and his goons with nothing but his belt if he had to. But that dream had been *really* persuasive. Fighting now would doom his mission to failure.

There were two options besides surrender. One was to run away, but there wasn't enough time for that. The doors were almost fully open now, and he could hear footsteps approaching.

The second option was to hide. This was more doable. Eisenhorn grunted as he rolled an unconscious guard over and slipped between that guard and another one. *Men shouldn't have to be this close together,* the general thought, finding that he was doing a lot of things lately that went against his sensibilities. He grabbed a jacket from a nearby guard to conceal himself further. It was far from a perfect hiding place, but as long as nobody looked too closely, he could easily be missed in this sea of bodies.

Thirty guards poured out of the throne room. They scanned the area and poked several of their unconscious comrades to see if they were okay. One snooping guard came close to uncovering Eisenhorn, almost pushing off the jacket that covered the general with the barrel of his rifle. Eisenhorn forced himself to stop breathing, but he had no voluntary control over his pounding heart.

Someone yelled at the guard, who yelled a reply in Mandarin and went to join his comrades. Eisenhorn let out a small breath as his heart slowed.

A man with a rifle and a conical hat emerged from the throne room. Eisenhorn recognized him as one of the cyborgs, Poppy. A group of soldiers came out after him, surrounding an imposing figure carrying a frail figure. It was Pansy, another Black Lotus agent. Eisenhorn had never seen the frail figure but guessed correctly who it was.

Poppy yelled something at Pansy, who shook his head in response. Poppy yelled again, getting impatient, judging by his tone. The emperor screeched like a crow. All the guards looked uncomfortable now. Poppy noticed this and switched to English.

"Let us use this foreign tongue so the men cannot overhear us," he told his brother. "We might as well. I have a feeling we will all be speaking it by the time this ordeal is over."

The emperor screeched again, this time like an alley cat with tuberculosis.

"We cannot stay here any longer," Poppy continued, ignoring his decrepit father. "The Helmet Man made it this far. He would have been in the same room as our emperor if Mother had not been here. Who knows how long she can hold him off? Even if she does defeat him, Incognito is likely close by. We must head for the pods."

"No, we shall head to an underground shelter," Pansy said. Eisenhorn was taken aback by the man's utter lack of accent and the sureness of his voice.

"Brother, I have a better handle on the situation," Poppy snapped.

"The enemy will be guarding the pods."

"I cannot believe this. Are you a coward?"

The emperor gurgled and screamed simultaneously, producing a unique noise that revolted and frightened the guards.

"I am not a coward," Pansy said. "You are merely foolhardy."

Poppy drew a pistol from his belt, walked up to Pansy, and cocked his weapon.

He pressed the gun between the emperor's eyes.

The guards were not quite sure what they were looking at. Neither was Eisenhorn as he watched from his hiding place. Never before had he seen such defiance against the emperor. It made him smile.

The response of the guards was slow and unremarkable. Pansy was the only one who could comprehend and almost moved to get the emperor out of the line of fire, but Poppy pressed the gun into his father's skull, a cool warning.

Pansy remained still. "What are you doing?" he asked neutrally.

The emperor was not sure what was going on himself, only making more animal noises. The guards were starting to get a handle on the situation and aimed their weapons at Poppy.

"I cannot stand it," Poppy hissed. "All my life, I have tolerated this nonsense. My mother, my siblings, all of you have such devotion to this creature, but I see no reason why you should. He has no respect or love for us. He would throw us all away if it meant he could live for an extra minute. But I was tolerant. I was tolerant because it meant so much to my family."

"Then why the change of heart?"

"Cloak was the last straw. My father's acceptance of those foreigners was him throwing away all his values. The only modicum of respect I ever held for him was his utter rejection of Western civilization, yet that creature of the West, that chrome beast, was standing behind his very throne only half an hour ago."

"You cannot kill him, brother."

"And why not?" Poppy put more pressure on the gun, making the emperor cry out in mild pain. Eisenhorn felt like nodding in approval.

"Because I have too much admiration for our mother to let you kill him," Pansy said. "If she believes in him, I shall too. I admire her more than anyone else. From her seemingly subservient position, she has carved a slice of power for herself."

"So, you also see what our father really is."

"I see you threatening the life of my mother's true love. You believe Cloak is behind the attack. Tell me, is what you are about to do part of their plan as well?"

Poppy examined his brother. Pansy was the quiet one, the one who was always vigilant, who seldom spoke but made his words count when he did. Because of this, Poppy had always respected him. That may have been the only reason he holstered his gun.

The emperor started laughing.

"I leave him to you," Poppy said, ever so tempted to take his gun out again. "I cannot be near this husk for a moment longer. Take him to the pods."

"Where are you going?" Pansy asked.

Poppy took his rifle off his back. He loaded a round into it. "Hunting."

He left his brother and father, pushing his way through the stunned guards.

"You always made Mother proud," Pansy told him.

Poppy did not look back.

As Pansy and the remaining guards took the emperor away, Eisenhorn lay still in his hiding place, contemplating the conversation he had overheard.

"Not my problem," he concluded. He got up when the emperor and his posse had left, but a whimper kept him from taking his leave. He recognized it and staggered into the throne room. It was more massive than he had ever imagined. Two dead guards were on the floor. One had stabbed himself. The other had a hole in his head. The general knew what had killed the latter and retched in remembrance. Then he saw a woman curled up in one corner, the source of the whimpering.

"Shu..." he whispered, walking up to her.

She stood up to face him. He saw the swelling and the tears. He also saw the shame. She covered her mouth. More tears came.

Eisenhorn didn't waste any time with words. The general put his shriveled arms around her frame and let her cry. To him, it was the only thing that had felt right in a long time.

***

"You sure you don't want one of these guns, Gilda?"

"No, keep them for yourself," she told Straper. "Your aim is better than mine, and each one of those guns is only good for one shot. We need to be careful not to waste them. Besides, I can't fire a gun while I'm busy piloting my walker."

"That's what I get for being a gentleman," Straper said. He was crouched behind a stack of metal boxes with two of the special guns propped up next to him. His rifle was aimed at the entrance to the loading bay, a stairwell that had been barricaded with containers.

Magenta stood near where he was crouched. It had been a real spectacle to see the compact walker unfold to its proper size, doing so like those toy cars that turned into robots. Then Magenta had barricaded the entrance with four large steel containers. It would take a lot to budge them, but Straper still didn't feel all that secure.

Xing had left soon after Slate and the others. He planned on lying low until the fight for the Forbidden City was finished, stashed away in some cramped shelter out of harm's way. In Straper's opinion, this strategy was not manly.

Incognito was still with Gilda and Straper. He hadn't bothered to take cover, resigning himself to pacing around the room until his talents were needed.

"Thank goodness we're back together again," Tim told Gilda. "I was worried that you forgot all about your autopilot pal."

"Yeah, how could I forget?" Gilda said, having forgotten his existence on multiple occasions. "Just keep the conversation to a minimum. We must stay vigilant."

There was a muffled explosion, which sounded like it had come from the surface. The loading bay shook. Dust floated down to coat them.

Incognito glanced up, squinting. "Fang has begun to break into the tunnel from above. I believe that is my cue to leave." He checked the tunnel entrance, which blast doors had sealed off. "Those doors will only hold off Fang's soldiers for a few minutes should they gain access to the tunnel."

Another tremor sent a slab of concrete falling from the ceiling, bouncing off Magenta's armor and breaking into a hundred pieces on the floor.

"Ouch!" Tim yelled. "That would've hurt if I had been human."

Incognito twirled his scythe. "They are certainly persistent."

"Get moving already!" Gilda shouted at him from her walker.

"Your ribbits have no effect on me, little toad. I will leave when I am good and ready." A third tremor came. More dust rained down. "Very well, I am ready now."

Incognito flew through the blast doors and disappeared. Gilda made a rude gesture. Straper felt like making one of his own, but a loud boom distracted him.

"That one sounded close," Gilda said, raising Magenta's arms in a defensive posture.

"It wasn't from above," Straper said, aiming his rifle at the barricaded stairwell. One of the steel containers had toppled over.

Someone was trying to get in.

"Crap, where's Incognito when you need him?" Straper asked.

***

Naomi was having a harder time dispatching the guards compared with Slate. She was also having more trouble not killing them. The temptation was ever-present. It wasn't as if she had bloodlust, but mercy was just so much work.

Five more guards came at her with swords. She snatched the blades from their hands telekinetically; the guards were flabbergasted by their floating weapons. Then she knocked their heads together, bent their swords, and bound them with their ruined instruments.

Oscar watched from a distance and only approached when Naomi was finished with her handiwork. She was covered in a thin sheen of sweat.

"It should be just down this hallway," he said. "Good work, by the way."

Naomi heard a muffled explosion. Had that come from outside? "Let's just get this done. It'll be one less thing to worry about."

The ceiling collapsed in front of them. Naomi stopped several planks with her mind from falling on Oscar's head. Then she waved her hand, telekinetically clearing the hallway of floating sawdust, just in time to see a young woman drop down from above and land on the floor with a harsh thud. The young woman straightened herself out and grinned.

"Look like I got here just in time," she said in fractured English. "Helmet Man not here? Even better. Just us girls now."

Swords extended from her hands. Naomi readied her special gun.

Oscar took several steps back.

CHAPTER 48

The Helmet Man had never had a ton of bricks dropped on him before. However, lying on the ground, he felt like his recent experience came the closest to it.

"Hurts to breathe..." Slate wheezed. "And I don't even breathe..."

"I did not anticipate our fight would be so short," his opponent said.

Slate got to his feet. He had landed in the courtyard surrounding the palace. The grass had just been cut, so bits of it clung to his outfit. The sky was electric blue from the force field. Distant explosions could be heard.

Snipers were positioned on the outer wall, the man with the silver helmet in their sights. Guards from inside the palace surrounded Slate from a safe distance. Mistress Lotus herself waited fifteen feet from him, passive and unmoving.

"You're one tough cookie," Slate told her. "But you just caught me by surprise. Your goons won't last the first round, even if you do."

"You will find that many of your tricks are of no use here," she replied.

"How about this one?" Slate prepared to bump his fists.

But before they could touch, a wave of pain overtook him, a pain that boiled through every one of his veins. There was no apparent cause. His entire body was afflicted. The Helmet Man collapsed, unable to use his devastating technique.

"Hurts..." Slate croaked. "What ... what shit are you pulling?"

"All water within my vicinity bends to my will," Mistress Lotus boomed. "Even the water within your body does my bidding. I can only weakly control such a small amount of fluid, but it is enough to cause immense discomfort."

Mistress Lotus pulled on the Helmet Man like a black moon tugging on the ocean. Slate could move, pushing himself off the ground, but that hurt even worse than not moving at all. He got on his hands and knees. Electricity sparked off him savagely.

"Getting up was an unwise decision." Mistress Lotus switched to Mandarin. "Sniper Eighty, leg!"

A bullet tore through Slate's calf. He swore and fell again.

"Who else is here with you?" Mistress Lotus demanded.

"None of your business, bowling ball…"

"Sniper Seventy-One, arm!"

Sniper Seventy-One did as he was told. The bullet didn't do as much damage as the last one, only taking a small chunk out of Slate's shoulder. It was still an excruciating experience.

"I only take mild pleasure from this," Mistress Lotus said. "Who gave you access to the pod tunnel?"

Slate sensed a pillar nearby. It held up the balcony he had fallen from.

"Sniper Eighty-Two, torso!"

Slate wasn't stupid enough to let himself get shot again. He sent a surge of energy through the earth, setting the grass alight. The smoke obscured the sniper's view as he pulled the trigger. The bullet missed Slate by a good foot.

With great effort and agony, Slate lifted his right arm and fired a beam. It hit the pillar, which burst into a shower of woodchips. The balcony groaned as gravity ripped it from its perch. Mistress Lotus and the guards had no time to move. There was a loud crash, screams from the guards, and a cloud of sawdust, further impeding the snipers. Some of those guards were likely killed.

Slate shrugged weakly. "Meh, I deserve some leeway."

The pain left him. He was sore in places he never thought could get sore, but that didn't keep him from getting up and limping away. If he was going to have a fighting chance against Mistress Lotus, he had to stay out of her range, whatever that was. Maybe then he would get lucky and nail her with a beam.

A black metal ball, three feet in diameter, smashed out of the palace, leaving a gaping hole in the wall as it sped toward the Helmet Man. Slate jumped out of the way. The ball hit a thin tree instead. A loud snap was how the life of the tree ended. It fell into a pond and made an undramatic splash. The black ball revved up, ripping up the grass and kicking up dirt before accelerating at its target once more.

Slate was confused. That couldn't be Mistress Lotus. Had she dug herself out of that wreckage already? No, that ball wasn't her. It didn't have a face.

Regardless, the ball was still dangerous. He leaped out of its path. The ball passed him and made a U-turn, coming back for a third time.

"Wait, what am I doing?" Slate wondered. All this dodging was starting to make him look like a wimp. He needed to act. He charged his fist. The ball was closing in now. It had serious momentum.

Slate punched the ball, letting the blasted thing drive itself into his fist, and tore a hole through it. Steam billowed out of the back of the deadly sphere, its outer shell shattering into sizable metal fragments. He expected to see wires or guts spill from the ball, but there was only a puddle of water and lots of steam left over.

Slate realized it was just a big old water container. It must have been some kind of decoy controlled by Mistress Lotus. Were there more?

Two more black balls appeared, answering his question. They were coming from opposite directions. He jumped. They bounced off each other instead and became seemingly disoriented. Slate landed away from them.

At least twenty more black balls appeared. They circled around the Helmet Man like hungry sharks. He didn't like these odds. Perhaps it was time to fly away.

Before he could even get his feet off the ground, pain overcame him. He didn't collapse this time, but he lost his balance and stumbled backward.

"I created these containers to give my children practice in dodging," Mistress Lotus said. She was among the herd of black balls, but Slate was in too much discomfort to determine which one was her. "None of them have ever lasted more than five minutes. I doubt you will be able to break their record." The balls rolled faster around him now. "I have been working on a new technique. It is more intimidating than practical but lethal all the same."

The balls began to pile up onto each other. Some water leaked from them and coated their surfaces. The pile of balls started to take shape, turning into something resembling a mind-boggling piece of modern art.

They had come together into a humanoid form. Three balls made up each leg, four for each arm, and the rest for the torso. The black ball with the face, Mistress Lotus, took the position in the center of the chest. The water kept them all fused together. This amalgamation towered over the Helmet Man, over twenty feet in height, larger than an average walker.

"I give you points for creativity," Slate grunted, suppressing his hurt. "But your form leaves something to be desired."

The air was clearing. The snipers were finally able to get a clean shot at the Helmet Man. Meanwhile, at least fifty guards armed with machine guns ran to aid Mistress Lotus.

"Have any more tricks at your disposal, Helmet Man?" she spat.

***

High General Fang was out of his league.

This was something he would never admit to himself, let alone anyone else, but it was the truth. He had only vague ideas on how to handle this situation, and they were all long shots.

Fang stood on the back of a truck, holding binoculars. A small microphone was attached to his coat so he could give orders through the loudspeakers positioned throughout the endless Tiananmen Square. Besides him, there were only a hundred normal men. The other three hundred thousand were all victims of the nanobots. They obeyed simple orders well, but their movements were sluggish and their wits dim.

Thistle sat next to Fang with her arms wrapped around her folded legs, whispering to herself. Fang felt tempted to kick her. He only refrained from doing so because he knew Mistress Lotus would not tolerate that, even if he was a high general.

Things had begun to go wrong when he got a radio transmission from the palace. Intruders had broken in using the pod tunnel. Fang had alerted all his troops. They responded robotically, raising their weapons in a jerky manner, the walkers even more clumsy. Fang couldn't help but detest the hand he had been dealt. These creatures could barely pull a trigger. How could they operate walkers effectively?

More radio transmissions came in. Dozens of guards inside the palace were being taken out, nonlethally to add to the strangeness, a concept that confused and annoyed Fang. The latest transmission informed him that the emperor had fled his throne room and was now attempting to escape in one of the pods.

This had convinced Fang beyond a reasonable doubt to act. The Black Lotus said they were going to take the force field down, but who knew how long that would take or if they could even do it? He would not wait any longer.

"Detonate all the land mines within Sector Fifty-Two!"

"Sir, there are still troops stationed there," a human officer said.

Fang yanked out his pistol and put a bullet through the officer's head. He turned to another officer who quickly carried out his orders by pressing some buttons on a portable control panel inside the truck.

Ten mines near the Forbidden City went off. The brainwashed soldiers standing directly on them were vaporized while the ones standing close by were torn to shreds. They all took this in good grace, which further annoyed Fang. Smoke choked the air. Debris sizzled as they hit the force field. A large crater now marred Tiananmen Square. More mines went off, killing more soldiers and even destroying a valuable walker.

There seemed to be little logic to Fang's strategy at first glance. In reality, he was using the mines to help begin the excavation process. With the force field in place, there was only one way into the Forbidden City, and that was the pod tunnel. One would have to dig in order to reach it, since there were no maintenance shafts within a hundred kilometers, a security measure that was now proving to be a major hindrance. As soon as Fang set off enough land mines, he would order his troops to dig the remainder of the way—by hand, if necessary—until they broke through to the tunnel.

As for why he didn't move his troops safely away before setting off the mines, he believed that time was of the essence and any meandering could mean endangering the emperor. In any event, he didn't care much for these lifeless soldiers anyway, and only a few hundred would perish. That still left thousands upon thousands.

The mines stopped exploding. Smoke cleared. Corpses smoldered. Hocking a loogie, Fang was about to order his troops to commence the excavation.

Then five hundred soldiers sank into the ground.

It happened so fast that Fang thought his eyes were playing tricks on him. He peered through his binoculars to confirm his initial observation was accurate.

Countless arms and heads were sticking out of the concrete. All the men appeared to be dead, but Fang could never tell with those freaks of nature. Had the exploding mines caused the concrete to collapse beneath them?

Another five hundred soldiers sank into the ground, as did several walkers. The soldiers next to them sank too, followed by more nearby soldiers. It was like a terrible game of dominos. Fang was sweating now, as were the officers standing near him. Something was gobbling up his men, and it sure wasn't quicksand.

Within a minute, ten thousand soldiers were gone.

"Sir, you have a call," said a trembling officer. He gave Fang a handheld radio. Fang snatched it up and pressed it to his ear.

"I see you've run into a little snag," Sebastian said, static lacing his voice.

"What am I looking at?" Fang demanded. A hundred more soldiers vanished.

"Incognito, I presume. That's usually the go-to explanation for such bizarreness."

"My men are sinking into the earth!"

"Our common enemy must be making the ground intangible beneath their very feet. How clever. I always wondered if he could do that."

"Explain this to me!"

"Incognito can walk through walls much like a ghost. He can also make other objects intangible by touching them. However, whenever Incognito passes through solid matter, he runs the risk of accidentally becoming solid. Doing so would cause his molecules to fuse with the wall or whatever object he's going through at the moment. But it seems he has turned his weakness into a weapon. He's probably gliding through the ground as we speak, making sections of the square intangible as he passes under them. Your men sink almost all the way under before the ground is made tangible once more and their molecules fuse with the concrete, killing them. My goodness, just imagine the mess..."

"How do I kill this specter?"

"Energy, such as heat or electricity, is his weakness. You have land mines, don't you? Use them to flush him out. When he's out in the open, have your men use explosives and flamethrowers. Maybe get that Black Lotus girl to help you out. I shall be along in an hour or so. Hang tight until the cavalry arrives."

Fang tensed up. How did that grinning serpent know Thistle was next to him? The girl had been crying ever since the men started sinking into the ground. Fang gave her a sour look and turned the radio off, not bothering to hear what else Sebastian had to say, though he got the feeling the blind man had already said everything he wanted to.

"Be ready, girl!" Fang barked at Thistle. "Kill the foreigner when he appears!" He turned to the officer manning the control panel. "Detonate all land mines within Sector Forty-Five and Thirty-Five! Force the mongrel out of hiding!"

Dozens upon dozens of guards poured into the loading bay, half of them waving swords, the other half firing their guns. The boxes that Straper hid behind kept him safe from bullets, at least for now. He poked his head out occasionally either to shoot guards with tranquilizers or knock them out with rubber bullets. But more guards simply came, stepping over their fallen comrades. It was getting harder by the minute for him to keep up this non-lethal approach.

Gilda was having just as much trouble, using rubber bullets and nets to ward off the guards. Sometimes, she got Magenta to sweep its leg to knock over the guards who got too close. But even with her walker, she would soon be overrun.

"Ms. Gilda, be more conservative with your ammunition," Tim told her. "You're spraying it all over the place."

"That's because the guards *are* all over the place," she snapped.

A bullet ricocheted off her walker. Despite the warning from Oscar about the weaker armor, Magenta was holding up pretty well. However, these guards were only armed with machine guns. If heavier artillery arrived, she might be in trouble.

And that was exactly what happened.

"Gilda, check it out," Straper said into his earphone. "The Black Lotus is here."

Gilda had already noticed the large bald man entering the room. It was Pansy. She recognized him from the sketch. It had to be him.

"Straper, use the gun!"

He shot another guard in the leg. "Not till he gets closer."

Pansy raised one of his arms. His hand fell off, something that made Straper yell, "Seriously, brah?" There was no bloody stump at the end of Pansy's arm.

Just the barrel of a rocket launcher.

Magenta maneuvered out of the way as a rocket came out. The project-ile struck the concrete wall. The explosion was small yet hot enough to make Straper sweat.

"Man, this guy deserves a real bullet." Straper aimed for Pansy's forehead and nailed him between the eyes.

It didn't even break the skin.

"Maybe an eye, then!" Straper shot Pansy's left eyeball.

Pansy squinted and rubbed his face. His eye was unharmed.

"What's this guy made out of?" Straper yelled.

"Something expensive," Gilda said. She fired her cannon arm at the in-coming guards. It was a concussion shot, so they were only blown back and rendered unconscious.

Pansy fired another rocket. This one blew up right in front of Magenta, which staggered back and nearly toppled. Gilda steadied her walker, only to find that Pansy had sprinted over to their side of the room. He now stood in front of Magenta, unmoving and stoic.

Magenta threw a roundhouse kick. Pansy raised his arm to block it. The walker's leg hit him dead-on, but he did not budge an inch. If anything, the walker's armor was dented.

"Now would be a good time to use the cannon!" Straper yelled.

Gilda fired a shell directly at Pansy. It hit his chest and exploded loud enough to deafen several nearby guards. The smoke obscured a lot, but it was clear that she had not missed.

Pansy walked out of the smoke. His clothes were in tatters. He cleared his throat with a cough and waved smoke from his eyes.

Gilda scowled. "Shit, it didn't work... Straper, I'll let you take care of this one!"

"Hey, I thought I was supposed to be the fraidy-cat!"

"You have that special gun! Shoot him! I'll keep the guards occupied for you."

Pansy snapped his head toward Straper and aimed his rocket-launcher arm.

"Dude, he just heard our conversation!" Straper cried. "He knows about the gun!"

"Damn it! He's been listening in on our communications this whole time!"

Pansy fired. The resulting explosion knocked over the boxes Straper had taken cover behind. Straper rolled out of the way, his own protection almost flattening him. Pansy was approaching him now, implacable to his very core, raising his lethal arm again.

Straper scrambled to his feet. He was out in the open with an indestructible man coming to kill him. He saw that the special gun was ten feet away to his left. There was no way that he could get to it without Pansy blowing him up first.

Wait, indestructible...

"Gilda, fire some tear gas over here!"

Gilda didn't question him. She was too busy warding off the guards and had an implicit trust in Straper forged by numerous battles together. She simply fired a tear gas canister, which hit the floor near Pansy. At the same moment, Pansy fired. The gas distracted him, however, and he missed Straper. The rocket flew and destroyed several pods along the wall, turning them into burned-out shells.

Straper pulled up his shirt, covering his mouth as best as he could. Pansy started coughing up a storm, as did many of the guards in the vicinity. Straper's eyes teared up as he ran over and picked up his plastic gun.

With watery eyes, he aimed the gun at Pansy and pulled the trigger.

Pansy froze as if Straper had hit a pause button. Then the cyborg fell backward and hit the floor with a metallic thud. The loading bay started getting quiet now. No more guards were entering the area, and Gilda had nonlethally taken out the rest of them. Straper ran over to a panel on a wall and turned on the vents to clear the bay of tear gas. Then he flushed his eyes out with some water from his canteen and gulped the rest down.

"You all right, Straper?" Gilda asked.

"Just give…" Straper coughed. "Just give me a sec…"

An indestructible man… Straper knew someone who was just as sturdy as Pansy had been: Thomas. The young prince, however, was vulnerable to weapons attacking the respiratory system. Straper had seen Pansy coughing on smoke, so he figured the cyborg was also vulnerable to tear gas. It was too tempting not to exploit such a weakness.

Straper grabbed another canteen and flushed his eyes out a second time. He blinked rapidly and glanced at Pansy. The cyborg was dead. The vacant stare and lack of color were obvious signs. Straper had set his gun to kill. It seemed logical at the time.

"Guess we couldn't spare all of them," he mumbled.

"Straper, there was no other way," Gilda said. "He was too dangerous. Even if we had only stunned him, he could have gotten up later and kept on fighting."

"It's okay," Straper said. "I killed that pirate before, remember?"

"I know, but you…"

"I'm going to gather up the guards' weapons, you know, in case they wake up or get out of their nets. Don't want to kill anybody else, right?"

He began to confiscate firearms. Several unconscious guards mumbled as they were disarmed but made no move to retaliate.

Gilda sadly watched Straper. "I worry about him."

"Yes," Tim told her. "Just like I worry about you, Ms. Gilda."

***

Lily made the first move.

Naomi made the second. She pulled out her plastic weapon as Lily charged, planning to make her one shot count.

Naomi heard a bang. A bullet would have buried itself into her back had she not caught it with her mind. Five guards had shown up and were firing at her from behind. She swept her leg, producing a powerful gust of wind that knocked the guards' legs out from under them. They all fell into a pile, moaning.

But Lily had kicked the special gun out of her hand while she wasn't paying attention. It shattered against the wall. Naomi swore. Oscar groaned.

"You going to have to fight me old-fashioned way!" Lily told her. She swung both her swords. Naomi ducked, a few strands of her hair getting cut instead, and sent a barrage of telekinetic punches into Lily's torso.

Lily grimaced but was unharmed. She kicked Naomi, who could not dodge in time. Naomi flew back and hit the wall. If that kick had been slightly higher, it might have crushed her windpipe, but she had gotten away with only a sore chest.

Lily came at her again, but Naomi was prepared. She focused on her opponent's head.

Skidding to a stop, Lily's snakelike smile was replaced with an irritated sneer as invisible hands twisted her head to the right. The resistance Lily gave was unexpected. Not only was her neck nearly unbreakable, but she was also ludicrously strong. A spasm of pain went through Naomi's skull as she fought to snap Lily's neck.

"Oscar, get to the generator already!" Naomi commanded.

All this kinetic violence had thrown Oscar off. He wiped his sweaty forehead and ran for the generator room at the end of the hall. He thought of staying to help Naomi but realized he would just get in the way, maybe even be taken hostage.

"Think you already won, missy?" Lily snarled. She punched the wall and tore out a metal pipe. A stream of water erupted, hit Naomi in the chest, and slammed her against the wall, soaking her.

She had lost her hold on Lily's neck. Now the Black Lotus agent was free to chop her to pieces. Lily ran at her, feet splashing on the wet floor. She ignored the fleeing Oscar. She was too pumped to care.

Naomi got to her feet. Noticing a wooden panel had recently been put up, she kicked the wall to her right, smashing it open. She saw a big black power cable embedded within. The Forbidden City had once been devoid of technology, but ever since the conductive mesh had been installed, electricity now flowed through the palace.

How fitting that this modernization would be a cyborg's undoing, Naomi thought. She ripped the cable in half and dropped both ends on the wet floor, making sure to levitate slightly to avoid getting shocked. Sparks spewed. Water even sizzled. Lily convulsed, but not as violently as Naomi had anticipated. Lily just gritted her teeth and kept walking.

"Electricity ... no kill ... stupid lady..."

Lily kicked the tiles. Her repulsion pad accelerated her so fast, she no longer touched the floor. Her sword was aimed at Naomi's head.

Naomi quickly leaned to the side. The sword cut her ear and was embedded in the wall. Smirking, she used her powers to bend the sword around a metal girder. Lily dropped back on the floor, getting electrocuted for a second time. She convulsed as she tried to yank her weapon from the wall.

"Stupid sword," the cyborg seethed. "Not supposed to break again..."

Naomi flew away. Lily attempted to swat her out of the air with her other sword arm, only cutting Naomi's ankle. Naomi landed on a dry section of floor and used her powers to obtain one of the beaten guard's guns. Using all her strength, Lily broke her sword to get free and retracted what remained of her ruined blade into her hand. She only had one functional blade left, but she planned to make good use of it.

Naomi fired her machine gun. She didn't expect it to inflict much damage, but perhaps the cyborg might reconsider her course of action.

She didn't. At least twenty bullets hit Lily as she sprinted toward Naomi. Half of them bounced off her metal skeleton. The rest struck her fleshy parts. Her wounds bled steadily, but she was not deterred. If anything, she was starting to get a bit of a high.

"I cut you, lady! I cut you really good!" Lily shrieked maniacally, foaming at the mouth. Her eyes had lost their fox-like quality and become those of a jungle cat. She wasn't cunning anymore. She was savage, and it felt heavenly.

Naomi ran out of bullets. She threw the empty gun at Lily, who knocked it out of the air easily. When Lily got within range of Naomi, she swiped her last blade as many times as she could muster, trading accuracy for frequency and persistence. For Naomi, it was easy to avoid one sword swing. It was not so easy to avoid a hundred. Lily increased her pace, making Naomi move backward. She soon found her back pressed to the wall.

Lily pulled back for a finishing strike. "Gonna cut you, lady! Gonna watch you bleed!"

The blade pierced the wall. It missed Naomi, though it did cut her hip. She felt blood trickling down her leg and ignored it, focusing her mind instead on the power cable. It came to her, and she caught the insulated part with her hand.

"Give up," Naomi warned.

"I kill you!" It was unclear if Lily said these words out of anger or euphoria. Her face was stretched as only plastic should be able to. She tugged her sword out of the wall, preparing for another attack.

Naomi kicked Lily in the stomach, using her telekinesis for an added wallop. Ripples went through Lily's body, her mouth opening in reflex and surprise.

Naomi shoved the live power cable into Lily's mouth and down her esophagus. The sound Lily made was that of a walrus drowning in acid. Her lips blackened and shriveled into raisins. Fumes escaped her nostrils. Her arms twirled about, the sword almost slicing Naomi in half. Naomi was smart enough to move out of her reach. Lily attempted to pull the cable out, but Naomi forced it farther down with her mind until it reached the cyborg's stomach.

Lily's clothes caught fire, as did her skin and hair. Sparks came off the end of her sword. She fell to the wet floor and bashed her forehead on the tiles until she broke them. The floor gave out beneath her. Lily was now falling into a hallway on the floor below. The cable, with a snap, stopped her descent. What was left of Lily twitched for several seconds before ceasing movement altogether.

The remains hung in midair from the power cable as if she had died at the gallows. The corpse was burnt flesh with the occasional glint of the metal endoskeleton. Water from the floor above rained down over the dead cyborg and pooled on the floor below her.

Naomi staggered over and glanced down through the hole in the floor. She gagged, wishing the cyborg had died easier. She knelt down and started wringing out her wet hair.

"I've finished," Oscar said, walking out of the generator room. "There were guards in there, but I took care of them with some knock-out gas. Nobody should be able to turn off the generator now unless they have my password." He was about to say more but almost tripped when he saw the fallout. There was a huge hole in the floor, more holes in the walls, water everywhere, moaning guards, and a burnt body dangling from a cable.

Naomi sighed. "And we haven't even found Temple yet."

"This doesn't look familiar," Eisenhorn said. "Do you really know the way? No shame in admitting you're wrong. Plenty of shame in wasting valuable time."

"I am sure," Shu said. Her face was still swollen, but she didn't seem to be as rattled as when he found her. Shu had decided to help him get to his room, despite betraying the empire. They had been walking for twenty minutes now, navigating the labyrinth that was the Forbidden City.

There were few guards. Most of them were either busy fighting the invaders or had already been neutralized. Shu yelped whenever she saw guards lying on the floor. Eisenhorn repeatedly had to assure her that they were only unconscious. It got to the point where he grabbed her hand and put it next to an unconscious guard's nostrils so she could be sure he was still breathing. As for the other servants, Shu said they were supposed to go to a large bunker below the Forbidden City in the event of an attack and hole up there until the palace was secured. This was done so they wouldn't impede the guards.

Eisenhorn picked up one of the guards' machine guns from the floor. He found another and gave it to Shu, but she was obviously not comfortable with it.

"It is all crumbling," Shu said as she stared at her gun. "Maybe it was already crumbling before these invaders got here. You know who they are?"

"Yeah, one's the Helmet Man. He's a real character. I don't think you'll be able to wrap your mind around him. His father and girlfriend came along with him. Two of my old cadets are here too. Then there's Incognito, up to who knows what."

"I have heard of Incognito and how the West fears him."

"Hey, there's a difference between fear and caution!"

"Oh, sorry."

"Don't worry about it. I shouldn't have snapped. What do the Chinese think of Incognito and the United Third anyway?"

"We were ambivalent. He was an enemy of the West but seemed to share none of the Chinese Empire's interests either. Now it is clear he is our enemy."

"Who are you rooting for?"

"I simply want to get out of here alive."

"Tall order."

The sounds of footsteps and harsh whispers halted them.

"Quick, hide!" Eisenhorn whispered loudly, grabbing Shu by her arm. They dashed through the nearest door. The room they entered served as barren living quarters for servants, containing several thin mattresses on the floor and a row of small chests for clothing. They kept the door open a crack and peered out. Shu covered her mouth with trembling hands when she saw who approached. Eisenhorn saw too and emitted a low growl.

Five guards were escorting the emperor. One pushed him on some elaborate wheelchair. It cost more than a Western sports car judging by the jewels decorating it. The guards were scared, but the emperor himself was downright petrified. He tore imaginary cobwebs off his head and scratched at his face with unkempt nails. Eisenhorn felt his stomach turn. The guards, meanwhile, talked to each other nervously.

"What are they saying?" Eisenhorn asked in his quietest tone, which wasn't much better than a normal one. Hatred dripped from it.

"They say that the Forbidden City is lost," Shu said. "Pansy and the other guards failed to take the loading bay. They are going to put the emperor in his personal bunker until High General Fang gains access to the palace."

As the guards passed the room, Eisenhorn felt every muscle in his body urging him to jump into the hall and tear that so-called emperor a new one. Cloak may be the true enemy, but this dingleberry had done his share of foul things. He was an enemy of the Western Union. He had tortured him, oppressed his own people, and waged war on the world. But somehow, in Eisenhorn's book, Shu's battered face was the emperor's worst crime of all.

Eisenhorn raised his machine gun.

"What are you doing?" Shu gasped.

"Stay out of my way."

"You can't fight them all! What about your room? Don't you wish to go there?"

The syringe… Eisenhorn knew it was his ultimate goal, but that didn't seem to matter anymore. That dream had been convincing. However, his outrage was even more convincing at the moment.

Shu gulped. "Please, do not fight the emperor. His word is law."

Eisenhorn gritted his teeth. "I can't believe it. You still think your emperor shits gold."

"You do not understand…"

"How can you let that man get away with so much? How can you still worship him after he had you beaten to a pulp just for kicks?"

"Please, Randolph…"

The general swung open the doors and dashed into the hallway.

"Randolph!" Shu screamed.

***

Incognito lost count of how many soldiers he had killed.

They weren't really human anyway, but he didn't doubt for a moment that the Helmet Man and his allies would find some way to demonize him. They were always coming up with ways to elevate themselves over everyone else. Fine, let them feel superior. Such was his burden.

Flying through the ground had its difficulties. Incognito couldn't see anything, and he had to go up periodically to breathe, like a whale. None of the soldiers had noticed his head poking out of the ground in those brief instances when he needed to catch his breath and get his bearings. They were not a bright bunch, much to his advantage.

Hundreds of soldiers sank into Tiananmen Square as he made the ground beneath their feet intangible. They fused with the concrete as soon as he turned it solid again. He didn't know how long he could handle this, but the pain in his chest had been increasing ever since he started fighting. Even if his body could hold out, this whole endeavor was getting boring. Maybe there was another way to handle this situation.

A mine detonated. Incognito got out of the way in time. Another mine went off. He made a sharp turn to avoid being incinerated. Then all the mines within his vicinity detonated. Some even went off below him. Having no other alternatives, Incognito was forced to surface. Perhaps these foes were clever after all.

He flew out of the ground and went up about fifty feet before stopping. The mines had killed at least five hundred soldiers. His enemy clearly had little concern for collateral damage.

The brainwashed soldiers spotted Incognito. They reacted without fervor, but they worked quickly. Those with flamethrowers and explosive projectiles shot at him. The walkers also let loose their arsenal. The sky was now on fire.

Swerving and darting at supersonic speeds, Incognito managed to avoid being consumed by the dozens of explosions or the streams of flame that reached up almost a hundred feet. It was hard to avoid all their attacks, so he decided to use one of his tricks. He reached in his pocket and tossed out seven metal balls. They levitated, started projecting prerecorded images of himself, and went off in separate directions, drawing away enemy fire. Incognito snorted. The scene was spectacular, but it was child's play all the same.

Something shocked him. He felt his heart give out, a familiar experience that was just as painful as the last time. Was it the Helmet Man? No, it was something new and malicious. He started falling to the ground, solid once more and now a victim of gravity. His vision blurred. The explosions sounded fainter. The scythe was slipping from his fingers.

His prosthetic arm then restarted his heart. His vision cleared. The grip on his scythe tightened. He was still in pain, but he was also fully conscious now. He returned to his ethereal state and flew upward. His eyes caught sight of what had almost killed him.

A cloud of black smoke flew at him. He hadn't noticed it earlier due to the already smoky air. A missile exploded near him. He could feel the heat and went faster. The living smoke matched his speed. Bits of static coursed through it like a thundercloud.

"Nanomachines," Incognito muttered. One of the cyborgs must be controlling them, presumably the girl. The nanomachines were rubbing up against each other to create a charge. If that cloud got close enough, it could stop his heart again. He wasn't confident that the prosthetic arm could restart his heart for a third time, and he didn't want to put it to the test. The cloud was gaining on him, buzzing with energy.

The holograms impersonating Incognito were still distracting many of the soldiers, but they were getting picked off fast. Only three were left, swooping down at the soldiers like falcons. High General Fang saw these technological illusions through his binoculars. Then he saw that Thistle was in pursuit of one particular Incognito.

"SOLDIERS, AIM AT THE ONE THE CLOUD IS FOLLOWING!" Fang shouted, the loudspeakers sending his voice across the square.

The soldiers obeyed and turned their attention to the real Incognito. Much of their fire hit the force field covering the Forbidden City, but it held up to the bombardment. Now Incognito really had to work, both dodging the soldiers' volley and the cloud of nanomachines. The soldiers kept their eyes on their target, ignoring the holograms.

That was their big mistake.

The remaining three holograms dove toward the ground. Upon impact, the projectors exploded. Each explosion ended the lives of at least fifty brainwashed troops. One of the blasts knocked Fang off the back of his truck. He hit the concrete hard. Thistle also toppled off and was rendered unconscious after banging her head.

The cloud pursuing Incognito dissipated. He noticed this and realized one of the hologram projectors that blew up must have disabled the Black Lotus agent. With that information, it only took him a moment to spot Thistle lying next to a stunned officer who was likely High General Fang.

It was time for a direct confrontation.

Fang raised himself up on his forearms, his back aching. He saw Thistle sprawled next to him. The useless brat...

"What are you fools doing?" he yelled at his officers. "Help me up!"

The blast had disoriented the officers. They were not quick to help and came close to fainting when they saw the specter land near Fang.

"I grow tired of this," Incognito said. He jammed the butt of his scythe into Fang's neck, causing him to wheeze. The soldiers were no longer firing at the sky. They pointed their weapons at Incognito. They could not shoot, however, for Fang was in the way.

Incognito took some pressure off the scythe. Fang gasped, covered in sweat.

"Tell your soldiers to stand down," Incognito said. "Make no more attempts to enter the Forbidden City. Wait here like a good boy and stay out of my way. Do this and I might not disembowel your emperor. We can bargain over his life later."

He lifted the scythe off Fang's neck, whose face was beet red, both from the lack of oxygen and sheer fury at being humiliated.

"STAND DOWN!" he wheezed over the loudspeakers.

The soldiers lowered their weapons, their faces blank and uncaring.

Incognito picked up the unconscious Thistle. "I'll be taking this one off your hands. You should be thanking me. I get the impression you're not very good with children."

Incognito floated away with Thistle. Fang got on his knees and spat on the pavement. The slack-jawed officers stood back as he roared obscenities and beat at the square with his fists.

***

Ever since he was a toddler, Poppy had only cried twice in his life.

The first time was when he had his eyes surgically removed and replaced with prosthetic ones. His tear ducts were still intact, but he was a hard and unfeeling man. When he did feel, it was usually anger and the rare instance of amusement.

This was the second time he had cried.

Lily's corpse hung from the ceiling, charred so badly that it was nearly unrecognizable. It was the soot-covered blade extending from one of the hands that made identification possible. Poppy allowed himself to let loose two tears before burying his emotions. He aimed his rifle at the cable suspending Lily's remains and put a bullet through it. The cable snapped. The burnt cadaver fell. It made a loud clunk when it hit the floor.

Poppy relieved one of the unconscious guards of his coat and put it over his dead sister. She had not been a good person, but she had been a good sibling, the only person he had ever felt comfortable confiding in. Perhaps he could have understood if they had just killed her. But this... This had been gruesome and humiliating. For that, he would put down Lily's killers in an equally foul fashion. His hate was cold and calculating. He would go up to the next floor and see if the intruders had left a trail.

The Chinese Empire does not forgive. A fine motto...

CHAPTER 51

Mistress Lotus's new look may have been impractical, but it was certainly intimidating. The humanoid amalgamation of metal balls would be difficult for Slate to beat, even if the snipers, guards, and the ever-present discomfort that made moving painful weren't present. He only had one option left, the only thing anyone could do in such a situation.

"Well, I know when I've been beat. I'll just be going now."

"I did not paint you for a coward," Mistress Lotus spat.

"No, but I'm an opportunist." The Helmet Man raised both palms. "Say cheese!"

A bright flash went off. The corneas of the guards and snipers sizzled like bacon. Those who still retained some vision were in too much pain to care that Slate was hobbling away.

But Mistress Lotus merely got angry. The amalgamation went after him.

"Ah, I forgot!" Slate yelled. "Bowling balls don't have eyes!"

The amalgamation didn't run but rolled. Its balls for feet spun in place for a moment, tearing up the manicured lawn, before the entire thing was propelled forward. It gained on Slate and punched the ground near him. The other arm tried to deck him with a backhand. The Helmet Man crouched down as he ran, the arm passing above his head. He noticed a small bamboo forest and ran into it. His indelicate movements broke a lot of stalks.

In favor of maneuverability, the amalgamation separated itself back into numerous black balls. They sped through the bamboo, managing not to knock down any stalks. The balls sometimes tried to ram Slate from the side, usually missing by only a few feet. The pain still gripped him, which meant Mistress Lotus remained nearby.

The bamboo forest was coming to an end. Slate broke more stalks before crashing into a statue. He shook the impact off and planned to keep on running. However, he skidded to a stop. Something had latched on to him. Teeth sank into his neck. The limbs that gripped him were weak, but they were rigid enough to restrain him. Slate attempted to shake the creature off, only stopping when he became aware of the other hundred statues.

He had entered the Traitors' Garden.

The creature that had been former Prime Minister Mao Long was now a living skeleton. All its ribs were showing, paper-white skin stretched over bone. It only wore a small undergarment to conceal its private parts, as if modesty mattered to such a wretched life anymore. Long plastic tubes hung out of its malnourished flesh. They had supplied it with only the bare minimum needed to live and suffer. It did not bother to form words or engage in complex thought. It had not helped Mao Long, and it would not help this creature. Viscous fluid oozed from the tubes and got all over the Helmet Man's clothes. He was slipping all over the place, the thing on his back still clinging and biting.

"Fricking house of horrors!" Slate electrocuted the feral creature until it dropped off him. The dead creature's limbs curled like those of a dried-up insect.

The black balls emerged from the forest, merging together again into one imposing form. The amalgamation punched at Slate, who took a step backward to avoid the blow. Another swing came. The black ball barely missed its mark. Slate was in full retreat now, working his way through the Traitors' Garden. He could hear the screams of the statues now and wanted to get out of there fast. The amalgamation followed, stepping over the statues. Armed guards were arriving at the Traitors' Garden. They spotted Slate and fired at him. He ducked as he ran. One bullet bounced off his helmet. The rest flew overhead.

More guards came. Now they had the whole garden surrounded. A few snipers who hadn't been blinded shot at Slate, getting closer to hitting him each time they fired. Blood oozed out of Slate's bite wound. Flying away would make him an easier target, and he was still unable to use his heart-stopping attack. The amalgamation was also getting nearer, its thundering footsteps making the statues shiver each time.

Hang on ... the statues! It was probably either the dumbest or the smartest idea that Slate had ever conceived, but the great thing about impulsiveness was that you didn't have to waste time philosophizing over every little thing. The Helmet Man simply went for it.

Slate pounded his fist into the ground, sending a good deal of his energy into it. The statues around him shattered. Shriveled things that had dared to defy their emperor fell out. Half of them were unable to walk and simply twitched on the ground. A few of the creatures even died of shock as the many stimuli of the world hit their deprived sensorial systems. Some condemned men, however, were able to stand. Tubes dangled off their pathetic bodies and dragged behind them. Their eyes were black pits and their bodies were weak. Their faculties were those of starving animals.

The guards stopped their assault and moved back from the creatures. Mistress Lotus only paused for a moment to access this development before continuing to make her way toward Slate, uninterested in anything else.

The creatures staggered around for a moment, unsure of what to do. Then one of them saw a nearby guard. The red uniform grabbed its attention, as did the scent of meat.

The creature went into a sprint and bared its teeth.

Everything turned to chaos. All the creatures able to walk attacked the guards. Most of the guards stayed where they were, but a few were wise enough to flee. They fired their weapons. Only a few creatures got hit, and only a fraction of those that did were killed. Five creatures pounced on a guard, feasting on the poor soul until one of his comrades was merciful enough to shoot him. Another guard knocked a creature back with the butt of his gun, only to have another tackle him from the side. Two guards tore a creature off their comrade and strangled the abomination with its own tubes.

The snipers did their best to help out their countrymen, but Slate fired a clumsy beam at the palace wall. A section of the wall collapsed, though the snipers had ample time to get off it. Slate was trying his best not to kill anyone, but he supposed he had already broken his promise by setting loose those creatures on the guards.

The amalgamation had caught up with him and attempted to stomp him flat. He rolled out of the way. Then it separated into dozens of balls. He danced out of each ball's way, brushed by only one. One ball killed a creature while another maimed a cowering guard. The balls came back together again into one horrible whole. The amalgamation raised a ball that served as its fist and struck Slate. He flew back and collided with a creature. It tried to eat him, but he grabbed the sides of its head and snapped its neck. A few creatures jumped on the amalgamation. Mistress Lotus shook them off as a dog would fleas.

"You're a feisty one," Slate groaned, the unnatural pain still gripping him. "Didn't think anyone was tough enough to take me on anymore, except maybe Incognito or that Temple. Look, I don't like killing worthy opponents. There aren't many of them around to make life interesting, so I'll give you this one chance to surrender."

"You sound as if you have already won this fight," Mistress Lotus scoffed. "Surrender is not an option for either of us."

"Crap..." Slate decided to take another route. "You know, I'm not usually attracted to bowling balls, but you honestly got it going on."

"I am impervious to your flirtations. Even if I were still able to copulate, the love for my emperor would never be befouled by your lecherous paws."

Slate grabbed his aching side with one hand. "Rejected... At least nobody can say I never took pity on an ugly chick."

Mistress Lotus was not one to be easily irritated, but the Helmet Man had a special way with people. The amalgamation threw another punch. Slate threw one of his own, using the arm that wasn't holding his side in pain. The fist was filled with energy and slammed into the black ball. A shockwave went through the amalgamation. All the water in the ball went to a boil in less than a second, causing it to explode from the pressure.

"I'm starting to think you're all show!" Slate yelled.

But Mistress Lotus had a trick up her sleeve. One of the balls had detached itself from the main body while he was distracted. It circled around and rammed him from the side, sending him flying at least twenty feet.

The Helmet Man smashed into the wall surrounding the palace. His beam had already weakened this section, so he went right through it without breaking his neck. He splashed into the moat surrounding the Forbidden City. There was rarely a time when Slate truly experienced panic, but he did experience it mildly right now, only because he was unable to swim and because water dampened his powers.

"Ah! Someone throw me my water wings!"

Nobody did. Slate splashed around for a few seconds before sinking. His helmet weighed him down, so floating on his back wasn't an option. On the other hand, he didn't need to breathe. Drowning wouldn't kill him.

But Mistress Lotus might. The water took hold of him and bashed him against the side of the moat several times. Then a whirlpool spun him around like a top and spat him back out. It was by no means a fun experience.

Slate was lifted from the water. A pillar of water wrapped around him like a python, threatening to squeeze him until he popped. The amalgamation had also returned. It stood on the outer edge of the moat, near where the force field touched down. The legions of possessed soldiers could be seen through the semitransparent barrier, quiet and waiting.

The water pillar slammed Slate against the force field. The amalgamation also lent a hand by leaning hard against him. Touching the force field would have electrocuted anyone else to death, but Slate only felt slight discomfort from the heat. The amalgamation leaned in, increasing the pressure. Slate did his best to wiggle from its grip, but his foe was strong. Water spilled from the moat and wrapped around the amalgamation, making it even more resistant to his electrical attacks. The liquid turned to steam as soon as it hit the force field.

"Why are you here?" Mistress Lotus questioned. "Why have you desecrated my home?"

"I'm here for Cloak, not you!" Slate shouted. "Temple's the one I should be fighting. You're just getting in the way!"

"Temple is a subject of the emperor and shall be protected. You are an enemy of the emperor and shall be obliterated."

"Fine..." Slate grunted, putting his hands against the force field. "If you want me as an enemy, I'm gonna be your worst one!"

Slate allowed the energy of the force field to flow through him. He started to gather it. The water around him got hot enough to start steaming. He even glowed a little, the entire force field flickering. Mistress Lotus did not like this and decided to kill him right then and there. She commanded the amalgamation to crush the Helmet Man until he was paste.

Too late. The water went to a boil in the blink of an eye, causing a steam explosion. The amalgamation was blown apart, most of the black balls exploding as well. Mistress Lotus herself shot backward like a cannonball and went through the broken wall. She knocked down several guards and freed creatures before hitting one of the pillars supporting the palace. She bounced off it and rolled to a stop near the ruins of the Traitors' Garden.

The pain left Slate. He landed near the edge of the moat on wobbly legs. After shaking some water off himself, he flew to find Mistress Lotus. Only a few guards were still around. Most were either near death or already dead. The remaining creatures had left the area with no real goal in mind. Corpses, shattered statues, and bits of broken wood littered what had once been a beautiful courtyard. At the same time, the area now had a newfound peace, for the screams of the Traitors' Garden had been silenced forever.

Mistress Lotus was not in good shape. The explosion had cracked her shell, revealing electronic innards and a brain suspended in amber-colored fluid within a clear container.

Slate shook his head, the silver helmet reflecting the pathetic scene. "Look what you've reduced yourself to. I never had a choice, but you did. Even worse, you did this to your own children. And for what, a little bit of power and some fancy moves?"

"You would not understand," Mistress Lotus said. "A creature like you knows nothing of loyalty. My emperor is divine, yet he chose someone as unworthy as me for a lover."

"Ah, geez… You call that loyalty? Lady, that's obsession. Your hubby treated you like crap, and you liked it because you got self-esteem issues. To make it all worse, you dragged your kids into this icky mess you call a relationship and turned them into weapons."

"I did it out of love. The Western Union created you out of greed. Is that any better?"

"No, and they're gonna answer for their nonsense one day. So will your husband and the Mentor. But first you gotta answer."

"It is *you* who will have to answer, Helmet Man." Something clicked inside Mistress Lotus. "I gave everything to my emperor. My love, my body, my children…"

A loud beep pierced the air. Slate had no time to run.

"Now I give my life…"

Not knowing what else to do, Slate shoved his hand inside Mistress Lotus and released enough energy inside her to power a hospital. The fluid suspending the brain boiled, killing her. She felt no pain because the brain lacked the necessary receptors.

The Helmet Man was lucky. The bomb's circuits had fried before it could detonate.

Smoke belched from the metallic corpse. Slate tore his hand from his ruined enemy. After taking a moment to make sure Mistress Lotus was down for good, he fell on his rear and turned his head to the sky, the silver helmet reflecting indifference back.

"That's a shame," he said. "That's a real shame…"

Naomi and Oscar were surprised they had not encountered any other guards since their confrontation with Lily. It made their lives simpler yet tenser. Oscar had tended to Naomi's wounds, but they were minor. It was the fatigue that was beginning to bother her, and if Incognito and Slate were feeling the same way, how could they possibly handle Temple?

"I'm concerned," she said. "Why hasn't Cloak shown itself?"

"Maybe they're letting the Chinese do the fighting for them," Oscar suggested.

"I don't like it. I'm starting to get jumpy."

"Then why don't you check and see if the others have spotted Temple?"

Naomi decided this was a good idea. She took her communicator out and talked into it as they kept walking. "Naomi here. What's your status, Gilda?"

"We're doing just fine," Straper's voice crackled. "Thanks for remembering me too."

"I knew you were there. Don't be so sensitive."

"Whatever. Why are you calling?"

"Do you two have any idea where Temple is?"

"No, but a bunch of soldiers and a Black Lotus cyborg tried to get past us."

"Which cyborg?"

"Pansy. It was insane. I killed him, though. Don't worry."

Straper had killed a Black Lotus agent? Naomi had expected Gilda to do something like that. "Good work. We secured the force field generator, and I defeated Lily."

"Righteous. That's two less cyborgs to worry about. What now?"

"I'm heading to your location with Oscar. After I drop him off, I'm going to help Slate capture the emperor."

"Okay, can I come with you?"

The request surprised her. She had always painted Straper as a bit of a coward. "Perhaps. I appreciate the offer."

A gun went off. Naomi raised her hands on reflex and deflected the bullet. It burst into a wave of blinding light, however, and knocked her and Oscar backward. She dropped her communicator, and it hit the floor the same time she did.

"What was that?" Straper yelled over the communicator. "Are you guys all right?"

Poppy picked up the communicator and switched it off.

Naomi had banged the back of her head on the floor. She was barely conscious as the barrel of a rifle pointed straight at her face.

"You plucked Lily's petals," Poppy seethed. He hated speaking in this foreign tongue, but he wanted this woman to understand his words. "Now I will pluck yours…"

Oscar was too stunned to help. He was also old and not a fighter. He only had it in him to sit up so he could see what was happening. It was one of the cyborgs, Poppy, and he sounded unpleasant. On some level, Oscar couldn't blame him. How would he feel if he found his sister's burnt body hanging from a ceiling?

"One of the guards you attacked told me what you did," Poppy mused, brushing his weapon against Naomi's cheek. "Strange how you let them live but decided to slaughter my sister. I believe I shall blow off your ears first. Then your toes. Then your nose. Then your—"

Something tackled Poppy from the side. It was thin and seemed to have tentacles growing from its back. Oscar then realized those were tubes. Poppy wrestled with the creature. He managed to kick off the shriveled menace and put a bullet in it.

Five more creatures came from around the corner. They spotted Poppy and ran at him, snapping their teeth and making monkey noises. Oscar didn't know where these things had come from and didn't care so long as they didn't come after him.

Poppy loaded an explosive round into his rifle's chamber and fired it at whatever those things were. The bullet exploded, killing three of the creatures and setting another aflame. Then he put in a regular round and used it to easily kill the fifth creature.

But the one on fire was still mobile. The flaming creature threw itself at Poppy, who shielded himself with his rifle. The two of them danced for a least half a minute, the creature snapping its jaws and spraying saliva. Naomi was still out of it. Oscar ran to her side.

"Get up, Naomi!" he yelled. "Poppy won't be distracted for long!"

Poppy finally threw off the creature and shot it twice in the head. The fire still ate away at the corpse. It reminded Poppy of his dead sister, which made his left eye twitch. He turned to Naomi. Oscar was still trying to wake her. Poppy bashed Oscar in the head with the butt of his rifle, knocking the old-timer to the side. He pointed his gun back at Naomi.

"Now, which part of your body was I going to remove first?" he whispered.

But there was one more surprise for Poppy. He noticed a shape moving behind him. On instinct, he twisted around and shot before asking questions.

Straper darted behind a pillar as the bullet whizzed by his head and hit the wall, spraying bits of wood at his face. He bled a little but ignored it. After having his communication cut off, he had decided to play hero and rescue Naomi and Oscar. So far, the fantasy wasn't playing out like he had thought it would.

Loading an explosive round, Poppy shot the pillar Straper was hiding behind. It disintegrated in a flash of light. Straper was already running. He fired his rifle four times before hiding behind a new pillar. One bullet came close to nailing Poppy in the head.

"Impressive shooting, Westerner," Poppy said. "But skill has no sway here, not when I have superior eyes and weaponry."

Straper heard another projectile fly by, but it hadn't even come close to hitting him. What was this guy playing at?

Then he saw a cloud of gas spurt from the bullet hole in the wall. It seemed

Poppy was trying to smoke him out with a bullet filled with compressed tear gas. Already having his fill of tear gas for one day, Straper dashed out from behind his pillar and aimed his rifle. Poppy aimed his rifle too, having loaded another explosive round.

They both fired.

An invisible hand grabbed Straper and yanked him to his left. Poppy's bullet exploded, but Straper was safely out of its blast radius. Naomi had come to at the last moment and used her telekinesis to save her foolhardy friend.

Poppy did not have the same luck. Straper's bullet went through his neck, making a deep gash. Trying to stop the flow of blood with his hand, Poppy swayed to the side and tumbled off his feet. His tailbone broke as he hit the hard floor. The pain wasn't quite felt, the blood loss already that severe. Straper hadn't made a perfect shot, but it had won the fight.

Groaning, Oscar sat up and crawled to Naomi's side. "How is your head?" he asked. "That was a serious bump."

"I can handle it," she said. "Everyone needs a concussion now and again."

Oscar touched his own head gingerly. "Can't say I feel the same way..."

Straper got off the floor and picked up his rifle. He approached Poppy, careful not to take his eyes off the cyborg. He was now only six feet from his opponent. Straper knew better than to get any closer. He aimed his barrel right at his target's head.

The blood would not stop flowing, no matter how much pressure Poppy put on his wound. His strange eyes were unfocused. Then they gained traction, focusing on Straper's face. What he was trying to communicate, Straper did not know. Perhaps he was vowing revenge. Maybe he was pleading. It was not clear.

Straper pulled the trigger.

Naomi's eyes widened.

"Straper!" Oscar cried.

Poppy's body went limp, a hole where his left eye used to be. Straper lowered his rifle and licked his dry lips. He let his weapon slip through his fingers and fall on the floor.

"What the hell happened to you guys?" someone interrupted. Slate had sensed the commotion and went to investigate. Now he found himself standing before six dead creatures, one dead cyborg, his dad and girlfriend lying injured on the floor, and a shell-shocked Straper. The dots did not connect easily.

"What happened to *you?*" Naomi asked. She saw the bloody gashes and tattered clothes covering the Helmet Man. He probably had other hidden injuries too.

"The emperor got away," Slate said. "Had to fight Mistress Lotus. Killed her, though. I think I killed a few guards too. Sorry, I wasn't able to keep my promise."

"That's okay. Where's Eisenhorn?"

"I have no idea. He must have run off somewhere." Slate pointed at Poppy's body. "Who killed that one?"

"Straper!" Oscar shouted. "What was that?"

Straper smiled. It was forced. "Hey, I was doing my job. Isn't this why we're here?"

"Wait, what exactly did he do?" Slate asked.

"Straper killed that cyborg in cold blood!" Oscar exclaimed.

"What?" Slate turned to Naomi. "Is this true?"

She nodded. "It was uncharacteristically brutal of him."

"You're kidding," Straper scoffed with a queasy grin. "No, you *must* be kidding. Hypocrisy, that's what this is. You and Slate both murder people all the time. Now I do it, and you want to chastise me? I can't believe it."

Slate moved fast, pinning Straper against the wall with his forearm. "Don't even use that line of argument, pal. We did what we had to. We never chose this life for ourselves. You just killed out of your own free will. Think you're a man for what you just did, huh?"

"What's the matter? The guy was dangerous! Keeping him alive would've been stupid. I saved Naomi from being mutilated by that psycho. You should be thanking me. I already killed another cyborg in the loading bay. What's another, huh?"

"That's the kind of talk Cloak uses."

"I'm just trying to be like you!"

"I'm your role model? That's a mistake."

"If you know killing is wrong, then why don't you stop?"

"Because I gotta kill the Mentor first."

Straper scoffed. "Then you'll change your ways? Is that right?"

Slate let go of him. "I think the world won't need me to be a killer after that. Maybe. I don't know. I guess we'll see when we get there."

The Helmet Man walked away. Straper stood for a moment. He made several attempts at laughing, each time producing a muffled sob. Gulping his feelings down, he sat down and stared at a spot on the floor.

With Oscar's help, Naomi got to her feet. Then Oscar decided to check if his equipment was damaged, and Slate walked up to Naomi.

"You find Temple yet?" Slate whispered.

"No," Naomi said. "I suppose you haven't either."

"Nope. Do you think he's hiding somewhere?"

"Could be, or maybe Temple isn't here right now. Maybe Xing lied to us."

"Why would he do that?"

"Maybe he really is trying to swindle Incognito."

"That'd be stupid."

"It could also be Temple was here but left right before we arrived, so Xing is just trying to buy some time, hoping that Temple will return."

"The other Gifted aren't here either. You might be on to something."

"If Temple isn't here, what then?"

"We move on to Incognito," Slate told her. "He'll be weakened by the battle. Now is the best and only time to take him out."

"But we're in pretty bad shape ourselves, and how are we going to defeat Temple later without his help?"

"It's two on one. We also have Gilda and her walker."

"But Temple..."

"Guess who's back?" someone yelled.

Slate, Naomi, and Oscar looked at where the voice had come from. Straper did so too, though more sluggish than the others. Then a jolt of recognition went through his system.

What the hell was *he* doing here?

"Nice to see my cadet has turned into a man!" Eisenhorn yelled, noticing Straper. An anxious Chinese woman holding a gun followed the general. Eisenhorn, meanwhile, was dragging something behind him, something that squirmed and squealed and reeked worse than a compost heap.

Slate stumbled back. "Holy crap!"

Naomi and Oscar shot each other looks over this unprecedented development.

General Eisenhorn had captured the emperor.

"Now, will *someone* take me to my room already?" he beseeched.

CHAPTER 53

Slate, Straper, Oscar, and their prize headed back down to the loading bay where Gilda still stood guard with Magenta. Slate told her what happened, giving her the short version. It took Gilda a few minutes to come to grips with the fact that General Eisenhorn, the guy in charge of the Bunker and their former commander, was here at the Forbidden City with them. Even stranger was how he ended up being the one to capture the emperor.

Only five guards had been protecting the emperor, but the feat was still impressive for a normal human. Eisenhorn had taken the guards by surprise and killed two of them before they had a chance to react. The other three engaged in a brief firefight with him and would have likely killed him if it weren't for Shu. She had come out at the last minute to help. Her aim was terrible, only shooting one guard in the leg, but it had given Eisenhorn the edge he needed, shooting the remaining guards while they were preoccupied.

The Helmet Man dropped his captive on the loading bay floor like a sack of potatoes. Rope bound the emperor's hands and feet. He shrieked and wiggled on the floor.

Slate stood over the wretch and cocked his head in puzzlement. "This guy is supposed to be a world leader? Man, politics doesn't make any sense."

Straper sat on a container, brooding. Oscar had attempted to speak to him, but the young man remained unresponsive. Gilda climbed out of her walker, taking a brief break now that Slate was here to help, and went over to see if Straper was okay.

"You got a minute?"

"Leave me alone," he mumbled.

"I won't," she snapped. "Straper, we've all done things we aren't proud off. I got the feeling we're going to do lots more of those things before this is all over."

"That guy needed to die. I ain't sorry."

"You sure seem like you are. Look, we can't have you moping your way through this mission. Learn from your mistakes and suck it up. We're going to need your help, Straper. We may have the emperor, but we haven't even encountered Cloak or Temple yet."

He gave her a fake smile. "Nice talk. Can you just go now?"

Gilda was ticked but decided not to provoke an argument. She just patted his back and went over to join Slate. "Where did Naomi and Eisenhorn go?" she asked.

"Eisenhorn is itching to get to his old room," Slate said. "Don't know why, but he is. That servant lady is gonna lead him to it, and Naomi is going with them as protection. It's the least we can do. The old guy did capture the emperor, after all."

"So, what now?"

"We wait for everyone to get back together. Then we look for Temple."

"Have you asked him about Cloak?" Gilda asked, pointing at the emperor, whose smell made her plug her own nose.

"He's pretty out of it," Slate said. "I doubt he'll be of help."

"Couldn't hurt to ask."

"Guess not." Slate kicked the ancient ruler, not so lightly. "Hey, divine leader who doesn't shower, where's Temple?"

The emperor literally coughed up a hair ball. Gilda hadn't thought that was possible for a human. She could only go green.

Slate kicked the emperor again. "Gross! How you managed to get over a dozen wives is beyond me. Come on! Tell me where Temple is! Where's Sebastian? Where's the Mentor?"

The emperor perked up at the mention of the Mentor. He rolled his head and eyes. "Mentor! Mentor! Mentor!"

"Now we're getting somewhere," Slate said. He decided to switch to Mandarin, silently thanking Shifu for his lessons. "Where is the Mentor?"

Gilda was surprised to hear Slate speak a foreign language. It sounded like he spoke it well too. Oscar may have been right about his son's intelligence.

"What's going on here?" Oscar demanded, approaching Gilda as if he somehow knew she was thinking about him.

"We're trying to get information from the emperor," Gilda said.

"Your efforts are in vain," Oscar told both of them. "That man has been nothing but a demented figurehead for over a decade."

"Where is the Mentor?" Slate shouted in Mandarin, grabbing the emperor by his beard. He pulled it until the old man squealed.

"Slate, quit being so impulsive!" Oscar snapped.

The emperor spat some words out. Slate managed to get their gist and got even madder. He let go of the emperor's beard.

"Say that again!" Slate bellowed. "I dare you!"

"Hey, take it down a notch!" Gilda warned.

The emperor grinned and spat out the same words again.

"You're blaming your children for this?" Slate yelled back in Mandarin. "After all the Black Lotus sacrificed for you? They gave up their bodies and dignity, all to please Daddy! How could you be so heartless?"

The emperor snickered, wagging his tongue.

"Mistress Lotus, the other cyborgs, your men, your own people are nothing but trash to you. You treat them all like dirt. You use them up and throw them away. I don't care if you made this empire with your bare hands. People can't be treated that way!"

"Please, calm down," Oscar urged. He was sweating. Gilda was too.

"Do you remember your son, the one you exiled?" Slate snarled. "I found him in a prison at the bottom of the sea, starved to death by someone almost as depraved as you. He really did care about the Chinese people, about his homeland. But you don't care about him or your people. I almost hate them too. To think they ever let you get into power. This is all a farce. You're no father or a leader or a god. You're a disgrace!"

The Helmet Man grabbed the defiler by the throat with one hand. He only had to squeeze a little before the emperor began choking.

"Stop it!" Gilda shouted, grabbing Slate's arm. He shoved her away. Oscar covered his mouth. He was too unnerved to be of any help.

"Hey, Slate."

The Helmet Man released the defiler. He turned to see that Straper had come over. Straper wore a blank look, but that didn't mean he was apathetic.

"Is this what you didn't want me to become?" he asked.

Slate didn't have a good response to that. Gilda and Oscar were stunned to see Straper so in control of the situation.

Straper sighed. "I can see why you wouldn't want that now." He walked away and sat back down on his container.

Slate growled, fuming for a moment before coming to a decision. He kicked the emperor one more time, tempted to do it until there was nothing left to kick, and turned his back on the senile monster. The emperor snickered but stopped when Gilda started kicking him too. Oscar quickly made her stop.

"We need this man alive," Oscar told her, still pale over what he just saw. "Let's just wait for the others to come back."

They didn't have to wait long. Naomi entered first, followed by Eisenhorn and Shu. A fourth companion had joined them. Xing was no longer in hiding, deciding to come out when he confirmed that the emperor had been captured and the Black Lotus was neutralized.

"What happened to the emperor?" Xing asked, shocked at seeing his ruler beaten and tied up with some filthy blanket.

The emperor saw Xing and went into a fit of fury. "Traitor! Traitor! Traitor!"

Shu hid behind Eisenhorn, fearful of the emperor's words, as if they were magic. She had been jumpy ever since they captured him. She was expecting some agent of Heaven to come down at any time and smite her for her transgressions. None did.

"I got what I wanted!" Eisenhorn cheered. He reverently held a syringe, which was filled with some clear fluid. "Right where I left it. Finally, some good luck!"

"Sir, it's good to see you," Gilda said. In truth, she had never liked the general, finding him rude and unbalanced, but she was happy to see a familiar face and did have a grudging respect for him. She even gave a small salute.

Eisenhorn returned the salute. "Glad to see you still know protocol."

Oscar cleared his throat. "Excuse me, General, but I must have a moment with you."

"That can wait. Missy, tell the people what we found!"

Naomi didn't care much for his misogyny. She would deal with it later. "We came across something concerning. A room filled with electronic equipment was trashed. Servers were burned, wires were torn out of walls, and all the guards there were killed."

"That is concerning," Oscar said. "What was the room's purpose?"

"It served many functions," Xing said. "But it was mainly a communications center."

Gilda scratched her head. "Why would anyone destroy that room?"

"There could be a number of reasons," Xing said. "Perhaps they are trying to cut off contact with the outside world."

"But that's not the most concerning part," Naomi said, lowering her head as she kept her emotions under control. "The guards all had holes in their bodies, all cauterized. Some even had their limbs ripped off. No blood, though, only burnt flesh."

"Oh, lord," Oscar said.

Gilda glowered. "That must mean…"

"Temple," Slate snarled. "He's here."

"Is he really?"

Everyone jumped in their skins. It was a new voice only to Eisenhorn, Shu, and the emperor. Everyone else recognized it and groaned.

Incognito had arrived, having appeared out of nowhere. He used his scythe as a walking stick while carrying a small girl with his free arm. She emitted an unnatural buzz. When he reached the others, he put the girl on the floor and gestured to her.

"This is one of the Black Lotus's cyborgs," he told them. "I don't care for personally murdering children, so I'll have one of you do it."

"Like hell we will," Slate said. "Do your own dirty work."

"Fine, keep her alive. I may be able to turn her into a useful slave."

"Who's this clown?" Eisenhorn scoffed. "Another circus freak?"

"Allow me to introduce Incognito," Naomi huffed. "Believe it or not, this is him on his best behavior."

"Incognito!" Eisenhorn cried. He grabbed Shu's gun. "Die, terrorist!"

He fired all his bullets. Each one harmlessly went through Incognito as though he were a hologram. Eisenhorn actually thought he was for a second until Incognito flew up and nailed him upside the head with his scythe's wooden handle.

"Randolph!" Shu shrieked, running to his side.

Eisenhorn didn't fall, but he felt a tooth had been knocked loose. He spat out blood. "I'd like to see you try that again!"

Incognito pulled back for another blow.

"Would you two stop it?" Oscar snapped. "Eisenhorn, you aren't going to win against this opponent, I guarantee it. As for you, Incognito, show this man some mercy. The Chinese have tortured him for a full year, and he caught the emperor for us."

"Ah, yes. I've been anxious to have a meeting with divinity." Incognito approached the emperor with methodical steps. The emperor howled, trying to slither away from this incarnation of death. It was the enemy the Mentor was supposed to protect him from, but now this phantom was right here in front of him. He howled again.

"Mentor! Mentor! Mentor!"

"Hush your squawking," Incognito sneered, smacking the emperor's head with his scythe's handle. The emperor's howls turned to whimpers.

"I'm rather disappointed by what I see," Incognito said. "This is the man who single-handedly created an empire and defied the West for decades? To think there was a time when I admired you..."

The emperor screamed something at Incognito. No translator was needed to tell these words were especially foul.

"I believe we share much in common," Incognito said. "Yes, we're so similar, it revolts me. But the important difference between us is you sought to rule whereas I only wish to conquer. I have no plans to prolong my life or live in the world I am about to create. You, on the other hand, suffered from hubris and wished to bask in your creation. That's when you began to fester and rot until your empire turned into something that was not a tool of liberation from Western civilization but something perhaps just as foul as the West itself."

Incognito knelt next to the emperor, his cold eyes gazing into the crusty, manic eyes of China's lord and master. "I will never rest. I will never allow myself to become a shade of my former self. And I will *never* abandon the people I swore to protect. I will hand over the Saladin Federation to someone who won't end up like you, someone who can serve my people, who can resist temptation and his base desires."

The emperor snapped his teeth. Incognito shook his head and stood back up. He looked at Eisenhorn. The general growled, putting his fists up.

"Quit acting ridiculous," Incognito told him. "This is no boxing match. I am merely trying to figure out why the Western Union would send someone so mentally compromised to act as an ambassador."

"I have a way with people. Now get out of my face before I chew yours off!"

"What is that you have in your hand?" Incognito demanded. He snatched up the syringe before Eisenhorn could even answer the question.

"Hey, give that back!" the general shouted.

"You are a diabetic, a drug addict, an assassin, or merely insane. Those are the only reasons you would covet this syringe so passionately."

"I'm only two of those things, pal. Now hand it over!"

"Quit torturing the guy and give his drugs back," Slate said. "He's earned it."

"Yeah, haven't you had your fill of bullying?" Gilda snapped.

"Please, Incognito," Shu begged. He shot her a look that made her squeak in fright, but she had enough courage to go on. "It is very important to him.

If you have any kindness in your heart, give the syringe back to him."

Incognito examined the syringe absentmindedly. "That was a terrible plea. And incidentally, I don't have any kindness in my heart."

"News flash," Gilda snorted.

"Give it here!" Eisenhorn charged. Incognito sidestepped him with almost no effort.

Then the general really had a fit.

"Give it, you snake! I didn't put up with Klara's bullshit for a year just to be shafted now. When I get that syringe, I'll make sure to blow you up right along with Temple!"

Eisenhorn didn't realize what he had said until he saw everyone else's reaction.

"What did you just say?" Naomi whispered.

"It was pretty clear what he just said," Slate said. "He's got a bomb."

"Does that syringe activate it?" Xing asked. "Is that why the Western Union sent you here? Have you been fooling me all these months?"

"Now he wants to use it to destroy Temple!" Gilda exclaimed.

Straper didn't budge from his container, but he did raise his head to hear the conversation better. Oscar almost fainted. Incognito examined the syringe more intently.

Shu turned to Eisenhorn. "Randolph, what's going on? Do you have a bomb?"

"I didn't know jack about it till Klara told me," Eisenhorn told her, finding himself attacked from all sides. "The Western Union put a bomb in my head so they could kill the emperor if they felt like it. But Klara... Yeah, she came to me in a dream and warned me about the assassin. The one with the syringe, you see! Now she wants me to kill Temple with my bomb, and if I see that monster anywhere near me, I definitely will!"

Eisenhorn saw his explanation only further concerned the others.

"So, who's Klara?" Gilda asked, not sure if she wanted to pry more.

"Klara is one of the Gifted," Oscar croaked.

CHAPTER 54

Nobody knew how to react to that revelation. They all exchanged glances. Eisenhorn was running all this through his head. "Hang on... Just ... hang on..."

Oscar was moist with sweat. "Eisenhorn, I wanted to speak with you earlier because we've met before. Over twenty years ago, after you were deemed mentally unfit to command, the higher-ups decided they had one more use for you..."

Incognito kept a good distance from Eisenhorn. That was the cue for everyone else to be worried.

"They wanted to implant some brain tissue inside your head," Oscar went on. "This brain tissue belonged to one of the Gifted. We theorized it could create psychic energy if stimulated properly. Klara ... she had the ability to erase things from existence."

"What does that mean?" Gilda asked.

"She could utterly destroy matter, not even leaving any trace of energy. It was a terrible power, an uncontrollable one too. But after she died, the Western Union was interested in utilizing it. They tasked me with harvesting her brain and implanting the parts responsible for her powers into Eisenhorn's head."

"What ... that ... makes no sense..." Eisenhorn had to lean on Shu's shoulder. She supported his weight, even though she was almost as shaken as he was.

"We needed to put it in a living human brain," Oscar said. "The technology didn't exist yet to keep brain tissue alive outside a body. Putting it inside General Eisenhorn was a stroke of sadistic genius too. As a general, they could make him an ambassador and use him to smuggle the bomb into the Forbidden City should the need arise. The fact that he suffered a mental breakdown did put his reliability in question. However, it also meant he was more expendable."

"Those Westerners are more devious than I ever imagined," Xing said.

"I did not know this," Incognito hissed. "How did I not know this?"

Oscar shrugged. "Only several people knew, including Powell, Hynes, and myself. Cloak must not know either, or they would have killed Eisenhorn. Even Eisenhorn himself was unaware. We pruned him before the operation and kept him uninformed after we finished."

"So, who's this Klara chick?" Slate asked. "I never heard of her before. Just how many supersoldiers did you geezers make?"

"Klara is merely a name she gave herself. You met her before, Slate, and fought her to the death. She's the reason you had to hibernate for twenty years."

"Holy crap... Klara is Void!"

"Klara is Void," Oscar confirmed.

"I thought Void was a guy!"

"I don't know how you could have made that mistake."

"Oh..." Slate calmed down some. "Guess it was all those mismatched clothes she wore. Couldn't tell what team she was on."

A desperate laugh escaped Eisenhorn's parched mouth.

"She was a strange one," Oscar said. "But I didn't think she was capable of such violence until she went on that rampage of hers."

Eisenhorn had now lost full use of his legs. Shu couldn't hold him up anymore and had to rest him on the floor.

"I got me a supersoldier in my head," he mumbled. "I got a chunk of someone else's brain in my noodle..."

"That must be why the Western Union was keeping Eisenhorn at the Bunker," Gilda said. "They probably wanted to stash him away until he was needed."

"Then why is he having dreams about Klara?" Naomi asked. "Is she still alive and communicating with him? He wouldn't have known her name otherwise."

"I think those are just suppressed memories he had or some other bizarre psychological phenomenon," Oscar said. "But there is no way she could still be alive, not when all that's left is a bit of her neural tissue in Eisenhorn's skull. The rest of her remains were dissected and later destroyed after the Gifted rebelled."

"You should have told me this sooner," Incognito scolded.

"How could I know that General Eisenhorn would be in the Forbidden City?"

"Fine, weasel out of your responsibility." Incognito eyed the syringe in his hand. "The question is what to do with this thing."

"I vote we toss it," Slate said.

"Too bad this isn't a democracy." Incognito presented the syringe to Naomi.

Eisenhorn woke out of his trance. "Huh? Wait, give it here! It's mine!"

"That would be like giving a grenade to an infant," Incognito said. "You might kill us all if I allowed that to happen. At least this wench has some common sense."

Naomi took the syringe, not pleased at all with the responsibility.

"It is a last resort," Incognito emphasized. "We can't allow Temple to escape, but let's try not to be martyrs unless absolutely necessary."

"Is Eisenhorn okay with being your bomb?" Naomi asked icily.

The general huffed. "I made up my mind long ago, missy. I'm willing to throw my life away for the good of the Western Union and the rest of the world, especially if it means killing that animal and kicking Cloak in the crotch. Whatever. I guess I'm all right with you having the syringe. If that helmet moron thinks you're okay, you probably aren't completely evil."

"You cannot sacrifice yourself like this," Shu told him, touching his shoulder. "Let these people do the fighting. You already helped them capture the emperor."

"Shu, you don't know a thing about men." Eisenhorn got to his feet. "A man makes the sacrifices. A man gives up everything to protect what he loves. A man trudges forward until he can't trudge no more. As long as this world has evil in it, true men like me will always be needed. And right now, sister, I'm needed."

A loud beep, like someone flatlining, echoed throughout the loading bay.

The emperor started to laugh.

"Better shut your mouth," Slate growled.

"That beep…" Xing went white. He rushed to the emperor and shoved his hand down his filthy robes, only vaguely aware of the stench, and took out a small object that looked like a golden egg. It had a detailed dragon carving on its side.

Xing opened up the egg. His breathing became rapid to the point of hyperventilation. He only took one glance inside the egg before dropping it.

"The world has ended," he declared.

Oscar picked up the egg and glanced inside too. He could see a screen that displayed some text. He was able to translate with a handheld computer and began to read. Incognito looked over his shoulder to see what all the fuss was about. They both were confused by what they saw. Then they began to comprehend. Then they began to understand Xing's fear.

The egg slipped from Oscar's fingers and struck the floor with a clunk.

"It *really* is the end of the world," he whispered.

***

Alphonse Schmitt sat in a well-equipped bomb shelter, drinking straight from the bottle. He imputed the last of the emperor's launch codes and closed his laptop. Schmitt had waited for Sebastian to alert him when Incognito and the Helmet Man had captured the emperor. They ought to be finding the Dragon's Egg right about now.

Taking another gulp of whiskey, Schmitt's bottle was at last empty. Killian was supposed to be getting him more Western liquor. Schmitt wouldn't drink any of that rice water.

The Mentor was almost never wrong. Even when one of Schmitt's dreams was somewhat inaccurate, it usually worked out in the end. But what Sebastian had asked him to do had really put his faith to the test.

Meh, whatever. Even if it all went to shit, he was nice and cozy in this fancy bomb shelter beneath the Taj Mahal. He had spent twenty years underground. What was another couple of decades? Maybe the fallout wouldn't be that bad.

Maybe he could repopulate the world with females of his choosing.

As long as Killian got that booze, Schmitt would be content.

***

"Great, what now?" Slate asked. "Don't keep us in suspense or anything."

"What–what we were just looking at wa–was the Chinese equivalent of the Western Union's nuclear football ... the Dragon's Egg..." Oscar stammered.

Gilda and Naomi felt their knees weaken. Shu cowered until she almost turned herself into a ball. Eisenhorn sneered in annoyance at the whole situation.

"I guess what you saw wasn't good news," Slate said.

Straper moaned, covering his face with clammy hands.

"This device just told us that fifty nuclear missiles are preparing to launch," Incognito said. "Their target is Seoul."

"It's in South Korea," Oscar added. "Western Union territory..."

"No..." Gilda said. "If those missiles hit..."

"It may start a nuclear war," Naomi finished.

"It *will* start a nuclear war," Incognito corrected. In one swift action, he put the point of his scythe's blade underneath the emperor's chin.

"Be careful with him!" Xing warned.

"Did you fire those missiles, wretch?" Incognito spat.

The emperor chuckled. Mucus bubbled out his nose.

"Those commands weren't sent from the Dragon's Egg," Oscar said, blotting his head with a handkerchief. "They were sent from somewhere in India."

"It's Cloak," Slate spat. "Those turds are at it again. Great, this makes that whole reveal about Klara seem like nothing."

"Speak for yourself," Eisenhorn grunted.

"The emperor must have given Sebastian his launch codes," Xing said. "How unprecedented... Temple truly does have a hold over the emperor's mind."

"What could Cloak gain by blowing up the world?" Gilda asked. "I know they're evil, but they're not *mindlessly* evil."

"I beg to differ," Incognito said, pulling his blade away from the emperor's throat. "However, I do believe there is some reason behind this whirlwind of madness. Cloak is attempting to split us up. They want me to prevent those missiles from hitting their target. That's why the scope of their attack is so limited and near where we are. It's just within my abilities to stop those missiles. They probably even counted on us finding the Dragon's Egg so we could anticipate the attack. Cloak would then use this opportunity to kill the rest of you. Divide and conquer: an old strategy. But there's a reason it has stuck around so long."

"Are you telling me Cloak is flirting with nuclear war for the sole purpose of keeping *you* occupied?" Naomi questioned.

"What a narcissist," Slate scoffed.

"It only makes sense," Incognito told them. "Their fear of me runs deep. It is the very basis of their actions."

"Yeah, you're definitely a narcissist. I should know."

"We have to stop those missiles," Oscar said. "Xing, there must be a way."

"Cloak has likely changed the launch codes already," Xing said. "Even if we coerced the emperor, he would not be able to help. It would take the authorization of three high generals to override any new launch codes. We would also need a functioning communications center, but there was only one in the Forbidden City, and Temple destroyed it."

"Can't you use the Dragon's Egg?" Oscar asked.

Xing shook his head. "That will not work."

"There must be something."

"I do have one idea," Xing said, talking more to himself now. "The secondary palace in Nepal has a communications center capable of carrying out such a command. High General Lee is there right now too, so I could get his authorization."

"What about the third authorization? Could we convince Fang to give his own?"

"Not under these circumstances, but before High General Duan met his untimely death, he did give me his own codes should anything happen to him. That makes three."

"Are you planning to take one of the pods?" Incognito asked.

"Yes, it is the fastest way to the palace in Nepal, and the tunnel connects directly to it."

"But this High General Lee might be suspicious if you just suddenly show up and tell him to stop an attack that the emperor may have ordered," Naomi said. "And he probably also knows by now that the Forbidden City is under attack. How will you explain your escape?"

"Have no fear," Xing said. "I have quite the silver tongue. I have already made up several plausible stories to tell him."

"Even if you manage to convince High General Lee to give his authorization and use his communication center, it will take you an hour to get there," Oscar pointed out. "Those missiles will have reached Seoul by then."

"I shall have to buy Xing some time, then," Incognito said. He glanced at Gilda. "Brat, you will accompany me. Your walker will be useful for dealing with enemy aircraft."

"What, are you joking?" Gilda asked.

"Enough with this bull!" Eisenhorn shouted. "Don't you idiots get it? You're doing exactly what the enemy wants you to do!"

"I agree," Naomi said. "Temple is still lurking somewhere inside the palace. He could attack us while Incognito is away."

Oscar frowned. "Cloak has put us in a dilemma. Does Incognito stay, condemning millions to die and risking global nuclear war? Or do we let him go, putting ourselves at risk and giving Cloak a greater chance of victory?"

Incognito banged the butt of his scythe on the floor. "We're wasting time. You can all last for a measly hour without having to hide in my shadow."

"Yes," Oscar agreed. "We have no choice."

"You don't have to go with him, Gilda," Naomi told her.

"Well, I'm no use here," Gilda said. "I'm not excited about it, but I'll go."

"Those remaining behind will guard the emperor and the tunnel," Incognito said. "Try not to engage Temple either, but you could always set off the bomb in the blowhard's head if push comes to shove." He snapped his fingers. "Woman, put a spare pod on the tracks. Xing needs to depart immediately."

Naomi gave him a sour look but complied, levitating one of the spare pods onto the tracks. Xing quickly got in, already fiddling with the seat belt. The blast doors opened. The pod was clear for launch. Gilda climbed into her walker and activated it.

Incognito grabbed Magenta's leg and gave Oscar one final look. "Radcliffe, make sure they conduct themselves accordingly."

"Be quick about it," Oscar told him. "Conserve your strength."

"I will use only the bare minimum."

"See you, Gilda!" Slate shouted. "Don't get nuked!"

"Screw you," Gilda said, smiling. She made eye contact with Naomi, who returned the smile. Straper didn't say much of a farewell but did nod to Gilda.

Incognito turned to Naomi. "Woman."

She didn't want to acknowledge him but could feel his gaze and decided to look his way. She saw his eyes and almost gasped out loud.

These were not the cold eyes she was so used to. She saw sadness in them.

"We will put an end to Temple," Incognito told her. "I will fulfill my word."

Incognito and Magenta became intangible and flew down the tunnel. Then they ascended, disappearing into the tunnel's ceiling.

Naomi was lost for words.

"I hope you aren't going soft," Slate said. "He's a danger to us all. One emo moment doesn't redeem him of all the trouble he's put us and the world through."

"I know that," Naomi said. "I know that all too well."

"I'm ready to leave now," Xing said.

Eisenhorn saw there was an empty seat next to Xing. A way out of there. Some part of him wanted to hop in and forget this whole mess.

But that wasn't manly at all.

"Shu, I want you to go with him," Eisenhorn said.

Shu looked innocently at him. "I beg your pardon? What about you?"

"I gotta stay. They might need that bomb in my head."

"Your government has done so many terrible things to you. You have given everything you had, only to be treated horribly in return."

"Sounds familiar, but I'm not doing it for my government. I'm doing it for you. I'm doing it for Johnson. I'm doing it for all my cadets who died at the hands of Cloak. I'm doing it to avenge all their deaths, to remind those murdering bastards that our lives are worth a damn."

A few tears escaped Shu's eyes. "Randolph, you have been so good to me."

"That's supposed to be my line."

Shu leaned in and pecked him on the cheek. Eisenhorn's smirk melted away, his whole face going beet red. For once, this color change in the general's complexion did not happen out of anger or inebriation. Shu giggled at his reaction and left him where he stood, getting into the pod and sitting next to Xing.

"I am still not sure what my opinion is of you," Xing told Eisenhorn. "Nevertheless, I am glad to have known you."

"You're acting like we're all gonna die. Get outta here already!"

Shu gave Eisenhorn one last fragile smile before the pod door sealed shut. There was a loud humming. Then the pod moved forward at a leisurely pace, getting faster as it went along. It entered the tunnel and picked up speed. The pod soon became nothing more than a white dot to Eisenhorn. He felt his eyes water.

Naomi went over to him and touched his shoulder. "I think you'll make a fine addition to our team."

The general found himself grinning. "Lady, I was always part of this team. If anything, you're the newcomer."

Slate, Naomi, Eisenhorn, Straper, and Oscar were all that was left, not including their two prisoners. The emperor swore as he saw Xing make his escape. A whimper came from Thistle. Naomi went to the child and gently shook her. Thistle did not budge. That made Naomi worry, even though this girl was a foe.

"What are we going to do with you?" Naomi wondered. "I suppose we could leave you in Xing's capable hands. He'll find a good home for you if he's as merciful as he appears."

"We still have one more of those swanky guns left," Slate said. "I don't wanna have to use it, but we shouldn't turn our backs on this one either."

"Your suspicion is healthy," Naomi said. "If it comes to it, I'll pull the trigger."

"Suit yourself."

There was a small tremor. The loading bay shook.

Naomi tensed up. "You feel that?"

Slate nodded. "Yeah, was that a bomb?"

A second tremor came. This one was more violent. Everyone standing up was thrown off their feet, even Slate and Naomi. Two big concrete slabs fell from the ceiling and shattered on the floor. The emperor squealed as a chunk of rubble hit the side of his head, leaving a nasty wound.

"They must be bombing us from above!" Naomi shouted.

"No!" Oscar yelled. "The force field would have protected us!"

"I AM HIGH GENERAL FANG!" a bombastic voice announced over loudspeakers in English. "SURRENDER, FOREIGN ROACHES! I HAVE YOU TRAPPED!"

They were able to hear him this deep underground because the last explosion had created an opening that led all the way to the surface. Naomi and Eisenhorn looked up through the opening and saw a sliver of clear blue sky.

There was no force field to be seen.

"Should've gotten in the pod," the general groaned.

***

The Chinese servants let out a collective scream when the tremors began. Over two hundred men, women, and children were gathered in a large one-room bunker. It had a low-hanging ceiling, poor ventilation, and no toilets, making for an uncomfortable stay. To make matters worse, there was no light. A few guards were there to keep the peace. They had their work cut out for them.

"Keep quiet!" a guard yelled. "Do not fear. The emperor is safe. He would want us to stay out of the way and let us guards handle the situation."

"We should help our emperor!" hollered an older man who worked in the kitchen. "If foreigners dare set foot in the Forbidden City, it is our duty to take up arms."

"What about food?" a woman asked. She cradled a toddler who wouldn't stop crying.

"Food is here," the guard lied. "Just be patient and wait for us to distribute it."

"And I think we figured out the gas lighting," another guard reported.

"Finally! Turn them on."

The guards turned on the gas and lit the lamps, the sudden light momentarily blinding everyone. Despite that, everyone welcomed this illumination. The toddler stopped crying, a few people sighed, and the guards became less tense.

A lone woman screamed. The guards turned to see where it had come from. Then they screamed too.

Temple stood in the center of the room. All the shrieks merged into one. How did they not notice him until now? Everyone scrambled to get as far from the beast as possible. Even the guards fled. Several people broke their shoulders trying to knock down the door that led to the surface. In their terror, they forgot the door had been sealed from the outside. The toddler was crying so hard now that someone went partially deaf in one ear. Nails clawed at the walls, breaking against the metal. Blood was smeared everywhere.

Temple raised a glowing finger.

Young Powell had no desire to come here.

But this was too important to leave in the hands of a clone. He only knew the gist of the situation and already felt he must see to this himself. Western Union forces, including *Leviathan*, were making their way to Syria to confront the United Third. Now this new fiasco had popped up. Today was going to be a busy day.

He had flown from Cheyenne Mountain directly to Washington, DC, and was now seated in the White House Situation Room. For obvious reasons, Young Powell had taken up a fake identity, posing as a presidential adviser. Quinn had arranged for him to be seated next to the clone so Young Powell could subtly give orders to the faux president if the need arose.

Familiar faces began entering the room. Astrid Herman was thin and exhausted, the stress of dealing with the Occupied Territories taking its toll on her. Next came Ivan Kazakov, who also looked ragged. Bartley Reynolds shuffled in, chowing down on a greasy burrito. Unlike the other leaders of the Western Union, Reynolds had bloated rather than thinned, his obesity reaching Falstaffian levels. His chair let out a cry of pain as he rested his ample rear on it.

The recently promoted Lexington made himself comfortable in a chair next to Young Powell. The scrawny man with the pencil-thin mustache was eying Herman from across the room with wandering eyes. He had replaced Redwood as fleet admiral. Lexington wasn't cunning or likeable, and that was just the way Young Powell wanted it. Another loyal lackey rather than a rival. Young Powell was already considering replacements for Herman and Kazakov, but maybe he was getting ahead of himself. He hadn't even found a replacement for Cromwell yet.

"I haven't had the pleasure," Lexington whispered into Young Powell's ear. Young Powell was comforted by the fact that this rodent couldn't recognize him.

"My name is Robert Mitchell," Young Powell lied. "I recently caught the eye of the president and have been advising him for several weeks now."

"A newcomer, eh?" Lexington simpered. "I'm something of a newbie myself. Only a few weeks ago, I was just another vice admiral. Now I'm running the whole navy. That Redwood looked down on me for years, but he got what was coming to him."

A female intern with a tray of glasses walked up to them. "Water, gentlemen?"

"Anything you're serving, I'll drink," Lexington breathed, winking at her.

The intern smiled politely and gave him a glass, but she quickly turned her attention to Young Powell. "Water, sir?"

"No, but thank you." He noticed the intern's nervousness. "Something the matter?"

"I'm sorry. It's just that you look exactly like Cary Grant."

"A compliment?"

"An observation. I really like old movies. Oh, better get going! Sorry if I was too casual."

"Not at all. Have a good day."

The intern blushed and bounced away. Young Powell grinned inwardly. That was the fifth woman who'd flirted with him since he got off the plane. This new body came with all sorts of perks. He was reminded of Natalie, which ruined his good mood. Lately, she was becoming too clingy for her own good. Maybe a pruning was in order.

"How did you get her to eat out of your palm like that?" Lexington asked him. "You must be wearing one of those new colognes. I thought they were only in the test phase. I've been trying to buy some for ages."

"Sorry, my friend. There's no secret to my success. I'm all natural."

At last, the man of the hour arrived. Or rather, the man of the hour's clone arrived. Everyone stood upon his entrance. The clone was a spitting image of

Powell's former self, old and plump. Now Powell was Young Powell. Now he would rule the West for eternity, along with the rest of the world. Now it was only a matter of winning this measly war.

Fake Powell took his seat next to Young Powell, neither acknowledging the other. Everyone sat back down. The doors were sealed. The lights dimmed. Holographic people materialized, two of them the British and Japanese prime ministers. It just warmed Young Powell's heart that Redwood was nowhere in sight.

A holographic screen popped up. All eyes focused on it. Satellite photos of the Forbidden City were displayed, showing multiple angles of the palace. Some photos depicted a force field surrounding the palace, while more recent photos that had come in only moments ago showed no force field around it any longer.

"Approximately four hours ago, a disturbance began inside the Forbidden City," Kazakov said from his seat. The holographic screen switched to a blurred image of a man with a scythe flying through the air. "We believe Incognito is responsible."

"That goes against all our intelligence reports," Herman interrupted. "The United Third was supposed to be brokering an alliance with the Chinese. If what you are saying is true, then intelligence has let us down once again."

"Mere speculation," Reynolds grumbled, devouring the last of his burrito. "Just because both groups are foreigners doesn't mean they like each other any more than we like them."

"Our enemies are killing each other," Fake Powell mused. "Seems to me that's a good thing. Well, except for the fifty nukes aimed at Seoul. What's their status?"

"They have not yet launched," Kazakov said. "However, it would only take ten minutes for the missiles to reach Seoul. The only consolation is most of the Chinese Empire's ICBMs are poorly maintained and constructed before the Great Choke, hand-me-downs from the former communist government. There is a good chance half of them will fail."

"Only one needs to work," the Japanese PM told them. "Our civilians do not know about this threat yet, but we may have to begin evacuations. Those short-range missiles could easily be rerouted to target Japanese cities instead of Seoul."

"Why in the hell are they targeting only one city?" the British PM asked.

"I believe they are concerned we might use the disturbance going on in the Forbidden City as an opportunity to attack," Herman said. "They are flexing their muscles, so to speak, to keep us from doing anything reckless."

"And what if they nuke Korea?" Fake Powell asked. "How am I gonna respond to that? Do I blow up one of their cities? Do I blow up all of them?"

Reynolds burped. "Damn nukes... This is why we can't have world wars anymore."

"Sir, force is the only appropriate response to force," Young Powell counseled his clone. All the others had no idea who the newbie was giving the president such bold advice, but they let it play out. The president had invited him for a reason.

"How much force are we talking about here?" Fake Powell pried.

Young Powell grinned. "All of it."

"I agree," Lexington added. He sensed a rapport between the so-called Robert Mitchell and the president. If he agreed with everything this Mitchell advised, it would undoubtedly get him in the president's good books. "You can't just ignore a nuclear strike. If those Chinamen are stupid enough to antagonize us, we'll incinerate them."

"If we take that course of action, at least a dozen of our cities will be destroyed," Herman warned. "That's the best-case scenario."

"I'm well aware of the costs," Fake Powell snapped. He turned his eyes down at the table. "Yeah, all of it... I like the sound of that."

Herman gave Kazakov a concerned glance. He returned one.

An army officer walked up to Kazakov and whispered to him. Kazakov whispered back. A new satellite image then appeared on the screen. It depicted a magenta walker cruising two thousand feet above China.

Flying next to it was Incognito.

Fake Powell pounded his hand on the table. "What's that freak up to now? And why is the Plato girl with him?"

"They are headed toward the predetermined flight path of the missiles," Kazakov said. "This photo was taken four minutes ago."

"Is he attempting to obtain another nuke?" Herman asked.

Young Powell had no idea what to make of this. Was Incognito trying to play the hero? If that was the case, Cloak must be involved. More and more, Young Powell was regretting not doing away with those mutant pieces of shit already.

Another officer ran up to Kazakov. Young Powell rolled his eyes. *Where do these idiots come from?* Kazakov listened to the man's words, his eyes growing wider as the conversation progressed. *Fantastic,* Young Powell seethed, *what now?*

An alarm rang. The holographic screen brought up a map with moving red dots on it.

They were all heading to the Korean Peninsula.

"Sir," Kazakov said. "The Chinese have launched their missiles."

Everyone in the situation room was quiet, their fear only apparent through their facial expressions. They waited to see how their commander in chief would respond.

Fake Powell remained stone-still. Something brewed within his skull. Young Powell frowned. Was this clone falling apart on him already?

"I am not pleased," Fake Powell said finally. "Not one bit."

***

Camilla Ryder sat in her walker, waiting for anything.

This was how she had spent most of the past week. She was on constant alert, her walker ready to take off at any time. The airfield she was staying at had no choice but to tolerate her presence, since she now wielded authority only dwarfed by President Powell's.

She had told the navy ships patrolling the East China Sea to lay more underwater sensors. If Incognito was going to the Forbidden City to organize an alliance, he would likely get there by traveling through these waters in his stealth submarine. There were also unconfirmed reports of the Helmet Man being spotted doing battle off Mumbai's coast. Ryder was curious, but the reports were too vague to act on. She and her subordinates would remain here for now.

She had checked in with Hank Powers the day before. A small hologram of the beefy man had appeared inside the cockpit.

"What is Keito's condition?" Ryder had asked him.

"Well, he ain't on death's doorstep anymore," Powers said. "Still unconscious, but he'll be back to his feet soon. Kennedy is still recovering at the other hospital. She's not answering my calls. I have to get updates from the nurses."

"Is Asami Kusanagi behaving herself?"

"Getting restless. She wants to roam the city. Told her it wasn't a good idea. People are nervous with the war going on. A lot of Asians have been getting harassed by gangs, and the police are too often looking the other way. I know she can defend herself and all. I'm just worried she's going to snap somebody's neck."

"Things are deteriorating in America, I assume."

"Not just America, boss. All of Europe is pretty uptight too, though they're more concerned about the United Third and their Saladin Federation. And I heard our troops are about to move in on Aleppo. They're calling it the deciding battle. Everyone's on the edge of their seats."

"The citizens of South Korea are also anxious," Ryder said. "This is understandable, considering their proximity to the Chinese Empire. Anything else to report?"

"No, except that I'm bored. Just be careful, boss. You sure you don't want me to come over there and help you out?"

"Stay where you are, Powers. That is an order. York and Patel will assist me."

"All right," Powers muttered. "I'll be waiting here for you." Then he stroked his handlebar mustache. Ryder wouldn't have been surprised if it had purred. "Boss, I was hoping that after all this was over, you'd like to eat out or something, you know…"

"It will never be over," Ryder said. "Goodbye, Hank."

Ryder now thought back on that conversation. It struck her as odd that she had called Powers by his first name. She had never done that before. It also forced her to review why she had benched him. He had redeemed himself during the failed invasion, so why did she not want him around anymore? Did their awkward encounter have anything to do with her decision? Was her opinion of him evolving? Did she wish to keep him safe?

Or was she ashamed?

Her radio cried annoyingly. Someone was trying to contact her.

"This is Ryder," she answered.

"Quinn here! Ryder, do you have any idea what's happening right now?"

"Anything relevant to me?"

"Lady, this is relevant to everyone. Nukes have been launched and are headed for Seoul. We're on the verge of a nuclear holocaust."

"I happen to be in Seoul. Should I evacuate?"

"If you're sane. Incognito's trying to intercept these missiles, along with Plato's brat. A squadron of Chinese fighter jets is now pursuing them. And before all this, Incognito and his stooges attacked the Forbidden City."

"So, Incognito isn't seeking an alliance with the Chinese. Are these missiles the only ones that have been launched?"

"Yeah, but we're still screwed! Damn it, why'd this have to happen?"

"Either these missiles were launched as a show of force to the Western Union or as a way to keep Incognito occupied."

Quinn calmed down. "Guess even Incognito doesn't want the world to end."

"No, he only wishes to see the West end. He needs the world in order to build his own ideal one. Having it turn to a wasteland is not in his best interests."

"Ryder, we're hoping to have *Excalibur* in range soon so it can intercept any nuclear missiles heading this way, but we need to stall for time until then."

"Very well, then. Should I focus my efforts on capturing Incognito or delaying those missiles from reaching Korea?"

"The president expects you to do both. Now hurry!"

The world was a blur to Gilda. They moved so fast that it hurt her head just looking out her window. Incognito kept his eyes locked on the horizon as he dragged Magenta behind him. Despite her negative feelings for him, Gilda had to admit that Incognito was a true professional, and for a situation like this, there could be no fooling around.

The one time they slowed down was when a squadron of Chinese fighter jets nearly crossed their path. Incognito dropped down near to ground level and decreased his speed in order to avoid detection. He had no desire to waste time on small fries.

During this period, Gilda saw in the distance the decaying remains of a once-great metropolis, the skyscrapers crumbling and gray. Then they passed over small villages and vast fields of crops. Meek farmers busied themselves with harvesting. They were hunched over, attending to their work, most not even noticing the magenta walker passing overhead. Those that did notice made a serious effort to forget they ever saw it.

It dawned on Gilda that most of these farmers were women and children, while any adult male was old or disabled. All the able-bodied men had become soldiers. She wondered how many of the mind-controlled victims in Tiananmen Square used to have families like those below. Seeing these submissive people go about their daily lives also gave her a whole new appreciation of the emperor's evil. He wasn't the people's protector. He was their slave master. Gilda had thought the Chinese would be better off than the people in India or the other subservient nations who worked in those ghastly factories. It was now obvious the only benefit the Chinese had over other citizens of the empire was cleaner air.

Once the squadron passed, they flew up to their original altitude and accelerated.

"We're almost above the East China Sea," Tim said. "Why are we here, Ms. Gilda?"

"To stop a nuclear war," Gilda said, realizing how preposterous it sounded.

"Oh, is that all?"

"Are you being sarcastic?"

"Of course I am!"

"Hush up, toaster," Incognito spat at the autopilot through the radio in his mask. "We've reached our destination."

He let go of Magenta. Now it floated in midair on its own, weapons ready. Every muscle in Gilda's body felt like it was about to snap from the tension. They had to stop a whole arsenal of nuclear missiles before the apocalypse was triggered. She kept thinking this, but it all seemed so theoretical to her. The fate of the world literally rested on their shoulders. Failure was not an option, or at least it was a catastrophic one.

"I'm picking up an incoming missile on my sensors," Tim said. "We're not the target, Ms. Gilda, but we're in its way."

"You hear that?" she asked Incognito.

"Yes, and I already see it," he said.

Sure enough, a long and deadly projectile glimmered in the distance, heading toward them faster than sound itself.

Incognito was gone. Gilda gasped at his speed. The glimmer in the distance vanished. Incognito appeared again before her.

"One missile down," he said. "And we've got company, a squadron of Chinese fighter jets. You deal with them. I shall attend to the missiles."

He disappeared again. More glimmers appeared along the horizon. A few of them went out. Incognito was already making fast work of them.

"A squadron of jets!" Tim cried. "Incognito's right! They're approaching our location!"

Gilda could see them with her naked eyes. Crimson aircraft were coming her way. They were worn-out things, built before the Choke. Gilda knew she would probably end up killing the pilots and wasn't looking forward to it.

Something else was also flying with the jets. It left behind a trail of flame.

"Ember," Gilda whispered.

Tim was confused. "Who?"

"One of the Gifted."

"Can we defeat her?"

"At the very least, we'll keep that psycho occupied. What do you think?"

Tim didn't respond.

"Tim?" Gilda was worried that he might have malfunctioned right when he nearly blew her eardrums out with his wailing.

"Ms. Gilda, a squadron of fighter jets!"

Gilda wished Tim had teeth so she could kick them in. "You already told me that. I can see them coming a mile away."

"No, a different squadron!"

Another squadron? Gilda scanned the sky and checked her radar to see where they might be coming from. Then she saw a group of fighter jet drones fast approaching.

Three flying walkers led them.

"It's the Western Union!" Tim shouted.

"No," Gilda said. "It's Ryder."

***

"What's our strategy, ma'am?" York asked Ryder.

"Allow Incognito to continue destroying the oncoming nuclear missiles for now," Ryder said. "However, when you spot an opening, take him down."

"Got it."

"But again, do your best to capture him alive."

"Ma'am, I don't know if we can do that."

"Like I said, do your best. Now hurry."

Obsidian accelerated, leaving the two other walkers behind. York leaned forward as he eyed his target in the distance. They were being asked to do the impossible, but if he could capture Incognito alive, he would earn Ryder's trust for sure.

But first, he had to survive the battle.

"Ready, Patel?" he asked.

"Roger that," she said, sounding flat and unenthusiastic.

"Cheer up, Patel. We're about to take down our greatest enemy."

"Then we can go back to conquering the world?"

York didn't have a reply. He only gunned his blue walker forward.

***

Geppetto couldn't help but whistle when he saw all those drones and the black walker going after that purple-haired brat. *Good, one less enemy to worry about,* he thought.

"Ember, come in," he said into the radio. Geppetto was seated inside a Chinese fighter jet. The pilot sat in front of him and spoke half-decent English. The aircraft continuously rumbled. Geppetto worried this old piece of junk would fall apart mid-flight.

"The view is breathtaking!" Ember sang into her radio. "The only thing that could make it prettier is a radiant mushroom cloud."

"Change of plans. Let's leave Plato to the Western Union and go after Incognito."

"I thought Sebastian just wanted us to keep him busy, and I'm not exactly eager to get chopped in half by a scythe."

"You got me with you, remember? All you and the other fighter jets have to do is distract Incognito for a bit. Then I'll swoop in and take control of him. I don't care how dangerous his powers are. He won't be able to resist my influence for long."

"That's right! Your ability is quite the trump card. Once you take control of him, can I deliver the finishing blow?"

"By all means." Geppetto then spoke to the pilot. "Tell the other jets to attack Incognito. Wait for my go-ahead before going in yourself. You just have to get me within a couple hundred meters so I can lock in on him."

The pilot nodded, stoic and obedient, and yelled into his radio. The other fighter jets broke out of formation and made a U-turn, beginning their pursuit of Incognito. Ember followed, giggling so loud, Geppetto had to turn his radio off to preserve his hearing.

For over a year, he had not been quite sure what he wanted anymore. With Atlas dead, there didn't seem much point in living. Revenge wasn't a very strong motivator either. Who was responsible for all this pain and sorrow? He was tempted to say the Mentor, only to realize the Mentor was not the first evil but the final evil, the last great sin. Everything seemed to lead up to the Mentor. Sebastian told him there was purpose to his pain and that the Mentor knew the answer. For some reason, Geppetto was kind of buying into it.

In the end, Schmitt had convinced him. Or rather, his existence did. His cruelty was limitless, yet he lived on. There had to be a reason why someone so evil could live for so long, allowed to commit so many horrible acts. Wasn't there justice in this life? Don't psychos get what's coming to them? Then how come Schmitt was still alive? How come Emperor Long had been allowed to abuse his subjects for so long? Why hadn't the Western Union been toppled yet after forcing its will on the world? Why did Atlas have to die? Why were the Gifted forced to live this existence?

The Mentor knew. The Mentor had the answer. The Mentor had *all* the answers. The Mentor would teach the world. The Mentor knew the purpose of evil, the meaning of life.

Geppetto had become a believer.

Had this been a part of Sebastian's plan, to send him on a bizarre odyssey and force him to interact with one of the vilest men alive in order to be converted? That could very well be. Sebastian was clever like that. Geppetto found he wasn't angry with Sebastian, however. If anything, he felt a little grateful.

That was why he would kill Incognito, the one man who was a legitimate threat to Cloak and its plans. Geppetto didn't even care about sucking up to the bosses or any worldly gains. He only wanted the answer, the reason for suffering.

If that meant starting a nuclear war, then so be it.

***

That was the twenty-fifth missile.

Incognito's scythe had cut it through the middle. The two halves spiraled downward, crashing into the sea. There was no need to worry about accidentally setting off the nukes. They were only meant to detonate once they had reached their target.

Incognito coughed. Blood spattered the inside of his mask. He ignored it, but he couldn't ignore the relentless pain in his chest. He was reaching his limit. It was a stroke of luck that he had made it this far on such little steam.

A syringe full of yellow liquid weighed heavily in his pocket. Incognito contemplated injecting himself with it but decided to wait until later. Once he injected himself, he would have a brief burst of power before crashing, perhaps never to recover. He couldn't afford to use it now, not until Temple showed himself.

A wave of flame almost cooked Incognito alive, but he was fast and alert, clearing the area. More flames came at him. He avoided the attack, getting irritated fast.

"Let's see if you live up to your reputation!" Ember shrieked. She twirled, flinging a dozen fireballs. They didn't even come close to hitting him.

"Your flamboyant antics are tiresome," Incognito said. "Of all the depravities excreted by the West, you rank near the top."

"A charmer, aren't you?" Ember threw more flames. Incognito dodged again. He decided to kill her right then and there. The only thing that stopped him was the five fighter jets that fired twenty missiles at him. The projectiles exploded. Incognito flew back immediately. He felt the heat on his back, not getting hurt but at the same time realizing it had been a close call. Wasn't the brat supposed to keep these foes busy?

Numerous glimmers on the horizon were now visible. More nuclear missiles.

Incognito sighed. How long would this go on for? The Chinese Empire had around five thousand nuclear warheads. There was no way he could take them all out.

Ember threw more fire. "Prepare to burn, Incognito!"

"Like I would die at the hands of a harlot."

***

The drones never went in for the kill. They were content with buzzing around Magenta like flies. Gilda knew these aircraft weren't occupied by people and planned to blow them to bits the moment they made a bad move.

"What aren't they attacking, Ms. Gilda?" Tim asked. "Are their intentions friendly?"

"Maybe," Gilda said. "But I'm never that lucky."

The drones lost interest in her, flying off in favor of a new target.

"Now where are they going?" Gilda asked no one in particular.

The radio beeped. Someone was trying to reach her. She could guess who. The question was whether or not to answer. Ryder might try to play mind games, but Gilda could also use this opportunity to reason with her. At the very least she could stall for time, so she answered.

"I did not expect to find you here," Ryder said over the radio, her voice empty.

"Look, quit being a freak and listen," Gilda said. "The Chinese aren't behind this. It's Cloak. Some of the Gifted are here right now."

"What would Cloak gain from starting a nuclear war?"

"They're not trying to start a nuclear war. They're trying to stop Incognito."

"I believe you."

Whoa. Gilda had not expected that, but she recovered. "Then help us."

"After careful consideration, I have sent the drones to combat the Chinese fighter jets," Ryder said. "Incognito is doing a service for the Western Union, strange as that may sound. My forces will not intervene. However, we will capture him the moment the missiles cease coming or he grows too tired to be of any more use."

"You're welcome to try."

"You clearly feel no loyalty toward Incognito. Perhaps there is some hope for you."

"Thanks, I guess."

"I had a conversation with your father. We discussed you and all the sacrifices he made so that you could be happy. It would be a shame to waste his efforts."

"What's between my dad and me has nothing to do with you," Gilda snapped. "I'm going to keep doing what I'm doing till Cloak is put down once and for all. They've managed to take over the Chinese Empire. They can't be left alone."

"I do not wish to fight you, Gilda Plato. That is why I request your assistance in capturing Incognito as soon as he is vulnerable."

"What? No way! We need Incognito's help to destroy Cloak."

"Do you?" Ryder asked. "The Helmet Man is one of the strongest opponents I have ever faced, and he is only getting stronger. With his help, I have no doubt you could overcome any challenge Cloak throws your way."

"Thanks for the vote of confidence, but I'd rather be safe than sorry."

"You and your friends must have considered going against Incognito at one time or another. Now is the optimal time to do so."

"But the nukes—"

"As I said, we will wait until either Incognito succeeds or fails. The Western Union is preparing *Excalibur* to target any nuclear missiles approaching Korea. Incognito only needs to hold off the barrage until *Excalibur* is in range."

Gilda was starting to regret turning on the radio. Ryder was getting to her.

But wasn't she right? Slate and Naomi were planning to kill Incognito the moment he became a liability. Gilda didn't like the idea of killing anyone, but she probably wouldn't feel all that guilty if it was Incognito.

Then she remembered the reason they came to China in the first place. Temple. If he was as dangerous as everyone said, they would need Incognito by their side.

And what about Slate? What would he say if she decided help Ryder kill Incognito? Gilda realized he would probably say it was a dumb idea. Slate was exceedingly smart in one major area, and that was combat. If he thought they should hold off on killing Incognito until they defeated Cloak, then she would wait too.

"Listen up, Ryder," Gilda said. "I—"

Her vision faded, as did her own voice. She slipped into unconsciousness like one would a pool. It was refreshing. It was welcoming. Ryder's voice echoed over the radio, but it was unintelligible. Gilda was soon submerged.

You naughty girl, her mother cooed. *You cannot deny the lord.*

CHAPTER 57

There was no island this time.

Gilda was floating. The water licking her body was black as coal. The starlight sky gave her skin a holy glow.

Look at yourself, her mother said. *That temple was made to be toppled.*

"I was awake..."

Now you're with me. Did you really think you had any control? I can take you whenever I wish. You cannot resist the pull of the moon.

"You're a liar..."

We're anything but.

"I hate you..."

As was meant to be.

"I want out of here..."

You'll never be free. Not as long as you have my blood.

"Shut up." Gilda closed her eyes to the heavens, hoping her own indifference would make it go away. She opened her eyes again. The stars were gone.

The moon was full.

What gives the moon its light? The voice came from everywhere and nowhere. *The answer is it can only reflect the light of the sun.*

The moon was set on fire.

The endless sea began to boil. Limbs emerged, shriveled and black, grasping at the light. There had to be millions of them. The arms nearest Gilda grabbed her. They were not gentle. They tore at her flesh, using their nails, making her bleed. She thrashed and screamed, but her struggling was useless and her screams mute.

Gaze into the reflection. Behold the lord of evil.

***

"Ms. Gilda, please wake up!"

Tim's shrill voice broke the spell. Gilda woke with a start, the air in the cockpit moist and foul. How long had she been unconscious?

"You talked in your sleep!" Tim wailed. "You told Ryder that you didn't agree to her terms, that you wanted to confront Incognito immediately. When she disagreed, you started shooting at her and Incognito!"

That made Gilda sit up. "Tim, why didn't you stop me?"

"I couldn't! Oscar made it so I couldn't take control of any essential functions during mid-flight anymore. Remember what happened when Cyphrus took me over?"

Gilda took inventory of her surroundings. The drones and Chinese fighter jets were fighting each other. There had to be at least seven dogfights going on. One drone collided with a Chinese jet, the impact destroying both. Ember was tossing flames at nearly everything. As for Incognito, he kept reappearing and disappearing, the planes always one step behind. He was so preoccupied with the missiles that the jets now actually stood a chance.

Obsidian fired a laser at Magenta. Gilda didn't have time to dodge. The laser pierced her walker's shoulder. The entire mecha shook so hard that she thought it was about to fall apart.

"I thought you were a reasonable girl," Ryder said over the radio. "It is clear I was wrong. I believe you have undergone some sort of psychotic break."

"You're one to talk!" Gilda spat.

Ryder fired more lasers. Gilda avoided these and fired her cannon. Obsidian moved to the right, the shell zooming past it.

"Your father would be disappointed."

"Ryder, I'm back in control! Let's stop now, please!"

"I finish all my fights, Plato."

They fought on. It was repetitive and tiresome. They dodged when they had to and fired when they could. The two machines were an equal match, and so were the pilots.

However, what determined the outcome of the fight was a lone drone falling from the sky. Gilda eyed it for a moment before coming up with a plan.

"How tough would you say that drone's armor is?" Gilda asked her autopilot.

"Not tough enough in the end," Tim said.

Gilda went for it anyway. She sped her walker to where she thought the drone was going to fall. Ryder shot her lasers, but Gilda maneuvered out of their path. Magenta caught the falling drone by one of its wings and held it like a shield.

"Let's see how well the Western Union makes these things," Gilda said.

Magenta flew right at Obsidian. Ryder fired her lasers. They all struck the makeshift shield. One of the lasers went through the drone's hull and clipped Magenta's wing. Gilda struggled for control as her walker twisted around, destabilizing. She pulled up. Her walker's flight path straightened as she braced for impact.

The drone smashed into Obsidian. Ryder's wrist broke. Her brain was rattled. Magenta dropped its shield, the crumpled drone plummeting a thousand feet down. Magenta then grabbed one of Obsidian's wings and snapped it like a twig.

Ryder had no chance. Her walker ceased to be airborne. It went down as fast as the drone had. Gilda gasped. Had she just killed Ryder?

Parachutes emerged from Obsidian's back, slowing the walker down. Gilda let out a breath. Ryder wasn't dead, and she was out of the way.

"I've wasted enough time here," Gilda told Tim. "Let's help Incognito now."

"Ms. Gilda, what happened? It's not normal to pass out like that."

"Tim, not right now."

"Ms. Gilda, you may not believe a machine can feel, but I do have a vested interest in your well-being. You can't have someone ride inside you without getting attached."

"I don't know about that..."

"Please, Ms. Gilda. What happened?"

Gilda thought back to her dream and shivered. "You wouldn't understand. I don't think *I* really understand."

"I care about you, Ms. Gilda," Tim told her. "You're my mistress."

Gilda smiled. Tim was getting to her. "Thank you, Tim. I appreciate your concern."

"Thank you, Ms. Gilda."

"Just don't ever call me your mistress again."

***

Incognito was not in a good mood. First the missiles, then the jets and Ember. Now it appeared the Plato brat had betrayed him. Her walker had flown in and fired its weapons at him. Now Magenta was preoccupied with Ryder, who had also decided to show up for the party. Would he never be rid of all these annoying gnats?

He sliced his fortieth missile in half and then tore the wings off three jets, the pilots using their last moments alive to gasp and scream.

A few fireballs flew at Incognito.

"Forgot about me, old-timer?" Ember shrieked. She was having loads of fun. Incognito wasn't and found he couldn't tolerate this woman any longer. He stabbed his scythe into a passing fighter jet, taking it for himself.

"Energy is your weakness!" Ember yelled. "Sebastian told me!" Flames curled around her, forming a giant protective orb of flame around herself. "Try to get me now, geezer!"

Incognito tossed the jet at her.

Ember squealed at the sight. The jet collided with her protective orb, creating an explosion that knocked her out of the air. A piece of the jet's wing stabbed her in the lower abdomen. Her protective orb dissolved. She squealed harder and descended until Incognito could no longer see her. Good riddance.

Geppetto watched this scene from a distance, shaking his head as he saw

Ember fall. He almost felt sorry for the crazy gal. Now it was his turn. For some reason, he hadn't yet been able to use his powers on Incognito. Geppetto could usually start controlling people's gross functions once they came within two kilometers of him. Maybe Incognito was moving too fast for his powers to hone in on. But now his pilot had brought him within a kilometer of his target. He was close enough now. He reached out with his mind.

Nothing.

Geppetto saw the pilot's head fly off.

The scythe then stabbed Geppetto in the chest.

The specter lifted him out of the jet, which started to fall from the sky as soon as the beheaded pilot slumped in his chair. Incognito floated in midair, Geppetto hanging off the scythe. The blade stuck out of his back. Blood filled his left lung. He could not scream, only dribbling red from his ajar mouth.

"A clever plan, dwarf," Incognito seethed. "You might have succeeded had I not anticipated your meddling."

"My powers..." Geppetto gurgled. "They don't fail..."

"Wrong. They just did. Thank Radcliffe for that. He surgically implanted pandorium mesh underneath my scalp years ago. Radcliffe wasn't sure this protective measure would work, but confidence has never been his strong suit."

"Clever..." Geppetto coughed. He took a small aerosol can from his pocket and sprayed vapor at his opponent. Incognito squinted but had no other reaction.

"I hate Schmitt beyond reason," Geppetto told him. "But he's a smart cookie ... I'll give him that..."

At the mention of Schmitt's name, Incognito knew Geppetto had done something devastating. If there was one thing Schmitt was good at, it was making weapons.

Incognito started to feel weak. Even worse, he felt heavy.

"Guess I'm taking one for the team..." Geppetto whispered. "Even better ... I get to take a Keymaster with me..."

Geppetto slipped off Incognito's blade, producing a grotesque squeaking noise. Then he hurtled toward the water far below.

But he wasn't the only one falling. As gravity began pulling him downward, Incognito had come to the horrid realization of what had just been done to him.

His powers were gone.

Schmitt had put small particles of his patented superconductor material into a spray can. One whiff of the stuff and Incognito's powers became null. It was a little something Schmitt had provided should Geppetto have a close encounter with the intangible terrorist.

Incognito kept a grip on his scythe. How could he let that little troll get the better of him? More nuclear missiles were approaching. Who would stop them? His vision started to blur. He found himself too weak to do anything as Armageddon approached.

Sapphire dove after him.

"Now's our chance!" York yelled. "Cover me!"

"Roger that," Patel said. They had both been waiting on the sidelines for this very moment and had even stood by as Ryder plummeted toward the ground in her walker. There would be no distractions. Nothing could stop them from completing their mission.

Or so they thought. A disabled drone slammed into Garnet. Grimacing, Patel fought to stabilize her walker. York was just within reach of Incognito when Magenta crashed into Sapphire. He fought to shake it off, only to have one of his wings damaged. Sapphire spiraled through the air as alarms blared inside his cockpit. York could only curse his luck.

Incognito was just about to pass out when a large metal hand caught him and stopped his descent.

"What an ... unusual tomboy you are..." Incognito wheezed. "First you attack ... now you save... What is your endgame...?"

"I wasn't myself," Gilda said through her radio. "But don't expect an apology. I don't feel sorry for you in the slightest."

"So be it..." Incognito took out his syringe of yellow fluid, rolled up his sleeve, and shoved it into his arm. He squirmed and hyperventilated for a moment. Then he relaxed. He turned immaterial and slipped from Magenta's hand, floating like the world's deadliest balloon.

"Looks like Schmitt's trickery has worn off," Incognito said. "But that injection will only last for a few hours at most. I shall be lucky if I live through this ordeal."

"My sympathies," Gilda spat.

"Ms. Gilda!" Tim screamed.

"What is that infernal contraption yammering about now?" Incognito snapped.

"What is it, Tim?" Gilda asked.

"I detect a nuclear detonation! One of the missiles reached its target!"

"What!" Gilda shouted. "That's impossible! Incognito stopped all of them."

"Not unless one got past us when Geppetto sprayed me and you were preoccupied with Ryder," Incognito said.

Gilda's mouth went dry. "No, that's a load of shit! Cloak wouldn't be stupid enough to do something like that. They just wanted to distract us."

Incognito didn't respond.

"But Ryder..." Gilda went on. "She told me that *Excalibur* was going to take out any missiles that got past us."

"It clearly wasn't in range yet," Incognito told her. "Look over there."

Gilda turned her head and let out a muffled cry.

A dull glow radiated from the east.

Seoul was no more.

CHAPTER 58

"**S**ir, we have just confirmed that Seoul has been destroyed."

The Situation Room was still. Kazakov's words had been so simple for something so unthinkable. Herman covered her mouth. Reynolds looked stupefied. Lexington seemed to be having a silent nervous breakdown.

Young Powell folded his hands. He observed images of collapsed skyscrapers and charred bodies popping up on the holographic screen like internet ads. There was only one way to respond to this kind of carnage.

Fake Powell leaned back in his chair. A dark shadow fell over his face, making it look hard and ugly. The clone knew what to do on instinct.

"Prep the nukes."

***

Gilda gagged. Millions of people had just been snuffed out. Those numbers were ludicrous, having no meaning to the average human mind. It would take looking into the face of every burned corpse even to begin comprehending what just happened.

"It can't be," Gilda whispered. "All those people are—"

"You won't get away!" Patel screamed as her walker sped at Incognito. She slammed her hand down on a button. The air around her walker instantly shimmered from the intense heat. Incognito would have been incinerated if he hadn't sped out of its range, taking Magenta with him. He also managed to avoid the lasers that Garnet fired.

But then Sapphire came from the left. York had his walker draw its sword, fly forward, and take a slice at Magenta.

Frozen in her horror, Gilda could not find the will to block it.

But Incognito could. He plucked a passing nuclear missile and used it as a shield. The sword went halfway through it before stopping. York swore and yanked it out. Incognito, however, then bashed Sapphire with the missile. The walker spiraled backward.

Patel continued firing lasers. She forced herself to shove thoughts of the nuclear blast out of her mind. Even so, tears filled her eyes. They had let a whole city die. But they couldn't let Incognito escape. This whole endeavor had to be worth—

And then the fight was over.

Patel didn't even hear Sapphire's sword go into the back of her walker. She also didn't feel her lower half get cut off. Blood splattered the inside of her windshield.

"Incognito!" York tried to fathom why his walker was stabbing an ally. Had Incognito forced the sword into Garnet? Had the fiend swung Garnet into the blade? Either way, the result was the same. With this critical battle lost, York realized with a neutral expression that his ambitions of becoming squad leader and a war hero were dead.

And so was Patel, but not before the phantom floated next to her.

"Any confessions?" Incognito asked.

She managed to open her mouth a crack. "I ... I almost thought ... you were right..."

Incognito pressed a button on her panel.

Garnet superheated.

Sapphire's blue armor melted within seconds. York screamed as his flight suit caught fire and his sunglasses shattered. The pain plunged him into unconsciousness. Both walkers began to fall down into the sea with the other wreckage.

Having flown away before Garnet heated up, Incognito glided toward Magenta as he watched his foes descend faster and faster.

Gilda remained unresponsive.

With unblinking eyes, Incognito turned to stare at the glow emanating from the east. He did this for a moment before noticing glimmers coming from the west.

"More missiles," he said.

"More?" Gilda screamed, breaking out of her catatonic state. "Did you just say *more?* Hasn't Cloak done enough? Can they be any eviler?"

"Girl, go back to the Forbidden City. You and the others take refuge in a bomb shelter. The Forbidden City has many of them, I'm sure."

"Are you staying here?" she cried. "Why? What's the point?"

"Nuclear war is not guaranteed. Perhaps if I prevent the remaining missiles from reaching Korea, I might be able to avert catastrophe."

"But I ... I can't just leave! I have to help!"

"In your shell-shocked condition? No, you must ensure the Helmet Man's survival. Believe it or not, some part of me still has high hopes for him, even though the buffoon and the treacherous wench have been plotting to kill me ever since we undertook this ordeal."

"You ... you knew?"

"I have been at this far too long to be fooled by such amateurs. I simply played along in order to get them to come with me."

"You still think Slate will lead your Saladin Federation? You can swindle and threaten us all you want to, but we won't ever give in!"

"If you say so. Now leave. Save the Helmet Man."

Incognito vanished. A few glimmers on the horizon disappeared as well.

Gilda didn't know how to feel at that moment. She could only release a ragged breath. "Let's head back now, Tim. We need to help the others."

"Without Incognito, the return trip will be longer."

"I know... I'd like to say there's no rush."

Magenta flew away, turning its back to the nuclear glow.

***

What an odd way to die, Geppetto thought. He felt lightheaded. Understandable, considering his hemorrhaging chest wound and the thousand-foot fall. The sea was so perfect and blue that he couldn't tell if he had five hundred feet or only twenty left until he hit the water. He supposed it didn't matter. This moment felt like an eternity anyway.

Warmth overcame him. Was he dead? No, it was the heat of flames. Not the flames of hell either, but earthly ones.

"Gotcha," Ember said, not in the best shape herself.

Geppetto grimaced. "Get your hands off me..."

"So ungrateful," Ember huffed.

They landed on a small iceberg Ember had created. The waves rocked it like a cradle as Ember put Geppetto down. She examined her comrade's chest wound before placing her hands on it. Geppetto's flesh started to burn. The wound was soon sealed.

"I'm no doctor, but that might do the trick," Ember said. She turned to the mushroom cloud. "Ah, beautiful... The whole world may soon glow like that."

"I can't believe you're the last face I'll see," Geppetto said. "Guess I deserve it... I was too weak. Maybe I could have left Cloak ... like Repulsa. I could have tried to act normal. I could have done the right thing."

"That hussy's living a lie," Ember told him. "She can't change who she is any more than we can. At least we know who we are."

Geppetto hadn't felt Ember burn his wound closed. That wasn't a good sign. "Does that make it any better?"

Ember shrugged. "Nothing makes it better, at least in the long run. That's why I always live in the moment and make sure to enjoy all the little pleasures."

"I figured it out..."

"Figured out what?"

Geppetto smiled. "What the meaning of life is..."

Ember's eyes became hungry. She grabbed Geppetto by his blood-soaked shirt, lifting his small frame off the ice. "You know?"

Geppetto nodded.

Ember laughed, letting Geppetto go. "The Mentor be praised! I can't believe it. You figured it out! Not even Sebastian has done that. Oh, you must tell me! Please, I'm desperate to know. The pain must have purpose. All these screams that titillate me must be crying out for a reason. These are the answers humanity has been aching to know for eons, and *you* get to figure it out first. What a privilege! What an honor!"

Ember laughed so hard that she felt sick to her stomach. She kept laughing until she saw Geppetto again. Then her laughter dried up.

Geppetto was crying. "It's horrible... It's so horrible..."

Ember felt herself shiver too.

"The Mentor... The Mentor is eviler than anything we could have imagined... Gonna commit the worst crime of all... And we helped, Ember. We helped... Sebastian doesn't know what he's doing. He's a fool ... a murderous fool. We all are ... murderers ... fools..."

Geppetto vomited black blood. His eyes rolled into the back of his head, becoming pure white orbs. Then he died.

Ember found herself shaken, something that didn't happen to her often. She gulped as she tried to smile down at the small corpse. White orbs stared back at her.

Ember had enough. She set the body on fire. It burned away in less than a minute. Then she lay down on her back and watched Seoul flicker on the horizon as it burned. She thought she could hear the screams. Maybe it was just the wind.

"Guess I'll have to find out for myself," Ember murmured.

***

Xing almost hurled as the pod slowed to a crawl. Somehow, Shu didn't look as bad off as he did. What was that woman made of?

"Stay close to me, and do not utter a word," Xing told her. "High General Lee is no fool. Deceiving him will not be easy. That is why I shall mainly tell him the truth."

"I understand," Shu said.

They got out of the pod. This hangar was identical to the one in the Forbidden City. Xing wasn't surprised to find the pod surrounded by fifty Chinese soldiers with machine guns, all of them aimed at Shu and him.

"The Forbidden City is under attack," Xing told them, though he suspected these men knew that already. Why else would they give this warm welcome? "Cloak has used this chaos as an opportunity to launch our nuclear missiles at South Korea. If they succeed, it could mean the end of us all. The invaders sent me here in hopes of stopping it. Even they do not wish to see the world perish. Please, take me to see High General Lee."

"You needn't be taken anywhere," a man in his fifties said. He walked past the soldiers with his hands behind his back. The high general of the west had a thin face and hollow eyes. Among the high generals, he was considered to be as moderate as Duan or Xing, but he was fully capable of ruthlessness when needed.

"High General Lee, I have codes for both Duan and me," Xing said. "All we need is your code, and we will be able to stop the missiles."

"And what if the emperor himself ordered the attack?" Lee asked.

"Those missiles were launched from India."

"Either way, you came fifteen minutes too late. One of the missiles has already reached its target. Seoul has been destroyed."

"No!" Xing yelled.

Shu cried out, covering her mouth.

"The Western Union will launch its own nuclear missiles at any moment," Lee went on. "We must take the initiative."

"That is fool's talk," Xing said.

"It is the only way. I will not sit idly by and wait for our empire to be turned into a smoldering wasteland. If we fire all our missiles at the West, at least there is a chance they will be completely wiped out first. Part of the empire may yet survive."

"You are talking about the extinction of humanity."

"This discussion is fruitless. I need those codes of yours to launch our attack."

"Lee, there is no way we can take part in that."

"You will give your codes, Xing, one way or the other."

The soldiers began closing in. Shu backed away in fright until her rear hit the pod. Xing was too busy thinking to do anything else. There had to be an alternative, some way out of this mess. How could they prevent the Western Union from launching its missiles? The only way that would happen is if the West thought the Chinese Empire wasn't a threat anymore.

The soldiers were only a few feet away from him now.

"Lee, I have a solution!" Xing yelled.

Lee raised an eyebrow. Then he raised his hand. The soldiers stopped.

"Because I respect you, Xing, I will give you one minute to explain yourself."

Xing nodded. "Thank you, Lee. I believe there is only one way to avoid nuclear war at this point. We have already destroyed one of their cities. The Western Union won't be satisfied if we only stop our remaining airborne missiles."

"What do you suggest, then?"

Xing took a breath, marveling at his own audacity. "We must disarm our entire nuclear arsenal. This is the only way to avoid nuclear war."

High General Lee didn't know whether to laugh or be furious. "Xing, do you realize what you are saying?"

"Yes," Xing said. "We must surrender to the Western Union."

Half the soldiers almost dropped their guns in shock.

"This is the most preposterous thing I have ever heard," Lee said. "You want us to bare our belly to the Westerners and pray they do not take a stab at us? We will not be able to reactivate our nuclear arsenal if we do this."

"I know," Xing said. "But a simple ceasefire will not suffice. Only unconditional surrender will appease them."

"I will not give it to them. What would the emperor say?"

"The emperor put us in this situation when he gave his launch codes to foreigners."

"Impudence! The emperor is divine. Do not question him."

"Lee, you are an educated man. Do you believe the emperor to be divine? Do you think he is not capable of error or that his judgment has not eroded over the years?"

"He built this empire. He saved us from the Choke while the West turned its back on us. Without him, we would just be another occupied territory of the Western Union."

"That was seventy years ago. Now look at our country. Starvation is rampant. The literacy rate is less than thirty percent. Most areas have no electricity or running water. Do I even need to remind you of the Traitors' Garden? Even the previous communist government was better than the nightmare we are living in now."

"If that is what the emperor believes is right, who are we to question him?"

"You have not been to the Forbidden City recently, have you? All the Western technology that the emperor has denied his people now litters his palace. He clings to that helmeted monstrosity like you now cling to him. He serves the creations of the Western Union. It is hypocrisy at its finest. He is not trying to help our people. But we are."

Lee almost opened his mouth again, but he could find no voice. He only stared at a wall to his left. Perspiration coated his face.

Shu then spoke, which surprised everyone. "Please, High General, I know it is not my place to speak up, but I believe the situation calls for it. Xing is correct. The emperor does not care about us. He has not for some time. Now he is being manipulated by our enemies and is putting his people in danger. I could not believe it myself. Even as I saw him squirm on the floor, I worried that the worm would turn into a dragon and smite me. But now I realize that he is merely an ancient and broken man. I do not hate him. I pity him. I was looking at what might have once been a great leader, but power and time turned him into something ugly and unrecognizable. He became a god. He became weak."

High General Lee heard blasphemy, but he also heard truth. Conflicting loyalties fought within him. It looked like he was about to explode. His soldiers moved away from him as though he really would.

Xing stared his fellow high general in the eye. "Lee, we need to show the world we have not lost its humanity. We must stop this carnage. We must prevent the end."

CHAPTER 59

Sunlight reflected off the silver helmet.

"COME OUT SLOWLY!" High General Fang yelled over his loud-speakers. "ANY SUDDEN MOVEMENTS AND WE WILL OPEN FIRE!"

The Helmet Man walked over the bridge spanning the moat. He did so cautiously but showed no fear. One of his arms was wrapped around a squirming husk of wrinkled flesh. The emperor's struggles could not even begin to break the Helmet Man's hold on him.

Slate pointed with his free hand at the emperor's head. Sparks spat off the tip of his finger. "You boobs better keep back! I got me a hostage!"

Naomi came after him, stiff and paranoid, carrying an unconscious Thistle. She had been unwilling to leave the girl alone in a collapsing palace. Oscar kept close to Naomi, rubbing his arms like he had a rash. Eisenhorn and Straper took up the rear, both of them armed. The general was apprehensive, but at least his enemies were out in the open. Straper was still in a funk. Nevertheless, he had his rifle ready and kept his eyes peeled. The last remaining special gun was strapped to his back. They may have a use for it yet.

Slate got off the bridge, taking his first steps onto Tiananmen Square. An endless horde of brainwashed soldiers had their weapons trained on him, several hundred clunky walkers loaded their cannons, and the mines beneath his feet were ready to blow. If a fight did break out, there was little doubt who would win.

After realizing the force field had been disabled somehow, Slate and the others knew they could no longer hold out in the Forbidden City. Naomi had suggested they escape in one of the pods. However, the tunnel collapsed right after she said these words. Perhaps she and Slate could have flown out of there, but even if by some miracle they avoided being blown out of the sky, how would they bring along the others? Naomi couldn't carry them all that far, and Slate would unintentionally electrocute anyone who held on to him while he flew.

Left with no alternatives, Naomi told Slate they should comply with Fang's demands for the time being. The emperor was their greatest asset. As long as they had him in their possession, Fang would hesitate before making any bold moves.

The first rank of soldiers stood about four hundred feet away from the moat protecting the palace. Their eyes were red and doll-like. Slate walked half that distance before stopping. Naomi and everyone else stopped as well when they reached him. Never before had the Helmet Man felt so exposed. Thousands upon thousands of his enemies had a clean line of fire at him. He made sure to keep his electrified finger pointed at the emperor. The others huddled together around him as if that could provide them with additional protection.

"HAND OVER THE EMPEROR AND I SHALL GRANT YOU A SWIFT DEATH!" Fang bellowed, his tone suggesting he would probably break such a promise.

"Some negotiator you are!" Slate yelled. "I'm keeping hold of this golden goose till I'm a hundred fricking miles away from here!"

"I WILL NOT HESITATE TO BLOW YOU AWAY!"

"You want to put your emperor's divinity to the ultimate test? Be my guest!"

"Don't pick a fight with them," Naomi said.

"Hey, since when do I pick fights?"

"Maybe I should handle the negotiations."

"YOU FOREIGN DEVILS WILL—WAIT, WHY ARE YOU BREAKING RANK? STOP THAT! GO BACK TO YOUR POSITION! I—STAY BACK! OFFICERS, OPEN FIRE! KEEP AWAY! AH, IT TRIED TO BITE ME! NO, STAY AWAY! I'LL KILL YOU ALL! NO, STOP! YOU ANIMALS! AH! KEEP AWAY! EH! NO! AH! EEEEEE—!"

The loudspeakers were cut off. Gunshots could be heard in the distance. Quiet followed.

Slate leaned back. "Spooky…"

The emperor stopped his wriggling. His confusion had petrified him.

Eisenhorn kept his weapon close. "Great, now we're in a horror movie."

"Dude, sounded like that guy just died," Straper said, the screams having forced a reaction out of him.

"How pleasant," Naomi said. "What does this mean for us?"

The sea of red soldiers began to part. Hundreds of mindless men marched sideways, creating a passage that stretched out farther than even Straper could see. This was done in less than twenty seconds, efficient and mechanical.

"How long do you think they rehearsed that?" Slate asked.

"I see a truck coming," Naomi said, ignoring his joke. She rested Thistle on the ground in preparation for a possible fight. The girl whimpered but did not awaken.

A silver truck drove down the passage that the soldiers had created. The vehicle was shiny and new, not something made in the Chinese Empire.

"It must be whoever attacked Fang," Oscar said, still sticking near Naomi. She frowned, starting to get fed up with him and his closeness.

"Have any idea who it is?" Slate asked her.

"Yes," she said with an iciness that unnerved Slate. "I have an idea."

The truck reached them a minute later. It came to a complete stop, its quiet engine turning off. The passenger door creaked open.

A yellow dog leaped out of the truck.

"Doggy!" Slate cried happily. In his excitement, he dropped the emperor, who broke his hip on impact. The ancient ruler was in so much pain that he couldn't even cry out. The yellow dog jumped on Slate and started licking his silver helmet.

He held the dog over him. "Man, dogs are the best! Dad never got me one."

Oscar didn't say how Slate had gotten a dog as a child and accidentally electrocuted it to death. He was too busy tasting puke as he saw the driver's door open.

"Forgive him," Sebastian said, stepping out of the vehicle, his cane tapping on the concrete. "It's been a long trip, and he's brimming with energy. I'm not used to road trips myself, but my driving skills are rather impressive for a blind man." He nodded to Naomi. "Hello again, Repulsa. I was hoping you'd still be alive."

Naomi raised her hand, almost breaking his neck right then and there. Then she remembered the thousands of guns pointing at her and forced herself to relax.

"It's you!" Eisenhorn cried, spit flying. "You slime! I'm not letting you get out of here alive!"

The general nearly fired his gun, but Naomi tore it away from him with her mind. She let it drop to his feet. He picked it back up, preparing to shoot again. Naomi raised her hand, warning him. He had a brief fit but lowered his weapon.

Straper shook off his funk. Hate was a powerful emotion. "So, we finally get to meet this dirtbag," he growled.

Sebastian grinned wider. "I see no introductions are required."

The emperor snickered, despite the searing pain of his shattered hip.

"Sebastian…" Oscar said. "You were stupid to show yourself."

"It's been a while, Radcliffe," Sebastian said. "Time has ravaged you almost as much as your guilt has."

"This your mutt?" Slate asked, the yellow dog still licking him.

"I suppose it is, yes."

"Tubular!" Slate sent a thousand volts into the dog, the canine smoking until its fur caught fire. Then he dropped the corpse and punted it, sending it smashing into the truck's windshield. After cracking the glass, the burnt carcass rolled to a rest on the hood.

"Holy crap!" Straper yelled, suddenly in a good mood. "That was awesome!"

"Exactly what I would have done!" Eisenhorn chortled.

Naomi and Oscar covered their faces in exasperation.

The Helmet Man followed his act of animal abuse by running up to Sebastian, grabbing his collar, and slamming him against his truck. Sebastian did not seem fazed by Slate's barbarism, maintaining his oily grin.

"You flaming turd..." Slate growled. "I've been itching to meet you. Now that I have, I ain't planning to let go till there's nothing left to hold on to."

Every soldier in Tiananmen Square cocked his weapon in unison, creating a singular sound that could have been mistaken for a violent gust of wind.

"Best rethink your strategy," Sebastian said. "Harming me would be a fatal mistake."

"Then I'll just have to take you hostage."

"I'm not the easy prey I appear to be."

A set of sharp teeth sank into Slate's calf. He yelled in pain.

"And neither is he."

The yellow dog, good as new, was tearing at the Helmet Man. Drool spilled out the sides of its mouth. Its black eyes were pitiless.

"Did you bring a whole litter?" Slate asked, knowing perfectly well this dog was the same one he had electrocuted to death only moments before.

Maybe two times is the charm. He shocked the dog so hard that its teeth exploded, bits of enamel going through the roof of its mouth and ripping through its brain. Then he kicked off the dead dog in irritation.

Sebastian did not stand idle. He broke Slate's hold on him with his cane and struck him square in the helmet with an open palm. The blow was delivered with such precision and force that Slate stumbled back five feet, almost falling over.

Naomi punched the air, her invisible blow making a hole in the truck right next to Sebastian's head. He did not flinch.

"Don't try anything else," she warned. "There are two of us and only one of you."

Eisenhorn did a double take. "She ignored the rest of us!"

Slate groaned. "That dog... Hey, where did its body go?"

Naomi glanced to where Slate had kicked the dog, only to find that its corpse was no longer there, just some blood and burnt fur. There was no body on the hood of the truck either.

The yellow dog appeared next to Sebastian. It had no injuries and panted happily.

Straper gawked. "It's a super dog... Oscar, is that mutt one of the animals the Keymasters experimented on?"

"All the animals were destroyed," Oscar said. "And I don't ever ... I mean *ever* ... remember making something that bizarre."

"This is not one of the Western Union's creations," Sebastian said, scratching the yellow dog's neck. "He goes by the name of Quantum. A few years back, Schmitt tried to create more Gifted, experimenting on many animals and an occasional human. But without the other Keymasters and the proper equipment, Quantum proved to be his only success."

Oscar almost had a heart attack. "What? You tried to make *more?*"

"So, Schmitt's alive after all," Slate said. "What's the dog's power?"

"Quantum's ability bears the most similarity to Houdini's," Sebastian said. "However, Quantum can only teleport when he has been killed. Once dead, his deceased body dematerializes. Then he resurrects himself anywhere he chooses, fully rejuvenated. His teleportation also has an unlimited range. Houdini could only teleport to an area within his field of vision, but Quantum could die in China and reappear in America instantly."

"Completely ludicrous!" Oscar exclaimed. "You've created an immortal dog!"

Straper scratched his head. "Whoa, trippy."

"How come your odious dog didn't resurrect itself right away?" Naomi asked.

"Quantum is unable to dematerialize when someone is observing his body," Sebastian said. "Schmitt speculates this is due to psychic energy interference. Or maybe he's just shy." The blind man laughed. He stopped scratching Quantum, much to the dog's disappointment.

"You killed High General Fang and his officers just now," Naomi said. "Why?"

"I didn't want him getting in the way. He was merely here to hold down the fort till I arrived. After all, these mindless soldiers can't command themselves."

Sebastian reached into his truck and pulled out Fang's severed head.

The emperor howled when he saw the head of his high general being presented like a hunting trophy. He writhed in protest.

"The soldiers devoured him alive," Sebastian said. "I had them leave the head for your benefit. Look, you can see the nibble marks they left on his neck."

"You could have made his death quick," Naomi hissed.

"I suppose, but he really was an unpleasant man." Sebastian tossed the head back into his truck. "Speaking of unpleasant men, I would ask that you hand over the emperor now."

The emperor squawked. He tried crawling away, not even getting a foot. A few of his long nails broke clean off. Blood squirted from his fingertips.

Slate scoffed. "As if! This guy is our ticket out of here."

"My dear Slate, do you honestly think I care if he lives or dies?" Sebastian asked.

The emperor was whimpering. Tears poured down his wrinkled cheeks.

"In fact, I believe this centenarian has officially outlived his usefulness," Sebastian said, jabbing his cane into the ribs of the decaying sovereign. "How about I let you kill him, Helmet Man? You seem the most eager to do away with the old man."

Slate tilted his head as if looking down on the emperor. A reflection of the pathetic wretch was visible upon his silver helmet.

"No," he grunted after a long pause.

"Are you sure? I know you want to."

"I said no."

"As you wish." Sebastian snapped his fingers, his everlasting smile at no time faltering.

Quantum started growling. His teeth were bared.

"Mentor..." the emperor sobbed.

The dog pounced.

"Mentor!"

The sounds of flesh being torn were somehow louder than the screams, which themselves lasted far too long. Oscar and Straper covered their eyes. Naomi and Eisenhorn made sure not to look away. The Helmet Man stayed still.

The screams went on for half a minute before Slate raised his finger and electrocuted the whole mess, slaying both creatures.

Only one of them came back from the dead.

"Looks like you ended up killing him after all, Helmet Man," Sebastian told him.

The revived Quantum took a seat next to Sebastian, barking three times contentedly. Two soldiers broke rank and cleaned up their former ruler's remains, though they couldn't get the bloodstains off the concrete. It was several minutes before the long-awaited confrontation resumed.

"I still have a hard time believing it," Sebastian said. "I finally get to meet the Helmet Man face-to-face. I've known about you my whole life. Your existence has played such an integral part in the Mentor's plans, yet this is the first time we've ever come in contact."

"It'll be the last," Slate promised.

"You really are a humorous individual. I too think the best way to face adversity is with a smile. How about you tell us all a joke to lighten the mood?"

"Don't have to. I'm looking at one."

Sebastian laughed, a little too loudly. It felt off.

"We didn't come all this way to banter," Naomi said. "Just listening to you reminds me why I left Cloak."

"Your betrayal did come unexpectedly," Sebastian said, settling down. "I thought we nipped your rebellious streak in the bud a long time ago, but that lesson was obviously forgotten. My word, Repulsa, how many mothers must we kill before you finally give in?"

"You're digging your own grave, pal," Slate warned.

But the woman once known as Repulsa did not rise to the bait. "Please, call me Naomi."

"Call yourself whatever you wish," Sebastian said, waving his hand. "Names are arbitrary anyway."

"It's time you started explaining things," Oscar said. "For starters, where's Temple?"

"Temple... Yes, you are correct. No more idle chatter. It's time to talk about the bigger picture." Sebastian tapped his cane rhythmically for a few seconds, contemplating his next words. "I should start by telling you all why I have submitted myself, body and soul, to the Mentor."

"Life under the thumb of the West was not pleasant," Sebastian said. "Slate and Repulsa can attest to that. I'm sure they gripe about it all the time."

Neither of them acknowledged him.

Sebastian snickered. "You only remain quiet because you don't want to agree with me. Childish but understandable. Do you remember when you severed my optic nerves, Radcliffe?"

"You were having seizures," Oscar said. "I did what I had to do."

"I distinctly recall that I was given no painkillers."

"We needed to monitor your neural activity to ensure your safety. Painkillers or anesthetics would have interfered with the readings."

"Why am I not satisfied with that answer?" Sebastian asked. "Helmet Man, you and I were both blinded by this man. Was his explanation enough for you?"

"It wasn't just his call," Slate said. "Don't blame it all on him."

"Yes, I know that. I'm asking if his explanation made you *feel* better. Did it?"

The Helmet Man did not reply. Oscar lowered his head.

"I thought not," Sebastian said. "Such shallow reasons did not satisfy me either. Surely, my pain had a higher purpose. The more I brooded on these questions, the more I realized how these questions did not plague just me or my fellow supersoldiers, but all of humanity. Why do we bleed? Why does evil exist? Is there a point to life, to suffering? Where did we come from? What is this all leading to?"

"People have been asking those same questions since the dawn of time," Oscar said. "Brighter minds than yours have tried and failed to answer them. Any answers provided are debated and poked full of holes. It's all a fool's errand."

"Gotta think about something in the shower," Eisenhorn said.

Straper almost went cross-eyed. "This is some deep stuff."

Naomi snorted. "Let me guess, the Mentor is looking for these answers too."

"No, Repulsa," Sebastian said. "The Mentor *knows* them."

Slate made a variety of rude noises before giving his opinion. "If your Mentor really does know the meaning of life, then go ahead and tell us. Or maybe the Mentor is full of it, and you were dumb enough to buy into all this shit."

Sebastian shook his head both in amusement and disappointment. "If the Mentor were to simply tell us, we would be unwilling to accept the revelation. No, this lesson must be taught the hard way. I have seen mere glimpses of the Mentor's vision, and even I am having a hard time comprehending it. Such ambition... You see, over twenty years ago, I started to have peculiar, vivid dreams. I didn't know what to make of them. Then the dreams began to command me. Had I gone mad? No, for Alphonse Schmitt was having these very same visions. The Mentor had contacted both of us. More importantly, our leader had contacted Temple. Tell me, have you had the dreams?"

"What's the Mentor planning?" Slate yelled, energy radiating off him. Quantum started barking.

Sebastian raised his hand. Quantum stopped barking. "In order to make humanity submit to the Mentor's philosophy, the world must first come into Cloak's possession," Sebastian said. "Then the Mentor can begin not only to teach us the purpose of life but also help us fulfill it."

Naomi smirked cynically. "So, your goal is world domination. How cartoonish. Is such a thing even possible?"

"It's certainly no easy task. Talented, charismatic men such as Alexander the Great, Genghis Khan, Napoleon Bonaparte, and Adolf Hitler have all attempted to do this, but no one has ever succeeded in having complete control of the entire globe." Sebastian's smile grew bigger, grotesque and unnatural. "But if the Mentor were able to play a direct role in our earthly affairs, world domination would become a trifling matter."

"Then where's the Mentor?" Slate asked. "If that coward really is powerful enough to take over the world, how come it hasn't happened yet?"

"The Mentor does not exist here. Our lord can only act through Temple as of now. In fact, Temple is the only anchor binding the Mentor to our reality. Without Temple, the Mentor would simply drift back into oblivion."

"This is all nonsense," Oscar said. "You're trying to bring a dream to life."

Sebastian leaned forward. "We are trying to bring a *nightmare* to life, Radcliffe. For that, the Mentor requires your Helmet Man."

"Me?" Slate asked, gesturing to himself. "Is that why Cloak's been wanting to capture me all this time? You want me to help bring your boss to our reality or whatever?"

"Yes, that is why you have been our primary objective from day one. However, shortly after the Gifted rebelled, you disappeared. The Mentor was not pleased but knew you weren't dead, for your energy could still be felt by our lord. So, we looked, even searching near the Bunker where you had been buried. Yet somehow the Mentor was not able to sense your presence. You must have friends in high places, Helmet Man."

"If all you wanted was me, what have you nincompoops been up to for twenty years?"

"We've been preparing for the day the Mentor reigns supreme. Making political connections, gathering resources, basically dealing with the practical aspects of the Mentor's plan. That is Cloak's true purpose."

"Sounds like you guys were just praying I'd show up. Pretty desperate."

"The Mentor knew you would reappear one day, and you did. When I found out from Houdini that you had resurfaced, I was pleased but not surprised.

"So, Houdini caught you, as I ordered him to. I was filled with such strong feelings that I fear my judgment may have been a bit clouded. Attempting to capture you so soon was a mistake. I did not know that you had protection."

"Incognito..." Slate said. "You didn't know he was a Keymaster."

"The affairs of the United Third and the identity of Incognito had little bearing on our plans till he started meddling with them. I was admittedly surprised to hear that one of the Keymasters was still alive and had made himself Gifted. After we found this out, Incognito became our main concern. We could not get close to you with Incognito around. He might also be the only individual in the world who can stand his ground against Temple.

"I knew he had to go, but how could I kill him? I couldn't wait for the Western Union to do the deed, if they were even capable of it. I didn't want to send all the Gifted to their deaths, so using them wasn't an option either. Then Cyphrus teamed up with the Chinese Empire and began to make her move against me. But I was not concerned by this. In fact, that's when a proper plan began to form in my head."

Straper groaned. "I don't like where this is going."

"Those nuclear missiles…" Slate growled. "Was that you?"

"That was Schmitt," Sebastian corrected. "He was the one that launched them from India, all nice and snug in the Taj Mahal's bunker, with the launch codes I gave him. Yes, Alphonse Schmitt is the one man who wouldn't hesitate to end the world if I asked him to."

"This is all one elaborate trap," Naomi realized. "You wanted us to come to the Forbidden City. Does that mean Xing was working for you?"

"No, he believed he was acting of his own accord. He was inspired by a dream that the Mentor planted in his head. It wasn't brainwashing per se. He was simply misguided by a seemingly reasonable plan. It's brilliant, really. Why chase after you when you were all more than willing to come to us? I considered breaking into *Tortuga* and kidnapping Slate while he was incarcerated, but I'd rather fight on my own turf, far away from any Western Union interference or any of your potential allies."

"We decided to come here, not you," Oscar said. "Slate almost didn't come himself. What made you so confident we would?"

"Because the Mentor has been watching all of you for some time now, prodding you, caressing you, converting you… The Mentor knows you … how to use you…"

"We aren't your slaves!" Eisenhorn shouted, his malnourished body shaking from all the stress it had undergone over the past several hours.

"No, you are the *Mentor's* slaves," Sebastian said. "We are all servants of the lord, whether we want to be or not. You have no choice. Submission is mandatory."

"If you wanted us to come here, why did you attack us in Mumbai?" Oscar asked.

"I needed to heighten the emperor's paranoia in order to obtain his nuclear launch codes. As an added benefit, I weakened you all."

"I'm still strong enough to snap your neck," Slate snarled.

"How did you know we were going to be in Mumbai?" Oscar pried. "Another dream?"

"No, an informant. Ember met with him."

"Who?"

"Does it matter? Just another tool."

"You launched those missiles to lure away Incognito," Naomi said. "You also had the Black Lotus and imperial guards fight us in order to exhaust us." Her muscles ached even as she said this. "You're willing to put the entire world at risk, all for the sake of your delusions. Even you should know better."

Sebastian chuckled. "Clearly, I don't."

"What if we hadn't found the Dragon's Egg? What if those nuclear missiles were launched without us knowing?"

"But you did find it, and we only launched them once we confirmed that Incognito had left the Forbidden City."

"The force field deactivated right after Incognito left," Oscar said. "How come I didn't notice anything amiss when I hacked into its system beforehand?"

"I believe there was a hidden program or some such hoo-ha. Honestly, you'd have to ask Schmitt. But are you really surprised you were tricked by him? He *did* invent the machine. I also suspect he's a little smarter than you."

Naomi stared with murderous eyes at her former employer. "So many variables, so many unknowns ... yet here we are."

"Yet here you are. The Mentor is truly a miracle worker."

"You separated us from Incognito, wore us down, and have us surrounded by thousands upon thousands of mind-controlled soldiers. So, what are you planning now? I hope you didn't do all this just so we could have a little chat."

"You are impatient, as am I. Take a look behind you."

Naomi didn't like the idea of turning her back to Sebastian or obeying any of his orders, but then she felt the heat behind her. She spun around, as did the others, all of them wondering how they hadn't noticed the inferno until now.

The Forbidden City was engulfed in yellow flames. The faint cries of burning guards were barely audible over the sound of burning wood. The palace's walls stood tall but were soon scorched black. The gas lighting only made everything burn faster.

"There were people still in there," Straper said emotionlessly. "Women, kids, regular Joes... You just burned them all up."

Naomi shook her head. "After all that effort to keep them alive..."

"At least you still have your self-righteousness," Sebastian said. "But it cost you dearly. You would probably be much less fatigued if you had just outright killed those guards. Their deaths would have been much less painful too."

Slate let sparks fly off his fists. At that moment, all the soldiers pointing guns at him didn't mean anything to him. He couldn't take any more of Sebastian's taunts. There was no point in capturing him alive. He was too dangerous, too smug, too good at what he did.

The Helmet Man twisted on his heels and charged at the blind man.

Temple stood in his way.

Slate tripped and fell, caught off guard by the sudden appearance of the second Helmet Man. The dark cloak hung from Temple's shoulders, fluttering in the wind. The red horseshoe, the symbol of Omega, stood out brightly on his garment.

And the blood had dried on his silver helmet.

The others turned around as well. When they saw Temple towering over their savior, the light ceased to illuminate their faces, their expressions *that* dark and helpless.

They saw their death. They saw their Mentor.

"You are about to fulfill your purpose, Helmet Man," Sebastian said, the corners of his mouth curling into the foulest sneer ever seen on a human face. "You *will* be broken."

CHAPTER 61

Oscar dropped to his knees, slightly injuring one of them. He felt nothing. His eyes were transfixed by the elongated silver helmet, which made Slate's look like a child's plaything. The silhouette of the helmet fell upon Radcliffe. He trembled in its wake.

Straper started to shiver. Then he started to convulse. He dropped his weapon and couldn't help but cry. "Dude... Oh, man... Oh, geez..."

This wasn't the first time Eisenhorn had encountered this foe, but that didn't make any difference. The thing's presence was still as overwhelming and crushing as he remembered, though even his memories could not accurately recall the iciness he felt wriggling in his colon. Klara ... where was she? *Please,* he thought, *help an old man out.*

Naomi bowed her head until her bangs covered her eyes. Her mouth was a thin line. Her already pale skin was now as white as Temple's.

"Why do you all look so glum?" Sebastian toyed, taking his place next to Temple. "Didn't you come all the way here for this very moment?"

Quantum yipped and started licking between its legs.

Slate got up from the ground, dusted himself off, and started chuckling. "Yeah, I guess you're right. This is what we asked for, so thanks for holding up your end."

Sebastian's lips curled, some of his teeth now showing as his smile became manic. "I admire how you keep your sense of humor even now."

"It'll take more than a doppelgänger to shake me up." Slate slapped his knee. "Man, you're really making things too easy! Not only are you killing Incognito for us, but you're handing over this bozo on a silver platter."

"I did not do it for your benefit, Helmet Man, I can assure you."

"If you say so." Slate turned his attention to Temple. "You keep the quiet routine up all the time, pal? Ha! You must really be my opposite."

Oscar couldn't help but gape at his son. Was Slate joking at a time like this? Even more concerning, was he telling jokes to Temple? Why not pull out a red cape to taunt the bull while he was at it? Eisenhorn and Straper wore similar expressions, showing that Oscar wasn't alone in feeling this way. Naomi said nothing, her bangs still concealing her eyes. Thistle remained unconscious, but she was whimpering now, feeling the sudden weight of evil crushing her, even in her dreams.

"I don't see what the big deal is," Slate scoffed, strolling up until he was mere inches from Temple. "You're big, I'll give you that. But if you're so tough, how come you're so scared to fight Incognito, huh?" He jabbed Temple in the chest with a finger. "How come you've been hiding until now? I think you get away with a lot by intimidation only. You know what you are? You're a peacock! One big fat pea—"

Temple grabbed Slate by the throat. It was done with one hand and with such speed that Slate didn't know what was happening until he started feeling the fingers burn into his flesh. They had already broken through the skin, the black nails now digging at his tendons.

"Slate!" Oscar shouted.

"Let him go!" Straper yelled, taking hesitant aim with his rifle. Eisenhorn did the same with his weapon. Beads of sweat ran down their foreheads.

Slate grabbed on to Temple's arm and pumped electricity into the limb. Temple's body shuddered for a second, a few burns now on his arm, but he took no other damage. Temple lifted Slate off his feet. The Helmet Man's legs kicked frantically and aimlessly.

"If you don't drop him, I'll drop you!" Straper warned for the last time.

Temple did not acknowledge him. Straper gritted his teeth and fired a bullet right at his neck. Eisenhorn also pulled the trigger several times. Temple raised his free hand, creating a wall of light that blocked the bullets. He lowered his hand. The wall disappeared.

"Didn't even make him flinch," Eisenhorn muttered.

Straper looked down at his weapon, realizing how useless it was.

Temple held Slate for a few more seconds before tossing him fifteen feet with one arm. The Helmet Man hit the concrete hard and skidded to a stop. The burns on Temple's arm glowed momentarily before healing. Fresh blood dripped off his fingers, making a scarlet puddle near his feet. Quantum scurried over and was more than happy to lick it up.

"You've made an awful mess," Sebastian observed. "Allow me to assist."

Temple presented his bloodied hand. Sebastian cradled the hand and put the first finger in his mouth. He made sure to suck the appendage clean before moving on to the next one. Straper and Eisenhorn exchanged disquieted glances. Oscar blinked, the rest of his face not knowing what expression to make.

Sebastian and Quantum finished their cleanup duty, moving away from Temple with reverence. Temple flexed his fingers and concealed his limb beneath the cloak once more.

"An impressive specimen, isn't he?" Sebastian said, using a handkerchief to wipe up the blood from his lips. "He has no vestigial characteristics whatsoever. Since he doesn't require food, water, or oxygen, he has no need for internal organs either. That means you can't use that heart-stopping technique of yours, Helmet Man. Temple truly is as perfect as a life-form can be. However, for the Mentor, that's not perfect enough."

"Bunch of sickos," Slate growled, standing up again. He shrugged at Temple. "I guess you are a tough one. But that's no problem. Not if Naomi and I—"

"Do you remember?" Naomi whispered. Her voice was so low that no one would have normally been able to hear it, yet her words somehow carried a weight that ensured nobody could miss them. Slate, Oscar, Straper, and Eisenhorn all twisted their heads to look at her. Sebastian also seemed intrigued, raising his chin.

"Do you remember?" Naomi asked again. "I wouldn't be surprised if you didn't. That must have been just another day for you."

Temple was stiller than stone. His towering silver helmet glowed with the light of the burning palace.

"What you did destroyed me," Naomi said. "You made my mother say things no mother should ever say to their child. I don't know what kind of philosophy you've created that allows that to happen, but it's a corrupt one. Only desperate fools would ever follow it."

Eisenhorn and Straper had no idea what she was talking about. Oscar only knew some of the details from Incognito, his throat tightening as he heard her speak. The Helmet Man, meanwhile, listened with great care.

"Mentor," she seethed. "I know you're listening. That puppet in front of me is revolting, but it didn't kill my mother. It was you. It has always been you."

Temple neither confirmed nor denied her claim. He was apathy incarnate.

"My mother called me a pig. But you're the pig, aren't you?"

She raised her head. Her eyes were wet with tears and wide with rage. There was insanity in that gaze. It perturbed even Sebastian.

"You're the one with pig's blood flowing through you!" she screamed at Temple. She threw a psychic punch. It slammed into Temple, his body jerking from the impact. "You're the pig!" She punched him again. "Pig!" Another punch. "Pig!"

Now she threw a hundred punches.

"Piiiiiig!"

Temple was struck dozens of times per second. His whole body thrashed about. Bones snapped. Joints were dislocated. Several invisible punches struck his helmet, making hollow thumps as they struck. His neck came very close to snapping.

Yet the beast stayed on his feet.

Naomi stopped throwing punches. Temple stopped jerking. Sebastian's smile had thinned. Quantum barked, not knowing what else to do. Naomi was crying now. The sobs came out in waves with brief pauses of dismal silence separating each one. Slate wanted to go to her side but found himself unable to move. A feeling of powerlessness overcame him.

Temple straightened himself out, popping his joints back into place.

Then he vanished.

Naomi's sobs stopped. Her eyes were the size of moons.

Temple appeared in front of her. His cloak tickled her legs.

He gave her an uppercut, hitting her jaw with such force that she went up in the air. Blood spurted from her mouth. She fell on her back.

"Naomi!" Slate yelled with more panic than Oscar had ever seen him express.

Her flesh would be badly bruised, but her jaw somehow didn't shatter. Temple didn't hold back. He kicked her in the chest. She cried out, rolling back five feet.

"You'll pay for that, creep!" Slate fired his beam. Temple erected a wall of light. It took the beam, but Temple had to raise both his hands to keep the barrier up.

The wall went down. Slate fired bolts of lightning next. They hit Temple's bare chest, only making light scorch marks that mended in a second. Temple fired beams of light in retaliation. They were thinner and weaker than Slate's beams, about the width of his finger, but they were also more accurate, and Temple had a faster firing rate. Slate dashed to the right, the yellow beams making little holes in the concrete as they missed their mark.

Zigzagging to avoid being hit, the Helmet Man made his way to Temple, charging up his fist full of energy. Temple kicked at him. The leg flew over Slate's helmet. He could feel the heat radiating off the limb. Whatever Temple was, he was giving off a ludicrous amount of energy. For some horrible reason, Slate suspected this energy was just the tip of the iceberg. If Temple was getting his power from the Mentor, Slate couldn't even begin to speculate how powerful the real deal was.

What was he doing? Was he afraid of this guy? Slate had been in plenty of nasty situations before, but he had never been truly terrified of any opponent. Maybe that was about to change. Maybe he was afraid not for himself, but for Naomi, his father, Straper, and even Eisenhorn. Either way, he found hesitation within himself. It wasn't a good feeling.

No, he wouldn't be afraid. He would joke around and get the enemy riled up like always. Then he would find some kind of weakness and exploit it. There was no need to be scared of Temple, only cautious.

"Try blocking this!" Slate threw his punch. Temple caught the fist, making sure not to let go. He began to squeeze it.

Slate chuckled. "Pathetic sadist... I knew you'd try to make me hurt."

The Helmet Man released all his energy from his charged arm. Temple's fist exploded. Severed fingers flew in all directions.

"Didn't think that through, did ya?" Slate charged up his fist and punched Temple in the stomach. Temple hunched over from the blow. Giving him no time to recover, Slate threw as many punches as he could muster into Temple's torso, his arms becoming a blur of static and ferocity. He felt a few of Temple's ribs crack. It felt all too good for the Helmet Man.

Temple didn't seem keen on being a punching bag forever, so he brought his knee up and hit Slate in the head with it. The silver helmet offered some protection, but Slate felt his neck strain from the impact. He moved back a few steps, disoriented and annoyed. Temple created a wall of light. It then accelerated forward, blackening the ground behind it. Slate jumped out of its path. The wall surged past him and disappeared soon after.

A beam skimmed past Slate's buttock, scorching flesh. The pain threw him off, and he stumbled upon landing. He expected another attack to quickly follow, but Temple hadn't moved from his spot. The stump of his arm was glowing. Bone was the first to grow, followed by the flesh, and finally the skin and nails. Temple's hand had regenerated. His ribs healed as well after his chest emitted light for three seconds.

"How are we supposed to kill this guy again?" Straper asked.

"Beats me, kid," Eisenhorn said. "Leave it to the helmet moron. He's not out of it yet."

"This is getting out of hand, Sebastian!" Oscar yelled. "Tell Temple to stop!"

"I've never commanded Temple," Sebastian told him. "If anything, he commands me. All I can do is watch—well, so to speak."

"Naomi!" Slate decided to ignore Temple for now. He ran to Naomi and knelt beside her. She wasn't unconscious, just dazed and humiliated.

"Hey, get your act together!" He grabbed her shoulder and shook her a bit. Naomi looked up at the silver helmet and flinched.

"It's just me," Slate told her. Temple had left a nasty mark on her jaw. Otherwise, she seemed okay physically. Mentally was a different story. She had a gaping, dead expression. Had she worn that same look when Temple killed her mother? He decided not to think about that too much. "Listen, I might need some help on this one. Get up!"

Naomi seemed to gather herself somewhat. She managed to form words. "Temple... He's quick... Strong too..."

"Yeah, he lived up to the hype all right."

"We need Incognito..."

"No way. Let that douchebag get blown up by a nuke. We can do this ourselves if you just get off your sweet tushie and pull yourself together."

A few idle tears came out. She wiped them away with her sleeve and smiled. "Help me up, you hunk."

"Hunk? Never heard you call me that before. It sounds just about right!" Slate helped her to her feet, though she didn't need all that much help. She touched his shoulder before stealing a glimpse at Temple. Her smile melted away.

"Let's strategize," Slate said, hoping to get her mind to a more logical place. "We need to pin down that bad boy and get underneath his helmet. Destroying the brain is the only way to kill him. One of us needs to keep him occupied while the other disables him."

"Right," Naomi said, hardening herself. "You can distract him. I'll attack."

"That shouldn't be too difficult. If I'm anything, it's distracting."

"What are you two conspiring over there?" Sebastian inquired.

"None of your business! Go suck your boyfriend's fingers!"

Sebastian raised his hand. His army responded by lowering their weapons simultaneously. The soldiers' movements were coordinated with machinelike precision.

"I won't intervene in this fight," Sebastian said. "Neither will Quantum or the soldiers surrounding us. We'll even keep your friends out of it."

"How thoughtful," Slate scoffed. "Now shut up!"

"Straper, Oscar, Eisenhorn, do not help us under any circumstances," Naomi ordered. "Temple will not be merciful. Neither Slate nor I will be able to help you if he gets his hands on you. Keep to the sidelines."

"You sure about that?" Straper asked. "I can't just sit here and watch."

"Best listen to the lady," Eisenhorn said. "We'd just get in their way."

"Sebastian might not keep his word," Oscar told his son. "If the fight looks like it's about to turn south for Temple, Sebastian and his soldiers will likely attempt to help him. They may even try to take us hostage. Be careful."

Slate nodded. "Thanks, old man. We've got this handled." He turned to Naomi. "Let's put an end to this shit right here and now."

Naomi nodded back. They stood side by side and faced their foe together.

Temple remained silent and still.

Sebastian snickered. "Yes, let us end this 'shit' for good."

Temple glided toward the duo.

CHAPTER 62

Temple's fists glowed as they swung at the Helmet Man.

Slate ducked and weaved. He had difficulty finding an opportunity to hit Temple with anything. He did manage to punch the brute in the stomach twice, but the damage was minimal. Slate kept retreating. Temple kept swinging, floating after him.

Naomi had flown away somewhere. If Slate didn't know better, he might have thought she was running away. But he did know better. Naomi cared too much.

Slate had fallen back so far that he soon passed the first rank of brainwashed soldiers. They did not blink or impede him in any way. Sebastian had kept his word so far. Temple jabbed his fist at him, but Slate ducked behind a stationary soldier. The fist barely grazed him. Temple punched again, going right through the chest of the soldier Slate was hiding behind. Temple yanked his fist out. The soldier dropped without a peep. Temple didn't care about killing these guys, Slate observed, so why should he? They were pretty much brain-dead anyway. Might as well use them for something important, like saving his own ass.

The Helmet Man ducked behind another soldier. Temple disintegrated this one's head with the back of his hand. Slate kept navigating the ranks, sticking close to the soldiers and even pushing some in his foe's way. Temple was persistent. He continued to deliver punches. The inanimate soldiers took most of the brunt.

Slate fired a beam. Temple twisted out of its way. The beam burnt through a walker and seven soldiers instead, all of them collapsing afterward. Temple fired beams of his own. Slate used a walker as cover. The mecha soon became riddled with more holes than a colander, killing the pilot and leaving the machine dead on its feet. They were leaving a sizable trail of destruction and bodies behind them. Slate hoped this game of cat and mouse would wear out Temple, but the juggernaut wouldn't quit. He was gaining on him, plowing down at least two soldiers per second, well over a hundred bodies by this point.

Something profoundly stupid then happened. Slate tripped and fell. He had accidentally got his foot stuck in a chamber pot. Even brainwashed soldiers needed to use the restroom. Slate growled. The foul liquid was all over his pants.

"Ah, shit!" he yelled.

Temple was almost on top of him.

"One hell of a way to die!" Slate cried, kicking the pot off his foot.

Temple stopped before Slate, the black cloak concealing his Herculean form. The red horseshoe on his back seemed to pulsate. A white fist emerged from the cloak. It reeled back for a finishing blow.

"Mentor!" Naomi cried.

Temple snapped his head to the left.

A walker aimed its cannon at his chest.

The cannon fired. The shell hit its mark, tearing Temple off his feet and propelling him backward almost ten yards. An explosion followed, which knocked over dozens of indifferent soldiers and set them on fire. They made no attempt to put themselves out. Smoke obscured what fate had befallen Temple. Slate doubted the freak was done yet. He got up, wondering if he should throw out his befouled pants.

"Nice one!" he yelled at Naomi. "Wondering where you were!"

Naomi floated out of the rusty walker's cockpit. Her intense expression indicated she was far from done. She waved her hands, blowing away all the smoke in the area.

Temple was sprawled out, burnt from head to toe. His chest was caved in. His legs were also gone. The rags that had once been his cloak did little to conceal the damage.

Two swords shot through the air. They pinned Temple's charred hands to the ground, going through the palms and coming out the back.

"Reminds me of an insect collection," Naomi spat. She floated high above him. Then she spread her arms out and raised them. At least two hundred guns floated up. She had taken them from the uncaring soldiers below. The firearms were all trained on Temple.

"Let's put your regeneration to the test," she hissed.

All the guns fired at once. The sound would have deafened Naomi if she hadn't stopped the air from vibrating around her head. Any soldier standing near Temple was ripped to bloody shreds. Temple himself soon didn't have much of a body left to speak of. The swords kept him from moving around too much until the innumerable bullets severed his hands. The helmet deflected a fair amount, making pinball-machine-like noises.

The guns were soon empty. Naomi dropped them all at once. Most of them broke on the concrete below. She looked at her handiwork. There was almost nothing left of Temple but black blood and a whittled-away torso, the helmeted head still somehow attached.

The torso twitched. It gave off a weak glow.

"You're still alive," Naomi spat. "I'm going to pierce that brain of yours and put you down for good." She summoned a sword from a soldier's sheath and caught it by the handle. It was definitely sharp enough to finish the job.

With wild eyes and her blade pointed forward, she dove down toward her foe.

Temple's torso glowed brighter.

"Watch out!" Slate yelled.

Naomi noticed too late. An explosion of light came from Temple. The turbulence it caused caught her by surprise, forcing her to descend. She almost had a serious mishap, but Slate caught her with open arms. Naomi wriggled out of his embrace and grimaced.

"You went for the kill too soon," Slate said. "Don't be so rash."

"I can't believe you of all people are telling me that."

"Let's make sure we destroy every scrap of his body before we go for the brain. Even in the state he was just in, he's plenty dangerous."

They glanced at the yellow inferno that was already dying down. They tensed up, expecting their enemy to walk out of the flames at any time.

They weren't disappointed.

Temple emerged from the fire, not a scratch on him. His cloak had burned away. Now he wore only his helmet and a tattered pair of skintight black shorts. His massive muscles rippled.

"Where are his nips?" Slate had to ask.

Naomi did not so much as crack a smile. She couldn't look away from the towering silver helmet. The blood had been scorched clean from it.

Temple required more.

***

Oscar turned away. "I can't watch anymore. It's too much."

"They'll be fine," Eisenhorn said. "They have that animal on the ropes."

"I hope so," Straper said. "But what are we gonna do after they win? We still have Sebastian and those soldiers to worry about. And possibly nuclear war too."

Oscar gulped. "Eisenhorn, should Slate and Naomi fail, there's always *that* option."

The general didn't have to ask what he meant and knew better than to do so. That blind looney might overhear them. The syringe… It always came back to the syringe. The thought of blowing everyone here up was an unsettling one, but Eisenhorn would if it came to that. The world wouldn't be safe so long as Temple remained standing, and if what Sebastian said was true, something far worse would come into being should Temple have his way with the Helmet Man. No, they had to succeed. But didn't that woman have the syringe on her now? How would he get his hands on it if she was busy fighting? Had it broken already?

"This fight is going on rather long," Sebastian said. "No matter. Let Temple have his fun. Slate needs to be utterly demolished before the Mentor can join us mere mortals."

Eisenhorn raised his fist. "You better shut your trap, creep. I've had it up to here with you and that mangy mutt of yours. Betsy wouldn't have sniffed that thing's hindquarters for all the kibble in the world."

"I totally forgot about Betsy," Straper said, smiling in anger. "I wish Marker were here to run over this dog too."

"Now that's no way to talk about a man's pet," Sebastian said. "Keep it up and I may have to punish you."

"It's two against one, pal!" Eisenhorn yelled, shaking his gun. "Just try it!"

Sebastian laughed. "I think I will."

He drew a sword from his cane.

"Boy, get ready!" Eisenhorn barked.

Straper did, aiming his rifle with pleasure. Oscar backed away.

Sebastian dropped the shaft of the cane on the concrete with a clatter and walked toward his quarry, slicing his blade through the air. "I won't kill you. I'm content with simply humiliating you. It doesn't feel right to deny Temple fresh meat. He'll do away with you three once he has subdued the Helmet Man and the traitor."

Eisenhorn readied his gun. "Wish you could see this coming... Fire!"

Both of them blasted away. Straper's bullets were fewer and more accurate. Eisenhorn was content with spraying all of his in the blind man's general direction.

Sebastian's sword became invisible in its quickness. His wrist and elbow were doing most of the work while the rest of his body remained stationary. A loud ding was made each time the sword blocked a bullet, the dozens of individual deflections almost musical when combined. Straper's and Eisenhorn's guns soon ran out of ammo. Sebastian stopped swinging his sword. Spent bullets dotted the ground around him.

He had not been hit once.

"He can really do it!" Oscar squawked.

"Had to see it to believe it," Straper groaned.

"Let's try fighting him the old-fashioned way!" Eisenhorn shouted. He charged at Sebastian, screaming and holding his empty gun like a club.

"Are any of you trying to figure out how I just did that?" Sebastian asked. He moved aside. Eisenhorn's blow missed him by mere inches. The general took another swing with his gun. Sebastian hopped back out of its range.

Straper came running, wielding a hunting knife hidden in his boot. He took a stab. Sebastian leaned to the side. The knife missed. Both Eisenhorn and Straper kept attacking Sebastian for a full minute, waiting to get lucky. But luck was not on their side.

"How about I show you something else?" Sebastian snatched up a bullet casing from the ground and flicked it. The casing struck Eisenhorn in the temple. He stumbled back, seeing stars. The casing then struck Straper, having ricocheted off Eisenhorn's skull. Straper almost felt himself black out. Blood dripped from his head.

"My senses are superhuman," Sebastian said. "I get so much data from them that Radcliffe had to render me blind all those years ago so my brain wouldn't overload."

His sword cut Straper's wrist. The young man howled and dropped the knife. Sebastian then slashed at Eisenhorn's ankle. The general collapsed with a pained cry.

Sebastian bounced in place as he slashed the air a few more times. "But even without vision, my other senses provide me with more than enough information, so much information that I know exactly what's going to happen."

"You can predict the future?" Straper cried.

"The immediate future, yes. I knew precisely where your bullets were going to fly, how to flick that casing so it would disable you both, and where you two would attack from. My predictions have never failed me before. I also know that you're about to pull a gun on me, Radcliffe."

Sweating, Oscar stopped drawing the compact submachine gun from his coat. Straper retreated back and started applying a growth patch to his bleeding wrist. Eisenhorn crawled away, giving Sebastian all the dirty looks he could muster.

"Humiliated yet?" Sebastian asked them.

"Just wait till Slate's finished with your pal over there," Straper said. "You'll be sorry once we beat your Mentor."

Sebastian chuckled. "Then it seems I'll never be sorry."

***

Slate wondered if they would have the advantage in the sky.

They didn't. In fact, Temple was even faster. All three of them were well over a hundred feet up. Naomi threw her ineffective punches of compressed air at Temple. He pursued her with such speed that the chase soon became nothing but a series of close calls for her.

Slate had to be careful about where he aimed his beam, since Temple kept close to Naomi. Temple dodged his first beam and blocked the second with a barrier. Naomi got in a lot of good blows while Temple was preoccupied. One of them even dislocated his shoulder. Perhaps her punches weren't so ineffective after all.

A disk made from yellow light then materialized in Temple's hand. He flung it at Naomi. After that, he popped his shoulder back into place. She stopped flying, letting gravity take over, and dropped fast enough to avoid the disk. It went over her head but came back around like a boomerang. The disk cut her arm, the wound already cauterized. Naomi screamed more from surprise than the injury itself.

"Seriously, how many tricks do you have up your sleeve?" Slate yelled at Temple. "You know, if you had sleeves!"

Temple caught the disk and threw it at Slate.

"Getting repetitive, I see! How the hell do you expect to take me by surprise?"

The disk was fast, but Slate was faster. He flew to the right, planning to let the disk pass him. But then the disk exploded, and he was thrown back.

Temple appeared above Slate, faster than lightning, and elbowed him in the back. The Helmet Man, already shaken by the explosion, began to spiral downward toward the burning palace.

"Hold on, Slate!" Naomi cried. She threw a few futile punches, but Temple shrugged off the invisible strikes and flew down after his prey.

Slate hit the roof of the palace, which had been weakened by the fire. He crashed through it somewhat painlessly and thumped onto the tile floor. He had landed in the throne room. The flames had turned it into the sixth layer of Hell. It was so hot, the throne itself had begun to melt. He didn't need to worry about smoke inhalation, but the heat was still deadly to him.

Temple smashed through the roof, preparing to stomp on his chest. Slate rolled out of the way. Temple missed, his foot making a hole in the floor. He yanked it out. Slate scrambled out of the throne room and shot a bolt of lightning at the ceiling as a farewell present. Flaming wooden beams landed on Temple, immobilizing him. His pale body caught fire. Slate sensed the rest of the throne room collapsed around Temple. There was little doubt in his mind that Temple would survive. He just wanted to buy some time so he could meet up with Naomi.

A large piece of wood almost crushed Slate. A section of floor gave out near him. He had to get out of this death trap. Running outside, he jumped off the very same balcony that Mistress Lotus had pushed him out of only hours before. The aches from that fight were still fresh. That devious Sebastian had made sure he and Naomi were worn down before Temple even showed himself. Both their movements and reaction times were suffering as a result. They had to end this fight soon, or Temple would end it for them.

Slate touched down in the courtyard, which was now completely ablaze. All the birds had flown the coop. Any animal that couldn't fly had long since suffocated. The bamboo forest was almost all ash. What now? Temple, with his preposterous endurance, would have the advantage in this hazardous environment. Aerial battles were also a no-go. It was best to get back out on

Tiananmen Square again and hide among the soldiers.

Before Slate could fly out of there, Temple burst out of the burning palace. He was on fire but made no effort to put out the flames. Temple threw a flaming fist, and Slate ducked out of the way, grabbed a sharp piece of wood off the ground, and stabbed it into Temple's side. Black blood trickled from the wound. Temple ignored it and elbowed his opponent right in the helmet, disorienting Slate. Then Temple lifted a finger, preparing to shoot a beam.

A floating support beam bashed him from behind, sending him flying so far that he went through a collapsed section of the palace wall and into the moat. Naomi dropped the support beam and gave Slate a look that told him to get ready.

Temple levitated out of the moat and up into midair, no longer on fire thanks to the water. His burns had healed almost immediately.

But Slate already had his arm charged. He fired a blue energy beam.

Temple created a shield. The beam struck it. He strained to keep his barrier up. Naomi sent a variety of projectiles at him, including discarded swords and bamboo stalks. They struck his sides and back, some going right through his limbs and chest, turning him into a living pincushion. His barrier started to flicker like an old fluorescent light. Slate pushed harder. He devoted all his energy to increase his beam's power.

The beam broke through, burning a plate-sized hole in Temple's chest and shooting out his back. Once again, Naomi telekinetically lifted a wooden support beam and hit Temple with it. Weakened by Slate's attack, Temple was knocked out of the air. He landed on two feet near where Sebastian and the others were. Bamboo stalks and swords were still sticking out of him, not to mention he now had a massive hole in his torso. He seemed to be having a difficult time standing, swaying on muscular legs.

Slate and Naomi gave him no time to heal. They had flown after him and were already on the attack before they even landed. Naomi used her powers to channel water from the moat and spray it at him like a fire hose. The stream of water was powerful enough to take someone's face off. She would have done

Mistress Lotus proud. Temple raised a wall of light with his right hand. The liquid hit it and produced a cloud of steam. Naomi kept the water coming. There was plenty in the moat to spare.

Meanwhile, Slate fired a beam. Temple erected another wall in front of him with his unoccupied hand. This wall seemed flimsy compared with the previous ones. Dark blood dribbled down his frame. Not only did he have to block two continuous attacks, but his injuries were not healing. All his energy was devoted to sustaining his barriers.

"Look at them go!" Straper exclaimed.

Eisenhorn touched his damaged ankle, wincing. "One of them walls is about to give. Just a question of which one."

Oscar knew the fight wasn't over, but he still felt a sense of profound satisfaction as he watched Temple weaken before his eyes. They only needed to keep hammering away at him until they severed his head or destroyed his body. Then they could kill the putrid brain nestled within that pandorium helmet. Death was at Temple's door.

Sebastian's smile then took on a wickedness that dried up all the good cheer. "It seems the fight has been won," he declared.

Temple dropped his front wall. Slate's beam quickly disintegrated Temple's entire left arm and burned the side of his torso until the ribs themselves showed. The beast buckled. It seemed as though Temple was on his last leg.

But then his remaining wall morphed, taking on a curved shape.

Slate realized their mistake too late. "Naomi, stop the waterworks!"

She didn't hear him over the sound of roaring water. She also didn't notice that Temple's curved wall had redirected the stream of water. It collided with Slate. He fell on his backside, soaked from head to toe. It was the worst state he could have been in.

Temple then used his energy to evaporate the puddles of water around them. White steam obscured Naomi's vision. The heat of it forced her back a few feet. She wanted to smack herself. They had been clumsy. Temple had used her own attack against Slate. Now she couldn't even see. How could she defend? How could she—?

She saw the glow. Then she felt something enter her. Blood ran down her legs.

Temple had stabbed her.

CHAPTER 63

Temple's left arm had regenerated some, but there was only a jagged bone poking out where his hand should have been. However, it was sharp enough to serve as a makeshift weapon. Temple had been quick, quicker than he ought to have been in his condition. Swords and bamboo still stuck out of him. His body was full of holes large enough for a bird to build a nest in. But his legs were still mostly intact. They had carried him well.

Now the bone on his stump was buried deep in Naomi's gut. Her white outfit was soaked in red. She wore no expression, almost as stoic as Camilla Ryder. And she felt no pain.

Temple would fix that. He lifted her off the ground. The bone dug deeper. Naomi gasped, her shock wearing off. Temple's body gave off a heavenly light. The bamboo in his flesh went up in smoke, the swords melting away soon after. His torso was soon repaired.

The last thing to heal was the stump inside Naomi. The heat it gave off made her barf up a mix of blood and breakfast. As Temple's hand regenerated inside her, Naomi's wound grew wider. By the time his fingers were complete, she was starting to black out from the torment. Only thoughts of her mother kept her from doing so.

"You maniac!" Slate ran up to Temple, his arm glowing with passion. Being soaked kept him from powering up properly, but he couldn't wait to dry off. He had to kill that thing.

Temple held Naomi between himself and the Helmet Man.

Slate roared. "A hostage? Coward!"

But the human shield proved to be effective. Slate's arm stopped glowing. He did not, however, stop running. If anything, he picked up speed.

"I'll just beat you bare-handed, then!"

Temple tore his fist out of Naomi. It made a squishy sound. She dropped hard enough for her head to bounce off the pavement. Temple reapplied his war paint, using his victim's blood to do so. The three red lines on the helmet only fueled Slate's outrage.

"Stop playing with my woman's blood!" Slate made a fist full of energy and nearly nailed Temple.

But in Slate's anger, he had become predictable. Temple sidestepped the attack and jabbed him in the ribs. Two of them broke. Slate got angrier. He kicked at Temple's legs. Temple hopped over the swinging leg and punched his adversary in the chest.

The Helmet Man gripped his injured breast. He threw two more punches. Temple weaved out of their way and punched him in the helmet. Slate's head rang. He delivered a few more blows. They had force behind them but were poorly aimed. Temple didn't even need to dodge. He punched the silver helmet again. Slate staggered back. Temple hit the helmet twice more. Slate's neck almost snapped. Temple hit the helmet one last time, breaking his own fingers and producing a loud crack. Slate fell and grabbed the back of his neck in pain. Temple flexed his hand, his broken fingers healing instantly.

"You can't win," Slate moaned. "You can't get away with what you did…"

Temple shot a beam through Slate's back. It came out the other side near his belly button. A four-toed foot then kicked Slate over on his side and stomped on his ankle, breaking it.

"Slate!" Straper screamed.

Eisenhorn and Oscar also watched with quivering lips as Temple proceeded to shoot the Helmet Man full of holes. Slate shrieked.

"My boy!" Oscar cried, running forward a few steps before realizing he had no way to fight Temple. He turned to Sebastian instead. "Have a soul! Please, get that thing to stop hurting my boy!"

"I already told you, Temple doesn't take orders from me," Sebastian said with false sympathy. "Don't bother begging either. He will not heed your words in the slightest."

Oscar went to his knees and kissed Sebastian's polished shoes with tears in his eyes. Sebastian was snickering so hard that he had to cover his mouth.

"Sebastian, I'm sorry!" Oscar cried. "It was my fault! The Gifted were abused because of me, because of my inaction. That's why I'm here, to make amends. I stole your sight and your pride. You are the victim! I am slime! I am the villain!"

Sebastian raised his sword. "You're right, Radcliffe. Thanks for the reminder."

He stabbed one of Oscar's outstretched hands. Blood squirted out. Oscar screamed almost as loud as his son just had.

Sebastian tore the blade out. "That was for blinding me."

But Sebastian was not finished. He ground his heel into Oscar's wound. Oscar could only mewl like a tortured kitten.

"And that was for not using anesthesia..."

"I can't watch this anymore!" Straper shouted. He loaded his rifle, not sure whom to aim it at. Another scream from Slate convinced him. Straper didn't think he had ever heard the Helmet Man cry out like that before. It was incomprehensible. The ear wouldn't accept it. Straper felt sick. He pointed his rifle at Temple, aiming for the neck.

Temple was suddenly in front of him. Straper hadn't even seen him move. Out of fear, he pulled the trigger, but Temple batted the barrel away before the bullet came out.

Straper dropped his weapon. He felt his bowels void.

"Get away, kid!" Eisenhorn bellowed.

Temple grabbed Straper's wrist. It took only a moment to burn through it. Straper shrieked as he saw his hand fall off.

"My hand! You're evil! You're evil!"

Two large white hands then clasped themselves around his head and lifted him off the ground. Straper's neck strained from the weight of his body. Temple began to squeeze. Straper shrieked again, clawing at Temple's arms with his one remaining hand. The scratch marks vanished with a dull glow. Straper's skull cracked in three different places. Trickles of blood ran from his eyes and nose. His voice finally gave out.

"I'll tear you to pieces!" Eisenhorn yelled, knowing in his heart that he would fail but also knowing he couldn't back away. He picked up Straper's hunting knife and ran up to Temple. The general went for the neck. Much to his surprise, he actually got the blade in there. A cascade of black blood poured out.

But Temple merely let go of Straper, who fell in a heap, and yanked the blade out. It disintegrated in his grasp. His wound healed too.

Eisenhorn knew what was coming next. Temple punched him straight in the face. His nose bled. Then Temple gave him a hook, knocking five of his teeth out. Temple focused on the torso from then on. Eisenhorn lost count of how many blows struck him, but it had to be around twenty. His knees gave out. The general crumpled beneath the weight of the agony. Temple reeled his leg back and kicked him in the gut. He gave another kick. A third was given, this one harder than the other two. The barbarity seemed endless.

A sword came flying. Temple caught it before it could pierce his chest and melted it.

Naomi was still bleeding, but she focused on her wound to keep herself from hemorrhaging too badly, willing her blood not to drip out. She limped toward her tormentor.

"See me now, Mother...?" she spat. "You see me now...? This is how you should've gone out ... like a human ... not a pig..."

Temple left Eisenhorn to his suffering. He took his time walking toward Naomi. They were moving toward each other now. Naomi threw an invisible punch. It hit Temple but barely made a mark. He kept walking with clenched fists. Naomi didn't have enough energy to use her powers anymore. The blood was flowing now. That didn't stop her from limping forward, her eyes unblinking and focused on Temple.

"Don't forget about me..." Slate said. He limped after Temple, unable to keep up. Raising a shaky arm, he fired a beam. Temple raised a rectangular light barrier that stopped it easily. He only had to use one hand to block that attack. Slate now found he couldn't shoot any more beams. He resorted to lightning, sending a few bolts. Temple didn't even bother to turn around when they struck his back. The burns healed as he walked on.

Temple reached Naomi and nailed her in the eye. She moaned and tried punching him too, a physical blow rather than one with her faltering powers, but it was an infant's punch. Temple hit her face again, this time smashing her nose. Naomi's face was swollen and ghostly pale. She felt like swooning. Another punch brought her back to reality, this one hitting her gut. Temple then bashed her cheek. She let out a sob.

Slate finally caught up with Temple. He was half dead. "I never ... I never hated someone ... so much in my..."

He punched Temple in the shoulder. Temple backhanded him. Slate didn't fall over. Bad for him. Temple kicked him in the shin and twisted his arm. Slate yelped. Temple let go of him. The Helmet Man went down.

Temple returned to Naomi. She was almost down herself. Temple had to hit her face a few more times before she too fell. Temple then put his deformed foot on her chest and started pressing down. She gasped, feeling the air being pushed out her lungs. Temple increased the pressure. Her chest was about to cave in.

Sebastian and Quantum watched on. The dog panted stupidly, in good spirits, while Sebastian occasionally laughed when either Slate or Naomi made their pathetic noises. Straper was on the verge of death. Oscar sniffled as he cradled his bleeding hand.

Only Eisenhorn had any real fight left in him. He had a hard time moving, but his usually crippling temper was now giving him much-needed strength. Temple had to die. The Mentor could not win. Who knew what would happen if Cloak got its way? Klara had been vague about what was awaiting the world, but it was obviously bad. Now it seemed he was the only thing standing in the way of Cloak and its heinous goals. There was no other choice.

He would have to use the syringe.

Eisenhorn had no qualms about killing himself or taking his comrades with him. They were all dead anyway. The very least he could do was make sure these monsters also died and the Mentor was defeated. And Shu had gotten away. That was something.

But didn't the helmet moron's girlfriend have the syringe on her? Temple was busy killing her, so Eisenhorn couldn't get it even if he had been able to walk. For all he knew, the syringe had already broken during her fight with Temple. The general was just about to give up when he saw a glimmer from the corner of his eye. It was rolling toward him. A surge of hope, unlike anything he ever felt before, overcame his being.

The syringe stopped near his hand. That woman must have rolled it over to him with her mind as she was being torn apart. The lady had guts. Eisenhorn was almost envious of her inner strength. With a shaky hand, he reached for the syringe. Suicide was a coward's way out in his book, but this could be seen as admirable. He had no regrets. He went for it.

The syringe shattered. Its contents evaporated.

Eisenhorn felt all the hope that had welled up in him expire.

"You didn't think I'd see that coming, did you?" Sebastian asked, having just destroyed the syringe with a well-flicked bullet casing. "Well, you were right, but I have my other four senses to compensate."

The general felt no anger. He felt nothing at all. All those months of trying to get his hands on that cursed syringe, all so it could shatter within his reach.

"I am curious what purpose that syringe served," Sebastian said. "Maybe it has something to do with why the Western Union sent an incompetent geezer to China as their ambassador. I suppose it really doesn't matter at this point. Judging by your demeanor, your plan has clearly failed anyway."

Sebastian then heard something far beyond the normal range of the human ear. Even Quantum only picked up the sound ten seconds after him.

Temple lifted his foot off Naomi and turned toward the noise.

"An aircraft?" Sebastian guessed out loud. Quantum barked, seemingly disagreeing.

After a moment, Sebastian put two and two together. He licked his curled lips.

"No ... it's a walker."

CHAPTER 64

Gilda didn't know how she would deal with those legions of soldiers guarding the palace, especially without Incognito to help her. She would have to be quick and lucky. Maybe Slate would sense her coming and escort her back to the Forbidden City. She could only hope.

Neither Gilda nor Tim could see that the palace was on fire until Magenta was above Tiananmen Square. Her guts twisted up. "Tim, what do you think is going on?"

"The force field is down," Tim said. "The Chinese may have started the fire in order to force Slate and the others out of the palace."

"The Chinese wouldn't put their emperor at risk like that. This must be Cloak."

"How do you wish to proceed, Ms. Gilda?"

"We'll try reaching the Forbidden City and see if Slate and the others are still hanging around there. Prepare for suppressive fire, Tim."

"Against this many enemies, I doubt that will help us, Ms. Gilda."

"Do it anyway."

They were now above the hundreds of thousands of soldiers surrounding the burning palace. The soldiers made no move to put out the flames. What was keeping them from helping? More importantly, why weren't they shooting at Magenta?

"Ms. Gilda, this is disconcerting."

"No duh. Keep flying."

"Ms. Gilda, behind you!"

Gilda spun her walker around and found that she couldn't breathe anymore.

Temple floated before her with his powerful arms crossed. There was no mistaking him. He did not make any hostile moves, but Gilda could feel his brutality. It made her skin crawl. That silver helmet made her skin crawl even more. Naomi's stories had understated just how terrible of a being Temple was.

"Tim ... we can't fight this guy."

"I know we can't, Ms. Gilda."

"I don't want to die either..."

"I know, Ms. Gilda."

"What do I do?"

Temple vanished.

"Flee, Ms. Gilda!"

Beams of light came from every angle. Magenta performed a variety of maneuvers, getting hit a few times regardless. One almost pierced the cockpit.

"He's moving too fast!" Gilda shouted. "I can't get a lock on him!"

Then she heard a thump. Temple had landed on Magenta. The walker tried to tear off the fiend with one of its arms, but he was grabbing on to the middle of its back, a place it could not reach. Gilda made Magenta fly violently from side to side, but Temple kept his grip.

"Tim, electrocute him!"

A surge of electricity went through the armor. Temple endured it. He punched the walker's back with a glowing fist, making a sizable hole.

"Communications are down!" Tim cried. "Another hit could end us!"

Gilda panicked. Curse Oscar for making her armor weak. Magenta couldn't withstand this barrage for long. There was only one real option. She flicked a few switches and slammed her foot down on a pedal.

Magenta went in reverse at maximum speed. Temple, who had been trying to hold on, now found himself unable to move. Even with his superstrength, he could not fight Magenta's inertia. He was pinned to the walker's back.

Gilda tilted her walker. Now it was headed in reverse toward the ground.

"This will flatten the freak," she snarled.

"Ms. Gilda, we're still high up! Hitting the ground at these speeds will kill us."

"I'll ditch before then, and your CPU is housed in a black box. It'll survive the crash."

Magenta was descending at nearly supersonic speeds. The walker would hit Tiananmen Square in half a minute. Temple strained but could not move his arms an inch.

But that did not mean he was helpless.

His arms began to glow, growing so hot that they started melting through the armor.

"Hull breach, Ms. Gilda!"

Two arms broke their way into the cockpit, one on either side of Gilda. She cried out as they wrapped around her and began to squeeze.

"Ms. Gilda!" Tim wailed.

"Eject..." she croaked, her face turning almost as purple as her hair.

Tim complied. Her seat ejected from Magenta, ripping Temple's arms off. Everything became a jumble. Gilda felt the wind slap her hard, but being released from that crushing grip was all that mattered to her.

The parachute opened up. The seat was floating down now. Gilda's world wasn't a jumble anymore. Now she could see Magenta crashing into Tiananmen Square below her. Thirty soldiers were turned to pudding. A cloud of debris billowed up.

After a moment, the dust settled. The crash had created a large crater. Even from up here, Gilda could tell Magenta was toast, reduced to a crumpled mass of metal. But if her walker looked that bad, Temple must be an absolute mess. She sighed, though it pained her injured chest.

Her seat landed near the crash site between two ranks of soldiers. Her parachute deflated, settling over several statue-like soldiers. Gilda unbuckled herself and took her time standing up on rubbery legs. The soldiers around her made no move to apprehend her. This only made her more nervous.

Gilda approached her walker, which looked even worse close up. Its legs and wings had been smashed to bits. Only one of its arms looked intact, and its body was completely squashed. She felt like crying. Oscar wouldn't be able to fix this.

Then the walker moved. Gilda grew tense and took a compact handgun from her belt, never expecting she would have to use it.

A white hand burst from the metal. It squeezed into a fist.

Gilda didn't give herself time to fear. She fired all her bullets. Not being as good a shot as Straper, she only managed to hit the arm twice and blow off its ring finger. That did little to help her. The metal got torn open even more. The wounded white hand dragged out the rest of its owner. The vile silver helmet worked its way out of the wreckage.

Now the fear came. Gilda dropped her empty gun, her feet telling her to run away from this place as fast as she could. But that wouldn't do any good. She had to think of something else. Temple was still regenerating and struggling to get out. He was as vulnerable as he would ever be. She had to act.

Gilda ran to what was left of her walker's cockpit, trying to keep a good distance away from the emerging Temple. "Tim, you still alive?"

"Affirmative," Tim buzzed, the speaker damaged.

Temple's upper body was now free. His chest wounds were almost healed.

"Tim, what works still?" she asked.

"The cannon arm is operational and loaded, but I am unable to reload."

"I've got one shell, then." Gilda slipped her wrist into the sleeve, taking control of Magenta's arm. The arm made a variety of creaks and groans, but it moved reluctantly.

Temple was now free and fully healed. Gilda felt her blood go cold. The arm was moving too slowly. It wouldn't make it in time.

He aimed a glowing index finger at her.

A cloud of black smoke then wrapped around his ankle and yanked him off his feet. He crashed onto his side, firing a beam into the pavement rather than at Gilda.

A short distance away, Thistle discreetly controlled the smoke, hoping not to rouse Sebastian's suspicion. She had woken up several minutes ago and had feigned unconsciousness ever since. Cloak was the reason her family was dead. The blind man had pitted the Black Lotus and the foreigners against each other. Now it appeared that one of the foreigners was on the verge of killing the beast, only needing a little help to do so. Despite her timidity, Thistle was proud to provide this assistance as she held back her tears and anguish.

Gilda saw the smoke, realizing that last remaining cyborg was helping her out. She would have to thank her later. The cannon was now aimed at Temple.

Then her world faded.

How dare you defile this temple...

Gilda could hear the voice of her mother in the back of her mind. She could feel the hands crawling all over her. She tried pulling the trigger but couldn't control her limbs. She couldn't control anything anymore.

"Temple..." she whispered. "He's been causing these dreams..."

Yes... Our Mentor has been peeling away the layers of your mind. The others were not as sensitive to the probing, but you felt it every time the lord entered you...

"Get out of my head!"

Have faith... Have fear... The deed is done...

Gilda snapped out of it. Her hand was still in the sleeve, her finger wrapped around the trigger. She was about to pull it when she realized the cannon was aimed at herself.

"Ms. Gilda, ru—!"

A beam put an end to Tim, cutting through the black box like cheese.

Gilda felt an immense shadow loom behind her.

Temple grabbed her throat.

***

Thistle felt the sword stab her.

A sharp squeak escaped her tiny mouth. She had still been pretending to be out of it. Sebastian had clearly not been fooled.

"Your breathing pattern changed," he told her in Mandarin. "An obvious sign you were awake. It seems your betrayal has failed to pay off."

Sebastian removed his sword and cleaned it off with his tongue. The blood flowed even faster now. Thistle only lived for a few more seconds before slipping away.

"You murdered a little girl..." Slate said. "She deserved another chance ... the chance we never got... I won't forget this..."

"The life of this one child will be a mere drop in our ocean of blood," Sebastian told him. "What use is there to fret over such a measly life?"

"Someone has to..."

"If you say so. Ah, Temple approaches. And he brought a playmate..."

Temple emerged from the sea of red soldiers dragging a young woman by her purple hair, needing only one arm to do it. Gilda clawed and cursed. Temple ignored her resistance. He released her where the Helmet Man lay.

Gilda saw all the abuse Slate had taken. Her heart broke.

"What are you doing here?" he asked in a withered voice.

"Slate ... you can't be..."

"Run..." Slate addressed Temple next. "If you hurt one hair on her..."

Using glowing fingers, Temple impaled Gilda in the lower back. She let out a silent scream, her face doing an adequate job of expressing her torture on its own.

"Animal!" Slate cried with renewed vigor. He gave Temple a hook. Temple caught it with one hand and twisted, breaking Slate's wrist. The Helmet Man cried out.

Digging around for several never-ending seconds, Temple at last got hold of Gilda's spinal cord. He tore out one of her vertebrae. Gilda passed out from the pain, a small mercy. Temple tossed her ten feet away, finished with the removal. Quantum wandered up and marked its territory on her. Temple inspected the blood-covered vertebra like it was a diamond. Then he turned it to ash and wiped the powder on Slate's silver helmet, drawing a horseshoe right where his forehead should have been.

Slate spoke as the ash was applied. "Mentor ... I know you can hear me... What is it you want? Face me... Face me now..."

After finishing, Temple stood up and left him and headed toward where

Naomi lay. She somehow clung to consciousness, enduring reality. She searched herself for any remaining strength to use against this unearthly enemy. She found none. Temple grabbed her long hair and towed her to the Helmet Man. He placed Naomi beside Slate so the two of them were facing each other. Naomi saw her battered reflection on the silver helmet. She felt like crying.

"Sebastian…" Slate whispered, knowing full well the blind man was listening. "What's Temple planning to do with us? What's he gonna do to Naomi?"

"You're barking up the wrong tree," Sebastian told him. Quantum barked, causing Sebastian to let out a laugh.

"Temple…" Slate moaned. "Mentor … whatever you are … let these people go… It's me you want… Use me… Throw me away… Just leave them alone…"

Temple put a foot on Naomi's head.

"I give up…" Slate went on. "I surrender… You've won…"

Every soldier on Tiananmen Square began to march in place, a thunderclap sounding each time the synchronized feet hit the pavement.

Temple started to press down. Naomi's eyes were full of shock.

"No!" Slate tried to move, but his injuries were too grave. "Show her some mercy! I'm begging you! I'm groveling here! I've never asked for anything harder in my life!"

The pressure increased. The marching grew faster. A mewl left Naomi's lips.

"Mentor, don't do it!" Slate cried. "I'll do whatever you want! I'll be your slave! Just don't kill her, please!"

Naomi's skull fractured. Blood leaked from her orifices. The marching reached its peak.

Sebastian stifled laughter. "Like mother, like daughter."

"Mentor!" Slate bellowed.

Then his prayers were answered. Temple stopped, but not by his own volition.

A blade had stabbed the beast through the back. It came out his chest.

"Reduced to begging already, Helmet Man?" Incognito scoffed. "How unbecoming."

"Sir, we need your final authorization," Kazakov said.

Young Powell leaned back in his chair. The idea of a nuclear war was an unpleasant one, but he was pretty sure most of the Western Union would remain intact. In the long run, this whole affair might be a good thing. Powell would be known to the world as the man who led humanity through the dark days of Armageddon. Powell the Savior didn't quite roll off the tongue, but it definitely had its appeal.

Fake Powell nodded. "Let's do it."

Kazakov nodded back. "Preparing to launch."

"Wait, what's with the dots?" Lexington asked.

Everyone turned to the map on-screen. Sure enough, all the red dots were disappearing one by one. The entire room started chattering, except for Young Powell, who kept silent.

A red phone rang. Kazakov picked it up and listened to what the voice on the other end had to say. The whole room was silent as he put down the phone. His expression was a mix of confusion and cautious relief.

"What is it, man?" Fake Powell demanded. "Spit it out!"

"Sir, it appears the Chinese have disarmed their nuclear arsenal. I am told they are unable to reactivate it, at least not in time to launch a counterattack."

"The Chinese have surrendered?" the Japanese PM questioned. "Impossible."

"Did we just win the bloody war?" the British PM asked.

Reynolds was sweating more than usual. "This is all very fishy."

"Are we still planning to retaliate, Mr. President?" Herman asked.

The entire room turned to their fake president. Young Powell brooded. He wasn't sure exactly how they had managed to avoid a nuclear holocaust, but it seemed as though the dice had come up in his favor. He would be a fool to ignore this good luck.

Young Powell turned to Fake Powell. "Sir, we have to show them we're civilized. I advise you accept the surrender."

"I concur," Lexington chimed in. "No point in killing them all now, especially since the fallout from our own missiles could come back to bite us."

Fake Powell pretended to think for a moment, having already made up his mind the moment Young Powell finished his sentence.

"Kazakov, keep our missiles on standby," Fake Powell said. "Let's be cautious and see what the Chinese do next. Like Lexington said, no point in killing them now."

***

High General Lee stared at the control station with the deepest sadness that Xing had ever witnessed. A few tears even escaped Lee's eyes. Xing and Shu stood behind him, well aware of the sacrifice they had all just made.

"We will now live under the rule of the West," Lee said. "I have betrayed my emperor and forsaken all my beliefs."

"It is not easy to face the truth," Xing told him. "Trust me. I know."

Shu touched Lee's shoulder, perhaps overstepping her bounds. Lee allowed it. He needed human contact. He needed to be reminded what this was all about.

"With time ... will I feel better?" Lee asked.

Xing had to smile, tearing up himself. "You will feel wonderful."

***

Temple was slow to react. The scythe lifted him off his feet.

At supersonic speeds, Incognito smashed him hard into the ground, breaking half the bones in Temple's body and making a sizable crater in the pavement.

Oscar let out tears of joy. "Incognito, you came! You finally came!"

"Of course I did," Incognito said, yanking his blade from Temple. "Such a minor distraction could only keep me occupied for so long."

"You have to stop them! You have to kill Temple! Cloak set up this entire confrontation so Temple could get his hands on Slate. Sebastian told me that if Temple has his way, the Mentor will come into being and take over the world. And I believe it!"

"You don't say?"

"Kill Temple! Without him, the Mentor will disappear forever!"

Incognito glanced around. The carnage left a bad taste. His eyes rested on Naomi, then on Thistle. Both their conditions left an even worse taste.

The soldiers had stopped marching when Incognito first appeared. Now those with guns cocked their weapons and aimed them at the phantom. He only sighed.

"It seems the nuclear attack has been canceled," Sebastian said. He was still smiling, but it was strained. Quantum growled, arching its back.

"Sebastian..."

The second-in-command of Cloak heard this whisper escape Naomi's lips. She was still conscious but sounded like she was about to black out.

"You thought you knew people..." she said in her quietest voice. "You thought you knew the Chinese... You thought they were docile servants... But you were wrong... Xing stopped those nukes... He didn't do it alone either... Others helped him..."

Sebastian did his best to ignore her, but her words cut deep.

"People aren't tools of a higher power... They beat you and your Mentor..." Naomi gave her weakest smile. "Now you have nowhere to run..."

Naomi passed out, the smile still on her lips.

"Incognito..." Slate said with difficulty. "Kill these punks... I'll kill you later..."

"Do not give me orders," Incognito said. "I shall proceed at my own pace. And refrain from making threats you can't back up."

Slate had no witty response. The pain clouded his mind. Gilda and Straper were still unconscious, but Eisenhorn was awake. He had trouble believing that Incognito was really here. It was too good to be true, yet here he was, an oasis in this insanity. He had an even harder time believing he was actually relieved to see the terrorist bastard.

Temple was getting up now, his bones healed. He made no move to attack Incognito and stayed far back from the newcomer.

"I see you like to play with your food," Incognito told Temple. "No table manners whatsoever. And why is it I feel no fear when I'm in your presence? Everyone else seems to quiver in their boots when they're around you. Is it because you know I'm stronger?"

"Incognito, the bane of my existence," Sebastian said. He snickered. It came off as forced. "I never thought I would meet you in person, though I never had any desire to. It wasn't enough that you experimented on children. Now you have to interfere with our betterment."

"Spare me your guilt trip," Incognito snorted. "That tactic might work on a self-effacer like Radcliffe, but it'll take more than that to pierce my psychological armor. You think your cause is just? I am the one who is trying to punish the evildoers that defiled you for all those years. But you are still a slave. You merely have a different master now."

"Your limited worldview amuses me. Do you honestly believe the West is the ultimate source of evil? A childish belief."

"You simpering fool, my belief is childish only in the sense of how graspable and plainly obvious it is, even to the feeblest of minds."

"I'm not interested in debating philosophy at the moment. Just stay out of our way."

"You are in no position to be making such demands."

"I beg to differ. Temple, Quantum, and I are still in fine form. Also, let's not forget the three hundred thousand brainwashed soldiers pointing their guns at you."

"Yes, I might end up breaking a sweat if I have to fight you all. I suppose I'll need to thin the herd out."

Incognito reached into his white jacket and pulled out a control panel covered in numerous buttons. One of them was big and red.

Sebastian struggled to keep his smug demeanor. "May I ask what that is?"

"I picked it up just before I arrived here. It was portable, much to my convenience."

"I'll ask again. What is it?"

Incognito refrained from answering. The answer soon became obvious.

Sebastian stopped smiling.

Incognito pressed the big red button.

Every mine under Tiananmen Square went off.

***

Thousands of explosions combined to create something resembling an atomic blast. Even if the mind-controlled soldiers had cared, they would have had no time to feel any pain.

Hundreds of thousands of puppets were blown away. The walkers and other equipment fared little better, torn apart or even melting in some instances. The burning palace was also destroyed. Not even a splinter of the Forbidden City was spared.

The explosion burned itself out, lasting only a minute. The destruction birthed great plumes of smoke that blocked out the sky. The square was now a gloomy twilight realm.

Sebastian had covered his sensitive ears, but that hadn't helped much. They rang like fire alarms. He felt as if his entire body was covered in first-degree burns.

Yet he lived. Quantum barked, Sebastian barely able to hear it. Temple was next to them with one of his arms raised. A dome of yellow light had protected all three of them. The smoke still swirled outside Temple's barrier, resembling a reverse snow globe.

Temple took down his semitransparent dome. Before the smoke could consume them all, his pale form pulsed with light, creating a gust of wind that nearly blew Sebastian's sunglasses off his head. All the smoke was pushed back three hundred feet, giving the trio breathing room. Quantum continued to bark.

"Hush up!" Sebastian ordered. His smile had returned, though it was a shadow of its former self. The ringing in his ears was starting to fade. From what he sensed, all of Tiananmen Square had gone from being a smooth concrete expanse to a craggy field of rubble. The pavement had shattered like springtime ice. There wasn't much in terms of human remains, only the occasional limb of a dead soldier that still smoldered. A few chunks of walkers were also lying around but nothing that could be salvaged.

It was all a junkyard now. Incognito had swiped the control panel that Fang had been using and set off all the mines. How clever. Sebastian realized he should have had those soldiers destroy the panel, but he never imagined Incognito would make it here.

Speaking of which, where was Incognito, or the Helmet Man and his friends for that matter? Sebastian had no doubt that Incognito was still lurking about. Had he rescued the others at the last second or left them to die? Was the Helmet Man no more? Were the Mentor's plans foiled? Sebastian grew more concerned with each passing second.

Quantum was still barking.

"I told you to hush up," Sebastian seethed, his smile twitching like a half-dead cockroach. "Why do you feel the need to—?"

A bus-sized slab of concrete hit Temple from behind. The rush of wind knocked over Sebastian and Quantum and stirred up a cloud of debris.

The concrete skidded to a stop with Temple crushed beneath it.

Sebastian got up. He didn't bother dusting the grit off his blue suit. "Mentor," he prayed. "Give me the strength to—"

Having already drawn his sword, Sebastian was able to block the blade in time, but it nearly beheaded him. He was sweating now, his normally well-kept hair a rat's nest.

"Not even your Mentor can save you now," Incognito said. He struck with his scythe again, Sebastian almost failing to counter. Incognito's speed was unmatched. Sebastian also had trouble predicting Incognito's moves since his moments of intangibility made it so he gave away few if any nonvisual cues.

"I doubt you'll be able to keep this up for long." Incognito struck four dozen more times in a three-second period. The last strike sliced Sebastian's stomach, spilling out a great deal of blood and ruining his suit.

"That little girl, you murdered her," Incognito told his opponent. "I didn't spare her life just so you could take it."

Incognito bashed the blind man in the mug with the scythe's handle, breaking his glasses and his cheekbone. Sebastian squealed.

"Filth..." Incognito hissed. "I should have aborted you when I had the chance."

Quantum leaped from behind, but Incognito would not be taken unawares. He sliced the dog's head off in one smooth stroke, the furry corpse flying past him and to the ground.

A beam of light came. Incognito flew out of its path, knowing his vulnerability to energy would be his greatest disadvantage. Temple had gotten up and healed his flattened body. He fired more beams. Incognito zigzagged his way toward Temple, the beams unable to hit. He sank his scythe into the ground and yanked out another massive piece of concrete. He tried bashing Temple from above with it, but Temple had already brought up a rectangular energy barrier to protect himself. The concrete disintegrated on impact.

Flicking his hand, Temple sent the barrier upward. Incognito moved out of its way. However, his jacket caught fire as it went by, so he had to ditch it. He wore a sleeveless shirt underneath his jacket, his non-bionic bare arm covered in track marks and cancerous flesh.

Incognito landed and made the ground around himself intangible. Temple partially sank into the concrete before catching on to what Incognito was doing and attempting to fly upward, but Incognito quickly made the shattered pavement tangible. Temple was now stuck, struggling to free his feet, which were fused with the ground.

Incognito would not pass up this opportunity. He sped toward Temple.

But then a set of teeth took a bite out of his shoulder. Incognito stopped in his tracks, grimacing. Quantum hung off him and wasn't planning to let go. How had that dog snuck up on him? And how had it reattached its severed head? *It must be Gifted,* Incognito determined. He made himself intangible, the dog losing its grip, and stabbed it in the side. The mutt went limp. Incognito grunted. His bite wound was shallow, but it would still slow him down.

While Incognito had been preoccupied, Temple ripped himself free of his fused feet. Black blood painted the concrete. He flew at Incognito, his feet already regenerating, and threw numerous glowing punches.

The specter weaved out of each blow's way, eyeing Temple with disgust and impatience. "Pathetic brute... Only the West could create something as foul as you."

Temple reeled back for another blow. However, it was at this moment that all his limbs fell off. Numerous lacerations also covered him, all of them leaking black blood. Incognito had chopped up Temple countless times while dodging the beast's blows. Temple hit the ground and rolled to a stop, too damaged to fly.

Incognito was tempted to finish the job when a yellow dog went for his throat. The scythe sliced Quantum's thigh. The dog landed on its feet, snarling and snapping. Incognito snarled himself. What were this mongrel's abilities? The dog seemed to both teleport and regenerate, but seeing as how it had been unable to teleport to avoid attacks and wasn't healing its leg wound, the dog clearly couldn't do either of these things on a whim. It likely could only teleport or regenerate whenever it was killed.

Quantum lunged for Incognito.

"If that's the case..." Incognito muttered. As the dog came at him, he slammed the handle of his scythe onto its upper back, breaking the mutt's spine. Quantum landed in a heap, unable to move its limbs anymore. The dog was immobilized yet still alive, so it couldn't use its powers again to cause any more trouble.

"Just two more dogs to cripple," Incognito told himself.

Analyzing the scene from afar, Sebastian now realized how much he had underestimated the masked man. Just how much had Incognito held back until now? Was he giving his all fighting Temple right now, or was he still restraining himself?

Sebastian squeezed his hands into fists. No, Cloak could not fail. The Mentor *must* become a reality. They had to get their hands on the Helmet Man, and they had to do it fast. Otherwise, Incognito may end up killing Temple. The Mentor would lose, and everything would have been for naught. Sebastian had to find Slate. All else was secondary.

But where had Incognito taken him and the others? Even Incognito had his limits, so he couldn't have taken his subordinates too far. He also would have liked to keep them within his reach but far enough that they wouldn't get in the way. They were likely still somewhere on what was left of Tiananmen Square. He just had to use his senses to find them. He opened himself up to the world. His ears had stopped ringing, which helped some. Fires were burning. Ash was falling. Lots of smoke. Breathing—wait, breathing? Yes, breathing... Sebastian heard a small group of people breathing about a kilometer away, still on the square. They sounded injured and tired. Only two or three of them were conscious. It must be them.

"The Helmet Man is to the west!" Sebastian yelled.

Temple had only partially regenerated himself, but he managed to levitate and fly toward his new destination.

"Fleeing is futile," Incognito spat, flying after him. Incognito would already have caught up with Temple had Quantum not injured him, but Sebastian knew Temple wouldn't make it. Even if he did, there wouldn't be enough time for him to break the Helmet Man. Sebastian had to figure out a way for Temple to gain the upper hand. He needed a miracle.

Then something caught his attention. A small metal object lay where Temple had erected his dome. Holding his bleeding stomach, Sebastian made his way over and picked up the object. It was a locket. One of Slate's comrades must have dropped it, and Temple's barrier protected it from the exploding mines. Sebastian sniffed it. He knew that smell anywhere. It belonged to Repulsa. He opened it up, unable to see the picture of her mother, but he did notice with his sensitive fingertips a name etched inside. The name was something Sebastian had learned from Schmitt when he asked the Keymaster who Incognito might be.

Jericho.

Sebastian's grin returned in full.

Oscar's hand stopped bleeding. He sat up, getting his bearings in the surrounding hell.

Smoke was everywhere, but it was letting up some so he could make out a few things. Incognito had made a reckless move that saved them all. As the mines had exploded, he gathered up everyone, an easy task with his super-speed, tied all their feet together with a steel thread to keep them in physical contact with him and remain intangible, and brought them underground for a minute to weather the fireworks above. During that minute, Oscar had been weightless and unable to breathe, hear, or see. It was like drowning with a blindfold on, a feeling he had no desire to experience again.

After the fire had died down, Incognito brought them to this section of Tiananmen Square, which had suffered less due to faulty mines, and left them there without so much as a goodbye. Still in awe of Incognito's resourcefulness, Oscar undid the steel thread from everyone's feet. Nobody was spared injury, and all of them save Oscar were sprawled on the pavement. Gilda, Straper, and Naomi were all passed out and near death. Slate and Eisenhorn were the only ones besides Oscar who were still conscious, albeit barely. They remained quiet and humorless. Oscar found this to be a true shame. He could have used a joke right about now.

A yellow glow grabbed his attention. It was a tiny pinpoint of light, but it grew with each passing second. His guts twisted up. Temple was coming. Had Incognito somehow failed? Oscar realized that, if that were the case, he was the only one who stood between Temple and his goal. No way could he allow Cloak to succeed. He needed redemption.

"Dad, get out of here..." Slate said. It drained him just to speak. "You can't fight that thing... You'll die if you stay..."

Oscar shook his head. "There's nowhere to run anyway."

Temple was now visible to the naked eye. He had regenerated, flying head-first for the Helmet Man with clenched fists and bulging muscles. Oscar reached for the gun in his coat, but he knew it would be of no use.

Only thirty feet away, Temple was at last stopped. Incognito bashed him on the back with a charred walker's arm. Temple spiraled down and landed on his hands and knees. Incognito swooped down at him, slicing off one of his back muscles. He made a second pass. Temple tried backhanding him, only to lose a hand.

Making another U-turn, Incognito went back for the third time and cut off Temple's left bicep. Temple swatted at the air with glowing limbs, never coming close to hitting Incognito, who continued to carve him up like a turkey. Dark blood splattered everywhere. Body parts littered the ground around Temple, his regeneration abilities unable to keep up with Incognito's speed. After Incognito had made a hundred slices within five seconds, Temple was barely standing on his feet, drenched in black blood with most of his muscles cut off.

Once again, Incognito came, this time to remove the monster's head.

But Temple glowed. He unleashed a burst of yellow energy. Incognito dove into the ground, avoiding the blast.

Temple sank into the pavement, all the way up to his waist. His lower body fused with the ground. He tried to tear himself out, but Incognito appeared behind him and stabbed him in the neck. The scythe worked its way underneath the silver helmet. Temple had only one hand left, and it had only three fingers. He grasped the scythe's handle just as the blade started to pierce his brain. Using all his might, Incognito strained against Temple's grasp, which was still strong despite his diminished state. Temple could not heal himself or use his energy in any way since he was too focused on healing his neural tissue to do anything else. If that blade caused enough damage to his brain, it was all over.

The scythe went in another inch. Temple's grasp weakened, his fingers slipping. Black blood pooled around him. Oscar watched with hunger in his eyes.

Yes, kill him, he wordlessly urged. All his years of penance were about to end.

"Death comes to us all," Incognito whispered to the ruined Temple. "With all your power, you are still no exception."

Two of Temple's fingers lost their grip. The beast now only had one finger on the scythe. His power waned, as did his life.

Incognito got ready for the grand finale. He tightened his grip on his scythe. "There can be no snakes in my Eden..."

He began to pull. Temple's glow started to fade.

"Stop right there, Jericho," a voice warned.

Incognito stopped. His eyes widened. Temple continued to keep his one remaining finger wrapped around the scythe's handle, though he still had trouble healing.

Sebastian stood ten feet from Incognito, wearing a grin more revolting than Incognito thought one could ever be. Sebastian wore no sunglasses, which had been broken earlier, revealing his unfocused blue eyes.

But what truly infuriated Incognito was the blind man's hostage. Sebastian had one arm wrapped around Naomi, who was still unconscious. The blade of his sword poked her neck.

Too busy witnessing the fight, Oscar had been unable to notice Sebastian in time. He now found Incognito and Sebastian facing each other, each one with a hostage whose life was threatened by a blade. If Incognito attempted to kill Temple, Sebastian would bleed Naomi out in a second. On the other hand, if Incognito let go of Temple and tried to save her, Temple might use the opportunity to escape or shoot Incognito in the back. Oscar never would have suspected that Incognito would allow his personal feelings to get in the way of his mission. The entire scenario didn't even seem possible, yet he was staring right at it.

"So, this is your weakness," Sebastian taunted, the silver locket dangling from his wrist. "Love is a luxury neither one of us can afford. You should've known that."

Incognito contained his rage, though a shiver managed to escape him. "I could kill you and this beast before your blade even pierces the wench's skin."

"You'd have already done that if you thought your chances were good. I'm too fast, and you're too weary. You can't save Repulsa and kill Temple. You can only have one."

"I can have it *all*."

"What's going on...?" Slate asked. "What's happening to Naomi...?"

"What are you waiting for?" Oscar cried. "Kill him already!"

"Be silent," Incognito spat. "I have the situation under control."

"No, you don't! There's no way to keep Naomi alive. Let her go! It's her or the world. That's no contest. If Temple gets hold of Slate, it'll all be over!"

"I said be silent..."

"What about your people? What about the Saladin Federation? Have you forgotten about them? Are they all less important than the life of one woman?"

"You oversimplify the matter. Now hush!"

Oscar wanted to throw a rock at the idiot. Since when did he grow a heart? Sebastian really had found Incognito's one true weakness.

Something glittered, a gun attached to Straper's back. Oscar saw it. An idea formed. He grabbed the weapon and aimed it at Sebastian. Incognito noticed what Oscar was doing and made no move to stop him. Sebastian also noticed but felt no concern. If Radcliffe was planning to shoot him, he could easily deflect the bullet.

However, in his confidence and exhaustion, Sebastian had failed to recognize the particular type of gun. It wasn't a regular gun. It was the special gun used to take down Black Lotus cyborgs, firing blasts of energy.

That meant he couldn't deflect it.

Before Sebastian could respond in any adequate way, Oscar pulled the trigger. Sebastian convulsed, releasing Naomi and his sword. The locket flew from his wrist and landed near Oscar. With Sebastian disabled, Incognito was able to finish off Temple once and for all. He forced the blade into—

A beam of light came down from the sky. It struck where they all were.

Excalibur had just been fired.

***

"Did we kill them?" Fake Powell barked.

"We will have confirmation in a moment," Kazakov told him. "It will take a minute or so for the heat and debris to die down enough that our satellites can make out anything."

Fake Powell nodded. Young Powell clasped his hands, smirking. First the Chinese had surrendered, and now all his remaining enemies had gathered in one place. Incognito, the Helmet Man, Sebastian, and that repellent Temple may have all just been wiped off the face of the Earth with one blast from *Excalibur*.

After hearing about the surrender, Fake Powell had received a report that the Forbidden City and the rest of Tiananmen Square had been destroyed. Satellite photos were then sent to him showing Incognito fighting the second Helmet Man. *Excalibur* happened to be in range at that time, and it wasn't like the Chinese could retaliate anymore if they fired *Excalibur* at Beijing. Hell, they might actually be grateful for killing those nuisances.

The only downside was Incognito could not be captured alive. This trade-off did not thrill Young Powell. A small bolt of static came off his fingertips as he thought this. He pocketed his hand, wondering if anyone had seen.

Kazakov got another message from an officer. "Sir, it seems our troops have begun to engage United Third forces in Aleppo. With the help of *Leviathan*, we have already taken half the city. Victory appears imminent."

Everyone clapped for that, Young Powell included. Another piece of good news.

"Are we aware if Emperor Long has perished or not?" Herman asked after the clapping died down. Young Powell scowled. Leave it to that killjoy to ruin everyone's good time.

"Perhaps that's why the Chinese surrendered," Reynolds said. "Without their divine ruler, they're probably nothing more than a headless snake."

More conjecture was offered. The tension decreased. Young Powell started to feel at ease again. Let the fools speculate. All that mattered was that the world now belonged to him.

***

Incognito did not know how injured he was, but his condition was likely severe, seeing as he could barely move. He lay on his back. His burnt clothes smoked. Cracks ran through his mask, making the Arabic calligraphy on his mask unintelligible.

"Western scum..." Incognito groaned. "Could they not leave me to my work?"

As *Excalibur*'s beam impacted the ground, Incognito had let go of Temple and pushed Naomi out of the way. He also ended up pushing Sebastian to safety, definitely not his intention. The shockwave had blown them back, Incognito catching fire at one point. Now he lay near a massive crater. Naomi was next to him. The blast had not injured her, though her other injuries were still very real and kept her in critical condition.

Sebastian got to his knees. He wore a stunned smile. "Exhilarating..."

Incognito ignored the slime. What about Temple? Had *Excalibur* destroyed him? He found the strength to raise his head, attempting to see if anything was inside the crater. The smoke was heavy. It took some time for him to see anything. When he did, a jolt went through his system. Then he relaxed. It seemed there was no more threat.

A lone silver helmet, scorched clean of its bloody war paint, rested at the bottom of the crater. Temple's body had been incinerated. Not even a pile of ash remained. Incognito snorted weakly. At least those Westerners did something right.

Then the helmet twitched.

Incognito thought he had imagined it, but this was wishful thinking on his part. A spine grew from the bottom of the helmet, followed by nerves and flesh. Then came the ribs and the limbs, and lastly the skin and nails.

The attack had knocked over Oscar and momentarily blinded him. The others were unharmed, though no better off than before. As Oscar saw a hulking figure walk out of the crater, he felt a sob escape him.

"Please be a dream," he begged. "Oh, just be a dream..."

Temple wore nothing, his shorts incinerated by *Excalibur*. To Oscar, his nudity somehow made him even more fearsome than before.

Temple stopped near Incognito and kicked him in the ribs to see if he would respond. Incognito felt the pain, but it was nothing compared with his other aches and burns. Not only had *Excalibur* severely injured him, but the injection he took earlier was also wearing off. He tried reaching for his scythe but barely had the energy to lift his hand. Temple made no move.

"Be done with it," Incognito told him.

Temple considered him for a moment. Then he began to walk away.

"Get back here, vermin," Incognito whispered. "I will not be ignored."

Temple reached down, grabbed Naomi by the hair, and dragged her. She let out a mild, involuntary squeak but was still out of it.

"Put that down this instant or—" Incognito stopped midsentence, a spasm going through him. He felt warmth in his mouth, his own blood.

Sebastian stood up. He turned to Temple with clasped hands and crossed eyes. "We best hurry, my lord. *Excalibur* will likely fire again soon."

Temple struck him with his free hand. Sebastian took it in good grace.

"Forgive me..." he said with bloody lips. "I should have kept Incognito better occupied... This should have gone more smoothly..."

Temple did not respond. He merely continued to drag Naomi away.

Slate could sense Temple approaching. There was no way he could escape. Anyone who could have taken on this foe was incapacitated. The Helmet Man schemed with all his might. He needed to come up with some crazy idea, something that could save them all, but the thought of Naomi's crushed head and the cries of his tortured friends clouded his mind.

"Nothing I can say," Slate mumbled. "Nothing I can do..."

"I won't let you," Oscar croaked. "I won't let you win." He took out his compact submachine gun and pointed it at Temple. It didn't take a genius to figure out that Oscar didn't stand a chance. Even he knew that it was futile and lowered his gun. Temple was getting closer to the Helmet Man, closer to victory.

Slate reached out to his father. "Dad..."

Oscar's eyes were red and watery. His lips quivered in uncertainty. Something had to be done. The Mentor could not win. Oscar knew he had committed too many sins. He couldn't bear another. He needed to atone. He needed salvation.

Looking at his gun, a strange calm overcame him. What needed to be done became clear. It was revelation. It was salvation.

Oscar aimed the gun at his son.

Slate lowered his hand. "Dad?"

His father let loose a hail of bullets.

But they did not hit the Helmet Man. Temple had dropped Naomi, appearing next to Oscar as if flying down from above, and yanked his gun arm to the side as the weapon fired. Oscar's aim was compromised. The bullets struck the pavement instead.

Temple let go of Oscar's arm.

The gun fell from Oscar's limp hand. His trigger finger now had nothing to squeeze. "Slate..." he whispered.

"Dad ... no..."

Incognito had been watching, still as stone. Eisenhorn was only vaguely aware of what happened, but it was enough to make him weep.

Sebastian began to laugh. "This is it! This is the Mentor's plan. It all came down to this moment. Have you learned, Helmet Man? Have you *learned?*"

Temple walked toward Slate. He did not bother to grab Naomi again. The deed was done. The Helmet Man had been broken.

Oscar finally spoke. "I sacrificed everything... I did everything I was supposed to do..."

He stumbled after Temple. After catching up, he went onto his belly and grabbed Temple by the ankle. Sebastian's laughter grew.

"I did everything I was supposed to do!" Oscar cried. "I just want to feel clean! Make me feel clean! That's all I ask! Make me feel clean!"

Temple kicked free of his grip. Oscar beat his hands on the ground and sobbed. Sebastian was now laughing so hard that he threw up and fell to his knees. His unfocused blue eyes popped out, making him look like a deep-sea fish.

Temple reached his goal. He towered over the Helmet Man, who lay beaten and broken before the beast. He grasped his helmet by the sides with two open palms and lifted him off the ground. Slate's feet dangled, his body limp and his spirit shriveled.

There was no sound. Sebastian still laughed, but either his voice had gone hoarse or it simply didn't matter to anyone anymore. Only Temple stood. Everyone else had fallen.

A spark flew off Slate's fingertip.

It seemed so innocent that it would have gone unnoticed had it not been followed by another. More sparks came after, growing in intensity. They soon turned into lightning bolts. But rather than strike the ground, they flowed into Temple. More energy came off Slate, a whole storm of it. Incognito felt his eyes burn from the brightness. It was a sun. That was how bright it was. There was heat too, as hot as a furnace. The light of Heaven... The fires of Hell... They had become one and the same.

The light stopped. So did the lightning. Temple kept his hold on Slate. He was waiting.

Then it happened.

Slate's helmet broke.

There was a sharp snap. A diagonal crack was suddenly there, down the face of the supposedly indestructible silver helmet, right through the horse-shoe drawn in ash.

Temple dropped Slate. Oscar still cried, not noticing or caring about what just occurred. Incognito, however, could not look away from the crack on the silver helmet.

After that, Temple knelt and dipped his fingers in Slate's blood. He stood back up and redrew the three horizontal lines on his helmet.

Then he drew one vertical line through all three of them.

The wind began to blow. It started soft, like the kiss of a lover. Then it grew harsh and hot. It picked up dust fast, making it hard to see, but only a blind fool would not be able to notice the unspeakable glow that came off Temple. The wind swirled around him. He was the pale eye of the storm. Sebastian rolled on the ground and held his stomach in hilarity.

There was another sound too, the chopping of air. Incognito thought he was hallucinating. Then the chopping became louder, more distinguished.

A tandem rotor helicopter landed, a group of armed men hopping out. One of them was much faster than the others and reached Incognito first by a substantial margin.

Abrafo wrapped his arms around his leader. "Incognito, how could this happen? We must get you to a doctor!"

"Is this a trick?" Incognito grumbled. "How are you here?"

"We got this helicopter from those twin monks at the monastery. Good thing you took care of those mindless soldiers for us, or we would have been blown out of the sky for sure."

"The monastery's location… You weren't privileged to that information."

"I overheard you talk with Radcliffe. Forgive me, Incognito."

Incognito had no reply except to spit up some blood.

"Men, save the others!" Abrafo yelled.

Abrafo's men quickly gathered most of the injured, who all had to be carried. The one exception was Oscar, though he still needed to be dragged away as he had his breakdown.

"Slate! Oh, God! Oh, God, help me!"

"Is that Temple?" Young-Bum asked, trying to ignore the battered bodies and Oscar's wails. The submarine captain and his men had decided to tag along with Abrafo. He felt a certain camaraderie with the Helmet Man and his friends. He also wanted to save Incognito. Someone needed to pay for a replacement submarine.

Abrafo saw what Young-Bum was pointing at, although it was hard to miss. Temple was glowing brighter by the second. Abrafo also noticed Sebastian rolling around and laughing, smiling and crying all at once.

"Blow them away!" Abrafo ordered without hesitation.

The men fired. The bullets disintegrated in bursts of yellow light before even coming within five feet of Temple or Sebastian. The heat was excruciating now. Abrafo noticed that the Helmet Man was still lying near Temple's feet. And he had just caught fire.

"I'm on it!" Young-Bum shouted. His metallic hand flew off his arm like a grappling hook and grabbed Slate's ankle. He retracted the cable, pulling Slate to safety. Two men put out the yellow flames that had almost devoured the Helmet Man before loading him onto the helicopter. Young-Bum stared at his prosthetic hand, which was hot to the touch. He also felt the temperature of the air rise another ten degrees.

"We must flee!" the captain yelled.

"No, we can't leave," Incognito seethed. "I've come too far to…" He started coughing. The argument ended right then and there.

Abrafo jumped onto the aircraft and placed Incognito on a stretcher. Sanjay piloted the helicopter, his good cheer no longer apparent.

Incognito's coughing abated. He had enough strength to raise his head for one last look. Sebastian was out of his mind, clawing at his face. He was even worse off than Oscar was. Temple seemed to be made of light. The wind was nearing hurricane levels now. The heat was that of an oven.

The doors to the helicopter closed.

CHAPTER 67

"Fire *Excalibur* again!" Fake Powell ordered. "They'll get away!"

"It is almost recharged," Kazakov told him.

"Almost isn't good enough! That helicopter is taking off as we speak."

"Sir, what about the second Helmet Man?" Herman asked. "Are we going to focus our efforts on killing him or Incognito?"

Fake Powell hadn't made up his mind, which meant Young Powell hadn't. The satellites were having a difficult time seeing anything due to the swirling storm that had abruptly appeared. However, the light of Temple was strong enough to pierce any hurricane. Young Powell felt his throat tightening. He did not know why, but the light made him feel ill. Judging by the looks of everyone else in the room, he wasn't the only one who felt this way. Incognito could live another day. Young Powell wanted him alive anyway. But he had no use for Temple. The memory of the monster, slipping in a puddle of his own making, and Schmitt's laughter only reminded him why this animal needed to die.

"I believe the second Helmet Man is about to do something dangerous," Young Powell said. "We must act now."

"Agreed!" Lexington added. "Incognito is half dead anyway!"

Fake Powell nodded. "You're both right. Do it, Kazakov."

Kazakov was about to convey that order when the satellite image on-screen turned to static. Nobody was amused.

"Now is not the time for a technical failure!" Reynolds bellowed.

"Sir, I just received a message from the astronauts on *Excalibur*," Kazakov said. "Their instruments are no longer functioning. They cannot get a lock."

Fake Powell went red. "Then fire a missile!"

The situation room vibrated. Fake Powell's face stopped being red. He looked around in confusion. The room shook harder. A water-filled pitcher smashed on the floor.

"Have we been nuked?" Reynolds cried.

"No need to overreact," Kazakov said. "A message on my terminal just came up. It was an earthquake. Nothing more."

"At a time like this?" Herman questioned.

The Japanese PM stood up abruptly. "Gentlemen, I have just been informed that minor earthquakes are occurring all over Japan."

"Bloody hell, we've got one on our end too!" the British PM yelled.

"This isn't a coincidence!" Lexington yelled. "This must be some sort of secret weapon the Chinese cooked up!"

"Be quiet!" Kazakov snapped. "Your conspiracy theories have no place here."

Another tremor occurred. This one sent a section of the ceiling crashing down. Several people fell from their chairs, including Lexington and Reynolds.

"Help me up!" Reynolds ordered some aides. "This is so undignified!"

Young Powell felt electricity flow from his limbs. Luckily for him, everyone was too distracted to notice the electric flash. More tremors came. Secret Service agents carted away Fake Powell. A coldness entered Young Powell. He felt a sudden need for someone to comfort him. Where was Natalie when he needed her?

The world shook, as did he.

***

Obsidian had inflatable pontoons, so it made for a passable lifeboat. Ryder awaited rescue, not expecting any to come for at least a few more hours.

Once again, she had let the Helmet Man slip through her fingers. If all had gone well, she might have convinced Gilda Plato to act against Incognito, maybe even defect back to the Western Union. But she had failed to salvage her. York and Patel weren't responding to her radio messages either. Ryder suspected they had perished.

Now she was alone once more. No emotions tortured her, but the void was more noticeable than usual. Perhaps she could talk to Powers. She called him up as she stared at the sky.

"Boss, can you feel it?" Powers answered.

"Feel what, Powers?"

"The quakes! They're happening all over the world! I woke up because of them. Asami says she's used to them, being from Japan and all, but I'm scared stiff!"

A violent wave hit her walker. Ryder was jolted to the side, restrained only by her seat belt. Another wave quickly followed.

"You all right, boss?" Powers asked.

"I will call you back." She hung up on him, bracing herself for the next impact. These were not normal waves. Korea and China must be getting hit with tsunamis.

A third wave struck. A surge of fear went through her. She screamed in pleasure. Feeling! To the West, in the heart of China, there was something being erected. It was tall and cold. It was horrible, but it was something. Ryder was hit by a fourth wave and screamed again.

The Helmet Man was nothing compared to this.

***

"Do you know why I changed my mind?"

Jeff Springer shook his head. He wasn't just trying to give a nonverbal answer but also hoped to shake his blindfold off. His hands were also tied behind his back.

"I was at an impasse," Taylor said as he drove their Jeep through the jungle. "Both options were not appealing. If I had let Thomas stay at the United Third's headquarters, he would have become a pawn of Incognito's once again. Even if Incognito were to die soon, someone like Barir could still hold the boy hostage. And like you said, the Western Union could bomb the United Third's headquarters at any time."

Thomas listened in, sitting in the back seat. He was hunched over in thought.

"What if I brought him to his mother, then?" Taylor asked. "Could she keep him safe from Cloak? If she knew about his powers, would she still want to take him back? Would I even be able to get him there?"

Taylor breathed in. "What swayed my decision in the end was Aleppo. From what I've overheard, the battle is not going well for the United Third. Whether it's because of Incognito's absence or the Western Union's technological superiority, I do not know. All that matters is this revolt is about to come to an end. The West will dominate once again."

"So, you realized the United Third is losing and that their base is bound to be discovered and bombed any day now," Springer said. "Yeah, that makes sense."

"I also realized something else," Taylor said. "I can't trust Slate. I can't trust Gilda or Kevin either. I will always care about them. I hope they come back from their mission alive. But I don't think Slate has Thomas's best interests at heart. His war is all-consuming. Slate can't act as a parent to this boy and fight Cloak at the same time. Of course, I also wished to escape from the United Third, but I couldn't bring myself to leave Thomas behind."

Springer smiled with lots of teeth. "And you decided to save me as well? Shucks, I knew you were all right."

"I'll need your help getting Thomas to England. However, I'll have to keep you on a tight leash so you won't be tempted to hand us over to the Western Union."

"What, me? Never!"

Taylor sighed. He looked back over his shoulder to see how Thomas was doing. The young prince looked sad, but he had given his consent. Not only did he not want to be a burden and wanted to meet his real mother, but maybe he too was starting to realize that Slate and Naomi wouldn't make for good parents.

And yet, with all these justifications, Taylor couldn't help but think he merely wanted to hurt Slate, to make him pay for humiliating him in front of Gilda and Straper, for leaving him in the claws of Incognito while he went to his death.

But Taylor dismissed such notions. No, his reasoning was sound. He wouldn't take Thomas away like Peter Pan on a mere grudge alone. The boy belonged with his mother, away from Incognito, away from Cloak, away from the fighting and cruelty. Taylor had sought to escape anyway. Why not do this kindness?

"Up ahead!" Thomas shouted.

Taylor saw a truck blocking the dirt road with several armed men crouching behind it. The United Third must have discovered their plot.

"Hey, what's going on?" Springer yelled. "I can't see, remember?"

With the United Third preoccupied with holding Aleppo, Taylor had thought this would be the best opportunity to flee. Maybe he should have waited for the cover of night.

"That truck looks sturdy," Taylor said. "I doubt we can ram through them. They have a lot of firepower too."

"Are we giving up already?" Thomas asked.

"No, but we'll have to stop. We just need to wait for opportunity to strike."

The Jeep stopped ten feet from the barrier. The armed men were all in their late teens, not really men at all. All the older men had gone off to Syria. Taylor stiffened. He didn't want to fight teenagers unless he had to. Even then, he would likely hesitate.

"Cradle-robbing, Dr. Taylor?" someone asked over their Jeep's two-way radio. Taylor and Thomas nearly jumped in their seats. "I did not expect someone so logical to pull a stunt like this. The Helmet Man must have had a bad influence on you."

It was Barir. Judging by the gunshots and explosions in the background, he was in Aleppo, commanding what was left of the United Third's forces.

"Let us go, Barir," Taylor said. "It's over. You're finished. Incognito isn't going to change anything. The Saladin Federation was a pipe dream."

"The tides of war may yet again turn in our favor."

"Barir, Incognito is a genocidal racist. He cannot be trusted. Can't you see this innocent child is in danger so long as he stays here?"

"That child is too valuable to allow you to take away. Even if he wasn't, you all know too much, and that Springer is scheduled to be executed."

Springer squirmed in his seat. "Get this blindfold off me! I don't want to die like this!"

"What now?" Thomas asked Taylor. "Do we fight?"

Taylor had made a lot of difficult choices recently, but he didn't have to make this one. An earthquake struck them hard and fast. Half the young men lost their balance and fell. Palm trees snapped and fell. A section of the road even collapsed. The truck blocking the road slipped backward. The young men stumbled back to avoid being crushed. The truck came to a rest at the bottom of a ditch. The road was now clear.

"What was that?" Barir yelled, having felt a quake on his end too.

Taylor floored it, and the Jeep kicked up lots of dust, providing good cover. A few of the young men shot at the Jeep as they choked on the air. One bullet hit a taillight. Two bullets would have hit Taylor had Thomas not acted as a shield, blocking the gunfire. His bulletproof body was unharmed, though he did cough from the dust.

"Get us out of here!" Springer yelled. "I think I almost got shot that time!"

A palm tree started to topple. Taylor twisted the wheel. It missed them by a foot. The young men kept shooting, but the Jeep was already out of range.

"Did we make it?" Springer asked.

"It appears so," Taylor said. Then he laughed. Thomas laughed too.

"Hey, this isn't funny!" Springer yelled. "We almost died back there!"

"Better get used to close calls," Taylor told him. His laughter abated as he mused on the earthquake that had saved them. Shouldn't he be happy it had come? But for some reason, the more he thought about it, the more anxious he became.

Thomas stopped laughing. "Was that a good thing that just happened?"

Taylor gulped, expecting another quake to come at any time. "No, I don't think it was."

It started to get dark. Taylor found this odd. There hadn't been a cloud in the sky earlier. He casually glanced up.

The Jeep started to swerve off the road.

"Watch where you're going!" Thomas yelled.

Taylor stopped the Jeep. He swooned in his seat.

"Why'd you stop?" Springer snapped. "Have you forgotten about the guys with guns?"

Thomas squealed, having just looked up himself.

"You too? Don't keep me in suspense! What's going on?"

Taylor, petrified and transfixed on the sky, yanked off Springer's blindfold. Annoyed, Springer looked up as well, wondering what all the fuss was about.

It was a solar eclipse.

The moon was smothering the sun.

Springer started sweating. "I'd like that blindfold back now."

***

The battle in Aleppo ceased. All the soldiers lowered their guns. Walkers stopped firing shells. Even *Leviathan* was not attacking anymore.

All eyes were focused on the sky. The eclipse had caught everyone's attention. Whether they were loyal to Incognito or the Western Union, all were equally damned.

Several smoldering buildings collapsed due to a combination of bombs and earthquake tremors, but nobody so much as budged. Fear had struck all their hearts. For five minutes, no one fought. Whether they knew it or not, they were staring at pure evil.

The battle soon resumed, but the fear remained.

***

"What are you doing under there?" Asami Kusanagi asked.

Powers was hiding under a table. "Get under here! I learned this in school!"

"This quake is nothing," Asami Kusanagi told him, sitting next to her comatose husband. "What about Ryder? She ended her call abruptly."

"I don't know, but I'm getting worried about her."

A tremor larger than the last one hit them. The lights flickered. The hospital was now running on emergency power. Asami screamed. Powers jumped at the sound of it, banging his head on the table above him.

"Ouch! What's your deal? I thought you weren't afraid of a little—"

Powers then saw why Asami had screamed.

Keito Kusanagi had sat up in his bed, pale and moist. Asami couldn't believe her eyes. She grasped his shoulders and shook him.

"Keito, you are awake!" she yelled in Japanese.

"Sky..." Keito croaked in English.

"Keito?"

"Look at the sky..."

Powers got out from under the table. "The sky? What's he talking about?"

A series of shrieks hit Powers' ear, making his blood run cold. They weren't just coming from inside the hospital but from outside as well.

Asami rushed to a window and yanked it open. She looked up at the night sky. Her knees gave out as she let out a gasp.

Powers rushed to her side. "What is it? Are we under attack?" He moved her out of the way and poked his head out the window. Washington, DC, had gone into a state of panic. Down on the streets, people got out of their cars to stare at the sky. Some of them screamed, a few fainted, and far too many of them laughed. A man stood on top of a truck. It was Mr. Preacher. He'd had some sort of fit that could have been mistaken for a religious experience. Then he started to do what he did best.

"Behold! The Omega is upon us! Have you had the dreams?"

Powers looked at the night sky. He didn't know what the big deal was at first. There didn't seem to be anything obviously wrong with the heavens. But when he did figure out what everyone was staring at, all the color left his face.

There were no stars in the sky. As impossible as it seemed, they had gone out. The stars shined no more. Was light pollution responsible? No, most of the lights were out due to the quakes, and there wasn't a cloud in the sky. The stars had indeed gone out.

There was only the moon. And it was full.

Once again, Hank Powers felt puny.

"Yes," Keito whispered. "I have had the dreams."

"It's time to dream again."

General Eisenhorn felt the sand against his cheek, knowing on reflex where he was. "Klara," he muttered.

"Eisenhorn..."

"The syringe... That eel broke it. I'm worthless."

"Open your eyes."

Eisenhorn did. He was in his usual dream spot on a white island with a black ocean surrounding him, an impossible star-filled sky above. Klara stood over him. He got up off the sand, not knowing what to expect.

Klara's eyes were filled with tears. "Eisenhorn..."

The general saw they weren't alone. At his feet, a young boy was curled up in the fetal position. He was shivering and weeping.

On the boy's head was a silver helmet.

"Is that...?" Eisenhorn had no time to finish that thought. He saw two others nearby. One was a familiar face. The other was a woman.

"See the family resemblance?" the woman jeered, holding Gilda up by the armpits.

"Klara, what's happening?" Eisenhorn whispered.

No answer, but he saw another person on the island, a young girl with black hair.

"Mom..." the girl whimpered. "Mom, why did you hand me over like that? Why did you offer me up to that *thing?* Mom, do you hate me? Mom, help me! *Help me!*"

Eisenhorn started crying. "Shut up! Just shut up, all of you!"

A young man appeared. He was missing a hand and looked deathly pale. "I just want to be strong..." Straper wheezed. "I just want to be tall..."

"I'm so ashamed…" Eisenhorn croaked. "I don't know why, but I'm so ashamed…"

Then the arms came. Millions upon millions of them reached up from the black water. These limbs were each pitch-black in color and covered in a film of mucus. They clawed at the sky, ravenous and humiliated.

Eisenhorn slipped and landed on a squishy surface. The island was no longer made of sand. It felt soft and organic, but it also felt cold, like a dead fish. It smelled like a thousand corpses.

The island had become a giant white eye.

One by one, the stars went out. The planets turned to dust, the one looking like Jupiter the last to go. The sky was soon dark. Only one source of light remained, dead center in the sky.

The hands stopped clawing.

Now they pointed.

Countless hands were accusing the light, belittling it. Eisenhorn raised his own hand, but he did not know why, at least not yet. An unparalleled anger welled up inside of him. The others on the island also raised their hands. They all pointed to the sky, to the light that seemed so pure and innocent that it practically mocked them. Only Klara didn't point toward the heavens. That didn't stop her from weeping, though. Eisenhorn could not understand his anger. He could only feel it. But he was starting to learn. Yes, he was starting to learn…

Eisenhorn fell to his knees. The anger was gone. Now there was only despair. Gilda fell too. Straper covered his face. The girl grabbed the sides of her head in torment. Even Gilda's mother, who had haunted and abused her daughter incessantly in her dreams, was down and weeping. In the end, there was only one defiler. All others were victims. There was no semblance of justice. Endless suffering. Evil for all.

The boy with the silver helmet was the last to point.

When this happened, a horrible cackling came from the ocean.

The white eye glowed a horrible yellow. Eisenhorn's hands burned. He was on fire. Everyone was on fire. The light was blinding. The cackling consumed him. He begged for release. He begged for it to all be over.

Oh, lord... Oh, lord... The sun is no more...

Oh, lord... Oh, lord... The moon is full...

***

Eisenhorn had finally gone under, only to writhe and spit out obscenities. He was not alone. Gilda, Straper, and Naomi did the same. Abrafo, Young-Bum, and their men kept far away from these seemingly possessed souls. Incognito merely lay awake with tubes in his arm. His men had given him as much medical assistance as they could, but he would need a real doctor if he were to stay alive for much longer.

"Wake up," Oscar pleaded with basset hound eyes. He sat by Slate's side, shaking his son incessantly. "Wake up... I didn't mean it. I swear I didn't mean it... I was used. We were all used. Wake up, Slate. Just wake up..."

Incognito didn't bother to console his former friend. He didn't even bother to explain the obvious. Oscar should have known by now.

The Helmet Man would not wake. He had gone into hibernation.

Incognito fingered the locket, opening and closing it with no purpose in mind. He had grabbed it before Abrafo carried him to the helicopter.

He sighed. "If only I hadn't cared..."

The helicopter jolted. Young-Bum nearly fell on his face, but Abrafo caught him.

"Can you pilot this thing straight?" Abrafo barked.

"We are experiencing turbulence," Sanjay informed everyone from the cockpit. "The storm has only grown bigger."

"Then fly faster!" Abrafo ordered.

The helicopter kept being jolted, the frequency of the jolts increasing at an alarming rate. It got to the point where everyone who wasn't lying or sitting down was thrown off their feet. An instrument began to beep. Sanjay swore and flicked some switches.

A bright flash of light hit them from behind. It was yellow and stung the eyes. A shockwave slammed into the helicopter. A nuclear explosion might as well have gone off. They spun out of control. Sanjay fought to keep them in the air with all his might. The windows blew in. Shards of glass struck Abrafo's arm, making him bleed.

Sanjay finally got them level again. The wind died down. There was no more light either. Abrafo pulled glass from his arm and looked over at his boss. Incognito had not enjoyed the experience, but his condition was stable.

"Look outside," he told Abrafo. "What do you see?"

Abrafo checked out the back window. What he saw was devastation. There was a massive mushroom cloud. It was black as night, though yellow light continued to radiate from its center. Abrafo had no idea how to describe this scene.

"You don't have to answer," Incognito said. He coughed and saw that Eisenhorn, Gilda, Naomi, and Straper were now all resting quietly. Their dreaming had stopped. Maybe it was a blessing. Maybe it was a sign of more horrors to come.

Oscar was still trying to wake his son, starving for forgiveness. He paused only to brush the tips of his fingers along the crack on Slate's helmet, wiping away the ash.

"I thought you would have wanted it that way," Oscar said. "I thought you would have chosen death over Cloak's victory. Isn't that what you wanted? Oh, please wake up…"

Oscar then grasped his son's shoulders and mewled. Incognito watched this pathetic scene, not sure if it was his place to judge. He wasn't even sure if what Radcliffe had done was right or wrong. But it was certainly cold.

Incognito's grip tightened around the locket. "I have failed… Cloak has won."

"**T**wenty years," Alphonse Schmitt mused. "Twenty years of my wonderful life spent in a frozen hole, wasting my time slaving away and getting plastered. Now, at long last, here is the fruit of my labors."

The unicopter soared above the endless waste. Whatever explosion had occurred had scorched the Earth clean. Not a tree or blade of grass was in sight. Blackened ground was all that remained. It was like this for ten miles in every direction from the center of the blast.

"What if Sebastian really is dead?" Ember moaned, sitting on the opposite side of the unicopter from Schmitt. "What if Temple's dead too? That would make us the last of Cloak, and I have no interest in being a part of Cloak if you're the only other member."

"I'm flattered," Schmitt snorted. "Why don't you hand me another beer?"

"You've already drunk them all, you inebriated scoundrel."

"Don't make me get my ring out, girl."

"We're a minute away," Killian said from the copilot seat. Ten other mercenaries were also on the unicopter, none of them wanting to be there. They'd had to wait three days for the air to clear up and the heat to die down. There was no radiation to worry about. That was the only plus.

The Chinese Empire was in complete disarray. The death of the emperor and the disarming of China's entire nuclear arsenal had effectively ended the war and perhaps the empire itself. High General Xing and High General Lee were attempting to take control of the government, but numerous rivals opposed them. Most of the Chinese military was preoccupied with maintaining control over the subservient nations as news of the emperor's demise had spread fast. It didn't help that Western Union ships had entered Chinese waters and were now demanding that the Chinese send an emissary so the surrender talks could begin.

Because of all these political factors, the Chinese had yet to search the ruins of the Forbidden City. Schmitt had little doubt that the Chinese would eventually get around to coming here. They loved their emperor too much to ignore his ashes for long. But he wanted to visit the remains of the Forbidden City first, so he had ordered Killian to fly him out here.

Ember had shown up at the last minute, having just come back from fighting Incognito. She didn't enjoy the prospect of having to share a unicopter with Schmitt, but her curiosity and concern for Sebastian and Temple were too overpowering to resist for very long.

"I hate this flight," Ember whined. "I almost wish Geppetto was here."

"I'm going to miss him," Killian said. "The man was a realist. I admire that."

"So, the dwarf is dead," Schmitt said. "About time. Didn't think his little heart would last as long as it did. Just wish I had the body. I could've dissected it."

"Take a look down there!" Ember yelled.

Schmitt did so. There was still a lot of smoke, so it took a while for him to make out the thousands of people moving toward the Forbidden City.

"They don't seem very organized," Killian said. "I think they're civilians."

The unicopter dropped down some. Now the people could be made out better. They were all Chinese farmers, mostly women and children, with callused hands and shrunken bodies. Years of hard labor and poor nutrition had not served them well. They all seemed to be in some kind of trance, unable to resist the voice that called to them.

Ember sighed. "The poor wretches..."

"Hope they aren't going to cause us any trouble," Killian said.

"How many do you think we could kill?" Schmitt asked.

"With our weapons, not even a quarter."

"Then pedal to the metal, Killian. I want to make it there before those animals do."

The unicopter was now above Tiananmen Square, which was difficult to tell, seeing as there wasn't anything left of it. But the air was clear here. Schmitt had no trouble seeing a yellow dog running around amid the ruin.

Schmitt grinned. "Land the unicopter near the mutt, Killian."

Killian obeyed. As the unicopter decreased in altitude, Ember spotted something near Quantum. A lone figure was sitting on his knees with limp arms.

"Sebastian!" Ember squealed. "He's alive!"

"Keep that voice of yours down," Schmitt snapped, fingering one of his ears. "Your womanly emotions shouldn't be *my* problem."

The unicopter touched down. Ember was the first one off. She petted Quantum vigorously as soon as she got her hands on the dog.

"Bad boy! Did you make sure to eat plenty of people? Who's a bad boy?"

Killian and his men got off next. They held their weapons tight. Schmitt stumbled out after them, still a bit tipsy. His stomach hurt too. When was the last time he ate something solid? He should at least have brushed his teeth.

"Nothing but burnt offerings here," he muttered.

"Sebastian, what's wrong with you?" Ember screamed.

Schmitt glanced over to where the exclamation had come from. Ember and Quantum had gone over to where Sebastian supposedly was. Killian and his men ran over as well. In no mood for running, Schmitt walked there at his own pace.

Something in his pocket grew hot. Schmitt only realized it was his ring when his pants caught fire. Cursing, he smacked the flames out. The implications of what had just happened made his mouth go dry. That ring should have been able to soak up even the Helmet Man's massive reserves of psychic energy. Just how much energy was needed to make the ring melt down? What could possibly produce that amount? Schmitt was hungry for answers.

When Schmitt finally joined the others, he saw that Sebastian really was there. However, it was more accurate to say it was a statue of Sebastian. He wore a frozen smile and didn't seem to breathe or blink. Sebastian's eyes were locked on nothing in particular, but his attention appeared to be entirely on one thing.

It took a moment for Killian to notice. When he did, he almost had a heart attack.

"Oh, sweet—!" He took a step back and raised his gun, unable to finish that sentence. His men had similar reactions. Ember saw what they were looking at and let her jaw drop. Schmitt's mouth made words, but no actual sound came out. All of them, like Sebastian, were transfixed by what was floating in front of them.

A silver helmet floated upright before Sebastian, ten feet in the air. It didn't bob up and down but stayed firmly in its position. It was Temple's helmet, its owner no more.

But this helmet was different. No longer was there blood on it, having become sterile in appearance. As well, the helmet now had two holes.

They were eyeholes.

The Chinese farmers had reached their destination. Thousands of them surrounded the scene. None of the farmers dared venture any closer than a hundred feet. They watched the silver helmet from afar. Schmitt, Ember, Killian, and the mercenaries were too transfixed by it as well to notice the sea of tortured souls that now encircled them. The helmet evoked a multitude of emotions from its witnesses: fear, ecstasy, and obsession. But the one that stood out among them was despair.

The eyeholes stared at the endless waste.

In a seamless transition, the helmet was no longer vacant.

White eyes peered from the silver prison.

They had come out of nowhere, seamlessly brought into existence. They had not come alone. A body came with them. It was tall, black, and oh so terrible. It loomed over Sebastian and the others. It did not acknowledge them. Its thin, long arms were crossed over its chest.

The Chinese farmers all went to their knees. The human sea submitted itself to the demon, gaunt eyes cast down, hands and foreheads pressed against the ground. Even the children did so. It came naturally to them all.

Ember went to her knees too. She clutched her chest and hyperventilated, now wearing a grin similar to Sebastian's. Killian and his men also went down. Some of them even cried. Quantum whimpered, covering its eyes with both paws. Schmitt was the last to give in, doing so willingly, wearing a twisted sneer. *Twenty years well spent,* he thought.

"My lord..." Sebastian said. "When you arrived ... when you came into being ... I ... I felt the earth tremble."

The demon used one of its taloned hands to caress the side of its silver helmet.

"No..." the Mentor declared. *"You felt God tremble."*

It took a moment for those words to sink in. A shrill cackle then escaped the silver helmet. The white eyes began to glow yellow. The cackling grew. The helmet melted and formed a smile. Light shined from the grin. Then the sun went out. They were plunged into darkness. The only light left came from a pair of glowing eyes and one shining smile.

It had finally happened.

The Omega Lord had risen.